THE

DISTANT
LANDS

JULIAN GREEN

THE
DISTANT
LANDS

a novel
translated from the French by

Barbara Beaumont

Marion Boyars
New York • London

First published in trade paperback in 1996
First published in hardcover in the United States and Great Britain in 1991
by Marion Boyars Publishers
237 East 39th Street, New York, N.Y. 10016
24 Lacy Road, London SW15 1NL

Distributed in Australia and New Zealand by Peribo Pty Ltd
58 Beaumont Road, Mount Kuring-gai, NSW 2080

First published in France by Editions du Seuil in 1987
under the title *Les Pays Lointains*
Copyright © 1987/1990 Editions du Seuil and Julian Green
This translation copyright © 1990 Marion Boyars Publishers

CIP catalogue records for this book are available from the Library of Congress and
the British Library.

ISBN 0-7145-3022-0

Typeset by Ponting-Green Publishing Services, London

About the Author

Born in 1900 of American parents living in Paris, Julian Green has spent most of his extraordinary literary career there, writing in French (and occasionally English) for a wide and enthusiastic readership. He has published over sixty-five books in France: novels, essays, plays, a four-volume autobiography, and, so far, fifteen volumes of his Journal. Many of his books have been published in English in the United States and in Britain, and have been translated into most other languages.

As an American, Julian Green is the only foreign member of the Académie Française. He is also a member of the American Academy of Arts and Letters, winner of the Harper Prize, the Prix Marcel Proust, the Prix France-Amérique, the Prix Cavour, the Benson Medal and numerous other international awards. He is one of the few living authors to have their collected works published in the prestigious Gallimard Pléiade series.

Many of Julian Green's experiences recounted in his four volumes of autobiography form the basis of his Southern novels, of which *Moïra*, *The Distant Lands* and *The Stars of the South*, among others, as well as his play *South*, pay tribute to his Southern heritage. His mother came from Georgia, his father from Virginia. Julian Green grew up with his *Southern belle* mother's tales of her aristocratic family before and after the Civil War. Julian Green lives in Paris.

To the memory of my mother,
daughter of the South.

Contents

CHARACTERS IN
THE DISTANT LANDS
IN 1850

ENGLAND   GEORGIA

Kent   Savannah

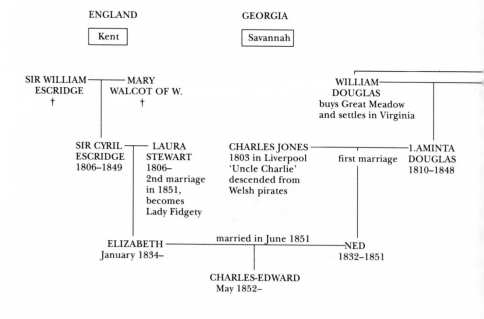

SIR WILLIAM ——— MARY
ESCRIDGE | WALCOT OF W.
† | †

WILLIAM——
DOUGLAS
buys Great Meadow
and settles in Virginia

SIR CYRIL —— LAURA
ESCRIDGE | STEWART
1806–1849 | 1806–
2nd marriage
in 1851,
becomes
Lady Fidgety

CHARLES JONES ——————— 1.AMINTA
1803 in Liverpool   first marriage DOUGLAS
'Uncle Charlie'   1810–1848
descended from
Welsh pirates

ELIZABETH ————— married in June 1851 ————— NED
January 1834–   1832–1851

CHARLES-EDWARD
May 1852–

GEORGIA

Dimwood

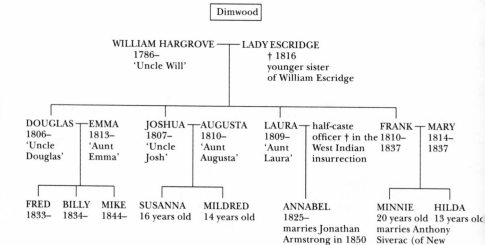

WILLIAM HARGROVE ——— LADY ESCRIDGE
1786–   † 1816
'Uncle Will'   younger sister
of William Escridge

DOUGLAS ┬ EMMA   JOSHUA ┬ AUGUSTA   LAURA ┬ half-caste   FRANK ┬ MARY
1806– | 1813–   1807– | 1810–   1809– | officer † in the   1810– | 1814–
'Uncle | 'Aunt   'Uncle | 'Aunt   'Aunt | West Indian   1837 | 1837
Douglas' | Emma'   Josh' | Augusta'   Laura' | insurrection

FRED   BILLY   MIKE   SUSANNA   MILDRED   ANNABEL   MINNIE   HILDA
1833–   1834–   1844–   16 years old   14 years old   1825–   20 years old 13 years old
                                           marries Jonathan   marries Anthony
                                           Armstrong in 1850 Siverac (of New
                                                       Orleans) in 1852

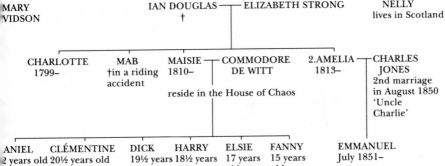

VIRGINIA

Prince William County

(Douglas clan, of Scottish descent)

MARY
DVIDSON   IAN DOUGLAS —┬— ELIZABETH STRONG   NELLY
                      †   lives in Scotland

CHARLOTTE   MAB   MAISIE —┬— COMMODORE   2.AMELIA —┬—CHARLES
1799–   †in a riding   1810–   DE WITT   1813–   JONES
            accident   2nd marriage
                     reside in the House of Chaos   in August 1850
                                                  'Uncle
                                                  Charlie'

DANIEL   CLÉMENTINE   DICK   HARRY   ELSIE   FANNY   EMMANUEL
2 years old   20½ years old   19½ years   18½ years   17 years   15 years   July 1851–
                           old   old   old   old

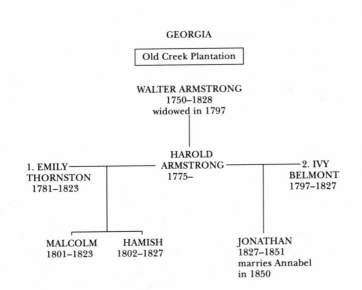

GEORGIA

Old Creek Plantation

WALTER ARMSTRONG
1750–1828
widowed in 1797

HAROLD
1. EMILY ——————— ARMSTRONG ——————— 2. IVY
THORNSTON   1775–   BELMONT
1781–1823   1797–1827

MALCOLM   HAMISH   JONATHAN
1801–1823   1802–1827   1827–1851
                             marries Annabel
                             in 1850

1
DIMWOOD

1

*E*lizabeth had just turned sixteen when she saw the plantation for the first time. It was on an April night full of the
song of tree-frogs. At first she was afraid. Holding the hand
of her mother who was in tears, she went timidly up the long
steps of the verandah flanked by two giant magnolias. It
seemed to her that the climb would go on for ever, and that
she would never reach the gentleman dressed in black accompanied by a black servant carrying a torch. He was tall and
upright and much of his pink face was taken up with thick
side-whiskers that merged into his mustache; smiling generously, he opened his arms.

'Welcome to Dimwood,' he exclaimed, as he took both of
Mrs Escridge's hands in his own and, leaning towards Elizabeth he kissed her. 'My little English violet, you'll just love
the South,' he said as his face rubbed against those cool
cheeks that were trying to get away from the tickling of so
much whisker.

Suddenly, in the doorway, a kind of joyful outburst welcomed the newcomers. Ladies in white dresses thrust themselves forward, and endless kisses were exchanged in a jostle
of words. Elizabeth felt in a daze faced with all those eyes
shining with curiosity, looking at her as if they were fencing
her in.

She felt happy and bewildered at one and the same time.
Now and then laments and exclamations in her mother's
voice filtered through to her, and she recognized fragments
of tales of their journey and their family misfortunes.

Like a nocturnal bird flung into the daylight, the girl
found herself almost immediately in a room lit by lamps on
sidetables in front of large mirrors that reached up to the
moldings of the cornice. She was overcome with a sudden
urge to escape and made for an open door, but already two
young men were at her side.

'No use trying to run away!' one of them shouted with a
laugh. 'You're our prisoner.'

Barely taller than herself, he seemed almost like a schoolboy, with his dishevelled hair and turned-up nose.

'I'm your cousin, Billy Stevens,' he said.

And without ceremony, he placed his huge, damp mouth on Elizabeth's cheek making her shudder. Turning towards his less exuberant companion, he said:

'Come on, Fred, what are you waiting for?'

Indeed, Fred had stopped a few paces short of the girl and was looking at her with a half smile. Either surprise or admiration had made the large black pupils of his eyes visibly larger in his long, handsome face, and he hesitated for a second before advancing to proffer clumsily his lips to the nose, ears, eyelids or any part of that frightened little face other than the mouth, but it was the mouth that his lips inadvertently brushed against. Both of them blushed while, behind them, the ladies gathered around Mrs Escridge, who was almost fainting amidst a flurry of tears and words.

'It's too much,' she kept saying. 'How shameful! I've never behaved so badly in my life.'

There was a medley of polite protests, and she was carried to a vast red sofa where she lay down.

She had dropped her bonnet, and her thick brown and gray locks were flopping around her long face with its premature wrinkles, furrowed by her forty years and more, yet there was a certain nobility in her features. Her large, thin nose alone bore witness to her being the last of an extinct line, and despair cried out from her huge, gray, cavernous eyes.

'I'll tell you everything,' she cried as she roughly rearranged the folds of her skirt that revealed her ankles. 'The discomfort, the bad roads, the endless nightmare of the carriage.'

'Tomorrow,' said the firm voice of Mr Hargrove who came to stand before her. 'We all know you have suffered. Now we are going to show you to your room and young Elizabeth to hers. You are both in need of rest. You must go to bed.'

'When my husband died,' she continued in an aggressive tone, as if she had not heard, 'I wanted to die as well. I loved him. All that is quite beyond tears. His enormous debts — did I tell you how much he owed?' she asked suddenly.

'Yes, Cousin, I have all the details. We'll talk about it tomorrow.'

'And our house in the country that I had to sell . . . Ah, that day was the end — my heart broke.'

'You'll soon forget all that here with us.'

'Forget! Never. I kissed the walls of every room before I left. But note that I wasn't crying. I'm not a woman to cry. We leave that to the men.'

With a movement of his finger, Mr Hargrove summoned Billy and said a few words in his ear. The boy disappeared immediately.

Then Mr Hargrove took Mrs Escridge by the hand with a mixture of gentleness and authority:

'Allow me to help you up,' he said.

She brushed him aside.

'Leave me,' she said, 'and for Heaven's sake don't interrupt me. Talking about my agony brings me relief. With the house mortgaged a hundred times over, Elizabeth and I had barely anything to live on, and so I sought help.'

At that moment she sent in his direction such a look of unambiguous supplication that, turning towards the women gathered most attentively around him, he nodded in the direction of the door. There was a moment's hesitation, but the message was received, and they withdrew with as much dignity as they could muster. Only Elizabeth did not move. She had been standing to one side during the preceding scene, in a corner of the vast room where no one had noticed her.

Mrs Escridge hid her face in her hands and whispered, as if making a confession:

'Cried for help . . .'

'You did the right thing,' he said, as the door closed.

'But the letter I wrote you from that wretched room in that black and icy lodging house in London, barely knowing what I was doing in that black London, dying of shame . . . begging!' she exclaimed. 'Yes, me begging.'

'Cousin Laura, I entreat you,' Mr Hargrove said. 'Begging is a meaningless word. Your husband was related to me. You are one of the family.'

'No,' she said wildly. 'I'm not one of your family, I'm the object of your charity. I have a horror of charity!'

He took a chair and sat down next to the raving woman.

'Dear Cousin,' he began as he took her hand.

She pulled away her hand immediately as if he had tried to steal it from her.

'Cousin Laura,' he began again, 'charity comes more from above than from men.'

'Oh no!' she exclaimed, 'don't talk to me about religion, or else I'll leave.'

'And where would you go, poor Cousin?'

She leapt at this word in a joyous fury.

'Poor cousin! You're right, Mr Hargrove. I'll be the poor relation, the one kept hidden away, apologized for, the spoilsport.'

'Laura Escridge,' he cried, getting up suddenly, 'allow me to say that I find you intolerable.'

And he added in a cutting tone of voice:

'I order you to be quiet.'

To his great surprise he saw her raise her head in his direction and look at him with something approaching admiration.

'Alright,' she said, suddenly calmer, 'but I take back nothing of what I said, and I ask to be left alone.'

'You'll be left alone,' he replied with a forced smile that got lost in the thickness of his mustache. 'We'll make peace now. The South is famous for its hospitality. I'll take you to your room. I hope you will like it. It's one of the most comfortable in the house. Be so good as to take my arm.'

Haughtily, but submissively, she obeyed, and placed a talon-like hand on a robust arm clutching at his alpaca sleeve. It was not without some effort that he helped her up, and the two of them headed for the door, as if he was taking her to a ball.

'Your charming Elizabeth will be your neighbor,' he said courteously. 'I suppose she stayed with the others. I'll give orders.'

A small, firm voice brought them to a halt.

'I'm here.'

'Elizabeth,' exclaimed Mrs Escridge, 'that's very bad of you, you hid so as to listen.'

With unhurried steps the girl crossed the long room and the big mirrors attentively counted each Elizabeth as she passed by in her kilt.

'I wasn't hiding,' she said. 'I was over there in a corner.'

'You should have left the room when you saw the others go.'

'I was better off on my own.'

These words, spoken in a firm manner, put an end to the questioning.

'Alright,' Mr Hargrove said softly, 'follow us, and I'll show you to your room.'

A few steps further and they found themselves at the foot of a wide curved staircase, which was shaped like a palette. As if to soften the rather austere elegance of the entrance hall, armchairs with red upholstery were lined up along the walls like people sitting and waiting patiently.

Mr Hargrove clapped his hands twice, and a black servant followed by another came immediately through a doorway, both wearing red livery and white gloves. On seeing them, Mrs Escridge could not hold back a slight cry of alarm.

'I don't want them to come near me,' she whispered.

'There's nothing to be afraid of. They're quite harmless.'

And having settled her in an armchair, he ordered the servants to carry her up to the first floor. With her eyes closed, she let them carry her, but at every step she let out a mild groan of horror and repeated under her breath:

'I swear the crossing was no worse than this . . . Oh, I hope we're nearly there.'

'Open your eyes, Cousin Laura,' Mr Hargrove said gaily after a few minutes, 'we're there.'

They were entering a room where the last rays of twilight extended something of a melancholy softness and, without a doubt, the charm of this half-light had its effect on Mrs Escridge's spirit, for at the very moment that Mr Hargrove ordered the lamps to be lit, she said something that betrayed a sudden and deep insight.

'Wait a moment,' she said.

Large and with a high ceiling, the room was lit by two windows overlooking the verandah, the white columns of which could be made out through the muslin curtains. A four-poster bed occupied the center of this room, transformed by the shadows in the failing light into the kind of place one sees in dreams.

Mrs Escridge ran her eyes for a moment over those walls where fate had brought her, then she gestured to Mr Hargrove.

'Can we put the light on now?' he asked.

She nodded and soon an oil lamp was shining on a round

table covered with an oriental rug. Here and there, mahogany furniture gleamed elegantly. The dreamlike impressions of the previous moment now gave way to an atmosphere of unostentatious but solid prosperity.

There was silence.

'I hope this room strikes you as acceptable,' said Mr Hargrove, 'but if there is anything that doesn't suit you . . .'

Mrs Escridge did not answer. With discreet thoughtfulness, he leaned towards her a little and said in a low voice:

'I too know what exile is like.'

Less spacious than her mother's, Elizabeth's room also overlooked the verandah that circled the first story as well as the ground floor of the house. The girl contemplated this room with a look of wonder, for it seemed to her, after the very ordinary rooms of her childhood, to be the sumptuous apartment of a lady. She felt herself becoming grown-up at a single stroke. In the newness of her joy, she directed a smile at the black servants, who returned it with such obvious good humor that she felt like saying something to them, but could not think of anything and blushed as she opened her valise, which they had placed on a chair. After the interminable wailing of her mother throughout the endless journey, her arrival in the New World, where she was encountering the unexpected at almost every step, acquired in Elizabeth's eyes the dimensions of an adventure.

2

A moment later they were offered a light supper in a small drawing room whose walls were covered with enchanting Italian landscapes which delighted Elizabeth: fascinating volcanoes against an azure sky, vines festooned with bunches of grapes and heavy hayricks were drawn by oxen with enormous horns along roads where boys and girls were dancing. Mrs Escridge, on the other hand, gave them no more than an indifferent glance and suddenly announced that she wanted to go back to her room and sleep.

'Don't you want them to bring you something to eat in your room?' asked Mr Hargrove.

She refused with a movement of her hand, but a certain feeling of shame must have come over her as she remembered the nervous outburst that she had been unable to control, for she made an effort to appear pleasant, and the shadow of a smile drifted across her exhausted features.

'Tired,' she whispered, 'ready to drop, you do understand?'

'We will have you carried up in an armchair, Cousin Laura.'

'No,' she said in a sudden surge of pride, 'I'll go alone.'

'At least allow me to accompany you upstairs.'

'No,' she said, and by an effort of will added: 'but I thank you for that and . . . yes . . . for everything.'

When she had gone, Mr Hargrove settled himself in an armchair not far from the table at which Elizabeth was sitting. He was aware that she was intimidated, and that everything produced this effect, primarily himself. But so did the black servant wearing a white jacket standing behind her, the candles in a small lamp at her elbow, the very chair she sat on, the back of which was so tall it gave the impression of a throne for a queen.

He signalled to the servant to withdraw.

'I am glad to have this chance to talk to you, my dear Elizabeth,' he began in a serious tone which terrorized her more than anything that had preceded this encounter.

'If only he didn't have those whiskers,' she thought. In all he said she could only make out shreds of sentences. 'While it's hot . . . don't let my presence stop you . . . you'll not be bothered this evening . . . everyone is fond of you . . . corn fritters . . .'

On that subject, explanations were becoming superfluous. Several of these small golden delicacies had already disappeared and, as her fears progressively left her, the young traveller saw Mr Hargrove emerge, as it were, from a cloud.

'Water,' he said, 'we drink nothing else at meals, but there is still this little almond cake . . .'

Now she was eating without inhibition and the cake

joined the fritters, but she was suddenly worried when she noticed the attention being paid to her hands. Out of the corner of an eye, her handling of spoon and fork was being observed.

'You'll not speak to the servants,' continued Mr Hargrove, 'except to ask them for something you need, and always nicely. What I'm telling you now is of the greatest importance. It is essential that they like you. They are in many ways like children. Would you like some fruit? No? In that case I shall wish you good night, dear Elizabeth. Go up to rest and sleep well.'

They both stood up and he leant over the girl who again quivered and shuddered beneath the tickling of the ornamental undergrowth.

Lying now under a sheet in place of a blanket, for the night promised to be warm, Elizabeth did not sleep. The croaking of the tree-frogs would on its own have been enough to keep her awake, but as the ear eventually became attuned to it, the sound of it finally merged into silence, becoming a fluid veil. With her eyes open, Elizabeth was looking straight ahead. Who could tell what apparitions might emerge? She must keep a particular watch on the phantom-like whiteness of the muslin hanging at the window.

Despite her tiredness she was determined not to give in to the growing heaviness of her eyelids, yet somewhere in the back of her mind things were becoming confused. A vast, green English field spread itself suddenly beneath white clouds, and she felt herself falling down into a black hole. Then she took a grip on herself again. She was in her bedroom back in Devonshire with the sun shining on the chest of drawers. Her mother was feeling sorry for herself while emptying the drawers when, suddenly, the monotonous breaking of waves and the rocking of the boat brought a brusque end to these images. She came to again, fearing that something in the shadows was waiting for her to close her eyes in order to prowl around her bed and, for a moment, she struggled, then slid unawares into the depths of sleep.

The following morning, in her room now exorcized by daylight, she waited hesitantly, not daring to open her door.

A sustained, dry, whispering sound in the distance filled the air outside, but she took no notice of it. Up and dressed early, she wondered how she could have been afraid within these walls where everything was welcoming, the rocking chair generous and full of giddiness, and the vast muslin curtain, so worrying by night, so innocent by day, as well as the great gilt-framed mirror in which Elizabeth could see her reflection. Mentally she was asking herself what the girl who was looking at her in this kilt ought to do; her uncertainty did not last long.

There was a gentle knock at the door, and a young woman came in laughing.

'Dressed already! Am I too late?'

Wearing a white lawn cotton dress with pale pink stripes, she was carrying over her arm a light blue dress which she placed carefully on the bed, then, turning towards Elizabeth, kissed her, saying:

'Don't be afraid, I'm your cousin Minnie come to your rescue. You would be in danger of suffocation in that Highland wool! Can't you hear the cicadas?'

'The cicadas?'

'Oh, don't you know? There is so much to explain to you! But for Heaven's sake, get that pretty skirt off quickly.'

As she spoke she moved about with a vivacity that made Elizabeth feel light-headed, but there was gracefulness in all her movements and her black eyes, shining with gaiety, seemed even larger as her face was small like a little girl's, and her pale complexion hinted at a delicate constitution. Her frequent smiles revealed teeth of an admirable whiteness of which she was obviously very proud. Her hair, which was brushed back into a chignon with auburn highlights, rested on the back of her neck.

She helped Elizabeth get out of her kilt and to put on the blue dress which was just a little too ample around the bust, but a stitch would suffice to make everything perfect, and there was an excellent seamstress to be found amongst the inhabitants of the house: Mademoiselle Souligou Trottereau, an old French Free-woman who had never forgotten her mother tongue.

'You'll see,' she said, as she pulled down the folds of the dress and then stroked them as if to comfort them, 'that here we have a world in miniature. First of all the family, with Mr Hargrove right at the top, Uncle Will, he likes all the young people to call him that. He is very good, everyone agrees on that. Then his two sons, the brothers of my father who is no longer with us, and Aunt Laura. There's Joshua, known as Uncle Josh, and Douglas, Uncle Douglas, the eldest — turn round — both of them married — won't you turn round — so that makes for an army of younger cousins, boys and girls; the baby of the family, Mike, terrorizes the ladies who avoid him like the plague as he always has dirty hands. It's all very confusing. You'll feel lost a bit at first, there is always someone turning up unexpectedly. In any case, I'm your cousin Minnie. And then the slaves, but we call them servants, remember that. There, you look ravishing in sky blue. The dress belongs to your cousin Mildred who is a bit bigger than you. Don't you feel more comfortable? For sure, now look at yourself in the mirror, but quickly, because it's nearly time, and making Uncle Will wait brings on a thunder storm.'

The room where breakfast was taken was considerably less spacious than one might have expected, but the house, which dated from the end of the eighteenth century, was not built to accommodate a great many people. Its proportions were so exact and beautiful that William Hargrove, an incorrigible man of taste, refused to disfigure it with the addition of a wing. In consequence, fifteen people, excluding Mr Hargrove, were squashed around a long, narrow table when Elizabeth made her entrance with Cousin Minnie.

'Sorry for being late,' the latter implored. 'I got Elizabeth to put on one of Mildred's dresses, as it's going to be hot today.'

'I excuse you from explanations that were not asked of you,' said Mr Hargrove in an Olympian tone. 'No,' he added, 'don't make Elizabeth sit over there. My little English violet will breakfast at my right this morning.'

That place had indeed been left empty. Flushed with embarrassment, the English violet slid into it, avoiding brushing the walls that were painted with scenes containing mysterious characters. Again her heart was gripped by fear when she found herself at the corner of the table the end of which was reserved in its entire width for the master of the plantation. Sitting next to her, he gave her the impression of a great quantity of Tussore silk exuding rivers of eau-de-Cologne.

Having surveyed the entire room with a long gaze, he got up slowly and solemnly, and all those present simultaneously bowed their heads towards their plates. Then in a voice that seemed to issue forth from some distant cathedral with its deep and muted resonances, he said the usual grace, to which he appended a succession of personal and specific intentions. It was slow and complete in every detail. Nothing was omitted, neither the favor of a day that promised to be fine, the well-being of the plantation's inhabitants, the good behavior of the servants, and the prosperity of the country and the wisdom of the government, not forgetting, but this in a more discreet tone, a blessing for Her Gracious Majesty over the seas, the sovereign of Mr Hargrove and her agreeable little subject newly arrived under the family roof, together with her beloved Mama, confined to her room with a slight indisposition. A general *Amen* brought to a whispered close this speech which gave the impression of having settled everything between Heaven and all the people of the world.

During this time the delicate little rye pancakes were growing cold and the butter was melting in the English china platters. And so there was a polite rush for everything that could decently be devoured. The silver coffee pots seemed to fly through the air in the white-gloved fists of the servants, who, until that moment, had remained as still as statues but were now running around the table. The great teapot reigned as sole sovereign over that part of the table which was Mr Hargrove's domain as he savored his eggs and bacon and drank his Lipton tea and, to judge by appearances, he was satisfied with himself and with God, for presently he gave a big smile as he wiped his whiskers.

'Your dear Mama is recovering from the fatigue of a long journey,' he finally said as he bent slightly towards Elizabeth. 'Don't be anxious. Tomorrow morning you will have your place among the young people of your own age. It will be more fun for you. But today we are getting to know each other, aren't we?'

'Yes,' she answered in a whisper.

'Yes who?'

'Yes, Mr Hargrove?'

'Oh no, my pretty one. "Yes, Uncle Will". Say it aloud so I can hear.'

'Yes, Uncle Will.'

'Nearly there, but we'll make progress. Your dear Papa must have spoken to you about his Uncle Will Hargrove.'

She remained silent.

'Come now, I see you are still a bit shy, my little English violet. And I think you are a little frightened of me, aren't you? That's a pity.'

At that moment a servant came up and whispered something in his ear.

'Good,' said Mr Hargrove in a low voice, 'you will go and let Miss Llewelyn know and she will take care of her. I want everything to be perfect.'

Not one of these remarks had escaped Aunt Laura, Mr Hargrove's daughter. Seated on his left because Elizabeth, albeit against her will, had taken her usual place, she was sitting upright and attentive, nibbling at little slices of toast that she put back on her plate barely touched. Her forty-odd years seemed not to have wilted the classic beauty of her face, despite its elongated cheeks, a defect that was compensated for by the singular charm of her dark eyes whose softness gave them poignancy, for they gave one the impression that they were looking far into the world of memories, at some spectacle of endearing melancholy.

Her seriousness and silence contrasted with the jovial nature of Mr Hargrove's two sons, which consisted of ironical comments on a little local electoral campaign which neither seemed inclined to take seriously. One felt that they were by nature indifferent to these political matters, whereas their father's eloquence became grandiose as soon as problems took on wider dimensions.

As for the wives of these two brothers with facetious opinions, they exchanged, without risk of being overheard in the general chatter, their impressions of Elizabeth, whom they esteemed to be 'adorably English' and even quite simply adorable. In whispers that they believed discreet, they wondered about Mrs Escridge, who seemed to them to be psychologically much more complex and consequently of a certain fascination. Their lips hesitated over the word 'hysteria' before it burst forth as confidentially as possible in the closeness of their chattering profiles. Emma, the more excitable of these two ladies, was also the prettier. In the fineness of her features and the perfect oval of her face she retained something of the grace of the young women of the South, despite her approaching fortieth birthday. Beneath the elongated arch of her painted eyebrows, her deep black eyes burned with restrained passion, and her fleshy little mouth retained something of the greediness of childhood.

Her partner in conversation, who was her elder, compensated for the fact, so to speak, with a natural air of majesty that was permanent protection against masculine yearnings. Her air of distinction condemned her to a much calmer existence than her neighbor who was born to wreak havoc in the domain of the heart. With Aunt Augusta, in fact, the size of the nose gave her profile a quality that was generally accepted to be regal, an impression borne out by the haughtiness of the look in her admirably green eyes, which, like those of an eagle, rarely blinked.

'I don't deny that she comes from a good family,' Emma repeated, 'but she won't let us forget it.'

'It's true that without breathing a word she lets it be known by her expression . . .'

'. . . treating us to an aristocratic nervous collapse,' said the little cherry-red mouth.

The bird of prey stifled a cry:

'She's cheating. I know about her ancestors, but let's lower our voices, it seems we're being overheard.'

'Let them,' exclaimed Emma. 'I'm very fond of Cousin Laura, but I feel sorry for her. So unhappy . . .'

'So weary after that cruel sea journey . . .'

'Her soul torn apart from leaving her native land.'

The echo of these lamentations reached the ears of Billy, the younger of Uncle Douglas's two sons. A tall, pink-cheeked boy of fifteen, he pushed aside a lock of brown hair tickling his forehead as he spoke.

'They'll both end up getting used to things right enough,' he maintained. 'After all, they'll be as well off here as over there.'

'Young man,' said Augusta, 'you speak in ignorance of

what the pull of the old country means.'

'Oh, it's not my old country,' answered Billy as he forcibly swept the rebellious lock aside.

'One day you'll come to see things differently and you'll visit the place yourself.'

'Me. Never, Aunt Augusta! No desire in the least.'

And with a flick of his forefinger, he despatched England along with that stubborn lock of hair.

Emma gave him a bewitching smile.

'I hope you will be more agreeable with Elizabeth.'

'The little one over there? She'll not be bad one of these days. We'll go and comfort her when she's a little older.'

'Shame on you!' exclaimed Emma with a laugh. 'It wouldn't take much for me to tell your father.'

Augusta's dry voice shattered the air:

'He deserves to be whipped.'

'Forgive me, Aunt Augusta, but there is no whip here at Dimwood,' Billy answered in a falsely sententious tone of voice.

Augusta turned her eyes to the ceiling with a martyred look and turned away.

'That's what's meant by shutting them up. You have to admire it,' Billy whispered to his neighbor.

This latter, less pink and a little less attractive to look at, but more serious, responded with no more than a smile. There was between the two brothers a kind of natural complicity that had its own customs and laws and interdictions. In contrast to the frivolous Billy, Fred took everything seriously, especially his role as the eldest. A promise of corpulence to come rounded the lower half of his narrow, matt, white face with its energetic features, a strong nose, a thin mouth and uncompromising jaw. The intelligence of his eyes was striking, but they gave away no tenderness.

'If I were you,' he said eventually in a calm voice, 'I'd watch my language. Otherwise you risk a little sermon from Uncle Will on sacrosanct Southern courtesy. Aunt Augusta tells tales and bears grudges.'

'Bah,' Billy said with a laugh, 'don't you get fed up of playing the Southern gentleman with his unassailable good manners?'

'No.'

'What do you mean, no?'

'No, because that's the way it is.'

'Fine, fine. Let's not argue, but I've often dreamt about free Tomo Cha-chi who had Savannah under his protection. I would have liked to have Indian blood in my veins.'

'Or Negro, perhaps.'

'It's not at all the same thing. If you think that's funny . . . Pass the jam down this way.'

Fred obeyed immediately.

'Here's the pot of Georgia syrup to make peace with my little brother as Tomo Cha-chi did with Savannah. If I were Tomo Cha-chi II, I would smile and compliment the squaw. Augusta looks as if she's on the warpath.'

'I'd rather die first.'

As if she understood what the two whispering boys were saying to each other, Augusta enveloped them in a look of fury, and then once more turned her back on them.

'No mistaking it,' Billy breathed into his brother's ear, 'she's trembling in advance for one of her little girls over-excited by food. Just look how they're jumping up and down in their seats as they whisper . . . I wonder how she managed to give birth to our most agreeable little cousin, for the mother is no Venus.'

'There is a majesty about her.'

'Do you think majesty attracts men?'

'You think too much about such things, Billy. You have a fire in your veins.'

'Agreed on the fire, not on the rest.'

The young ladies in question were three in number and their *joie de vivre* was not in doubt. As if to take part in the celebrations, their curls jostled around those chatty, charming little heads. Mildred, the daughter of Augusta and Cousin Josh, was blonde and distinguished by the peremptory tone of her high-pitched voice and the warlike confidence of two forget-me-not blue eyes. It was she whom Billy considered the most interesting, but the two others in their youthfulness were close rivals and he declared that they would pass muster in a year or so.

Suddenly Mr Hargrove's bass tones rang out and dominated the conversation and, with a common accord, everyone fell silent.

'Young ladies over there,' he began, 'you forget that at table children should be seen and not heard, not even in whispers. This little liberty is of no consequence, or my name is not William Hargrove, but today is no ordinary day. We are welcoming your cousin from overseas. Show her around the house in accordance with all the rules of Southern hospitality.'

With the slowness which was part of his character, he then got up as if by degrees and said grace, the brevity of which found favor in the ears of all, for a speech addressed to the Lord was always a possibility to be feared.

There was a scraping of chair legs on the tiles and all went their separate ways amidst a chatter of soft and drawling voices that Elizabeth was happy to hear, because to her they seemed reassuring. She was used to the sharper, more clear-cut intonation of her native land, and the somewhat languid music of the speech here made her smile. She followed her companions in their pale frocks. Elizabeth was a little ill at ease but gracious nevertheless in hers, which needed a few alterations, and they walked straight ahead, doubtless res-embling four flowers, towards the beginning of the great avenue.

There her gaze became lost between two rows of giant oak trees whose topmost branches merged to form a vault. Here and there in the distance thin rays of sun filtered through the dark greenery, casting golden patches on the gray earth as if to measure the improbable length of this tunnel. It was in vain that the little English girl's eyes searched in wonder-ment for the end of it. It seemed like a dream walk to the ends of the earth. One could walk for days on end under the protection of the almost motionless foliage. Between herself and this density where life rustled imperceptibly, between these enormous trunks and the little outsider, there existed a mysterious affinity that she was aware of in the depths of her being without being able to explain it to herself.

They walked for a quarter of an hour between the trees, all chattering at once; but Mildred's voice carried more authority than her cousins':

'This is the finest avenue in the district. Uncle Will has had all the moss torn off to make it look exactly like an avenue in England.'

'But we have moss in England,' said Elizabeth vivaciously, 'and it's very beautiful, it's like velvet.'

Laughter greeted this protestation.

'Our moss isn't at all like yours. You'll see.'

Having arrived at a path that turned away from the avenue and plunged into the grass, they stopped, as if with regret.

'It's forbidden to go any further,' Susanna said.

'Because this little path crosses over all the meadow and goes as far as the wood.'

'No one goes to the wood,' said the timid and piping voice of Hilda, who blushed as if betraying a secret.

Mildred explained in a professorial tone:

'No one except Uncle Will, alone or with Miss Llewelyn. He on horseback, she in her donkey cart. Miss Llewelyn is afraid of horses. But they don't go that way very often.' A few seconds' silence followed, as if to accommodate some mystery, then Mildred resumed: 'If you look over to the right, you can see the wood, all gray and almost without leaves.'

'It's called the Wood of the Damned,' Hilda suddenly blurted out, unable to restrain herself any longer.

'You'd do better to hold your tongue,' said Mildred.

'Why the Damned?' Elizabeth asked.

Mildred supplied the answer immediately in an angry voice.

'It's the servants who call it that, we don't know why and Uncle Will isn't very keen on our talking about it. Let's go back to the house, shall we, Elizabeth?'

Slowly they resumed their way, less talkative than on their way out, for the heat was becoming more powerful. Birds exchanged distant calls; the gap between question and answer made them sound rather melancholy.

And suddenly the vengeful cry of the cicadas rose up in the pale blue sky.

Hilda sighed and touched Elizabeth's hand.

'You should have come sooner,' she said. 'The days were still so cool three weeks ago.'

'They arrived last night,' said Mildred. 'I heard them early this morning, but they quiet down a little at sunset. It's like that everywhere in the South, you'll get used to it.'

'You'll be offered all kinds of ices,' Hilda said. 'My

favourite is blackberry. What's yours, Elizabeth?'

Elizabeth answered in vague terms that she was not very sure. As she approached the plantation, she kept her eyes fixed on the house; until now she had not seen it from a sufficient distance to be able to see what it was like, but now, from the end of the avenue, it seemed to her a dwelling of fairy-tale gracefulness. On its right, as on its left, plane trees that were twice its height skimmed the roof with enormous branches, making it appear minute. But with each moment that passed as they came closer, its increasing size revealed the perfect beauty of its simplicity. Completely white, it consisted of a single cube-shaped building girded with two verandahs, one of which ran round the ground floor and the other, supported on slender columns with Greek capitals, round the single upper story.

Never had Elizabeth seen such a house and the effect was such that her admiration was mingled with feelings of confusion that she did not admit to herself. The least talkative of her companions, Susanna, with jet-black curls, came up to the young foreigner. She was tall and slim and looked at people and things with a seriousness beyond her years, and her deep black eyes seemed almost always motionless.

'Are you pleased, Elizabeth?' she asked softly.

The answer did not come immediately.

'Yes.'

'Pleased, but a little apprehensive, aren't you?'

'Oh, everything is so different . . . That's all, I'll have to get used to things.'

'Everyone is very fond of you. If you have any little problems tell me. It seems that Mademoiselle Souligou is coming this afternoon to fix your dress until they take you to Savannah.'

'Mademoiselle Souligou?'

'Yes, the seamstress, a very nice old Free-woman.'

'Souligou is a witch,' interjected the peremptory voice of Mildred, who had overheard the last words. 'All West Indians are witches.'

'She's not a witch,' Susanna said, 'but she is nosy and you must not talk to her. Uncle Will doesn't wish it. What's more, she expresses herself so badly in English . . .'

'She mixes up English and French,' said Mildred, 'but she ends up by knowing what she wants to know. Do you speak

French, Elizabeth?'

'No, not really.'

'She'll jabber away in her own language. Her parents were from over there. She'll ask questions.'

'I shan't answer.'

As she came close to the great black outline of the magnolia, she furtively pressed her mouth to one of the flowers whose perfume made her smile. A thought that she did not dare to express aloud went through her mind:

'Who knows if I won't be happy here?'

3

M ildred had decided to go for a ride on horseback in the countryside, so it was her sister Susanna who took upon herself the task of helping Elizabeth explore at least part of the house. Hilda wanted to join them, but was dissuaded with difficulty.

Without pausing, they crossed the gallery, the tall, narrow mirrors of which reached up to the complicated scrolls of the cornice. Semi-darkness reigned everywhere and their eyes could only make things out as if they were somehow shrouded in mystery, for from early morning onwards these treasures had to be protected from daylight by drawing heavy dark green blinds. Consequently Elizabeth held Susanna's hand, and she guided her steps, speaking in her low and quiet voice.

'You'll gradually get used to the rather weak lighting. The door near the stairs . . . you can't see it properly yet, but that's where Uncle Will's office is. You won't go in there very often. No one is allowed to disturb him, except for a lady in gray whom we occasionally see in the corridors. Maybe you've already met her, not terribly young, rather fat, but she walks quickly.'

'Was she at breakfast? There were so many people there.'

'No, she never has meals with us. It would take time to explain, but she has always been here. She doesn't belong to the family. We'll go upstairs now. Can you see the bannister?'

'I don't need it. I can see now. My room is up there on the right.'

'Very good, but I'll keep hold of your hand just the same. We won't make any noise as we go past your mother's door which is next to yours.'

'I know. Mama must be sleeping. This morning she told me she didn't feel well. In such cases she takes laudanum.'

'I hope she doesn't take too much.'

'Oh no. The ordinary dose the apothecary prescribes.'

'Naturally she's very tired.'

'She's unhappy.'

The simplicity with which this sentence was spoken seemed to strike Susanna, for she fell silent. The steps creaked so loudly beneath their feet that the two girls stopped from time to time as if breaking the silence would have frightened them.

When they finally came to the top of the stairs, they slid past Mrs Escridge's door, then past the following one and reached the end of the corridor that was so dimly lit because its windows looked out onto the verandah.

'You would think the house was empty,' said Elizabeth. 'There isn't a sound.'

'It is more or less empty for the moment, on this side. Nearly all the bedrooms overlook the great avenue. You were given the quietest ones.'

She almost regretted this sentence as soon as she had said it. And indeed she added almost immediately:

'. . . The quietest and also the pleasantest.'

They had reached a right angle in the corridor.

'Would you like to go round via the verandahs? Everyone is downstairs at this time. It will be more fun than walking along corridors of closed doors.'

Elizabeth had not been able to comprehend the itinerary she was being made to follow, and becoming progressively more intrigued, she gave her consent.

'We'll go through my room.' Susanna said. 'It will certainly not have been done, but it doesn't matter. This is my door. The next two are Mildred's and Hilda's. All the girls on one side,' she added with a laugh.

'What about the boys?' Elizabeth asked innocently.

'Downstairs. On the ground floor, next to Uncle Will,' said Susanna laughing more loudly. 'He likes to keep an eye on them. But does that interest you?'

'Not at all,' said Elizabeth, her cheeks red.

'I was joking,' said Susanna, 'but let's go in.'

The sun was not yet beating down on this side of the house, and the shutters of the high windows were sufficiently open to allow light to pass through the whiteness of the curtains. With great delicacy Elizabeth released her hand from Susanna's.

'And where shall we go now?' she asked.

'To see one of the prettiest rooms here, right down there we'll turn right.'

From their gilt frames, at regular intervals along the wall, immobile personages watched them like inquisitive people at their windows. Many were dressed in the old-fashioned style with wigs which powdered the velvet of their shoulders with hoarfrost. Some were in black, with their necks swathed in wide silk scarves.

'The family,' Susanna said lugubriously.

Elizabeth slowed down attentively before all these unknown people.

'Oh,' said her companion, 'you'll see them so often . . . all English. They become boring after a while. Uncle Will will tell you about them.'

'Oh, that one!' Elizabeth stopped and suddenly said. 'I think he's very good-looking, don't you?'

'Don't admire him too much. He was handsome in his youth, then he became one of the hardest judges in the whole of England: what they used to call a hanging judge.'

'Oh!'

'Yes. A distant cousin. He made fun of the condemned before sending them to the gibbet. That's something Uncle Will won't tell you, but the family knows about it.'

'Uncle Will looks so kind,' Elizabeth said with a slight hesitation in her voice.

Susanna looked at her with a smile.

'I can reassure you on that, Elizabeth, Uncle Will is very

good.'

'I didn't say I was afraid of him,' Elizabeth said crossly, 'I'm not afraid of anyone.'

'Of course. People only have to see you to be convinced of that. We're there.'

They had in fact come to the very end of the corridor and now found themselves in the spacious area that led on from it. Light filtered through the muslin of the curtains as if through a mist, but fully lit up a door smaller than all the others and painted light green.

It was in front of this door that Susanna stopped.

'You won't tell anyone I brought you here, will you?' she asked her with her hand on the brass knob. 'It isn't exactly forbidden, but Uncle Will prefers us not to talk about it. Do you promise?'

'Promise.'

They went in. The room was oval, of modest proportions, but decorated from top to bottom with delicate branches of gilded foliage running along the cornices and framing panels in which mirrors dulled with time barely shone. There was no window, a single rounded opening in the middle of the ceiling was blocked by a thin layer of alabaster and in the pale yellow light that was shed from this height the detail of the decorations could be gradually made out.

Susanna closed the door without a sound and then said aloud:

'You could scream in here and no one would hear you. Even with their ear to the door.'

Elizabeth was looking around her, given over to quiet amazement that consisted in part of a vague feeling of insecurity but also the pleasure of a mysterious adventure, when a surge of good sense raised an objection:

'People would hear if there were a window.'

'There has never been a window.'

'What about the keyhole? You could listen through the keyhole.'

'Can you see a keyhole?'

'Oh no, I can't. I hadn't noticed that.'

'The silence comes from something else. There's a secret.'

'Then what is this little room used for?' she asked after a while.

'Nothing. Uncle Douglas says that's why it's so pretty.'

'I don't understand.'

'Oh, that's the kind of thing Uncle Douglas says, strange things.'

'So anyone can come here when they want? You need only push the door.'

'Yes, but no one comes in. You couldn't stay here five minutes.'

Elizabeth's eyes began to shine.

'Ah, a ghost, perhaps?'

Susanna burst out laughing.

'No. You'll be disappointed, but there is no ghost in this house.'

'I should like to know why one couldn't stay in this room if one wanted.'

'You wouldn't want to, and that's all I can tell you. And then everyone has seen it as you can imagine, it's of no interest to anyone, but we don't talk about it. We must go now. I'd be sorry if we were found here.'

Returning to the corridor, they followed it as far as a place that was darkened by closed shutters, and they slowed down a little as if plunging into darkness.

'The sun is on this side now, but the house will stay cool until evening.'

After a slight uncertainty that doubtless came from the effort of getting used to the half-light, she took Elizabeth's hand and the two of them moved on rather quickly past a door almost indistinguishable from most of the others.

'This is Miss Llewelyn's room,' Susanna said. 'She lives a little apart. She has her meals in her room.'

'I haven't met her yet.'

'You'll see her for certain. She's the lady in gray I was telling you about. Don't speak to her too much – you won't feel like it, what's more.'

'You sound as if you don't like her very much,' Elizabeth said with a laugh.

'Oh, I've nothing against her, but it's true I don't like her very much.'

'Why not?'

'I don't really know. She's a bit strange. But you're inquisitive, Elizabeth!'

'Excuse me.'

Susanna suddenly burst out laughing and gave her a kiss on the cheek.

'I feel we're going to get on well,' she said.

Elizabeth smiled politely and did not answer.

There was a brief silence during which Susanna ran her fingers through her shoulder-length black curls and re-arranged them.

'Perhaps we'd do well to go back down,' she said. 'People will be wondering where we are. My mother especially. She always wants to know what I'm doing — as if I were still a baby. It's a bit ridiculous.'

'My mother's a bit like that with me.'

'Shouldn't you go back to her?'

'I think she's sleeping.'

'In your place . . .'

'Right, but you'll have to take me as far as her door. I should get lost in all these corridors.'

'Oh, you'll find your way quickly enough, come on.'

Together they retraced the way they had come, but without exchanging a word. It was only at Mrs Escridge's door that Susanna opened her mouth and whispered:

'You must find me a bit too much . . . Elizabeth?'

Elizabeth raised her eyes and looked at her seriously but in a way that was still rather childlike.

'Oh no, Susanna.'

'That's the first time you've called me Susanna.'

'Really? I wasn't aware of it.'

'Yes, really. Don't take that nice present away from me.'

'A present . . . I don't understand.'

'Forget it. It's my way of speaking. Everybody gives me to understand that I'm different from other people. Here you have to be like other people. See you later.'

She moved quickly away and, as if rooted to the spot with surprise, Elizabeth listened to the hard, harsh sound of the steps beneath her feet.

4

She knocked at the door with two fairly discreet taps in the secret hope that they would remain unanswered and that she too would be able to go back downstairs with a quiet conscience, but she did not have long to wait. Mrs Escridge's voice, harsher than usual, ordered her to enter.

At first Elizabeth could make out nothing in the half-light. The closed shutters allowed only a faint light to filter through, a ray of which fell on Mrs Escridge's slippered feet. The girl moved in that direction:

'Mama' she said.

'"Mama,"' Mrs Escridge imitated. 'You've remembered you have a mother and that she is here. I have been waiting for you for hours. What is the meaning of all this conspiratorial whispering I've been hearing at my door? Who were you with?'

'With Cousin Susanna who showed me round the house.'

'While I die of sadness between these walls you go for a walk, chattering in the corridors. I love you very much, Elizabeth, but you are heartless.'

'Forgive me. I thought you were asleep.'

'I did sleep.'

'Did you take something?'

'Yes indeed, as you say, I took something, thirty drops. It didn't prevent your mother from narrowly escaping death last night.'

'Oh!'

'Yes, "oh!" Didn't you hear me calling you?'

'I was asleep.'

'You were asleep, naturally. I don't hold it against you. Don't stand there looking at my slippers like a half-wit. I know they are frightful. Find a chair. I need to talk to you.'

The girl's eyes got used to the uncertain lighting; gradually she saw the furniture emerge from the shadows and become solid forms: a vast chest of many drawers, and in a corner a four-poster bed adorned with white lawn hangings. After her mother's dramatic summary of the night she had spent, she had expected to see sheets and blankets in tumultuous disarray, but everything was in place and the bedspread carefully arranged.

Finally she came across a heavy chair that she pushed to a respectful distance from the imposing rocking chair where Mrs Escridge sat enthroned among cushions.

'Come closer,' the latter said.

Elizabeth drew nearer.

Leaning towards her, Mrs Escridge suddenly cried out:

'What on earth is that dress you are wearing?'

'Cousin Minnie made me put it on, on account of the heat.'

'On account of the heat! Go and open the blinds and let me see.'

Her insides gripped with fear for what might ensue, Elizabeth went over to the window and pushed the shutters a little, allowing a thin ray of light to get through.

'More than that,' Mrs Escridge ordered. 'Don't try to hide.'

The small trembling hands obeyed and light rushed into the room with a vengeful fury.

Mrs Escridge looked at her daughter for a moment without saying anything.

'I would have been too hot in my kilt,' Elizabeth said as if to exorcize the worrying silence. And she added:

'There are alterations to be done.'

'Turn round.'

The girl obeyed, holding in the pleats around the waist with her fingers.

'Alterations to be done,' Mrs Escridge repeated through clenched teeth.

'A seamstress is coming shortly,' Elizabeth whispered plaintively.

She feared that her mother would demand a return to the hard-wearing warm skirt of good British wool, but she was in for a surprise.

'Not bad,' Mrs Escridge said in a gentler tone.

There was a silence and then she sighed.

'Evidently you could not refuse.'

'It was offered so kindly.'

'An act of charity. The first, Elizabeth. From now on everything will be given us out of charity. Tactfully, of course, but that doesn't change our position at all. Charity down to the last morsel of bread.'

'Oh Mama!'

'There's no "oh Mama", that's the way things are. The polite condescension of the rich . . . They themselves don't realize it. You'll see. And then their pride in these regions, their South . . . You can feel it just as you can smell the earth.'

Her features hardened in her elongated face framed by wisps of black hair, and she continued her speech with a somber air.

'Tell yourself that you come from a family that is more ancient than theirs on your mother's side, and don't let yourself be put upon. But we are their poor relations.'

Dressed only in a nightdress that covered her completely down to her feet, she might have looked comical if the volume of this white fabric had not made her look vaguely like a tragic actress expounding on her misfortunes.

Her voice became quieter.

'I'll not conceal from you,' she continued, 'that I dislike this country. I already feel as if I've been here for years. I'm suffocating. Can you hear the cicadas? It's enough to drive you out of your mind. Doesn't it ever stop? Everything is unfamiliar here. This morning a big fat black woman came to make my bed. A slave. I could tell from looking at her that she would have slit my throat if she'd dared, like in the West Indies.'

'In the West Indies?'

'Leave off the West Indies. After the black woman came a white one.'

'Doubtless it was Uncle Will who sent her to you.'

'Well built and low slung, playing the lady in her gray dress, but common with it.'

'Miss Llewelyn?'

'She introduced herself, but I've already forgotten her name. Have you seen her?'

'No, but they told me about her.'

'Who is she?'

'I don't know. She doesn't belong to the family.'

'I should hope not, but she made herself at home in my room and never took her eyes off me. She said she'd have an English breakfast sent up to me. I don't want her and don't need her. At one point she tried to ask me questions.

Me! And she has a way of looking at me that I cannot abide. I want to see no more of her.'

She took a palm-frond fan from a small table at her side where a glass, a carafe of water and a red-labelled bottle were to be seen. She began to fan herself with a sharp gesture.

'This stupid fan. It only stirs up the hot air. Close the shutters, close them completely.'

Elizabeth obeyed immediately, but not without some difficulty as the heavy shutters moved slowly on their hinges. Again there was darkness in the room and the girl groped her way towards the rocking chair, guided by the large white mass of her mother's nightdress.

'You can go,' the latter said. 'No, don't kiss me, I'm all sticky. Tell them downstairs to leave me alone.'

'But what if you need something?'

'I don't need anything. I have all I need.'

'Mama, be sensible.'

'That's enough, Elizabeth.'

Step by step in the shadows, the girl moved away and finally stopped with her hand on the door knob. In the silence she could hear the slight sound of the palm fan that her mother was waving, and the strange thought crossed her mind that summer after summer, until the end of her days, she would hear that barely perceptible rustle of a palm frond.

'Are you still there?' her mother suddenly asked.

'Yes. I'm going.'

'Don't be late going to bed. You'll come and kiss me before you put your light out.'

'But of course.'

Having closed the door behind her with consummate care as if leaving a sick-room, Elizabeth went down the sumptuous curved staircase; this alone spoke of opulence. 'Poor relations' . . . Those unforgettable words accompanied the girl who was terrorized by the least thing in this new life of hers, and at each step she felt like apologizing for putting her foot down on the red carpet.

Her first concern however was to set about finding Uncle Will to tell him that her mother would not put in an appearance all day. She found him settled in a corner of the long gallery behind a newspaper. After hesitating for a moment, she went up to him.

The paper fortress was lowered and thrown to one side with a big smile and the usual jollities. There then followed what the little English violet feared. With her eyes closed in horror, she again had the impression that her face was disappearing into a thorn bush.

When he had let her go she blurted out:

'Mama wishes to remain in her room all day.'

Mr Hargrove nodded his head anxiously.

'Very good, my dear. I'll let Miss Llewelyn know. The best thing for you would be to join your young companions until it's time to go to dinner. They are scattered about.'

5

*L*uncheon (which was called dinner) was taken at two o'clock in a very large room, so long that it called to mind a gallery. With the shutters three-quarters closed, the high windows gave the room only just enough light, pleasantly filtered through the impalpable muslin of the curtains. The floor, paved with smooth tiles, gave an impression of coolness, and on the damask tablecloth the profusion of silverware cast a note of celebration and magnificence.

This was Elizabeth's impression also. Used as she was to the old, more modest dwelling where she had spent her childhood, she was rather taken aback for a moment at the entrance to the dining room, and Cousin Minnie had to take her by the hand and lead her to her place at table.

Seated now between Mildred and Hilda, she looked around her like some animal caught in a trap, for if the breakfast had disconcerted her a little, the 'dinner' promised to be more intimidating yet. All this ceremonial was for a purpose, but there were new faces making their appearance:

a slim young man dressed in black who was the boys' tutor. He was on Aunt Augusta's right, having bubbling young Billy as his neighbor. Opposite him, on the girls' side, sat a woman of about forty with a serious and gentle expression who was evidently in charge of the girls.

There was mild excitement amongst the others present, who began to speak almost all at once. The newspapers from the capital had just arrived. Elizabeth's naive eyes were dazzled as they ran over the precious stones, emeralds and sapphires that sparkled on the women's fingers, then she wondered why at each diner's place an ice cube floated in a large crystal glass full of water. Each one had his own, and the little cubes were beginning visibly to decrease in volume. That was amusing.

The conversations ceased all of a sudden when two servants in white placed before their master a joint of meat in a great blue and gold porcelain dish. Mr Hargrove then stood up as if for some religious ceremony, took up an impressively long knife and, as was the office and privilege of the master of the house, set about cutting up the sirloin of beef with a delicacy and adroitness that all the family admired. In a flash of memory, Elizabeth thought she could see her father at the far end of the table, going through the same motions, with the same gravity, and was surprised by a terrible yearning for her homeland.

'As thin as lace for me,' said Laura's soft voice.

'As if I didn't know,' muttered Mr Hargrove.

The tastes and demands of each had always been known to him, and people were silent as they watched him. But when everyone was served, tongues were loosened as the rice came in, steaming and as white as snow in a silver dish.

'Father,' Uncle Douglas said, 'do you have any news? We'll never get anywhere with these chatterboxes from the North. For them action mostly means preaching to us.'

'Let them make their speeches. The Constitution looks after our rights,' said Uncle Josh serenely.

In their turn the women let their voices be heard.

'The Union, that's the only word on their lips!' exclaimed Emma.

'The Union has been in a bad way for fifty years, and it certainly won't last to the end of the century,' declared

Augusta in a peremptory tone.

Uncle Josh shrugged his shoulders:

'Why all this emotion? We have the right to leave whenever we like. I'd like to know who could stop us.'

'They'd try force,' said Douglas.

'What force? They don't have an army.'

Once more Emma launched forth into the debate as she cut up her meat:

'South Carolina has already threatened to leave the Union.'

'Secession, they're talking about it everywhere in the South.'

'Secession!' exclaimed Billy suddenly with his cheeks aflame. 'Why not? I'm in favour of Secession.'

'Billy, be quiet!' roared Mr Hargrove who had said nothing until this moment.

In the silence that followed this unexpected explosion, he continued to cut slices of beef with a somewhat majestic slowness and in a calm voice he added:

'The way I see things, the Union seems to me necessary. Don't tell me that I'm an Englishman and that I think like an Englishman . . . A slice, Augusta? . . . No? There is some truth in it, I grant you, but my heart is with you.'

'No one doubts it, sir,' said Uncle Josh whispering approval.

Fine flights of oratory were a Southern weakness and something of that nature seemed imminent in William Hargrove's voice, which had acquired a gentle tremor.

'Despite everything,' he continued, 'let us imagine the secession of Georgia. How could she face the world alone?'

There was a general shout in reply:

'Not alone! All the South with us!'

Mr Hargrove did not flinch, but his usually pink cheeks turned white. Very deliberately he put the long knife back in the great dish and said to the servants standing behind him:

'Take it away.'

'Frankly,' he said, 'I don't care much for dinners that turn into parliamentary sessions. I am of the opinion that we should take advantage of the good things that Providence has put on our plates. Billy, I shall have something to say to you at five o'clock in my library.'

'I'll be there, sir,' he answered resolutely.

'Today,' Mr Hargrove resumed with a smile, only part of which could be distinguished beneath his mustache, 'today is not just any day. It is the first young Elizabeth will spend under our roof and I fear you may have frightened her with your shouting, but we are going to try and make her forget that and make her feel happy amongst us. An indisposition deprives us of her mother's presence. I deeply regret that.'

'We too,' politely interjected a few scattered voices.

The cake that came at the end of the meal to put the seal on this casualty of a celebration was appreciated down to the last crumb, a generous portion having been put to one side for the cook. It was in truth enormous and it had taken two servants to carry it on its silver dish. Round and covered with white icing, it was welcomed amidst a buzz of admiration from the ranks of the young.

'My word,' said Uncle Douglas, 'it's dreadfully like a wedding cake.'

'Or rather a birthday cake,' said Mr Hargrove in a lively manner. 'What is your exact age, Elizabeth?'

'Sixteen,' said a voice half strangled with emotion.

'Well, we shall celebrate Elizabeth's sixteenth birthday,' the master said, wielding a giant-sized knife.

'Come on, Father, short and to the point,' said Uncle Josh with a forced laugh, for he felt that all this jollity had a false ring to it. 'We are all sufficiently greedy as you very well know.'

'I obey,' said Mr Hargrove, and he started to cut slices in which multicolored candied fruits shone in icing that looked likely to be heavy.

A sweet wine was served at the same time, so light that the children were granted the pleasure of it along with the adults. A product of the local area, it was made with wild plants in accordance with a recipe that had been a jealously guarded secret for generations, and its taste was not recognizable to even the most discerning palate, but the older people politely drank a quarter of their glass and the young ones asked for second helpings, which were not granted through fear of seeing them fall into drunkenness. Mr Hargrove's principles were as strong as his beverage was weak.

When he judged that the moment had arrived, Mr Hargrove got up as if to make a speech, but he simply said these few words:

'Ladies, you will be pleased to take a rest, I am sure. Josh and Douglas, you'll not refuse to join me in the smoking room. I received a port yesterday that has been round the Cape and is waiting for us.'

'Children,' called out Mr Hargrove in a schoolmasterly tone, 'you can go your separate ways, but I want no damage done. Elizabeth, my dear, remember that before supper you are to receive a visit from Mademoiselle Souligou.'

6

The smoking room, panelled with dark wood, was lit by a wide window overlooking the great avenue of moss-capped oaks. The half-lowered blinds concealed only a little of its grandiose beauty and it invariably attracted the attention of those who entered this low-ceilinged, smallish room. A mahogany table and four heavy armchairs in plum-colored velvet constituted the entire furnishings, not counting a kind of shepherd's crook made out of mahogany and placed on the table and used, as in England, for passing the port without having to get out of one's armchair.

The port was declared without equal, and cigar smoke was already swirling above the three silent men when William Hargrove opened his mouth and began:

'I've been thinking about what happened just now. That outburst . . . In future we should avoid talking about our problems at table, in front of the servants.'

'They didn't understand a thing,' said Douglas in a lively manner.

'Have no illusions,' Hargrove responded, 'they are more aware of what is going on than you think. This word 'secession' is most unfortunate.'

'Father, I would defy the most intelligent of our servants

to tell us what secession means. Negroes are like children.'

Uttered with tranquillity, this remark from Josh dropped into the silence.

'Perhaps,' Hargrove finally said, 'but they understand that something serious is going on.'

'So what? What are you afraid of?' asked Douglas.

William Hargrove put down his glass of port and assumed a majestic air.

'I'm afraid of nothing, my boy. The servants will keep calm whatever happens.'

'That's what everybody in the South is saying,' said Josh quietly. 'There will be no slave revolt. There will be no slave revolt,' he repeated as if to reassure himself.

'No one needs reassuring,' said Mr Hargrove in a firm voice, 'but we don't have to put our own eyes out in order not to be able to see. Slavery is a curse.'

'Undoubtedly,' said Josh, 'but it's not our fault. It was a gift to us from Europe, slave traders from France and England.'

'I know, I know,' continued Mr Hargrove, 'slaves were needed to put up with our climate and work in the cotton fields.'

Josh shrugged his shoulders.

'Slavery will die out gradually. At the moment there is a kind of fashion among some people, even the Russians, for setting their slaves free . . . In twenty years you won't see a single slave in our parts.'

These words provoked some emotion in Mr Hargrove, who raised his voice:

'But you need to have very great wealth to be able to give your slaves their freedom. It would mean ruin for many planters. We know of cases very close at hand. Don't you think that I too have been tempted to free my slaves?'

'Father,' Josh said, 'we're convinced of it, but your slaves love you, you know it. Everybody knows it. You do everything you can to alleviate their condition. You have an enormous family on your hands.'

'Freedom, what would they do with it?' Douglas asked. 'And where would they go? To the North to die of tuberculosis?'

Mr Hargrove's face darkened.

'There was one who ran away three years ago. He was a living reproach.'

His two sons could not restrain themselves from bursting into laughter at these words.

'The living reproach came back after a week!' exclaimed Douglas. 'And you didn't hold it against him.'

'Indeed. I ordered my steward to leave him alone. I was accused of weakness when I wanted to be humane.'

Josh lent towards him.

'Let people talk. Not a single one followed the fugitive's example. What more proof do you need of their attachment?'

'Very well,' Mr Hargrove suddenly said, a little annoyed. 'My personal problems are of no interest to the world. Let's talk about something else. I make no secret of the fact that Mrs Escridge's presence in the house causes me some concern. She will be a difficult person.'

'She's been here barely a day,' said Josh. 'Give her the chance to get used to everything here.'

'She is still full of England,' said Douglas maliciously. 'You ought to be able to understand her. She owes her presence here to your generosity.'

'Oh, she would have managed to sort herself out more or less in London, but I was thinking in particular of the future of her little girl. I tremble at the idea of her being under the guardianship of that irresponsible woman.'

Mr Hargrove put out his cigar and stood up.

'It's nearly four o'clock; I am going to rest in my library. We'll see each other again at supper.'

Having said these words, his heavy tread reached the door and he disappeared.

'He's not pleased,' said Douglas.

'Neither am I, Douglas, but I keep my thoughts to myself.'

'I'll follow your noble example, Josh,' Douglas said with a loud laugh. 'Let us go and rest too.'

7

Much against his will, young Billy remembered that at five o'clock he was to go and find Mr Hargrove in his library. The temptation to forget was very strong, but, fearless as he was, he did not dare take on the master of the house. Although the latter never raised his hand to anyone, a dressing-down from him was in itself something to fear. The cutting tones and the language of classic precision used on these occasions inspired in the victim a desire to be swallowed up into the earth. A stormy outburst of blows would have been less humiliating, but such was not the style of this man, whose apparent gentleness was actually like that of iron. There was nothing inviting about appearing between those walls. Nevertheless, Billy flicked away with his hand the lock of hair that swept across his forehead and strode resolutely down the corridor that led to the library door, but he stopped short.

The sound of voices reached him, muffled somewhat by a thick layer of padding that, from the inside, protected the silence of this place that was ordinarily forbidden to all except Miss Llewelyn.

Billy immediately recognized this privileged person's Welsh accent shouting out something, of which only shreds containing the word *proof* reached his ears.

Now more attentive, he made out the end of a sentence repeated with angry obstinacy:

'. . . always proof . . . what proof? you always need . . .'

This verbal torrent that nothing seemed likely to stem did not cover up the sustained but dull rumbling of another voice, and suddenly there was a silence that was more alarming than what had preceded. Seized with terror, Billy leapt backwards and moved off down the corridor along which he had come. This instinctive movement was fortunate for him, for the library door suddenly opened and William Hargrove appeared red-faced in the doorway.

'Billy!' he called.

With the artfulness of his years, the boy turned on his heels with an air of innocence.

'You can go,' said Mr Hargrove drily. 'I'm busy at the

moment. Go and walk in the avenue. I'll let you off this time, but never behave at table again as you did today.'

These words were barely uttered when the door was slammed shut and Billy was able to withdraw, relieved but highly intrigued.

While this was going on, quite a different scene was taking place at the other end of the house, in a room furnished with a large work table and two heavy wardrobes supported on ball feet. In addition to that there were two upright chairs on which Elizabeth and Miss Pringle, the girls' tutor, sat facing each other.

Amidst a shuffling of slippers on tiles a little old lady in a flowered cotton dress appeared. Rather bent with age, her head was nevertheless upright, revealing a face where wrinkles ran in all directions forming complicated patterns around a long pointed nose and a mouth elongated by a big motionless smile. In this gaunt, brown face shone two black pupils constantly darting back and forth out of curiosity, and her head was swathed in a thick kerchief of indigo blue, the pointed ends of which rose triumphantly like wings atop this tiny person who was evidently proud to be Josephine Souligou, West Indian and seamstress from Pointe-à-Pitre.

She stopped in the doorway with her eyes fixed on Elizabeth.

'Good evening, Mademoiselle Souligou,' said Miss Pringle with impatience, 'come in, don't stand there.'

'Good day, Miss Pringle, I've just got here, as you see.'

The accent was French and the voice gentle with an almost childlike inflection which would suddenly break and become harsh. She moved forward without taking her eyes off the English girl.

'Miss Elizabeth is a relation of Mr Hargrove's,' said Miss Pringle. 'She is going to live with us from now on and today you have to adjust her dress for her, which is a bit too long. Elizabeth, Mademoiselle Souligou is the seamstress of the household. I am sure that you will get on. I'll see you tomorrow morning, but if you have any questions . . .'

'None,' said Elizabeth.

'I have thousands!' exclaimed the West Indian woman.

'I'm sure you do,' said Miss Pringle, 'but that will be for another time, Mademoiselle Souligou. Good evening.'

'Miss Pringle's not talkative,' said Mademoiselle Souligou when she found herself alone with the girl.

She pronounced Miss Pringle's name in such a curious way, rhyming almost with *angle*, that Elizabeth would have been amused in other circumstances, but she felt ill-at-ease with this strange-looking old woman.

The West Indian woman suspected as much straight away.

'Don't be afraid,' she said broadening her smile. 'Here I'm known as "good old Souligou", because I'm always ready to lend a hand. And so this evening I'm to alter your dress a little.'

'But it's not my dress,' the girl said, not without some effort to get the upper hand of her discomfort.

'I can see that. Miss Minnie told me everything. She is very fond of you. Will you come a bit nearer . . . There, that's enough.'

Her shaky though fast-moving English finally removed Elizabeth's anxiety in spite of herself and she lowered her head to hide a smile. The seamstress noticed it despite all and exclaimed gaily:

'Laugh, Miss Elizabeth. If you laugh it means that you're no longer afraid of Souligou and we're going to be friends.'

Elizabeth blushed. This familiar overture disconcerted her.

'I assure you I was not making fun,' she said animatedly.

'There, there, Miss Elizabeth, I know that. I know everything. You're the young English lady they have been talking about for weeks. Mr Hargrove himself announced your arrival.'

'I came with my mother,' Elizabeth explained as if to minimize her own importance.

'I know that as well. Miss Liouline informed me.'

'Miss Liouline?'

'The lady in gray who's looking after her.'

'Oh, Miss Llewelyn!'

'Say it as you like. If I were you I wouldn't talk to Miss Liouline too much. But I'm chattering. We must get to work. Your dress is a disaster.'

This remark was followed by a worried silence in which only the rustling of material in the dressmaker's hands was to be heard.

'Not much to do,' she finally said, 'unless you take it off and I take it to my room.'

'I don't want to take it off.'

The firmness of her tone made the West Indian woman give a mischievous little laugh.

'Not English for nothing,' she whispered in French.

And she concluded aloud in English:

'Well, Miss Elizabeth, we'll try and put it all right here and now, but you'll have to be content with a big hem at the bottom, whereas I could have taken it in and made you look elegant.'

As she chattered away, she rummaged in the depths of the pockets of her multicolored skirt and pulled out a pair of scissors in a case and a small box.

'Turn round a bit. Are you patient?' she asked as she knelt down in front of the girl.

'I will be.'

Pins were inserted where they were needed with surprising rapidity.

'Turn round ... turn round,' ordered the West Indian woman as if playing some game, and Elizabeth, whose face had become a little pinker, obeyed and bit her lips.

Now the thread was running through the pale blue lawn and the seamstress found her tongue again.

'It seems that they're going to take you to town the day after tomorrow to a certain Madame Clementine from Paris,' she said, 'but she's never set foot in France, the little thief. But Paris, you see ... people round here are such *gobeurs* – how do you say that in English?'

'I don't know.'

'Never mind. She has a reasonable choice of models that she says are copies from over there. It's young Billy's Mama who is to take you to Savannah in the carriage, for she has a shopping list as long as your arm. I heard that from Miss Susanna who is very fond of you, what's more everybody at Dimwood likes you. I hope they won't forget the presents.'

'The presents?' Elizabeth asked.

This word retained a certain magic in the ears of the little girl she still was in some respects.

'What! Do you imagine the servants don't expect a little

something from the big city? Not all of them, of course, but each one has the right to a present in turn. Mr Hargrove doesn't want to see any discontented faces at Dimwood. Last time old Bessie got a fine cotton skirt with every color in it and a big pack of tobacco for her pipe, because she smokes a lot. They call her the farm grandmother. Be kind to her. Be kind to all the servants and they will like you, they'll smile at you, but if you're proud . . .'

'I'm not proud,' exclaimed Elizabeth, who thought she detected the shadow of a reproach.

'Don't move, please, else I'm likely to prick you. I didn't say you were proud, I said: "if . . ." And what I'm telling you is important. The servants will judge you quickly.'

'How will they judge me?'

'Try and understand: they will form a good or a bad opinion of you. If their opinion is not good, they will always be respectful, but there will be no place for you in their hearts, and when contempt slips into a black man's heart, that's bad. I know, I'm a West Indian and Mr Hargrove knows it too.'

She fell silent. Her silence seemed just as worrying to Elizabeth as the flow of words that had been suddenly interrupted. What was going on in that old head bent before her? The two wings of the indigo kerchief pointing upwards no longer seemed comic. The girl had the feeling that everything was changing around her, and that a vague threat hung over this still mysterious plantation. The Negroes . . . They frightened her mother.

'You say nothing, little one?' said the somewhat gentler voice of the dressmaker.

Elizabeth was too disturbed to notice the shift from 'Miss' to 'little one'. She was in need of reassuring words. The dressmaker was ready with them:

'There is nothing to fear from our servants here because no one upsets them. Mr Hargrove is very strict on that point.'

'Cousin Susanna told me that he is very good.'

'Good? Yes. Good because he is prudent. Everyone learns to be prudent in these parts. There, I've finished. Turn round. Again. Not too bad. No longer ridiculous in any case.'

'Was I ridiculous?' exclaimed Elizabeth.

'Not you, my beautiful child, but that skirt that was flopping round your heels.' She got up with difficulty and sat down. 'As I see you now,' she continued, 'you'll have the boys after you in less than a year.'

'The boys?'

She said this in the same way that she had said: 'Presents?'

'Yes indeed. The boys. Any one would think I was talking about strange beasts.'

'No, I assure you.'

'Did you know any over there in England?'

Elizabeth hesitated.

'Yes, one,' she said with a laugh. 'A childhood friend, from the nursery. We played together.'

'And was he fond of you?'

'Oh yes. Me too . . . well, yes.'

'Did he cry when you left?'

'Cry? No, what a strange idea, Mademoiselle Souligou! Boys don't cry. Not in England.'

'I was forgetting. What about the girls?'

'No. It would be ridiculous. And in any case, all that was just for a laugh!'

'Here you'll find boys who might make you cry, Miss Elizabeth.'

'I should like to see them try!'

'I know about things, my dear. I have premonitions at certain times.'

Instinctively Elizabeth, who had remained standing, took a step backwards and sat down in her turn.

'You have relations throughout the South and more cousins than you can count. Did you know?'

'Not at all.'

'They've told you nothing. On your father's side you're related to the Siveracs of Louisiana. Some of them come this way sometimes. There are others too. All the great Southern families are related. I've seen young and old come to Dimwood. The Siveracs have the reputation of being amongst the finest.'

'"The finest",' Elizabeth repeated mechanically.

'Ah, that interests you, Miss Elizabeth! It's all very well to be English, but you're still human.'

This last remark was made in French with a smile that completely filled the lower half of the old face. Guessing at a hint of irony, Elizabeth blushed.

'I don't understand,' she said.

'But you speak a little French.'

'Very little. What I learnt at school.'

'Well, if young Siverac comes on a visit to Dimwood, he'll teach you a few words. The whole family has remained French. But he's dangerous.'

'Dangerous!' exclaimed Elizabeth naively. 'I have no desire to see that gentleman.'

'Oh, he's not a murderer! He won't hurt you.'

Now the failing light was making way for great expanses of shadow which seemed to be coming down from the ceiling and the girl was almost unable to make out the features of the West Indian woman.

The latter bent over towards her a little and said softly:

'They'll bring a lamp and we shall take leave of each other, but we shall meet again, and if anything goes wrong, ask kind Souligou's advice. Be careful with the boys. Listen. I'm going to teach you a little French song that could still be heard at the court of Louis XVI.'

And in a voice imitating the tones of childhood, she sang a tune in an old fashioned style of which Elizabeth could only remember the last verse:

> End is here
> And wolf doth wait
> My pretty little one
> At his gate.

In the twilight, these words lodged in the back of her mind and without knowing why she felt a tug in her heart.

A servant came in and placed a lamp on the table.

8

'Supper' was at sunset and was less lengthy than 'dinner', also calmer. The heat of the day had rather wearied everyone and even their appetites seemed languid. Only the turtle soup, served cold, received acclaim and little attention was paid to most of the rest of the meal. Faithful to a custom he never broke with, Mr Hargrove said the evening prayers and said them at length, to the song of the tree-frogs timidly announcing nightfall.

In a voice he kept in reserve for such moments, he thanked Heaven in an abundance of words, and a multiplicity of repetitions which ended on an impression of mystery, for the more he went on, the more subdued and almost plaintive his voice became in the presence of the elaborate dessert that remained uneaten by these fifteen people with their hands folded, fixed in the immobility of boredom, each one lost in the private dreams of his own heart and senses.

In her dress shortened by Mademoiselle Souligou, Elizabeth again felt ill at ease amongst these men and women dressed for the evening with some care, the women in white frocks, the men in black, their necks imprisoned in stiff collars and heavy silk ties. And all around the table jewels shone in the soft light of the oil lamps.

The final *Amen* liberated the diners, the 'children' into a kind of desperate rush towards the door, the ladies with their customary dignity that led them to the drawing room, while the men headed with slow steps towards the verandah where the usual political conversation awaited them, amidst the smoke of long cigars.

Seated between his two sons, Mr Hargrove kept silent for a moment, and the floor began to creak beneath the rocking-chairs. The night was dark, but the trees in the great avenue stood out against the sky where the first stars glittered.

Almost in a whisper, Mr Hargrove dropped the name Calhoun, which had a sinister ring to it. A long pause ensued, then Douglas muttered:

'I admire him, but I find him more and more worrying.'

There was no immediate comment on this sentence, the

chairs continued to rock and the tree-frogs to weave the thin veil of their incessant song. It seemed that the great peace of the night was seeking to silence the lips of men.

'Why worrying?' Mr Hargrove asked finally.

These words fell into the black hole of silence as if in search of oblivion, but this time they were rescued by Josh who gently asked the awful question:

'Can't you see that he's tearing the country in two? His speech in the Senate was a provocation.'

'He was defending our rights magnificently,' said Mr Hargrove on reflection.

'As early as 1811 he thrust America into a war with England,' said Douglas rather more animatedly.

'All that was long ago,' said Mr Hargrove, and the faintness of his voice made the long ago seem even more distant. 'Things are settled because they have to be settled. But let's talk about something else. Can you see Orion's shield above the trees?'

'Yes.'

'Well, when I am travelling and think of home I say to myself: "Our dear Dimwood is under Orion's shield."'

'I wonder how it could be any different tonight,' whispered Douglas, annoyed by this display of sensitivity.

'What did you say Douglas?' asked Mr Hargrove.

'Nothing, sir. I think that Dimwood is indeed situated beneath that constellation.'

Either because she was still ashamed of her dress on account of Mademoiselle Souligou's stern judgement on this borrowed outfit, or because she wanted to be alone in order to reflect on all that the West Indian woman had told her, Elizabeth did not join the 'children' who ran off towards the great avenue.

Avoiding the drawing room where the women were chattering, she took a few steps along the verandah, but suddenly heard the grave, slow voice of Mr Hargrove and retraced her steps immediately. Undecided and unhappy, she ended up getting lost in the corridors. What she feared above all, without wishing to admit as much to herself, was meeting a black servant, but she also dreaded the moment when she would have to go up to her room and see her mother.

After a few minutes' coming and going she found herself in the large entrance hall and took refuge, as she had done the day before, in that corner of it which was least well lit. There she tried to recall certain details of the day. She had the confused impression of having been passed from hand to hand, from one person to another, each one revealing to her something about the life of the plantation. Sometimes it was Susanna's somewhat sad voice that she heard, but more often and more insistently it was the name Siverac and the warning about that dangerous man. It seemed to her that since her departure from England everything had been conspiring against her desperate desire for happiness. It was in vain that people smiled at her. She was afraid at Dimwood. Only pride prevented her from bursting into tears.

For several long minutes, she remained motionless and as if transfixed by the silence and solitude in the position of one who waits, when suddenly she was seized by a kind of panic. Horror welled up in her, such as comes from the abyss and takes possession of every human being at some time during his time on this earth. Aged barely sixteen years, she had a brief but shattering intuition that the world around her was merely an illusion, concealing something else, a reality that it was impossible to grasp and impossible to deny. This lasted the length of a heartbeat and seemed interminable. She wanted to scream but remained dumbfounded, falling almost immediately into the deep sleep of total exhaustion.

The sound of steps woke her, and she saw Aunt Laura coming towards her. In her pale gray dress with a ruched bonnet on her head, there was a singular dignity about her and she would have seemed intimidating were it not for the gentleness of her regard.

One could not say she was pretty. Her face was too long and her features too large for that word to be appropriate, but her nose was very straight, dividing her serious physiognomy in two and creating a perfect symmetry. The dimness made her look beautiful and a less kind light sometimes conferred on her an almost masculine ugliness, but at no time could one take one's eyes off that face, radiant with a profound goodness. For all this she remained the most mysterious person at Dimwood. She spoke exceedingly little and although she sat on her father's right at meals, he paid no attention to her at all. His only insistence was that she be near him, but it was rare for them to exchange even a few words. For a long time now the particularity of these circumstances had ceased to be a source of surprise. People accepted without comment both the silence that separated these two and their places at table that brought them together. It was probable that she suffered on account of it. As for him, it was impossible to know. He was judged summarily: good and, in other ways, incomprehensible in his motives. Aunt Laura was liked, but there hovered around her an atmosphere of melancholy smiles, and on the moral plane she lived a solitary life that was respected by all.

'Elizabeth,' she said with a laugh, 'I woke you up! Forgive me, but I've been looking for you for some time. I didn't expect to find you there, curled up like a cat in an armchair. You're tired?'

'No, oh no. I don't know why I fell asleep.'

Nothing of what had preceded her falling asleep remained in her memory, other than an inexplicable sadness, and she looked seriously at the smiling woman.

'Is there something worrying you?' asked Aunt Laura.

'Nothing,' said Elizabeth, smiling in her turn. 'I think I must have been dreaming.'

'If that's all it is! We'll chase your dreams away with a walk, would you like that? But I have something that's worrying me. I went up to your mother's room to see if she needed anything. I knocked at her door and she would not let me in. She called out that she wanted to be alone.'

'I'm not surprised. She told me the same thing this morning.'

'It's only natural that she refused to let me in. She barely saw me last night, but do you not think that you could have a try? I admit I am rather worried.'

'She told me that she would see me when I went up to bed. It is useless trying to talk Mama round.'

'I'll not insist. So let's go for a walk around the verandah.'

'Mr Hargrove is there with his sons.'

'I know, but we won't go that way. But you shouldn't be afraid of my father. He is very fond of you.'

'I am not afraid of Mr Hargrove,' the girl said proudly,

'but I don't want to disturb him. I think he's talking about the news . . .'

'Ah, the district is buzzing with news and it's been going on for thirty years. People are fond of political discussions in these parts – shouting. All that noise at lunch . . . I felt sorry for you, I fear it may have upset you.'

'No.'

She was lying. Pride kept her mouth shut.

'Very good,' said Aunt Laura, 'I'm proud of you.'

As they chatted, they had crossed the great entrance hall and come to the north side of the verandah. The air was cooling down and smelt good.

'We're on the garden side. You can't help but notice our gardens even without seeing them . . .'

She took the girl by the hand to guide her in the semi-darkness.

'It will be lighter in a few moments,' she added, and they went forward on to the verandah.

With their elbows on the balustrade, they remained silent for a moment, then Aunt Laura lowered her voice and said:

'There are so many flowers down there that their perfume reaches up this far. Roses, jasmine . . . Can you smell them?'

'Oh yes,' said Elizabeth, made as happy by these exquisite perfumes as if her own Devonshire had been given back to her. 'But why are the gardens so far away?'

'Ah, that's the way it is. Can you see them now? The moon is lighting them up a bit, but it doesn't allow you to see the beautiful colors. It all seems very dark, a great mass of green.'

'You might almost think it was a little wood.'

'Yes, a little wood. The plants are amazingly high at that point and there are paths going in all directions. You could get lost in it.'

'Cousin Susanna told me that she would take me there before supper, but I was with Mademoiselle Souligou.'

Aunt Laura remained pensive for an instant.

'Before supper,' she finally said. 'The best time is at nightfall when the sun is not so hot. All the same, I should like you to go there with me. Susanna is charming, but I know all the varieties of flowers better than she does, and there are so many of them . . .'

'Couldn't we go there now?'

'It's too dark now and you'd see almost nothing. And then we don't go into the gardens at night. My father doesn't like it.'

'What a shame!' Elizabeth could not help whispering. There was no reaction to this exclamation.

'Would you like us to go and sit down?' said Aunt Laura gently. 'We'll be fine in these rocking chairs. I hope you like them.'

'A lot. I have one in my room, I never tire of rocking in it.'

The naivety of this remark made Aunt Laura laugh.

'You're already quite American,' she said gaily. 'Sit down there in this chair close to mine and here we are . . . The air is still warm.'

She handed her a palm fan, of which there were many on the verandah.

With vigor and childish pleasure Elizabeth began to wave the fan close to her face. The anxieties of the day faded away and now everything seemed pleasantly new to her. For the first time since her arrival she experienced that mysterious joy of complete confidence in a human being. Aunt Laura's charm had such an effect on her that she would have liked to divulge to her both her disappointments and her confused hopes, but an instinctive reticence held her back. As if in answer to that mute appeal from a still arid heart, the voice spoke out in the shadows:

'I should like to see you happy, because that was not the case with me.'

She was silent for a moment and then continued:

'The world is a cruel place, Elizabeth. I shall be here to protect you if I can.'

'But Aunt Laura, what is there to fear here?'

She hesitated for a second and then added, forcing a laugh:

'Mama is afraid of the Negroes.'

'My dear girl, it's not a question of Negroes. They are simple souls. If you like them, they'll like you, and they can tell straight away if you like them. Smile at them. Each one will end up telling you his name. And then you mustn't forget it. If you forget a servant's name, he'll be hurt. I know them well. They won't do you any harm. But I wasn't thinking about the servants.'

'Oh, I'm not afraid of anything, you know!' Elizabeth said joyfully, getting bolder as her confidence increased.

'You're talking like children from your part of the world. Like myself at your age. We're both of English stock. So many people here are. Nevertheless, you'll find that cruelty I was talking about everywhere. It's not limited to Dimwood. The whole world is a dangerous place.'

'Dangerous . . . It seems we have a cousin from Louisiana who is dangerous.'

Aunt Laura quivered and looked worried.

'Who told you that, Elizabeth?'

'Mademoiselle Souligou.'

'That's absurd. I know him, a gentleman just like everybody else. What's more, I shall be here to protect you. I shall speak to Mademoiselle Souligou.'

She got out of her armchair with a brusque movement.

'It's getting late, dear Elizabeth. The moon is coming up and we shall be able to look out over a good part of the plantation. You can see a lot better now. After that I think you should go to your mother, don't you think?'

'I'd have preferred to stay longer with you, Aunt Laura.'

'That's very kind of you, but we shall see each other often.'

Once more they stood with their hands on the balustrade. The moon's cold light fell on to a vast expanse of garden, woods and ground faintly colored by the first growth of spring. Whereas the sun's glory is triumphant in a burst of sound, in this light that seemed to give voice to the silence, everything took on a phantom-like appearance but was as precise as in a pen-and-ink drawing. One's first reaction could only be to remain silent, so as not to disturb a sleeping world, then lips formed timid words.

'How big it is,' Elizabeth whispered.

'Yes, always a bit more than I remembered and more . . .'

She interrupted herself with a sigh.

'More what?' the girl asked.

'It doesn't matter, my sweet. It's the moon that makes you see things differently, more seriously. You can see the gardens clearly now.'

'Yes indeed. The long paths and the spaces surrounded with trees. Grass everywhere and big flowers. How beautiful they are!'

'The servants water them when the sun goes down. A delicious coolness lingers ... You'll hear the tree-frogs singing tonight. They come from the water over there, and go up into the trees, can you see?'

Elizabeth could indeed see a long pool whose surface shone with metallic reflections in the moonlight. The funereal magnificence of cypress trees could be made out in the depths of the stillness.

'Those trees are so old we don't know their age,' Aunt Laura said. 'The Indians lived over that way.'

'How do you know?'

'There is in the vicinity a little tree with a trunk twisted into a spiral. The Indians used to do that. They would choose a very young tree, barely upright, and make it into that shape. Later it would serve as a marker in their explorations all over the country. The tree would grow, deformed but no less vigorous. They'll show it to you in the daylight.'

'But I can see it quite clearly, it's at the end of the pool, on the right-hand side. It's very ugly. You'd think it was a dwarf.'

'Elizabeth,' cried Aunt Laura, her voice changed and full of emotion, 'what eyes you have! How can you see as far as that? It's true, at your age I could as well.'

She let a few seconds pass without saying anything, then said gently:

'It's late now. We'll go back and you'll go and wish your mother good-night.'

'Yes, but first of all tell me what that big black wood is over there.'

Her question was somewhat cunning, for she had recognized the Wood of the Damned that had been pointed out to her in the distance that very morning.

'That's Dimwood,' Aunt Laura said rather rapidly.

'Dimwood? Like the house.'

'Yes, they kept the name, I don't know why. The dark wood. Nobody goes there. It's very ancient, but the trees aren't that fine. They should be cut down, since nobody ever walks in that direction.'

'But Aunt Laura, there are people in that wood, I can see them very clearly.'

Suddenly taking the girl by the hand, Aunt Laura began to speak impatiently and in a low voice:

'There is no one, Elizabeth, it's an illusion caused by shreds of moss hanging from the trees that move about in the least breeze.'

'Yes, but I can see men walking up and down as well.'

Aunt Laura uttered a nervous little cry:

'My girl, I tell you it's an illusion. Everybody knows about it. There can't be anybody there. In the thirty years I've been on the plantation, nobody has ever been seen over there. So I beg you, let's say no more about it and go in.'

Without another word they left the verandah and went into the house where not the slightest sound was to be heard.

'They are all taking the air in the great avenue,' said Aunt Laura. 'Do you want to join them or go upstairs now?'

It seemed as if she wanted to make up for her earlier severity, for as she spoke, she stroked Elizabeth's hair.

'I prefer to go to bed,' she said. 'I'm tired.'

'Well, I'll go with you as far as the stairs to be sure you don't get lost. It's a real maze . . .'

They went through several small rooms that Elizabeth did not know, then the long entrance hall where she had slept. At the bottom of the stairs Aunt Laura stood still and said seriously:

'I'm very fond of you, my girl, and if ever you're in distress, I mean distress . . .'

This unfinished sentence echoed strangely in the silence, and the girl raised a worried face towards the woman whose great dark eyes were shining with tears.

'Come to me,' the voice almost implored, 'but for the love of God, always tell me the truth.'

Elizabeth's cheeks were suddenly suffused with red as if they had been slapped. She immediately understood that Aunt Laura had not believed her when she had spoken about the men in the woods.

'I always tell the truth,' she said without hesitation.

Without answering, Aunt Laura touched her cheek with a kiss, smiled at her and went away.

9

*E*lizabeth had barely entered her room when she heard her mother calling her.

Mrs Escridge was sitting up straight in the rocking chair. In her hand was a palm fan that she put down on her knees as soon as she saw her daughter come in. Her hair was carefully arranged, and she was wearing a dress of puce-colored taffeta that she put on only in exceptional circumstances; she remained perfectly still and looked at Elizabeth in silence.

'What have you been doing today, Elizabeth?' she asked in a calm voice.

The girl was seized with emotion and felt her throat tighten, for there was something unusual about her mother's behavior that made her anxious, but she overcame this worry and gave a calm account of her day, taking care not to include certain details. In substance she told her everything: meals, conversations, the dressmaking session, and the short night-time walk on the verandah with Aunt Laura.

'And who is this Aunt Laura?'

'Ah, she is Mr Hargrove's daughter.'

'So it was she who came to knock here. She did give her name, but that is of no importance. She may very well be the daughter of the master of the plantation, but I had given orders not to be disturbed. But why are you still standing there looking guilty? Try to be more natural with me. I hold nothing against you. Come on, sit down.'

Elizabeth took a chair and sat opposite her mother, who was looking at her attentively.

'So all in all,' the latter continued, 'you didn't leave the house except for a short walk in what you call the great avenue. Did you feel happy to be here?'

'In all sincerity, not very happy yet, but I think I'll get used to it.'

'As for me, I shall never get used to this country and I feel so unhappy that I should like to be dead.'

These last words were launched like a cry and she stood up brusquely. Standing immobile and in full regalia while the rocking chair behind her swung to and fro all alone with a kind of frenzy, like that of an animal ready to pounce, she began to speak slowly without looking at her daughter, but with her eyes fixed on the door.

'I've been thinking a lot in the course of this interminable day', she began. 'My great mistake was thinking that we would find a bit of our homeland in this country that once belonged to it.'

She held in one hand a handkerchief with which she wiped the corner of her mouth from time to time. Her whole character had something majestic and rather frightening about it, and her daughter contemplated with horror this woman who was her mother and whom she believed to be going mad.

Mrs Escridge did not raise her voice, rather she expressed herself with precision and restraint. Elizabeth would have thought that she was reciting a text learnt by heart, if those well articulated sentences had not disclosed the chaos of her thoughts.

'I want to go back to England,' she continued with assurance. 'I have countless friends there who will be only too happy to put me up. And whatever you do, don't let them tell you that I'm going out of my mind. That's the reason they'll give you for not supporting my efforts. But I shall do things myself and I shall leave. You see that I dressed for a party this evening. I'm celebrating my flight to freedom, my escape, in advance, Elizabeth. For I am already being treated like a prisoner. There is that woman in gray with her keys, who springs up from nowhere to keep an eye on me, and all those Negroes hovering around me. On heavy silver trays they bring me things I wouldn't touch for anything in the world.'

'But Mama, they would so much like you to come down and dine with us all. Mr Hargrove . . .'

'Be quiet and listen. Be on your guard against William Hargrove. He is a cruel man. Your father told me some terrible things. In Haiti . . . But never mind about that. I only wrote to him because he was under an obligation to come to my aid. I knew too much, you see? Now, do you see this little bottle?'

'Yes, Mama, it was half full yesterday evening.'

'I've no need of your remarks. I must have another one. I feel ill. If I'm going to die, I want to die in England. So, you're going to get me another bottle like this one.'

'Laudanum . . . '

'Yes, laudanum, and if you tell me again that the bottle was half full yesterday evening, I'll slap you. You can tell them that I have pains in the head enough to make me scream. So I want you to bring me another bottle tomorrow morning. Do I make myself clear?'

'I promise to do all I can.'

'I want none of your promises. You must obey and bring me another bottle. Last night a black servant came in here with a saber. He didn't dare touch me. I looked him straight in the eyes and he disappeared, but I am in danger. I want to leave. As for you . . . if you have the heart to let your mother go without you, I can't stop you. Think about it.'

'Oh Mama, do stay!' exclaimed Elizabeth.

'Don't argue with me. I am determined to leave this frightful country. You think it over, I'll give you all the time you need. If you stay, you'll be brought up in luxury like a little American Republican, they'll find you a planter for a husband and you'll live surrounded by slaves in a suffocating climate. And now go to bed. You may kiss me.'

Elizabeth made as if to throw herself into her mother's arms, but the latter did no more than proffer a cold cheek and said:

'No emotion. You'll say your prayers. Did you read your Bible this morning?'

'No, Cousin Minnie came to my room . . .'

'I don't know who Cousin Minnie is, but you can read a whole chapter before going to sleep. And I shall know if you don't. Good-night.'

These last words were spoken in the clipped tones that Elizabeth knew well and, far from affronting her, restored her confidence, giving her hope that her mother was regaining control of herself. Indeed, behind this woman's severity was concealed an unreasonable attachment to the only child she had by a husband she had loved too passionately.

If you have the heart to let your mother go . . . — she gave herself away there, Elizabeth thought with an intuition beyond her years when she was alone in her room.

Her throat was gradually becoming less tense. She undressed and flung far behind her the blue dress that she was starting to dislike. Now, in the long nightdress that covered even her feet, she sat on the edge of her bed and read a chapter of the gospel, but her attention wandered.

In accordance with the principles handed on by her mother, she was looking for words that she could apply to herself and that could be discovered by reading attentively, but she found nothing, whereas usually the book spoke to her. So that cross which was to be carried every day was not for her, just as she was beginning to feel its weight without recognizing it. Only the verse about reading the signs of the times struck her by its strangeness. If her mother questioned her tomorrow, she could quote that passage.

Her Bible closed, she knelt at the foot of her bed and, with her head in her hands, buried her face in the blankets. In a muffled voice she recited the Lord's Prayer in that archaic English that enhanced its mystery: . . . *and lead us not into temptation* . . . What temptation? . . . *but deliver us from evil.* Deliver her from evil? Why deliver her? Was she a prisoner of evil? What did it mean, that black, frightening word? She didn't dare ask herself what it meant, but a long inheritance of tormented faith raised questions inside her at times of uncertainty, and she had felt alone and worried since leaving England. Aunt Laura had reassured her for a moment, but those sudden curt words about the men in the wood . . . And after that her mother's solemn and icy delirium . . .

She got up, blew out her lamp and, in a kind of panic, rolled herself in the sheets, childhood's ultimate refuge against the forces of darkness that she imagined to be surrounding her. With the blankets pulled up around her ears, she slid almost immediately into the depths of dreams.

Suddenly she found herself on a road bordering a field where sheep were grazing. Lambs were leaping in the air and making her laugh. Big white clouds were moving across an intensely blue sky with majestic slowness, and she recognized her own Devonshire home from one of those fine summer days when joy descends to the earth. Her father was holding her by the hand and talking to her as they walked, but she couldn't grasp any of his words. She understood only that the house was still theirs and that they were going there never to leave it again. It was not yet visible. It was hidden behind a long, low hill, crowned with a thick wood, and the treetops barely moved in the warm breeze. Although she did not feel in the least bit tired, it seemed to her that they had been walking for hours, that the hill was not getting any closer, and that the same lambs were frolicking gaily around the same ewes. The clouds were not making headway either, although they were still moving. What reasssured her was the gentleness of the hand that held hers and squeezed it every now and then. Only her father had this way of telling her he loved her, with affectionate little squeezes. It was a kind of secret language that he had adopted. Words were superfluous. Moreover, his voice was becoming so indistinct that she was not listening. She waited for the hand to transmit another message, and suddenly she raised her eyes towards him, but saw no one, and that hand that had sent waves of happiness through her whole being was invisible.

She woke up soaked in sweat and threw off the blankets. The moon lit up half of the room with its icy light, loaded with silence. The dream continued with an appearance of reality.

Seized with a fear that penetrated to the very depths of her being, Elizabeth remained motionless for a long time, as if fascinated by fear. No effort of memory could restore to her those happy moments on a Devonshire road she had experienced a minute earlier. All that remained was the vague memory of the strong and gentle hand in which her own had rested.

Gradually the feeling of having left one world to enter another of tangible reality, cleared itself from her mind, and again she wondered why she found herself in this household where not a single object was familiar to her, where everything told her with blunt precision to leave. The walls wanted nothing to do with her, nor the furniture, nor those proud columns. Faces smiled at her in vain and voices sounded caressing; behind all that hovered the unspoken word "foreigner". They were fond of her, but did not accept her. They would have loved her all the more if she were not there . . . This thought made her laugh in spite of herself in her confusion. From her mother, from her breeding, she had inherited a relentless irony that helped her to get through difficult times.

All of a sudden she was tempted to find out what was going on in the room next door: whether her mother was asleep or, if awake, if she were reading or doing something else. She felt awkward about listening at the door. How many times had it been said in her presence that that was something to leave to the servants. She did it nevertheless, with her ear glued to the door frame . . .

Silence. Such was the humiliating reply.

Without making a sound, she got as far as the big French window that opened onto the verandah and, with her heart beating, she pushed the shutter with precaution. She thought she would die of fear at the slightest creak, but the hinges made no noise. Prudently she took one or two steps and, leaning forward, was able to see her mother's window: light showed through the slats and even more so through a gap between the shutters that Mrs Escridge had not closed completely. The curiosity of her daughter could thus be easily satisfied, but what audacity would have been required to take on someone who guarded her private life so jealously . . . ?

Elizabeth hesitated. She had the idea that if she bent herself double, there was less chance of her being seen, and even less if she crawled along. This was the solution she adopted, and a minute later her head was almost down at ground level, with her golden curls touching the floor and her gaze plunging forward into the bedroom.

First of all she saw the bottom of the puce-colored taffeta dress that her mother had not taken off, but a little shiver of horror ran down the neck of the young spy when she saw that the pointed toes of the boots, however little they extended from under the dress, were pointing straight at her. The golden curls were suddenly whisked aside.

There was a long silence and perfect stillness. Only the

timid, crystalline sound of the tree-frogs could be heard as it merged with the silence of the night. Then a whispering of taffeta announced that Mrs Escridge was moving, and then, as this noise became more distant, Elizabeth took another exploratory look around the room.

What she saw intrigued more than frightened her. Standing in front of the large mirror, her mother was putting on a lace-trimmed bonnet, the ribbons of which reached down to her shoulders. A clearly discernible smile lit up that face that was usually so serious. She seemed to be very attentive in arranging her black hair with her thin fingers beneath the rim of the fine cloth. From time to time she turned her head to one side as if talking to someone who could not be seen. Perhaps there was no-one there, for not a sound emerged from the room that Elizabeth could hear. Suddenly a great mocking laugh burst forth from the sycamores that surrounded the house. The strident tone froze Elizabeth's heart and made her mother turn towards the window.

The girl had just enough time to escape. She returned to her room in a tremble and flung herself on to the bed. A minute went by and then again the great croaking sound of merriment echoed above the roof. With her head under the blankets, Elizabeth remembered that Susanna had told her about a sinister bird that was often heard at night but was ignored. Now, in the imagination of the English girl buried in her bed, it was the starting point for crazy excursions into every possible domain of nocturnal horror.

She tried to still the beating of her heart by reciting softly the Lord's Prayer, but there again those strange words about deliverance from evil only increased her unease and, quite overwhelmed by the burden of emotion, she lost consciousness.

A hand stroking a tuft of her hair protruding from the blankets dragged her gently from a deep sleep. For no reason she guessed that it was her mother and did not move. Far from trembling, she felt herself overcome with a surge of childish tenderness, the like of which she had not experienced since those far-off years in Kent, and in the silence she heard these few words whispered sadly:

'My poor little Bessie.'

That was what her father called her.

She kept herself from stirring and waited for her mother to withdraw before stifling her sobbing in her pillow.

10

At dawn the birdsong from the woods reached her like some great call of delirious happiness. Almost at a stroke the great confusion of voices fell silent. The magic ceased. Like a disappointed child, Elizabeth embarked on her day. After she put on once more the humiliating blue dress, and, as eight o'clock struck, she stood at her mother's door and let a minute go by without knocking. Who would she find? She had not forgotten those words of whispered affection in the night, but she both loved and feared her mother at one and the same time. However, the calm voice that bade her enter restored her confidence.

Lying in bed propped up on three pillows, looking well and with the Bible at her side, Mrs Escridge greeted her in a calm voice. The room had not yet been tidied; but the puce-colored taffeta dress was carefully laid out on a sofa, like some grand lady feeling unwell, and revealed a certain degree of care and attention.

Elizabeth had barely entered when she noticed on the rug that little phial that she knew only too well, but the label was of a different color. She pretended not to have seen it.

'I suppose you slept well,' said Mrs Escridge. 'Come closer, so I can look at you. Good. I hope you keep for a good while yet your pink, healthy complexion from home, instead of that waxy white you see in Southern belles. But come closer. My word, anyone would say your eyes were red as if you'd been crying. Answer me.'

'Yes, perhaps a little.'

'Well, that's your business. It's no crime to cry so long as it is not in self-pity, which is a most ridiculous thing. I shan't question you. Now you're going to tell me the truth. You see this phial just by your feet?'

'Yes, I see it.'

'Empty, of course. Was it you who placed it on my bedside table in the night?'

'Oh no.'

Mrs Escridge took her Bible and put it on the sheet within Elizabeth's reach.

'Put your hand on the Bible. Obey me. Tell me again that it wasn't you who brought that phial of laudanum while I was asleep.'

Elizabeth placed her hand flat on the black book. How many times had she gone through this procedure, which was the only way to quiet her mother's misgivings?

'As you require it of me, I affirm that it was not I who put that phial there. What's more, I've never seen one with a white label. When will you believe me, Mama? I'm not a liar.'

'I know, but I like to be certain of things. This phial contains only a few drops. Barely the normal dose. The same as the port, which I swear has never been round the Cape.'

With a scornful movement of her hand, she pointed to an elegant crystal decanter, also empty, near her bed.

'All of it stintingly measured out, as if for a sick person to whom one gives medicine with prudent charity. So if it wasn't you, who came here?'

'I know nothing about it.'

'That woman who knocked at my door yesterday afternoon? Aunt Laura, you call her.'

'I know nothing about it.'

'Who then?'

'I really know nothing about it.'

'There's nothing to be got out of anyone in this house where lies abound.'

'I'm not lying.'

'I know, I know, don't keep on saying so.'

'I'll try.'

Suddenly she seemed to get a grip on herself and continued more slowly as if talking to herself:

'Moreover, why argue with people who have taken me

into their home with no obligation to do so? It is for the poor relation to keep quiet. They have good manners, that's something. You will make my excuses to William Hargrove, Elizabeth. I shall not put in an appearance today or tomorrow. Too tired. That's what you must tell them. Go and have breakfast and don't disturb me all day. There were too many people here in the night as it is.'

'Too many people, Mama?'

'You wouldn't understand. I was over there, I know, I'm sure of it. No, don't try to kiss me. I hate sentimentality. You'll ask them to give you some writing paper for me, some ink and a pen. A thick-nibbed pen like in England. You'll bring them to me this evening. And don't stand there like a statue. Off you go, my girl, but first pick up my fan which has slid under the bed. Then I can at least feel on my skin a tiny amount of air. Do storms never break in this hell of theirs? But off you go. I want to be alone!'

That morning, breakfast was fortunately much quieter than the day before. Elizabeth brought out the commonplace sentence about her mother's extreme tiredness and Mr Hargrove expressed his regrets, then launched into the prayer which was unusually long. The exchanges that followed were remarkable only for their inoffensive emptiness. Except for one or two attempts by Billy that were instantly quashed, nothing occurred to liven up the conversation, and the word 'politics' was not uttered. One needed to be an innocent like Elizabeth not to suspect at least that this most engaging subject had been banned by the master of the plantation for specific reasons, but the newcomer to Dimwood did not care to know about it.

Just as everyone was leaving the dining room, Mr Hargrove came up to Elizabeth and said:

'Would my dear little English violet do me the honor of talking with me in the library?'

And as he leant towards her, the girl was enveloped in the smell of Russian eau-de-Cologne with which he perfumed his whiskers, and this made her forgive Mr Hargrove the inane wheedling with which he addressed young people. This fresh, masculine smell brought her instantly into the presence of her father who used to cover his hands with it.

'Yes,' she said with a smile.

She was led to the library, which was an inviolable holy of holies for everyone except the severely guilty awaiting their punishment, Miss Llewelyn for reasons unknown, and Job, the servant responsible for tidying it.

Elizabeth had never seen a room like this, and for a moment her stupefaction took her speech away, as she turned her head from side to side at the sight of so many books.

Like walls of dark leather sprinkled with tiny gold letters, they occupied the whole of the space between skirting board and ceiling, producing a strange effect of suffocating beauty. The half-closed shutters and the big blind on the verandah assured the coolness of the air and darkened the room, but one soon became accustomed to the half-light that enhanced it all.

Mr Hargrove made Elizabeth sit down in a round-backed armchair while he seated himself on a more severe ecclesiastical kind of throne from a bygone age, and straight away he adopted a jovial tone to start off the conversation.

'Here we are, the two of us face to face, young lady, both of us English and so likely to get on, don't you think?'

'Oh yes,' she said politely.

'Don't be too surprised by all these books, don't get the wrong idea, I haven't read for years now. I like their company, but they've taught me to do without them. Do you understand?'

'Not completely . . .'

'I'll explain it to you some day. There's just one short row of poets from home and the Bible, naturally. I'm certain you read your Bible.'

Rather annoyed by this indirect question, Elizabeth let it drop into the silence.

'Don't you?' he asked with a kindly smile that turned up the corners of his mustache.

'Oh yes, Mr Hargrove.'

'Dear me, not Mr Hargrove, I beg you, but Uncle Will.'

Silence.

'Don't you?' he insisted.

Then something strange took place in this sixteen year-old girl, who had been so obliging until then: exasperation suddenly transformed her into someone else.

'You shall be Uncle Will, since you wish it,' she exclaimed in a fiery manner. 'But in my turn I insist: I shall no longer be your little English violet.'

A flash of anger came into William Hargrove's eyes; his pride had been wounded, but he gained control of himself immediately and burst out laughing:

'Good shot!' he said. 'I like the rebellious streak in you. We are indeed from the same stock, Elizabeth. Now listen to me. Do you know why you are here?'

'Because my mother asked you. I know all that.'

'Better and better. We are talking man to man.'

'Why man to man?'

'Well, like a man and a woman if you prefer. I'll watch my language. You and your mother are part of the family here. My only regret is that you arrived at a time when things are going badly and likely to get worse.'

'All that shouting at breakfast yesterday morning made me suspect as much.'

'That won't happen again but, for your part, do you know what caused that outburst? Have you any idea of the situation in this country?'

'None at all. How could I? I've only just arrived.'

'Your mother told you nothing?'

'No, nothing. I've never seen her with a newspaper.'

Mr Hargrove stood up and, with his hands behind his back, took a few paces to the far end of the room. Elizabeth had time to observe him unhurriedly and noticed the elegance of his pale gray suit, the jacket of which was edged with narrow black piping, opening on to a white waistcoat. Despite the irritation that this grave, graying man provoked, she admired him for remaining slim. In a way, this was the first time that she had looked at him.

He came back towards her and sat down again.

'I'm going to explain our problem to you – oh, as simply as possible.'

She put on her little girl look.

'I'll try to understand,' she said.

Thereupon he fell silent and looked at her attentively.

'Sometimes I feel that you don't like me very much, Elizabeth.'

'Oh, I never said that.'

'No, but as we are of the same breed and blood relations even, we understand each other without things being spelt out.'

This time she contented herself with turning an innocent face towards him and fixing eyes void of all thought on the deep, black eyes of her interlocutor.

'Be at ease,' he said. 'I'm going to give you a brief account of things. I can feel already that it will be inadequate, but here goes: the North and the South, which together form the Union, are in spite of everything, separated not, thank God, by a border, but by their climate. That's one factor.'

'Less hot in the North, I hope. Very, very hot here.'

'I believe that, like us, you'll become accustomed to it, my dear girl. You will see that this house remains cool even in the strongest heat. Dimwood is a kind of refuge.'

He was speaking rather more slowly; one felt he was anxious about what he was going to say, and bending his head a little, he lowered his eyes as if to examine the toes of his shoes. Elizabeth followed his gaze and noted the perfect shine on the leather and the well-turned foot. She discovered that she was curious about these details because she was bored.

'The South's wealth comes for the most part from growing tobacco and cotton. The North is industrial and needs what the South produces. Do you understand me?'

'More or less, but I must say that these questions do not interest me greatly.'

'Well, let's move on a bit more quickly. In order to grow cotton you need Negroes who tolerate the heat better than white people. They came from Africa, were shipped here by French and English companies. Did you know that?'

'Oh no. Those things were never talked about in England.'

'It's time that you knew about it. It was Europe who sold us the slaves.'

'Sold them!'

'Yes. There's no other word for it.'

'But what if they didn't want to come?'

'They were not asked. They were taken by force. There was no other way.'

Elizabeth's cheeks turned from pink to red.

'It's shameful!' she exclaimed.

'Well,' he said with a kind of rising intonation in his voice, 'I think so too. And I believe that nearly everyone here thinks the same way. For its part, the North bought them and then resold them to the South, on account of the climate, which was not suitable for black people. The North has forgotten that. Trading in slaves has been forbidden for a long time, but they are here and it's a nightmare for the South.'

'So why not send them home?'

'Everything leads us to believe that they wouldn't want that at any cost. With the succeeding generations, they have become attached to the land that they cultivate. They have to work, but they are well fed and looked after if they fall ill. They are cared for like children, and they end up loving us if we don't ill-treat them. Their savageness is lost through contact with us. All that can be summed up as the advantages of civilization. They are taught our religion and it becomes dear to them. In many cases, they add it to their own, that of their ancestors. Do you follow me, Elizabeth?'

'Just now you were clearer. I've lost sight of the problem.'

'They are dreaming about freedom, that's the problem. The freedom that we took away from them. You'll hear people say that there won't be an uprising, but they say it too often for it not to be always on their minds. They don't entirely succeed in convincing themselves.'

'So let them give the slaves their freedom back!'

'Some planters are doing so more and more. But you need to be very rich. Freeing ones slaves means ruin.'

He stopped. He evidently did not want to say any more, but Elizabeth's presence impelled him in a way that he did not understand. He had asked her to come into this room, and now he was wondering why. The image of a path blocked off by a gate kept coming forcibly back to him and he found the situation incomprehensible.

Elizabeth, for her part, remained motionless and, for the first time, felt intuitively that she was in the presence of an unhappy man, whose good humor was a show and his imposing confidence a pose. She looked at William Hargrove with a feeling akin to pity and gave him a timid smile. He trembled.

'Why do you smile, Elizabeth?' he asked with sudden severity.

'Did I smile at you?' she said. 'I hadn't even realized. What is wrong in a smile?'

'One doesn't smile without reason as you very well know. Is it something I said? Something amusing? I want to know.'

'I don't understand.'

He looked at her somberly.

'You are not being as open as you were earlier,' he said slowly. 'You're not the same person.'

'May I go?' she said, standing up.

Seeing her move towards the door, he seemed to emerge from a dream.

'Elizabeth!' he exclaimed, 'I have frightened you unintentionally. Stay, I beg you. I expressed myself badly. I thought you were making fun of me because I said that some planters were facing ruin through freeing their slaves.'

'Not at all,' she said rather curtly. 'On the contrary.'

'On the contrary?'

'Yes, on the contrary, I thought that was good.'

It was his turn to smile, almost as timidly as she had done a moment earlier.

'Sit down,' he said in a gentler tone. 'I have something to tell you that will make you understand everything in just a few words. I won't keep you long. People might wonder where you are, and look for you all over the house,' he added with a laugh as if making a joke, whereas this sentence revealed all that he sought to conceal from himself.

Elizabeth did not share his jollity but patiently returned to her place.

'Not far from here,' Mr Hargrove continued, 'there lives a man of constricted circumstances, or more exactly, who lives in shameful poverty. His house, which was formerly much admired, becomes more dilapidated with each passing year, and the surrounding land is reduced as he sells off plots in order to have something to live on. Together with his son he lives in the old homestead known as "Old Creek" that still retains some vestiges of its former splendor. His name is Armstrong.'

'He needs help.'

'You can imagine that we thought of that, but he won't

hear of it. Too proud. An Armstrong accepts charity from no one.'

'Charity!' said Elizabeth, remembering her mother's comments on this point.

'Why yes, charity. People don't like the word, but charity is out-and-out Christianity. Take away charity and what is left of the New Testament?'

Instinctively she felt that he was going to launch forth into a sermon, and she was right, because holding forth on religion provided relief for his conscience at critical moments.

'What about the son?' she enquired in a lively manner.

The reply came immediately, dry and to the point.

'The son is a good-for-nothing.'

'Can't he do something?'

'I told you the son is a good-for-nothing,' replied Mr Hargrove, slightly annoyed. 'We'll talk about him another time. What I want you to know is that where these two men live, there once prospered one of the finest plantations in the country. It was worked by nearly a thousand slaves, then one day, under the influence of an idealist . . .'

'An idealist?'

'A fanatic if you like . . . that crazy Armstrong decided to set free all his slaves, almost overnight. The price he got for his cotton allowed him to live comfortably for some time. His son, who was barely of age, helped himself liberally to indulge his pleasures, and then one day they had to think about giving up the land in ever larger plots. Having got over his noble act, Armstrong saw poverty advancing towards him, step by step, like the man dressed in iron that the Bible tells us about. He had never had any business sense and his lack of will-power was unbelievable. His steward, who had become superfluous, though competent and loyal, could doubtless have saved him if Armstrong's pride could have bent a little in dealings with an inferior. He was dismissed. Armstrong preferred to give in to his son Jonathan whom he adored. But I'm being long-winded, I'm boring you.'

'Not at all. How old is Jonathan?'

'That's a strange question, Elizabeth. Why do you want to know?'

'It makes the story more interesting,' said Elizabeth

candidly.

'Jonathan is a man devoid of all moral sense. He has stolen more than half of his father's fortune, lost it gambling or in the lowest forms of dissipation. All the families of the county find him odious on account of his pride. People avoid him, and with reason. I regret not having neighbors. May your paths never cross.'

Elizabeth lowered her eyes and murmured:

'I hope so, if he is as wicked as you say.'

'I'll make sure of it,' he said gravely.

Once more he was the William Hargrove of the slow voice and serious, but rather sad, eyes.

At that moment the tall, narrow clock filled the room with ten deep and well spaced chimes. With the final vibrations, Hargrove placed his fingers gently on Elizabeth's head.

'Off you run, my girl,' he said. 'You've been here too long.'

He opened the door, then, after hesitating:

'If they ask you why . . .' he suddenly said. 'But no, they'll ask you nothing. Try and find the "children". Off you go now.'

A little surprised at the brusque dismissal, she raised her clear, blue eyes towards him, and he found their innocence difficult to bear.

'Quickly now,' he said as he touched her shoulder, as if to push her away.

11

With the door closed once more, he went and sat down at his desk and put his head in his hands.

His stifled voice rose up in the silence:

'Oh God!' he uttered repeatedly, 'Oh God!'

Terror was the dominant tone in this prayer, but also

relief at a danger passing, as Elizabeth's steps moved down the corridor.

Until that moment his opinion of himself had not been over-flattering, but reassuring, insofar as he believed himself safe from upsets of a passionate nature. Transitory temptations did not succeed in disturbing a state of moral well-being as carefully arranged as a Victorian interior. People told him so often that he was good that, in the long run, he came to believe it, and was persuaded of being liked. Once or twice a month, when what he secretly called his 'natural impulses' emerged, to unbalance his equanimity (or his good mood), he would disappear from the plantation and spend a few days in New York, where there were always things to be bought for Dimwood. He would then come back home calmer and always affable.

Three days earlier, however, the arrival of Mrs Escridge and her daughter had dramatically upset everything. A carriage had gone to fetch the travellers from Wilmington station and, in the mauve light of dusk, that radiant little face had come as a surprise. In his confusion, he had failed to go down the steps towards the newcomers, as even ordinary politeness demanded. Instead he was rooted to the spot in stupefaction, and, with an unacknowledged joy, he watched that victim of fate climb up towards him like some prey offered up by the forces of darkness. This impression was so strong that he had to make an effort to watch Mrs Escridge, bowed by extreme fatigue, her heart full of resentment, mounting the steps of her benefactor's house. The whole body of this humiliated woman held his excessive generosity against him, crushed as she was by his gifts. And as if in a brilliant flash of light, he caught a glimpse of hell climbing up towards him, embodied in these shipwrecked souls, the one as much to be feared as the other, but for strangely different reasons.

Now, in the solitude of the library, he wondered with horror why God was leading him into temptation when he had sought to follow the Gospel in coming to the aid of a widow and an orphan.

His habit of seeing signs in everything made his heart beat faster, confronted with such a risk of condemnation. Throughout his conversation with Elizabeth he had for the first time in his life been aware of something or someone that was never talked about, because no one believed in it any more. He would not have been able to describe what he felt, except that he was not alone with that sixteen-year-old girl. On account of that, she made him afraid. He had never suspected that a man might tremble on the edge of the void at any moment whatsoever of his life . . . Indeed what other name could be given to the brusque intrusion of a non-being? The abyss . . . no. It was worse because nothing moved in that setting of old books and the tall clock patiently counting out the minutes that remained to be lived. Suddenly the indescribable was everywhere, consuming the air . . . Finding oneself on the edge of a precipice would not have been as hard as this. An eternity of damnation was settling itself where time had flowed freely an instant earlier.

In the monstrous theology based solely on the fear of God that he had constructed for himself over the years, he believed himself to be barricaded in against the devil, and preserved from divine wrath. He forgot that God is good. Unconsciously all his wild religious ideas were in turmoil. He had never been in love. His wife, who had given him three sons and a daughter, had inspired in him no other feeling than a somewhat satisfying indulgence. She was obedient and sensible and ran the house well. He asked no more of her. Her sudden death had not been a source of sorrow to him.

Solely by the power of a sick imagination, he had come to see a place of horror in this peaceful library where a girl had been listening to what he was saying. He did not dare to admit the stirring within himself of an attraction that he had no wish to understand. It was especially at that moment when Elizabeth smiled at him that he rose in fury against what he took to be a diabolical plot, and in it he saw a sign of what awaited him in the next world if he did not disentangle himself in time. Suddenly he saw Elizabeth as the instrument of a destructive power, and everything around him became an illusion of the senses concealing the reality of eternal fire, which he thought he could already feel burning into his soul.

He would have been incapable of saying how long this mental anguish lasted, nearly depriving him of his sanity. He measured time by the intensity of his suffering, but infinity is immeasurable. Through a kind of startled inner movement, he came back to his senses and his decision was taken. The hell he had invented for himself immediately faded away and the obsession calmed down for, as has already been noted, he had forgotten that God is good.

After supper that evening, he asked his two sons to follow him into a small sitting room reserved for the exchange of confidences. It was a charming, circular room in late eighteenth-century style, with chaotic garlands of flowers elegantly entwined around the cornices. This masterpiece of Italian stucco did not quite harmonize with the plum-colored, lavishly upholstered Victorian armchairs. The trees of the great avenue could be made out through the muslin drapes at the tall windows.

Josh, the more handsome of the two brothers, was wearing, despite the heat, a black velvet jacket that showed off to advantage his slim waist and the pale gray trousers, the latest thing in male fashion. His face with its bright complexion was witness to fresh air and a good digestion, rather than to intellectual or political preoccupations, but his blue eyes shone with a zest for life and a naturally carefree temperament, responsible for his good humor. With his upturned nose and perfectly white teeth, he still looked like a student, making it difficult to believe that he had a sixteen year-old daughter.

Douglas, his elder by one year, was of severe appearance and usually bore the look of a man disturbed in the flow of his thoughts. His slightly balding forehead elongated his narrow face with its dull skin stretched over an ascetic bone structure; this impression was intensified by his black pupils, shining from the depths of his shadowy and cavernous eye sockets. Tall and with the leanness of good breeding, he always held his head erect. A well-cut black suit was the final element marking him out as the aristocrat of the family, something expected of him, as if to compensate for the somewhat countrified appearance of his younger brother.

Between the two of them, William Hargrove's person spoke of prosperity, bearing the burdens of his state with a ponderous majesty, but there was something painful in the way he looked at things that raised him above the commonplace.

It was precisely what was to be read in the depths of his brown eyes that made his sons love him; on that point they were in agreement. They alone had an idea of the tormented state of this secretive man's soul, he who seemed so calm and so self-controlled.

Thus they listened after he had begged them to be seated.

'I need your advice,' he said in a voice rendered somewhat faint by emotion. 'From now on it will be you who will take care of young Elizabeth. As for me, I'm forced to admit that I'm incapable of it. I have the impression that I frighten her. It's not good for me to talk to her.'

At that moment the two brothers exchanged a glance that concealed the same thought.

'You already have too many worries,' said Douglas animatedly. 'It's quite natural for us to take charge of Elizabeth, isn't it, Josh?'

'I quite agree,' answered Josh. 'We'll look after her.'

'That has taken a great burden from me, and I thank you for it, but I owe you an explanation.'

'It's not necessary, we understand,' exclaimed Josh bemusedly, fearing a speech.

A change came over William Hargrove's face.

'What do you understand?' he asked, blushing somewhat.

Douglas intervened immediately:

'We understand that the girl's entire upbringing needs to be tackled afresh and that she has to be trained in the ways of the South. That needs patience – and time.'

'You will not find her easy,' Hargrove said, reassured. 'Her well-behaved look conceals a determined character. She has her own ideas and sticks to them. In my talk with her I came to realize that she's a little abolitionist through and through. Maybe she does not know the word, but there is no doubt about her opinion on the matter. Slavery makes her indignant.'

'We'll take her to see the Bishop of Savannah,' said Douglas.

'The Reverend Elliot comes across very well on that particular institution of ours. He'll be able to enlighten the girl's religion. He brings out first-rate arguments.'

'But she's no longer a little girl,' said Hargrove, turning his head a little to one side. 'She speaks like a woman.'

Joshua felt a surge of affection that was perhaps unfortunate.

'Don't worry, Papa,' he said. 'She's not stupid, she'll adapt almost without noticing it, for she is kind, charming even . . .'

'Charming,' Hargrove repeated with a martyred look.

Somewhat haughtily and disdainfully Douglas let a few notions drop into the conversation.

'In good time we'll dig out some presentable husband for her. The South is full of well-bred, handsome young men.'

'Not just anybody,' Josh exclaimed. 'She's as good as us.'

'Better,' Hargrove murmured sadly. 'On her mother's side she comes from an older family.'

'There is her mother too,' said Douglas sententiously.

Hargrove uttered a groan.

'Was I right to have her come?'

They were of a single voice in replying:

'You couldn't do otherwise, after that letter . . .'

'Oh, I could just as well have sent her all the money she needed to live comfortably in England. I easily have the means to do so . . . The riches of the South are inexhaustible, thank God, and she is dying of homesickness.'

'You'll never be able to give her back her little Tudor mansion,' said Douglas crisply.

'We'll make her forget that Tudor mansion,' exclaimed Josh. 'By being considerate and attentive . . .'

'You are even more naive than usual this evening, Josh,' said Douglas. 'She's wandering about in her mansion all the time. That's what the laudanum is for.'

'I'm not against the use of laudanum in moderation,' said Hargrove. 'It's not forbidden.'

'Indeed, Scripture never mentions it,' said Douglas sarcastically.

'Douglas,' his father said, 'you are talking like a fool . . . The woman is suffering. If she finds relief in a few drops of laudanum, she'll get what she wants. I've taken it myself in bad times.'

There was silence. The sun was going down, casting through the trees its last rays that skimmed over William Hargrove's tormented face and made him turn his head aside. Josh got up and closed one of the shutters. In the neighboring woods, birds were singing with a kind of panic, as if to hold on to the daylight that might disappear for ever, and a sudden melancholy filled that moment with the light's dazzling farewell. Hargrove got up out of his armchair.

'You'll help me,' he said, without making his thoughts any more specific and, as he moved towards the door, he wished his sons a good-night.

Left alone, the two men looked at each other for a moment without saying a word.

'I wasn't expecting such an honest admission,' said Douglas finally.

'It'll be the first he's given in a long time,' said Josh. 'Being a widower doesn't suit him. That little foreigner has changed him.'

'Foreigner?' said Douglas. 'Here in Georgia an English girl is no foreigner. You forget to what extent Savannah was influenced by England. Something of it still remains.'

Josh made an impatient gesture.

'I know all that. Despite everything, Elizabeth is not from these parts. She comes from elsewhere.'

'Like Papa, then. And to a certain extent like us, who were born in the West Indies. Anyway, what are you driving at? Were we accepted, yes or no?'

'Accepted if you like. It was not very easy for Papa. Accepted, yes. Adopted, not completely. Don't you feel it?'

'It's of no importance,' exclaimed Douglas. 'Marriage will set everything to rights for that little one in any case.'

'As for Papa, he will remain in his invisible solitude in which we share.'

'Bah,' said Douglas, 'we're getting morose. Let's go and smoke a cigar in the great avenue.'

Beneath the oaks, whose enormous trunks could be made out indistinctly, cooler air disturbed the foliage and they breathed in the night air with enjoyment. Talking amidst these shadows made their words seem confidential. One did not say the same things in daylight.

'I admire our father's courage,' whispered Douglas, as if he feared being overheard. 'He understood that he had to make a clean break, otherwise there would have been scandal. He has more suffering to come.'

'I always thought that was his principal occupation. Suffering.'

'Perhaps you are right. Conscience . . . what tortures it will have subjected him to . . .'

Josh gave a rather devious little laugh.

'A pity he can't dampen it down with chloroform! "Conscience makes cowards of us all . . ." '

'So you still read Shakespeare.'

'Oh no,' said Josh, making excuses, 'just a vague memory from school.'

'But he's not a coward. He's simply afraid of the plantation, he is afraid of war, and above all, he is afraid of himself. And he faces up to it all. You don't understand him properly.'

'I do, but he's inventing a nightmare for himself. The plantation is solid. War is impossible and he himself is the Rock of Gibraltar of respectability — which does not prevent, moreover, our dear Papa making a few escapes over New York way.'

The answer was instant and dry.

'I don't concern myself with Papa's personal affairs.'

Josh laughed mockingly.

'How you take umbrage! I've been put in my place by the family moralist. But don't let us squabble when it's so good to be under these big trees which wonder what we're talking about. The problem about Elizabeth seems more urgent to me. Do you feel capable of dealing with her? Frankly, I don't at all.'

'It's less difficult than you imagine. Do you wish to entrust things to my good sense?'

'With all my heart!' Josh exclaimed.

'In that case, I shall confide my ideas on the subject to you, and the decision I took last night without consulting Papa.'

The rest of the conversation was lost in the great concerto of crystalline voices rising from the foliage to greet the coolness of the night.

12

The day was long and trying for Elizabeth. Barely emerged from William Hargrove's library, she ran to look for her female cousins in order to find out at what time they were to leave for Savannah, but neither Mildred nor Hilda had waited for her before going off in a tilbury to the big shady wood that stretched to the north of the plantation. There shelter could be found from the heat that promised to be severe, and there too the solitude was propitious to the little confidences that girls of their age delight in.

As for Billy, set on independence, he had headed off on his young chestnut horse for an unknown destination.

Having explored the environs without daring to go too far, Elizabeth decided to return to the house. But, before going up the steps of the verandah, she stopped for a moment beside the great magnolia, from whose heavy white flowers spread a delicious perfume, as if to stop her in her tracks and console the girl with disappointment in her face. Her fingertip touched the wide, shiny leaves, and, with an instinctive movement, her lips brushed one of the corollas. From her very first moments at Dimwood, she had felt an inexplicable affinity between herself and that fragrant tree. The magnolia was becoming a person. She lightly caressed the bark and whispered sadly in that voice used for speaking secrets into someone's ear:

'They've forgotten me.'

Indeed, what had become of the visit to the renowned seamstress in that big town noted for its elegance? William Hargrove had given his agreement, Aunt Laura was to take Elizabeth there. There had even been talk of a carriage . . .

She lowered her eyes to the blue dress that made her ashamed, in spite of Mademoiselle Souligou's alterations, and fought back tears of resentment and humiliation. With a heavy heart, she climbed the steps of that house for which she was beginning to feel an aversion, and came to the large deserted entrance hall which she crossed without lingering. Perhaps they were looking for her in one of the ground-floor rooms – or in her bedroom, but she felt she did not have the strength to face the risk of seeing her mother, who would question her endlessly.

As usual at that hour, the house was plunged into semi-darkness in order to conserve some semblance of coolness until evening, and it was easy to get lost in what was still for Elizabeth a worrying labyrinth. Yet she carried on, stopping at each door, frightened of seeing it open, but wishing for nothing better, feeling more and more that she had strayed into some dubious quarter, where an invisible presence hovered, as in days gone by in the little Tudor manor house, where some nooks and crannies were to be avoided after nightfall.

Her steps led her to a verandah where light filtered through half-open shutters. A glance sufficed for her to see that there was no one about on this side. Where were they all then? In their rooms, or far away on some walk? She felt ill-at-ease realizing that she was alone in this silence, yet another form of solitude. She thought of calling. Calling who? She did not dare. Without much hope, she resolved on completing the circuit of the ground floor and, moving away from the window, she returned to the corridors' shadowy domain, where Susanna had told her the big linen cupboards were situated. She knew that if she went straight on she would come to the entrance hall and there, she told herself, seated in one of the big armchairs, she would think things over. She would have been quite incapable of explaining what she meant by thinking things over, but that sounded reasonable and she headed resolutely towards the wider but dark central passage, guided by the light at its end.

She had barely gone three yards in that direction when she was startled and let out a cry. There was a white apron standing in front of her. That was all she could see at first, until her name was spoken in a conspiratorial whisper:

'Miss Lizbeth.'

'Who are you?' she cried.

'Don't be afraid now,' the white apron said. 'I's Betty.'

At that moment Elizabeth could make out a black face in which the whites of the eyes stood out.

'I'm not afraid,' she said. 'I'm looking for someone.'

Her instinctive fear of Negroes made her heart pound.

Betty moved a few steps away and opened a door. Through a shaft of light, filtered here as in the other rooms, emerged a woman with a face the color of shining dark mahogany. It was full and round and exuded a disarming goodness.

Elizabeth could not remain silent faced with such a look brimming over with gentleness. Her fears faded away. But it was Betty who spoke first.

'I's the maid for Miss Hilda and Miss Mildred.'

Elizabeth noticed her ample and solidly built body supported by a sturdy pair of legs, which were concealed by a red cotton print skirt. Her bare feet were encased in sandals. From this imposing and ponderous personage rose a melodious sing-song voice.

'Miss Lizbeth, don't go bein' afraid of me.'

'But I'm not at all afraid, I told you so.'

A brief silence, then she heard the following words, accompanied by a smile that revealed dazzling teeth:

'I's goin' to tell you a secret.'

'Ah?' said Elizabeth intrigued.

'Yes'm, my name's Betty.'

'But you already told me that!'

'Yes'm, but I just wanted to be sure you done heard it right.'

Elizabeth caught her meaning straight away.

'Very well — Betty,' she said.

She hesitated slightly, then asked:

'Is there no one in the house?'

'Oh, they's all here, 'cept Mass'r Billy and Miss Hilda and Miss Mildred.'

Elizabeth wondered if it was proper to ask a question, but was not able to resist:

'Then why is there no one to be seen?'

'It's always like that 'bout now.'

'Why?'

'Oh, Miss Lizbeth,' said Betty, 'they's resting.'

'They're resting . . .'

'The heat, Miss Lizbeth, they's tired.'

Elizabeth did not pursue the matter, but other questions that she dared not ask occurred to her. She selected the one that had been tormenting her for over an hour:

'Aren't they going to Savannah today?'

'Savannah? Oh, I don't think so. Savannah is a long ways

off, a mighty long ways.'

The girl's throat tightened.

'By carriage?'

'Not by carriage. First you takes the railway at Macon. The carriage leaves very, very early and waits there at Savannah.'

'The carriage . . .' Elizabeth repeated nervously.

'The carriage is here, Miss Lizbeth, why is you sad?'

The English girl, usually mistress of her emotions, let out a groan that made her ashamed:

'Oh Betty . . .'

She got a grip on herself immediately.

'I'll go and wait in the entrance hall. Someone will come.'

'Why don't you wait here in Miss Susanna's room? She was lookin' for you before. She'll be right pleased.'

As she said these words, she moved away from the door to let the hesitant Elizabeth pass through. To appear to obey even a suggestion made her feel awkward, but it was hard for her to get the upper hand of her natural curiosity. Simply glancing into the room as she passed did not seem a fault in her eyes. She moved forward and stood for a moment in the doorway of a square room where the light, softened by the verandah, caressed the peach-pink walls and gave a kind of simple and secret identity to the furniture. She was struck by the bed with its delicate little columns. Beneath the light, white canopy with fluted hangings, the cream-colored bedspread could be seen to have tiny tufts of fluffy cotton sewn on to it here and there at regular intervals. Big mirrors in mahogany frames and a rocking chair were all she permitted herself to take in as she looked around furtively, but with great accuracy.

'Very pretty,' she said.

'Miss Susanna, she like everything real pretty. She's a real lady.'

This last word struck a particular chord in Elizabeth's ear. She was on the point of saying something, but had second thoughts and restricted herself to an imperceptible nod.

'I'm going down there, Betty.'

'I'll tell Miss Susanna you is in the entrance hall.'

'It's not worth it, I'll only be passing through there.'

And, finding the phrase somewhat abrupt, she added:

'Thank you, Betty.'

The only answer was a smile, but of such kindness that she was obliged to return it.

The entrance hall was empty, as she expected, and she did not linger. She might meet Susanna there. That brief glance of a moment directed at her room had revealed something that threw her into a daze: she did not like this tall girl, who, for all that, was keen to please her. It seemed like a revelation, but with nothing to justify it, and contradicted by a first, entirely favorable impression.

It would be better to shut herself in her own room while praying to Heaven that her mother would not hear her. She went up the stairs with steps as light as a kitten's and, once arrived at her door, seized hold of the brass knob which she turned slowly. Finally she found herself beside her bed where she lay down and, with her face buried in her pillow, she gave herself up to her grief without restraint, not caring about creasing the hated sky-blue dress. Mrs Escridge's door was closed. Abandoning herself to big stifled sobs was a desperate means of relief for Elizabeth, a lamentation upon the stupidity of her mother who had led her into a trap. In the tears that shook her shoulders, she felt herself becoming a different person, resolute and free from illusions. She could change nothing about the fact that she was becoming the prisoner of this plantation, where she had been told a dozen times that she would be happy, that she would get used to it. In spite of herself, a deep cry emerged from the depths of her being.

She felt ashamed once the crisis was over. The pillow was all wet, and she took a corner of the sheet to wipe her eyes and her cheeks. Earlier on she had wondered what it meant to reflect; now she knew. She no longer had any confidence in anyone at Dimwood. The only thing that shone through her despair, and for a reason she did not properly understand, was the smile of that colored woman, that Betty who at first had seemed to her absurd and terrifying. But there again she must be wary of illusion. That ponderous creature with childlike speech had seemed good to her. Was she not like all the others, veritably dripping with pleasantries and compliments? Mr Hargrove was no exception. She hoped never to speak to that man again. She found him repulsive. Why? Oh because . . . "because" was her angry inner answer to everything.

She turned round sharply. Standing in the doorway, like some figure in a painting, her mother was watching her in silence. On account of the heat that she could take less and less, she was wearing a nightdress that covered her completely, hiding her feet. Far from looking comic, dressed in this way she was like an apparition. Her loose hair spread on her shoulders added to this worrying appearance. However, she began to speak in a calm voice:

'You're crying, my sweet, and I understand you more than you think, but you know that in such cases, ladies don't cry. Yes, yes, I heard you. In silence I too have shed tears here, enough to bathe in. What's wrong?'

Elizabeth made an effort to regain her calm and an ordinary conversational tone, but her throat was choking:

'They were supposed to take me to Savannah today to have a dress made for me to replace this one that's not mine. I think they've forgotten me.'

'I see no subject for a tragedy in that. Life is made up of disappointments. You are vain, Elizabeth. That dress is not bad. A bit worn, it seems to me. Is that all?'

Elizabeth did not answer.

'Have they cut out your tongue?' her mother asked. 'Tell me all about it, but no more tears, I beg you.'

The girl looked straight at this woman whose features retained something of their nobility, despite the ravages wrought by worries, and she could not but admire her.

'I don't like it at Dimwood,' she said simply.

'You chose to stay here. I'm going back to England. Come with me to my room.'

Elizabeth followed her. As she walked behind her, she found it impossible to brush aside a sudden alarm on seeing that dull, brown head of hair which covered the whole of the width of the back of the nightdress, like a curtain. She would have been incapable of identifying the source of this unease that was something of a mystery to her.

Mrs Escridge's room had been tidied with particular care. There was nothing draped over the furniture nor flung on the floor, which was painted black, and the bottle of port was still in its place on the bedside table alongside the little phial of laudanum and the Bible. There was, however, a surprise in store for Elizabeth: in a corner, near the window, the cabin trunk, which had been put away once it was emptied, had reappeared and was now open. Linen and a few belongings could be seen in it.

The suspicion that her mother had gone mad once more crossed Elizabeth's mind, and she stood still, her eyes fixed on the trunk. Mrs Escridge apparently read her thoughts, for she exclaimed crossly:

'Take your eyes off that trunk, you little fool, and don't imagine I'm thinking of leaving tomorrow. It's there because it's a comfort to me to know that it will be full one day and that it will be carried to the coach that will take me to the station. I have all my wits about me, my girl.'

'Of course, Mama!' exclaimed Elizabeth, somewhat re-assured by the vigor of that final sentence.

'Sit down.'

She herself sat down in the rocking chair, started it rocking and began:

'Several letters that I wrote last night are already, I hope, on their way. I gave them to Laura who undertook to get them away.'

'Aunt Laura came here?'

'Yes, Aunt Laura as you call her. Her good manners and gentleness more or less got the better of my prejudice and I allowed her in. She was standing there on the verandah insisting so courteously through the open window ... I thought she might be useful to me, do you see?'

'She's charming.'

'Charming,' repeated Mrs Escridge with a dreamy air. 'Have you spoken to each other?'

'Yes, yesterday on the terrace. She told me some amusing things about the plantation and the gardens.'

'Did she perhaps broach the subject of religion?'

'No ... not entirely.'

'Not entirely ... I see the subtlety,' murmured Mrs Escridge. 'She and I also spoke,' she continued aloud, 'not about the garden, not about the plantation, but about religion, as it happens. She confided in me. Elizabeth, there is something you must know. She's a Catholic.'

'Oh!' said Elizabeth.

'Yes. She makes no secret of it, she talks about it discreetly and tactfully. In spite of everything, she's a lady, but she goes to mass. They have a little timber church in the neighborhood, and they are tolerated. There was one in your father's family.'

'A Catholic!'

'We don't talk about it. What's more, Queen Elizabeth had him hung. Let's leave it at that. As for Aunt Laura, she was born in the West Indies and was brought up there by nuns. We need to be careful.'

'What do you mean, Mama?'

Mrs Escridge stopped rocking the chair and assumed a fearsome voice:

'I mean that I'd rather see you dead at my feet than know you were a Catholic.'

'But it's impossible, Mama,' exclaimed Elizabeth full of emotion.

'I hope so. But those people always have conversion in the back of their minds, and they're clever, ingratiating. I hear there are quite a lot of them in the area. If you stay here, be on your guard.'

'I no longer have any desire to speak to Aunt Laura.'

'Don't go too far. She's a Christian, in her own way.'

'An idolatress, Mama.'

'Let's say immersed in the darkness of superstition. She can't do anything about it. She was born into it. But she's good.'

'Good?'

'Yes, I have to admit it. To me she has been good. But dangerous nevertheless.'

'I'll be careful.'

A short silence settled between them, as if to allow them to get their breath back, for this conversation stirred up their emotions. Elizabeth, seated on an upright chair with a back taller than herself, was trying to face up to her mother's attentive gaze, but she could not manage it. In spite of herself, her eyes rested on the open trunk, speaking its silent language of flight, and by dint of looking at it she ended by believing in it.

'Mama,' she exclaimed suddenly, 'I'm leaving with you!'

Mrs Escridge stretched out her arms towards her.

'I've found my little girl again. I was waiting for that cry.

Your silence hurt me, because I've always loved you and I could see you letting me, your mother, go without a word.'

Elizabeth flung herself towards her, and felt a cold mouth placed on her cheek burning with girlish emotion.

'We'll be happy over there,' she said. 'We won't be rich, but it'll be home. Anything is better than living as poor relations in a rich man's house who gives you alms out of charity.'

'This old dress they gave me!' said Elizabeth furiously.

'If that were all, my child!'

Mrs Escridge suddenly became pensive.

'It's my fault,' she said in a sudden rush of humility. 'I thought I was doing the right thing, I was thinking of your future.'

'I don't want a future here.'

'You'd have been rich one day. Married . . . '

'I don't want that.'

'Elizabeth, do you remember the little lodging house where we spent weeks in one of the gray streets of London? The meals, the stew that made us feel sick and that was served up day after day in a damp and icy dining room?'

'Oh no, no, Mama. It's not possible.'

'Yes, it's possible. And do you remember that night when you were crying in your bed because you were cold? I got up and spread one of my blankets over you, only to go back shivering to my own? It will mean the same gruesome little lodging house. "Modest charges, home cooking" the prospectus said. In case you've forgotten, I can remember it.'

'But somebody would help us. You've written letters.'

'To our cousin Joe Anderson who is a lawyer. He's the best man in the world, but he is not very well off. To your godfather, Philip Grey, the architect. He can do anything, he is successful, but having started off from nothing, he is still afraid of going without, and it's hard for him to give up even a sovereign. We'd have to work at it. Do you want me to go on?'

'No,' Elizabeth said with a firmness that surprised her mother. 'I'm sure there'll be someone, and I want to see England again, with you.'

'With me?'

'But of course.'

'So you love me a little bit, in spite of my strictness?'

Elizabeth looked her in the eyes:

'Don't you know?' she asked.

Upset and moved more than she cared to let on, Mrs Escridge turned aside.

'My little girl,' she said simply.

In the long silence that followed, she began to raise and lower the tip of her foot to impose on her chair the rocking rhythm that favored her thoughts and her dreams. Sitting almost opposite her, Elizabeth tried to make out in those impeccably regular features some of that violent tenderness that she had seen a moment earlier, like a flash of lightning, but the face had an absent look about it, like that of a sleeper whose thoughts are elsewhere. The gaze of the pale gray eyes was fixed on a point above Elizabeth, as if looking for the answer to a difficult question on a panel of the door. Suddenly she spoke in a gentle, distant voice that was un-familiar to her daughter and seemed to prolong aloud the direction of some secret meditation:

'I've never been really maternal. Perhaps I gave too much love to the one who has left us. But I loved you, Elizabeth, I loved you because you had in your eyes that glimmer of light that I used to watch for in his last months, a thirst for life . . .'

'I still have it,' Elizabeth said in an outburst of which she was not in control. 'I know what you mean.'

Mrs Escridge stopped rocking and sent in her direction a look with a hint of a reproach:

'But he is no longer there,' she whispered. 'However, when you are near me, I'm sometimes aware of his presence. You mustn't leave me, my sweet. I did what I could for you. Dimwood isn't my fault. We'll clear a path for ourselves amidst the corpses.'

Elizabeth suddenly got up, seized with alarm, as she had been on seeing the open trunk.

'Mama,' she exclaimed.

'Yes,' said Mrs Escridge quietly. 'You're leaving?'

'Lunch . . . They don't like it if I'm late.'

She stammered a little and blushed as she saw her mother look towards the clock that showed a quarter past one.

'You won't be late today,' her mother said with a smile

that relaxed her face, 'but you look quite overcome with emotion. Rest for a moment in your room . . .'

And she added almost immediately:

'Come here first and let me kiss you for just now.'

Without clarifying what she meant by 'just now', she turned towards Elizabeth and, taking her in her arms, hugged her silently and placed her mouth on her forehead, amongst the tousled golden locks, and then several times on her cheek in a kind of random tenderness.

Back in her room, the girl sat down on her bed, disturbed and perplexed at one and the same time. This maternal effusiveness was radically changing her notion of a woman usually so reserved and so much in control of herself. Always ready to love, Elizabeth had received a revelation of another's mysterious being, and she felt herself borne, as if on a wave, towards her mother whom she was getting to know.

Her mind was made up now. She would leave Dimwood with her, she had promised, she would do it. One morning the door of her room would open and she would pass through it for ever. 'For ever . . .' Those words that she kept repeating under her breath were changing her life. Her blue eyes were already looking around and saying goodbye in a way that suddenly transformed beyond description the furniture, the walls and the whole decor that she was not even beginning to get used to after three days and, through the secret magic of things, the room took on an unknown beauty.

The suspicion crossed her mind that she was unconsciously becoming attached to this place that she thought she hated, and worry seized hold of her, as if, having fallen into a trap, she could see the trap closing over her.

The minutes went by. She had almost half an hour left. She went to comb her hair in front of a mirror and saw fear in her eyes. The words of the Lord's Prayer came to mind, full of meaning: 'Deliver us . . .' She said them aloud, then put her hand over her mouth in a childish gesture, as if to seize hold of them before her mother could hear them, for the door of her room was ajar.

She listened. Normally the creaking of the floorboards beneath the rocking chair reached that far, but she heard nothing.

Out of curiosity and with her heart beating a little faster, she slid to the slit of the door and saw her mother kneeling before her bed with her face buried in the sheets. Against the white fabric, the great dark wave of her brown hair was spread out, more alarming than a cry of despair. The girl moved promptly away, as if she had seen something she ought not to, and sat down in a distant corner of her room.

Torn with indecision, she wondered what she might do, but she did not have long to wait. After a few minutes, the door opened wide, and she saw her mother appear. Her pale, elongated face had taken on the beauty of a Fury from the ancient world. Her eyes, made larger by violent emotion, were looking for Elizabeth without seeing her. Her hoarse, dull voice uttered three words:

'She has gone . . .'

'But I haven't, Mama!' the girl exclaimed advancing towards her.

'Elizabeth,' Mrs Escridge said, 'listen carefully to what I'm going to tell you. I ask you, in the presence of God who is my witness, to forget for ever what I told you just now. If, out of weakness, I should go back on my decision, you would remind me of my word. Stay here. Your only chance of happiness is on the plantation. That doesn't seem possible to you now, but it will one day. Do you promise me not to try and follow me when I leave?'

Elizabeth looked at her dumbfounded. Too many different thoughts were whirling around in her head for her to be able to utter a word. The slowness with which her mother spoke, her almost religious seriousness turned her into some intimidating personage, come from some higher realm and chasing away all thoughts of madness. At the same time all the fields, trees, flowers and streams of the distant land that she was dying to see again were tumbling through her daughter's imagination with nightmarish precision. So forceful was the shock she received from this imperious discourse, that she felt dizzy and had to lean on the back of a chair.

'Mama . . .' she said.

Mrs Escridge waited for a moment with a stillness that by itself was enough to provoke fear.

'If you hesitate,' she said finally, 'if you refuse, I shall leave secretly, at night. I could do it. You'll come into my room one morning and you'll find me gone.'

After a brief silence she said:

'I shall go alone.'

Upset as she was, Elizabeth noticed the glazed look that enveloped her whole person with the muted violence of an adieu.

'I'm waiting for you to promise to stay here,' said her mother in a firm voice.

The minute that followed was like death agony for Elizabeth. She found the strength to force back her tears and finally said:

'I promise to try.'

To her great surprise, Mrs Escridge gave her a strange smile:

'You are your mother's daughter,' she said. 'You don't give in easily. In any case, I'll have done what I could. Go and have lunch now. You'll be late.'

'Let me kiss you, Mama!'

'This evening, before you go to bed, but I want no tears.'

'Very well, this evening,' she said in a strangled voice.

As the girl went to open the door, her mother stopped her:

'You'll make my excuses to Mr Hargrove. He's a man I dislike, but he has a right to respect.'

With the door closed again behind her, Elizabeth was obliged to lean on the wall to avoid falling. Another dizzy spell made her close her eyes and she had to let several minutes go by without moving and with her chest shaken by a dull thudding.

Suddenly a frightful noise coming from Mrs Escridge's room reached her, it was like a stifled howl. She had heard that cry once before, the night her father had died.

13

*E*veryone except Mr Hargrove was at table when she arrived, rather windswept, as in her confusion she had forgotten to comb her hair again. 'Fortunately Uncle Will isn't here yet,' she thought to herself.

'Late! Late!' cried Billy gleefully.

'Billy, stop teasing her,' said Uncle Douglas. 'We have just sat down. You are not late, but we were just waiting for you before saying grace. It is I who say it in my father's absence.'

'It'll be short, I hope,' said Uncle Josh.

A whisper of approval went round the table.

'I shall do it according to my inspiration,' replied Uncle Douglas drily.

'And that of the Lord perhaps,' added Uncle Josh in a pastorly voice.

Douglas looked at him furiously and stood up. After an effort to recollect himself, he assumed an appropriately grave tone of voice. All the heads were bowed and he said a prayer of reasonable length.

Having sat down again, he said with annoyance as he unfolded his napkin:

'There is a time for laughing, and a time to be serious, and I say this for the benefit of all those present.'

'It's frightful,' said Uncle Josh, 'you're starting to sound like Papa, ready to replace him.'

Douglas recovered and said calmly:

'No one can replace him and, besides, he isn't dead.'

Aunt Laura made a furtive sign of the cross.

'Come, Douglas, don't be angry,' Uncle Josh continued. 'You know you'll never stop me laughing. And your prayer was very good. I can be serious when necessary. It's not so hot today. And life is good. What else?'

'Enough, enough!' they said on all sides. 'Let's have lunch.'

The two servants who were now going round the table with the serving dishes gave toothy smiles as their contribution to the general good humor. With the blinds down, the room was plunged in a gilded half-light that lent added beauty to everything: the tablecloth was snowy white, the silverware shinier, but above all young Hilda and Mildred seemed prettier and Elizabeth even more so. A little taken aback by all this excitement, she held her knife and fork clumsily and could not manage to cut her meat. She had no appetite, but she felt that the chatter around her was gently drawing her out of the tense atmosphere that reigned in her mother's room. She tried to follow what was being said, but without success. Uncle Douglas's careful voice could be heard again.

'With all the respect that I owe my father . . .'

'Who is so good and whom we love . . .' chorused Uncle Josh and all the women, except Aunt Laura.

'What's the matter with you?' Uncle Douglas asked in exasperation.

'Isn't that what you always say when you're about to criticize him?'

This question, asked so innocently, brought Douglas's irritation to a peak and he suddenly became stony-faced.

'If you carry on, I shall remain silent,' he said coldly.

'Oh, Douglas,' his brother said, 'can't you see that with all this respectfully etc. we are like school children when the schoolmaster has left the room? Have a laugh with us. We're teasing you kindly.'

Uncle Douglas made an effort to take himself in hand.

'Well,' he said with a forced laugh, 'when I was so rudely interrupted, I was simply going to remark that he whose place is empty paralyzes the conversation somewhat. Which means you're going to be able to talk about the war.'

'As there isn't going to be a war,' Uncle Josh replied, 'it would be more interesting to talk about something else. For example, what does Papa's sudden disappearance mean?'

Aunt Augusta who was always majestic, even in her intonation, let drop these disconcerting words:

'He usually gives warning. I don't care for this mystery.'

Aunt Emma tossed a charming little head, and her brown curls seemed to be dancing for joy at the idea of the dizzy thoughts that were about to come from her mouth:

'I hope the same thing hasn't happened to him as happened to Mr Armstrong. I tremble to think of it.'

'Well, don't think of it,' said Uncle Josh.

Mildred's clear voice rose up from the back of the room:

'What happened to Mr Armstrong, Aunt Emma?'

Uncle Douglas let out a groan.

'You're not going to bring out that old story, Emma! It'll frighten the children.'

'But I love stories that scare me!' exclaimed Mildred.

Hilda and Susanna joined in:

'Me too.'

Elizabeth suddenly became very attentive. Inside herself she was pleased that Mr Hargrove was not there and, even deeper down, she wished that he would never come back. Timidly she whispered:

'Me too.'

Aunt Emma assumed a disdainful air:

'If that story can scare them in broad daylight, we must be dealing with a generation of sissies.'

'There are no sissies in the South!' Billy exclaimed.

'Let's have some quiet!' his father said. 'You're dying to tell your story, Emma. I can't stop you, but at least get it right.'

The steaming rice was brought in at that moment, and the servants were no longer smiling. A vague anxiety could be made out on their faces, and their hands trembled imperceptibly inside their white cotton gloves.

Aunt Emma began in learned tones:

'It was in 1825 . . .'

Uncle Josh corrected with a smile:

'1823.'

The narrator continued with a sigh of impatience:

'So one spring evening in 1823, young Armstrong was having dinner with his father in this house where we are now, and where his family had lived for a century. He was just finishing restoring it. It was already admired by the various local planters, and Mr Armstrong himself was proud of his new dwelling.'

'And with reason,' Uncle Josh remarked. 'The work of one of the good English architects.'

'Proud but anxious,' continued Emma. 'No, I won't have any rice in this heat. Yes, anxious . . .'

'Why anxious?' Uncle Josh asked.

'A crisis of conscience. They say he often had them.'

'A bit vague,' remarked Uncle Douglas. 'and there is

nothing as overbearing as people who have crises of conscience. But carry on.'

'In the middle of the meal, a servant came to tell him that someone was waiting for the young gentleman in the entrance hall. The latter, without asking who it was, without even saying a word, but with terror all over his face, got up and left the dining room.'

At that point Jonah, one of the two servants who were serving at table, put down his dish and headed for the door.

Aunt Augusta could not hold back her indignation.

'Did you see, Douglas? Jonah! What insolence! Do something.'

'I shall do nothing at all,' replied Uncle Douglas, 'and Jonah will not be reprimanded.'

Uncle Josh sent a highly ironical glance in Emma's direction: ·

'That's what is meant by frightening the servants! You're undermining our social structure from the base.'

The reply was delivered in a single burst:

'Our social structure is the most solid in the world, but if you annoy me I shall not continue.'

At these words four young heads straining forward united in a single cry:

'Oh yes, Aunt Emma, do go on!'

Emma pouted as if offended, let a few seconds go by and resumed:

'In the entrance hall was a man of medium height, wrapped in a black cloak that concealed the bottom half of his face up to his eyes.'

Jeremy, the second servant, who had held out until this point, closed his.

'Young Armstrong asked no questions of the stranger, but when this latter turned on his heels and went out, he followed him. They were never seen again.'

There was a short silence.

'Is that all?' Billy exclaimed.

'Isn't that enough?'

'In any case, it's all we know,' concluded Uncle Douglas. 'More experienced narrators usually add that the stranger in the black cape had eyes of fire.'

'I forgot the eyes of fire.'

'You did well, for if he did have them no one saw them except Mr Armstrong. You disappointed your young listeners there.'

At the end of the table, the 'children' were looking at each other in silence, open-mouthed.

'Eyes of fire!' Billy exclaimed, 'but someone did see them: the servant who opened the door.'

'Quite right, my boy, and you can imagine that he was questioned, but his nerves went to pieces and they left him alone. And they never managed to get him to talk about the visitor in the black cloak.'

'It was . . .' (a long silence) '. . . the Devil,' declared Aunt Emma resolutely.

Almost making an attempt at concealment, Aunt Laura made the sign of the cross again.

Uncle Douglas clapped his hands:

'I think this frivolity should stop and we should move on to the dessert. Jeremy, you are braver than Jonah. If you can get to the kitchen without fainting, go and bring us the ice cream, and quickly.'

Jeremy went.

Aunt Emma felt deprived of the success she had expected, so she resumed speaking in the hope of making up for lost ground:

'After a year of fruitless searching throughout the district, they finally gave up. Mrs Armstrong had died of grief.'

'Let's cut it short,' said Douglas in a rapid, authoritarian manner. 'The house remained in Armstrong's hands until 1827. It became dilapidated without anyone realizing, like all houses that aren't loved enough. Our father, who had just arrived from the West Indies . . .'

At that moment, Aunt Laura got up and said almost in a whisper:

'I beg you all to excuse me, the heat wearies me, I'm going to rest in my room.'

'You are quite pale,' said Uncle Josh as he got up in his turn. 'Wouldn't you like me to go with you?'

She smiled and shook her head, then went towards the door. In her plum-colored cotton dress, she gave the impression of gliding over the ground without touching it.

'I'm sure she'll make a detour via the kitchen to see

what's going on,' said Uncle Josh.

'And why that ice cream hasn't been brought,' added Aunt Augusta . . .

'. . . or if the servants aren't ill, that would be more like her,' Uncle Josh continued.

At that moment Billy's mocking voice pierced like an arrow the air that was becoming heavier:

'You might think that our charming English cousin has had her hair done by a strong wind.'

The blood rose to Elizabeth's cheeks and she trembled, raising two distraught hands to her untidy hair.

Uncle Douglas gave a gesture of irritation.

'You are behaving badly, Billy. Leave Elizabeth alone. You should speak to your son, Emma.'

Billy began to yelp:

'But I wrapped my remark in a compliment. Elizabeth is very pretty.'

'What impertinence!' exclaimed Aunt Augusta. 'I always said that boy should be whipped.'

'Aunt Augusta, I would not emerge alive from your hands if you were to take on the job, but corporal punishment is forbidden throughout the Dimwood estate. And you very well know it.'

Uncle Douglas gave a sharp knock on the table with his fingers.

'I request silence. It is hot and that is making us all uncomfortable, but from this evening we shall have fans. Tomorrow will be a more interesting day for Elizabeth, whom my brother is going to take to Savannah.'

A cry greeted this news:

'Savannah!'

Uncle Douglas turned towards the back of the room:

'How is it that you didn't know, Elizabeth?'

'I forgot to tell her,' said Uncle Josh. 'This little trip has already once been put off . . . You'll come with us, Emma. We shall need your advice.'

A little gleam of triumph immediately began to shine in Aunt Emma's eyes, but she took a grip on herself and assumed a modest air.

'Delighted to be of use. I thought it was Aunt Laura who was to . . .'

Uncle Douglas interrupted her:

'My father did not wish it. He suddenly changed his mind.'

'Ah, why?'

'No questions, I beg you, Emma. I cannot tell you any more and, as there are no servants present, I will remind you that we should never talk about the Devil or diabolic intrigue in front of them. There are reasons for it. I'm sorry that you told that story, Emma. I should have opposed it, but though I know it by heart, even now it fascinates me.'

'All the more so,' said Aunt Emma in a dramatic tone, 'as that notorious, interrupted dinner took place on this very spot.'

Uncle Douglas corrected her gently:

'Wrong. At that time the dining room was in the big room where we've put the billiard table . . . on purpose.'

'I didn't know.'

'There are many things that you don't know about the place.'

These words fell into a great silence, then Billy, who could hold out no longer, remarked in his turn:

'I too think that the dessert is a long time coming.'

He had barely spoken these words when the object of his longing appeared, a voluminous, deep red ice surrounded by pineapple slices protecting it like ramparts. It was carried in a great silver dish with solid handles by Jeremy, whose normally mahogany face was verging on gray from the effects of terror.

'Put the dessert down in front of me and go away,' Uncle Douglas ordered. 'But first of all, where is Jonah?'

'Jonah not well, Mass'r Douglas.'

'Tell him to keep calm. I'll come and speak to you later.'

With unsure hands, he placed the great dish in front of Uncle Douglas and ran off like a hunted animal. For a moment, Uncle Douglas looked with perplexity at the ice cream, then pushed the dish towards his brother sitting opposite him.

'Josh, you serve us, please. I'm too clumsy. The plates will be passed round one after the other. It'll be like when we were children. But I call you all to witness that there are subjects which must not be broached in front of the servants. I am as much to blame as you, Emma.'

Standing up, Uncle Josh began to slice the ice cream, and Aunt Augusta was served first; she received a slice of a reasonable thickness.

'I don't understand why our servants are so fearful,' said Aunt Emma who got her slice of ice cream immediately afterwards.

Uncle Douglas seemed to be hesitating but finally said:

'I'm not betraying any secrets. It was the two or three slaves who came from the West Indies with our father who poisoned their minds.'

'The West Indies!'

This cry from the end of the table rang out like an explosion of curiosity, and Uncle Douglas's face clouded over at the same time.

'The West Indies are very well as they are,' he declared with severity, 'we're going to talk about something else.'

To the general surprise, Billy voiced his opinion somewhat sententiously:

'We mustn't frighten the children.'

'What is it to do with you, Billy?'

'I've read a very interesting book about the West Indies, sir, in which you can learn all about what goes on, backed up with the aid of pictures. There are some passages that make you shiver.'

'Well, you can keep your little store of knowledge to yourself. I don't know what's stopping me from not giving you any dessert, like a six year-old.'

'It's not worth it,' said Uncle Josh. 'His portion has just arrived and he has already demolished it. You know his voracious appetite.'

Uncle Douglas took a grip on himself so as not to raise his voice, but let out a cutting phrase, full of anger.

'I'm most displeased with you, Billy.'

'I'm sorry for it, sir.'

'Don't think you've got off so lightly. Where did you get that book?'

'In the bookcase in the drawing room.'

'What a mistake not to keep it locked!' Uncle Josh sighed.

'You will return that book to its place immediately.'

'I've done so. I read it last night.'

The two brothers exchanged glances.

'What can have put that idea into his head?' muttered Uncle Douglas through his teeth.

Uncle Josh shrugged his shoulders.

'How can you stop the servants gossiping among themselves and Billy listening in without appearing to do so? It's always the same when Papa goes away from here. Disruption, disruption . . .'

'I assure you that I shall not listen to the servants,' said Billy, cut to the quick. 'You meet them everywhere in the house. You'd have to be deaf not to pick up bits of their stories as you go by.'

Uncle Douglas resumed that authoritative tone suited to a head of a family.

'Come, come, let us leave all that. Tomorrow morning — do you hear, Elizabeth? — Aunt Emma is going to Savannah with you.'

'And me!' said Billy.

'You? No, you're not included in the plans.'

'But I want him,' said Emma. 'I shall need my boy for my errands. I absolutely insist on it.'

'Me too,' said Billy. 'I'll be there. There must be a man to look after Elizabeth.'

Uncle Douglas turned to his brother:

'A man! Did you hear him? I'll not argue, as Emma wishes it . . . You'll have to get up early. You'll leave in the carriage for Wilmington station at eight o'clock. Breakfast at seven o'clock. Aunt Laura will see to everything. I'm sorry she won't be going with you, but Papa has his ways of thinking . . . You'll spend the night there, rooms have been booked at the best hotel, the De Soto. And you'll come back the following day late in the afternoon.'

Thereupon Billy stood up, eyes shining and mouth open, ready to speak.

'Be quiet and sit down,' his father ordered. 'Naturally there will be someone to welcome you at the station, Mr Charles Jones.'

'Charles Jones!' echoed Emma joyfully.

Aunt Augusta raised her chin.

'What a character! He is the most British of all Victoria's subjects.'

'Indeed,' explained Uncle Douglas, ' it appears that he is

very keen to be the first to greet his young compatriot.'

Elizabeth looked around in bewilderment and blushed for the second or third time, but this time even more than before, for all eyes were turned towards her. It was as if, at that very moment, she had begun to exist at Dimwood and she wished desperately to vanish under the table.

The last remnants of the strawberry ice having disappeared from the plates as from the serving dish, Uncle Douglas stood up and said a short prayer, imitating his father's tone as best he could, then proposed that they go and rest; this advice was by way of a ritual and quite superfluous.

'Elizabeth,' he added, 'Aunt Laura will take care of you and the necessary preparations for your little journey. As soon as she has recovered, she will come to you in your room.'

'Oh, not to my room,' exclaimed Elizabeth.

'Why not?'

'It would disturb Mama. She can hear everything.'

Josh and Douglas exchanged a wondering look.

'It's true that we almost forget that she is there,' whispered Uncle Douglas furrowing his brow.

'But she could just as well be in England, as she seems determined not to see us.'

Aunt Augusta, whose ears had been flapping, spoke up in her precise voice:

'Be under no illusion. Mrs Escridge is present in a way that is . . . importunate. We are all aware of it.'

'"Importunate" is unkind,' said Uncle Josh insistently, 'especially in front of her daughter. She is not inconveniencing anyone.'

'Alright, I withdraw "importunate",' said Aunt Augusta in a regal tone.

While this debate was going on, Hilda and Mildred were pestering Elizabeth to get them invited to accompany her to Savannah, which meant that she heard none of it.

Uncle Douglas turned towards the end of the table and assumed an affectionate tone:

'My little Elizabeth, I'm sure that one of your cousins will be happy for you to rest in her room.'

'In mine!' exclaimed Susanna authoritatively.

'In mine, in mine!' responded the voices of Mildred and

Hilda.

'Or in mine,' said Aunt Laura gently, having suddenly appeared in the doorway.

Beneath her fine lawn bonnet, her face was still pale, but retained an expression of perfect serenity. Parrying all likely questions, she immediately said:

'I think I've reassured the servants, but it would be better not to mention certain things in front of them. I'll take charge of Elizabeth. Do you agree, Josh, and you, Douglas?'

A great sigh of relief was Josh's answer.

'Wholeheartedly!' he exclaimed with a laugh.

'Agreed,' said Douglas. 'We're sorry that you missed dessert, but you know that ice cream won't wait.'

In her usual even, calm voice, Aunt Laura replied:

'I am in need of nothing at all. Elizabeth, will you come with me?'

In the general silence, Elizabeth looked desperately around her, as if calling for help, but she encountered only a semi-circular wall of smiling faces counselling compliance. Only Billy's fiery face launched a mute call to revolt.

She had a moment's uncertainty, then followed Aunt Laura.

14

*I*n the half-light of the corridor, Aunt Laura took the young English girl's hand and began to speak in whispers, anxious not to disturb the silence or the shadows.

'My room is at the end of the house, set apart from all the others. That way I have a kind of solitude. Don't expect to find in it the refinement you see elsewhere. Coming to my room is a bit like giving yourself up to me out of affection; do you understand that, young as you are?'

Elizabeth hazarded an agreement, for she did not wish to hurt this woman whom she could not manage to like, despite her effusiveness the day before on the terrace. And then there was her mother's revelation: a Catholic . . .

When they reached her room, Aunt Laura turned the key in the lock and opened wide the door. They went in. Elizabeth was surprised to discover a charming room whose walls were hung with flower-strewn fabric. The eye quickly lost itself amidst every possible variety of rose, peony, lilac and a multitude of forget-me-nots and daisies. The girl smiled in wonder.

'Do you like it?'

'It's much prettier than my room . . . much gayer.'

'It's different. When I was little, in England, my mother wanted me always to have flowers before my eyes. Now I don't notice them any more, as I have seen so much of them. Sometimes, when I think of my childhood, they re-appear. You'd say they emerge from the walls.'

'She's mad,' Elizabeth thought, but inwardly corrected herself. 'No, she's English.'

And turning towards Aunt Laura she told her:

'I would have liked to have a room like yours.'

'Provided you're happy in it. That wasn't the case with me.'

The word 'why' paused momentarily on Elizabeth's lips, but she held it back and, casting her eyes around, she noticed the straw chairs, the deal table and a rocking chair made of a black, shiny wood that was new to her. Its back was of plaited willow and seemed enormous, spreading out like a giant palm leaf.

'Yes,' said Aunt Laura in response to her silent questioning, 'it comes from abroad. It's the chair my mother left me. She had little benefit from it here, she died after eighteen months, didn't like Dimwood. Over there, behind the white curtains, is my bed.'

Elizabeth went over to that great snowy cube that occupied one corner of the room, but Aunt Laura's gentle voice prevented her from going any further:

'Don't disturb the curtains, there's a good girl.'

Short and to the point, the answer was not long in coming:

'I would not have done so without your permission.'

'I know. I'm sorry.'

And without further ado she added:

'Tomorrow you'll go to Savannah by carriage. It's not very

far: you'll be there in two hours. The man who will meet you is someone people like on first sight. A little too sure of himself, perhaps, he is one of the leading merchants in the town.'

'A merchant . . .'

'You must understand. In Savannah, a merchant of that importance is the equal of a lord. You'll be showered with generosity. Don't accept everything . . .'

Elizabeth's impatient little voice broke into this sentence:

'But I know all that. Mama told me dozens of times in England: "A lady never accepts . . ."'

'Very well. My advice was wasted, I suppose. You'll be taken to the great Savannah seamstress. Aunt Emma will guide your choice. Be careful about colors that are too bright, and everything that they say comes from Paris . . .'

'From Paris!'

'Yes, from Paris, but it's doubtful if they do come from there . . .'

'My father went to Paris. I too shall go there.'

'When you're grown up, perhaps, but those are dreams.'

'Oh, I'd give anything . . .'

'In the mean time you'll be satisfied with Savannah which is reckoned to be the most elegant town in the South . . .'

She hesitated a moment and added, as if reluctantly:

'. . . after Charleston in South Carolina. But let's leave that. I've made a complete list of what you'll need. It's a long list. You have nothing. Why are you looking at me like that?'

'You sound like my mother. We have nothing.'

'There was nothing offensive in my remark. My father is only too happy at the chance to give, to give everything. His generosity is without limit – as far as money is concerned.'

That sentence about poor relations went through Elizabeth's mind like a refrain, and she felt incapable of holding back words that she did not want to speak:

'And what if you don't like to be obliged for anything, like my mother . . . or like me?'

The emotion made her tremble a little, confronted with the stupefaction and consternation in Aunt Laura's eyes. Finally the latter simply asked:

'And how do you expect God to help you, other than by human hands?'

Elizabeth did not answer. Neither could take her eyes off the other and several seconds went by, then Aunt Laura said in a flat voice:

'For years I was as proud as you. Finally one gives in. One comes to terms.'

'Comes to terms with what?'

'Everything. Life . . . You have to know how to bend.'

Elizabeth's startled expression seemed to impress her, and she made an effort to speak gently:

'Be reasonable and everything will be easier. You are much liked here, you have everything going for you to be happy.'

She added brusquely:

'I hoped to go to town with you, but that will be another time. You'll get up an hour earlier tomorrow morning. You'll have breakfast in the little room where Mr Stoddard and Miss Pringle take their meals. They will doubtless be there. I think they are very keen to see you. I shall let you go now, and I shall stay here, I have kept you too long. Will you kiss me?'

'Certainly,' whispered the girl.

As she remained motionless, Aunt Laura bent towards her a little and with her colorless face stroked the pink cheek that took no evasive action.

15

With the door closed behind her, Elizabeth wondered what she was going to do. Too much disturbed by her talk with that woman whom she did not understand, she wished, above everything else, to be alone, to seek refuge in some corner of the plantation where no one would find her. She went towards the door of the house, but there she saw Hilda and Mildred suddenly appear, prettier than ever in their dresses, one in white, the other in lilac, and their little faces flushed with excitement beneath big, floppy straw hats.

Both of them were talking at once, jabbering with so much to say:

'Elizabeth, you're coming with us to the wood by the river.'

'Two carriages are ordered for tomorrow. Two! Try and guess what that means.'

'Mama is lending us her gig. Don't stand there looking so forlorn. Come on!'

And they each took one of her hands.

She let herself be dragged off to the bottom of the steps, but put up a show of resistance near the magnolia tree. Out of this tall, dark, shiny mass, from which the big white flowers seemed to emerge like inquisitive faces, she felt a kind of amorous power coming towards her, holding her captive in some gentle tutelage.

'Why have you stopped?' asked Mildred.

Elizabeth was stroking a magnolia leaf with the tips of her fingers.

'Oh, do you like that magnolia? We all love it. The gardener says he doesn't know how old it might be.'

'It might have been here before the house. We're very fond of it.'

These words disappointed Elizabeth, who wanted that tree's love all to herself.

'Hilda,' said Mildred, 'run off quickly and fetch a nice straw hat for Elizabeth. Susanna has a whole lot of them.'

'She'll want to come with us.'

'Oh no, she mustn't come! Elizabeth is just for you and me,' said Mildred impetuously. 'Say anything. She always gives in.'

Hilda was already bounding up the steps in front of the house.

'For one thing you're not comfortable in the gig if there are more than three of you,' she shouted as she disappeared.

Alone with Mildred beside the magnolia, Elizabeth, already half in agreement, would have liked, in spite of everything, to remain loyal to Susanna whom she barely liked, but who had been affectionate towards her.

'Susanna is very kind,' she said suddenly.

'Yes, of course she's kind, but boring. And she's not the

same age as us.'

'That's true. She already talks like the others.'

The others . . . that term embraced all adults as far as the extremes of decrepitude, all those beyond comprehension, impossible to listen to.

'That's it,' exclaimed Mildred. 'The others. How clever you are! Just imagine, Hilda and I are dying to go to Savannah, because there are shops in Savannah. Shops, that's what's missing at Dimwood. Do you understand?'

Elizabeth understood vaguely. In the village near her father's mansion, she could only remember, as far as shops were concerned, a baker's and a grocer's: those in London she remembered only in a nightmarish haze.

'It really is marvelous to talk to you,' continued Mildred, 'because you understand everything. So you'll only have to say one word to Papa for him to take us with you, as there are two carriages.'

'Two carriages and a gig!' cried Hilda, who had heard these last words as she arrived waving a large hat decorated with a green ribbon. 'I had trouble getting it from her. She wanted to come – with the hat! Isn't the gig here?'

'As you can see.'

'I bet Tommy has fallen asleep again. It's hard to get orders obeyed. That's what comes of speaking gently to the servants as our grandfather insists. It makes you cross.'

Just as her anger was blowing its little worst, the sound of wheels could be heard round the corner of the house, and soon an elegant gig came into view, drawn calmly by a placid old mare who looked on the point of dozing off.

She stopped a few paces short of the three girls without even a 'Whoa!' being said. Tommy came down from his seat and took off his straw hat with its frayed edges. Dressed in white cotton, he looked hardly more awake than the mare, but he stood before the three young ladies with a natural dignity that struck Elizabeth. His gray, curly hair softened his rugged features, and he smiled as he greeted the three girls.

'Hello, Tommy,' said Mildred and, turning her head towards Elizabeth, she added briefly: 'Elizabeth, this is Tommy.'

The young English girl was undoubtedly touched by the humility of the old man standing before her with his hat in his hand, for she returned his smile and said:

'Hello, Tommy.'

The reply came immediately and surprised her:

'Why, thank you, Miss Lizbeth – good mornin'.'

'Tommy,' said Hilda, 'what's this old granny mare that you've brought us? I asked for Rumpus.'

Rumpus was a petulant and vigorous pony who would break into a gallop at the slightest crack of the whip.

'Mass'r Douglas, he say Rumpus is too dangerous. He don't want y'all to take Rumpus!'

'It's unbearable,' said Hilda, 'Uncle Douglas is so careful, he takes us for babes in arms. Alright, Tommy, we don't need you any more.'

He bowed, put his hat back on and went away, but not without having glanced towards Elizabeth.

'Why did he thank me?' she asked Mildred.

'Oh, the servants are like that. He wasn't expecting it. You made a conquest, but don't forget his name is Tommy when you see him. Otherwise he won't like you.'

'And so what?' said Hilda annoyed. 'What does it matter if they like us?'

'Grandfather thinks it's important. Come on, get in, Hilda. You take the reins. Get in, Elizabeth, you can sit between the two of us.'

All three of them settled into the elegant gig with its upholstered black leather seat, but it took a minor downpour of cracks of the whip to persuade Granny to move. She then set off at a well-behaved trot along a road that went straight through the fields.

They had not got very far when a small brick house caught Elizabeth's attention. Situated almost at the edge of the gardens, it seemed intentionally isolated, although its green shutters and a red-tiled roof made it look attractive.

'That's where Joe Dickinson, the bailiff, lives,' explained Mildred. 'We don't like him very much.'

Hilda immediately had to have her say:

'He gives himself airs because he's from South Carolina, but he is awfully common. Uncle Douglas is the only one who speaks to him. Use the whip, Mildred, or we shall never get there.'

The whip was brought into action and Granny pricked up

her ears, made a small effort which lasted for a few yards, and then resumed her usual pace. Hilda let out a great sigh of impatience:

'We'd be there already with Rumpus! I suspect Tommy of speaking to Grandfather.'

'He's not here.'

'That's true. It's one of those days when he goes away. We never know where, he doesn't say anything. You need to tell him something, you go to his room, and it's empty.'

For a quarter of an hour she chatted with Mildred across Elizabeth, who said nothing. In fact, the cry of despair that she had heard two hours earlier had repeatedly come back to her, but the activity at dinner made her forget it. Now, with her eyes on the furrows of the fields under cultivation, fascinated by their straightness, it seemed to her that she could hear it again like an adieu that tears through the soul, the same adieu as at the death of her father. She was on the point of telling her companions that she wanted to go back, when a phrase of Mildred's caught her attention:

'I don't find anything surprising in these absences. It's to do with the house . . .'

She noticed that Elizabeth was listening and stopped.

'We shall frighten our cousin,' she said.

'Oh no,' the latter replied somewhat irritated. 'I'm not afraid.'

'That story Aunt Emma told . . .'

'I know quite a few like that.'

And in a sudden surge of national pride she added:

'At home nearly all the houses have something like that.'

'You mean ghosts?'

Elizabeth shrugged her shoulders.

'That or something else,' she said with a superior air.

Mildred lent forward a little towards Hilda and they looked at each other with the same expression of curiosity mingled with anxiety. Suddenly Elizabeth stopped thinking about her mother. She found it amusing to terrorize these proud Southern misses with their plantation and their slaves.

'Tell us, oh do tell us!' exclaimed Mildred.

'Oh yes, do tell,' begged Hilda. 'A good crack of the whip, Mildred, the woods are in sight. It'll be marvellous to hear all that in the shadows.'

The long, black shape blocking the horizon was indeed drawing closer.

'What do you want me to tell you? There are so many stories . . .'

Hilda took charge of things.

'Your father had a manor house.'

'I don't like talking about our house very much.'

'Do it to please us, won't you? Surely there was a badge over the door . . .'

'You mean a coat of arms? Yes, you could hardly see it, the manor was so old. A portcullis . . .'

'What's a portcullis?'

'Oh, of course, how could you know? An iron gate behind the drawbridge.'

'A drawbridge! Oh Mildred, pass me the whip, that animal is falling asleep.'

'Not on your life, you'd kill her.'

'Two lions looking at each other from each side of the portcullis,' the young English girl continued unperturbed.

'And of course your manor was haunted,' said Mildred.

'Horribly so.'

'And you saw . . .'

'Oh yes.'

This answer, so short and so full of terror, was greeted with a weighty silence that neither of the cousins dared to breach, but the same question was going round in their heads. Mildred finally burst forth:

'In any case, there's nothing at Dimwood.'

Elizabeth knowledgeably made a worrying distinction:

'Some people see them, others don't, which doesn't mean that there's nothing there.'

'Have you seen something in the house?' asked Mildred in a voice that was less sure.

'When I see something, I keep it to myself. It is impolite to confide in people.'

'I'm sleeping in your room tonight, Hilda. I think I'd rather not know, Elizabeth.'

'You idiot,' exclaimed Hilda, 'she's going to frighten us. It'll be delightful in the woods.'

Elizabeth contradicted her drily:

'It won't be delightful, because I shall keep quiet.'

Even as she spoke these words, the oaks on the edge of the wood enveloped them with all their shade, and they instinctively fell silent. Even for the two cousins who knew this place well, the impression of entering some silent kingdom maintained a magical force. Here another world began. The great trees mingled their branches, stretching them out like gigantic arms, laden with heavy foliage, through which the sun could not penetrate; and rows of cypresses contributed to the thick darkness. As the carriage advanced, the light from the road melted away and there remained only that special gleam found in the depths of the forest, with a softness too full of mystery not to give rise to a certain unease.

The mare stopped and Hilda got down to tie the reins to the trunk of a sycamore.

Now the girls ventured on to a path leading them towards a clearing where there lay a tree that had been struck down by lightning a long time ago. There was obviously no question of moving it, as a path circled it lazily on each side. They sat down on the trunk stripped of its bark and, almost without thinking, they held each other's hands to reassure themselves, for not a single bird sang at that hour. They would have preferred any kind of insect buzzing to the solid stillness of the air and the space around them, an oppressively real presence emanating from this centuries-old vegetation. The dread of what is ancient reigned here as in all places where time seems to have taken flight and sought refuge. The three girls dizzily felt that their souls were as old as the world.

They remained motionless, not daring to open their mouths, the blood rushing in their ears.

After a moment, they were ashamed of their apparently groundless fear, and Mildred ventured to speak:

'Today the wood isn't like it is on other days.'

'Perhaps,' said Hilda in the same tone, 'it's because of what we said just now about ghosts.'

A short silence served as commentary on this explanation, then, in quite a calm and slightly sarcastic voice, Elizabeth spoke in her turn:

'But you were saying that it would be delightful to listen

to ghost stories here, weren't you?'

She gently released her hands from theirs and waited a few seconds, hoping for an answer, then she said amiably:

'I've changed my mind. I'll tell you one if you like.'

'I'd prefer it some other time,' said Mildred.

Rather embarrassed, Hilda attempted a diversion:

'Perhaps it would be more fun to walk by the river . . .'

Elizabeth laughed to herself.

Mildred leapt to her feet:

'Oh, you must see the river. You can guide us, Hilda.'

'It's not difficult, you only have to follow the path, but don't wander away from it. You can get lost very quickly, and then . . .'

'And then?' Elizabeth asked.

'Oh, I don't know, but you shouldn't wander off too far, you'd never be found.'

Elizabeth did not insist, but these woods, which she had found so intimidating at first, now attracted her with all the unknown things they concealed. She could sniff something that they didn't want to tell her. She began to walk behind her companions in silence. Out of kindness they sought to brush aside from her path the giant ferns that bent over at head height and flapped gently against their cheeks.

She lingered on purpose and there came a moment when Mildred realized that she was no longer following them. Gripped with anxiety she called out:

'Stop, Hilda, Elizabeth's not there any more.'

Hilda turned round, and both of them began to call:

'Elizabeth, where are you?'

Somewhat shrill and already quite distant a voice reached them through all that greenery that closed in like a wall:

'I'm here.'

'Where's here?'

'Here, where I am. I want to know where you come to if you go too far.'

'We don't know.'

'You know very well, so if you don't tell me, I'll leave this spot and go somewhere else. And if you try to catch up with me, I'll run off straight away.'

The two cousins looked at each other, their eyes enlarged with fear.

'Tell her anything, Hilda.'

With her hands cupped around her mouth, Hilda thrust out this sentence:

'You come to a crossways of old trees where snakes and branches fall on you as you go by.'

A silence for taking stock ensued, then the voice with the transatlantic intonation reached them:

'I think that's very interesting, but snakes might drop on to our shoulders just as easily where we are now. It's still the same woods. So what's at the crossways?'

'You were wrong to talk about the crossways,' said Mildred.

'Never mind. If you swear to come back to us, Elizabeth, we'll tell you.'

'I won't swear it, but I'll promise you.'

'Fine, we have your word.'

'As an Englishwoman!' cried Mildred to add a serious guarantee to the verbal agreement.

By way of an answer all they heard was at first a distant rustling, then an ever more audible swishing, finally the tall ferns began to wave and parted brusquely to let Elizabeth emerge, looking determined.

'Here I am,' she said. 'Your story, quickly.'

'Here? It would be better by the river, it's not comfortable, standing up among all these plants.'

'Here and now, or I'll disappear. You don't know me.'

'Start, Hilda.'

'No, you. Souligou told it to you.'

'Well, here we go,' said Mildred with a sigh. 'It seems that some distance from here, right in the depth of the woods, there is a great circle of trees, giant oaks covered in curtains of gray moss.'

'Green, rather,' Hilda corrected.

'Anyway, curtains of moss like you see everywhere. And in the middle, nothing, grass.'

'Is that all?'

'No. On certain days, you can hear a dull noise coming up from the ground. It's not known what it is. Grandfather has heard it and doesn't want to talk about it. He forbids us to go that way. He is the only one who knows the way, what's more.'

'You told me that Souligou had heard it too, that dull

sound.'

'That's what she says. According to her you can make out a cry; it's always the same. She's full of stories like that. What is for certain is that a lot of Cherokee Indians were killed over a hundred years ago, when the Whites arrived. The English . . .'

Elizabeth did not react.

'Carry on,' she said. 'Why have you stopped?'

Hilda intervened with authority:

'Englishmen, Americans, Frenchmen. The Indians used to scalp their prisoners, then finished them off with hatchet blows.'

'Tomahawks,' clarified Elizabeth.

'How do you know that?' asked Mildred.

'Do you take the English for fools? They taught us all those things at school. Colonial wars . . .'

Goaded on by this badinage, Mildred continued:

'Well then, a massacre. The whole tribe was done away with, and ever since there has been that cry from down below. All of these woods were full of Indians. They didn't fight in the open fields. They fired their arrows from behind the trees. This was their domain here, their woods.'

Elizabeth looked at her with a friendly smile:

'You are on their domains everywhere, dear Mildred.'

'Goodness,' exclaimed Hilda, 'you sound like Uncle Josh. He's mad about the Indians.'

And to create a diversion she added:

'I've no idea what time it is, but I have the impression that the light is failing. We've only just got time to go and see the river.'

In silence they returned to the meandering red earth path. Suddenly Elizabeth's voice made itself heard:

'Mildred, you've forgotten the snakes that drop on to passers-by. Are they only in the trees?'

'Oh no, the grass is full of them.'

This answer must have seemed satisfactory, for Elizabeth fell silent and they soon reached a spot where there was a wide space between the trees, revealing a gray sky. The murmuring of the river already reached their ears, and they could smell the perfume of hyacinths in pink and blue clumps amongst the bushes.

The young Englishwoman's heart began to pound at the sight of the flowers, and she ran to the edge of the water with a cry of delight. Bordered by willows, the river ran deep green, its swirling flow lazily and slowly intertwining in mysterious, whispered chattering.

Mildred and Hilda caught up with her and enthused in their turn. Mildred, closing her eyes, nuzzled her pretty face into the syringas and declared that she would die of pleasure, while Hilda took on a grave air, face to face with the wild irises whose royal beauty was at its fullest in these solitary places.

In her greater simplicity, Elizabeth sighed:

'Why didn't you bring me to this paradise straight away, instead of making me walk through those oppressive ferns?'

As she spoke, she turned her head to right and left as if to see everything at once and carry it all away within her. Pale yellow orchids were climbing up the pine trunks and along the creepers, scattering specks of mauve light in the shadows. Red and white azaleas, vigorous and invasive, grew as tall as trees, spreading themselves into a canopy of deep red, shining with pink and white.

She breathed in, becoming intoxicated with the fragrance of jasmine, which brought back to her all those English and Scottish gardens, wrapping her in exquisite sadness. Full of emotion she lay stretched out gently on the grass and began to laugh as she might have begun to cry.

Mildred knelt beside her immediately:

'You're happy,' she exclaimed. 'I was sure of it. Let's stay here, all three of us. Come on, Hilda!'

Hilda looked at them with her large, penetrating black eyes, which heralded the woman she would grow into and, abandoning her irises, she came and sat down beside them. Full of love, Mildred leant over Elizabeth and gave her a kiss on the cheek.

'I hope,' she said in a surge of affection, 'that you're a little bit reconciled to our South now. It seems you wanted to run away . . .'

Elizabeth did not answer, but Hilda spoke in her place.

'She'll be completely captivated by Savannah when she sees those marvelous houses . . .'

'And the marvelous shops!' added Mildred, 'it's enough

to make your head spin.'

'We'll show you everything,' said Hilda, 'and better than Aunt Emma who will be taken up with her calls and her friends and the innumerable relatives we have there. Mildred and I will look after you. The second gig is for us who are accompanying you.'

As if in a dream, Elizabeth's voice said softly:

'But Aunt Laura didn't say you were coming too.'

The two cousins had the same irritated reaction:

'Oh her! She is always against us, and she interferes with everything.'

'You need only ask Papa. He adores you. Everyone adores you, darling. So you only have to ask.'

Hilda assumed an imperious tone:

'You ask. You'll get your way with Uncle Josh.'

'Rather than with Aunt Emma. Papa always gives in. But never with Aunt Laura. If I were you, I'd be wary of her.'

'Why, Mildred? Mama is fond of her.'

'Your Mama doesn't know her the way we do. She is strange.'

'Haven't you noticed,' inserted Hilda, 'that she and Grandfather never exchange a single word?'

'Even at table,' added Mildred.

Elizabeth had not noticed.

'No,' she said. 'Don't they speak to each other at all?'

'Not at all. I don't advise you to ask them why. It's one of those questions that are never asked here.'

Elizabeth contrived a little laugh:

'How mysterious you both are!'

'Mysterious! Do you hear, Hilda? Me, mysterious!'

She stretched out on her back beside Elizabeth and flung an elegantly shod foot into the air:

'Look at this pretty red leather shoe. They'll buy you some just like it in Savannah. Don't you like them?'

In spite of herself, Elizabeth looked at that little foot vainly waving itself about and, although she judged the gesture to be vulgar, she admired the shoe.

'Not bad,' she conceded.

'Not bad? I should hope not. It's Russian leather, my dear.'

Hilda made an effort to adopt a more languid pose.

'It's simple enough,' she said to Elizabeth, 'in Savannah, you have only to choose, they'll give you anything you want, all that you want.'

These words, spoken with a kind of ceremonial nonchalance, had a singular effect on the young stranger. Something was changing deep down inside her. She might well have been vaguely shocked, but she became attentive.

Without lowering her leg, Mildred raised the edge of her skirt a little.

'While I'm at it, I'll show you the lace of my pantaloons.'

Elizabeth was startled and without being able to stop herself, she let out a remark that struck her as ridiculous as she said it:

'That's not the done thing!'

Hilda raised her head to share a glance with Mildred.

'An innocent,' she whispered.

Speaking that word made her fifty years old. Her wrinkled eyes seemed to be sending a message to her cousin.

The latter burst out laughing:

'You sound like our parents, Elizabeth dear. A lady doesn't even let her ankle be seen. You'll see later on, at the ball, when you have a crinoline on, and your crinoline is swirling in the air, whether people don't see the lace of your pantaloons. In any case, mine are of Belgian lacework.'

Pulled down further, the skirt did indeed reveal a flounce of a spidery fineness. Elizabeth blushed. The leg was lowered.

Hilda ventured a comment in a learned tone:

'The lacemakers work in cellars over there, and that gives a special quality to the thread.'

'And, of course,' said Mildred in an offhand manner, 'they go blind.'

In a voice trailing away and with her eyes closed, she suddenly added:

'These flowers, all these flowers, are you breathing in their perfume, Elizabeth? Aren't you glad to be with us in this secret garden?'

'Where nobody comes,' Hilda clarified.

Elizabeth restricted herself to a smile. For some minutes now, she had vaguely guessed that she was not with girls younger than herself, but with grown-ups whose motives eluded her. Only that word 'innocent' that she had caught

— 126 —

on the wing shed some dubious light. Mildred and Hilda, especially Hilda, knew things that she did not, and she felt uneasy on account of it.

Orchids whose stems clung to one tree after another, like creepers, attracted Elizabeth. She admired these garlands and, drawing close, breathed in a delicate fragrance of vanilla. Unusual, these flowers with pale orange petals spotted with red, opened out generously around a brownish pistil.

Hilda followed the young stranger's eyes.

'Are you interested in those orchids?' she asked. 'Have you never seen any in England?'

'No, never.'

'Oh, you're lucky. Do you see that pretty blue and gold butterfly flapping its wings above the flower? Can you see it?'

'Where? There. Oh yes. It's charming, you'd think he was dancing.'

The butterfly was fluttering, touching the pistil.

'Look,' said Hilda. 'Look! He's not moving any more, he looks as if he's melting, as if he were turning . . . liquid.'

'But it's disgusting!' exclaimed Elizabeth horrified.

'It's not at all, the petals close up slowly.'

'Hilda!'

'This orchid is carnivorous. It waits for its prey.'

Hilda turned upon Elizabeth a serious countenance with her black eyes aflame:

'Its prey, do you understand?'

'I think that flower is horrible.'

Hilda gave a mysterious smile:

'Yet it is beautiful,' she murmured.

The light was fading. In the ensuing silence, she could hear the song of a distant bird. It must have been hidden in the wood and, after two or three melancholy notes, it fell silent, then, a moment later, one or two more notes, sad and spaced out:

'The thrush,' whispered Mildred, as if she feared to silence its plaintive little voice, 'the hermit thrush.'

'It only sings when there's silence,' said Hilda, 'it needs solitude.'

Elizabeth was listening, straining towards that timid cry.

'It is heralding dusk,' whispered Mildred. 'We must go.'

They got up without opening their mouths. They walked for a little while in front of the orchids and the deeper tinted irises in the fading light. The water was still talking softly to itself. All the magic of the evening sought to hold them back at the first approach of night. The thrush was still singing with dreamy hesitation. Then other birds began to sing much closer and drowned its voice.

They became pensive and much less talkative than on the way there. Once more they cleared a path between the giant ferns that slapped against them, and they soon came upon the carriage and patient Granny nodding her head in static sleep.

It was Hilda who took the reins, naturally waving the whip about with a vengeful hand. She didn't have to use it much, for the old mare knew the way to Dimwood through the woods well enough and began trotting enthusiastically towards her blessed stable: Hilda accused her of hypocrisy as she cracked the whip above her ears.

Mildred laughed. Elizabeth said nothing.

'You look dreamy,' said Hilda. 'Are you not pleased with today?'

'She's thinking about her loves.'

'Shut up, Mildred. You don't care what you say.'

'But it's not a sin, my pretty cousin! One day they'll introduce you to some handsome boys in uniform who will court you.'

'Perhaps that doesn't appeal to her,' inserted Hilda.

Disturbed once more without knowing why, Elizabeth chose to laugh about it.

'Idiots! I was looking at the clouds.'

Indeed, the sky was turning an orangey yellow on the horizon and becoming streaked with long gray clouds that were gradually deepening, spreading darkness over the meadows. Only the strong red of the earth on the road still shone out.

Suddenly there resounded an explosion that was both loud and dull at the same time. Elizabeth let out a small cry and looked at her companions. Hilda burst out laughing:

'Don't be afraid. It's the crow.'

'The crow?'

'The crow that announces rain,' said Mildred.

'What an extraordinary crow! Not at all like at home.'

'Ours can only be heard in the South. It goes off boom, and then goes away.'

'We shall have a storm tonight,' Hilda announced. 'That will bring back the April coolness for a few weeks. We were suffocating, weren't we, Elizabeth?'

The answer was short, because Elizabeth never knew where these questions might lead, and she was wary.

'Yes, we were suffocating.'

Suddenly Mildred declared:

'Elizabeth has a sky-blue soul, like her dress.'

'Leave my soul out of it. And as for the dress, I hate it.'

'They'll offer you marvelous ones in Savannah. There is a range of pinks such as you never heard of. I can see you in pink with a hint of mauve.'

Mildred's over-excited voice rang out immediately in the breeze that had just that minute got up.

'Oh no, Hilda! Pale green, rather. With that golden hair, it would be stupefyingly beautiful. But we'll be there to help you choose, Elizabeth.'

'I seriously believe that you're both mad,' the latter said. 'I shall choose on my own. And it's not at all certain that you're coming tomorrow.'

'Awful girl!' exclaimed Mildred.

'No. Awful nice,' corrected Hilda. 'I'm sure she'll arrange everything with your father.'

Overcome with exasperation, despite these comforting words, she indulged the mare with a crack of the whip that almost made good old Granny burst into an unexpected gallop.

Without wanting to say so, all three were wondering whether they would reach home before nightfall. In the trees forming a high black wall to their right, the cicadas wove their grating cry into a web of sound.

Time passed while docile Granny continued her even trotting on the path she knew well, and they realized that their only hope of arriving at Dimwood depended on the old mare and her instincts. The whip remained inactive. A large lantern fixed to the front of the carriage would have helped them, if they had taken a box of matches with them, but their heads were full of other things when they left, and now they remained silent. Mildred was trembling shamefully. Suddenly she whispered:

'Can you see the road, Elizabeth?'

'I can see nothing and I'm taking charge of nothing,' said Elizabeth coldly. 'It was you and Hilda who made me get into this vehicle. I hope Granny bolts.'

Mildred groaned:

'Oh, Elizabeth, sometimes you are too British.'

'Not at all,' exclaimed Hilda, 'she's right. You'll see.'

Brandishing the whip, she brought it down with all her strength across the back of the mare who neighed, tried to rear up, then she calmed down and stood motionless. Cracks of the whip began to rain down on her, but she did not budge. A horror-stricken silence ensued.

Elizabeth's calm voice made itself heard once more.

'There's nothing to be done. I've known beasts like that. It's a mule. And it's tired enough to drop.'

'What are we going to do?' asked Mildred.

'Wait or go back on foot.'

'That's an hour's walk,' said Hilda, 'and we can barely see.'

'Twilight suddenly gave way to night, much more quickly than in England. In the same way, everything around the three girls appeared enormous. Instinctively Mildred and Hilda snuggled up to Elizabeth who fought them off in vain.

Since they had left 'paradise' the two girls had produced the worst of impressions on Elizabeth. She pictured them as two little witches in some fairy story. She especially disliked the display of lace underwear, the purpose of which escaped her. She had had so much drummed into her about the refined manners of the South.

'Don't push me like that!' she said suddenly. 'And don't be afraid. They'll send someone to look for us, for certain. So keep quiet, you cry babies!'

'We're not cry babies!'

Seized with the malicious desire to tease them, Elizabeth asked innocently:

'Would you like me to tell you about a mysterious discovery to pass the time while we wait?'

Mildred, who lacked prudence, exclaimed:

'Oh yes!'

Hilda remained silent.

'You asked me just now if there was anything at Dimwood. I hesitated to answer. There is something.'

'Oh, Elizabeth,' said Hilda reproachfully, 'you shouldn't have said so.'

'It's frightful,' groaned Mildred, and she immediately added, interestedly: 'Have you seen it?'

'There is nothing to see, it's everywhere. It comes up from the ground on which the house is built. There was fighting there . . .'

Remembering their own tales of the woods, she now served them up a dish of her own concocting to teach them – who knows? – to keep the secret of their frilly underwear to themselves.

'Think about,' she continued, 'a battlefield . . . not to mention the Indians you massacred . . .'

She waited a few seconds to assess the effect produced, but her words did not have the hoped-for success. In the almost total darkness, the sky seemed higher and the fields boundless. She heard Mildred sniffing gently, then Hilda whispered:

'You've spoiled Dimwood for us for ever.'

Elizabeth immediately understood what she had done, and she could not hold back the words that sprang into her mouth:

'Forgive me!'

She stretched out her hands to right and left. Her left hand was seized by Mildred who squeezed it uncontrollably, but her right hand was ignored.

'Too easy,' murmured Hilda.

Elizabeth felt all the humiliation of that answer. But she had asked for it and preferred to remain silent. Quite different from her cousin, Mildred revealed a generous heart, and the young English girl was moved by it, but she could have wished she were a little less weepy and let go her hand which she had tapped affectionately. Now she had to stomach Hilda's snub, and that was hard. The rough, dry sound of the cicadas seemed in harmony with the process.

Suddenly she heard a distant tinkling of bells, and a small, flickering light appeared on the road. It took a while until they finally recognized the sound of horses' hooves:

'They're coming from Dimwood!' exclaimed Mildred through her tears. 'It's for us.'

And she blew her nose.

Three pairs of eyes strained out of their sockets scrutinizing the darkness, until a cart brusquely emerged, seeming to rise up from the ground, so sudden was its appearance. A horse with bells on its harness stopped a few yards away from Granny, and old Tommy got down from his seat.

'Tommy!' exclaimed Elizabeth, bending over towards him.

He raised a face whose ugliness was softened by a smile, for the lantern's light cast heavy black stripes over his wrinkles.

'Miss Lizbeth, they's frightened up at the house. They's wonderin' where the three of y'all got off to.'

Hilda gave the explanation in an acid tone:

'We are here because your unbearable Granny is playing up and won't budge. I shall ask to have her put down.'

'Oh no, Miss Hilda!'

And without dropping his reins, he took two steps towards the mare and cradled its head in one of his arms. She did not flinch.

'Granny,' he said, 'You be nice now. I's goin' to hitch you to the cart and you goin' to follow real nice. You be nice, Granny, you be good.'

'Let's be done with all this, Tommy,' ordered Hilda.

Furtively, he leaned his cheek against the mare's muzzle and returned to his cart. The turnaround was effected with care, and with the reins of the gig tied to the rear upright of the cart, the latter was finally able to set off again at a fair pace. Restored to exemplary docility, Granny trotted behind it.

'We'll never get there,' Hilda sighed. 'I don't like that old servant. I advise you to avoid being familiar with the servants, Elizabeth.'

This remark provoked a glacial reply:

'Thank you, but I know how to behave towards servants, my little Hilda.'

There followed a heavy silence that threatened to last until the wheels stopped rolling, while Elizabeth, without opening her mouth, fought off Mildred who was trying to take hold of her hand. Each time she thought she had succeeded the angry hand would disentangle itself. And so all three had more or less fallen out with each other when they reached the house.

Uncle Josh was waiting for them on the verandah steps and scolded them with a smile:

'My dear young ladies, a little longer and you would have made us all late for supper.'

Hilda wasted no time in asking him if so many Indians had been massacred at Dimwood that their spirits rose up from the very ground on which the house was built, and if besides that, there was 'something' within its walls.

'It was I who said that,' said Elizabeth calmly, in contrast to the precipitous outburst of the talebearer.

Uncle Josh immediately understood the situation:

'I am not sufficiently Scottish to see or feel the presence of 'something' in our house, but, dear Elizabeth, this country has been a battlefield for centuries. We're living on top of a cemetery.'

'Papa, that's horrible!' exclaimed Mildred.

'Calm down, we have become used to it. As far as the redskins are concerned, those from whom we simply grabbed their ancestral lands, we Americans should plead guilty, but before us came the Spanish, followed by the English and the French. The indictment of the white races by the noble Indian race is a vast and disturbing subject for reflection. But ten minutes from now, I want to see three young ladies with clean hands at the dining room table. Do you understand?'

He gestured towards the front door and, in astonishment, they let themselves be swallowed up by it.

16

S upper was briefer than usual, and the redskins kept a discreet distance.

As everyone was withdrawing, however, Hilda signalled to Elizabeth that she wished to speak to her.

'Follow me,' she told her, 'it's important.'

Out of curiosity, Elizabeth followed her along the dimly lit corridor. Following in the resolute footsteps of that small creature, she admired, in spite of herself, all the authority of that narrow figure with her head tossed proudly back.

Hilda's choice of venue was the oval drawing room where the men customarily closeted themselves to smoke their cigars far away from the ladies, but that evening Uncle Josh and Uncle Douglas had announced their intention of taking a turn about the great avenue.

Once the door was closed, Hilda half drew the curtains at the tall windows and turned the lights out.

'We can see well enough like that,' she said, 'and people will leave us alone.'

'Why all this mystery, Hilda?'

'Be patient.'

They sat down some way away from each other.

'What childishness,' thought Elizabeth. 'She is even more of a little girl than I thought. What is she leading up to?'

There was a faint glimmer from the sky full of black clouds, and in the dramatic half-light, Hilda's deep and careful voice could be heard:

'Cousin Elizabeth, you have assured us in every possible way that you are English. That's all very well. As for me, you might say that I have all of the family's Scottish blood in my veins.'

'That's all very well. My turn to say it.'

'Thank you. Do they teach you in your lessons that the King of England sent the man they call the Butcher of Hanover to cut to pieces our army of patriots, the army of the Young Pretender?'

'At Culloden. But of course. Is that why you've made me come here?'

'Oh no, but to remind you that when we hate, we make a good job of it.'

'Are you not mad, Hilda? What's all this history lesson about?'

'It'll help you to understand me.'

'That's not difficult. You hate me. I'm leaving.'

— 134 —

'Not so quickly. Just now, on the road, you told us there was something here.'

'Yes, but I'm not afraid of it.'

'Perhaps because you don't know the whole story. I suspected that there was something. Grandfather maintains that they are old wives' tales, and I ended up thinking he was right. It took you to come and stir things up again for us, for Mildred and me, out of malice.'

'Not at all. I'm not malicious.'

'Yes, you are. You think you're good because you read your Bible and say your prayers. I know. Somebody told me. As for me, people think I'm malicious, and I'm not.'

These final words were pronounced with such a singular tone that Elizabeth leaned forward in order to see her a little better, but she could make out nothing in that stony white little face, other than the magnificent flashing of her big black eyes.

'Hilda,' she said softly, 'you forget that I asked both of you to forgive me.'

'You couldn't do anything less, but what is said is said, and for my part I shan't forget it. Aunt Emma didn't tell you everything. If you want to know the whole story, you only have to ask Souligou, then you won't ever sleep at Dimwood.' She let a few seconds go by and continued in a harsher voice: 'I asked you to come here this evening to tell you that I shan't speak to you for a month.'

Elizabeth could not hold back a laugh:

'My word, you are punishing me!'

'Oh, you're making fun of me because I'm only thirteen, and you're sixteen, but I know more things than you do. Keeping silent is my way of punishing people.'

There was so much seriousness in these naive words, that Elizabeth's gaiety gave way to a sudden compassion inside her.

'Maybe one day I shall return to England with Mama, Hilda. Then I shall be no more trouble to anyone on the plantation. We are homesick.'

These words dropped into the silence. Elizabeth, who had not taken her eyes off that little creature sitting opposite her, thought she could see two tears running down the colorless cheeks, then a shy voice piped up, a voice of childhood:

'I don't want you to go, Elizabeth.'

Elizabeth looked for something to say and found nothing. Without really knowing how, she felt herself face to face with a mystery and, in a sudden flash of memory, those moments spent in the 'paradise' at the water's edge appeared to her in a new light. She could sniff the presence of a secret, the deeper meaning of which eluded her, although she was on the point of understanding it. In the same way a name can foil our memory, while seeming quite close. As if to help her, the term 'innocent' came back to her, but in vain. It seemed as strange as the rest.

In a flash an idea came to her that she thought likely to extricate her. With her finger on her lips, she said with a smile:

'You're forgetting the punishment, a month's silence.'

Then Hilda gave her a look in which a blade of despair was unsheathed. Turning her head, she quickly went towards the door and left.

In some consternation, Elizabeth resolved to go up to her room and pack her case, making as little noise as possible. If her mother were to hear her, she would speak to her. What would she speak to her about? Again she was perplexed. She would watch her tongue, but it would do her good to talk.

On the stairs, indecision brought her to a halt at almost every step. Talking was dangerous. That little black-eyed Hilda, how could one so young contain so much that was shadowy? What was it about 'innocent'? Why no lamps and curtains drawn in the smoking saloon? Adults played tricks like that. Hilda was like an adult and already grown up . . . It was better to keep quiet about all that.

As she entered her room, she was surprised to see Betty there, leaning over a valise which she had placed on the bed. The big smile that showed her white teeth put Elizabeth at ease. She needed a human face to speak to her of goodness, and this black face seemed to dispel the enigmas in which she had been thrashing about for the last hour.

'Betty,' she said gaily, 'I wasn't expecting to see you here.'

'I's your servant now, Miss Lizbeth. Now don't you do

nothin'. Old Betty, she's goin' to do it all for you, Miss Lizbeth.'

'But why all this linen? I'm not going on a journey.'

'Miss Laura she say: pack Miss Lizbeth's trunk. Two days in a hotel.'

'In a hotel!' It took her several seconds to imagine a fabulous hotel with bedrooms decorated with flowers and busy waiters rushing to and fro.

'Do you know Savannah, Betty?'

'Yes, Miss Lizbeth, they done bought me at Savannah.'

'What did you say?'

'Yes'm, I was twelve years old when they done bought me at Savannah.'

'But by whom?'

'By Mass'r William.'

Elizabeth looked at her, vaguely uneasy. It was as if, having left some incomprehensible world with Hilda, she had dropped into another that was equally dark and incoherent. She suddenly had the impression that the black woman in front of her was no longer a human being, but an object. This crazy idea just flitted through her mind, and she tried to reason with herself. Didn't she know that all the servants on the plantation had been bought? It was that word 'bought' that disturbed her.

'Betty,' she said simply.

Perhaps the black woman guessed that the girl from foreign parts was upset.

'Mass'r William, he's real kind to all us servants.'

After some hesitation, because she knew that it was not permitted to ask certain questions, Elizabeth asked:

'What about the others?'

Betty raised her eyebrows in surprise and answered gravely:

'Everybody real nice to us.'

And she added with the same smile as before:

'Especially Miss Laura.'

'Aunt Laura?'

'Yes'm. She like all of us servants. When we's sick, Miss Laura come.'

Limiting her praise of Aunt Laura to that, she went to the mahogany wardrobe and took out the kilt.

'Oh no!' exclaimed Elizabeth.

Betty turned round, holding the skirt at arm's length like a trophy. From the whole of her corpulent personage, there emanated both great gentleness and maternal authority.

'Miss Laura she say that's a pretty skirt for you to go travellin' in. In Savannah you's goin' to find plenty of pretty things to wear. But you wear this to travel. You's too nice not to wear a pretty skirt like this.'

'Very well,' said Elizabeth.

The kilt seemed rather ridiculous to her, but she would be pleased to be rid of the hateful blue dress. And was Savannah not to provide her with every conceivable elegance? The very name of that unknown town was already beginning to turn her head.

'Very well,' she repeated, with a touch of impatience.

'Yes'm, Miss Lizbeth, but we can't see nothin'.'

Shadows had indeed invaded the room all of a sudden, and the rumbling of still-distant thunder rolled on, like the chariot wheels of some biblical army.

Elizabeth looked at Betty and saw nothing but the whites of her eyes.

'Are you afraid?' she asked.

'No'm, Miss Lizbeth. Is you?'

'Of course not, but we must light the lamp.'

In this room, where things were not yet sufficiently familiar to her, she could not quite remember where the lamp was. With the agility of a cat, she was moving off in the wrong direction when she heard a dull thud that made her ears prick up.

'Have you dropped something, Betty?'

'No'm, Miss Lizbeth.'

'Do you know where the lamp is?'

'No ma'am, I's hardly ever been in here.'

'I don't dare to wake Mama. There is usually light coming from under the door. She leaves her night light on.'

By waving a hand about in the void, she finally felt a wall beneath her fingers, but the fear of knocking over an occasional table or of bumping into a piece of furniture stopped her from going any further, and a vague disquiet seized her. Gradually the terror she had experienced so intensely in childhood, the fear of the dark that is our link with prehistoric times, made her call out:

'Betty!'

A voice answered somewhat uncertainly:

'Yes, Miss Lizbeth.'

Suddenly the whole room came into view in the unbearable flash of some dazzling light, scouring the room from the detail of the cornice to the cracks between the floorboards.

There was enough time for Elizabeth to see Betty on her knees with her hands glued to her face, near the table where the lamp was. Night closed in around them again immediately, and the girl let out a cry as in a shipwreck:

'Don't be afraid, Betty! There's no danger.'

A deafening crash was the only commentary on these words, and the thunder filled the sky with its long, vengeful unfurling.

Without hesitation, the girl made for the lamp, but for all her careful calculation of each one of her steps, she suddenly bumped into one of Betty's knees, provoking an animal-like howl.

'Don't be afraid, Betty, it's me,' she said. 'If you move, you'll knock the lamp over.'

A moment later, the soft light of the oil lamp restored an appearance of calm to the room, upset only by Betty's dramatic posture.

At that moment, a door opened and Mrs Escridge, wearing her long nightdress, asked calmly:

'What is going on? I heard a cry, Elizabeth.'

'It's nothing, Mama. Betty is packing my case.'

'On her knees? How curious.'

'We're leaving for Savannah tomorrow morning.'

'I know. Cousin Laura kept me informed, but I'll believe in that journey when you've gone. In the meantime, close the window immediately.'

'No, ma'am. I'll do it.' Betty said suddenly.

Rather shamefaced beneath the English lady's cold stare, Betty got up, went towards the big window and closed it.

'Elizabeth,' continued Mrs Escridge, 'when these preparations . . .'

Again a flash of lightning paid its respects to every nook and cranny of the room, isolating each object in a light worthy of the Last Judgement, making a terrifying momentary inventory.

Betty let herself drop on to the bed, invoking the Lord. As pallid and motionless as corpses, Elizabeth and Mrs Escridge awaited the clap of thunder. It came a little later than the first time, but was full of equal menace.

When silence was restored, Mrs Escridge, in a patient voice continued her speech where she had left it:

'. . . when these preparations for the journey are over, you'll come and have a word with me.'

'Immediately, Mama. The storm is moving away, Betty. Pack the case and leave the blue dress in the wardrobe.'

She had barely crossed the threshold of her mother's room when raindrops reverberated on the verandah roof. Mrs Escridge was smiling in a way that Elizabeth had not seen since their departure from 'the old country'.

'Do you hear?' she said dreamily, 'The rain. The air is already cooling down, we shall be able to breathe. Do you remember the smell of the earth in our garden at home after the storm?'

'Oh, I've thought about it. I've been thinking about all that since we've been here. Have you had an answer to your letters, Mama?'

'It's still too soon, my little one. They told me it'll take weeks, even if they don't keep me waiting. But I'm like you. Will time never end? It seems to me that we've been here for a year.'

'I think I shall leave with you.'

'No.'

'But Mama, there are times when I'm as unhappy here as you.'

'That's possible, but you'll stay. This little trip to Savannah will set everything to rights. Firstly, Savannah has remained an English town, it seems. Aristocratic, ha! ha!'

'But things are too sad here on the plantation.'

'It will be less sad when you have everything you want. But don't forget that everything is given to you out of charity.'

'Exactly. I hate their charity.'

'Listen, my girl. If ever I arrive back over there, I shall be living off nothing but charity, but I prefer our charity at home to their charity here! As for you, you'll be living in comfort and riches.'

'I'd rather be poor and living over there.'

'Don't talk like a fool. Have you forgotten the lodging house and the stew in the evenings?'

'Lord,' thought Elizabeth, 'she's going to serve up that stew to me again, and make it more horrible each time . . .'

'. . . thickened with a floury sauce and filled out with lumps of fat, all of it barely warm . . .'

'Mama, I beg you . . .'

'Good, I can see that you understand, so we shall talk no more about it, but when you're down in their aristocratic town, you'll get two phials of laudanum, like a good little girl. And don't kiss me this evening. I don't feel in the mood for sentimentality. Likewise, I'll say goodbye to you straight away. The formalities are over. Leave quietly to-morrow morning without waking me, that's all. No, draw the curtains so that I shan't see any more of those flashes of lightning that are annoying me. Then leave me. I'm going to listen to the rain.'

As she was going to bed, Elizabeth had the impression that all the pleasure of the trip to Savannah was melting away. She was especially saddened by her mother's baleful evocation of the evening stew and the disconcerting prospect of a poverty-stricken life in England. To cure her of her homesickness, she was being offered the poisoned gift of a life free from material cares in a country she disliked. A few hours earlier, the name Savannah still retained some brilliance in her eyes, but the sarcastic tone in which her mother had spoken about it cast a shadow over that town. The word aristocrats made her especially confused. How could Americans be aristocrats?

Rain fell all night, with a heavy, clearcut drumming on the verandah roofs. Elizabeth listened to it as one does to a long story. From time to time, flashes of lightning filtered through the crack in the curtains and sliced the darkness in two with a slash of steel, and the thunder rumbled as it moved further away. Elizabeth dreamt that she was sliding down into an abyss.

17

I t was still raining gently at dawn. The two carriages were waiting in front of the house. Elizabeth was dazzled by their elegance. Long and spacious, they were poised like skiffs on great wheels painted pale green. A tarpaulin was protecting the seats from the last drops of rain, for the weather was clearing. Black horses, splendid, shiny animals in fine livery, were proudly tossing their manes, and one felt that they were pleased with their good health and the care taken of their appearance.

The coachman had thrown a light box-coat over his dark red and gold livery, and vast green umbrellas were coming and going between the front door and the running boards of the vehicles. There was a joyful chattering amongst the travellers as they chose a place for themselves for the journey. The sun was coming through behind shreds of cloud, and the umbrellas suddenly snapped shut, having become redundant. It was decided that Aunt Emma would travel in the first carriage with Elizabeth and that Uncle Josh would follow in the second with Billy, who would have preferred Elizabeth's company, but he was made to keep quiet. Behind these luxurious vehicles, a hefty cart was drawn by a well-built horse with good muscles.

Moreover, their plans were changed, as often happens in the South. Elizabeth heard Uncle Josh telling Aunt Emma that they would go to Charlie Jones's. 'He had a message sent to me last night. No question of going to the De Soto, we're staying at his place. So, direct to Savannah.'

Uncle Douglas was standing on the verandah with Aunt Laura who was smiling a little sadly, and hands were waving as was proper, but at the first turns of the wheels, Elizabeth's attention was drawn towards one of the dining room windows, and behind the pane she caught sight of Hilda's white and serious face with its black eyes, full of reproach as they watched her.

Now the vehicles were entering the great avenue, and Aunt Emma, sitting next to Elizabeth, was chattering gaily, her head caught up in a delightful little straw bonnet with lilac ribbons. The noise meant that she could be heard only by the person sitting opposite her. For fear of the drips that might fall from the trees, she held a pretty little green silk umbrella that she was waving about in an unsteady hand. Elizabeth kept on her knees the great cape with soft edges that had had to be wrenched away from a reluctant Susanna, she too having been deprived of the jaunt to the big town. With her hair blowing in the wind, she was breathing in the sharp air as one drinks cool water, and was amused at the complicated sound of hooves, which, in its own way, spoke of a future free from material cares. With ferocious irony she recalled the London lodging house stew, but by the same process of association of ideas, a still more recent memory made her quiver, bringing her up with a start. A little before dawn, at that darkest hour, a flash of lightning tearing through the night had woken her, and she had heard her mother's voice in the next room, an imploring voice, stuttering prayers. Did she never sleep? Elizabeth had listened for a moment, surprised and a little worried, then she dropped back into sleep. In the sunlight piercing the foliage of that proud avenue, the voice, usually so curt, seemed to be reaching out to her, but sad and suppliant, trying to hold on to her, perhaps? She was so struck by it that she did not notice Aunt Emma's white-gloved hand, pointing out to her something on their left. Turning her head finally, she saw a long row of cabins with white-washed walls, each one separate from the rest and boasting a little garden crammed with flowers.

'The slaves' quarters,' Aunt Emma was saying, 'but remember, we only ever call them servants or 'coloreds'. It's Aunt Laura who looks after them, and they adore her. She'll take you to see them.'

'To see them!' exclaimed Elizabeth without enthusiasm.

'Yes, yes. They must see you, they must like you. It's like a big family that we take responsibility for. But you'll see, they're very kind.'

These last words were spoken in the hope that they would reach the young half-caste coachman, who was sitting up straight in his well-fitting blue suit, but nothing changed his haughty posture.

Aunt Emma drew close to Elizabeth in such a way that she seemed to want to imprison her stubborn pink face in the brim of her bonnet:

'There's nothing to fear from them,' she said in a confidential tone, 'they never rebel.'

'I know,' said Elizabeth drawing back a little. 'They told me everything.'

The problem having been settled once and for all, Aunt Emma flung herself back into her corner and admired the landscape. The plantation was already far away. Almost edging the road, a thick forest of giant pines afforded a glimpse of shadowy depths. Aunt Emma waved her hand:

'All that is ours,' she declared in an offhand manner.

Carried by the breeze, an intoxicating odor emanated from the greenery at the very top of the rust-colored trunks. Elizabeth closed her eyes in delectation.

'It goes on and on,' said the voice coming out of the bonnet. 'You'd say there was no way of stopping this invasion.'

'Why stop it?' Elizabeth thought.

But the carriage was going at full speed and the landscape soon changed. The pine trees became more spaced out, giving way to grassland, which stretched on as far as the eye could see, towards other forests, drawing a wide black band across the horizon. Suddenly Elizabeth opened her eyes wide: far from the road, she caught sight of a great expanse of water of an indeterminate color, neither gray nor brown, all spiked with monstrous sections of dead trees in a kind of primeval chaos that made the edge of the marsh inaccessible in this place where nature was damned. A strong and fascinating impression of evil sadness exuded from this place, where silence was tinged with malevolence.

Sinister words emerged from beneath Aunt Emma's bonnet:

'Dangerous,' she added, 'snakes, fever, mosquitoes, a lair for criminals on the run.'

She raised a perfumed handkerchief to her small nose, and said in a stifled voice.

'A scar on the face of the county.'

But Elizabeth found it interesting and was sorry that the coachman, with a click of his tongue, made his animals increase their pace. She would have liked to linger and become intoxicated with the unnerving, almost infernal, poetry of this place.

During the half-hour that followed, she remained victim to that uncanny landscape, given up to an inner contemplation of that stretch of water laden with secrets. All the ancestral piety that she bore within her barely weakened the attraction of the uncertain supernatural, where Scottish superstition reigned supreme. By one of those mysterious tricks of memory, the further away they went from the long expanse of water, the better she could make out its disturbing details which created a sensation of solitude. Then came horror. The premonition of forbidden zones, forbidden she knew not how or why.

Aunt Emma's somewhat irritated voice brought her back to her senses:

'What's the matter with you, Elizabeth? I've been talking to you for five minutes. You don't seem to be aware of the fact. What are you dreaming about?'

'Nothing, Auntie. I didn't hear.'

'Look at me. You're white. Do you feel ill?'

'No, I assure you.'

'We have been through two villages. Savannah isn't very far away now. Unfortunately we shall see some hovels.'

'Hovels?'

'My dear girl, you are not yourself. There's something wrong.'

They looked attentively at each other for the first time since Elizabeth's arrival at Dimwood. In the lilac-trimmed bonnet, the aged innocence of this charming, pretty face appeared to the girl like some revelation about a whole society. The wheels made a loud noise as they went round, the horses hammered hard on the road, and once more the sun bore down on the earth to devour it.

Elizabeth was growing up.

2
SAVANNAH

18

*I*mmersed in these all-absorbing thoughts, she was paying
no attention to Aunt Emma's discourse when, suddenly,
she suppressed a cry on seeing the hovels she had been
warned about a moment earlier. The ground was more sandy,
obliging the carriage to go more slowly, and she was able to
observe the wretched dwellings that lined the road. As if to
enliven hopeless poverty, they were painted in all colors,
and they tugged at the heart of the stupefied young Englishwoman, who could not hold back some exclamation when
she saw the children who ran up as the vehicles went by.
Their skinny bodies were barely covered by their rags, and
they raised faces towards the travellers where hunger silently
begged in its own mute tongue full of rancor. Scattered
about behind them, dressed in torn or badly patched cloth,
dirty and forlorn men and women of all ages watched without
opening their mouths, immobile and unperturbed.

'And I thought the South was rich!' Elizabeth exclaimed.

'It is, very,' said Aunt Emma, and she pointed to the
groups of curious spectators as she explained. 'But these are
the riff-raff, poor Whites.'

This time it was a loud cry of indignation that Elizabeth
uttered:

'Riff-raff! Why riff-raff?'

Shocked, she had stood up, casting her eyes over all
those faces that were amazed at her amazement, and all of a
sudden she heard the young coachman's voice launch forth
words with a hint of insolence:

'That's how it is, Miss. Those poor whites is riff-raff.'

'Nobody asked you for your opinion, Jehu,' exclaimed
Aunt Emma. 'Come now, faster.'

Catching Elizabeth by the arm, she obliged her to sit
down and once again drew her bonnet close to that shattered
little face.

'You ought to know, my girl, that these people are despised
even by the coloreds. Their very name is an insult in polite
society. They call them Poor White Trash.'

Elizabeth refrained from passing an opinion on what she
had just heard, which disturbed her even more than

anything else she had seen. Neither could she understand why, amongst all this poverty-stricken white humanity, Negroes were going about dressed in bright colors, mainly blue, but also red and green. They were all coming and going in complete freedom, singing and chatting with the liveliness common to their race, while the Whites all around seemed not to notice them and did not move.

'This is all very mysterious,' she thought.

The conventions she had absorbed in the last few days at Dimwood had been strangely toppled, but the picture was changing fast.

Now the horses' hooves were gaily clip-clopping over a wide street paved with pink brick. The fairy tale was beginning, wiping away those earlier impressions. To right and left, immense sycamores bent gracefully to mingle their foliage and form a light and impenetrable vault.

Once again, Aunt Emma used her loudhailer, that is to say, she turned towards Elizabeth and shouted to her:

'We have just entered the town via the Ogeechee Gate, and that name means nothing to you, because your mind is elsewhere, but I pointed out the Ogeechee River to you in the distance ten minutes ago when you weren't listening. I believe you are deaf.'

'Yes, yes,' the girl answered distractedly.

Her eyes were turning to left and right, not tiring of looking at the houses with white or deep red façades, overgrown with honeysuckle. Between wrought-iron railings, ten or a dozen steps led up to front doors of elegant simplicity. Masses of flowers smiled at passers-by: azaleas, rhododendrons, hydrangeas.

She vaguely heard Aunt Emma's shrill voice hurling directions at the coachman; the names Whitaker and Broughton struck the girl's ears, taking her back to England after her passage through Indian territory. It was indeed of her country she thought when, in a kind of daze, she crossed an area where houses with fine white columns formed a vast square. Divided one from another by little gardens that resembled bouquets of flowers, hundred year-old oaks covered them indiscriminately with their peaceful shade, as if to draw them closer together. Each one was distinguished by the perfect sobriety of its façade and, again, all the demands of refinement were concentrated on the doorway, ornamented with a slight pediment or even a rounded peristyle with five small columns.

At this point Aunt Emma assumed the didactic tone of which she was fond:

'You can admire these villas after a fashion, so proud of themselves for being here. It was a lad from your part of the world who built them. Remember his name. He was twenty-three years old and his name was . . . his name was . . . . Oh how annoying! I've forgotten it, but Douglas will tell you . . .'

'Twenty-three!' exclaimed Elizabeth in a daze. 'Was he handsome?'

'There's a fine question! I've no idea. There are times when I wonder if you aren't mad.'

And suddenly she exclaimed:

'Jay! William Jay. Remember that name.'

'I shall never forget it,' murmured Elizabeth, no longer really knowing what she was saying.

For a quarter of an hour now she had felt herself in transports of joy. The memory of Dimwood gradually disappeared from the horizon of her mind and belonged to a past already strangely distant. The plantation with its hours of anguish and tears was fading like some nightmare. It gave way to the delights of the present moment which permitted her to see, in the middle of the square on a shady walk between vast lawns, ladies in light-colored dresses, in an amazing diversity of the most delicate shades, lime-green, lilac, pale yellow, their heads lost under wide-brimmed sun-bonnets, sprigged with tiny clusters of flowers. Anxious about the harmful effects of the light, these elegant ladies held in their white- or mauve-gloved hands ridiculously small sun-shades that they waved nonchalantly about. The murmurings of their conversation laced with laughter reached Elizabeth's ears like a song of happiness and freedom from care. She would have liked to get down and join them, but the vehicles were already moving out of the square and turning east. She caught the name Abercorn that Aunt Emma was making some effort to hurl at her, when Uncle Josh's voice resounded from the second carriage that was overtaking them:

'We're there!'

Spacious and paved with pink bricks where rows of sycamores cast a gently shifting shade, the street was fragrant
with honeysuckle that decorated the houses and jasmine
bordered the pavement.

Set aside from its neighbors, Charlie Jones's dwelling
was endowed with a wrought-iron verandah reached by fifteen
or so steps. At first glance, Elizabeth took in nothing else,
for almost immediately ensued the joyful chaos of arriving,
akin to a riot. Servants in almond-green livery with handsome
gold braid ran down the steps two at a time, their coat tails
blowing in the breeze, while the travellers got down from
the carriages with all the customary exclamations. From the
top of the verandah, a man dressed in black hurried down
to the new arrivals, his hands outstretched and laughing
lustily.

'We have been expecting you this last hour!' he exclaimed.
'I thought the Cherokees must have been having fun scalping
you. Hello to you. Hello, Emma! Hello, Billy, you rascal!
Where is my young countrywoman?'

Elizabeth was still in the back of the carriage, intimidated
by this man who struck her as one of the most handsome
people she had ever seen, as much in his natural elegance as
in the regularity of his features, and especially in the flashing
of his large, deep blue eyes.

Seeing that she was not moving he made as if to take a
great leap towards her with the lightness of a dancer, and
seized her in his arms. She let him and blushed.

'I hope you are not afraid of English bogeymen, Cousin
Elizabeth,' he said.

She stammered:

'I'm afraid of nothing!'

'Well, I take that as permission to kiss you.'

She felt against her own his face, scented with eau-de-
Cologne, and closed her eyes so that he should not see her
emotion.

'Charlie,' Uncle Josh exclaimed, 'when you've finished
your indifferent rendering of *Romeo and Juliet*, what about
looking after your guests?'

But black hands were already picking up the luggage and
carrying it up to the verandah. Charlie let his voice be

heard:

'Aminadab, mint juleps in the green drawing room! Your arm, Emma, let me help you up these few steps. Octavia will show you to your room where you can rest.'

Leaning on him as she carried her crinoline, Aunt Emma let slip some incomprehensible niceties.

'What you say is so full of good sense!' said Charlie Jones, who had not heard a word of it. 'It's a pleasure to listen to you.'

Aunt Emma turned towards him a hooded face radiantly smiling:

'You're a charmer, Charlie Jones,' she declared, 'and I don't know if I should believe you.'

He protested, and this banter brought them to the door of a most agreeable bedroom, generously endowed with mirrors, overlooking the gardens.

Freed of Aunt Emma, he ran towards Josh who was holding Elizabeth by the hand, calmly following the servants loaded with heavy valises of thick leather. Charlie himself opened the door of the room reserved for his compatriot.

She went in and could not hold back a cry of wonder. The room was surely worthy of it, its walls hung with pale blue moire silk, and its pretty furniture upholstered in chintz with large flowers on a black background. In a corner a bed with delicately grooved columns was hidden behind white curtains and a sand-colored hessian blind filtering the light gave protection to a wide balcony. A little to one side, hanging on the wall in a black frame, a portrait made something of a contrast with the delicacy of the whole, but it did not catch Elizabeth's attention at first.

'There you are,' said Charlie Jones gaily. 'This will be Elizabeth's room every time she comes to Savannah.'

'A room fit for a princess,' Uncle Josh remarked.

'As I've never received a princess, I'm not qualified to comment on your opinion. Would you like to see the wretched broom cupboard reserved for you now? Don't run away, Elizabeth. As for you Billy, patience. I think there's still some rat hole left somewhere in the house that's being saved for you.'

'A rat hole!' exclaimed Billy indignantly.

'Don't complain, my boy, you should be able to sleep on a

bench at your age.'

Still teasing them with his inexhaustible joviality, he led his other guests down a spacious corridor, each one to his room. Josh let out a cry on seeing his. As masculine as the girl's had been cosy, it offered every guarantee of British discomfort, combined with dignity of the highest style: massive armchairs of genuine antiquity, a bed of regal proportions – one glance was enough to ascertain the marble-like hardness of it. The only concession to human softness was a sumptuous rocking chair, strewn with cowardly cushions, as well filled as anyone could wish.

'I was sure you were lying when you were talking about a broom cupboard,' said Uncle Josh with a laugh.

'A sample of our national hypocrisy,' said Charlie Jones modestly. 'I'll leave you for a moment. Us two now, Billy. Follow me.'

With his nose to the fore, ready for action, and his brow furrowed, Billy obeyed without a word, still ready to make disobliging remarks if the rat hole really did live up to its name.

He did not have long to wait. At the far end of the corridor, he saw a door to which had been pinned a sheet of paper on which the following inscription could be read in large letters:

PRIVATE RESIDENCE OF WILLIAM HARGROVE JUNIOR
KNOWN AS 'THE RAT HOLE'
ENTRY STRICTLY FORBIDDEN ON PAIN OF
IMMEDIATE EXECUTION

Charlie Jones went in first and leant against the wall in order to let Billy pass. As he did so, he opened his mouth and remained dumbstruck.

It was a broad, square room, with a high ceiling. On the walls painted with ocher were to be seen, in gilt frames, a series of colored engravings. Some offered, to those anxious to learn, instruction in the different stages of a boxing match, and this with ferocious realism, while others depicted fox hunting, where the pink of the coats was triumphant, together with hunting horns and the shiny hindquarters of the thoroughbreds. Elsewhere, a superb etching showed the final struggle of a sailing ship against a raging sea, but what amazed Billy above all else was a long Indian canoe hanging from the ceiling. A rope pulley made it possible to lower this craft that was equipped with a paddle.

'All made out of buffalo hide and available to enthusiasts, but I recommend gentle streams rather than those noble rivers that the alligators are so fond of.'

'Oh!' said Billy, looking delighted. 'I'll be careful, you can be sure.'

'Be equally careful about the girls you see in the town. I know you, I was your age once. As you know, alligators have eighty teeth. Young ladies have no more than thirty-two, but in both cases the smile needs to be approached with care. Understood?'

'Yes, sir.'

'Don't call me sir. From now on, you can know me as Uncle Charlie.'

'Right . . . Uncle Charlie.'

'When you come in at night, not too late and before cockcrow if possible, you'll be able to rest your shattered limbs here.'

He pointed to a black oak bed in a severe style, as narrow as a soldier's bed, pushed into a dark corner.

'Pleased?' asked Charlie Jones.

'Oh, yes!' said Billy with somewhat studied enthusiasm, for at Dimwood he slept in a curtained four-poster bed.

'In a few minutes, a servant will come and bring you to the small drawing room, where we can lay our plans. It is going to be a full day.'

He had barely spoken these words when he disappeared, leaving a perplexed Billy behind in the bedroom, trying to make out Charlie Jones and his irony. He thought he could detect in it a sort of secret complicity. The boy strove to see in it a subtle authorization to behave badly, within limits, for the easy living of Savannah had its reputation in the surrounding countryside. These profound considerations kept him busy until the liveried servant came to take him to the green drawing room.

For her part, Elizabeth was enchanted with her room. She sat in all the armchairs, then leant over the balcony and breathed in the flowers, whose perfume wafted up to her.

The portrait in its black frame received no more than a glance at first, but suddenly, as she walked past it again, she stopped. The painting, in a rather naive style, depicted a young man of about twenty, dressed in black and with a carefully knotted white scarf around his neck. The face had an imperious beauty. The stormy blue eyes had a tendency towards blackness, but a slightly mocking smile hovered on the fleshy lips. Just as he was, he stirred the girl's emotions, awakening thoughts of love.

For a few minutes she would not have been capable of telling whether it was pain or, on the contrary, joy that made her heart pound and, when the servant came to knock on her door, she felt so discomfited that she begged him to wait. What was tormenting her even more than this impassioned admiration verged on the most irritating of mysteries. It seemed to her that she had known this person, spying on her from his old-fashioned frame.

'You are falling for someone who is no more. Leave the dead in peace.'

Finally she came to her senses and, running towards the door, she followed the servant.

Alone in his room after Charlie Jones's departure, Uncle Josh cast a critical glance about him and looked at the bed with a connoisseur's eye.

'Interesting,' he muttered. 'In perfect taste. Circa 1600, I should say, and straight from some princely, if not royal, household, but I'm going to insist that they add a thick horsehair mattress, or even two of them.'

And he said aloud:

'There's always some trick or other in that joker's attentiveness. Let's have a look at this armchair.'

Settling himself in the rocking chair, he swung backward and forward for a few minutes with a beatific smile.

'Tolerable,' he said, 'pretty tolerable even. Our Charlie is still human, in spite of his success.'

He got out of the chair brusquely and continued his exploration of the room with a curiosity that left nothing unturned, until there was a knock at his door.

'I'll be down,' he cried. 'No point waiting for me, I know the way.'

19

The green drawing room, which saw them all gathered together a moment later, was notable for the relative simplicity of its refinement, set off by the delicate gilding on the moldings and the discreet rustle of the violet taffeta curtains.

Adorned with an imposing lace bonnet, Aunt Emma took her place in a substantial armchair, while the master of the house made Elizabeth sit down at his right on a long, lavender silk sofa.

'It is contrary to all Southern customs for a gentleman to sit next to a young lady on a sofa,' he declared with a smile, 'but I hope that our guest of honor will not chase me away, and that she will be good enough to share a welcoming julep with us.'

As he spoke these words, three servants dressed in white made their entry with trays laden with large glasses decorated with the traditional mint leaf on crushed ice.

'Charlie,' exclaimed Aunt Emma, 'don't you think Elizabeth is too young to drink a julep? She doesn't even know what it is.'

'You can rest assured, Emma, I myself prepared the julep destined for her. But then an English girl isn't afraid of anything, is she?'

'Not of anything!' said Elizabeth like an echo, but she blushed in spite of herself and felt ill at ease on account of her blue dress that clashed with the colors of this elegant room.

As if he had guessed at her unease, Charlie Jones added:

'A little mouthful of this beverage will change your view of the world and will make you smile. You'll find this straw useful.'

Uncle Josh, who was standing in the middle of the drawing room, was of the opinion that Elizabeth should be informed of what she was about to drink.

'I can explain to her,' exclaimed Billy suddenly, burning to get a word in. 'I couldn't say how many juleps I've made for my friends.'

'Well, let's see,' said Charlie Jones indulgently, 'but

remember that you're in the company of experts here.'

The boy ran a slightly nervous hand through his hair in order to give himself confidence.

'For each glass, a handful of mint leaves,' the orator began.

'A handful! He overdoes it!' said Aunt Emma.

'Don't interrupt him,' said Charlie Jones. 'He's a hot-headed son of the South who does nothing by halves. So, dear professor, here you are with your handful of mint leaves at the ready, and what are you going to do with them?'

'I crush them, I reduce them to a pulp.'

'As one crushes the enemy in battle,' suggested Uncle Josh.

'Exactly. When they are in the bottom of the glass, I fill it up to the brim with crushed ice.'

'Crushed to death, like the mint, unfortunate thing,' muttered Uncle Josh perfidiously.

'By no means. Just normally crushed, that's all.'

Charlie then assumed an innocent air.

'So far everything is going splendidly. And now comes the great moment for the rum that you pour over it all.'

Billy was scandalized and cried out:

'Rum, Uncle Charlie? What are you thinking of? Come now, whiskey.'

'Fine, my boy, but there are so many different whiskies.'

Aunt Emma's bonnet stirred itself.

'Oh, never mind which one! Let's be done with it. I don't want to drink before everybody else, but I'm dying of thirst.'

'Never mind which one,' said Billy sententiously. 'Every gentleman known that bourbon is the only one possible.'

'Bravo,' said Charlie Jones, 'but how does he know all that? I wonder if, young as you are, you don't already have a past. But we won't go into that. Have you finished?'

'Not yet. Last of all, the sugar.'

A renewed exclamation from Aunt Emma.

'Oh! Not too much, for heaven's sake, it's the sugar that makes you tipsy.'

Billy flashed his blue eyes at his mother.

'What else do you want it to do, Mama?'

'Logically, he's right,' said Charlie Jones giving his

opinion, 'but there is moderation in all things, my boy.'

'I hate moderation!' exclaimed Billy who was getting more and more dishevelled.

Then Uncle Josh gave a crafty smile.

'My word, you'd think the professor had drunk a julep by way of preparation in the kitchen.'

'I don't frequent the kitchen, sir.'

Uncle Charlie intervened.

'Be quiet, Josh. You're upsetting our expert. Carry on, Billy.'

'I stick a mint leaf into the ice, on the top, like a banner.'

'And that, of course, is the finishing touch,' said Uncle Josh wryly. 'It only remains now to drink your impeccable julep.'

Billy raised his hand:

'You're in too much of a hurry, Uncle Josh. First it has to spend the night on ice.'

Charlie Jones burst out laughing:

'Well played, my boy. He got out of all our little traps, Josh. Let's judge the result now. Elizabeth,' and here he made a pause, 'I drink in your honor.'

'To Elizabeth's happiness, and to the future,' Uncle Josh added.

The glasses were discreetly raised, and the straws activated. There was a brief silence, then Uncle Josh said simply:

'Delicious.'

'Absolutely,' said Charlie Jones. 'What do you say to it, Elizabeth?'

'I think it's quite good,' she said.

'Do you hear her?' exclaimed Charlie Jones. 'She is in that great literary tradition of understatement out of a horror for vulgar superlatives.'

'What's all this commotion?' said Billy, who had already emptied one third of his glass, and whose head was spinning. 'Doesn't she like my julep?'

'Calm down,' said Josh. 'In the first place, it's not your julep. It was made here last night. And then we should let Elizabeth get used to the taste.'

With her eyes closed, the girl seemed to be elsewhere. She methodically consumed the contents of her glass, which they had to take gently from her hands.

'Not so quickly, my girl,' said Charlie Jones, 'one has to learn to savor slowly the good things in life.'

'But I feel fine,' she said with an ecstatic smile and then, in a rather uncertain voice: 'Give me my glass back.'

Aunt Emma's voice made its presence felt:

'I told you to beware of the sugar.'

She readjusted her ample bonnet that was always slipping to one side.

'But I admit,' she said, 'that this julep is amongst the best I've ever drunk.'

Charlie Jones stood up.

'I suggest that we take our glasses to the dining room. You'll find yours at your place, Elizabeth.'

After a little unsteadiness, Aunt Emma was on her feet and held out her glass to a servant.

'Give me your arm, Charlie,' she said.

They left the drawing room together, followed by Elizabeth, whom Josh was holding firmly by the hand, and finally Billy whose eyes were shining even more than usual. They were all laughing and joking, even before they sat down at table, and such a good-humored confusion prevailed that a joyful meal was augured. Their voices were already rather loud.

The oval-shaped dining room was decorated with light wood panelling, simulating fine-grooved pilasters in the purest neo-classical Regency style. Scattered on the white tablecloth in very careful disarray, flowers of every hue lent a festive air to the somewhat severe decor.

Elizabeth, who could feel her head pleasantly spinning, found some support in contemplating Charlie Jones. He had placed her on his left, and she could not but admire him, as much for his perfect profile as for the freshness of his cheeks as brightly pink as if he had just been for a gallop in Devonshire on a fine winter's morning. She did not understand much of what was being said to her, but she was happy.

Uncle Josh called to her from the other side of the table and wanted to know if she felt all right. By way of an answer, she smiled at him. She felt like smiling at everybody, without realizing that the contents of her glass had been surreptitiously replaced with water colored with mint.

She had the impression that everyone was talking at once, and making enough noise for twenty. The white-clad servants passed by like shadows as they moved around the table, and their eyes lingered on the young foreigner. A delicious sensation of unreality took hold of her, despite the presence of Uncle Charlie, who was outlining the program for the day at the top of his voice, and she quivered a few times as she heard her name recurring, but nothing mattered in that moment of well-being. Suddenly a white-gloved hand placed in front of her a plate of cold soup, of which she raised a spoonful to her mouth, imitating her neighbors, but without recognizing the taste of what she compliantly swallowed. At that moment Uncle Charlie leant towards her and whispered in her ear:

'Turtle soup. Do you like it?'

She vaguely nodded agreement and gave him a smile.

Gradually she came to and turned her gaze away from Charlie Jones, realizing that Billy, who was sitting next to her, had been watching her for some time. Suddenly he gave her a dig with his elbow and said, in what he believed to be a whisper:

'They're simply trying to fit you out as they would like. Aren't you listening to what they're saying?'

'What they're saying, oh no . . .'

'Mama is choosing dresses that are too old for you. "Respectable" is the only word on their tongues. Uncle Josh is awful, as bad as the others.'

'Awful?'

'Terribly old hat. Fortunately Uncle Charlie is insisting that you have your say. So listen. I'll be there to tell you how young people dress.'

'Oh yes,' said Elizabeth, restored to complete lucidity.

'If you don't look out, they're going to turn you into a lady. Like that dress you're wearing, between you and me it's . . .'

'Frightful!' exclaimed Elizabeth aloud. 'But I'll stick up for myself.'

Suddenly there was a strange silence.

'She said something,' intervened Aunt Emma.

One might have thought that some kind of miracle had just taken place.

— 161 —

'Don't worry,' said Uncle Josh. 'She's quite all right.'

Sitting up straight like someone who is going to make an important declaration, Charlie Jones got ready to speak:

'Let's arrange things so that today will be Elizabeth's first real day of happiness in the South. She will choose what she prefers from all the things offered her. We will indulge her whims, we won't torment her with good advice. Let's spoil her . . .'

Mutterings could be heard from the direction of the adults, but Billy took it upon himself to applaud.

'Hurrah!' he said.

Charlie Jones gave him a steely look and continued:

'. . . because we suppose that she is too refined not to know where those elusive boundaries are situated.'

'What boundaries?' asked Billy.

'I'll explain that to you in private some day,' said Charlie Jones softly. 'For the moment let us think of nothing but joyfulness.'

'I'm trying to imagine the face my father would pull if he were here to listen to you.'

Josh's remark upset Elizabeth, who could sniff danger.

'What are you thinking of?'

'Appearances. He sets so much store by them as far as dress is concerned.'

'He'll accept anything that might make Elizabeth smile.'

Uncle Josh sighed without answering.

'Come now,' said Charlie Jones, 'don't take on this gloomy air. I know Willie Hargrove better than you, his son, does. We've worked together. I can convince him of anything I like.'

Aunt Emma assumed the subversive air that was her custom whenever she had in mind to amuse herself by scattering alarm in the conversation.

'I find it very odd that he's staying away from Dimwood for so long.'

'He'll be back, never fear,' said Uncle Charlie.

'Ah, and what if he doesn't come back for some reason?'

'You're dreaming, Emma,' said Josh. 'Let's move on to something else.'

Not to be put off, Aunt Emma continued calmly:

'It wouldn't be the first time a man leaves the plantation

for good.'

For the last few minutes, Elizabeth had been all agog, and this intensity hardened her features as suddenly she let slip a question, like a cry from her lips:

'Isn't Uncle Will coming back?'

This sudden outburst provoked stupefaction, and Uncle Josh immediately reassured the girl, but Charlie Jones was watching her closely: it was not fear that had cried out, but rather a hope that could not be admitted to.

'Cousin Emma,' he said at last, 'do you not see that you are frightening Elizabeth with your tales? Let us leave all that, don't you think? Let's do justice to this Virginia ham and to the sweet potatoes and corn fritters!'

A dish was put down in front of Charlie Jones who stood up once more, as if to salute this noble joint of meat, whose color was reminiscent of the dark red of the finest houses in the town. Caramelized sugar gilded parts of this fragrant mass which aroused a general murmur of satisfaction and put an end to the disagreements.

As he wielded his long knife with amazing dexterity, Uncle Charlie kept an eye on his young neighbor.

'Elizabeth,' he said, 'this ham comes straight from a little town in Virginia; it's modest, yet has almost a worldwide reputation. It's called Smithfield, and I'll take you there some day. You'll see an enormous barn, as dark and full of mystery as a wood, and you can walk about in it amidst the delicious aroma, in the shade of hundreds and hundreds of hams hanging from the beams. You'll think you're lost in a forest for the greedy, but everything there arouses your appetite. It's out of your reach, but not out of mine. I've selected the best for you.'

Uncle Josh suddenly interrupted him.

'We're hungry, Charlie. For Heaven's sake, have done with your eulogies.'

Unperturbed, Charlie Jones continued his skilful carving of thick slices and answered through his teeth:

'You doubtless judge my little speech to be frivolous.'

'It seems to me charming and entirely superfluous.'

Almost under his breath, with his head bent over his knife, Charlie Jones muttered:

'But you ought to know that I never do anything without

good reason.'

His task was completed with this phrase, and the servants held out one after another the large Meissen plates, rimmed in dark blue and so hot that they were burning to the touch. Soon they were host to the ham, the maize fritters in round discs and the sweet potatoes cut into pink slices all running with gold.

Intoxicated by the food as they had been by the julep, the guests gave themselves up to the pleasure of chattering amidst the clicking of cutlery on porcelain. Elizabeth had been fitted out several times in all the colors of the rainbow, in lawn, in silk and in cotton, in short skirts and in mid-calf skirts strewn with flowers, with ribbons, and with fluttering frills. Out of prudishness they skirted around the problem of lace fringes decorating her hypothetical pantaloons; and Billy, who attempted to venture an opinion on this matter, was firmly put in his place by the three grown-ups. She who was most concerned had not said a word since the beginning of this discussion. She ate in silence and took no second helpings.

Uncle Charlie leant towards her:

'You seem worried, Elizabeth. You haven't touched that wine in your glass, it's very light. Is something upsetting you?'

'Oh no, I assure you, Uncle Charlie.'

She looked at him with a smile, then asked all of a sudden:

'May I ask you a question?'

'Do not hesitate for a minute.'

'It is perhaps not very polite to reveal such curiosity, but I should like to know who is that gentleman whose portrait I have in my room.'

He burst out laughing.

'Is that what was making you so thoughtful?'

She turned quite pink.

'I never talk a lot, you know, I let other people talk. They have so many things to say!'

'Yes, don't they? And usually they leave nothing to spare. But you asked me a question and you haven't answered mine. That gentleman whose portrait you saw in your room . . .'

'Oh, I see I shouldn't have asked . . .'

'Oh yes, what do you think of him?'

'I think it's a fine portrait.'

'Don't try to play games with Uncle Charlie, my girl. Would you have liked to know that gentleman?'

'I didn't say that.'

'Perhaps not. But you'll never meet him.'

'Is he dead?'

'Not entirely. It's me when I was twenty.'

She started, then let out a nervous laugh. Her disappointment was so obvious that he himself was taken aback, and the two of them looked at each other for several seconds. Then Charlie Jones laughed in his turn, with great good humor:

'People change quickly with age, Elizabeth. Not the ladies, they are indestructible, but we men . . . I can understand your surprise.'

The girl guessed involuntarily that she had wounded him in that self-esteem that is always raw in men, and she sought for some word to soften the blow.

'No surprise,' she said in an animated tone of voice, 'I recognized you straight away.'

'Elizabeth,' said Uncle Charlie with a gleam of tenderness in his blue eyes, 'you're no good at lying yet.'

She exclaimed angrily:

'I never lie.'

'They'll teach you how, and it'll be a pity.'

She suddenly hated this man, for she had in fact lied to him, but, although in emotional panic, she admired him in spite of herself. How could she deny the likeness between the portrait in her room and that pink, regular face that was looking her straight in the eyes?

'I have angered you a little,' he said in a low voice. 'I hope you are not cross with me. I shall do everything to ensure your happiness here.'

She limited herself to a slight movement of the head by way of thanks.

'In a little while the carriage will take you to Mademoiselle Clementine's,' he continued. 'She is in receipt of my instructions to satisfy your every whim. Mademoiselle Souligou has sent her your measurements. That will help matters greatly.'

'Souligou . . .' said Elizabeth like someone remembering a dream, and at a stroke she saw herself back at Dimwood.

'I don't want to go back to the plantation,' she said.

Uncle Charlie did not answer straight away and began to drum on the table with his fingertips. His face clouded over:

'Can you tell me why?' he asked gently.

She shook her head.

'Later perhaps?'

Making an effort with the whole of her being, she looked him in the eyes.

'How can I confide in someone who doesn't believe me?'

This simply spoken sentence did not produce the effect she expected. Without the least protestation, he confined himself to a smile:

'I understand,' he said. 'I understand very well, but I think we are being overheard.'

Indeed, a great silence had settled around them for the last few minutes, and Aunt Emma's didactic voice rose up amidst the steam from the meal.

'Cousin Charlie,' she said, 'I think it is somewhat unfair for you and our dear Elizabeth to be speaking so softly for so long, and not a single word of ours seems to have got through to you. I'm sure you were saying some most interesting things.'

The pink of her cheeks had become brighter without her realizing it, and her great lace bonnet had slid down towards one shoulder. Uncle Josh set right this little irregularity in her toilette, then took a firm hold on a splendid cut-glass decanter, containing the precious Gruaud-Larose that Billy was keen to get his hands on.

'Charlie,' said Josh as he got up, 'if you are in agreement, I suggest that we cut short this delicious meal and tarry no longer before setting off for town. It's going to be a busy afternoon.'

'What about my siesta?' said Aunt Emma.

'And the dessert?' said Billy.

Uncle Charlie laughed good-naturedly in a way that settled everything.

'Just as you like,' he said. 'Let us first of all leave Aunt Emma to take a little rest on the drawing room sofa, and as for the strawberries and cream and other such consolations, they will be waiting for us when we get back at tea-time.'

With a nod, he called one of the servants:

'Go and tell Azor to get the horses harnessed.'

'Azor,' said Uncle Josh when the servant had gone out. 'There's a name I haven't heard since my youth when I was on holiday in Paris, but it was a dog's name.'

'Is it my fault, Josh, if my coachman is called Azor? That's the way his parents wanted it. But if the Reverend Ebenezer Tucker, their own pastor, were here, he would tell you to re-read the New Testament, and you'd soon come across your Azor with a blush.'

'Well I never!' said Uncle Josh. 'I'll check it.'

'I admit to having checked it myself. The Bible is full of surprises. In the meantime, let's help Aunt Emma up.'

'Aunt Emma has no need of help,' the latter said in a fit of pique. First holding on to the table, then on to her chair and finally to the arm of a servant, she managed to get to her feet.

With an impatient gesture, she shook out her crinoline to its full width and moved off towards the door with a dignified slowness. Although she was standing upright she seemed to be supported only by the hoop of her mauve, flounced skirt propelling her forward.

20

*H*alf an hour later, Uncle Charlie's two gigs were on their way to the shopping district. In a more fashionable style than Uncle Josh's, which had remained behind in the stables, they presented a somewhat ostentatious contrast between the jet-black of the coachwork and the bright yellow of the large wheels, spinning round like the sun. Perched on his seat in an elegant, light beige frock coat, Azor the coachman was constantly cracking his whip, but for no particular reason. One could feel that he was proud of himself from the way he wore a cylindrical little hat almost down to his eyes, setting off to advantage his bronze complexion.

The second gig was entrusted to Jehu, one of Uncle Josh's coachmen, the very one who had brought Elizabeth and Aunt Emma to Savannah. He competed in self-satisfaction and whip-cracking with his colleague, over whom, being a mulatto, he felt himself vastly superior. The brass buttons shone on his red outfit and, above all, his black boots with peach-colored lining added to his confidence. He knew that he was admired just as much as the magnificent chestnut horses, with their sensual beauty, their elongated shape and the refinement of their harnesses. In all of this a kind of impudence had the upper hand, and there was something provocative in the clip-clop of the horses' hooves on the stone roadway.

In this highly populated part of the town, admiration and envy watched this show of vanity pass by, and there rebounded onto the occupants of the vehicles a vague feeling of unease that was difficult to explain. Elizabeth did not know how to interpret the faces of those walking by, but she judged herself to be incomprehensibly in the wrong, and she would have liked to hide. As for Aunt Emma, she was afraid. Although she was well used to riches, she did not care to attract attention to herself in the streets with this display of opulence. For his part, Billy, of a simpler make-up, was taken with the desire to stick out his tongue at those showing such curiosity.

As on the previous occasion, he was seated next to Uncle Josh. The latter pretended not to notice the disconcerting interest that he and his companions aroused. The lowly people who could not take their eyes off them did not always keep to themselves the unfriendly thoughts inspired by the luxury and showiness of high society. And yet notable families had to give due consideration to their rank. A principle that had withstood the rigors of time was not in dispute: that there should be in the district some men and women who worked hard to earn a living and that others lived only on charity, was one of the mysteries of fate. On this point, Uncle Josh's views tended to concur with received wisdom, but there was something else that was more disturbing. Neither the laborer in the field cultivating the land nor the shopkeepers and tradesmen in the town had any value in the eyes of descendants of the English aristocracy. Those who worked constituted a single class, that of the *crackers*, a term of abuse. One had gone much further down the scale of the non-rich by the time one came to the real poor, to wretches with faces that made one anxious. They constituted the dregs, the *Poor White Trash*, openly despised, even by the Negroes, and in that area – like Aunt Emma, but for more precise reasons – Uncle Josh was afraid. It was not that he feared rebellion and violence; he simply wondered how much longer all this could go on. But he progressed no further in his cogitations.

Soon the two carriages entered a street shaded with syca-mores. It was not the main street, and the houses had no more than two storys, but its shops earned it a noteworthy reputation for respectability. In their windows were rare objects from Europe, sometimes furniture of the grandest style. A number of antiquarian bookshops offered to con-noisseurs rare works in fine old bindings. At the end of the afternoon, strollers would linger, and elegant ladies' parasols created a medley of colors which added to the charm of this quiet street. The clatter of the carriages made heads turn, and people immediately recognized the Jones's coach-work. No one was surprised to see them stopping in front of the fashion house where the name of Mademoiselle Clemen-tine of Paris was spread out in English-style lettering. The shop windows to the right and left of the doorway, took up almost the entire width of the building, the last in a long row.

In the downstairs room stood half a dozen wooden dummies dressed in the fashions of the day, but with that little some-thing extra in which the experienced eye of a Parisian woman would perhaps have recognized the style of her capital. Bodices boldly low-cut, covered with a lace kerchief, thus concealing what it seemed impossible to show off in any other way. Waists mercilessly pinched, allowing free and triumphant rein to the fussiness of the crinolines. Imagina-tion alone envisaged the legs, like the clappers of some monstrous bell. To help out the imaginative powers of passers-by, the wax heads that topped the bodies of these lifeless ladies offered them delightful faces, with smiles of radiant stupidity.

Billy was not unmoved by this artifice and was only sorry that no naked arms were visible, but the sleeves spewed out masses of embroidered fine linen down to the wrists of little hands in leather gloves.

As for Elizabeth, she was still quite dazzled by the splendor of the rich, deep-colored taffetas, by the delicate shades of summer fabrics, with frills that would quiver in the swirl of the dancing, that were intended for a ball . . . All she hoped was that, having come into this place tortured by her sky-blue dress, she would go back into the town dressed like everybody else.

Aunt Emma jostled her a little as she passed by on her way up to the first floor.

Mademoiselle Clementine welcomed her visitors with a marked politeness. She even gratified Aunt Emma with a discreet curtsey. Quite tall and filling out a pale gray dress, she faced up to her fifty years with cosmetics that brightened up the cheeks of a worn, pretty face. As light as a lace cloud, a bonnet was perched on her head, her heavy black hair parted and drawn back up just above her dainty little ears, of which one felt she was proud; but what struck one first of all were the deep, warm, black eyes beneath brownish eyelids. She was born, she said, in Louisiana, and often alluded to her creole background. Her very soft voice was pleasant to the ear, but she was known for being able to speak out. For clients from good society, she reserved a carefully rehearsed intonation, such as was to be heard in aristocratic circles.

Was she aware of the contrast between her own person and the setting she had so carefully dreamed up to play her role in? The straight-backed armchairs covered in sober, pale blue material, the absence of any superfluous ornamentation, even to the severe elegance of her gray dress, without the least flounce or the most modest of crinolines to bring life to its pleats?

She herself exhaled violence reined in, one could sniff out the passion that flowed through that wild and substantial body from which there exuded a kind of animal warmth. Less easily than the gentlemen who are given to indulgence, the ladies glossed over it, glossed over many things in favor of her prodigious talent with the needle.

Where did she come from? From what corner of Louisiana's vastness? People did not know, and she did not say. And where did the money come from to set herself up in such an exacting town as Savannah? Some mysterious protection had been involved. It was better not to know; there she was, with her magician's hands.

For the moment she was standing, against the daylight to conceal a few wrinkles, and her visitors, seated in front of her, awaited they knew not what pronouncement on the most suitable way to dress the new client, whom she was silently taking in with a somewhat merciless attention. Even pinker than usual, Elizabeth had difficulty bearing the weight of those dark looks, and she felt indignation welling up inside her. It seemed to her as if she was being examined from head to foot, and when a sing-song voice asked her to stand up, her reaction was one of rebellion, and she did not move. Uncle Josh had to explain to her gently that it was necessary to help Mademoiselle Clementine in her work and, with some ill feeling, she stood up.

Standing up now in front of everyone in her hated blue dress, she cast a despising glance at this large, indiscreet woman, who was walking around her as if around some monument, stopping, reflectively, at every step. And in the silence the latter could be heard to mutter in French:

'Souligou, Souligou, you have a long way to go before you make it to *haute couture.*'

Uncle Josh then spoke up in the same language:

'Mademoiselle Souligou does not pretend to be in the same league as yourself, as far as sewing is concerned, Mademoiselle Clementine.'

'Speak English, I beg you,' exclaimed Aunt Emma. 'I feel excluded when you speak French.'

Mademoiselle Clementine turned towards her:

'Excuse me, madam, it's my foreign blood speaking.'

And she continued in English:

'The dress of Miss . . . Miss . . .'

'Elizabeth,' said Josh impatiently, 'I thought we had told you.'

Mademoiselle Clementine bowed with a smile and continued:

'Miss Elizabeth's dress is charming, but it does not suit

her. I hope I can do better.'

As she spoke these words, she fixed an inquisitive look on the English girl. She was visibly asking questions about the newcomer of whom she knew almost nothing, except that she had a penniless mother and had been taken in by Mr Hargrove. Out of charity, according to those in the town who were well informed.

Out of charity . . . It was praiseworthy, but did Elizabeth come from that category of poor whites, that dross? To put it differently, was this little thing a lady or some common personage? From a modest background herself, she couldn't be sure, she lacked the *instinct* peculiar to those who just know quality; the curious thing was that this same instinct was infallible in the slaves, who could judge such things in a trice. Now she, Clementine, had not a drop of black blood in her veins, she came from a *somewhere else* that she did not reveal. Without knowing it, she had put her finger on the open wound of a whole society: that notorious Southern arrogance that exasperated the North.

In her uncertainty, an idea came to her. Raising her voice, she called out:

'Dorcas!'

A door immediately opened to let through a young half-caste woman. Clothed almost entirely in a long work apron of gray cloth, she was nonetheless graceful, and her face was striking for the delicacy of its features. Like a pedigree dog confronted with a rare piece of game, Billy immediately fixed an avid gaze on her.

'Stop it, Billy!' muttered Uncle Josh under his breath.

'Yes, Uncle,' said Billy, without turning his eyes away.

Covering this brief exchange with a gently authoritarian voice, Mademoiselle Clementine asked:

'Is it nearly ready, Dorcas?'

'In another hour, it'll be all done. One of them is ready, mademoiselle.'

The warm, rather slow voice completed the arousal of the adolescent, despite an imperious look from Uncle Josh who was trying to bring him back in line.

'An hour is a long time,' said Mademoiselle Clementine. 'Bring me Elizabeth's dress without delay.'

Dorcas disappeared, and at that very moment these words

struck the seamstress's ear, a sharp voice, like a slap of the hand, exclaimed:

'*Miss* Elizabeth, if it's all the same to you.'

There was quality in the voice that issued from Elizabeth's mouth.

A rather sheepish and secretly approving smile lit up Mademoiselle Clementine's face: now she could place her.

'Miss Elizabeth's, of course,' she said.

Suddenly all eyes were focused on the girl, somewhat in surprise and admiration. For the first time she felt that she had crossed a threshold and been accepted. Her eyes were still aflame with indignation, which added to her beauty. Billy nodded to her in complicity, as if he had suddenly discovered her.

Again the door opened and the dress appeared, carried at arm's length by Dorcas. Of pale green fine linen, the almost ethereal fabric was rendered even lighter by three scalloped flounces.

Uncle Josh, together with Billy, started up the whisper of connoisseurs. Aunt Emma remained silent.

'This pale shade should go very well with your golden hair,' said Mademoiselle Clementine. 'Do you like it, Miss Elizabeth?'

Unable to help but find it charming, the girl considered it fitting to restrain the compliments:

'It's not bad.'

'In that case, you could try it on straight away. In the small drawing room, Dorcas.'

The half-caste girl moved towards a door at the far end of the room, followed by Mademoiselle Clementine and Elizabeth, who had suddenly become more docile, for she was burning with impatience to get out of the sky-blue dress and to see herself in this interesting outfit.

A brief silence followed her departure, then Uncle Josh gave his opinion:

'I'm so used to seeing her in her blue dress that I'm expecting a surprise — a pleasant surprise. What do you say, Cousin Emma?'

'Nothing, I'm waiting.'

'As for me,' said Billy, 'I'm sure it will be perfect. If the skirt isn't too long.'

Uncle Josh gave him an ironic look.

'Really? In your case it's never difficult to follow the train of your noble thoughts. On that point, you are embarrassing that young coffee-colored person by your staring. A gentleman does not do that.'

'Dorcas didn't look embarrassed, Uncle.'

'My word, you already call her by her name. I shall keep an eye on you, my boy, don't forget it.'

'Oh! I remembered her name because it seemed pretty. That's all.'

'I admit it's charming. It's redolent of Greek mythology.' Aunt Emma shook slightly at these words.

'Don't you ever read your Bible, Josh? There's nothing mythological about Dorcas. She was a holy woman in the circle of St Paul.'

'Ah? I think that has escaped my memory.'

'If it was ever there to begin with. And do you know what trade she followed?'

'No idea. That of a holy woman, I suppose.'

'Seamstress, my dear.'

'Well, I never.'

'And she made clothes for the poor.'

'Good for Dorcas.'

'With skirts of a respectable length, you can be sure.'

'I take your word for it, Emma. But here comes the object of your solicitude.'

Indeed the door opened, and the English girl appeared, radiant with pleasure in her new dress. Brightened up by that shade of pale green, her hair created a halo of light around her face which was restored to the freshness of childhood. She took a few steps forward and stood in the middle of the room, seized with a sudden shyness, like an actress in her first role.

'Delightful!' exclaimed Uncle Josh.

'Oh, yes! Delightful,' said Billy in an echo full of warmth.

Much more in control of her personal reactions, Aunt Emma simply said:

'Let her turn round a bit.'

'If you would be so good, Miss Elizabeth,' said Mademoiselle Clementine.

Elizabeth obeyed. Judgement was not passed straight

away.

'In my day,' Aunt Emma began, 'it would not have been tolerated . . .'

Uncle Josh interrupted her without hesitation.

'Since your day, fashion and customs have become less narrow, my dear sister-in-law. And then, Uncle Charlie decided that today Elizabeth will have complete freedom to do as she thinks fit. Tell us if you're pleased, Elizabeth.'

A radiant smile was his answer.

'I must say,' remarked Mademoiselle Clementine, 'that Souligou was not an inch out in her measurements.'

Then a quiet but firm voice was raised:

'Josh,' said Aunt Emma, 'have them tell Jehu to take me back to the house. I'll not come with you into town.'

'We are all sorry about that,' said Uncle Josh as he helped her up from her armchair. 'Jehu is waiting downstairs with the gig. I'll come down with you.'

The lace bonnet shook a vigorous no.

'I'm sorry I was a little brusque with you just now,' Josh whispered to her.

She reached the door without answering, but her whole body seemed to express her angry displeasure. Her shoulders were shaking beneath the delicate mauve shawl.

When she had gone, there were a few seconds of polite consternation on their faces, and then Uncle Josh resumed gaily:

'It only remains to congratulate Mademoiselle Clementine and for us to withdraw to do our rounds of Savannah's shops.'

'I showed Miss Elizabeth four or five dresses,' said Mademoiselle Clementine. 'She selected one after some hesitation, which shows a sure sense of color and fashion.'

'I couldn't make a mistake, they were all delightful,' said Elizabeth politely.

'Send all five of them to Mr Charlie Jones's house,' said Uncle Josh immediately.

'You'll have them tomorrow afternoon,' came the immediate reply.

Before she could even say thank you, Elizabeth saw Dorcas come in carrying a large box wrapped in pink paper and all tied in green ribbon.

Her face clouded over. She could guess only too well what that box contained.

'Ah! The blue dress,' said Uncle Josh. 'I was forgetting that.'

'Dorcas will put it in your carriage,' said Mademoiselle Clementine.

'Let's go down. You go first, Elizabeth. After me, Billy.'

There followed a brief and silent scene. Billy, out of hypocritically scrupulous politeness, gave way to Dorcas, with an intent that was all too obvious for the young half-caste not to guess at, and she hung back. With her eyelids lowered, she did not wish to see the eyes he was making at her. Suddenly a discreet cough could be heard and Billy, in spite of himself, returned to the straight and narrow path behind his uncle. Mademoiselle Clementine kept an eye on her employee.

21

The gig driven by Jehu had just disappeared with Aunt Emma when they got into the one where Azor sat enthroned. Billy was hoping to sit next to Elizabeth, but Uncle Josh ensured that good order prevailed.

'Next to me, my boy, so that Elizabeth can spread her pretty skirt out without it getting creased.'

Leaning towards his nephew, he assumed a confidential tone and said to him:

'Let's speak man to man. Your dear Mama is an adorable woman, but she has this particular habit whereby a measure of claret puts her in a good mood . . .'

'A measure!' exclaimed Billy. 'Almost half a decanter, Uncle.'

'Come, come! In any case, she is taken with inexplicable remorse afterwards — as if she had done something wrong

— and things become melancholic. In such circumstances she becomes somber and sees sin in everything.'

'I don't.'

'Never mind that. I simply wanted to find an explanation for her severity just now. Conscience, do you understand? Your grandfather has the same scruples.'

'Oh, him! Everyone knows that. His conscience comes into everything.'

'Silence! I forbid you to talk about Papa in that tone of voice. Now you are one of us, Elizabeth, it is time I told you something about the history of our town. Straight on, Azor, and not too fast.'

'We should never get on, Elizabeth,' said Uncle Josh, 'if roses and jasmine held us up at every street corner. Savannah consists almost entirely of large squares which are like as many paradises. They follow on, one after another, in a straight line, and one always passes from one to the next by means of a shady avenue. Trees, trees, you'll see them everywhere. They call Savannah the forest-town. And flowers . . . Are you sorry you came here now?'

Stammering like someone in love, she answered:

'I should like to live here and never leave the place.'

Billy's voice dragged her from her dream like a clarion call:

'That's it!' he cried. 'Let's leave Dimwood. It's only in Savannah that a good time is to be had.'

'I charge you to put the idea to your grandfather,' said Uncle Josh sarcastically.

'Oh, Grandfather is far away. He must be fed up with Dimwood.'

'He'll come back one of these days.'

'Do you think so?' asked Elizabeth innocently.

'But of course. He must. And then Dimwood has its charm.'

'Not like here,' muttered Elizabeth.

Uncle Josh reacted a little impatiently.

'It's different. But I can see that I was verging on the lyrical in describing our town to you. There are some unpleasant facts of history. All of these squares were formerly strongholds, of which they have kept the general outline.'

This last sentence disillusioned Elizabeth.

'Was there fighting here?'

'Not against the Indians. Providence put two great men here, to prevent bloodshed. In the first place General Oglethorpe, who came from England to found a colony, to begin a place of refuge for the unemployed of the realm, but also for the youngest sons of families, who had no future at home. That involved a lot of people. Not enough, said the official Companies, so they opened the doors of the prisons.'

'Bravo!' exclaimed Elizabeth.

Uncle Josh turned towards her and gave her a curious look.

'Now then,' he said. 'I'm gradually discovering an Elizabeth I didn't know. But the prisoners sent to the New World were not great criminals. They were imprisoned for debt.'

'Even better then,' the girl said with feeling. 'No money to pay the men in black who come to the house with papers . . . I've seen them at Papa's.'

Uncle Josh took her hand.

'You must try not to think about all that any more,' he said gently. 'All that is over, do you understand? You'll see no more men in black. So shall I go on with my story?'

'Oh yes, Uncle,' exclaimed Billy. 'No more men in black, Elizabeth.'

'Oglethorpe arrived in South Carolina, at Charleston, in 1733.'

'Charleston people are stuck-up,' Billy observed.

'I beg you to keep quiet,' said Uncle Josh. 'So at Charleston in 1733, the English were already there.'

'Of course,' murmured Billy.

'Your remark is offensive to Elizabeth, and stupid into the bargain. The English had been there since Charles II, nearly eighty years earlier. And well before them, there had been the Spanish sent by Philip II. The English saw them off.'

The narrator suddenly shook slightly and cried:

'The cart . . . Azor!'

'It's still outside Mademoiselle Clementine's shop.'

'It's my fault,' said Uncle Josh. 'I completely forgot it. Most bothersome. All of the servants are counting on getting presents. It's a real tragedy . . .'

'Yes, mass'r Joshua,' said Azor gravely.

'Carry straight on to Broughton Street, and stop outside

the big store. We shall be there a good while if my calculations are right. Go back to Mademoiselle Clementine's and come back and wait for us with the cart.'

'Oh! Yes, mass'r Joshua.'

Beneath his wide panama that cast a shadow over the whole of the top half of his face, he cast an anxious look into the void and continued in a lower voice.

'Those who like moralizing in the North are always reproaching us on account of our peculiar institution. I should like to see them with dozens of families on their hands, like us. One day I'll tell you what happened to our great-grandmama who forgot the cook's present . . .'

'Oh! Why not straight away?' cried Elizabeth and Billy with one voice.

'No, and no. Where was I?'

'As far as the Spanish,' said Billy with resignation.

'Ah! The French before them. They went around the area, changing Indian names into French names, and left quite soon — through lack of interest — and came back two years later . . . A bit faster, Azor.'

'Oh, yes. A bit faster, Uncle!' exclaimed Billy.

'Insolent little thing! Came back, settled and were chased off by the Spanish. These latter were unforgivably cruel towards the Indians, whom they wanted to convert by force. These unfortunate Indians were sun worshippers, and at first they had admired the sumptuous ornamentation of the Catholic clergy, their processions, the sun carried under a canopy and accompanied with singing.'

'The sun?' asked Elizabeth. 'Do Catholics worship the sun too? I was sure Aunt Laura was hiding something from me!'

'Oh, no. What I call their sun is a great golden object with rays coming out of it, and you have to prostrate yourself before it. One of their favorite superstitions. The English came, as I told you, set all that to rights and established an outpost. Having cleared off, the Spaniards continued to roam around the area.'

'Very good,' said Elizabeth. 'I shall tell that to Aunt Laura.'

'My girl,' said Uncle Josh taking her by the hand, 'I advise you to keep quiet and never to embark on a discussion with Catholics. They have an answer for everything.'

'You sound exactly like my mother.'

'That's very likely. Finally, Oglethorpe arrived with twenty settlers. Leaving Charleston, he decided to look for territory suitable for his most philanthropic plans further south, and he stopped in the region where he was to found his ideal colony. Ideal!'

He raised his eyes to the sky as he said these words.

'For there was something of the gentle dreamer about that intrepid general. In advance he had banned two scourges from his colony: whiskey and slavery. He also added, so they say, Jews and Catholics. He got them all. But we're there.'

Indeed, a loud commotion heralded a world aggressive in its reality. Broughton Street, down which the gig was now proceeding, was sadly lacking in that poetry which adorned the town's fashionable neighborhoods. With its three-storied houses and grocer's shops, ironmongers, hardware stores, apothecaries and small banks, it came as a shock to the girl who was absorbed in happy reverie. There was no line of trees to soften with their shade the commonness of this wide shopping street. People came and went with more hurried steps than elsewhere, amidst the noise of traffic and the constant murmur of chattering voices.

Leaning towards Elizabeth, Uncle Josh explained:

'What you can see is what is known as the modern world in all its vulgarity. The big store where I am taking you was formerly the most elegant in Savannah and seeks to remain so, retaining its frontage of twenty years ago, but with renovations inside in an effort to conform to today's tastes. Have I made myself understood?'

'No,' said Elizabeth, 'I didn't hear a thing.'

He sighed.

'Never mind,' he said. 'You'll see. We're there.'

Confirming Uncle Josh's little speech, the big store, protected by awnings, extended over an impressive length its display windows framed in black wood with old-fashioned, primitive decorations. Thin branches of foliage in lighter wood climbed up and down these plain surfaces. An experienced eye could recognize mulberry leaves without difficulty, harking back to the early days when the silk worm reigned supreme, to be unseated later by King Cotton.

The gig had barely come to a halt when Elizabeth jumped on to the pavement and ran towards the shop, followed by

Billy and, more slowly, by Uncle Josh who called out:

'At least admire it as you go by, you little hot-head. Don't let her get lost, Billy, I'll catch you up at the gloves or shawls.'

As soon as she had taken her first steps inside the shop, Elizabeth was rooted to the spot. She had seen shops in London, but not quite like this one. The first hall, which seemed immense to her, opened on to another equally spacious one. They were high-ceilinged and the only daylight they received was softened by the awnings, but it was sufficient to light up the heavy counters that followed one after the other, like look-out posts, along the walls.

Indeed, one had the impression that the elegant clientele was attempting to besiege the shop girls who were defending their masses of precious rags, silk, velvet, lace. In her initial uncertainty, Elizabeth took to running from side to side, getting mixed up with the hordes of ladies. However distinguished these persons might have been, they had no scruples about pushing and shoving, and they ferociously elbowed aside the young lady who was resolutely trying to slip in amongst them. It took Billy's energetic grasp to pull her to a less encumbered space.

'What exactly do you want, Elizabeth?'

'I don't know,' she said in confusion. 'Everything, well almost. A shawl, shoes, gloves.'

'I don't know about the shoes. I never come here. As for the gloves, Uncle Josh will help us, here he comes.'

Rather red from the commotion, Uncle Josh was indeed approaching, fanning himself with his hat.

'Aunt Emma shouldn't have left us,' he groaned. 'I've been here several times with her, but I don't know the place very well. I can only remember that gloves are that way.'

Beating a path to the glove counter, which attracted fewer crowds, they managed to get Elizabeth's whims attended to. She lost her senses immediately. Incapable of choosing, she pushed her delicate little hands into twenty pairs of every imaginable hue, from white to gray, through the beiges, from pale yellow to eau-de-Nil. And this was only cotton, for when it became the turn for leather gloves, fine and light, she plunged into a dreaminess and a hesitation that exasperated Billy to the point where he was unable to keep his feet still.

'Oh, women!' he groaned under his breath.

His little hard straw hat was falling almost on to his nose and made him look just like a schoolboy. Then Uncle Josh exchanged a half-smile of complicity with the saleswoman, a mature lady with pale gray eyes.

'My boy,' he said with a laugh, 'what women will teach you some day is how to wait.'

And suddenly he declared in a confident voice:

'To have done with the difficult problem of gloves, madam, I request that you send two dozen assorted pairs to Mr Charlie Jones's residence. The young lady will make up her mind quietly at home. It's more than likely that she'll keep them all.'

Elizabeth was delighted, but she nevertheless pretended to be shocked:

'All of them, Uncle Josh? Do you think so?'

'Knowing human nature as I do, my girl, I'm sure of it.'

At that moment, Elizabeth leaned over the counter towards the lady with the pale gray eyes and whispered a few words to her. A conspiratorial little exchange followed and after several seconds, another pair of gloves put in an appearance. In fine leather, somewhat larger than Elizabeth's, they were of a beautiful plum color, tending towards mahogany. Elizabeth looked at Uncle Josh questioningly.

'Those as well?' he said. 'But of course, I understand.'

When they left that counter, lassitude came over Uncle Josh and Billy at the thought of what awaited them, but Elizabeth remained valiant and over-excited.

'Where to now?' asked Uncle Josh.

The answer came immediately:

'Shawls first, then hats, shoes and also . . .'

She hesitated. All around her customers were passing by so close that they could hear everything, and she had the feeling that some were lingering on purpose. Turning her back on Billy, she drew herself up a little towards Uncle Josh and whispered:

'. . . the unmentionables.'

Uncle Josh could not help laughing at this echo of English prudery.

'Of course,' he said, 'but Aunt Emma would have been

able to advise you better than me.'

'I don't need Aunt Emma's advice,' said Elizabeth crossly. 'I know very well what I want.'

'With pretty lace frills, I hope,' said Billy.

And he added with a smirk:

'As if we hadn't guessed!'

She gave him a furious look and was about to answer when Uncle Josh took her hand:

'Let's calm down,' he said, dragging her off in the general direction of the shawls, guided by a vague memory of his wanderings with Aunt Emma.

The air was getting heavier as more ladies crowded in. An animal odor hovered, for even the most distinguished of the customers smelt as strongly as the others under the effect of the implacable Southern heat.

'It's here,' Uncle Josh muttered to himself, 'that class distinctions become confused amongst these primitive bad odors of humanity.'

'Can't the shawls wait,' groaned Billy, 'for another day?'

'No,' said Elizabeth.

Uncle Josh wiped his forehead with a large handkerchief from which there rose a fresh and exquisite smell of eau-de-Cologne, and he waved the square of white cloth as if showering benedictions. Grateful faces turned towards him.

Finally the shawl counter was reached, and the indefatigable English girl could plunge her fingers into a rainbow of diaphanous lawn. An instinctive taste guided her in the choice of colors and she confined herself to pastels, but these threw her into indecision and she began changing her mind until her head spun. And as was his custom, Uncle Josh settled the matter by ordering a whole batch of twenty-five shawls to be sent to Mr Charlie Jones.

Embarrassed, but delightfully so, she gave Uncle Josh her best smile and asked in a little girl voice to be taken to the hats. Billy cried out rebelliously:

'Hats! There are loads of them at home.'

She answered him with calm obstinacy:

'That's possible, but I don't see mine amongst them.'

'Quite right,' sighed Uncle Josh. 'Charlie wants her to have her own way today. So this very last request is granted.'

'May I go off?' asked Billy.

'Of course. Go and see if Azor is there with the cart and wait for us in the gig.'

'Because there is still the cart to fill!' exclaimed Billy.

'Yes, but I've left written instructions for everything to be done in the afternoon. It was Aunt Laura who drew up the list.'

'No one will be forgotten?' asked Elizabeth.

Uncle Josh gave her a curious look.

'That's a strange question, my girl. Is that of interest to you? You must have been chatting to Aunt Laura. It's usually she who takes charge of that job, but her father did not want her to come to Savannah this year.'

Elizabeth sent an anxious look in his direction:

'Mr Hargrove? Is he going to come back?'

'Come now, Elizabeth! Why are you looking like that? He will certainly come back some day. He's not dead.'

She lowered her head pensively and let herself be led to the hat counter in the next hall. The daylight was fading and some people were already leaving. By some mysterious convention, voices were lowered as the light diminished.

The millinery department occupied a whole corner in which great oval mirrors gathered the last rays of the sun. In this softened light everything seemed, in Elizabeth's eyes, to move further and further away from everyday reality. She looked at the various models of straw hats exhibited and at first expressed no preference.

'You are being very good,' said Uncle Josh. 'Would you like the lady to help you decide?'

The shop girl, a tall, slim brunette, had been looking at the girl who could not make up her mind, wondering who the newcomer to Savannah might be.

'Something with a wide brim to protect your complexion,' she said as she picked up a vast, pale yellow hat with long green ribbons.

Elizabeth shook her head.

'Try it on anyway,' said Uncle Josh. 'With the summer likely to be hot, you'll be glad to keep the pretty pink of your cheeks.'

That was the first compliment Uncle Josh had paid her, and the pink turned to red. She accepted docilely, and soon, in the depths of an oval mirror, her face appeared to her beneath the straw wings like a face in a portrait. Again she had the disturbing feeling of venturing into another world. Was it homesickness? Two months earlier she had been in England, and now she was in Savannah. Why Savannah? She could hear Uncle Josh's rather flat voice, and then the shop girl's more rapid one, and she understood nothing of what they said. The big hat had disappeared, to be replaced immediately and with great care by a different hat. Smaller, narrow and decked with ribbons, it made her want to laugh, but the laughter did not get past her lips.

'Too serious,' Uncle Josh was saying. 'In a year or two perhaps . . .'

She had caught these words, and she found them threatening. Still here in a year or two . . .

Other models followed, each one carefully placed, as if it had been a crown. There were charming ones amongst them, decorated with flowers, one of them even embellished with an ostrich feather that hung down low at the back, regal fashion — that was the term the shop girl used.

'Regal!'

'Perhaps,' said Uncle Josh skeptically.

After twenty minutes, Elizabeth having been unwilling or incapable of deciding, Uncle Josh wearily asked for twelve of the models shown to be sent to Mr Charles Jones. Elizabeth had not opened her mouth, but as she reached the exit with Uncle Josh, politeness suddenly welled up inside her and she whispered:

'Thank you.'

'It's Uncle Charlie you have to thank, my girl, but the gig is waiting for us.'

It was indeed waiting for them, with a morose-looking Billy waiting on the seat with his legs crossed and his arms spread out in an insolent manner.

'Get out,' Uncle Josh ordered him, 'and let Elizabeth in. You're making yourself a spectacle for the whole street.'

Billy obeyed without argument, and the girl sat down next to Uncle Josh.

'Are you pleased?' asked Billy.

She looked at him as if she had never seen him before and again that strange unease took hold of her, the feeling that the outside world and everything around her was fading away. By an effort of will, she retreated into total silence for fear of hearing herself utter words devoid of meaning. Above her, high up, Uncle Josh's voice spread out its grave and measured tones, and from time to time there recurred a strange name that caught her attention:

'Tomo Cha-chi.'

The strangeness of the sounds aroused her curiosity and made her come back to everyday reality.

'You'll see that in a minute,' Uncle Josh continued. 'Just before the law courts. That's where they put it as a pledge of eternal fidelity.'

The carriage was rolling along beneath the cork oaks of an avenue of pink-bricked houses and waves of perfume from the gardens reached them, but here and there street lamps were coming on and the magic of that time of day faded away.

When they reached the square where the law courts stood, the girl cast around her a glance that was doing its best to be attentive, but perhaps she had seen too many white columns to be amazed or to admire.

'Look, but do look.'

Reluctantly she directed her eyes towards the place he was pointing to with an impatient hand, and she started with amazement. A few steps away from the carriage, she saw a rock of enormous proportions, angular, more or less well carved, as if to civilize what remained of its untamed wildness, but which in no way diminished its presence; an image of stubborn reality confronting the fragile elegance of a small English castle from bygone days.

'It was the Indians who brought it there, the Cherokees, whose chief, Tomo Cha-chi, was a great man. With a few of his warrior braves, magnificently dressed, he welcomed General Oglethorpe without any show of hostility, and there was no war.'

'So,' said Elizabeth, 'what are all those fortifications for that determined the shape of your big squares?'

'Oglethorpe had them built later. He was a man of foresight and reckoned on the possibility of invasion, either by the Spanish or the French. In fact, he crushed the Spanish who were out for conquest not far from Savannah, at the battle of Bloody-Marsh. Mr Stoddard will tell you all that.'

'I would have liked you to tell me about Tomo Cha-chi. You'd do it better than Mr Stoddard.'

'I do believe that nobody likes the Indians as much as I do, but night is falling and we are expected. So it will be for another time. Home, Azor.'

22

*B*ack at Uncle Charlie's, they were surprised not to see anybody. A servant, whom they asked, replied laconically that everybody was resting.

'That's one of the favorite occupations in the South,' explained Uncle Josh, turning towards Elizabeth, 'and I think I am going to indulge in it myself until supper time. If you feel like going by way of the dining room, Uncle Charlie will have had prepared for you what he calls consolations.'

Having stayed behind alone with Elizabeth, Billy took her by the hand and led her to the dining room. In the cool darkness of the big room, cutlery was indeed gleaming on the long white tablecloth, but nothing else. Billy pulled an impatient face and clapped his hands. A minute went by, then a rather sleepy servant appeared.

'The strawberries?' asked Billy looking imperious. 'And the cream . . .'

'Everything has been put in the cool, Mass'r William. They'll be brought to you straight away.'

Billy collapsed into an armchair and declared:

'These history lessons are exhausting. Uncle Josh and his Indians . . . We ought to get rid of all those people in one go and have done with them. Won't you come and sit beside me? While we wait for the refreshments . . .'

She looked at him warily:

'No,' she said. 'I'm ready to drop. I shall go and rest in the drawing room, on the sofa.'

'Never mind . . . I'm staying here. I'm frightfully hungry, but when we're alone for once . . .'

As he said these words, he stretched himself out lazily in a way that made her feel awkward without really knowing why. Dressed in white, he seemed huge in the half-light.

'Do I frighten you?' he asked in a sly tone of voice.

'Frighten me? Are you mad? Frightened of you?'

He began to laugh.

'Frightened of boys.'

She felt flaming anger rise to her face and was going to answer when a servant came in carrying a silver candelabra with four candles which he put down on the table, and almost immediately, another servant appeared laden with a dish of strawberries and a pot of cream.

The still light seemed to caress Billy's pink and mocking face. 'A child,' she thought, suddenly calmed, and she left the room to the accompaniment of Billy's little laugh and the sound of a spoon on a plate.

In the drawing room, an oil lamp was shining in the center of a small table without disturbing the great shadows on the ceiling nor allowing the furniture to emerge fully from the darkness. However, she quickly found the long, red velvet sofa and stretched herself out on it.

Too many things had disturbed her during the afternoon and she could find in herself none of the morning's happiness. Both worried and disappointed, she let her eyes wander towards the walls where gilt frames faintly gleamed. Portraits were lined up at equal distances, but almost nothing could be made out, except for the rather ghostly white of the faces.

The question she was asking herself unceasingly since the previous day came back into her mind: what was she doing in this strange town? It was like an enigma set by a suspicious stranger.

The fatigue of the day half closed her eyes and, as she was sliding from wakefulness into sleep, she saw a man dressed in black cross the room slowly and cautiously. When he got as far as Elizabeth, he stopped for a brief moment, continued on his way towards the door and went out, like a shadow.

It was only after his disappearance that she recognized

him with a groan of terror which wrenched her from sleep. She had seen William Hargrove.

'He's dead,' she thought without hesitation. 'He's haunting us.'

Sweat was running down her face, and she wiped herself with a little handkerchief. She had never before seen an apparition, and she began to tremble with terror, but suddenly she heard, coming from the dining room, the ringing of a spoon on porcelain and was grateful to Billy for this reassuring sound.

'Dead,' she said under her breath. 'I was sure of it.'

She got up, took a few steps and picked up a palm-leaf fan from the small table. 'Finished,' she said as she fanned herself, 'he's gone. They didn't want to tell me.'

At all costs she wanted to get out of that room and walk in the garden, but she was not keen to see Billy again, and she found it repugnant to use the door through which the dead man had disappeared. Which way had he come in? But what need did he have of a door to come in by? He had waited for her to lie down on the sofa in order to come and look at her. This thought renewed the fear in her mind.

Finally she was ashamed of her cowardice. If using the same door as the ghost upset her, the simplest thing was to go out via the dining room.

Leaning over his plate, Billy raised his head and exclaimed as he saw her:

'There you are! What's the matter with you?'

'There's nothing wrong with me. I slept a little.'

'You're all white. Look at yourself.'

'I have no desire to look at myself. I'm going to get some air in the garden.'

'I'll come with you.'

'No,' she said, fanning herself with the casualness she had observed in her elders, 'I want to be alone, thank you.'

'Oh, you can act like a lady if you like,' he said irritatedly, 'you'll be less fierce some day, when you're being courted.'

With his spoon in his hand, in front of a little heap of strawberries swimming in cream, he looked even more like a child than he had earlier on, but with traces of his greediness all over his face.

Without answering she reached the garden. She could

barely make out the paths between the flower beds that were becoming enveloped in shadows. The perfumes hovering in the cooler air kept her where she was. She would have liked to remain there and become intoxicated with them, when Billy's impertinent voice reached her from the dining room and dragged her from her dreams.

'Don't be too cross about what I said. You're not at all bad, and I love your English accent.'

Seized with fear at the idea that he was going to come and join her, she made for the steps and went in by the main door. Oil lamps lit the staircase and she found her room without difficulty. A surprise awaited her. Wrapped in mauve paper, big boxes were piled up everywhere in the corners, and on the bed two of the dresses she had chosen were spread out.

She admired them for some time and remained perplexed. Her eyes turned towards the handsome young man in the oval frame, as if to ask his advice, but he was dead. Worse than that, he was alive with the marks of age. Finally she rang. That at least was easy. A long strip of embroidered tapestry hung on the wall, ending in a brass ring.

After a moment, a black maid appeared in a white apron, her head tightly bound in a green kerchief. Despite her age, she gave a hint of a curtsey. Never had Elizabeth seen such a black face. The outlines of the features were blurred in that shiny mask, but in her eyes she read that gentleness common to all Negroes and their tragic need for love.

The old woman said in a quiet voice:

'Mass'r Charlie done told me to take good care of you. My name's Nora.'

A smile revealed her white teeth. Elizabeth, who at first had thought her rather terrifying, suddenly had a surge of feeling for her, as she had had for Betty.

'Nora,' she said.

'Yes, Mass'r Charlie done told me to help you to dress.'

'Oh! I can dress myself.'

'For dinner?'

'Oh . . . yes, I'll change my dress, that's all, but it's not time yet.'

'No ma'am. That's in an hour. Does you want me to put them new things in your armoire?'

'My armoire?'

'Ain't you seen it? Mass'r Charlie had it put there while you was in town.'

Crossing the room, she placed a large ebony hand on a maplewood wardrobe, pushed against a wall at the back. Long and heavy, the piece of furniture had three drawers fitted with brass handles.

'Mass'r Charlie said: "This here is goin' to be Miss Lizbeth's room".'

She reached up and ran her hand over the top of the wardrobe. Elizabeth saw that she was quite willing to talk, and to talk a lot.

'Yes,' said Nora, as if in confirmation of this intuition, 'that's what he say, Mass'r Charlie.'

'But Nora, I live at Dimwood. That's some way from here.'

'I know, Miss Lizbeth, I knows Dimwood, but he wants you to live in Savannah, too. You want me to put them things away?'

'But I shall have to take them to Dimwood.'

'That's a shame, Miss Lizbeth. You's fine here.'

'Why do you say that? Do you know Dimwood well?'

'Oh, yes! Real well. I's at Dimwood eight years. Then Mass'r Hargrove, he done sell me to Mass'r Charlie.'

'Sold you!' exclaimed Elizabeth with indignation.

'Oh yes. I was his. I wanted to come to Savannah. Mass'r Charlie, he real nice.'

'Mr Hargrove too, isn't he?'

'Mighty kind, real good, Mass'r Hargrove, but I didn't like Dimwood.'

A brief silence followed that short sentence. With her interest suddenly aroused, Elizabeth hesitated, in spite of everything, to ask questions. It was not done to question servants. One word however was burning on her lips, and she ended up saying:

'Why?'

'You ain't goin' to tell, Miss Lizbeth?'

'Come now, Nora, of course not.'

'I don't like Dimwood.'

'Were they unkind to you there?'

'Oh, no! Everybody was kind to me.'

'Well then, Nora?'

'I don't know.'

'You don't know why you don't like Dimwood?'

'Miss Lizbeth, I just knows I don't like Dimwood.'

'Well, as you don't want to tell me anything, you shouldn't have spoken about it.'

Nora gave a tearful look.

'Is you angry with me, Miss Lizbeth?'

'No, you're not telling me everything because you don't trust me.'

Standing up, they looked at each other in silence for a moment as if they were expecting something from the other. In Nora's eyes, Elizabeth thought she could discern a worry that was turning to anxiety and, moved to pity, she smiled at her. Doubtless encouraged, the old woman simply said:

'I's scared of that place!'

Elizabeth's smile faded from her face. She had the impression of having advanced too far into a dangerous zone. Nora's words had the effect of enlightening her as to her own situation. A truth against which she had been fighting since her arrival there suddenly seemed self-evident: she too was afraid of Dimwood, but even feared finding out why.

'That's all right,' she said. 'I understand, Nora, I understand very well, and I won't say anything.'

Then a glint of disappointment showed in Nora's eyes. She had undoubtedly been hoping for questions that would have permitted her to say everything that she was keeping to herself. But now that night had come, the shadow of both women was thrown on the wall and the girl felt a childish fear at the idea of disturbing revelations.

'You'll tell me about Dimwood later,' she said.

And she added with a little laugh, making fun of herself:

'When it's daylight.'

Disconcerted, Nora, in her turn, made as if to laugh.

'Now you can put my dresses away. I'll choose one for this evening.'

Without a word, the old woman pulled from her apron pocket a pair of steel-rimmed spectacles that suddenly gave her a wise old air, and the unpacking began. One after the other, with almost religious care, the dresses were first of all spread out on the bed so that Elizabeth might indicate her preference, then placed with a kind of respect in the great

armoire as if they were real people. That was what upset
Elizabeth, this fear of not being sufficiently meticulous in
obedience to their masters. 'You'd think she were burying
my dresses,' she thought.

She finally settled for the longest, of an aquamarine blue,
and she began to get undressed, when she let out a cry: how
could she have forgotten to buy herself some underwear,
the "unmentionables"? She did not want Nora to see her in
the austere pantaloons that her mother herself had made
for her.

'You'll turn round while I put my dress on,' she said
gently. 'No, don't look at me. I cried out like that as a joke.
Go on, turn round.'

Nora obeyed, but Elizabeth saw her make an indistinct
movement as if to drive away some misfortune. She recognized the gesture without being able to remember where
she had seen it before. Undoubtedly some superstition of
the Negroes.

. In less than two minutes, she had put on the aquamarine
dress and puffed out its pleats at the waist, then told Nora to
turn round:

'That sure is a pretty dress, Miss Lizbeth, nice and long,
too!'

'That's on purpose, I wanted it to be a bit long.'

Indeed she remembered what Billy had told her about
underwear that could be seen in the swirl of the waltz, and
with all her heart she hoped that they were not going to
waltz, but one never knew. And then there was the eternal
Aunt Emma . . .

She stood in front of the large mirror, but could make out
almost nothing.

'Bring the lamp closer, Nora.'

The old woman took the lamp and crossed the room, at
the same time sending great shadows as far as the corners of
the ceiling where they seemed to be looking for someone.
As she came close to Elizabeth, she stood still with the lamp
in her hand.

'Sure is a pretty dress,' she repeated.

Without admitting it to herself, the girl had been hoping
for something else, a real compliment. Sometimes doubts
brushed against her. Billy had called out to her that she was

not bad, but that was all. For her part, she considered herself to be pretty, but not more so than most girls of her age. It was especially her hair with its golden lights or the freshness of her complexion, her pink cheeks, that were admired. Was she not radiant? Too young, she was unable to discern in her small, worried face the promise of an indefinable charm, more insidious than the commonplace attraction of perfect beauty. However, she looked at herself for a moment with pleasure. At last she saw that she was elegant, like the others. The nightmare of the sky-blue dress was coming to an end.

When all the clothes had been put away in the chest of drawers, there followed a great display of shawls that prompted Nora to cries of admiration, whereas Elizabeth examined them with a slightly blasé eye. She was quickly getting used to luxury and already felt herself rich in her soul. With a careless gesture, she threw over her shoulders one of those strips of diaphanous silk, and turned towards Nora who looked at her in silence.

'Well, Nora?' said Elizabeth chancing her luck.

The answer came like a timid groan of adoration:

'Oh, Miss Lizbeth? Miss Lizbeth, you sure does look nice!'

'Can I go down to dinner like that?'

'Oh, yes'm. You sure does look nice. Mighty pretty.'

'I'm not asking you if I'm pretty,' said the delighted hypocrite, 'I want to know if I've done things in the proper way . . . Ah! my gloves. Should I put gloves on?'

Of her own accord the old woman ran to fetch her a pair of small white gloves with just a tint of pale blue. The choice seemed right to Elizabeth, her heart warmed by the naive compliment she had finally obtained.

'Where are you from, Nora?' she asked benignly and was almost immediately ashamed of this condescension copied from the tone of voice of certain Southern ladies.

'Me, Miss Lizbeth? Mass'r Hargrove he done bought me in Virginny, but my Mama she's from West Indies.'

The humility of this reply completed Elizabeth's embarrassment.

'Bought,' she repeated. 'Bought with your mother?'

'No, ma'am. My Mama, she stay in Virginia. We wasn't sold together.'

'But that's not possible, Nora! They separated you?'

'Yes, Miss Lizbeth.'

'What about your father?'

'Oh, I don't know, I ain't never seen him. Mama, she say: "Your daddy is a long long way away."'

Turning away suddenly, the girl went over to the window that overlooked the garden. This exchange had come as a shock to her, and she wished to conceal her emotion. Nora's voice followed her, somewhat plaintively:

'You ain't upset with me, is you?'

'No, not that. Nora is very good, very kind. You can go now. Will they come and fetch me at dinner time?'

'Yes, and there'll be the bell.'

'Oh, fine! Good night, Nora.'

'Good night, Miss Lizbeth.'

Elizabeth, alone, glanced towards the sky with the full moon rising. Normally this slow ascent would have held her attention for some considerable time, but this evening vague worries took a hold on her. She wanted to go back to England.

Her pretty room seemed threatening to her in the lamplight. Big patches of shadow hung in the corners of the ceiling like curtains, and in the middle of the room, the small table near the rocking chair was bathed in a sort of pale yellow little lake, an ordinary enough decor that invited rest, reading, or boredom. Soon, no doubt, the bell would ring and there would be a knock at her door. Did she feel like going down, like dining?

Again she went over to the window and leaned on her elbows. It was then that she heard a whisper of voices drawing nearer, and she recognized those of Uncle Josh and Charlie Jones.

Uncle Josh was talking animatedly, but Charlie Jones's calm voice broke politely into his sentences. At first she understood nothing, for they were talking inside the house, and her first reaction was to withdraw. If one should not listen at doors, was it permitted to listen at windows? She did not move: Charlie Jones had just spoken her name. A mutter followed, then Charlie Jones said more loudly:

'Let's go and smoke a cigar in the garden, we'll be able to talk more at ease there than in this drawing room where everybody can overhear us.'

Elizabeth blushed in the shadows, but remained at her post nevertheless.

'I'm doing exactly what is asked of me,' said Charlie Jones, 'I'm obeying as if it were a last will and testament.'

'There can be no question of a will, since there is no deceased. I find that clause of the agreement inhuman.'

'Me too.'

'So?'

'So I obey, in spite of everything, because that's the way I am. Calm down, Josh. Can I really not offer you a cigar?'

'No, thank you, I hate cigars.'

Charlie Jones gave a little laugh of amusement.

'It's me that you hate at the moment.'

'Don't be a fool. The whole story makes me indignant. Your generosity is being taken advantage of cynically. You lay out an enormous sum . . .'

'Excuse me, he's settling a quarter of the total.'

'Without having resources comparable to yours, he could do more. We are far from being poor.'

'Perhaps, but I'm supposed to be the most prosperous man in Savannah, *noblesse oblige*. All this talk about money is wearisome, do you not find?'

'I know, but I can't forget that you have twenty-three poor families on your hands. You're taking on another one.'

'Leave me alone with all my supposed good deeds. Let's talk instead about your family. If I were your brother Douglas, I should keep a watch on my wild young stallion of a son.'

'Billy!'

This name had an electrifying effect on Elizabeth. She left the window and took refuge as far away as she could from the window. Her heart was beating energetically. In her disarray, she felt like throwing herself onto her bed and burying her face in the pillow, but the fear of creasing her dress had the better of the urge, and she remained standing. In any case, she would have to remain standing if she wanted to keep the careful arrangement of the pleats. Even sitting down involved a risk.

Motionless in a corner, she could distinguish no more than an indistinct muttering of words and, as she began to think things over, she realized that she had been stupid.

Could it be that she was afraid of Billy? Billy with strawberries all over his mouth . . . It was too stupid.

Something else that she did not admit to herself troubled her. In the days when he had been rich, her father owned a stable. She used to ride, and knew what he meant by a stallion. The very word was horrible. In Charlie Jones's mouth it embarrassed her terribly.

When she felt calmer, she was ashamed of her timidity and returned to her post at the window. Curiosity got the better of her scruples. The garden, immersed in shadow, put her in mind of a well. She could make out only the red dot made by Charlie Jones's cigar. She listened.

'In my present situation,' Uncle Charlie was saying, 'you will understand that I can't. It's you who will open the ball.'

Uncle Josh burst out laughing.

'Do you imagine that I know how to dance?'

'No . . . well, you can try.'

'Think of what you're saying, Charlie.'

'Well, it'll have to open on its own and it will without difficulty after the champagne.'

'Let's hope so.'

'Do you think Elizabeth is going to like life in Savannah?'

'One gets used to everything,' said Uncle Josh more calmly. 'With the excursions, visits to neighbors, balls, perhaps some day.'

At this point Charlie Jones's jovial voice made itself heard and he exclaimed:

'I should hope so. Your family life is a bit on the serious side, if I may say so. I don't mean that your plantation is . . . mournful . . .'

'Go on, say it! Do you think I don't know it? Dimwood is a boring place.'

'Well then, some action, some fun, Josh, parties. Do you want me to take charge? Youth needs to be happy . . . and for all those people to get married. Two boys and four girls, plus Elizabeth.'

'Ah! She too, of course.'

At this point in the conversation, the one concerned had two reactions: she threw herself back, then leaned forward, running the risk of being seen.

'She's pretty,' said Charlie Jones.

— 197 —

'Quite pretty,' conceded Josh.

'I know about such things, she will drive all the suitors of the neighborhood mad. I can see them already.'

'I can't, but we'll keep her locked up.'

'She will make use of her charm, that unfair weapon. Can't you feel it?'

'The charm of innocence, perhaps, but that will pass before she can do much damage.'

'Wrong. She'll retain something of it. Your father, who is usually so strict, seems to have been affected by it, according to what Emma told me just now.'

'Oh, don't let's talk about that painful affair. Everybody could see, everybody could understand, everybody knew — except her.'

'I'm not so sure. During lunch today I talked to her about him, to see if really . . .'

The end of this sentence did not reach Elizabeth's ears. Giddiness overtook her and she had to hold on to the curtain before being able to move away from the window. Mr Hargrove . . .

She reached the rocking chair and dropped into it, despite her fear of creasing her dress. Downstairs, in the garden, they were talking about the man in black whom she had seen pass through the drawing room. She didn't want to know. She wanted to go away. For several long minutes she heard the whisper of the voices amidst a manly smell of cigar smoke that wafted up into her bedroom. To see her mother again and to leave with her . . . This thought kept coming back to her.

Suddenly the bell rang, discreetly, but clear and bright, like the chimes of a clock. The voices fell silent. Through an effort of will, Elizabeth got up and went to look at herself in the mirror.

'Quite pretty . . .'

She whispered these words sadly, as if in confidence.

'Very pretty,' answered the mirror.

There was a knock at the door, two or three knocks that were so gentle that they seemed to be apologetic. Opening it, she found herself facing a gigantic servant in a blue livery with gold buttons.

She trembled and shook her head.

'I'll go down on my own, I know the way.'

The servant bowed and disappeared.

She knew the way. At the end of the corridor, two paces from her door, there awaited her the handsome staircase with its long, pale gray marble steps and its elaborate wrought ironwork. An oil lamp fixed to the wall cast a theatrical light that made her blink, and she was pressing her hand against the bannister when she suddenly saw Billy coming up towards her.

An elegant black suit molded his slim waist and the whole of his person, so full of movement. Beneath his hair tamed by brush and comb, his face shone with devilment, and he exclaimed:

'As you can see, I'm hurrying to meet you. Did you find your unspeakables in the shop, or your innumerables, or your unmention . . .'

She slapped him with all her strength and he nearly fell over the bannister. They looked at each other in stupefaction. Elizabeth had the impression that her hand had flown through the air without consulting her. Billy, his mouth open, could not get over the suddenness of the gesture, and all at once, they both burst out laughing like children.

'I could feel it coming,' the boy exclaimed, making a joke of it, 'you go at it hard in England!'

'That's because we don't do things by half measures, and then it should have happened some time ago. Put your tie straight.'

'My tie? What's wrong with it?'

Elizabeth leaned forward and delicately set to rights the white silk neckerchief, skilfully knotted, which had swivelled to one side. Her fingers encountered the boy's skin and she withdrew them sharply.

'Will there be many people to dinner?' she asked.

'Perhaps. Men and women, it'll be a bore, but it will be good. It's always good at Charlie Jones's. Is my tie all right?'

'Perfect.'

'Well, thanks all the same. My cheek is still burning. Does it show? Is it red?'

'Let's just say you have a splendid complexion on one side of your face.'

He vigorously fanned his hurt cheek with his hand.

'Awful creature!' he said with a laugh. 'What shall I look like?'

'Like a gentleman slapped for impertinence.'

'Right. Let's make peace and go downstairs. You're really not bad in your blue dress.'

'Aquamarine,' she corrected with resignation.

'Ah? A bit long, isn't it? I can't see your legs. You've got nice legs, you know . . .'

'Stop it, Billy. And get down the stairs! You can already hear people.'

'Haven't you got a fan? All the girls have fans.'

'Oh! I haven't got one, what's the use of it?'

'To tease the men with, but never mind. I don't mind. What's this great lout of a fellow in braid?'

The servant in blue livery whom Elizabeth had seen a moment earlier had in fact just come up to them and stopped at the bottom of the steps.

'What do you want?' asked Billy.

'Mass'r Charlie ask me to come tell you they's waiting for you, Miss Lizbeth and Mass'r Willy.'

'We're on our way. What's your name?'

'Ebenezer.'

'I shall never forget you,' said Billy's mocking voice.

Annoyed, Elizabeth looked at the black man:

'Ebenezer is a very fine name.'

The servant gave a toothy grin:

'Thank you, Miss Lizbeth.'

23

The dining room, which was much more spacious than the one where they had had lunch, was painted entirely in pale almond green right up to the ceiling, which was in a slightly deeper shade of green. The whole gave a feeling of coolness that went well with the blue livery of the servants, who numbered six, standing upright, imbued with their sartorial magnificence while the guests chattered at the tops of their voices as they sipped their juleps.

There were so many of them that the girl hesitated in the doorway, recognizing no one in the crowd. With her head spinning, she could make out nothing but blue liveries, black suits and pale dresses. She looked around desperately for her companion, but Billy had disappeared, because he found it boring to make introductions. She had a premonition that she was going to fall down, when a warm, deep voice spoke into her ear, as a hand supported her at the waist.

'In such a state over such a little thing . . .'

It was Charlie Jones himself who was leaning over her, wafting the smell of cigar and eau-de-Cologne.

'I knew you would be a little perturbed and was waiting for you on purpose. How do you feel?'

Ashamed of her weakness, she made an effort:

'Fine,' she said.

'Perfect. Take my hand and stand up straight. I shall not introduce you to all my guests, it would take us until morning. They all know who you are. I'm going to take you to the place where you'll be sitting, next to Uncle Josh. Don't be afraid.'

'But I'm not afraid!'

'Smile, then. You have a delightful smile.'

She remembered secretly the young man with stormy eyes in her room. He might have spoken those words to her . . . And yet it was he who was leading her amidst all that babble of voices along a very long table. As they passed by, people moved aside with good-humored exclamations, and she realized that Charlie Jones's smart answers, and the discreet greetings that made her blush to the very roots of her hair, were all about her. She was aware of nothing but white blotches that were all the same, like in some interminable waking dream.

When she finally found herself next to Uncle Josh, she felt like kissing him, but the surprised look he gave her brought her back to reality.

'You are all pink, my girl. What's troubling you?'

'Nothing at all, it's the heat perhaps.'

'The ventilators will be put on later. You'll be offered a julep. Refuse it. You're not used to them yet. Have you met some interesting people? The best of Savannah is gathered together here, a little bit in your honor.'

Elizabeth let out a cry.

'Oh, no!'

'What's that? Oh . . . yes! Aren't you pleased?'

'Listen, Uncle Josh. I would prefer people not to take any notice of me.'

Uncle Josh put his half-full julep glass down on the table.

'Elizabeth,' he said seriously, 'you're not going to bring shame on us. You are a young lady from England who is doing us the honor of coming to live with us, in the South, and you'll behave like a lady.'

Cut to the quick, she riposted:

'But naturally.'

'Bravo! I like those eyes shining with anger much better than your fearful look just now.'

In his elegant black suit, finely tailored, and his magnificent snow-white cravat, skilfully knotted beneath his chin, with two little points like tiny wings, he suddenly looked rather grand in the eyes of the young Englishwoman, wounded in her pride.

'Nearly all the men here,' he continued, 'are descended from very old English families, grandsons of youngest sons who came to make their fortune in the crown colonies. To tell the truth, you'll find yourself back in what they call the old country. You'll be paid compliments. Don't set too much store by them. That's part of Southern politeness. What a noise they are all making! One has to shout to make oneself heard. Have you understood what I said?'

'Practically nothing, a muttering,' she said, forcing her voice, 'but don't worry. I know how to behave. I wasn't brought up in a farmyard.'

Uncle Josh looked at her scandalized.

'On a farm!' he exclaimed. 'Your mother never told us that!'

At that moment, a man of about twenty came up to them. Black sidewhiskers reached down to his chin, encircling his thin face in which grey-blue eyes of great gentleness rested on Elizabeth. Uncle Josh introduced him immediately.

'Alexander Moreland, one of our young architects, a very great friend of our dear Charlie Jones for whom he works occasionally. Alexander, our young cousin, Elizabeth Escridge, is from Kent where the family has its roots.'

Elizabeth held out to him her hand which he took hold of with a bow, without taking his eyes off the pink-colored little face that seemed on the point of smiling. As short as the ensuing silence was, it was nevertheless embarrassing. Josh decided to break it.

'Elizabeth was not afraid of the long journey to get to us.'

'Let us hope that she will find things here so much to her liking that she won't want to leave,' said Alexander Moreland in a low voice.

'Oh, I hope not!' she said without thinking.

She feared having misheard and wondered if she had not answered wrongly.

He smiled at Uncle Josh.

'The accent,' he said. 'What charming music comes to us from over there!'

'Yes, close your eyes, and you'll think you're in the old country.'

'In the present case, one has no desire to close one's eyes.'

This sentence was spoken slowly, the young man's eyes looking straight into Elizabeth's, as she forced herself not to blink. She was trying to understand what he meant, was it an impertinence or a compliment? In any case, she must not falter, but the words 'quite pretty' and 'not at all bad' were fluttering around in her head, and she was hesitating between wariness and the fascination that those handsome gray-blue eyes were having on her. What tenderness she thought she could make out in them . . . She liked him.

She had never known such joy mingled with worry, no one had ever spoken to her in this way, and she wanted to reply, to say anything at all, and smile, but her face remained frozen, and she suffered delightfully — a strange happiness — when a tall gentleman succeeded in sliding between the young people without appearing discourteous, for he excused himself with a refined politeness.

'Entrance ought to be forbidden to importunates of my kind,' he said in a melodious voice, 'I am without a doubt interrupting an agreeable *tête-à-tête.*'

'Admitting that you have assessed the situation accurately, what good news do you bring us to secure your pardon?'

'None. Negotiations continue.'

'It'll end with a compromise like last time,' said Uncle Josh.

'It'll have to, otherwise . . .'

'There is no otherwise that's viable,' interrupted Josh very firmly. 'The Congress will find a solution as always. Come, Harry, don't come casting concern into the heart of my young cousin who has come from England to live with us. Elizabeth, I introduce my friend Harry Longcope, one of the great hopes of the bar here. Miss Elizabeth Escridge.'

Harry Longcope bowed ceremoniously.

'Miss Escridge,' he said, taking care over his intonation, 'as long as you are amongst us, you shall know nothing but the sweetness of peace amidst the poetry of the South.'

Elizabeth understood more or less nothing of this speech, he annoyed her, but she did notice the beauty of his features which had a classical regularity. She thought, however, that they had an unfortunate resemblance to the plaster casts in the art room at lessons she had attended. Nothing was given away on that impeccable forehead and that perfect mouth. By way of compensation, the pale blue eyes shone with self-satisfaction.

She greatly preferred the face of her architect, in which she thought she detected a gently reproachful glance. Emotional complications were already beginning. They were brusquely interrupted by the arrival of a young soldier in a dark blue uniform, brightened up by a double row of brass buttons. The stiff collar forced him to carry his head high, and this resulted in a proud and resolute expression over the whole of his countenance.

It came as quite a shock to Elizabeth, and she felt a shudder of pleasure run down the back of her neck. The boy looked twenty and, to her, seemed to breathe courage. One might have said that an atmosphere of danger and daring hovered around those unobtrusive shoulders, and his person, tightly clad in government cloth, altered by a good tailor. Was he handsome? She could not say, she was dazed, but she noted the red hair cut very short.

'The army, now!' sighed Uncle Josh, and he took the girl's hand. 'Come and sit down, Elizabeth,' he added in a commanding tone of voice.

The moment could not have been better chosen. Charlie Jones's voice was, indeed, making itself heard loud and clear above the general buzz, begging his guests to take their places, which created an amusing confusion. Amidst peals of laughter, names were looked for on pretty cards decorated with flowers, and the juleps that had been immoderately drunk did not help matters. But soon everybody was seated and the blue liveries began to go round with dishes.

Silver candelabras spread pools of diffused light on the pale pink tablecloth, and violets bloomed in small cut-glass vases. One of these bouquets was just in front of Elizabeth, catching her attention without her knowing why. She was looking at it as in a dream, when she suddenly remembered that Mr Hargrove used to call her his little English violet, and it was as if he were saying to her: 'I'm here.' For several seconds, she felt the same terror as three hours earlier, in the drawing room, when she saw passing through the drawing room the man dressed in black, whose eyes she felt resting on her.

Instinctively she touched her neighbor on her left. Uncle Josh, who smiled at her, asked:

'What is it, my girl? Do you not feel well?'

She got a hold on herself and said, as she too tried to smile:

'I'm a bit hot, that's all.'

'You'll see, the air will cool down in a moment. And some advice, don't eat too much. Are you hungry?'

'Not at all.'

'They're going to pour out some champagne. Drink a mouthful or two, no more, it will do you good.'

The sound of this voice, and the commonplace nature of its advice, reassured her somewhat. Taking advantage of Uncle Josh's talking to a lady, she moved the flowers slightly.

On her right, a young man was trying in vain to engage her in conversation, but she was pretending not to hear, as he wore eye glasses. By way of compensation he had very fine hands, long and slim, and one of them was placed on the pink tablecloth like some precious object, right next to Elizabeth's knife and fork, as if seeking to be admired, saying, in its own language: 'Look at me, recognize breeding.' But the girl's attention was directed elsewhere. Her eyes were seeking out at one and the same time the young architect and the soldier, but could not find them straight away, for they were lost in the sea of pale dresses alternating with suits and uniforms. On the other hand, she could make out not far from her the hope of the bar of Savannah, and he gave her a little nod of the head that remained unacknowledged. In truth she was still too ill at ease to take in everybody as she would have liked. People were looking at her too much without it being obvious. She suddenly noticed a young officer, then another, and felt a blush mounting to her cheeks. With her nerves on edge, she broke with the tips of her fingers into the crust of the roll placed to the side of her plate. Her uncontrollable shyness played tricks on her that she was quite unable to understand. She was furious at blushing without knowing why. As if to mock her weakness, a royal-blue sleeve, from which a white-gloved hand emerged, made its appearance at her elbow, and a plate was put down in front of her. The smell of soup rose up to her nostrils, and she was suddenly conscious that she was being spoken to:

'Elizabeth,' Charlie Jones was saying to her, separated from her by Aunt Emma and Uncle Josh, 'don't let yourself be upset by all sorts of clashing opinions. It's a passion among Southerners to make speeches and shattering declarations.'

'But I don't understand anything,' said Elizabeth, making an effort to shout, 'people are speaking too loudly.'

'Well, it's better that way,' said Aunt Emma who was smiling now: rested, radiant, someone important.

Seated between her brother-in-law Joshua and Charlie Jones, Aunt Emma occupied, in effect, the place of honor. A fussy bonnet of plum-colored material, edged with lace, covered her head, and just above her left ear a tiny ostrich feather, fixed with a ruby broach, waved at the slightest movement. Wearing an ample dress of brown taffeta, Aunt Emma studiously held on to her role of grand lady. When she saw that Elizabeth was watching her, she gave a little wave with the tips of her fingers, as a condescending gesture of friendship towards the young foreigner.

Elizabeth pretended not to see this patronizing little greeting, and continued to look around the table; she discovered Billy leaning towards a young lady in pink with the same greedy look that he had had for his strawberries. She thought it bad manners, without being able to stop herself feeling a slight pinch of jealousy. In the hubbub of words around her, voices were becoming more animated, and she could make out the name 'California', which kept recurring.

Champagne was served.

'A mouthful,' said Uncle Josh to Elizabeth, raising his finger.

At that moment, Charlie Jones turned towards the girl.

'Josh allows you a mouthful,' he said with a laugh, 'you can add another one for me. Champagne never hurt anyone. This one is from Epernay, in France, and it comes to me carried gently on merchant navy ships. Do you understand what people are talking about at the moment? No? Of course not, but it doesn't matter.'

'The champagne won't do anything to calm them down,' Uncle Josh remarked. 'You'll hear them shouting soon.'

'Not too much, despite everything, on account of the ladies.'

'You're mad, Charlie, the ladies will be the chorus. What do you think, Emma?'

'The ladies will say what they have to say,' said Emma in her most professorial tone of voice.

Something in her voice heralded a storm. Putting down her half-empty champagne glass, she looked at Josh and Charlie in turn, her eyes already shining under the influence of the champagne, then declared:

'I think someone ought to tell Elizabeth what is going on.'

'Yes, but later,' Charlie exclaimed, foreseeing disaster.

Aunt Emma pressed an imperial forefinger on the table.

'Now,' she said.

'What's got into her?' Uncle Josh asked Charlie in an anxious whisper. 'She's not at all like that at Dimwood. I'm afraid the alcohol might be a mistake.'

Charlie gave him a crafty look and spoke into his ear.

'What does she drink at home?'

'Usually water or tea.'

'No need to look any further, but for this evening, we'll

have to limit the damage by preventing her speaking. Stand up and say something, no matter what. Propose a toast, for example.'

'It's up to the master of the house to do that. Come on, on your feet, Charlie, and good luck!'

'I'll get my own back for that,' said Charlie with a mocking whistle, then, getting to his feet, he assumed an affable air and proclaimed in stentorian tones:

'I want to have a word.'

'At last!' exclaimed Aunt Emma, who was fanning herself energetically.

'First of all, I propose a toast to our beloved South.'

A head-splitting shriek was let loose into the silence, as people made valiant efforts to get to their feet.

'Hurrah for the South!'

Elizabeth remained seated. The evening was taking an uncomfortable turn. She had a premonition that the worst was on its way.

Charlie Jones continued.

'I request a kind thought for our absent friend.'

Absent . . . Elizabeth's heart began to pound. There could be no question of a dead man here. And, as if to confirm her premonitions, affectionate whispers ran around the table, like a soft, caressing swell at sea.

'Dear old Willie Hargrove . . . We're missing you this evening . . .' She saw him again passing through the drawing room in front of her, giving her a long, sad look, but, mingled with the horror of this vision from beyond the grave, there was an undeniable relief, of which she was ashamed. It seemed to her that the master of Dimwood had come to dine with her. She did not, in any case, have leisure to linger over this momentary hallucination, for she moved from one horror to another as she saw Charlie Jones turn towards her with a broad smile.

'And now,' he said, pronouncing each word carefully, 'I propose a toast of affectionate welcome to Miss Elizabeth Escridge.'

Then a kind of chaotic hubbub broke out amongst the diners. They were all standing and trying to get a glimpse of Elizabeth, who had been somewhat ignored until then, and a roar suddenly filled the room:

'To Elizabeth!'

Without knowing what to do, the girl got to her feet too, and, in her bewilderment, turned to the neighbor on her right. He had removed his eye glasses and was looking at her with stupefaction. Each of them seemed to be seeking some refuge from their feelings in the other, and she had time only to notice a face that seemed to her like that of an angel. The young man, not knowing what was expected of him, lost his head and kissed Elizabeth.

A great clatter of applause greeted this unexpected expression of feeling. She waved her hand in the direction of all those faces that she could make out through her vertiginous shyness.

With the relentlessness of a wave, they seemed to be coming closer to her, then drew back, only to come closer again. She grabbed hold of Uncle Josh's sleeve with her left hand, and raised a look of distress in his direction, but he was content to squeeze her arm and say:

'Stand up straight, so we can be proud of you.'

These words caught her in her self-esteem, and she thought she could hear her mother's dry, careful voice making her ashamed: 'Don't make a fool of yourself in front of strangers.'

By means of a sudden surge of pride, she got the upper hand of her terror, but she was still a prey to giddiness. However, she could make out the diners more clearly; their faces, the pale dresses of the ladies, alternating with black suits, even down to the white silk cravats knotted beneath the men's chins. All these people persisted in coming close and then dropping back, as they had done a moment earlier, but with the difference that now they seemed to be dancing some enormous quadrille, with a forward movement full of fire, then a majestic retreat, followed by another conquering lurch. In the grip of the gaiety, she automatically raised her glass. Polite hurrahs greeted this gesture. This time Uncle Josh's voice demanded silence.

'Now that our Elizabeth has been adopted by the South, dear friends, let us give her some idea of the crisis it is going through.'

A low muttering ran through the assembled company like a buzzing of bees, and a lady launched forth in a firm voice:

'Why?'

It was the beautiful Mrs Harrison Edwards, widow and owner of one of the most flourishing plantations in the district. Her pastel-gray taffeta dress set off the gleam of her velvety white skin, of which she revealed as much as was decently possible, with a low-cut neckline that was prudently bold, a vague echo of Parisian daring. The caressing softness of her huge black eyes was famous and had her compared with a queen in exile. Out of concern for good manners, she had done no more than nibble at a piece of pork pie, letting the rest be taken away, not without regret, for she loved food, but the oval shape of her face was threatening to become rounded. A lot of men hovered around her.

'In the first place,' she added, 'there is no crisis.'

'Do you think so?' exclaimed a number of voices.

She continued with sovereign calm.

'What are those chatterboxes in the Congress upsetting our lives and our comfort for? Look around you. The South is up to taking on any crisis. The wealth of the South is inexhaustible. What other country can say as much?'

'But Lucile,' said Charlie Jones, 'it's a political crisis.'

She answered imperturbably:

'Political crises are always settled, because they have to be settled. That's what Congress is there for.'

In a very patient voice, with just a hint of exasperation, Charlie Jones declared:

'This enlightened exposition deserves some further explanation, Elizabeth. In the days when England ruled over the whole colony, people only talked about the North and the South in a general kind of way, but there were already disagreements about the territorial limits of the various provinces. It was long drawn-out between Pennsylvania and Maryland, for example.'

While all these words were being bandied about, the servants in their blue liveries moved around the table with heavy salad bowls of gold and white porcelain. On a bed of avocado pears and black mushrooms, the lobster salad wrenched a cry of delight from the beautiful Mrs Harrison Edwards, who was incapable of resisting.

'Wildly spiced! . . . Divine!'

The orator was being listened to with somewhat distracted ears as wine flowed into the glasses, and from the glasses into mouths with a kind of regularity that the girl found fascinating. All this made for a lively atmosphere, preventing her from becoming bored. She was, though, inattentive, and was not at all following Charlie Jones's history lesson. She had the impression of being in an unruly class and was amused at the whispering all around her.

'If he's only got as far as English rule, the sun will be up before the War of Independence.'

An old gentleman with a white mustache, Judge Pilgrim, raised his hand and held it in the air until there was silence. He began to speak in a broken and most polite voice:

'May I remind my worthy and respectable friend that the ball is to begin shortly, for I believe I can hear the musicians tuning up in the drawing room? Could he not hurry along somewhat the majestic course of the river of History? Impatient youth . . .'

'Say no more, Your Honor, I shall leap over the years.'

Nobody had heard any sound of instruments and impatient youth coped with its lot by patiently emptying its glass, but the Honorable Judge Pilgrim wanted to go off to bed. Charlie Jones continued in a flat voice:

'To put an end to recriminations from the provinces, two English surveyors were called in: Mason and Dixon.'

'Hurrah for Mason and Dixon!' the guests exclaimed with a single voice.

Charlie Jones, marble-faced, proceeded in a decidedly authoritarian tone.

'It was about 1730. They drew a long line on the map of the country from west to east, marking out the boundary between North and South. It took them thirty years and, as they had an imperfect knowledge of geography, the line went straight where it would have done better to zigzag. A frontier.'

To the general surprise, Elizabeth, who had suddenly become attentive, let out a cry:

'Oh, why?'

Her clear voice pierced the stifling air, and there was a moment of amazement. Her cheeks and forehead flushed, the girl turned her head towards Uncle Josh. The latter said calmly:

'I think there is some good sense in that exclamation.

There is nothing more dangerous to peace than a badly drawn boundary. The great Jefferson himself, straight after the victory over England, foresaw a war between the states making up the Union.'

At these words, the Honorable Judge Pilgrim, who had remained seated, stood up and said:

'My friends, it is late for a man of my age, and I am going to ask your permission to withdraw, but before I leave I beg you to remember that thirty years ago we thought we were pretty close to war with the North. It was on account of the entry of Maine and Missouri into the Union, Maine being a free state, and Missouri having slaves. And yet the country showed evidence of good sense. A great man, Clay, put forward and secured a compromise. Missouri took its place in the South as a slave state, and Maine entered the North as a free state, and a whole generation lived in peace and good neighborliness. This time too, on account of the difficulties surrounding California's entry into the Union, there will be a compromise, there won't be a war, but the frontier has its uses. I wish you a pleasant evening and good-night.'

Having spoken these words with imposing gravity, he was about to leave the room when Billy suddenly sprang up in his path, with his hair ready for battle and his face aflame from the food and drink.

'And if there had been a war, Your Honor, what would you have done?'

The judge stopped short and fixed him with his steel-blue eyes.

'My boy,' he said quietly, 'you will learn that such questions are not to be put to a man of my estate, but as you care to know, I should have run for my gun, whether the South were in the right or not.'

An extraordinary silence greeted this declaration. One would have said that in the light from the candelabras, some invisible presence was passing over the heads of these men and women. The old man left the room, walking with straight steps in his long black coat.

After a minute which seemed interminable, Charlie Jones spoke up:

'It is beyond doubt that a badly drawn border is

dangerous. In the case of Missouri and Maine, we saw a Southern state make an enclave in the North and a Northern state an enclave in the South.'

A man of about forty turned to Charlie Jones. His face was very brown and the hardness of his features betrayed something of the rigor of an officer.

'Mr Jones,' he said with studied politeness, 'we consider you to be one of us and you have succeeded in gaining our friendship . . .'

'I hope so,' said Charlie Jones patiently.

' . . . but you are English.'

'As your family has been for two centuries, Major Crawford.'

'I concede that, but I'm from the South, and no one will ever stop that frontier, be it rightly or wrongly drawn, passing through the hearts of all men from our part of the world. Now, you come from the old country that we don't turn our backs on, but, with all the respect due to you, you still come from elsewhere.'

'I come, in fact, from a small town on the border between Shropshire and Wales. That's not a secret. But where is all this leading, Major Crawford?'

This question was asked in a somewhat louder and more patient voice and, at the same time, Charlie Jones's nostrils flared ever wider.

The answer came with a more specific mark of politeness.

'Sir, to this, that nothing will ever enable you to experience the same feelings as we do, when it's a question of the honor of our nation. This is a soldier speaking to you who stood the test in the Mexican campaign thirteen years ago. Whether the Mason-Dixon line is properly drawn or not, we shall cross it in less time than it takes to say it, if the occasion arises.'

'Those are noble words, Major, but in my turn I shall ask you a question. When the town of Savannah made me an honorary citizen and endowed me with the same high office as the three merchants who ensure its prosperity, do you think, Major Crawford, that there was any doubt about my Southern sentiments?'

Major Crawford's dark complexion became suffused with a fine heated red that gave him a flash of youthfulness, and he declared firmly:

'I stick to my position, Charlie Jones, but I had no intention of offending you.'

Charlie Jones answered placidly and with almost imperceptible irony.

'If the offense evaporates, the opinion you hold of my sentiments becomes insignificant in my eyes; you are wrong, but we are all prone to error, it is part of our nature and is almost a right that is granted us. As for the frontiers, they are like snakes that it's better to leave sleeping if we don't have the means to exterminate them on the spot.'

As he spoke these words, he had progressively assumed an air of majestic disdain, turning him into a statue. The only things to move in his marble face were the magnificent, stormy eyes that scanned slowly from right to left, as if seeking some objector to be knocked down. In moments such as this, there emerged the fellow 'formidable companion', as Thackeray described the opulent merchants who ran the town. Listening to him then, one had the impression that his shoulders were becoming broader, and that in some indefinable way the whole bulk of his body was increasing. After several seconds of rather awkward silence, his features relaxed and he resumed a jovial tone.

'Elizabeth,' he said, 'you cannot have understood much of what we've been saying.'

'Nothing.'

He burst out laughing.

'I like these direct answers, but it is time for us to describe the situation to you. But before anything else, dessert. Come on now, you,' he said to the servant who had been listening more and more attentively to what was being said, 'clear away quickly, and bring us the next course.'

The servants immediately hurried about their business, and, as if the word 'dessert' had magical connotations, there appeared, one at a time, young men in uniform who at first slid along the walls, then stood behind the ladies, in order to engage in discreetly whispered conversation. They were students from a local military school. Charlie Jones had invited them to the ball that was to follow and, knowing exactly what they were doing, they had arrived too early.

24

*A*part from the grandmothers in their funereal furbelows of autumn-brown taffeta, most of the women offered for all to behold gentle, smiling faces that in the eyes of the world passed for the image of the South, with all the charm of a refined and fragile society. To the delicacy of the features could be added the voice with its sometimes exquisite drawling intonation. Some mysterious likeness gave them all a look of being related, which was not to be explained by the line of the forehead, the curve of the cheeks or the contours of the mouth, but by a hint of haughtiness in the carriage of the head, and a quiet deep pride in their eyes. The only thing lacking in this array of feminine gracefulness was the bloom of complexion, but the whiteness of the skin brought out more sharply the shine of the eyes, in which fire lay dormant. With the mischievousness of little girls and chattering broken by hysterical laughter, they remained strangely distant.

In spite of everything, Elizabeth admired their natural elegance and was comparing all her new dresses that were sleeping in their wardrobes to the cloud-like mauve, white, pale green and pink outfits of these flowers brought to life, who were happy enough to sink their aristocratic teeth into pieces of red meat. From time to time a joyful little wave reached her from the other end, accompanied by a smile full of benevolence. Her anger raged in her immense solitude. What put her silently beside herself was that these ladies were visibly making an effort to be simple with her, to put themselves on her level, whereas in her father's manor house, in days gone by, a coat of arms had hung over the entrance — and where was their coat of arms?

This little attack of nobiliary fever quickly regressed and she esteemed herself to be ridiculous. Incapable of finding her rightful place in a society so much closed in on itself, she began to look for some more accessible human nature amongst the military.

There were a lot of them now. In their severe uniforms, starred with brass buttons, she found them just as decorative as those privileged members of her own sex. Uprightness and a frankness that was a little on the rough side could be read in their open countenances, and she noted with equal pleasure the alluring gaucheness of their good manners. Standing up, they were bending stiffly over the shoulders of pretty ladies and murmuring things that prompted outbursts of gaiety, or, sitting near them, their tactic was for a strong hand to approach a forearm that had no serious means of defense. No one paid any attention, for all were behaving in much the same way, except amongst the clan of matrons and white-whiskered gentlemen. A noisy good humor set everything to rights, casting a veil over indiscretions. Elizabeth looked on with interest and wondered if she too would be importuned with compliments. The neighbor to her right was so quiet . . .

Brusquely she remembered him and turned her head in his direction. She had a surprise: he was looking at her gravely with his gentle, short-sighted eyes. His eye glasses were hanging from the end of a black cord. Doubtless out of a desire to be smart, he had not put them back after having removed them for a moment. What novelists call 'an interesting melancholy' had spread over his face, which was of a perfect regularity. Heavy black hair lay in waves on his rounded forehead, giving the impression of a young romantic, and the very weakness of his eyesight seemed a further attraction, conveying a mysterious look. One could not be sure whether he was looking at one or thinking of something else, but his red, sensual mouth rather violently undermined the poetry of the upper half of this motionless face.

'Miss,' he said after some hesitation, 'I know who you are, but you don't know who I am.'

'No,' she said.

'Well, my name is Francis Brooks.'

Elizabeth smiled politely and there was a pause, then he continued:

'You are perhaps surprised to see me amongst all these fine, handsome people. It was Mr Charlie Jones's wish.'

Somewhat taken aback, she said coldly:

'That's good.'

The boy's cheeks colored.

'I prefer you to know: I don't come from a great family.'

He had said this with such simplicity that she had a surge

of feeling for him which quickly she mastered.

'Well?' she said.

'My father is a tailor in a small town in Virginia.'

'In Virginia . . . I don't know where Virginia is.'

'Further north, and a long way from here but still in the South.'

Quite in spite of herself, Elizabeth's attention was drawn towards the movements of those moist lips, and she suddenly turned her eyes away, as if she had seen something she should not. She continued, however:

'So you are not from these parts, but you're from the South, like the Savannah people.'

'Quite right, but where I come from, people are less . . . agitated.'

She felt perturbed, without quite knowing why. The young man spoke with a pleasant slowness, and his voice was attractive, if a little high-pitched. He waited for her to make a remark, and as nothing happened, he resumed:

'Mr Jones has a number of properties in Virginia. One of them is built on a former race track. I have spent holidays there at Christmas and in the summer.'

'He must be very fond of you.'

'I think so. He has looked after my education. He is a very good man.'

'What trade will you follow?'

'Architect.'

She started.

'He already has one,' she murmured.

'Oh! He has several to build the great house on a corner of Madison Square. It'll be the largest in town. Tudor.'

'Tudor?'

'Yes. In the Tudor style, and all the materials have to come from England.'

She could no longer follow very well, because she was thinking of the architect from earlier on, who had spoken to her in such a singular fashion, as he fixed her with a long, deep look. Perhaps Francis Brooks was going to work with him and then . . .

The young man was becoming talkative, and again she set to watching the play of the lips that opened and closed unceasingly.

Giving in to sudden desire to say something, she let out a sentence that betrayed great innocence:

'I think you have a handsome mouth.'

He stopped short and looked at her, shocked. She immediately realized the enormity of her remark; she had brought herself down in his eyes. Laughing nervously, she exclaimed:

'I am just making conversation. Your mouth is like everybody else's.'

Young Brooks's face turned scarlet, and she herself felt the burning of blood rising to her cheeks. They both fell silent. In a gesture that seemed to be his custom, he had placed both of his hands on the table, like unused tools, and again she noticed the slenderness of the fingers, the narrowness of the wrist protruding from the sleeve. These were not, as people said in her circle, the hands of a common man. Raising her head, she saw that the young man had not taken his eyes off her, and in that look, where shortsightedness cast a kind of mist, she believed she could make out a reproach.

'Mr Brooks,' she said, 'pay no attention to what I said.'

He replied gently:

'Miss Escridge, people often make fun of my mouth which is too large.'

'Oh! That's not what I meant,' she cried. 'Forgive me if I have wounded you.'

He remained for a second with his mouth half open, then said in a quiet voice:

'If people could hear you, Miss Escridge . . .'

'So what?'

'They would not understand. With the difference between us.'

She felt ashamed: ashamed of herself, ashamed of society, ashamed of everything, and she answered vivaciously:

'I make no distinctions, Mr Brooks.'

His face lit up with a smile, and to Elizabeth's consternation he replaced his eye glasses on his pretty nose.

At that very moment, there was a slight commotion at the opposite end of the table which attracted everyone's attention. It was Major Crawford, who, suddenly and silently, was taking leave of everybody present. His chair, pushed back too sharply, had tipped over behind him, and was lying there like a victim of his displeasure. After parrying arms with Charlie Jones, he had not been able to make out whether he had received a snub or not, for he did not think very quickly, and he was heading for the door with military step, in order to go and fume in the street.

Calmly Charlie Jones watched him disappear from the dining room.

'Good old Major Crawford,' he said aloud, 'he'd be amongst the first to get a bullet in the chest for the South, if there were a war.'

'But there won't be a war,' declared Aunt Emma peremptorily.

In an optimistic atmosphere, helped along by the champagne, this affirmation had the effect on the guests of a signature at the bottom of a peace treaty, and there were a few sober hurrahs. These latter could just as well have heralded the entry of the desserts that the procession of servants was carrying in on three heavy trays of painted metal.

First came the Pantheon of Rome in multicolored ice-cream. Vanilla pillars and raspberry walls supported the weight of a pistachio dome, while a door that opened beneath the pediment gave a glimpse of a horde of sweetmeats looking like emeralds, rubies and topaz. An angelica shrubbery edged this monumental horror that aroused general amazement, and, on the part of the young people, a barely restrained ardor for gluttonous demolition work.

It was closely followed by a mountain of small biscuits, as thin as autumn leaves, in an amazing variety of three-cornered rolled-up shapes.

The Pantheon was barely placed on the table, when Charlie Jones announced that the guests were to help themselves, and ordered the servants to withdraw.

'You treat them like children,' Uncle Josh said to Charlie Jones.

'Can you hear their cries of joy at that absurd Pantheon? Do you think that those are the voices of grown-up people? I'm not cross with them for being light-hearted, but the truth is that we are short of adults. This enormous, and between you and me hideous sweetmeat will help me to let slip a few home truths that I'm hoping to serve up to them.'

'You're not going to talk to them about the war?'

'What war? There is no war, but for some months we've been heading towards a danger of war, and what does the South do when there is danger of war? It dances.'

'This,' said Charlie Jones to Uncle Josh, 'is the best moment to get them to swallow a corrective pill and put their ideas straight, while putting Elizabeth in the picture.'

'But you're not going to alarm them!'

'Alarm them? I should like to, for the space of a minute, but a blast of cannon fire would not suffice. On the contrary, it would elate them. Elizabeth!'

Elizabeth did not hear him. All her attention was devoted to her architect, whom she had finally located. This latter, who circulated a lot, had almost completed the circuit of the table. At that point he was directing his gaze at a very pretty girl, busy, like himself, eating ice-cream as she payed him back look for look: their plates were touching. Now he was no longer far away from Elizabeth, and she looked on with melancholy at what seemed like a betrayal.

'Elizabeth!' Charlie Jones called again.

She raised a martyred face towards him.

'What's wrong, my girl? Are you not having any dessert?'

She shook her head:

'Not hungry,' she said.

'Oh! One can eat ice-cream without being hungry, but do as you like. We're in the country of liberty.'

Raising his voice, then, like a teacher, and in a manner to be heard by all, he announced:

'Now I am going to try and instruct you, without boring you, on the subject of our present difference of opinion with the North.'

'They've already explained it to me,' she said softly. 'I've already been instructed.'

'The general outline, I'm sure, but it's the details that are curious. You'll see. You'll get some surprises. To start with, do you know where Mexico is?'

Silence.

'Well, Mexico is situated in Central America, between North America and South America. Do you follow me?'

All that Elizabeth could see was the pretty girl who was picking at her ice-cream to make it last, so as not to lose any of those fascinating glances. Very charming she was, too,

— 220 —

with her black curls with a reddish tint. Her magnificent dark blue eyes seemed to be drinking in everything that the rather fixed eyes of her interlocutor were telling her about her beauty without equal in the South.

'Just now,' the young English girl thought, 'it was me.'

'A former Spanish province,' Charlie Jones continued, 'Mexico finally won its independence. In the days of the Spanish reign, Texas, a slave state, was already attracting immigrants from the south-west and, when the country was free, the movement increased. The newcomers were made most welcome by a country that was short of labor. Are you still following me, Elizabeth?'

'I feel as if I'm there with you, Mr Jones.'

She had let slip this impertinence in spite of herself. In her embarrassment, she turned towards young Francis Brooks, the neighbor to her right, whom she had somewhat forgotten.

'I continue,' said Charlie Jones forcefully. 'In 1830, there were no less than twenty thousand of them, and the government of Mexico became alarmed. In order to put a brake on immigration, they began by abolishing slavery, which ruined the settlers who had been established in Texas for over ten years. There was some disruption and finally, in 1835, war. The most significant episode was the battle of the Alamo.'

This name, launched with a cry, brought a start to the guests who were thinking of other things, and with a single voice they let out a resounding acclamation:

'Remember the Alamo!'

Dragged from her sentimental dreaming, Elizabeth raised a horrified face to Uncle Josh:

'What's the matter?' she asked.

'Elizabeth,' bellowed Charlie Jones, 'at the Alamo, one hundred and eighty-three Texans held out for two weeks against four thousand Mexicans. When reinforcements arrived, the Mexican forces suffered a crushing defeat. Mexico found itself obliged to grant Texas its independence. The latter then asked the United States to admit it to the Union. Are you going to believe this? The United States refused.'

'Why?'

'Do we know exactly? Doubtless no one wanted a conflict with Mexico. It was in 1837.'

'Charlie,' said Uncle Josh. 'The musicians are waiting and are getting impatient. Can't you hear them tuning up?'

'Well, if necessary they can tune their instruments to the trumpet of the Last Judgement. I shall continue.'

However, the muttering interspersed with stifled laughter continued around the table, but they were beginning to listen. The remains of the ice-cream pantheon were lying in a pool of raspberries that no longer interested anyone.

'Finally, in 1845, Texas was annexed, in accordance with its wishes. Mexico contested the siting of the frontiers. War was a natural consequence of the dispute that followed. It could have been avoided, but the South wanted it, and the belligerent spirit even reached Massachusetts in the North, Elizabeth. But Washington dealt with matters in its own way. It was not at all a question of invasion . . .'

'Perhaps,' a guest remarked very loudly, 'but it looked terribly like it.'

'. . . but rather,' continued the orator, 'of a simple military occupation of the disputed territories. From the very first clashes, the Americans suffered a reversal, and a wind of anger blew through the whole country: American blood had been spilled on American soil. Warmongering fury was unleashed. The American army, fewer in number than the enemy's, nonetheless carried off seven memorable victories, and Mexico was taken. The war had been short. The commander-in-chief, Winfield Scott, covered himself in glory. Lee and Jackson, both from the South, likewise. At a stroke, the United States took from their adversary Arizona, New Mexico, as well as Texas, and, more important than all, California. In compensation, they purchased these territories, or rather forced Mexico to sell them.'

'Bought and sold with blood,' declared the same character, who a little earlier had picked up the term 'invasion'.

He was a small, graying gentleman, with an emaciated face and small, intensely black eyes. Dressed with extreme care, which gave him something of a clerical appearance, he was holding himself all the more erect, for he had been drinking and was watching his words.

'Blood,' he carefully pronounced, 'runs in an ever flowing stream along the frontiers, smudges the eternally provisional peace treaties, settles war debts . . .'

'. . . washes clean insults to honor,' said a pupil officer in a brief voice.

'. . . except when they are indelible, such as I have seen, and then all the laundering of duels can erase nothing.'

Expanding his chest to the full, the soldier made an effort to adopt an arrogant tone, but despite his furrowed brow and loud voice his face retained the features of early youth that undermine the desired effect.

'Sir, I see that your thoughts are not those of everyone,' he said, 'and that you are against . . .'

A firm voice put a stop to this speech that looked likely to be vehement:

'Pupil Butts, be quiet. Do you know to whom you are speaking? The best you can do for the moment is to keep silent. This is your commander inviting you to do so, this very moment.'

Pupil Butts turned round, saw as if in a flash of lightning the angered face of his captain, and fell silent.

'Charlie,' whispered Uncle Josh to his imperturbable neighbour, 'you don't give enough thought to your guest list: that little warmonger . . .'

'. . . slipped in with his mates and will not return because he doesn't yet know how to drink like a gentleman. As for the good Professor Horatio Brixton Brigg, he is a little madder than usual this evening, because the champagne liberates his conscience, but he is the glory of his little college and there are several people who listen to him.'

'Good, but for Heaven's sake cut it short, cut it short.'

'Agreed. In January 1848, peace was signed between Mexico and the United States,' Charlie Jones continued aloud. 'However, on the 14th of January of this same year, even before signing the treaty, there was a really dramatic turn of events. A man called Marshall, while digging at Colonna in California, found gold. They found more further on, and then more or less all over the place, and the news of this immediately began to spread all round the world. From every corner of America and from all the countries of Europe, migrants rushed to California. It was the notorious . . .'

'Gold rush!' yelled the guests. 'We know all that, Charlie Jones.'

'Perfect. By the end of '49, there were eighty thousand

settlers in California. In the same way that France had its 'forty-eighters', America had its 'forty-niners'. However, Congress found itself faced with the problem of admitting California to the Union. The South was insisting that California be admitted as a Southern state, which seemed reasonable. The eighty thousand Californians greatly wished for this entry into the Union, but on one condition, that no Negro, neither free man nor slave, be permitted to live there. The South, which saw this state as a slave state, thought she had been tricked, and demanded compensation. Congress favors California's entry and offers, by way of compensation, to prevent runaway slaves seeking refuge in the North, and to return them to the South and their masters.'

'A derisory proposition,' exclaimed a gentleman whose white hair was standing on end and whose large torso promised an orator. 'You can just imagine that the North won't send back a single runaway slave.'

To general surprise, Elizabeth spoke up as loudly as possible:

'But they'll be free, up there in the North.'

The orator swivelled round slowly in the girl's direction:

'My dear young lady, they will indeed be. Free to work for the Yankees, who will make them break stones in order to earn a crust, free to fall ill with lung disease, thanks to the hard climate. Many will die. Some, more fortunate, will escape and come back with tears of joy to their former masters. That happened with one of Mr Hargrove's slaves. He came back, only too happy to rediscover his cabin in the sun and a good master who did not even think of scolding him.'

Elizabeth turned pale at the name of Hargrove.

'We're not afraid of the North,' proclaimed a lady, getting to her feet.

She was a very handsome redhead in a taffeta dress which reflected the light in shades of green, and in an instinctive gesture she waved at the ceiling her two superbly powerful, fleshy arms.

The effect was electrifying. The men all leapt to their feet in unison and began to shout, letting out savage cries.

It was suddenly smothered by a victorious outburst that resounded like a call to arms, to fade away almost immediately and become lost in a turmoil of gentle amorous-ness and irresistible whirlwinds. The doors of the ballroom were opened wide, and the waltz filled the whole house. Hailing from Vienna, having triumphed in the great capitals of Europe, it was one of Lanner's latest successes, calling to mind the imperial court of the Hapsburgs, its sumptuousness and warlike splendor alternating with languorous sweet nothings.

In the dining room, chairs fell over all around the table; without a word, hands were gloved as if by miracle; and, without a shadow of uncertainty, the guests thronged to the magical call, caught up and sucked in, as it were, by the all-powerful maelstrom. In this general intoxication, every woman was beautiful, all the men became handsome.

Elizabeth did not have to wonder. Before she had even realized it, Francis Brooks's arm had taken her waist prisoner, and she saw him cast off his eye glasses which twirled gaily in the air on the end of their black cord.

'But I don't know how to waltz,' she groaned.

The boy's breath brushed over her cheek, and she felt his mouth near her ear:

'You don't have to know how to waltz to be able to waltz!'

She did not argue. She let herself be carried off. Her feet seemed to be fleeing from under her, and embracing of their own accord the airy beat that lifted her off the ground.

In the ballroom, she saw about twenty musicians in a gallery, with their instruments in action, strings, clarinets, cymbals, guitar, bassoon, kettledrums. The bow of the violin seemed king of the feast. Brandished higher than its brothers, it seemed to fly over the strings, sometimes singing like the voice of a girl in love over the mumbling of the double basses.

With her eyes half closed in an effort to avoid looking at her partner, Elizabeth gave herself up to the headiness of the moment. She was discovering the delights of spinning round that required no study, for the boy took charge of everything. She only had to place her hand in his and follow the swing of his body. Without having the elegance of more expert dancers, he was not lacking in natural gracefulness, nor in a surprising lightness, which sometimes made her take little leaps. He was happy, but she felt awkward that he kept trying to bring his face closer to hers, as if to sniff at it, and she turned her head from side to side. Then she realized that, without his glasses, he could barely see and was trying to make out her features.

In the vast round of the dance, she noticed that people were giving them rather surprised looks, and imagined that her lack of experience was provoking smiles, and at first paid no attention. She was satisfied with everything. Unquestionably Francis Brooks was holding her a little too tightly, but, she thought, he is dancing like a rather simple boy, and she suddenly understood everything. What he called 'the difference' was visible. Her joy disappeared at a stroke. She blushed with shame: by dancing with her, this boy of modest origins brought her down. She felt a surge of anger rising to her heart, and instead of moving her head away when he leant towards her she decided to look him straight in the face and smile. Did he think she was leading him on? He smiled in his turn, and abruptly drew his mouth close to the little ear that was still burning with indignation.

'May I be permitted to tell you something, Miss Elizabeth?'

The waltz carried them to a corner of the room, and through the long miaowing of the violins, she could hear him quite well. Instinctively she shook her head.

'I think it would be better not to talk to me here, Mr Brooks.'

'If I don't tell you now, I shall never dare to tell you, and if I don't tell you, I shall die. I love you, Elizabeth.'

'Oh! I had forbidden you!'

'You cannot forbid a man to love you, Elizabeth.'

'I implore you to be quiet.'

But still he persisted in a whisper of barely controlled vehemence:

'But I do, Elizabeth, I assure you, the moment I saw you, at table . . .'

At that moment, a young man of studied elegance, with lace cuffs and his neck tightly held in a black silk cravat that brought out the whiteness of his face, suddenly appeared alongside them and bowed to Elizabeth. His proud beauty was reminiscent of eighteenth-century portraits in which the English aristocracy is to be seen strutting like peacocks: the same self-satisfaction, the same haughtiness.

'Miss Escridge,' he said, 'I have an urgent message for you. The waltz is striking up again, will you grant me the honor of finishing it with me?'

His face flushed scarlet, Francis Brooks made as if to seize Elizabeth's hand.

'Sir,' the intruder said drily, 'I beg you to leave us alone. If you need some explanation, I'll give you as much as you like under the trees in the colonial cemetery. I shall be there at dawn, and I shall perhaps have the surprise of seeing you there, but I'm not counting on it.'

'It's not him you'll find there, but me, Mr Hudson,' someone said. 'Your behavior is unacceptable. You are bringing down the South in the eyes of two perfectly innocent people.'

This rather flat, but quite sonorous, voice belonged to a tall man, whose energetic face was adorned with small, black, comma-like sidewhiskers beneath protruding cheekbones. His suit, which was outrageously tight-fitting, suggested a vigorous and supple body. With his gray eyes he thrust a look in Mr Hudson's direction, as if aiming a shot, and waited.

'So I shall have two counts to settle, Major Burton,' said Mr Hudson quietly. 'They will be seen to one after the other, and first of all with this . . . gentleman, whose name is unknown to me.'

'Wrong, Mr Hudson,' replied Major Burton in an even quieter voice, 'by virtue of the rule of age, for it is evident that I am older than you two, I demand the first round, and, unless I'm sorely mistaken, Mr Brooks will not be troubled.'

Mr Hudson shook his head disparagingly.

'I agree to let you have the first round, Major Burton.'

During this barrage of false politeness, Elizabeth had been leaning lightly on the arm of Francis Brooks who remained speechless and looked drawn. Going from one speaker to the other, he was trying to make out in their features something that eluded him with his poor eyesight. He had a vague feeling that his death was involved in all this, without being able to find a reason for it. The blood had drained from his cheeks. Quite as white as him, the girl was wondering whether she was not going to cover herself with shame by falling down in a faint, but her inherited sense of irony came to her aid: it was her first duel. How should one behave in such circumstances? In any case, ridiculous emotion was to be avoided at all costs. Major Burton adroitly extricated her from embarrassment:

'Mr Brooks,' he said, 'I hold you to be an honorable man whom this discussion does not concern, whatever Mr Hudson may think. Would you, I beg you, escort Miss Elizabeth to her place?'

The music, which for some minutes had been miaowing amorously before dying away, was surprisingly restored to military vigor, and it was in a clash of cymbals that Elizabeth cried out in her clear voice:

'I can very well return to my seat alone, but if Mr Brooks would like to accompany me, that is up to him.'

Having spoken these words, she moved away, followed by Francis Brooks who, not daring to offer her an arm, walked docilely behind her.

Major Burton and Mr Hudson left the ballroom and went into a small adjoining room that served as a cloakroom, and there, amidst the heaps of coats and shawls, capes and top hats they began to shout to get the upper hand over the waltz's glorious racket, which the closed door did not completely stifle.

'Mr Hudson, you nearly caused an incident in the middle of this party, I insist that you explain why.'

'It's very simple. That Francis Brooks is the son of a Poor White, the vermin of our society. His presence at the ball is a scandal and an affront.'

'Mr Hudson, the reason you give is unworthy, and I esteem it an offense to honor. Fix for yourself the exact time and place of our encounter.'

'It is nearly midnight, Major. At four o'clock in the morning you will find me under the end trees in the colonial cemetery with my seconds.'

'I shall be there with mine.'

Having agreed on the procedure for the duel, a single pistol shot at twenty paces, they went into the street through the garden gate and took their leave as the first bars of the *quadrille* blared out in lively fashion.

Elizabeth, however, having returned to her place next to Uncle Josh, who had not taken part in the ball, remained motionless and seemed to be absorbed in the rise and fall of the dance, but her mind was elsewhere, and her heart was still throbbing with the excitement that she could not manage to still. Uncle Josh leant towards her:

'You left off too soon, you and Francis. There is still the final gallop, which is the most amusing.'

She smiled at him and said:

'I'm tired, Uncle Josh.'

'Would you like them to take you to your room?'

'No, thank you.'

Feeling that Francis Brooks was looking at her, she turned her head towards him and read horror in his face, the features of which seemed frozen, as in a statue. She instinctively placed her hand close to his. He did not see it. It was evident that he could see nothing.

'Mr Brooks,' she said.

No answer. She bent towards him a little.

'I hope that you have no fear.'

The word 'fear' dragged him abruptly from his silence.

'Fear!' he said in a flat voice. 'You don't understand, Elizabeth. That man insulted me.'

Elizabeth was seized with indignation, like a kind of violent form of pity, and, amidst the deafening noise of the orchestra, she raised her voice and said to Francis Brooks:

'He's mad, he had no right.'

'Why no right, Elizabeth? What was there to stop him?'

Now he was transfigured by anger, and the shortsighted, shy fellow was becoming an angry young man.

'Tell me what there was to stop him, Elizabeth.'

Taken by surprise, she said straight off:

'He had no right to want to dance with me while I was dancing with you.'

'That's not what it's all about. I had no right to be there. Mr Jones had advised me not to dance, but I wanted to so much . . . Elizabeth. I should have remembered the difference . . .'

'Oh!' she cried, 'I told you that between us it did not exist.'

'It exists for that man.'

'It's shameful. You heard what Major Burton said.'

'Perfectly, but that man who provoked me had no right to. I know why he did it and it's what you don't want to tell me: on account of the difference he provoked me.'

'So, what are you going to do, Francis Brooks?'

'I don't know. Farewell, Elizabeth.'

Before she could answer him, he had left his place and reached the door, groping a little, like a blind man.

Elizabeth's heart felt constricted. The music was hammering at her temples with unbearable regularity, and she put her hands to her head.

'What's the matter?' Uncle Josh asked suddenly. 'Don't you feel well?'

'I simply feel like going to sleep. I shall be able to find my room on my own. No, I beg you, Uncle Josh.'

But he was already up, standing next to her, and took her hand to lead her to the door.

Two or three servants were there, listening and watching the gallop. Their eyes shining and their teeth all white in a broad smile, they moved briskly aside when Uncle Josh appeared.

'One of you take Miss Elizabeth to her room,' he said.

25

The oil lamp was casting a feeble light that left the larger part of the room in semi-darkness. Only the small table covered with an oriental rug and the great rocking chair could be seen, as in a stage set. Conspicuously placed next to the lamp was a Bible.

The servant offered to turn up the wick, but Elizabeth did not wish it. From the big armchair in which she had flopped from exhaustion, she looked at that old Negro in his blue livery. His curly hair was graying, and he moved around slowly and carefully as he pushed a chair against the wall and drew the curtains at the window a little, a somewhat pointless gestures that betrayed a desire to talk.

'Miss Lizbeth,' he finally said very softly, 'can I tell you somethin'?'

He was standing in a corner of the room where she could barely see him, and this voice emerging from the shadows made her feel unsure. Without knowing what she was afraid of, she would have preferred the black man not to be there. Far away in another part of the house, the noise of the band could be heard, stifled by the distance, and it was for that very reason somewhat sinister.

'What do you want?' she asked abruptly.

'You's lookin' mighty pale. Can I go?'

'Yes. I don't need anything. You can go.'

'Yes'm. Good night, Miss Lizbeth.'

As he was heading for the door, he passed close to her and she moved slightly to one side. After some hesitation he stopped two paces behind the chair, and she took fright.

'Go away,' she said, 'I want to be alone.'

'Yes, Miss Lizbeth.'

She heard him move further away, then place his hand on the door knob. There, again, he stopped and said under his breath:

'Mr Hudson, he was askin' where you went off to when you left the dining room.'

'Mr Hudson? You mustn't tell him where I am.'

'Ain't nobody said anything.'

'Fine. Go away. Thank you.'

Once the servant had gone she locked the door. This precautionary measure surprised even Elizabeth, but she did not want to admit to herself that Mr Hudson had frightened her. She hated him. Despite his handsome profile and the elegance of his person, she guessed at a basic brutality in him, and she could not forgive him the humiliation he had inflicted on the unfortunate Francis Brooks who was incapable of defending himself.

She had been thinking of him for the last few moments and asking herself contradictory questions. When he brought his face very close to hers, in order to see her better, he looked like a blind angel. In those moments, she felt a sympathy she could not explain, for she was not, of course, in love. But there were those ridiculous eye glasses that made the situation absurd, and then she had never believed herself to be in love with anyone. In spite of everything, when he had carried her off in the whirl of the waltz, she had felt what the dizziness of happiness could be like, but she knew she was not in love, and she kept repeating it over and over to herself, in order to be sure.

Downstairs, the ball was breaking up and the guests were leaving amidst a great hubbub of laughter and compliments. For Charlie Jones, the evening had been a dazzling success, and his only regret was that his young compatriot had faded away, but Uncle Josh assured him that she had gone up to bed. No worry in that direction.

No worry and yet . . . The wheels of the last carriages were still echoing on the cobbles in the road when Charlie Jones and Uncle Josh went and shut themselves in the small drawing room overlooking the garden.

Beneath the appearance of a distracted and dreamy man, Uncle Josh concealed a natural curiosity. Not very talented at dancing, he had not wanted to give himself up to the collective head-spinning, preferring to observe the ball from a distance. It had not escaped his notice that four people had drawn to one side at a certain moment, and he sighed for his opera glasses that were useful in such cases.

A suspicion had come to him. Leaning towards Charlie Jones he said to him:

'Had you given Francis Brooks permission to waltz with Elizabeth?'

'I had advised Francis to keep to himself. Is he down there?'

Uncle Josh began to laugh:

'I suppose so.'

'But I thought you didn't want to budge from your place to keep an eye on things.'

'I keep an eye especially on Aunt Emma, from whom I'm constantly removing a champagne glass.'

'How crafty the two of them are! I haven't got the heart to stop them if they're enjoying themselves, but Francis disobeyed.'

'We'll see what he has to say. I can see four people

leaving.'

'Before the gallop? It's a bit soon.'

'Do you realize it is past midnight?'

The night air was cooling down as Elizabeth took off her clothes, the pretty dress first, a little crushed, then the 'unmentionables', straight, wide, edged with a grim flounce without lace. Had they been noticed? It no longer mattered to her. One might have said that the frightful scene of the provocation had changed her whole perspective on life, like in some giant kaleidoscope. In the middle of the party, there was suddenly the tortured face of Francis Brooks, like that of a man who had been slapped, but he had not been slapped. It was worse. The harsh and precise voice of Mr Hudson had struck him with the ferocious force of a horsewhip. And he was incapable of responding to those murderous words . . .

In her white nightgown that reached down to her feet, she went and leaned at the window. Never had she seen so many stars in the sky. With her head thrown back, she looked at them until she was giddy. Strange thoughts were going through her mind. What did her life mean beneath this frightful mass of stars? The ball, the whole evening, the band, the faces, it all seemed ridiculous, above all unreal, but in the colonial park men were going to fight, perhaps die, in a few hours' time. She could not believe it, she could not bear the idea that Francis Brooks would be killed, but the prodigious glittering was saying something else that was incomprehensible.

She no longer wanted to sleep. There was a fascination in this deep silence. All noise had ceased in the town for some time now. Only a dog was barking a great distance away. Suddenly she felt her legs go and she reached the big rocking chair, dropped into it and set it moving with a slight kick of the heel.

The rocking calmed her a little and sleep was on the point of gently taking over, making her eyelids heavy, when she noticed a sheet of white paper protruding from the gilt edges of the Bible placed beside her. Pulling it out of the book, she recognized Aunt Emma's large imperious hand: 'You left your Bible at Dimwood. I've had mine put in your room. Read the chapters you had got to: Matthew III in its

— 233 —

entirety, and the first chapter of Isaiah from verse 18, "Were your sins like scarlet, I shall make them as white as snow," as far as the end. I shall question you. Good night. E.'

'No,' she thought, 'I haven't the strength, but I'll say my prayers.'

Under her breath she began: 'Our Father', when the thought came to her that Francis Brooks was going to be killed, and she cried aloud:

'Oh, no! Not the blind angel! Stop them, Lord! Make it all right!'

Then she hid her face in her hands, she heard the noise of a vehicle in the street and left her chair to run to the window. She saw nothing at first, as the shadow of a sycamore hid the road in front of the garden, but she heard muffled voices. Someone was giving orders impatiently.

'Quickly! I'm in a hurry.'

Leaning out in order to see better, she could distinguish the head of a black mare, then the grating of a carriage, then the running board folding beneath the coachman's feet as he took his place. A whip cracked lightly almost immediately, and, emerging from the darkness, a gig with large yellow wheels rolled into the dazzling moonlight. Elizabeth just had time to recognize the silhouettes of William Hargrove and of Azor, who was pushing his horse to a gallop in the deserted streets.

Dragging herself to her bed, she threw herself down on her stomach. It was the pillow that caught the great cry of distress:

'I thought he was dead!'

26

The colonial cemetery was a large park crisscrossed with avenues where the finest trees in Savannah cast a constantly moving shade over paths of pink brick. Sycamores, catalpas, cork oaks, all bore in their foliage shreds of grey moss like long, torn veils, stirred by the slightest breath of air. Originally from Barbados and borne by the wind, this almost ethereal vegetation added a melancholy element to even the most cheerful countryside, and its strange attraction finally had its effect on the imagination. You could pull it out from the green depths, but it would come back, like some obsession.

At four o'clock in the morning, it was daylight, but the town was still sleeping and the cemetery empty. Rays of sunlight caught the surface of the stone slabs scattered at random in the grass, and those who were curious could read the names of soldiers from the time of the Independence, but also of duellers that a sabre blow or pistol shot had laid beneath these romantic shadows.

Mr Hudson arrived first, accompanied by his two seconds, whom he had sought out straight away, just as they were preparing for sleep. In consequence, both of them wore an air of sullen gravity. Arching his back in order to show off the slimness of his waist, and with a smile on his lips, Hudson was wearing a look of extreme satisfaction, his hat at a somewhat war-like angle which seemed to suit him. His hand, in a pearl-gray glove, was holding a whip with which he was striking himself lightly on the calf. Coming almost immediately behind him, Major Burton presented a quite different appearance. Ten years older than his opponent, his features bore the marks of tiredness, and his quiet face was that of a man attending a boring show. His seconds, clearly soldiers in civilian dress, maintained a profound silence. With the usual greetings exchanged, one of Hudson's seconds recalled the conventions: a distance of twenty paces, single pistol shots to be discharged simultaneously.

It remained to measure out the distance when an incident interrupted the operation. A galloping could be heard in the avenue at the edge of the cemetery, and Charlie Jones appeared on his bay mare.

Dressed in black from head to foot, he jumped to the ground with the suppleness of a young man and cried:

'I offer my excuses, gentlemen! I request your attention for a moment.'

As soon as he saw him, Mr Hudson changed color and,

in an instinctive gesture, he put his hand to his hat and dropped his whip, which fell at his heels.

Turning first of all to Major Burton, Charlie Jones said:

'Commandant, I have been informed of your difference of opinion with Mr Hudson by Francis Brooks, who will be here very shortly. His very poor eyesight is the sole explanation for his slowness in getting here. What is more, I think I can see him, running and out of breath, adjusting his eye glasses.'

'But I had told him that there was no point in his coming.'

'It seemed indispensable to him, however. Francis Brooks is as much a man of honor as we are. Mr Hudson,' he said briskly, 'if circumstances are not against it, I shall have a few words to say to you when you've settled matters with Major Burton.'

Mr Hudson nodded agreement.

At that moment, Francis Brooks appeared, wiping his forehead and trying, without success, to say something. His black hair was dishevelled and he was holding a stovepipe hat that was visibly too big for a man of his size. He stuffed his handkerchief into his pocket, and in the same way that people remove their hats out of politeness, he took off his eye glasses, then bowed. Everything in his appearance betrayed violent emotion, controlled with great difficulty.

'Pull yourself together,' Charlie Jones said to him, 'stand quite still next to me and watch. Watch carefully.'

The young man drew as close as he could to Charlie Jones and did not move, but his face was running with sweat and his eyes were darting from one of the adversaries to the other.

Each of them, in shirt sleeves and gripping his weapon, was waiting for the signal to be given, the usual exclamation. In an almost unbearable silence, birds were calling from every corner of the cemetery and their songs collided in a kind of teasing and mocking chorus.

'Gentlemen, are you ready?'

A few seconds passed which seemed never-ending.

Without his eye glasses, Francis Brooks could see nothing, although he strained forward, and his heart raced in his chest.

'One . . . two . . . three. Fire!'

A bullet whistled past the major's right ear, but he did not stumble, whereas a faint cry issued from Mr Hudson's mouth.

They hurried round them.

'Mr Hudson is so clumsy that he nearly killed me,' said the major with a smile, 'but either I am mistaken or he won't be waltzing any more this season.'

Mr Hudson had indeed had a bullet go through his arm, just below the shoulder.

When first aid had been administered to the wounded man, the two were asked if they wished to be reconciled. The major shrugged his shoulders.

'No objection,' he said with indifference in his voice, 'but the boy will not wish it. He's a firebrand. He aimed for the head, as was his right. If there's a war, he'll be good in a bayonet charge, he'll be a ferocious lover, but he'll never be a leader.'

As if he had heard these words, Mr Hudson cast a furious look in his direction that gave the lie to any hope of reconciliation.

Followed by Francis Brooks, who stuck to his side, Charlie Jones went up to him. They were dressing his wound. In a kindly voice, he asked him if he was in pain.

'It's bearable,' said Mr Hudson with a forced smile.

'The bullet passed through the arm and tore a muscle,' said the doctor who was taking charge of the wounded man. 'He'll have to wear a sling for at least three months.'

'An arm in a sling, there's something to earn you the esteem of the whole of Savannah,' said Charlie Jones gaily. 'A record has been made of this meeting. Honor is saved. A reconciliation is proposed to bring an end to this affair. What do you think?'

The young man shook his head to say no. Then Charlie Jones did something that was peculiar to him and which amazed his friends. In some indefinable way, he began to change his appearance. His shoulders seemed suddenly broader, his whole height was drawn up in such a way that he gave the impression of having grown taller, and his face became more serious.

'Hudson,' he said, 'some day I shall have the chance to speak to you at greater length. This morning, I ask you to think of the time when you used to work in my offices. You are free to act as you please, but in your place, I should not refuse the very honorable hand that is being extended towards you.'

The two men looked at each other for a moment, each one seeking to guess at what the other was concealing in his eyes. Mr Hudson finally said in a flat voice:

'I can only answer you when we are alone.'

Charlie Jones turned immediately to the seconds:

'Gentlemen, may I ask you to withdraw for a few minutes? Is the first aid sufficient, doctor, for you to . . .'

'Yes, but I should be happier if Mr Hudson could sit down. The pain can be very sharp.'

'Oh, I can very well remain standing.'

'Let them bring over that bench I can see in the path,' ordered Charlie Jones. 'You go off with the others, Brooks. But what are you hiding beneath the flap of your coat?'

'Later, if you please, Mr Jones.'

'All right. Off you go.'

One of the benches used by strollers was installed beneath an oak from which fluttered the fringes of the eternal moss curtain.

They sat down.

'Hudson,' said Charlie Jones, 'a simple gesture can change a life. Shaking Burton's hand will earn you the esteem of the whole of Savannah society and will confirm your situation, which can only be helped by it. Do I have to spell things out?'

'You must understand me, sir. I had asked Miss Elizabeth to dance with me because I could see her on the arm of a man whom I judged to have no place amongst us.'

'You can imagine that the people who were whirling around you did in fact overhear all that you were saying. After three minutes, the whole ball knew about it. Let's have it out, Hudson. Formerly you speculated wildly, and three times I saved you from complete ruin. Your furniture was seized, your house sold, you were in danger of prison for debt. Is that true?'

Hudson paled and did not answer.

'Right,' said Charlie Jones, 'when you'd come out of there, you would have got lost amongst the great and wretched hordes of Poor Whites. You had all the qualifications for it.'

'I beg you, Mr Jones.'

'The subject is not pleasant, I agree, but we must come to the case of Francis Brooks. Son of a Poor White and taken up by me, he has done his studies, and now he is amongst the best of my architects. As shortsighted as a mole, he manages to get by with a whole series of magnifying glasses and succeeds brilliantly. Don't you admire him?'

'I'm no judge, and then . . .'

'. . . and then you'd like to see me finish. Here you are. If you touch Francis Brooks, you'll have in me a tenacious opponent until the end of my days. I shall always be there to impede your progress. Do I need to remind you that, being related to none of the great Savannah families, it's better to set about things prudently if you want to — how shall I put it — climb?'

Mr Hudson started rebelliously.

'Do you not think we have said enough on this subject, Mr Jones? There comes a point when one cannot carry on being humiliated.'

'And that is the time for wise decisions. In your case, for example, to shake Major Burton's hand. Your seconds are waiting for you, with the major's.'

'With all the respect due to you, I beg you to note that you are exerting an unfair pressure on me. There is a name for it.'

'Don't be a simpleton, Hudson. You are perfectly free to act however you please. I have simply warned you of the danger that is lurking.'

In a voice trembling with annoyance, Mr Hudson answered:

'How can I do other than obey you? I shall go then, fuming in my heart.'

'Fuming in your heart,' Charlie Jones repeated philosophically as he stood up. 'Do you feel able to walk on your own? May I help you?'

Mr Hudson gave him an indignant look.

'You're joking,' he said.

With his left hand, he leaned on the bench and stood up. The doctor, who was standing some distance away with the group of seconds, ran up to him immediately.

'I'll accompany you, Mr Hudson. It's vital. Are you in pain?'

Mr Hudson turned a marble face towards him. All the vacuousness of his beauty emerged, lit up this time by the fires of anger.

'I am indeed in pain,' he muttered through his teeth.

'That's only to be expected, it'll pass.'

'Never. But leave me, I beg you. What should I look like if I had to be helped to take a few steps? They are coming over to me, what is more.'

The formalities were gone through in accordance with custom, beside the unraised grave of a soldier, twenty-three, who had looked askance at an officer in the heyday of the revolution. The major held out his hand with a somewhat indulgent smile. It was touched, rather than shaken, by Mr Hudson, whose furious look aimed more accurately than his right arm had done earlier.

During all this, Charlie Jones was waving to Francis Brooks to come over and speak to him. It was some time before the latter noticed him. They pointed him in the right direction and, with the help of his eye glasses, he came running up.

'Francis,' Charlie Jones immediately said to him, 'show me what you are hiding under your coat.'

The young man unknotted a bag tied to his waist and pulled from it an imposing pistol of a bygone age. The brass butt was inlaid with ivory, and the barrel unusually long.

Charlie Jones took the object in his hands.

'Be careful, it's loaded!' cried Francis Brooks.

'And you're carrying it around in a bag tied to your waist? What are you thinking of? And where does this formidable life-preserver come from?'

'It was my grandfather's pistol, when he was fighting for Independence.'

'It should be in a museum. We'll get the powder out first.'

Francis Brooks stopped him with a gesture:

'But it's there to defend my honor.'

Charlie Jones looked at him with an affectionate smile, but emptied the pistol all the same.

'Your honor has not been touched, dear Francis. You will never have to defend it by means of arms if I succeed in getting duels banned. Come with me.'

He took him familiarly by the arm, and the two of them walked beneath the trees. The pistol shots had drawn a crowd, and Charlie Jones found himself being greeted at almost every step. His companion had taken back his venerable pistol, now empty, and replaced it in its bag, but he felt no less important for that alongside Mr Jones – invulnerable too. For he had been afraid, and his nightmare was coming to an end in the soft light of morning filtering through the foliage and caressing the long, pensive gravestones, spread out here and there, in no particular order.

Charlie Jones stopped in front of one of them:

'Here lies a young man of twenty-three who died at the sword of a friend who loved him. Some insolence bandied in ill humor or in jest, no matter, it was an affront. An affront! That was the word that was always being heard. So swords were crossed. Over there, another grave. It is from 1820 or '22 and more tragic. It is the tragedy of a great medical man of the district, brought about by a young fool who was in love with his wife. It is not so long ago that all the young men in Savannah carried a pistol or a knife on them. Don't let yourself be provoked by anybody. Your infirmity makes it impossible for you to fight. But let's leave all that. See how good life is this morning. The park has never been more delicately lit. There is an invitation to happiness in the air. I'm going to go home on my bay mare. I'll see you later, Francis, come and find me on the building site.'

He moved off immediately, walking at a good pace towards the mare that was waiting for him beside a servant.

Just as he was going to put his foot in the stirrup, Francis Brooks's voice, high-pitched and a little strangled, reached his ears:

'Do you think there will be a war, Mr Jones?'

Charlie Jones seated himself comfortably in the saddle and said:

'Perhaps, if the politicians lose their heads, but not if we listen to Mr Clay.'

And, striking his mount with his cane, he took her away at a gallop.

Francis Brooks, with his hands stretched out in front of him, like a blind man, was trying to run after him shouting:

'Mr Clay! Mr Clay!'

That night Elizabeth barely slept. She had only just gone
off, when she was wrenched from her sleep by the fear that
pursued her into her dreams. She again saw herself leaning
at the window, watching the back of Mr Hargrove in his gig.
The night remained silent, and the horse was at full gallop,
but she could still see Mr Hargrove's back, wrapped in his
box coat, motionless. Seized with fear, she threw back her
blanket and began walking around her room in bare feet.

On the table, the lamp had gone out, and the Bible, open
at the eighth chapter of Isaiah, was waiting. The pages shone
faintly in the moonlight. She touched them with her hand,
irresolutely.

The memory of the ball came back to her with sudden
violence, and she had to lean on the table for support.
There were those three men around her, one silent, the
other two exchanging words of anger that she did not understand. She felt her heart pounding in her chest.

What time could it be? When it was light, they were going
to fight, and one of them would be wounded, perhaps
killed. Was it possible? In times of trouble, she convinced
herself that the only real world was what she could see and
touch. The walls, the furniture around her, the whole room,
all that reassured her, soothed her distress a little; but,
without daring to admit it to herself, what troubled her the
most was the fate of Francis Brooks. She trembled for him,
because he looked like a lost child between those two angry
men. At certain moments, the gaucheness of his movements
and an element of clumsiness about his person made him
seem comic, but this was in itself unbearable, because it was
like an insult to a vulnerable and quite defenseless creature.

On the mantelpiece, a small Swiss clock decorated with
forget-me-nots and edelweiss showed three o'clock. Elizabeth could only work out the time by feeling the hands with
her fingers, for the sky was still dark. She did not want to go
back to bed through fear of more nightmares. Again she
wandered amongst the furniture to pass the time. Daybreak
would bring news. She tried in vain to imagine the colonial
cemetery which she visualized full of palm trees bending
over the graves. To fight in a cemetery . . .

The thought came to her of pulling on the embroidered cord and asking for Nora, her black maid, who would fill the lamp. She did not dare nor did she want to. Nevertheless, she went over to the door beside which the cord hung and held it in her fingers, tempted in spite of everything, when her glance fell on a square of white paper, almost by her feet . . .

Another letter slid under the door . . . She seized it, turned it over. The envelope was stuck down. How could she read the name in the dark? Obviously the letter was intended for her. She remembered the old black servant who had hovered around her after dinner, saying strange things to her, and she spoke the name Hudson aloud. If it was from him, what a disappointment . . . She despised that man who had insulted little Francis Brooks. But despite everything, getting a letter was quite an event. She had only received four in her whole life: from her grandmother, from her old tutor, from her father while travelling, and from a mischievous friend who had written on behalf of an imaginary admirer. At the age of twelve, Elizabeth had wept with resentment, but this time, it was something different, she could feel it.

Suddenly, she turned the key and opened the door. How come she had not thought of that before? A night light burned on the staircase, shedding just enough light to enable the steps to be seen. It was a small bronze object, copied from Roman lamps, which consisted of a wick dipped in oil and was placed in a niche, at the feet of a marble statue of Hermes.

With the perfect eyesight of her sixteen years Elizabeth was able to make out the large, irregular hand and read this, standing on a step and leaning on the banister:

Elizabeth, if I may call you that, what is the point of writing this letter that a servant is going to slide under your door? When you read it in a few hours' time, I shall perhaps be dead. Tonight, at the ball, I did the most foolish thing I've ever done in my life, insulted a poor boy who could not fight with me, being my inferior, because it made me mad with anger to see you on his arm, you, whom I had been watching throughout the

— 243 —

whole of the banquet, you whom I love to distraction, because you are the one I have been waiting for since my earliest youth. How beautiful you are, Elizabeth . . . Do you know it? You are Juliet's age. How beautiful you are, Elizabeth . . .

She lowered the letter. Under the shock of such a sentence, she felt something give way inside her. Never had a young man spoken to her in this way; in a kind of magical double image, she saw herself in Hudson's sentence as in a mirror, as beautiful, very beautiful, with her golden hair spread over the whiteness of her nightgown, and her pink cheeks that spoke of English fields, and she stopped hating that man.

After a few seconds, she resumed her reading:

My opponent is one of the best shots in the district. I have myself been put to the test with a pistol. I intend to shoot him in the head, for I can no longer live if I do not silence that mouth that spoke the outrage. So honor will be saved and it will no longer be in shame that I shall come and tell you again of my love . . .

This time, the letter dropped from her fingers, as she did not wish to believe what was yet so evident. Marry Mr Hudson? She picked up the letter and put it back in its envelope, then returned to her room, locking the door in just as much haste as she had opened it.

Mr Hudson's face appeared to her suddenly, as in a hallucination. Smooth and beardless, it made her feel ill at ease in a way that she did not understand. Could a man be too handsome? A certain perfection of feature produced boredom rather than love. And then, there was no question of love, even less of marriage. Living with a model from an art class!

She cast the letter into a drawer with the impatience of someone with too many admirers, but deep inside herself she realized that she was acting out her role very badly. They were going to fight over her. There was reason to feel important.

Dawn was breaking behind the roofs. A vague grey glimmer

invaded the room. Leaning at the window, Elizabeth watched the shrubs emerge slowly from the shadows, then the borders of pink geraniums.

Suddenly she went and fetched the letter and waited for daylight to read the end of it. Perhaps at the very moment when she was casting her eyes over its final lines, he would fall dead, struck by a bullet in the forehead. In novels, there were gripping coincidences . . .

In the first rays of daylight, she was finally able to read these words:

> Forgive me for writing to you so extravagantly. I do not forget that you are still a very young lady and that you have perhaps never heard a man speak to you as I am doing now. Perhaps a man who is brushing with death has the right to press on. If I am to fall now, let it be in the intoxication of this avowal.
>
> Your unfortunate Philip

With her brow furrowed, she re-read the last lines without being sure of having properly understood them. In spite of the little attraction she felt towards Mr Hudson, she was beginning to view him differently. His letter frightened her. She could not help pitying him, and, by the same token, herself also. So young and drama already in her life . . . very romantic, this situation . . .

Now she could bear to wait no longer. She wanted to know how it was all going to end, if the two men were now standing face to face. Somewhat confused, she was holding the letter in her hand, and, in a moment of good sense, thought she could see her mother casting her very British eyes over it, and at the same time saying: 'Keep quiet, you little idiot, and don't make a fool of yourself.'

This time without hesitation, she pulled on her bell cord. There was no answer for ten minutes. One could have thought that the shocked silence had closed its waves around this impetuous ringing, waking people up at the crack of dawn.

Finally, in a great shuffle of shoes along the ground, Nora came in, with her hair hastily tied up, her eyes drooping with sleep.

'Good-day, Miss Lizbeth. Is you feelin' poorly, Miss Lizbeth?'

'Yes, Nora. Good morning. What time is it?'

'I ain't rightly sure. The sun's comin' up. I reckon maybe four o'clock.'

'Four o'clock! Oh, Nora, I'm worried. At four o'clock, two gentlemen are going to fight in the cemetery . . .'

'The colonial cemetery? Seem like they's always always some two gentlemen there, every week. It's somethin' terrible.'

'Nora, I hope they are not going to kill each other.'

Nora then made that gesture that intrigued Elizabeth. She looked as if she were wrapping the top half of her body in some invisible cloak that was pinned to her shoulders.

Elizabeth watched her:

'What are you doing, Nora?'

'A prayer, Miss Lizbeth, for them two gentlemen.'

'Very good,' said Elizabeth, too embarrassed to enquire any further.

She took a few steps towards the window.

'I should like it to be over, Nora. Does a duel last very long?'

'I don't know. Never wanted to see. Miss Lizbeth, I's goin' to remake this bed. Go on back to sleep now.'

'Certainly not. Lower the blind. The sun is beginning to shine.'

Nora obeyed, and the orange canvas plunged the room into a golden half-light.

The large woman had not taken the time to put a white apron over her black dress, and she was moving to and fro in the room, trying to tidy up, picking up underwear that Elizabeth had dropped more or less anywhere. In reality, she was curious to find out why the young English lady was interested in this duel. She did not dare to say anything, but she hoped for a sigh of sadness that would allow of some attempt at consolation, and she moved her heavy frame about, making the floorboards creak relentlessly beneath her weight.

Elizabeth, however, remained silent, and walked about in the room avoiding Nora whose presence was annoying her somewhat now. She stopped in front of the portrait of

Charlie Jones and raised towards him, once again, a long, tender look, full of reproach. Why had he not remained as he was then in the full flush of youth? Why did people change?

27

A little before breakfast, refreshed by late but restorative sleep, and by a bath prolonged as far as possible, she came down to the ground floor. In one of her new summer skirts, pale yellow that morning, she was restored to her usual looks, surprising everybody by the bright pink of her cheeks. Seeing no one in the hall, she was heading for the garden, when Charlie Jones came up to her, all in white, a smile on his lips and a gardenia in his buttonhole. Eau-de-Cologne enveloped him like a cloud. With a great burst of laughter, he seized Elizabeth in his arms:

'A little duel of no consequence!' he exclaimed. 'Nobody dead, nothing but a wound in the arm for Hudson, who won't be able to waltz again for the whole season. He was hoping to despatch Burton to the next world and nearly succeeded. He will be judged severely. He's not a gentleman. I hope I'm not upsetting you . . .'

'Oh, no!'

'Let's take a turn about the garden while waiting for breakfast.'

They walked for a few minutes beneath the sycamores on the big sandy paths that surrounded the lawns. Elizabeth plucked a jasmine flower as she walked by, and sniffed at it from time to time.

'Now that two men have fought over you in a duel,' Charlie Jones said gaily, 'you are no longer a delightful little girl, but a charming young lady. Can you feel the difference?'

'Perfectly.'

'I do not rule out the idea that Mr Hudson may have fallen in love with you, that seems more or less certain. Am I wrong? But I'm being indiscreet.'

'Not at all, but how can one assess the sincerity of a man one does not know?'

'Devil take it, you've matured during the night! You're already giving grown-up answers.'

'It may well be that, as you say, I have matured, Uncle Charlie. May I know now if Francis Brooks is safe and sound?'

'Safe and sound, of course. I was there. Apparently Hudson declared that he would set him right with a whip, as soon as his right arm would permit him.'

Stopping immediately, Elizabeth threw the jasmine flower to her feet.

'I hate that man,' she said.

There were people missing at breakfast. Aunt Emma, in the first place. As Uncle Josh sat down near Charlie, he said to him in a half-whisper:

'She had a great crisis of conscience last night. She is still in bed with a handkerchief soaked in ice on her forehead, and is groaning fit to rend your soul.'

'A grain of calomel will set her right,' said Uncle Charlie in a bantering tone. 'I'll go up and see her later on. Is Billy not here?'

'Billy left quite early, a little before midnight, when the ball was in full swing.'

'Perhaps he was bored.'

'Oh, no! He waltzed like a madman, and then feeling suddenly unwell he disappeared in a hurry. Desperate for sleep, no doubt, he went to his room with the help of a servant . . .'

'Who helped to put him to bed, I suppose.'

'Not entirely. Billy had the canoe that was hanging on the ceiling brought down, and he flung himself into it fully clad. And he is asleep. He's a great dreamer. Carried by the muddy waters of the Savannah river, to the edge of cloudy forests, he's drifting towards an ideal world where everything is permitted, where the most attractive persons . . .'

'Stop there, Josh. I'm going to give orders for a few drops of cold water to bring him back to reality.'

He signalled to a servant and whispered a few words to him. He smiled from one side of his face to the other and disappeared, at the same time as Elizabeth came into the dining room and took her usual place:

'I apologize,' she said as she walked past a mirror, 'I noticed that my hair was untidy.'

'That untidiness seemed some artistic effort to me,' said Charlie Jones. 'You don't have to, but as Aunt Emma is not with us this morning, take her place next to me.'

Elizabeth restricted herself to a smile, and without a word sat down next to Charlie Jones.

'Admire,' he said, 'the tidiness of everything. You can see the big dining room down there, and the ballroom further on. No trace of the banquet, nor of the great whirling of the waltzers. Everything passes; a party leaves nothing behind it.'

'Nothing except the memory of a duel with pistols in a cemetery,' said Elizabeth softly.

Uncle Josh and Charlie Jones exchanged surprised looks.

'You could, indeed, see things in that way,' said Charlie Jones, 'but a duel like that is quickly forgotten. Now a nice strong cup of tea will have us all back in good shape. Do you agree, Elizabeth?'

'Entirely, but I need black tea.'

'The same color as the teapot?'

'But of course.'

Indeed, in the middle of the table an enormous, aggressively British teapot was enthroned, reflecting in its completely black, round shape the three people sitting around it.

Only Uncle Josh declined, wisely taking a fruit juice instead of a brew he considered to be homicidal.

A servant brought on a tray a newspaper freshly arrived from Washington. Charlie Jones unfolded it and threw it to one side almost immediately.

'Toombs keeps on vociferating against Clay's attempts at appeasement. I fear he'll go a little too far some day, and then . . .'

'And then?' Elizabeth asked.

'And then the Northern preachers will warm things up and it will be a free-for-all as to who can find the best reasons in the Scriptures for invading us.'

'Do you think that our preachers are short of learned biblical quotations to put a shine on the bayonets of our soldiers?'

'What soldiers? We haven't got an army.'

'But armies can be improvised, Charlie, as soon as the first heroic proclamations are made by civilians standing on some platform.'

'It would be a defeat for the South, in spite of everything, Josh. The theory of free government for each state has the force of law.'

'On account of that, South Carolina nearly broke away from the Union ten years ago, when she thought the North was seeking dominion over her. Secession is in the air, we can smell it.'

'Come Josh, be calm. You're suddenly getting as worked up as a preacher in a pulpit.'

'Whose fault is that? It's all very well your being English, on the quiet you are one of the most stewed up about it.'

'Josh, if we launch into that subject, we're going to frighten someone.'

Elizabeth put her cup down.

'If it's me you mean, you don't know me very well. I don't know what it is to be afraid.'

'Bravo, Elizabeth!' cried Uncle Charlie. 'In order to think about something else, we'll go in the gig to the building site from which my new house will rise some day.'

'Some day?' said Uncle Josh. 'Have you fixed the date?'

'As I want it to be very beautiful, very spacious and highly decorated, ten years.'

'Ten years! Where shall we be in 1860?'

'Here, in peace. That's telling you what little faith I have in war.'

'Do you realize, Charlie, that the word "war" keeps cropping up *à propos* of everything in these parts?'

'Let's banish it; a fine for anyone who mentions war.'

'So,' said Elizabeth, who was bored by this discussion, 'tell me why there are no blackbirds to be heard in the South? Are there none? I listened to the birds early this morning, I was on the look-out for blackbird song — in vain.'

'It is sad to say,' answered Charlie Jones. 'I too noticed it when I arrived here in 1830. Blackbirds don't whistle in the United States.'

'But Uncle Charlie, there is no song gayer, happier, or with more variety . . .'

'More optimistic,' added Joshua. 'I heard them whistling in Paris. They would put courage into the most anxious man. Oh, Paris! I spent three months there in my youth. Such memories! Such charming memories!'

Charlie Jones cut him short.

'Don't start on that, Josh! You can tell me all that when we're alone. Can I give you some more tea, Elizabeth?'

'Thank you, Uncle Charlie, I've finished.'

'Very well. Since we've all finished, I propose to go and see how Aunt Emma is. As for you, Josh, I suggest you do the same for Billy. Elizabeth . . .'

'I'm going up to my room,' said Elizabeth without offering any explanation.

Her determined expression brought a smile to Charlie Jones's lips.

'The longer she's here, the more English she is,' he said to himself secretly, and bowed.

Elizabeth had good reasons for going up to her room. Mr Hudson's letter came back to her mind and she wondered where she had left it.

She rushed into her bedroom. The bed had been made, and everything was tidy. She observed that the portrait of Charlie Jones was still in its place, but at that instant, only Mr Hudson's letter mattered. The idea that it might have been found and read was unbearable. A man does not write such things without having received a hint of encouragement — a look, a smile, a squeeze of the hand.

In distraction she ran about opening drawers, looking underneath the furniture, unmaking her bed, sheets and blankets flung in a heap on the carpet, of which she had lifted up the edges, and suddenly she cried:

'Nora!'

How could she not have thought of it before? Nora had done the room, seen the letter and taken it away. To what purpose? All of these old black women dabbled in witchcraft, had dealings with the Devil . . . Or she had taken the letter in order to show it to Charlie Jones, out of malice?

She pulled on the bell cord and, sitting down in the rocking chair, made an effort to seem calm. She must talk to the awful old woman in such a way as to make her freeze with terror. She would know what to do. Her eyes fell on the black book, the Holy Bible that she did not have the right to question. At the moment, the Lord was punishing her, but what for? She had done nothing wrong. That man had written her a love letter. She should have torn it into a thousand pieces. There was a waste-paper basket near the small table. Empty. The book frightened her, she had had the temerity to make it speak by force, ordering a witch to ask it questions. 'Do not trifle with God,' the book had answered.

The door opened behind her.

'Nora!' Elizabeth said.

'Yes, Miss Lizbeth.'

'Come here.'

She had barely spoken these words when she noticed a white line sticking out from the edge of the black book. Bound in the old-fashioned style, it had wide flaps, intended to protect the expensive gilding, which, to tell the truth, was of no more than a hair's breadth.

With an abrupt gesture, she opened the Bible and pulled out the letter. Holding back a cry of horror, she looked at Nora who was standing in front of her, arms dangling and with terror on her face.

'What's wrong, Miss Lizbeth?' she murmured.

A heavy silence followed.

'But no,' Elizabeth said finally. 'I just found this letter in the Bible. One should put nothing in a Bible. Didn't you know that? Didn't they ever tell you?'

'No, Miss Lizbeth.'

'Where did you find this letter?'

'There, on the floor.'

She pointed to the carpet, almost at Elizabeth's feet.

'Well, that's all I wanted to know. Now, tell me why you haven't taken the portrait down.'

'I seen Mass'r Charlie when he come back this mornin', I say Miss Lizbeth, she want to keep that portrait, he say:

"Very well, leave it."'

'Oh, Nora! You shouldn't have told him! But never mind.'

'Mass'r Charlie seemed right pleased.'

'Good. I've unmade my bed, you can make it up again later. You can leave me now.'

Nora did not move and seemed to be waiting for something. With her back to the light, she looked even blacker than usual, her ugliness even more marked; but Elizabeth had been viewing her differently for the last few minutes. 'She is afraid of me who am only sixteen years old, and she is at least sixty,' she thought. 'It's strange . . . She is awful to look at, yet she seems so good and honest.'

'Nora,' she said with a smile, 'why are you standing there?'

'Miss Lizbeth you ain't angry with me?'

Then words that she could not restrain flowed from Elizabeth's mouth:

'Nora, you must never again ask me whether I am angry with you. I am always pleased with you.'

The old woman clasped her hands over her ample bosom and seemed on the point of saying something, but Elizabeth cut short what looked likely to be effusiveness.

'No,' she said, 'I want you to go away. I'm very pleased. Go away, go quickly.'

It was now Nora's turn to smile and she did so from one side of her face to the other as she reached the door without a word.

'A moment longer and it would have been tears,' said the girl under her breath when she was alone. 'Ridiculous!'

She took the letter, and with a kind of violence pulled it from its envelope, then unfolded it and read it, after which she left it open on her knees and looked at it in perplexity. Of course she must destroy it, as she did not love the man who had written it.

He, however, was in love; he had humiliated himself before her, recognizing that he had behaved badly in insulting poor Francis Brooks, but later on, after the duel, had he not said that he promised him a whipping? She despised him on account of that and decided to tear up the letter. He was lying. He was not a gentleman.

Did she imagine that gentlemen never lied? He was not

lying when he wrote that letter. How she would have liked never to have received it, never to have read it! What an embarrassment that sheet of paper was . . . Yet it was a love letter. Her first love letter. She remained looking at it for some time. Later she would perhaps receive others, but that one would still be the first, for ever.

Slowly, as if with regret, she put it back in its envelope and fetched a worn leather travel holdall from the back of a cupboard, a family memento that her mother had given her when they left England. The outside was like a very small valise, equipped with a handle and protected with a lock. Inside, metal-capped bottles shone. There was a mirror in a pocket under the lid, and it was there that she slid the letter, where no one would find it.

Thus she would have time to reflect on this problem that was quite new to her — what fate should be reserved for love letters. For the moment she felt relieved of the burden of this difficult question, and that should suffice.

In the drawing room, to which she went down a few minutes later, she came across Charlie Jones, who was reading a newspaper.

'Elizabeth,' he said, 'how do you manage to appear so pink and rested after a night full of little happenings? Oh, miraculous youth! But sit down. I want to give you news of Aunt Emma, for I can sense that you're burning with impatience to hear.'

The irony of this last sentence made Elizabeth smile.

'Moderately,' she said.

'Well, all is for the best. I suspect Josh of having given her a bit of laudanum. You'll see her at lunch, calmed down.'

'And her conscience at peace, I hope.'

'Everything points in that direction. She knows nothing of the duel, and, of course, she should never hear of it.'

'That would be best.'

'You've caught me reading the paper, a mournful occupation. The entire North is rekindling the fire of its indignation about slavery.'

'Uncle Charlie, I can't stop myself from thinking that they're right.'

'Charming Elizabeth, a good part of the South thinks as you do, in principle, for the slaves' labor is imposed on us because of the climate, but it's a curse. The North traded in slaves like us, until the day it realized that its climate was killing them. So they sold the remaining survivors off to us for a good price. I recognize that their argument carries weight. It makes for a union of detestation and good conscience, but I'm counting on Clay to get a compromise accepted, if Toombs will keep quiet. Let's leave that, Elizabeth. The subject becomes boring in the long run.'

'It is interesting, all the same.'

'We shall have all too frequent occasion to return to it. Would you like me to take you in the gig now to Madison Square, to show you the building site of my house which is starting to rise from the ground?'

'With pleasure,' the girl said politely.

'I think you will enjoy it, and if we have time we'll stop to pass the time of day with the Very Reverend Elliott, Bishop of Savannah, who has expressed a desire to see you.'

Elizabeth started.

'A bishop!' she exclaimed. 'I have never spoken to a bishop.'

'Well, it'll be your first bishop,' said Charlie Jones with a laugh. 'There has to be a first time for everything. But there is nothing frightening about this bishop, his courtesy is exquisite.'

'Anglican?'

'Episcopalian. That is the American version of Anglicanism, the most aristocratic, the most elegant Church.'

'Ah?'

As they were leaving the room, they saw Josh who was hurrying to meet them in the entrance hall.

'I announce,' he said, 'that Aunt Emma, quite recovered and in a severe frame of mind, has emerged from her room in a black dress, and is heading for the excellent breakfast that awaits her in the dining room.'

'Elizabeth,' said Uncle Charlie in French, '*filons!*'

'Sorry?'

'Forgive me, a memory of my Parisian days. It means: let's get away from this place without delay.'

'You're wasting time,' Josh said, 'she's moving slowly, but coming like the hand of destiny and full of moralizing.'

'We'll go via the garden. She'll have her tea with Billy.'

'Don't count on it. Billy is having breakfast served in his room, and fasting doesn't come into it.'

'Admirable the way order is restored to things here below. Elizabeth, you'll find a heap of bonnets and palm fans by the front door. Take what you need. The sun will show no mercy. I'm running off to get the gig brought round. I'll meet you in front of the house.'

He went and Elizabeth ran to the little cloakroom where she chose for herself a broad hat with long green ribbons, for she was beginning to fear for her pink complexion amongst the paleness of Southern belles.

An instant later, she was in the street and getting into the elegant black gig. Seated next to Charlie Jones sporting a superb panama, she felt happy as if on some spree. The gaiety of her compatriot made her forget the anguish of the night, and she cried out with admiration at the rows of houses of deep red brick, over which sycamores cast constantly curious shadows. With their tall windows, and the simplicity of their lines, the old dwellings retained something of the rather severe dignity of the first settlers. For the first time Elizabeth got an intuitive view of the Southern soul, that defies any attempt to define it, eternally incomprehensible to the outside world. She experienced a strange feeling, as sudden as impulsive love, but more confused.

The ever quicker trotting of the horse betrayed Charlie Jones's impatience. Every morning he hurried to the Madison Square site, as if to some passionate rendezvous, for in his eyes few pleasures equalled the thrill of pride in seeing his creation through the fresh eyes of an unprepared visitor.

Madison Square was reckoned as one of the most spacious and liberally shaded of the town. Cork oaks made it a favourite with walkers and ladies, in the late afternoon, perambulated with their tiny and almost useless sunshades.

For eighteen months now, however, a whole corner of the square had been given up to a kind of citadel with scaffolding by way of towers, and an enclosure of pinewood with a door that was not opened to the curious. This pinky-brown fence, erected with obvious concern for good looks and durability, had at first attracted attention and then an irrepressible curiosity. People wondered what treasures could be hidden behind these tall planks, so perfectly cut and fitted that not the slightest gap allowed a glance to slide through into the great square.

The gig stopped in front of the solid wooden door and, jumping to the ground like a young man, Charlie Jones held out his hand to help Elizabeth down. All this was done with extreme speed and, the key placed in the lock, the door was opened, and a servant dressed in linen toile immediately appeared. He had obviously been waiting, greeted Charlie Jones and went to take the horse by the bridle.

'Go and wait in the shade with the gig and answer no questions. Remember. I forbid it.'

'Yes, Mass'r Charlie.'

Still standing on the threshold, Charlie Jones assumed a serious air and made a little speech to the girl:

'Elizabeth, you will leave America for a moment, and imagine yourself in England. I'm confiding this to you and you alone, for you are English. You will only see the lower part of my house, but we are already a good way on from the first and second stages. Three windows are already in place on the ground floor. The whole of the paving will come later, but one corner is done. On this land, purchased at a staggering price, I am restoring to the Crown a little piece of the colony that remained loyal the longest in the unfortunate war that made her lose a continent. Do you think me mad?'

'Uncle Charlie, there are questions that one is not obliged to answer, but you are daring me to cross this threshold.'

He looked at her without saying anything for a brief moment and continued:

'Very well. I'm speaking to an intelligent woman. I'm building what, in pre-revolutionary France, they would have called a folly. Mine will be a Tudor folly.'

'Tudor!'

'Yes, and it will be surrounded with palms and banana trees. Now you think I'm really mad.'

'Yes,' she said laughing, 'but for Heaven's sake, let's go in!'

'Follow me.'

He went in and moved aside to let Elizabeth pass, after which the door was locked with a double turn by an energetic hand.

The sunlight fell straight down, like a waterfall, onto the building site, and at first the girl could see nothing. Lowering the brim of her hat over her forehead, she protected her eyes behind her fan. Suddenly she felt Charlie Jones's great silky hand rest on her arm.

'Allow me to guide you over to a wide, cool patch that will be a refuge for us.'

His voice was no longer the same as earlier, when it had been firm and slightly didactic. Now words fell from his lips with the softness of a caress.

Ten or twelve paces led them to a corner of the site where the light did not penetrate.

'Look,' he said. 'Eighty laborers work in shifts from morning till evening here.'

Indeed, she saw men dressed in overalls of blinding whiteness, and wearing enormous straw hats beneath which their heads disappeared, as under the shelter of a roof.

At the opposite corner rose a scaffolding at the foot of which were stacked enormous wooden chests banded with metal. One of them, which was being opened with care, was under the supervision of a man in black, whom Elizabeth recognized easily, in spite of the panama that concealed his face.

'You see your dancer from last night over there,' said Charlie Jones. 'He knows perfectly well that you are here, but I know him, he does not dare show himself to you. He is ashamed of his eye glasses.'

'The eye glasses don't stop people being fond of him.'

'If only he were there to hear you . . . He adores you.'

'I don't wish for as much, alas!'

'That's where his little drama lies. He told me just now that he is suffering.'

'I'm sorry for it, Uncle Charlie, but love doesn't come to order.'

'Don't think I don't know that, and I shouldn't want to see you become Francis Brooks's wife for anything in the world, but do you want me to have a bench brought over? Are you tired?'

'Not at all. What is so precious in those crates that they are opening them with such care?'

'Bricks from England brought in trading ships. The journey is long, but the contents of the crates are priceless in my eyes. Each one of these bricks arrives wrapped in several layers of tissue paper.'

Raising the edge of her bonnet, Elizabeth looked at Charlie Jones who did not flinch:

'Are you serious?' she asked.

'Ask Francis if I'm serious when I hear that a brick has been broken. Terror runs round the building site at such moments, although my anger shows in words only. I want everything in this house to be perfectly beautiful, and I want everything, down to the last bit of wood, metal or glass, to be given me by my native land.'

'The glass too?'

'Certainly. May light pass into every room through panes from over there. I know what you're thinking. Go ahead and think it, my girl. The French say: as mad as an Englishman. You have an Englishman before you. Do you begin to understand?'

'The evidence answers the question.'

'Excellent. I'll go on: the day will come when this house will be a refuge. Don't ask me how or why. I don't know, but I'm sure of it.'

Over the surface, little walls marked out squares and rectangles, the plan of the ground floor.

'The entrance hall will be long, decorated with statues and ending in a curved staircase,' Charlie Jones explained. 'The drawing room that opens off to the right is enormous, with stucco work along the cornices.'

With a broad sweep of the arm he pointed to the imaginary stucco work.

'Stucco brought from Italy in merchant ships,' said Elizabeth wickedly.

'No, wrong. Made on the spot by English craftsmen, and in the purest Grinling Gibbons style. At the other end of the ground floor, the dining room.'

'Vast, I suppose.'

'Wrong again, small. I hate banquets that prompt people to eloquence. Let's leave, Elizabeth. It's hot. Would you like me to call Francis over to greet you? He'll take his eye glasses off first.'

— 259 —

'Poor Francis, I don't want to make him suffer. With his handsome, violet-blue eyes, he could make more than one woman fall in love.'

'The eyes are not bad, in fact, and there is hope of curing his shortsightedness, but it complicates everything and will take a long time. He's turning his back on us. Let's go.'

28

The bishop received them with cordial charm. Tall, slim and dressed in black, he wore on his chest a plain gold cross at the end of a chain. It was the first detail to strike the girl and kept her silent throughout the first few minutes: no outward sign of this kind featured in her own religion, and, imperceptibly, it came as a shock, but the handsome pink face with its regular features that was bowing towards her reassured her a little. She smiled. The bishop asked his visitors if they wished for some refreshment, and Charlie Jones's voice refused politely.

On every side, rows of books reached up to the ceiling, speaking of immense knowledge which petrified Elizabeth. She turned her eyes towards the window which looked out on to the slender sycamores of Monterey Square. Ladies were walking by, chatting happily, free . . . How she regretted not being amongst them . . . Her first bishop was intimidating her . . .

They sat down. First, political news was calmly surveyed. Charlie Jones approved Clay's efforts to preserve peace and the Reverend Elliott could of course do nothing but give his blessing to such praiseworthy intentions. He was, in spite of everything, in favor of the strong-arm approach outlined previously by Calhoun. On this point, they both went into ecstasy over the tenacity of the old campaigner, who, being too ill to attend the Senate, had sent a substitute charged with reading his speech. As if there could be anyone to replace the man with the hawk-like eyes and hair constantly standing on end in anger. The speech had, nevertheless, had its effect, and negotiations had been halted since his death. This exchange of views remained charmless for Elizabeth who, calmer now, observed the Reverend Elliott and ended up finding him quite handsome, in spite of the long white locks that covered his ears. She had imagined him younger. The deep, blue eyes that doubtless concealed erudition, were not lacking in gentleness but betrayed affability in keeping with his state, and a certain human tenderness. There was something holy in those eyes, faith, the great virtues, she added inside herself, to put her Protestantism back in its rightful place, and love too, love for all people. He must have experienced it when he was young . . .

How talkative these two men were! Perhaps she would, after all, give up any idea of asking questions about slavery. They were already standing up as if to bring the visit to an end and she too leapt to her feet. They were talking about her, however. Charlie Jones was explaining to the bishop that she was descended from an old family in the county of Kent, and that the ancestral home, although passed into other hands, still bore the arms from the days of Henry VII above the entrance. His Eminence turned his eyes towards her and gave a slight bow of the head, accompanied by an approving smile, and she felt quite happy, when there burst forth, like a thunderclap, Charlie Jones's unlikely gloss:

'All that doesn't stop her being an abolitionist.'

'An abolitionist!' exclaimed His Eminence.

He leaned towards the young abolitionist with a smile, and the golden cross, moving away from his chest a little, swayed and glittered.

'My dear child, do you imagine yourself to be the only abolitionist here in the South? Deep down I am like you.'

'Slavery is a curse for which the South is not responsible,' said Charlie Jones in a trenchant tone.

'Do you not know,' the bishop continued without taking his eyes off Elizabeth, 'or have you forgotten that Abraham, Isaac and Jacob had slaves?'

'In the scriptures, Your Grace, there is only mention of servants.'

'That is what we call them, too,' said the blue eyes.

'Yet the particular institution that is inflicted upon us has lasted for such a long time that one could believe it to have some part in the divine plan of salvation.'

'Until we're told differently,' rectified Charlie Jones.

'One might indeed suppose,' conceded the prelate, 'that with new ideas, it could disappear in twenty years.'

In the gig, she worked her fan with agitation.

'I'm against slavery,' she declared suddenly.

'Splendid. Me too. If my servants want to go off to the North, they're free to do so. I've told them so, but they're not so stupid! They're very well off at my place. But then I don't have a plantation. I have my offices at the docks. I sell cotton to the whole of Europe, Elizabeth. I am a merchant.'

'A merchant!'

'Yes, a merchant. Are you shocked? Are you disappointed? There is no other term, all the businesses belong to us. Everything considered, the town's fate is in our hands. In times of financial crisis, and we do have them, there is a rush to my bank, I mean the one I founded here.'

'I didn't know,' said Elizabeth, with the degree of admiration she judged necessary for politeness's sake.

'It's not a bad thing for you to know,' Charlie Jones continued, 'not that I want to show off stupidly, but because, being wealthy, I have acquired a sense of responsibility, and that's where you and I meet up.'

'How's that?'

'In the catalogue of your indignation, I believe you share that high society's disdain for Poor Whites.'

'It figures high in the list.'

'This morning's duel — your first — is a blatant illustration of it. If you were in love with Francis Brooks, would you marry him?'

'In love . . . but I'm not really in love with anyone.'

'Not yet, but our Southern boys can be very seductive.'

'First of all, I don't know if I want to get married.'

'Let's leave that. Do you know of a race that is more exasperating than the English?'

'Yes, all the others.'

Charlie Jones burst out laughing.

'Learn, you exasperating little Englishwoman, what our aristocracy bequeathed to the South in settling here: its self-satisfaction, its condescending haughtiness which it passes off as politeness, its taste for luxury and the display of that luxury . . . and its elegance, its crazy gallantry, its refusal to accept defeat, its rock-like constancy in the face of misfortune . . . the disdainful look cast on poverty, because poverty equals failure, and it worships the Mammon of riches and success, its hypocrisy, for which it has an almost world-wide reputation . . .'

'Uncle Charlie!' shouted Elizabeth.

'Calm down, we're there. I would add that when Europe found itself dominated by a tyrant, England, with her usual stupid obstinacy, was there to say no for ten years, and she crushed him.'

Elizabeth gave him a look shining with triumphant joy.

'Napoleon Bonaparte,' she murmured.

'Gently, my little one. That's the name of the greatest man of our times. But England has never been a generous enemy, it's a luxury she can't afford. When her adversary was in her hands, she sent him off to die on a remote island, and there she began to admire him. It's still going on. People might respect us, but we'll never be loved — except in the case of isolated individuals with irresistible charm.'

'Like you, Uncle Charlie,' exclaimed Elizabeth, remembering the portrait in her bedroom.

'I was about to say so!' he said with a laugh.

He stopped his horse in front of the great sycamore that covered the entrance to the house with its shade:

'Do understand,' he continued seriously, 'the humiliation of the Corsican Ogre who was beaten by a soldier without talent.'

'The Iron Duke, a great Englishman in spite of everything.'

'Wrong, my dear Elizabeth, an Irishman, but it's of little consequence. Here, believe me, you've got the wrong England.'

'How do you expect me to understand such strange words?'

'You're right. It might seem extraordinary to you for me to say these things in the street. I'm giving in to one of those sudden intuitions I feel obliged to obey. I love the

South, ever since I decided to live here. It carries within it all the elements of a great nation distinct from the North.'

Elizabeth pulled the brim of her hat down over her forehead, in an effort to avert the midday sun.

'It's not the first time I've heard that said,' she offered patiently.

'Unfortunately,' Charlie Jones continued, 'it's living in a world that's on the fringes of modern times. The North is changing and modernizing. The South isn't shifting. The past, that it makes into its present, suits it. Cotton ensures its prosperity. It refuses to see that the North's power is increasing year by year in an alarming manner.'

'But I hear it said that the South is worried.'

'Worried or not, it is determined to stand up to that dangerous neighbor. It puts its confidence in cotton, which the North, like overseas countries, needs. The North is building factories. The South doesn't have a single one.'

'I don't see why there should be a war on account of that situation.'

'It can be avoided if the South makes concessions, but it doesn't want to give grounds for believing it's being intimidated. Its self-esteem is at stake, and it's plunging into a fearful adventure of which no one can predict the outcome.'

'So war is inevitable.'

'It won't be tomorrow, because the North isn't keen to risk such a costly undertaking. My conviction is that a more or less solid arrangement will be found to save face. Do you think I should be building a house if I thought the country on the verge of a conflict?'

'Frankly, if I could, I would go back to England.'

'Are you afraid?'

'Oh, no!' she cried in furious embarrassment. 'I said that because I'm homesick.'

'We'll come back to what I was saying just now. Your England is not in the deep South, it's in Virginia. You'll find it there, calm and green, with its fields, its woods and its great country houses, where everything is conducive to a happy life. But you're uncomfortable in the sun. Let's go and sit in the garden. There's something else I want to tell you.'

He touched the horse with his whip and the gig set off

again to go around the house. A servant came to take the chestnut horse by the bridle. A moment later, Elizabeth found herself sitting next to Charlie Jones in a grotto of greenery, where she took off her bonnet with a sigh of relief. All around her the branches of the trees reached down to the ground in curtains of foliage which gave this refuge the coolness of a cellar.

'I admit,' she said with a smile, 'that I'm more comfortable listening to you here than in the street.'

'Reproaches!' he said with a laugh. 'I deserve them, but you have to take me as I am. The mood of the moment gets the upper hand over politeness. Listen. I was talking to you about Virginia. Its name alone has a magical sound for me. It's the state that's given America its greatest men. It was called Virginia in honor of the Virgin Queen, the great Elizabeth. You'll think yourself at home in her territory. I've had a house built there, where I shall take you some day, and you'll never want to leave. My son spends his holidays there.'

'Your son! I didn't know . . .'

' They've told you hardly anything about me. I was married and have been a widower for two years.'

The simple word 'widower' came as a shock to Elizabeth, as if Charlie Jones were enveloped by funereal hangings.

'Don't look so horrified,' he said a little sadly. 'I loved my wife, and it was on account of my mourning that I did not open the ball yesterday evening. Perhaps you wondered . . .'

'No.'

'By marriage I'm related to all the families in the South.'

'All the families? You mean the best ones?'

'Let's say those that matter. I'm not crazy about nobility. But still, I hope to remarry next year.'

He hesitated for a moment and continued:

'My son has already turned eighteen. He is doing his studies at the University of Virginia, where all the sons of Southern gentlemen go. There. I've told you almost everything. Except the most important, which is the most embarrassing. In a word, when your mother, in her difficulties, appealed to my friend Hargrove, it was because of family ties between him and your father.'

'I know all that.'

'If she had turned to me, you wouldn't be at Dimwood, but here or in Virginia, and, I believe, happier. I'll try and make sure that your life is agreeable.'

'Thank you. I'm keen to see my mother soon.'

Again he hesitated, and looked at her seriously.

'I understand you, Elizabeth. Your mother is an admirable woman. We can go in now. Lunch is in an hour.'

And in an unexpected gesture, he leant towards her and placed his lips on her forehead.

'Stay with us,' he said.

She did not answer.

29

Leaving Charlie Jones in the entrance hall, she went straight up to her room. Everything was in perfect order, and a quick glance sufficed to establish that the portrait had not been moved. She rang.

The sun was no longer coming into her room, and the half-closed shutters broke down the harshness of the light, but not a breath disturbed the stillness of the long muslin curtains.

Elizabeth was splashing water over her face and arms when Nora finally appeared, breathless and shuffling in her slippers.

'I's comin' from the kitchen, Miss Lizbeth, I can't get up them stairs quickly.'

'That's all right, Nora,' said Elizabeth as she dried herself. 'Listen. Mr Charlie told you to put his portrait in his room, and a picture of flowers here, in its place?'

'Yes'm, but if Miss Lizbeth want the portrait . . .'

'You must do what he told you. You take the portrait down and I'll have — whatever he wants. Take it now.'

'All right, Miss Lizbeth.'

She obeyed and carefully unhooked the portrait, then slowly went to the door, which Elizabeth took the trouble to open wide for her. The old woman stopped in the doorway:

'Miss Lizbeth ain't angry?' she asked in a plaintive tone.

'Nora, I forbade you to ask me that. Once and for all, I'm never displeased with you, so take the picture away and mind how you go down the stairs.'

A little worried, her eyes followed the portrait's journey to the bottom of the steps, then she closed the door.

Her gaze was carried to the wall, where the portrait hung no longer, and she looked at the empty space.

'A widower,' she said to herself, 'and father of an eighteen-year-old son. All in all, an old gentleman. When he was young, he must have considered himself handsome to have himself painted.'

For a few minutes, she dreamt on the unfair changes made by age, then decided to change her dress for lunch, and chose the one she judged to be the most beautiful, although a little gaudy: eau-de-Nil, decorated with mauve ribbons. It seemed to her something amusingly audacious to do, changing her into a different person.

As she was admiring herself in the mirror, stroking the folds of the light material, there was a knock at her door, and without waiting for an answer, Aunt Emma made her entrance in a long, puce-coloured dress, trimmed with black bands.

Having reached the middle of the room, she stopped and remained silent.

'May I ask,' she finally said, 'where you got that extra-ordinary outfit?'

'There's nothing extraordinary about it,' Elizabeth answered firmly. 'Uncle Josh bought it for me yesterday, it's from Mademoiselle Clementine.'

Aunt Emma frowned.

'I'm starting to have doubts about the fashions of this town. There is a complete lack of seriousness.'

'Girls of my age often wear brighter colors.'

Aunt Emma tossed her head back:

'If you were my daughter, I would insist that you wore a more discreet dress. I wonder what your mother would say if . . .'

She suddenly interrupted herself and continued more calmly:

'I was simply passing by to collect my Bible. You've read, I hope, the chapters I pointed out to you.'

'No, not those chapters, but something else in St Paul.'

'St Paul, good. You should have read the gospel first, but let's see St Paul.'

'In the epistle to the Galatians.'

'An unexpected choice.'

'A sudden inspiration,' said Elizabeth in a somewhat frenzied attempt to tell the truth without giving herself away.

'I'm not against that kind of inspiration, I've had them myself. And what did St Paul say?'

'This, which struck me: "One should not trifle with God."'

Aunt Emma closed her eyes and said in a flat voice:

'It's true. I'd forgotten that verse. It has always frightened me.'

Her face had suddenly turned an unhealthy, yellowish white.

Elizabeth took a step towards her and took her hand.

'What's the matter, Aunt Emma? How can that verse frighten you? It's not addressed to you.'

'It is. You can't understand, you're too young.'

As she spoke these words, she suddenly appeared much older. Moved to pity, Elizabeth led her to the rocking chair into which she collapsed. Her weight immediately set it in motion and, with the irony of things, swung her back and forth as if setting off on a journey.

'Another crisis of conscience,' thought the girl, who could not repress a smile, 'we shall never get lunch.'

'Aunt Emma,' she said, 'St Paul was writing for simple people, with whom he doubtless had to be outspoken.'

Aunt Emma pulled a handkerchief from her sleeve and sighed:

'Don't say stupid things. The Bible always speaks to each one of us. Stop this chair.'

There was a knock at the door. A servant announced that lunch would be served in a few minutes.

'Let's go down,' said Aunt Emma, wiping her forehead shiny with sweat, and in a resolute tone that surprised Elizabeth she declared: 'I think I'd feel better at Dimwood than here. I'll speak to Joshua just now.' She only called him this in the most serious of circumstances. 'I hope you are agreeable to returning there. Taking everything into consideration, Savannah is no place for you.'

'I don't know what you mean by no place for me, Aunt Emma, but I shall be happy to see my mother again.'

At these words, Aunt Emma gave her a furtive look.

'Help me up,' she said.

In the dining room, plunged into semi-darkness, Charlie Jones and Uncle Josh were having an animated discussion and fell silent when Aunt Emma appeared, followed by Elizabeth. Crouching in one corner, a very young boy dressed in white was pulling on the cord of a fan, and the big square of canvas stirred up the humid air with a kind of groan.

'We kept you waiting,' said Aunt Emma in a preoccupied tone of voice. 'I was talking to Elizabeth about our return to Dimwood.'

'Already?' exclaimed Charlie Jones.

Billy, on his side, protested vehemently:

'We've only just got here and we're leaving already?'

'Be quiet. We're not leaving today, or tomorrow, but the day after tomorrow.'

'That makes for a short visit, but Dimwood is not so far away, and you are at home here, and my house awaits you.'

'Dimwood is boring and Savannah is fun,' grunted Billy.

'We'd rather not know what you call fun,' said Uncle Josh sarcastically, 'nor what you were doing during those hours when you mysteriously disappeared.'

'Leave him, Josh,' said Charlie Jones. 'You're only fifteen once.'

'Nearly sixteen,' said Billy.

The two men exchanged a look as if they were making mental calculations.

'Let's stay until Saturday, Emma,' said Uncle Joshua. 'That will give Elizabeth a chance to visit some of our friends. People want to meet her in Savannah.'

'Or perhaps you could leave with Emma,' said Charlie Jones, 'and I'll bring Elizabeth back to Dimwood myself later.'

'And me!' yelled Billy

But Aunt Emma proved to be intractable:

'Elizabeth is coming back with me and Billy. The children have seen enough of Savannah for the moment.'

'Mama!' said Billy.

'Be quiet. Elizabeth, you are in agreement, I think.'

'I admit that I shall be pleased to see my mother again.'

There was a brief silence during which the enormous fan's little lament could be heard.

'Well,' said Charlie Jones, 'sadly, it's agreed . . . Let's have lunch.'

A veil of melancholy covered the meal, despite Uncle Charlie's efforts to brighten up the conversation. Uncle Josh was worried. Aunt Emma, in a particularly moral frame of mind, disapprovingly ate slice after slice of toast dripping with marmalade. Even Billy, usually so full of chatter, only opened his mouth to facilitate the miraculous disappearance of a good dozen pancakes swimming in maple syrup.

Elizabeth barely touched her tea and remained deep in silence, watching the young servant. With a mechanical gesture, he pulled the cord of the fan, but the warmth of the air made him nod off, and there came a point when the fan remained motionless.

Putting her toast on a plate, Aunt Emma proffered in a flat tone:

'I'm suffocating.'

'Bah, the boy has fallen asleep,' said Charlie Jones, 'we'll wake him up.'

'He wouldn't die from a glass of cold water straight in the face,' declared Aunt Emma.

'Proposition adopted,' said Charlie Jones with a big smile, 'but we'll modify your style.'

And, dipping his fingers in a bowl of water, he flung a few drops into the servant's face. The latter opened terrified eyes, and seeing his master smiling, he answered him with the dazzling smile of adolescence.

'I's sorry, Mass'r Charlie,' he stammered, pulling on the cord with all his strength.

'If I were you,' said Aunt Emma, 'I'd sell that lazy bones, I'd sell him south, he'd find a buyer.'

'Emma,' exclaimed Josh, 'for Heaven's sake, what are you thinking of? Do you realize you can be heard next door? It's not at all the time to be speaking like that.'

'Calm down,' said Charlie Jones. 'I have no intention of selling Noah nor any of our servants. Stop looking like a hunted animal, Noah, and get the fan working.'

With its sad grinding, the machine began to move the air again, but everyone had finished eating, and Aunt Emma announced that she was going to rest in her room.

When she had retired, the two men exchanged a look and nodded. Elizabeth watched them, as if expecting some explanation. Never before had anything troubled her as much as Aunt Emma's attitude. Until then, she had felt only indifference towards her, and sometimes a certain pity when she believed her to be unhappy, but suddenly she took an aversion to her.

Faced with the girl's perplexed expression, Charlie Jones told Noah he could go, then, turning towards Billy, suggested he saddle a horse to set off and explore the district. Orders had been given in the stables, and the outing was expected. The offer was accepted, not without a last, languishing look in the direction of what remained of the pancakes and maple syrup.

'There goes an uncomplicated soul,' said Uncle Josh when Billy had turned on his heels.

'I don't understand how Emma can have produced such a simple creature. Emma is all confused.'

'Let's leave things to sort themselves out, Charlie. Elizabeth, I hope you didn't get upset over that rather absurd discussion about the fan.'

Elizabeth gave Uncle Josh a look of studied coldness:

'Upset? No, but I learnt something I didn't know.'

'Listen. Aunt Emma talks like people talked when she was young. Since then such inhuman language would not be used amongst us.'

And he added, lowering his voice:

'It's not that we fear an uprising . . .'

'There will be no uprising,' confirmed Charlie Jones.

'No, Charlie, but it's one of those possibilities that you can never quite get out of your mind and which haunt you. Those words you have just spoken, and which are heard every day: "There will be no uprising." We're sure of it, but we feel the need to keep repeating that we're sure.'

'You are haunted by the memory of San Domingo, Josh.'

'At San Domingo, things were very different. The slaves had a leader.'

'I can't see a Toussaint-Louverture rising up out of the ground in our area, but we shall frighten Elizabeth with our sinister remarks. Let's leave this stifling dining room.'

Elizabeth was sorry that nobody had commented on her eau-de-Nil dress and her mauve ribbons.

30

The temperature did not halt the various activities necessitated by imminent departure. Uncle Josh took charge of the assorted presents that the servants at Dimwood were expecting to receive. He set off in a gig, followed by the cart for the massive purchases, and only returned three hours later, exasperated but pleased to have behind him that chore that he described as killing.

The afternoon was belatedly given over to a few visits in the residential district, where the most elegant houses of the town were to be found. They all retained the appearance of family homes, in their façades and the ornamentation of the doors. Elizabeth was received with the charm of Southern hospitality. She could have believed herself the object of all possible friendship, and at first the rather formal aspect of the compliments and the good humour eluded her. Everything was done to make the young Englishwoman feel at home in this closed world, noted for its superciliousness.

Faced with these women in pearl gray and these men in black with white cravats reaching up to their ears, she had the impression that they were all doing violence to some natural seriousness in order to appear pleasant according to the strict rules of traditional manners. And she wondered whether, in her green dress with mauve ribbons, she did not look like some village girl in Sunday best. Aunt Emma's enraged opinion came to mind. She was troubled by it, because she was not yet aware of the attractiveness emanating from her whole person, from her clear voice, full of echoes of the homeland. She was judged to be delightful.

The following day was a bustling one. The imminent departure cast confusion, as if preparations were being made for a trip around the world. Billy helped matters by continual absences. He was suspected of hanging around Mademoiselle Clementine's shop. Amidst the constant comings and goings, he was on the look-out for some glimpse of Dorcas, the fascinating half-caste who was employed in the workshops of *Caprices de Paris.*

At Charlie Jones's house, the travellers' clothes were filling up trunks. Valises had to be added for Elizabeth's purchases. Nora was given this task, but left in the armoire the dresses, shawls and 'unmentionables' that the girl would find there on her next visit. For everyone was counting on her spending a good part of the year in Savannah, everyone except the object of their discussion who was asking herself innumerable questions.

A little before dinner, Billy reappeared, looking like a toff, and the description he gave of his excursion into the woods aroused great interest, especially on the part of Charlie Jones, who knew that those woods were impenetrable. 'But,' he whispered into Uncle Josh's ear, 'you're only fifteen once in your life.'

The following day promised to be hot, and departure was put off until four o'clock in the afternoon. They did what they could to fill in the interminable waiting, and the time was wasted. Having got over her acute crisis of conscience, Aunt Emma confidently declared to Uncle Josh that she felt happy to be leaving this immoral town and filled her enforced leisure with writing letters to her friends.

As he had done the previous day, Billy disappeared without giving details as to the purpose of his excursion, and Uncle Charlie taught Elizabeth to play chess. She understood it immediately, and her generous opponent let her win the first game.

Whilst revealing to her the knight's sly skipping-about

and the all-embracing power of the queen, he did not omit to give her prudent advice which she listened to politely.

'At Dimwood, you'll do well to let them talk without getting too caught up in the discussions. People talk much too much in the South. I fear there will be difficult moments, painful ones, perhaps.'

'Painful?' she said.

'There will be good ones too. Life is made up of such mixtures. There will be no shortage of balls with the onset of winter. Boys will come courting you. Don't commit the folly of believing a word they tell you. In your place I'd send my bishop straight to two squares short of the queen, to tease her. She is awkward and cowardly and won't move. If ever fate has too hard a blow in store for you, you'll remember that I'm always there as your best friend, and that your room awaits you here. I'm moving my king forward clumsily. With your rook you can put him in check, he is lost. Check mate. Bravo. But they're ringing for lunch.'

'Already?'

'Chess is magic. It doesn't help time to pass, it demolishes it, reduces it to nothing. It's very useful.'

Crossing the drawing room, he stood in front of Aunt Emma, who started and looked up in astonishment.

'Aunt Emma,' he said, 'you must put down your pen. We're lunching. Leave your paper, Josh. My word, you were all dreaming. Didn't you hear Jeremiah announcing luncheon? Where is Billy?'

'Behind you, Uncle Charlie.'

He was there, in fact, with his face rather red and beads of sweat on his forehead.

'I've just got here,' he said, 'I've been . . .'

'I'm not asking you where you've been. Don't let's wait any longer.'

In the half-light of the great room where the silverware shone on the white tablecloth, Noah, crouching down, was pulling vigorously on the cord of the fan, and the flapping of the canvas procured the illusion of a breath of fresh air, but the meal was rather half-hearted. It was too hot to eat or even to talk much. Only Billy retained his noble appetite and tried in vain to describe what he had seen that morning. Silence was imposed upon him, and he found his consolation in the garland of crayfish and, as he was the last to be served, in what remained of a coffee ice-cream of which he left only the smallest trace.

The siesta, which was declared compulsory, was prolonged by half an hour and delayed the departure. Uncle Charlie had to gently shake the sleepers on the sofas of the drawing room and entrance hall. Billy proved to be the most obstinate of the rebels and, in consequence, Uncle Charlie's vigorous hand upended the sofa. Sitting on the ground, the boy rubbed his eyes and did not dare protest, but expressed a wish:

'Uncle Charlie, let me take my canoe.'

'Out of the question. On your feet, my boy.'

Billy got up suddenly.

'They could have tied it to the cart with the presents . . .'

'Billy, you'll find "your canoe", as you call it, here, at my house, when you return, but it's Ned's canoe. Now get your-self ready. The carriages are in front of the door and have been waiting for half an hour. This time, you'll be in the carriage with Aunt Emma.'

'Oh! Uncle Charlie!' exclaimed Billy who took on a martyred air.

'There's no "Oh, Uncle Charlie" about it. You'll travel with your mother.'

The travellers were taking their places, when, at the last moment, Elizabeth appeared, followed by Noah. He was carrying an extra valise.

'I'm sorry,' she said, rather embarrassed. 'It's the shawls, the gloves, and all kinds of little things for Mama.'

Uncle Josh did not answer straight away.

'That's quite natural,' he said, 'quite natural.'

The parasols were opened, the whips cracked and the vehicles set off at a healthy trot, while Uncle Charlie waved in the flaming heat of a merciless sun.

3
SOLITUDE

31

*T*he carriages pulled up in front of the verandah and were
immediately surrounded by servants clutching torches.
The gleam of the light on the red liveries and gold braid
gave a party atmosphere to this arrival in the dark. Like
Billy, Elizabeth jumped down eagerly, but Aunt Emma, who
had slept throughout the journey, declared that she was
shattered with tiredness, and would have to be lifted out of
the carriage. With an arm around her waist, Uncle Josh
supported her as far as the verandah steps. He helped her
up with the aid of Jonah's strong arms. Once at the top, she
let out a tragic sigh and said in a faint voice that the journey
had killed her. She was taken to her room and there she
asked for a phial of that good laudanum that had restored
her to life at Uncle Charlie's, and which she had never tried
until then. She was put to bed and made a fuss of, and she
soon fell asleep, happy to feel far from the world and its
vain stirrings.

Secretly indignant at this faint-heartedness, for he knew
the reason for it, Uncle Josh set off to look for William
Hargrove, but no one could tell him the whereabouts of the
master of Dimwood. He had come back the day before and
had gone again.

Mildred and Hilda were the only ones to suddenly appear,
emerging from a dark corridor like pretty wild animals
coming out from the depths of the wood. They both took a
few steps forward towards Elizabeth, but held back from
kissing her.

The young Englishwoman began to laugh:

'What's the matter?' she asked. 'You're looking at me as if
I were a ghost . . . or had the plague!'

'Not at all,' exclaimed Hilda.

'We're so pleased to see you . . .'

Mildred's affirmation remained without an echo.

'You'd think I frightened you.'

At that moment, someone behind her touched her hand. It
was Susanna with the jet-black hair and beautiful black eyes,
the silent one, who had only once spoken at any length to
Elizabeth, on her first morning at Dimwood. She was hardly

older than herself, but the woman she would become was already evident: calm and gentle, with a slightly ironic smile.

'The blue dress,' she said.

'Oh, dear Susanna, I have not forgotten it. The seamstress in Savannah wrapped it up, it's in the trunk.'

There was a brief silence. Suddenly Susanna took a step towards her and hugged her convulsively. Tears ran from her eyes, wetting Elizabeth's cheek, who was too amazed to struggle.

Over Susanna's shoulder, she could see Mildred and Hilda running away down the corridor, and she felt struck with terror.

'Everybody is running away!' she exclaimed. 'What's the matter?'

Susanna's arms dropped abruptly and she wiped her eyes on her shawl, and then in a voice that she made an effort to make calmer:

'You won't sleep up there tonight,' she said.

'Something has happened. Mama is ill, you've kept it from me. I want to go up and see her.'

'Listen to me, Elizabeth, she isn't ill.'

Elizabeth ran to the stairs, but Susanna caught her by the arm

'I'll come up with you. You must listen to me. Your mother gave Betty a message.'

Elizabeth, who was trying to free herself, stopped short:

'A message from Mama . . . Betty . . . I don't understand . . . You're frightening me.'

Taking her arm by force, Susanna went up the great staircase with her, where the Greek god in his niche surveyed the scene with his unseeing eyes. Elizabeth tried to free her arm that Susanna was holding with an energetic grip. Suddenly a great cry was unleashed:

'She's dead and nobody wants to tell me!'

'I swear to you that she is not dead. Calm down for Heaven's sake.'

A door on the first floor opened. Betty appeared and raised her arms.

'Miss Lizbeth!'

'Light the lamp in Miss Elizabeth's room,' cried Susanna.

Not without summoning the Lord to her aid, Betty

plunged into the darkness, and her pious exclamations horrified the girl:

'I'm sure of it now,' she groaned. 'Stop clinging on to me, Susanna. Everything has been kept from me, everyone has lied to me.'

As they were going up together, a soft and gentle light began to shine through the open door. It was at that moment that a terrible thought, worse than all the others, devastated the girl's heart: her mother had gone mad. Several times Elizabeth had had the impression that she was losing her faculties: the death of her husband and this exile in a country she disliked had been enough to disturb her brain. Now she was being kept in a darkened room, waiting to be taken somewhere else . . .

Giving up all resistance, she turned her anxious face towards Susanna:

'Stay with me, will you? I'm worried, unhappy.'

'But you don't need to be afraid. Come . . .'

With calm steps they went to the top of the staircase.

In Elizabeth's room, the oil lamp gave a reassuring look to things. Everything was in order. The mahogany furniture gleamed discreetly, and outside the call of the tree-frogs seemed to merge with the silence.

Sitting on a chair, Betty was crying with her head lowered, and between her knees, spread wide apart, a white envelope could be seen in a fold of her black dress. When the two girls came in, she took the letter and stood up.

'Miss Lizbeth,' she murmured with the letter in her fingers.

Susanna intervened immediately:

'Yes, there is a letter for you, Elizabeth. You'll see, your Mama explains everything to you. She made us swear, swear on the Bible, that we would say nothing, neither here at Dimwood, nor at Savannah. No one was to say anything. She insisted, she insisted.'

She tried to smile as she spoke in a frenzied manner, as if to stifle the unhappiness, to eradicate it in advance, but Elizabeth was not listening any more.

Without a word, she seized the letter and went towards her mother's room, but the door did not open.

'Open it,' she said, turning back towards Susanna and Betty.

With the light of the lamp shining on her face, she seemed taller in the shadow that reached up to the ceiling behind her. Her suddenly pale features took on a hardness.

Susanna looked at her, stupefied by this transformation, while Betty looked in a drawer for the key that she held out trembling to this Miss Lizbeth whom she no longer recognized.

Susanna was at her side immediately.

'Leave me, Susanna, I want to be alone. Go away, Betty.'

This authoritarian tone made Susanna draw back and leave the room with the maid in tears. Elizabeth turned the key in the lock.

With the door opened, she moved forward into the dark and empty room. She remained motionless for some considerable time in that deserted room that spoke only of absence, telling her what no one had wanted to tell her. A faint odor of laudanum brought back memories.

After ten or so minutes, she went back to her own room and took the lamp which she carried into her mother's room and put it down on the little bedside table by the great four-poster bed. It seemed to her that in this light a presence rose up, holding her prisoner. Sitting on the bed, she opened the letter that she still had in her hand and read it:

Daughter,

I am leaving. Do not weep too much, do not weep at all. I have shed all possible tears. My departure will make your life easier, as it will my own. If you are as clever as I think, you will end up being happy. You will get used to this aristocracy, which, no longer having either its titles or its ancestral lands, has taken refuge in shadowy isolation. They have retained their nobility, but it is as if they no longer knew how to use it. A nobility descended from emigrants, attached to usages that are out of date these days, and a courtesy that is no longer the same as ours. Laura Hargrove, with whom I have spoken at length, put me in the picture on these particular points. It is not admissible here, any more than it is in England, to ask questions, but you know that. We leave that habit to the continentals who do not know how to go about life.

Although she is of the Roman religion, Laura Hargrove is worthy of our confidence, but with prudence. There is no way of ever knowing what is going on inside the head of a hot-headed Catholic, nor what ulterior motives of conversion might be lurking there. You'll remain on your guard through faithful reading of the Bible. With those reservations, you'll find in Laura Hargrove a kind woman, full of good sense. She has suffered greatly.

Never forget that you are English. Try likewise to be always human. The world esteems that it is an impossibility for us, but I do not share that opinion entirely, and what does the opinion of the world matter?

To return to completely material matters, you need have no worries on your mother's account. Charlie Jones, whom I knew in my youth when he was on a visit to England, and was almost too full of attentiveness towards me, has shown himself to be generous beyond limit. A considerable sum has been put at my disposal in a London bank. The rest has been more than adequately made up by William Hargrove, who did not wish to be outdone in the ways of Southern munificence. Ready to see the Lord's hand in all things, I accepted without the shadow of a scruple. By virtue of the same principle, I can now only advise you to act entirely likewise, tactfully, as from now on you are adopted by our lost colony.

You will hear from me in due course. And then you will be able to send me your news. I've never been in favour of effusiveness. Let it suffice for you to know that I have always loved you as a mother should love her daughter, perhaps even to excess in my case.

Laura Escridge

Elizabeth spent a good part of the night dressed, in her mother's room. Sitting in the rocking chair, she gave herself up to a steady rocking that helped her to think, and, through an effort of the imagination, she tried to remodel her life without her mother. From time to time she dozed. Several times someone came into the room without her being aware of it. Laura, then Uncle Josh. Neither of them wanted to wake her, and they withdrew almost immediately.

At daybreak, wrenched from her torpor by birdsong, she returned to her room, got undressed and slid between the sheets. There, with her head under the blankets, she suddenly burst into tears which shook her for several minutes, then she fell asleep, still crying.

There was a knock at her door for breakfast a little before nine o'clock. She washed hastily and came down just as everyone was taking their place at table.

She was asked if she had had a good night, and the answer came immediately, with a smile:

'Excellent.'

A finely tuned ear might have picked up a more or less general sigh of relief, lighter than a breath. Billy knew nothing of what was going on, and his only sigh was for the arrival of the pancakes with maple syrup.

Life resumed its normal course. Standing up, William Hargrove first of all thanked the Lord for the safe return of the travellers, and called down blessings on all those present, and on all the workers on the plantation, then came the nation, and more particularly the South, then the state of Georgia, and with a wonderful *diminuendo*, dear Dimwood.

As if in a dream, Elizabeth observed this man whom she had believed to be dead, and who had looked at her at such length when he thought she was asleep in Charlie Jones's house. She had taken him for a ghost at the time, and although she had seen him leave later in a carriage, the first, supernatural impression mingled strangely with evidence from reality. A night of anxious thought, and too little sleep, set free in her a tendency to see in the visible world a kind of hallucinatory phenomenon. Nothing was real, everything was concealed behind appearances. What mattered was going on inside herself. From what distant origins did this strange rejection come to her? Residual tiredness could be the explanation that morning. With all her strength, she would have liked to be able to give the lie to those certainties that caused her pain, to deny the presence of the people around her, to deny the plantation and the whole of the South, to deny the sea journey, and, through a superhuman leap, to find herself once more on English soil.

Aunt Laura, sitting next to Elizabeth, did not take her eyes off her, and seeing her look more pensive than usual, said under her breath:

'My father has had a very pleasant room made ready for you on the ground floor, it's cooler in summer.'

Elizabeth looked at her indifferently.

'I shall be your neighbor,' Aunt Laura added.

A rather mechanical smile greeted this news, and the short exchange finished there, but Aunt Laura placed her hand momentarily on Elizabeth's, in a gesture of unspoken affection.

They drank their tea in silence. Around them people spoke with unaccustomed moderation, as if out of respect for Elizabeth's grief, but the conversation gradually became livelier. Uncle Josh vaunted the beauty of spring in the wide avenues of Savannah, the charm of its squares, and the interesting visit to Mademoiselle Clementine of *Caprices de Paris*, which provoked noisy sighs on Billy's part, while Mildred and Hilda strained eager faces towards the speaker. Seeing himself commanding such flattering attention with his speech, Uncle Josh began to describe the banquet, then the rush to the ball, when an imperious coughing broke into his narrative flow, and Aunt Emma, eyebrows raised, indicated with a nod of the head the young Englishwoman, who looked unmoved.

The latter's attention was secretly directed towards William Hargrove, who avoided looking at her. He appeared even more anxious than usual, and occasionally exchanged a few words with his daughter-in-law Augusta, placed at his right. She did not look any happier either and at that corner of the table there reigned a certain unease that was becoming more and more apparent until Joshua abruptly stopped speaking.

In the thick silence that followed, Douglas's serious voice made itself heard:

'While people enjoy themselves and dance in Savannah, things seem to be taking a turn for the worse in the North. The agreement proposed by Clay has been violently criticized as being much too favorable to the South. Everything is back in the melting pot, and peace seems threatened once more.'

Elizabeth felt her throat tighten at these words. A reality whose existence she could no longer deny, was rising up before her like a granite wall. How could her mother not have taken her with her? The question presented itself to her mind with an insistence that boded ill. Until now she had never taken the problems of the North and the South seriously, because she understood nothing of them. But now the repetition of the same phrases seemed to hold a real threat. War emerged from words proffered millions of times, it sufficed for there to be sufficient of them.

For the first time she experienced an instinctive animal fear that turned her stomach, and drops of sweat ran down her forehead to her nose. Without opening her mouth, she leant towards Aunt Laura and touched her hand.

The response to this gesture was immediate. Aunt Laura repressed a cry and stood up:

'Come with me, Elizabeth. You are quite pale.'

The girl stood up without hesitation, and they left the dining room, where complete silence was the first effect. No one moved until the moment when, Elizabeth and Aunt Laura having gone, tongues again began to wag, and great exclamations began to strike the air. Then it was the turn of questions and explanations. The fatigue of the journey and the heat were posited.

'The shock of the empty room,' decreed Uncle Josh.

Only William Hargrove remained motionless, petrified with horror as his eyes rested on the wide-open door.

The two brothers met up beneath the trees of the great avenue. Uncle Josh viewed the situation calmly.

'The decision,' he said, 'had to be taken quickly. She didn't even wait for an answer to her letters. Moreover, what need did she have of an answer? She left here with all she required, and more besides.'

'Even so, arriving over there all alone will be hard.'

'Alone! One is never alone with a fortune . . .'

They walked for a long time in silence, this thought echoing inside them.

32

*T*he room to which Elizabeth was taken made her smile, in spite of her still feeling upset. Indeed, everything there seemed intended to make life pleasant for her and, more particularly, to make it calm and peaceful. A certain fortunate naivety seemed to have selected the means to this end. The walls, painted in pale yellow, were decorated with Italian landscapes, large watercolors, the work of a patient and enthusiastic hand that had omitted neither the smallest cloud in a blue sky nor a hint of smoke rising from Vesuvius. The silk curtains, of rainbow colors, draped two tall French windows opening on to the porch, sheltered from the sun by the verandah, beneath which it extended for its full width. A few steps sufficed to reach the balustrade and breathe in the perfume of magnolias.

'This is your room,' said Aunt Laura. 'It's the guest room. My father wants it to be yours from now on. Do you like it?'

Elizabeth indicated that she did. The sight of the magnolia alone was enough to calm her, as a reunion with a lost friend would have done.

'Do you feel better? Do you want to rest on the bed?'

'No, thank you,' the girl murmured.

And she added in a firmer voice:

'I'm alright.'

'You still don't have a very good color, but it'll come back. This room is more cheerful than the other one. We had put you there because the two rooms communicated with each other, but they were a little austere. Look at this little writing desk. Don't you think it pretty? It's made of camphor wood and comes from . . .'

She stopped. There was a feeling that she was hoping to distract the girl from her worried thoughts with a flow of words and, without wishing to, had said too much.

Elizabeth crossed the room. Placed between the two windows, the piece of furniture in question was of a fussy elegance, its curved lines adorned with frenziedly carved ornamentation: fruit and flowers, foliage climbing up and down in all directions.

Elizabeth's natural curiosity was suddenly aroused, and

she examined the writing desk with an attentive look that seemed to embarrass Aunt Laura.

'It is there to amuse the eye rather than to be used for letter-writing,' she said with a slight laugh. 'It's what they call the rococo style, but if you want a more practical one, something more serious . . .'

'No, it's funny . . . Where does it come from?'

'It comes from far away . . . the colonies.'

'The colonies?'

'I'll explain to you later. It's a bit complicated, and your Mama must have told you never to ask questions.'

At this, a flush of color brightened Elizabeth's face.

'Excuse me,' she said.

'I understand your curiosity. This little piece of furniture is so strange. I can't decide if it is pretty or rather awful. I was made a present of it when I was your age, and it has never left me. It has travelled a great deal.'

As she said these words, she looked so sad and pensive that Elizabeth felt the desire to wrench her from this sudden dreaminess.

'I think it's very pretty.'

'Well, I give it to you then. Usually it is in my room, but in a way I shall be pleased not to have it near me every day.'

Elizabeth thanked her and looked at the writing desk with renewed interest now that she knew it was hers.

Aunt Laura smiled and added mysteriously:

'It has a secret.'

'A secret!'

'It's up to you to find it out. I'll leave you now. I have to do the rounds of the servants. I'll take you with me one day. Today I'm counting on being reassured that there are no mistakes in the distribution of the presents. These coloreds are like children. Before I go, a word about what was said at table this morning. I hope it didn't upset you. From time to time, to look serious, they play at being afraid.'

A glimmer of hope lit up the girl's eyes.

'Do you think so?'

'There won't be a war. I'll leave you. Have a rest. Don't let the "children" disturb you.'

When she had gone, Elizabeth remained perplexed for a moment. Aunt Laura had undoubtedly reassured her by the conciseness and confidence of her statements: a few words had sufficed to brush aside the nightmare of war. How mysterious that woman still was ... Her mother's words came back to mind. Trust, but prudent trust. Why prudent? And this gift of the little writing desk, such charming generosity ... She, Laura Hargrove, must have been fond of such a strange and graceful piece of furniture. The girl still had in her ear the sound of the rapid and gentle voice, like a sudden decision to have done with it once and for all.

She set about the writing desk brusquely and with frenzied curiosity. She would wrench its secret from it. Perhaps it was a tiny drawer concealed in the convoluted foliage. Or perhaps, at the back of one of the visible drawers, another drawer released by some trigger mechanism. Or something else in the legs, a hollow, a groove containing a spring. Her delicate white hands were running over this cunning escritoire from top to bottom, and she was biting her tongue in exasperation, when Hilda and Mildred suddenly bounded into the room amidst peals of laughter.

They had come in through the porch and ran towards Elizabeth:

'Don't tussle with that rotten piece of furniture,' said Mildred as she kissed her. 'It's not worth it. Aunt Laura is the only one who knows.'

Hilda hugged her in her turn, perhaps a little too hard, for Elizabeth made an effort to shake her off.

'Aren't you pleased to see us, Elizabeth? You were awful going off there without us, but we missed you. Can we sit down?'

Without waiting for permission, they were already settled on a low sofa scattered with silk cushions.

Standing in front of them, one would have thought that Elizabeth no longer knew how to talk to them. Perhaps their manners surprised her.

'Sit down!' said Mildred.

Without a word, Elizabeth took an upright chair and sat down opposite the two girls who exclaimed:

'Come on, between us!'

'You're not going to sit there like a judge,' said Hilda.

'I think you're looking better than earlier on,' said Mildred. 'At breakfast you were as white as wax. Come on then . . . Look, we're making room for you.'

'Thank you. I'm alright like this.'

'She's afraid of us.'

'Shut up, Mildred!' said Hilda. 'Elizabeth is English, she's alright as she is.'

'When you really belong to the South, you'll be less . . . less . . .'

'. . . restrained,' suggested Elizabeth, annoyed.

'Oh, how properly she speaks, better than us,' exclaimed Mildred.

Hilda looked serious.

'If you knew what had happened here during your absence . . . After you had left in the morning, late that same afternoon, young Armstrong arrived in a carriage with a lady.'

'Ravishing.'

'I don't know how you managed to find her ravishing, with the thick white veil that was hiding her face.'

'You could guess, and an all-white dress too, but such elegance, such style . . . and I love yours, green with mauve ribbons.'

'Ah? I wanted to put a different one on for the journey, but we left in such a hurry. It must be creased.'

'Not at all. You didn't forget us, you must have some souvenirs for us in your luggage.'

'Yes. No. You can take what you like, but I don't understand anything of your story.'

'It's Mildred who never stops talking. Listen, Mildred, let me tell the story.'

'Oh! Tell it Hilda, do tell it.'

'Young Armstrong asked . . .'

Mildred could not hold her tongue:

'. . . to see Grandfather!'

'Not at all. He asked a servant if Mr Hargrove was there.'

'It's the same thing.'

'It's very different.'

Elizabeth had stood up, and drew her chair closer.

'Mr Hargrove?' she said.

'Yes. That seems to surprise you.'

'He wasn't there.'

'Quite right. That's what young Armstrong wanted to know.'

'But where was he?'

Hilda looked serious and her great black eyes were fixed on the young English girl.

'That's a question one never asks at Dimwood. He came back here after lunch three days ago, and that's all I can tell you. I advise you not to ask him where he went.'

Elizabeth was on the point of saying that she knew perfectly well where he had gone, but judged it wiser to remain silent.

'And what about young Armstrong?' she asked.

'So, does he interest you?' said Mildred maliciously.

'Not in the least, but are you telling this story or not?'

'Well, young Armstrong went very slowly round the house in his carriage with the lady. They went as far as the garden. He was pointing to things with his crop.'

'He always has a crop,' said Mildred.

'. . . with his crop, pointing out to the lady in white the windows, the porch, the verandah, and he was talking, talking.'

'He was explaining.'

'Be quiet, Mildred. You couldn't hear what he was saying. No one came out of the house to speak to him.'

'We hate him,' said Mildred.

'. . . no one came out, but everybody was at the windows . . .'

'. . . hiding behind the curtains.'

'Yes, behind the curtains — oh, Mildred, how exasperating you can be!'

'I don't understand why you were so afraid of him,' interrupted Elizabeth.

'We're not afraid. It's rather complicated. His father, who is still alive, sold Dimwood to Grandfather.'

'To Mr Hargrove?'

'Of course. When will you understand, Elizabeth, that our grandfather is William Hargrove? Sorry if I seem a bit impatient, but Mildred's interruptions set me on edge.'

'Alright, alright, Hilda, I won't do it again, but when you play the schoolmarm . . .'

'Enough, Mildred, else I shall go away. So old Armstrong sold the property on one condition. When the time was up, the property would revert to the Armstrongs, if they were in a position to buy it back.'

'They haven't got a cent,' said Mildred.

'At that time, the occupants of the house will be obliged to negotiate with the Armstrongs. If our parents are no longer alive, it will be us, brothers, sisters, cousins, who will have to have discussions with young Armstrong or his descendants.'

'That's still a long way off, you don't have to worry for a long time yet.'

'I hope so, but young Armstrong is keeping an eye on the house as if it were already his. He is so insolent . . . Sometimes he comes to visit us. A neighborly visit, as he calls it. We all flee, except Grandfather. He is in need of money, young Armstrong.'

'You're not going to tell me that he comes to borrow money from your grandfather. That would be the limit.'

'No. He comes to sell him another bit of land, bordering Dimwood. That enlarges our property, and young Armstrong undoubtedly thinks to himself that it will all come back to him in due course. Young Armstrong is a monster.'

'You call him young Armstrong. How old is he?'

'Oh, young is just a manner of speaking . . .'

'He's already old,' exclaimed Mildred. 'Twenty-two!'

'What's he like?'

The two girls answered with one voice:

'Frightful!'

'And added to that,' said Mildred, 'he has a reputation for seduction.'

'Some women have such poor taste . . .' said Hilda. 'But now there is this woman in white. Who is she? He was showing her the house as if she were going to live in it with him some day.'

'They stayed a long time. We could see them very well from our window, couldn't we, Hilda?'

'When they came round our side, we stood behind the lowered blinds. You could see clearly between the slats. And then, as the light was failing . . .'

'Miss Llewelyn . . .'

'Miss Llewelyn suddenly went out as far as the great avenue and stationed herself there, at the foot of a sycamore.'

'I hate that woman,' exclaimed Mildred. 'She frightens me.'

'Everybody hates her.'

'Why?' asked Elizabeth. 'My mother didn't like her either, and refused to talk to her.'

'There's only Grandfather at Dimwood who speaks to her. They often shut themselves up together in the library to talk. We shall never know what they say, but sometimes voices are raised!'

'If only we could listen . . .' said Mildred.

The cutting answer came immediately:

'Only servants listen at doors, and if Grandfather caught one he might sell him.'

Mildred blushed, and to hide her shame she asked impatiently:

'What next? Miss Llewelyn at the foot of a sycamore? In her dirty gray dress . . .'

'She was there, standing up straight and solid, with her hair screwed up on top of her head. The vehicle had just passed the verandah when they saw the horrible woman. She took a step towards them, and the lady in white let out a cry, and young Armstrong sent his horse off at a gallop with a great crack of his whip. They sped past her like an arrow. She looked down the avenue for a moment and came back.'

'Then what?' said Elizabeth.

'Nothing else. That evening, at dinner, hardly anyone spoke. Mildred, you said that you'd seen young Armstrong with a lady, and you were made to shut up.'

'I wonder what right they had,' exclaimed Mildred. 'Everybody saw them.'

'Everybody except Aunt Augusta, who was asleep.'

'She's always asleep.'

'She was in her room, and Uncle Douglas did not want to wake her.'

'Of course, it was he who scolded me. Uncle Douglas is hard. Aunt Augusta asked questions. He told her not to take any notice of what I said, and that I said any old thing. She gave me an awful look.'

'Oh, my little Mildred, you are exasperating with all your moaning.'

'Alright, Hilda. Silence. Nobody saw anything. In any case, Aunt Laura's eyes were red, really red . . .'

'So what?'

'Nothing else. I'm keeping quiet. The mysteries of Dimwood. A stone on the grave.'

Elizabeth, who was listening attentively, gave a hint of a smile:

'I'm sorry that Mildred is unable to say any more,' she said. 'I suspect she knows some interesting things.'

Hilda stood up.

'We've told you all there is to know, dear Elizabeth. It's wonderful being with you again, but we must leave you. If Aunt Laura finds us here, she won't be pleased.'

'Oh, why?'

Mildred leapt to her feet, and imitated Hilda's serious air:

'Why? Why? That word is banned at Dimwood, Elizabeth. One should never ask questions.'

Hilda grabbed her by the arm.

'Come on now, little wretch. Aunt Laura might turn up at any minute. We love you, Elizabeth, you are delightful, but there's no point in dressing up as if for a ball at Dimwood!'

They were already in the porch when Mildred cried out:

'But there will be balls!'

33

The drabness of Dimwood days contrasted sharply with the bustle of daily life in Savannah. It did not take Elizabeth long to realize that boredom had taken up permanent residence on the plantation. Only the meals broke up the persistent monotony. No reference was made to the events that had taken place during Elizabeth's absence, which she only learnt a little at a time. Between breakfast and dinner, as between dinner and supper, there was absolutely nothing to do.

Once the upheaval of the return and the fantastic news about young Armstrong and the lady in white had simmered down, everything returned to its normal pace. Restored to equanimity, Aunt Emma seemed to have rediscovered a little of the youth lost at Savannah by her crisis of conscience. Emeralds and diamonds again adorned her chubby fingers, which in her case were the accompaniment to perfect inner peace. At table, the men exchanged views on the political battles in Washington. Elizabeth did not listen.

She got used to her room, whose charm had an effect on her. The magnolias alone reconciled her to this country that was still full of mystery, but she suffered too much from the absence of her mother to seek out the company of the 'children', and she was discreetly left in peace. Hilda and Mildred no longer dared to burst into her room as on the first day. Someone had forbidden them, and the English girl showed no desire to see them. Instinctively she was wary of the so-called inseparables.

In order to forget her sadness, she immersed herself in reading novels that she found in the drawing room bookcase. The *Last Days of Pompeii* interested her a lot, but without her really realizing it, and, the heat playing its part, she was giving herself up to the languor of the South, taking long siestas in a huge colonial-style cane rocking chair.

Sometimes, but never too often, Aunt Laura came to visit her. She always announced herself by calling Elizabeth's name, and only entered after receiving an answer. She usually remained standing, as if to indicate that the visit would be brief.

'I come as a neighbor,' she would say in her soft voice, so special to the women of the South. 'I hope that all is well.'

In her mauve cotton dress, which reached almost to her heels, she would walk back and forth with a girlish gracefulness.

'You mustn't hesitate to give Betty orders. She is very obedient, but left to her own devices she does nothing; she won't give a flick of a duster, unless you tell her to. All servants are like that.'

'She is very kind.'

'Of course. She is delighted at the moment, because they brought back from Savannah for her the red petticoat she was dreaming of. It's frightful, but we have to give them these little pleasures, so that they'll be satisfied with us. It's very important!' she added with a little laugh.

Sometimes she would go to the back of the room, to the second window that only opened half-way up. Sometimes she would go over to the rocking chair where Elizabeth was sitting reading from which the English girl made as if to rise, out of politeness, but each time Aunt Laura made a gesture to stop her:

'Don't move, I'm only passing through.'

This sentence, that recurred quite frequently, made the girl feel slightly uneasy. A fleeting intuition kept on coming back to her: they were keeping a discreet eye on her.

'Are you reading a novel? I used to read them too, at your age, back home.'

'Back home, Aunt Laura?'

'Yes, I'll tell you about it another time. I was born in Virginia. My father took us a long way from there when I was ten, but I've never forgotten my native land. They'll take you there some day, but I'm chattering away. I hope you are not disturbed. I want them to leave you alone — for the moment.'

She stopped in front of Elizabeth and looked at her with her big, black, motionless eyes which lent a tragic beauty to her face.

'If you need me,' she said, 'I'm next door.'

And she left the room without a sound, as she had entered it.

Elizabeth did not know what to think of Aunt Laura. Her mother had told her that she could be trusted, even though she was a Catholic, but a certain reserve was still necessary. She remembered Aunt Laura's authoritarian voice on the subject of the gray men that Elizabeth was sure she had seen in the Wood of the Damned, while the Catholic lady denied such a thing was possible. How could she forget it? All the kind words and deep looks would not heal her wounded pride.

At table, she was spoken to, not as to an invalid, but as to someone convalescing. Naturally, Mrs Escridge's name was never mentioned; she might just as well never have set foot at Dimwood. Elizabeth would have preferred by far to have been kept informed. She must have reached New York. Was she at sea? When would she arrive on the other side? She was following her, she was with her, she could see the splashes of foam on the poop of the ship, the sickening sinking of the waves, and their sudden rising again, wrenching the stomach — she liked the violence of the water and its strong smell.

Sitting near her, Minnie drew her skilfully out of her dreaminess. In Elizabeth's eyes, this girl who hardly ever spoke retained, through her silence, a kind of peaceful mystery. A quiet cheerfulness shone in her black pupils, a playfulness that lit up a small face with a rather sallow complexion, due perhaps to a delicate constitution. Her heavy, auburn chignon, shot through with a reddish glow, covered the nape of her neck, and gave a romantic air to the whole of her countenance, but her charm undoubtedly came from her irresistible smile, which revealed teeth whose whiteness was rivalled only by that of the steaming rice that was served every day at William Hargrove's table.

That morning, as breakfast was ending, she took Elizabeth to one side:

'If you have nothing better to do, come for a walk with me, along the river. The sun hasn't reached there yet, but take your bonnet all the same.'

Faced with these amused, caressing eyes, Elizabeth could not say no, and a moment later the two of them were taking the path that edged the dark and silent waters. It was Mr Stoddard and Miss Pringle's favourite walk for squabbling with each other at dusk. Between Elizabeth and Minnie, however, there could be no difference of opinion; the latter's perpetual good humor was a disarming virtue.

'Time is going by horribly quickly,' she said. 'It's not so long since I brought you the blue dress, yet it already seems so long ago . . .'

'My first day at Dimwood, my first morning. I didn't like that blue dress very much.'

'Mildred sets as much store by it as the Queen of England would her coronation dress. She has asked Susanna for it several times. I prefer the one you're wearing today, white and pale green. *Caprices de Paris?*'

'No. It was Uncle Josh who chose it at the big store in the avenue . . .'

'I know, a very good address, good style. I bet you don't

even know who I am, Elizabeth. Don't say you do. Above all, never call me Aunt Minnie! But I'm old, you know, I'm twenty!'

They both laughed.

'I have the impression at Dimwood,' Minnie continued, 'of not really belonging to the group. It's a bit complicated. An orphan.'

'An orphan!'

'Like in a melodrama. My father died when I was seven, and my sister Hilda six months. He was the youngest son of the Hargrove family. Killed in a duel.'

That word made Elizabeth quiver.

'It seems that they talk of nothing but duels in Savannah.'

'Oh, there are a lot less now. A society was founded for the abolition of duels. But that won't give me back my father, whom I adored.'

For a few minutes, they walked in silence along the path carpeted with wild grass. Birdsong reached them from the depths of the wood on the other side of the river. Elizabeth swore never again to ask questions, although her head was full of them, and as if to satisfy this yearning to know a little more, Minnie began talking again:

'My mother died not long after my father.'

And in a strange tone in which an instinctive modesty could be detected, she added:

'She loved him too much.'

The walk continued as far as the edge of the forest which concealed the mysterious gardens that were already burdened with memories for the young Englishwoman. Not a word was exchanged for a considerable time. They walked slowly, their heads bowed, each one absorbed in her own reflections.

The sun was reaching the big sycamores when Minnie seemed to emerge from a dream and said suddenly:

'We've gone a bit far. Put your bonnet on and we'll go back, shall we?'

She began to laugh gaily:

'I have an idea we've been telling each other loads of things, without having opened our mouths for quite a while.'

'Perhaps,' said Elizabeth, caught by surprise as if robbed of a secret.

'Oh, don't take it seriously! I sometimes say scatty things. We'll cross the lawn. The cicadas are starting to chirp, it's going to be hot.'

She opened the little sunshade hanging from her arm, and soon they were walking over the thick grass, not yet yellowed by summer. In the beautiful morning silence, the grating chirrup of the cicadas burst forth abruptly, surrounding them with an intangible wall of sound.

'Listen,' said Minnie. 'I haven't told you anything about my sister Hilda. We're all very fond of her. She has grown up in rather a haphazard manner . . . I mean, not having her parents to look after her, to keep an eye on things. Our dear little Hilda has remained a bit wild. Oh, how should I put it? Charming, delightful even, but . . . secretive, mysterious. She's fine as she is, in fact, but don't take too much notice of her. Do you understand?'

'I think so.'

'I hope so.'

With a sigh of relief, Minnie gave Elizabeth a last smile, one of those bewitching smiles which, in her mind, set everything to rights. They took their leave of each other near the magnolia, at the bottom of the porch.

Elizabeth returned to her room. To her great surprise she found Hilda there, in a mauve dress, lying on the sofa, her face buried in a cushion. As soon as she heard the English girl's steps, Hilda got to her feet. Her cheeks were wet with tears.

'Elizabeth,' she said under her breath, 'I don't know what they've told you about me. You shouldn't believe what people say. Do I frighten you?'

In a lightning flash of intuition, Elizabeth foresaw a harrowing scene that would oblige her, she knew not how, to tell lies.

'You don't frighten me. No one has told me anything unkind about you.'

'Why don't you want to see me then? Don't you like me?'

Such an embarrassing question! Elizabeth felt that she had become someone she did not know, and yet there returned to her mind, like an image consciously forgotten, Hilda's face at the window, aged with grief, on the morning of the departure for Savannah. And now she was like that again, with sadness enlarging her black eyes which said everything she was unable to express.

Elizabeth remained dumbstruck for a good while.

'I never said that,' she murmured.

'Well, then . . . Listen, I'm not a bad girl, what they call a bad girl. At least I have the right to tell you you're pretty, don't I? You're not going to make me suffer, are you Elizabeth?'

'Oh, Hilda! I don't understand you, I think we should talk about something else.'

Hilda turned her back to the window when terror suddenly seized hold of Elizabeth: Aunt Laura's tall figure was standing erect on the porch. Motionless and apparently listening, perhaps she was a little too far off to catch words spoken with a pronunciation muffled by anxiety.

She gave a little cough and, in two or three steps, was inside the room. Hilda turned pale.

'I'm interrupting a little conversation, and I'm sorry for it,' she said cheerfully.

In her long dress of white cotton striped with gray, she retained her natural elegance, and her black hair, parted down the middle, softened the somewhat austere beauty of her face. There was something reassuring about her person.

'Hilda, my darling,' she said with a smile, 'it seems we are forgetting our agreements — secret ones,' she added with a false air of mystery. 'Should I recall them in front of Elizabeth . . . or not?'

With a nod of her head, Hilda indicated that she could do so.

Aunt Laura drew a handkerchief from a small white leather handbag, and began gently to pat the face that was raised up towards her in supplication:

'Don't cry, little girl, you've done nothing wrong, but I prefer you to go for a walk with Elizabeth in the great avenue rather than seeing her here, in her room, do you understand? Don't you agree, Elizabeth?'

Hilda understood, Elizabeth agreed.

'Some day I'll take you both for a ride in a gig, if you'd like that. We must show Elizabeth the surrounding area, don't you think?'

Again she received an affirmative reply, albeit with resignation.

'And now,' concluded Aunt Laura, taking Hilda gently by the hand, 'I shall take my charming niece into my room with me, where we can talk like two good friends. We'll see you later, Elizabeth.'

As they were leaving the room to return to the porch, Hilda turned her eyes to Elizabeth with a look of distress.

Left alone, the girl sat down in the rocking chair and tried to calm herself down by picking up *The Last Days of Pompeii*, but three minutes had not gone by before this interesting historical reconstruction was hurled at the ceiling. Elizabeth rarely gave in to such sudden bursts of temper, but, on the one hand, what she called Hilda's whimpering had annoyed her, because she could not make out the real reason for it. On the other hand, she thought she was discovering in Aunt Laura a woman whose moral cruelty was all the more revolting since she concealed it beneath a gentleness full of fair words and empty promises. Catholic cunning! To take Hilda off into her room on the pretext of a conversation between two good friends . . . Little as she knew of the treachery of the world, Elizabeth expected that some corporal punishment would ensue, accompanied by cries — as in England — but she heard no more than Aunt Laura's voice in a long mutter of words, and all of a sudden, stifled and spasmodic little sobs.

Several days went by without Elizabeth receiving a visit from Aunt Laura. The latter, too sensitive to be unaware of some misunderstanding between herself and her young neigh-, bor, preferred to let time pass before completing a moral education in which she suspected there were some strange gaps.

Sitting side by side at table, they exchanged no more than a dozen words on everyday matters, but smiles bloomed almost unceasingly on Aunt Laura's lips. It seemed clear that Elizabeth had withdrawn all her confidence from her. The reconquest of this foreigner would take the patience of a saint.

At Dimwood, time went by with a slowness that might lead one to believe that some clever mechanism held back the workings of the clocks. In a corner of the great drawing room, one of those venerable old timepieces known as grandfather clocks rose almost as high as the windows. It was rounded like a double bass. A full hundred years old, it had chimed every hour of the War of Independence, and still bore the English royal coat of arms in gilded wood. Now it measured out the boredom of endless afternoons, for there was nothing to do in William Hargrove's noble, colonial dwelling between dinner in the heat and supper at twilight. A dozen times, from morning till evening, Elizabeth came to examine the position of the hands, and to direct a look of hatred at the heavy pendulum, whose deep, slow tick-tock seemed to want to calm the beating of her heart, and she remembered her mother's cry: 'Will time never come to an end?'

Spring had lasted barely three weeks, and summer was already setting in with the grating sound of cicadas. It was necessary to await the first breeze of sunset in order to take the cool air in the great avenue, when the timid clamoring of frogs rose up in the trees. One of the customs at Dimwood was that the children should take their walk at this time separately from the adults. Eternally absent, Billy would leave the girls to their chattering and their little secrets. For strictly personal reasons, he preferred to find distractions elsewhere, his accomplice in his escapades being rowdiness.

That evening, Susanna and Elizabeth found themselves alone, walking slowly in the half-light, when Minnie joined them. They were all three in white dresses and appeared minute at the foot of the giant oaks that lined the avenue. For Elizabeth, this was the most cherished moment of the day, and she would emerge from her natural reserve and let herself go:

'I like walking with you,' she said. 'Why do they leave me alone during the day?'

'It's Aunt Laura's idea,' said Minnie.

And she added:

'She thinks you ought to be left alone on account of . . .'

'I know, on account of my mother's absence, but I'm not a baby. There's something else.'

'Something else?' said Minnie. 'I don't know. Do you know, Susanna?

'Oh, no. I don't know.'

They fell silent for a minute or two as they walked. One

might have thought they hesitated to disturb with their words the kind of fluid and persistent song that surrounded their every step.

'We shall see the stars in a minute, the moon is rising,' said Minnie in a lower tone as if to be in harmony with the night and the trees.

Instinctively, Elizabeth too began to speak less loudly:

'Couldn't Mildred and Hilda come with us?' she asked.

'They've gone off on some exploration,' said Susanna with a slight laugh. 'They believe that there are corners of Dimwood that nobody knows yet, mysteries to be unearthed.'

'Aren't they afraid?'

'Afraid of what?' said Minnie. 'There are no more Indians in the district.'

'Snakes falling from the trees . . .'

Susanna and Minnie burst out laughing.

'Not any more. The sparrow-hawks have killed them all.'

'Yes, they told me . . . They showed me the garden near the spot where the Seminoles were massacred.'

'They shouldn't have,' said Minnie. 'Grandfather is not very keen on us going there.'

'On account of Jonathan Armstrong,' said Susanna.

'Don't let's talk about that, Susanna,' said Minnie.

'But Aunt Emma told the story in front of Elizabeth.'

'I love stories of that kind,' the latter said, 'I suppose that Jonathan Armstrong is the one who got up from table and never came back?'

'No,' said Minnie, 'Jonathan Armstrong is the one who was seen at Dimwood the other day, but Aunt Emma got it all wrong, nobody knows exactly what happened.'

'Souligou knows,' murmured Susanna pensively.

'I know Souligou,' said Elizabeth, 'I met her when she came to shorten the blue dress. She was very pleasant with me.'

'Beware of Souligou,' said Minnie.

'Why?'

Minnie hesitated.

'Oh, nothing,' she said with a laugh. 'She makes me feel uneasy, that's all. She's strange.'

'She's supposed to be coming one day soon to mend our underwear,' said Susanna. 'If you have anything that needs mending, Elizabeth — and if you're not afraid of her . . .'

'I'm not afraid of any one. I'll see if I have anything.'

In her mind she searched among her possessions, one could always manage to find something . . .

'When is she coming?'

'She doesn't give warning, suddenly she's here. Betty will let you know. But be careful of Souligou's stories if you want to sleep at night.'

Susanna's drawling voice added to the mystery of these words that annoyed Minnie.

'Let's stop playing at who can be the most frightened. Look instead at the first stars, right up there between the trees.'

All three tossed their heads back. Through a long gap in the foliage, a black sky glimmered, raining down silence.

They stayed for a moment, not opening their mouths, motionless and fascinated. Then one of them whispered:

'Looking at them eventually makes you dizzy.'

'You end up all giddy.'

'We ought to go further on,' said Minnie, 'following the path that runs along the edge of the avenue, there is a spot where you can see the whole of the sky. The moon is rising.'

A white light on the ground defined the enormous shadows of the trunks of the oaks, like a solemn procession through a ghostly landscape. In the distance, beyond the bleached meadows, the Wood of the Damned spread out an amorphous mass of darkness.

Minnie took the girls by the hand and they began to walk very quickly under the trees, then along the grassy path, running almost, and seized with a childish inexplicable joy.

They came to an abrupt halt. The full moon seemed to be filling the sky all on its own, and they were struck by the uncanny strength emanating from it. Without saying anything, they looked at it as if they were seeing it for the first time; but each time is always the first when confronted with that orb of light that gives off waves of solitude. Minnie, no more than Elizabeth and Susanna, felt no desire to disturb the magic of these amazing moments. They experienced a vaguely haunting joy at finding themselves suddenly transported to another world. The spell needed to be broken gently.

'We'll greet it,' said Minnie in a voice like a whisper.

'One greets the full moon on high ground,' said Susanna.

'High ground? Where do you think we're going to find high ground at Dimwood? But there is a long stone bench just near here that we could stand on.'

Elizabeth was the first to set herself free from the enchanted atmosphere.

'To hear you muttering away, anyone would think we were in a cathedral,' she said in her careful voice, 'but I think the bench is a good idea. I hope the moon will understand.'

'It's true,' said Minnie, reverting to a normal tone of voice, 'we are a bit ridiculous, but it's fun.'

'It'll bring good luck,' said Susanna.

And, laughing, they began to run, happy to feel themselves alive.

The stone bench awaited them a little further on. Eaten away by a century of rain and half covered with moss, it appeared all the more romantic to these three girls, already light-headed from the supernatural lighting that enveloped them. Taken over by the nervous laughter of schoolchildren, they climbed on to the bench and stood on it, holding hands with Minnie in the middle. In their white dresses, they looked as if they had been dipped in silver.

'What now?' asked Susanna.

'Now,' said Minnie, 'you have to bow three times, all together, completely serious.'

'If we laugh, it'll think we're making fun of it,' said Susanna, 'and that will bring us bad luck.'

With some effort to restrain nervous gaiety, they bowed a first time, then a second, and suddenly became more serious, as if they actually believed in the reality of this strange act of adoration. Each one of them concealed within her some romantic secret. At the third greeting, Susanna lost her balance and fell forward, dragging her two companions with her. Together they rolled in the grass and the dead leaves, and, seized with an outburst of irrepressible hilarity, they uttered cries in the blackness, jerky expressions of joy. It took Elizabeth and Minnie some time to notice that Susanna was sobbing.

34

*E*lizabeth slept soundly that night and woke early. Her first thought was to ring for Betty. The latter appeared without delay, and her smile wiped away from the girl's mind the last remaining traces of the moonlit evening that had left her with so few worries. The woman's black face, softened by her good nature, restored calm to her heart.

'Betty,' she said, 'when Mademoiselle Souligou comes to do sewing jobs, I want you to let me know immediately.'

Betty's usual smile widened almost to her ears.

'Mamzelle Souligou, she been here since seven o'clock this mornin', but she work in another room, on the top floor.'

'Whereabouts? You can show me. You must tell her that I'll go up and see her after lunch.'

With an indefinably guilty air, she added:

'One of my summer dresses seems a little long to me, I want to have it shortened just a little. Do you understand? The width of two fingers.'

Betty nodded that she understood. Solid and round in her black skirt that reached her calves, she stood motionless and seemed to be thinking. Her great bronze-colored hands fingered her white apron, as if to smooth it out.

'Why do you say nothing, Betty? Don't you like Mademoiselle Souligou?'

Betty smiled again and looked at Elizabeth.

'I likes everybody at Dimwood.'

This simple phrase struck the girl as concealing something that eluded her. 'She is thoroughly obliged to say that she likes everybody,' she thought. 'It's the answer of a slave.' Yet she insisted:

'Do you think she's nice?'

The black eyes rested on her, and there were so many things to read in them that Elizabeth regretted her question. The answer came after a good minute or so:

'To me, yes'm, but it's better not to see her.'

The calm, firm tone with which these words were spoken sharpened Elizabeth's curiosity to the point where she was taken with a desire to shake that placid woman who knew so many things that it was painful to her not to know.

Betty's gentleness reassured her, and even more than her gentleness, a natural tenderness that led one to believe that she did indeed like everybody. It was unfair to question her.

As if in a flash of lightning, she saw herself standing before this woman waiting patiently for some order, some word. Suddenly the scene turned strange: in this room with furniture made of expensive, honey-colored wood, its tall windows through which the filtered light penetrated without violence and, with a kind of humility, a girl. She saw herself, Elizabeth, in a nightdress that reached down to the ground, assuredly very beautiful as was confirmed by a large gilt framed mirror — beautiful with her blond hair in disarray around her pink face — and, two paces away, the old black maid with her heavy shape, her pitifully ugly face, in complete contrast to the elegant surroundings. Her Betty, full of love. And Elizabeth felt suddenly diminished before her.

35

According to Betty, the best time for seeing Mademoiselle Souligou was towards the middle of the afternoon. By then she would have finished a good part of her work, and if Elizabeth wished to talk with her on the subject of the dress to be shortened, they were less likely to be disturbed. Betty suspected that this dress was no more than a pretext, and that the young foreigner wanted above all to get the old seamstress to talk. She did not approve, she feared the worst, but she gave in, out of love.

In a room on the top floor that served as a work room, Mademoiselle Souligou had been installed by a long table, on which was piled the linen for mending from the entire household. It was reminiscent of fairy stories where the imprisoned princess will be released only when she has completed some humanly impossible task. In the present case, the victim was nothing like a princess and was completely free in her comings and goings, but the heap of clothes and underclothes, handkerchiefs, towels, glass cloths and neckerchieves was nevertheless of demoralizing proportions. Yet the seamstress was accorded all the time she deemed to be necessary, and she was paid with a generosity that cut short any objection. Her weakness for splendid gold dollars was a pertinent fact.

Betty had led Elizabeth the length of a corridor to the bottom of a steep and narrow staircase that led to Souligou's work room, but she did not go up herself. Her conscience reproached her vigorously for having led the young foreign lady into ways that might pose a danger to her salvation. Such indeed was the terror that the seamstress inspired in her. Yet she could not find the courage to say no to Miss Lizbeth and, leaving her there, she took flight.

Climbing the fifteen steps with the agility of a panther, Elizabeth found herself up in the attic, and had no trouble finding her way. The broken voice she immediately recognized was an accurate guide:

'Straight on, Miss Elizabeth. Ten paces straight ahead and you'll be with Josephine Souligou, widow Trottereau.'

Turning to the right or to the left in the half light of the landing, Elizabeth would have entered a maze of poorly lit corridors, but a shaft of light reached her from a half-open door in front of her. With her back to the door, the presence of the seamstress was revealed only by the two war-like points of her dark blue check headscarf that protruded above the back of a big red velvet armchair.

'How did you know it was me?' asked Elizabeth with a laugh.

'Heavens, I was expecting you.'

'Did Betty warn you?'

'Come now, stop your questioning and sit down. Betty didn't warn me. Did I have need of her to know you were going to come? Do you think I don't know you? Take that chair.'

Although she was not used to receiving orders, Elizabeth obeyed immediately and took her place on a chair by Josephine Souligou, whose face she could now study at leisure. The black eyes that were never still brought life in a disturbing manner to that brown face on which the years had scribbled wrinkles in all directions. The nose was thin and pointed, thrusting forward, as if in search of something, a gold coin, some perfume, a scent, the future. The still-youthful teeth sometimes showed themselves under cover of a smile which retained an unexpected charm.

'When you've finished inspecting me,' she said, 'you will tell me what brings you here to see me. No, leave the dress for shortening that you have forgotten to bring me in any case. Worried, are you?'

'Oh, no.'

'Oh, yes. Make an effort and tell the truth.'

'I always tell the truth.'

'Bravo. I like a little skirmish, but you'll find that Betty has disobeyed orders in bringing you here. Aunt Laura, as you call her, forbade her to.'

'Why?'

'Ask her. We are going to have a forbidden conversation. That can be a thrill. Let's begin. This dangerous linen store in which you find yourself is my domain. Not being a slave, and not belonging to anyone, I have a right to a certain consideration. This armchair, which has seen better days, is nonetheless majestic. They want me to be comfortable, because I know how to make myself indispensable. I alter suits made too tight by good food, and I darn, darn, darn. Only the broomstick is missing to complete the image people have of me. This mountain of linen will keep me here for another four days. I'm not sorry about it. Josh Hargrove isn't stingy. His father doesn't care for me. I upset his conscience which is given to worrying. I know too much about the family, do you see? You've really been adopted by the South now, my little Elizabeth, buried up to your eyes in the aristocracy of this land. But your education is incomplete. You need to be trained.'

Elizabeth leapt to her feet:

'To be trained!'

'Calm down. The handsome young men of the South will set about turning your head with smiles. Do you already have a *beau*?'

'A *beau*?'

'Oh, a lover, an admirer if you prefer, they're called *beaux*, and people collect them. Now look around you. The room is worth it.'

The work room did indeed have some singular features. The ceiling was so low that a tall man would have been forced to stoop in a standing position, but, on the other hand, its unusual length and width were surprising. The vast work table occupied the middle part of it, and was surrounded by fourteen chairs with high, straight backs in the Dutch style of the previous century. There was a kind of dignity about this setting that made one think of a gathering of important personages, come together to discuss politics, or simply to take part in a banquet. In some indefinable way, the patches of shade, settled in the corners, took the place of the absent seats and sofas and, in their own way, furnished the empty spaces where the eye did not linger. There was nothing surprising in this trick of the light, for the windows were reduced to long, narrow openings extending all around the room, like half-closed eyelids, casting only a parsimonious light on to the black painted floorboards.

'Don't you find my work room unusual?' asked the seamstress. 'There's just enough light to sew on a fine day. By way of compensation, it's a wonderful place for observing what's going on at Dimwood.'

She gave a sly laugh and elaborated:

'To spy on people. That's one of the many enigmas of Dimwood. There are nights when this room is full of people, but that's enough about things bordering on the supernatural. Are you interested in the supernatural?'

'If you mean ghosts . . .'

'For example . . .'

'Well, frankly, yes.'

'I have a unique range of them, but let's keep that for nightfall. Pass me that shirt.'

From the top of the heap Elizabeth took a roomy shirt of fine linen, decorated near the collar with two tiny red letters, just like drops of blood. She could not resist bending her head forward to read them.

'W.H., you nosy little girl,' said Mademoiselle Souligou. 'You can't imagine what he looks like in this austere nightgown.'

'Not Mr Hargrove!'

'Yes, of course. Why that horrified look? You'd take him for some ecclesiastical dignitary without his cross. But he's still a good-looking man for all that. Don't you think so?'

'No.'

'Ah, I'm teasing you, I shouldn't. How did he manage to tear the sleeve? But are you wondering how I was able to see him in his nightwear? One very hot evening I was passing through the porch, breathing in the perfume of the jacarandas. He had left the shutters of his room half open, and I disappeared into the shadows, but I saw him.'

'I'd rather you talked to me about something else, Mademoiselle Souligou . . .'

'Just call me Souligou, like they do mostly at Dimwood. For my part, I'll call you Elizabeth. People don't need to look at you for long to realize that you're quality. The servants immediately and instinctively know who is quality and who isn't. Generations of servitude have taught them that, at least. If you're not quality, they despise you. The contempt of the servants is awesome. Hard to follow?'

'Yes. No. I'm not very interested in that.'

'Perhaps you would have been interested if, like me, you'd seen young Armstrong the day you left for Savannah.'

'Young Armstrong . . .'

'Yes, little one. Young Armstrong, hated by women, but they look at him and look at him. Young Armstrong is quality.'

'That's all the same to me.'

'You're like me. These distinctions are idiotic. I have creole blood in my veins, and I'm worth just as much as any those arrogant "quality" people, but you finally end up thinking a bit like everybody else. When I saw young Armstrong, I said to myself, in spite of my better feelings, that the blackguard held himself as only an aristocrat can — that straightness of the back . . .'

'Don't you find that that word "aristocrat" becomes exasperating when it's used over and over again?'

'It unleashes revolutions, and right now it's cooking up a nice little war for us . . .'

'Mademoiselle Souligou!'

'Souligou, at your service, *ma petite*. You can be reassured that the war won't be tomorrow, but the threat is there, like a big black cloud that won't go away. We've been living in the shadow of a disaster for years. You get used to it, people dance, drink, fall in love. Young Armstrong, you can be sure, is thinking much more about his love affairs than about the war. He's an incredible scoundrel, but a handsome beast, despite a wicked face. Keep away from him.'

'Is he as dangerous as that?'

Souligou raised her eyes from her work and looked at Elizabeth attentively:

'Elizabeth,' she asked, 'do you believe in the Devil?'

'Naturally, since it's in the Bible.'

'I don't need to look in the Bible. I only have to see that man's face to believe it.'

The girl kept silent.

'In any case,' continued the seamstress, 'I see you're not one of those who run away from men, but be careful.'

'I've never run away from anyone.'

'Little innocent, we're playing at hide and seek. Aunt Laura knows what she's doing by making lots of little visits to your room.'

'How do you know?'

The seamstress leaned back to laugh in comfort.

'I know it all, because Negroes have tongues and Souligou has ears.'

'There are times when I hate Aunt Laura.'

'You are wrong. She is perhaps the most upright soul at Dimwood.'

'A Catholic!'

'Let's leave that and be serious. Have you looked at these windows properly, tall and narrow? They make me think of somebody who half closes his eyes so as to be able to see better in the distance. Thanks to this feature, I was able to follow the movements of young Armstrong and his companion in white all around the house. They went at a walking pace, the two of them, she in her elegant yellow gig, harnessed to a gentle, piebald horse, he on his chestnut mare pointing out to his *belle* all the parts of the house with his whip, and leaning towards her to give all the necessary explanations. I was going along the windows in order to get a good view and I remember everything. I can say that in those thrilling moments, I felt as if I were turning the pages of a novel, and never has that boy seemed more hateful to me, nor, I have to say, more interesting to watch. Dressed with care, in spite of financial difficulties that have become legendary, he was wearing a tight-fitting, very short bright red jacket, his legs were shown off by white pants, with beige leather boots. You'd have said some young lord was setting off for the hunt, his hair blowing in the wind, his small face with its bewitching ugliness, such as makes sensitive ladies pass out. And, do you see, all his physical and moral insolence manifested in the exaggerated straightness of his back.'

'As you describe him to me,' said Elizabeth, 'I have not the least desire to meet him, but I can't make out the lady in the gig from your story. She seems more like a ghost.'

Once more the seamstress let herself go in peals of mirth, and her white teeth shone suspiciously in the twilight.

'You amuse me, little one. A ghost. The ghost of the white lady, that's all that was needed to complete the legend of Dimwood. But have no illusion. The white lady in question is a woman of flesh and blood, and a most beautiful creature behind the veils in which she is wrapped. Where does she live? Elsewhere, because she's always elsewhere, whether in the North or the South, but invariably amidst some luxury. Men have faced ruin on her account, and young Armstrong is following their example, but he clings to her like some animal, and so long as he has money, she will let herself be loved . . .'

'Is he rich then?'

'Oh, no! But he knows how to get what he wants, and he's counting on making her a present of this house some day and living here with her. That's why he came with her the other afternoon, to get her to admire their future love nest.'

'Is he mad?'

'Not quite as mad as you would think. You see, the house is old and stylish. It used to belong to the Armstrongs, from whom William Hargrove bought it when he arrived from Jamaica to settle in the South. Young Armstrong's grandfather had lost all his fortune in disastrous speculation, and Dimwood was for sale, but he couldn't find a buyer because of its bad reputation. Hargrove didn't look too closely. He was wrong — or perhaps he didn't know everything.'

'He didn't know everything about what?'

'We're getting there. I think he had his suspicions. Hargrove is a hard businessman. In any case, he soon understood that he had before him a man on the brink of despair, and he took advantage of him. The Armstrongs are well known for the misfortunes that pursue them from one generation to the next. They'd sell themselves to the Devil to get out of it, but the Devil too is very hard in business, and he despises an easy catch. He's only really interested in souls that refuse to give themselves up to him.'

'Why do you keep talking about the Devil?'

'There's a lot for him to do at Dimwood.'

'Are you hoping to frighten me, Souligou?'

'Not at all, but there are too many West Indians amongst the slaves. One of them came from over there with William Hargrove, it was a mistake, but let's leave that. Let's come back to Harold Armstrong who sold his plantation for a price way below its real value, but enough to give him the illusion of being rich. He sold it for a period of twenty-five years. It was the old English custom that was still in use here in 1827. That means in 1852 . . .'

'Harold Armstrong repossesses Dimwood and comes back home here. I know that law. Two years is a long way off.'

'Oh, my dear! Two years is tomorrow. Harold Armstrong was worn out by excesses of all kinds. There remain his heirs. Two have already died. The last one is no other than Jonathan, whom you do not wish to see, and that's for the best.'

'If things turn out badly, I'll go and seek refuge in Savannah. Charlie Jones hopes that I'll come and live there.'

The seamstress took on a dreamy air and remained silent. A feeble ray of sunlight pierced the gloom and cast a pool of pale gold on the black floor. The great pile of linen in the middle of the table was just an indistinguishable white mass, but William Hargrove's vast nightshirt was spread out between Elizabeth and Souligou like a field of snow. The seamstress came to herself brusquely:

'I'm not going to ruin my eyesight mending this inexplicable tear . . . Savannah!' she said. 'I can just see you there. The trouble is, you end up getting fond of Dimwood, and quite quickly too.'

'That's not at all the case with me, but you were talking about Jonathan and his two brothers who died. Aunt Emma told us the frightening story of the two owners of Dimwood who mysteriously disappeared. She said nothing about the father.'

'Aunt Emma gets everything wrong, because it was not thought right to tell her the whole truth. Emotional as she is, she might well have left Dimwood for good. Are you inclined to listen to the revelation of what happened here, even if your beautiful blond hair stands up on end?'

'Do you take me for a softy, Souligou?'

'I don't need to tell you that you'll repeat nothing of what I'm going to tell you. It would bring you bad luck. Do you hear me?'

Elizabeth's look spoke pages.

'*Fillette*,' Mademoiselle Souligou began, 'I call you that in French, because you are nothing but a little girl in my eyes; when you are afraid, I'll stop.'

'Carry on,' said Elizabeth, who already felt a pleasurable shudder.

'You must know, then, that the house always belonged to the Armstrongs until the arrival of William Hargrove. It seems it was very expensive. It was built by the English, and they knew how to do things properly. It saw the revolution of 1776, and there was fighting all around here. You must know, too, that many Indians were killed in these parts. Remember that.'

'Many Indians . . .'

'Yes, quite warlike, Creek Indians, they call them. They'll scalp a man like you peel a peach.'

'But that's horrid, Souligou.'

'Shall I stop?'

'Oh, no, I beg you.'

'Apart from that, everything was calm at Dimwood around 1800. The plantation had hundreds of slaves, who worked hard in the cotton fields, under the eyes of an overseer with a whip.'

'Hateful!' exclaimed Elizabeth.

'Calm down. The whip was only there to frighten them, the overseer's voice and looks were enough. In the society of those days, like now, a planter who ill-treated his slaves was not socially acceptable. But the overseer was wicked. Poisoned to death later on.'

'Oh, that's interesting.'

'That's nothing yet, *fillette*. In 1800, Grandpa Armstrong had been a widower for three years, and he preferred reading to tending his plantation. He hated figures, and gave his overseer, Silas, responsibility for everything. All the Armstrongs had a reputation for being studious. Over-studious, perhaps. If you're studious, reading makes you too inquisitive about things. You get to want to know too much about things it's better to leave alone.'

'Such as?'

'Don't interrupt me so much. You'll find it all out. Silas used to cheat a bit with the accounts, not unskilfully. Old Armstrong didn't look that closely. I say old Armstrong to distinguish him from his son, but he was fifty and was called Walter. His son Harold was twenty-five that same year, 1800. Do you follow me?'

'Yes, I see we're going to get caught up in family trees.'

'Impatience! You want the horrors straight away, when you don't even know if you'll be able to bear them. I'll try to go quickly, however. Harold was courting a girl from a neighbouring plantation, Emily Thornton, who kept him hanging on for as long as was necessary, so she thought, but she was madly in love.'

'Was she pretty?'

'Ravishing. She was nineteen, and now, *fillette*, you have to understand. One day, her admirer, her *beau*, announced to Walter Armstrong that he had to marry Emily as soon as possible, without waiting. She was pregnant. Are you still following me?'

'Yes, I think so. Usually, marriage comes first.'

'The marriage took place, and the child was born at Dimwood, seven months later after a honeymoon in Cuba. After a furious outburst, Walter Armstrong had a stroke at Dimwood. It left him alive, but enfeebled. They kept quiet about it. People guessed and kept quiet, except in private.'

'Why so much mystery? I don't really understand.'

'Ah, devil take it. You're more of a novice than I thought. Didn't your mother tell you anything? But after all, a child can be born at seven months. Let's move on. The child, a boy, was given the name Malcolm. He was not baptized.'

'Why?'

'Go and ask somebody else that. There are Protestants who don't believe in baptism. His mother adored him. Old Walter too. He lapsed into childishness with the baby. Only Harold, the father, didn't care for the newcomer. He found children troublesome. He was strange in any case. Since he found Dimwood a sad place, he used to invite all the plantation owners to dine. People accepted because he kept a good table, wines especially, so they say.'

'Was that enough to make people come?'

The seamstress leaned forward, then backwards as if rocking with laughter, but her laugh, like the cackling of a hen, had nothing cheerful about it. Mockingly she answered:

'You'll find out, *fillette*, that it's enough to hang a chop over your front door, and the guests will come running. And if you wave a good bottle about, they'll arrive in droves.'

'That's not a very nice thing to say, Souligou.'

'No, it's not very nice, but you'll have to get used to it. Something happened one day, however. Invitations were turned down — politely, of course — but more and more, and then eventually no one came. It wasn't on account of the Armstrongs. There was something else.'

'Something else? Oh, don't stop Souligou.'

'I'm stopping because we're coming to more serious matters. It was on account of this house.'

'Didn't they know it?'

'Not very well. You must know that Grandfather Walter had never gone in much for entertaining, what's called entertaining. His son Harold knew how to play at being a lord, but his wife, especially Emily, was dazzling. She was refined, amusing. And then there was always the food. They ate in princely fashion.'

'Then what?'

'Then, as I told you, it was the house. People didn't like the house. Masses of flowers in every room, all the chandeliers alight, a little orchestra playing softly during supper, lively conversation, charming ladies dressed fit to kill, in short a party, a great aristocratic to-do. People had a good time eating and drinking too much, but they didn't come back.'

'But why didn't they, Souligou?'

'There was something that disturbed them, frightened them.'

'Frightened? In this house?'

'Yes, *fillette*. In this very place.'

At that moment, a little bell rang out outside, giving five or six rings at intervals, but in an imperious manner. Elizabeth looked at the seamstress anxiously.

'That's not the supper bell?'

'No, not yet. It's the bell ordering the servants to get ready, to set the table and put their liveries on. You're not familiar with all the sounds of the house. We've still got a good half hour. Shall I continue?'

'Oh, yes please!'

'This house, you see, is badly positioned. It was built on a bit of land where too many Seminoles were massacred. The Seminoles are as wild as the Creek Indians, but they were on their own territory, and the ground is damned for a dozen miles around. In the wood near here, there's a spot where you can hear them at certain hours of the night. A dull sound coming up from the ground, cries.'

The young Englishwoman swallowed her saliva and murmured:

'I know, not far from the river, at the spot where there are a lot of flowers . . .'

'Yes, how do you know that? It's forbidden to go there.'

'Hilda took me there with Mildred.'

'The inseparables. You'll be careful, won't you? Do you understand?'

'Yes . . . No.'

'Let's move on. Harold Armstrong was strange, as were all the men of his family. In his handsome house, where hardly anyone came calling any more, he was getting bored, all the more so since his wife gave him a second son, Hamish, a year after the first. Having adored his Emily, he now began to hate her, perhaps because of the children. Their crying put him in a rage. He would have liked to leave Dimwood, but there was the plantation. It wore him out, and he could see that things were going badly, but it was still bringing in money, and the house kept him here. When his boys were old enough, he sent them to private schools, then to university, a long way away, a very long way away, in Virginia.

— 318 —

Emily, who still loved him, suffered to see him change. His father, old Walter, had shown him books that taught how to communicate with the dead.'

Elizabeth could not restrain a cry:

'That's not possible!'

'Oh yes it is, *ma petite*, it's very possible, and a lot of people go to a great deal of trouble to do so. If they don't succeed, it's because they don't have the gift. Harold had the gift. At night he would go out into the garden where you were with Hilda. He would spend hours listening. An old slave from the West Indies would go with him. Between the two of them they managed to pick up sounds, words that they didn't understand, voices calling.'

'I shall never go over that way again, Souligou.'

'You'll undoubtedly be more at peace in the house, or very close to the house, but even so ... You'd do better walking with Aunt Laura, and if you want me to finish my story in good time for the first supper bell, let me speak without interrupting me. Neither Harold nor his slave knew the Seminoles' language, but they understood that these Redskin words were meant to tell them something. Don't shudder too much at this point, *fillette*. I'm telling you what I was told. The years went by. The boy Malcolm came back from Virginia in 1821. He'd been expelled from the university. I don't know why. He was a damned soul. You could guess that just by glancing at him. I've seen that myself.'

'What was he like?'

'Odd! Handsome with an icy look, Jonathan's look.'

'Oh, I shall never see that one!'

'Don't be so sure of that. If he came the other day, it wasn't only to show the house to his lady friend, it was because he hoped to catch you by surprise. Shall I carry on or shall I stop?'

'Carry on.'

'When Emily saw her son, she thought she would go out of her mind with joy. She clung to him like a drowning man clings to a life raft. She didn't dare look him in the eyes, but she loved him. She informed him of his father's nocturnal excursions. Everybody knew about it, what's more. He went on his own to the Indians' wood. He had no trouble making himself understood there, for if anyone had the gift he did.

By beating on the ground, he invented a kind of language. Soon there were answers. Don't ask me what they were. He imagined all kinds of things. Sometimes secret ceremonies, sometimes a tribunal where the dead were judged, Whites, of course. He believed in it so much that he went off his head. He would describe all that to his father who, in his turn, ended up believing in it. The guilty dead had to die a second death.'

'That's horrible, Souligou.'

'You wanted horrors, didn't you? Is that enough for you?'

'Carry on.'

'The father became frightened. The son didn't. He was convinced that the Indians considered him a friend and were inviting him to their territory, to go down, as he used to say, to go down under the ground to see.'

'He was mad.'

'Completely. One night, he told his father that the Indians had arranged a meeting with him in the leafless wood, the wood with the moss curtains, you know, the Wood of the Damned. Harold tried to hold him back, but there was nothing to be done. If he wanted to *go down*, it had to be via the Wood of the Damned. He told his father: "Do you not hear them? They're calling, they're waiting for me." Harold grabbed him by his arms. Malcolm flung him to the ground and leapt on to his black mare. The animal broke into a gallop as if stung by horse flies. Of its own accord it went off towards the wood, and Malcolm could be heard shouting with terror. It was old Harold who recounted all this, long afterwards. The black mare galloped as far as the wood and well beyond. The next day they found Malcolm upright, three feet off the ground, at the end of a low branch of one of the old trees.'

Elizabeth let out a cry.

'He hung himself!'

'Oh! He didn't have to go to the trouble. The noose was waiting for him, knotted in the Indian manner apparently.'

Elizabeth stood up without a word, her face white.

'Souligou . . .' she murmured finally.

The answer came, calm and slightly mocking:

'It's all very well being English, I can see you're upset. Sit down again, I've nearly finished.'

Elizabeth sat down immediately.

'When Emily heard the news, she died on the spot. Her heart gave way. Harold's nerves were of sterner stuff. He buried his wife and his son in a distant cemetery. Malcolm's death passed for suicide. It was talked about a lot, many questions were asked. Not many days went by before the slaves started seeing Malcolm. He *walked*. That means he used to appear, more or less everywhere, in the Wood of the Damned, around the house, and even in the house. The Whites couldn't see him, the Negroes would tremble and groan in horror. Of course, some people had made it their duty to visit Harold, but his coldness was not favorable to expressions of sympathy. There was, however, one woman of English descent, like you. He was no longer in the first flush of youth, but they saw each other several times. Like all the Armstrongs, Harold was attractive to women. After a few weeks, she had fallen in love. He was in need of a woman's company, and the marriage took place a year later, almost in secret, in the presence of two witnesses, Grandfather Walter and Harold's second son, Hamish, who had come back from university with his degree and his mortarboard. You're going to ask me what Hamish was like.'

'No, I'm not,' said Elizabeth somewhat vexed.

'You'll find out, for all that. A serious face, with glasses.'

The memory of the blind angel flashed through Elizabeth's mind like a shaft of light in this sombre story.

'In appearance a good boy, with a smile, but taciturn. A bit strange, very sly. And learned with it, of course. He wanted to be an architect, and at first he had certain rooms of the house fixed up, which were in need of it. Harold had been neglecting things and confidently left everything up to Hamish, together with all the necessary funds. The work was coming on when Hamish seemed to take a dislike to the handsome dwelling, then began to hate it, as if it were alive. It was very evident that he wanted to go away. It was the first time a man of his family wanted to leave Dimwood. Perhaps he felt that if he stayed any longer he would never get away. The house always ends up bewitching you.'

'Not me,' said the girl in animated fashion. 'I could leave Dimwood without any difficulty.'

'You haven't been here long enough. In a year or two

you'll be a prisoner, but listen to the rest. Normal life resumed at Dimwood. Harold and Ivy got on well. She was expecting.'

'Expecting?'

'Do I have to teach you everything after all, *ma petite*? She was expecting a child and had reached the eighth month. That's when the event took place. One evening when they were all three at dinner . . . I say all three because Grandfather Walter dined alone in his room.'

'That was hard.'

'He preferred it. A kind nurse fed him. So, all three of them in the dining room . . .'

'The one where we dine?' asked Elizabeth, suddenly worried because she thought she could see what was coming next.

'Yes, miss, the one where you are going to dine this evening. An old servant came in, his knees knocking with terror, and announced that a gentleman all in black was waiting in the antechamber. Harold let a moment go by, then got up to go and see.'

'Oh, he shouldn't have. Aunt Emma, who told us this story, said it was the Devil waiting in the antechamber.'

'Aunt Emma sees the Devil everywhere, because she is afraid of going to Hell if she doesn't behave herself; she ought to see him in her champagne. It wasn't the Devil. Harold came back, and said with a laugh that there was no one there, except the old servant hiding in a corner with his hands over his eyes. Hamish got up in his turn. The servants' whims got him down. He was going to teach that one a lesson. The servant told him everything. Hamish slapped him and said: "Fool, you saw nothing." — "I see Mass'r Malcolm with eyes of fire." — "You're drunk. I'm going out on my horse to get some air." He never came back.'

'It's horrible, Souligou. Don't you think his brother came to fetch him?'

'To go where?'

'Where he is for all time.'

'That would be interesting, but I think it's simpler than that. He was equipped with a comfortable bedding of bank notes, the money for the repairs, a considerable sum, for men from the South don't stint even when they're in difficulties ... No sense of money, through having too much of it ... Where had I got to?'

'You'd got to Hamish, who never came back. '

'Quite right. They looked for him in every corner of the estate, then further afield. Time was wasted. The sheriff offered to help, bloodhounds followed the tracks. It was impossible to find him in America. I can see him in Europe for my part, perhaps in Paris, I hope so, on the boulevards ...'

'Why the boulevards?'

'Ah, you don't know Paris! I had a stay there when I was still with my dearly beloved husband, Captain Trottereau. I still dream about my passion sometimes. At Dimwood, Hamish's disappearance was such a blow to poor Ivy that, when her time was due, she gave birth to a boy and died, in 1827. The boy was Jonathan, who came snooping round here with his beloved swathed in white.'

She fell silent.

'Is that all?' asked Elizabeth.

'My goodness, yes. They must have told you the rest. Mr Hargrove arrived here in 1827. At that time, Grandfather Walter had gone senile and Harold was living alone, like a savage, with one or two black nurses who would have faced death for their master.'

She fell silent again and appeared thoughtful. The light was imperceptibly fading, and all around the house birds were beginning to sing at the tops of their voices, as if in some frenzied farewell to daylight. A sudden sadness invaded Elizabeth's heart.

Mademoiselle Souligou's voice suddenly brought her back to herself:

'That's all for today. I hope you are pleased and that you had a good shiver. Don't go seeing Malcolm with his fiery eyes. That would be too much.'

'I've never yet seen a ghost, but England is full of them,' said Elizabeth in a rush of patriotic pride.

'Ah, do you imagine we don't have them in America? If you could count them, it would double the size of the population. But you are doubtless keen to know what happened to Harold, Jonathan's father?'

Elizabeth was not keen at all. It was the son she was interested in, in spite of herself.

'Yes, of course,' she said casually.

'Harold had always drunk, but after Ivy's death he began drinking seriously. So as not to hear little Jonathan's cries, he had him put in a nursery. Silas, the overseer, was still there, barely affected by age, as active and as dishonest as in the good old days of Grandfather Walter. No one knows how Harold got the notion of looking into the accounts and found out. Then . . .'

'Then?'

'Then he began by breaking his walking stick in two over Silas' back, he grabbed him by the heels and tipped him out of the first-floor window. That was in 1827, the year Mr Hargrove came to live here. You know the rest.'

'What about Jonathan?'

The seamstress raised her eyebrows as she looked at her, as if to sharpen her basalt-black gaze.

'Watch out, little one. The wolf is lurking about. His name is Jonathan, and he is keen to get to know you.'

'Oh, I don't want to see him! I should like to know what happened to him,' said Elizabeth with the blood rushing to her cheeks.

'Well, well. Jonathan grew up first of all in a world of angelic black nurserymaids and white babies. Then lessons caught up with him and taught him nothing. He finally ended up on Old Creek, his father's modest plantation ten miles from here. He is hated at Dimwood, and his visits are dreaded. He comes from time to time, as they explained to you, to sell Hargrove a bit of land to make something to live on, to drink and all the rest. You've seen how it works.'

'Yes, but I don't want to see Jonathan.'

'An excellent resolution. Now to serious business.'

Opening a drawer, she took out a pack of cards that were much longer than ordinary playing cards, shuffled them and fanned them out on the table, but in such a way that only the backs could be seen.

'Tarot,' she said. 'Do you know what it is? No? You don't know anything. Choose a card.'

'Isn't it forbidden?'

'Forbidden! Forbidden by whom?'

Elizabeth did not dare to say by the Holy Bible, and her hand hovered uncertainly over the cards that were soiled by long use. She finally took one at random. The seamstress turned it over with an eager hand:

'The Juggler,' she said.

Indeed, a drawing in a primitive style showed a man playing with goblets.

'The Juggler. That can be good, just as it can be bad.'

'Why?'

'It would take too long to explain to you. It depends on what comes next. Another card then.'

With a hesitant hand, a hand that felt guilty, Elizabeth took a card.

'The Lover,' announced Souligou. 'That might be alright if it wasn't for the Juggler. He's a problem, your Juggler.'

'Couldn't we change him, swap him?'

The seamstress raised her head and again the black eyes plunged into the blue ones.

'And what about fate, *fillette*? Can you swap fate? Come now, don't look so horrified. Another card, the last one.'

Elizabeth drew a card which was turned over slowly. There was silence. In the large room where the light was sinking, the girl's voice piped up like the cry of a bird:

'Isn't it good? Tell me, even if it's not good.'

'I can't, but you believe in it all the same, eh?'

'No!' exclaimed Elizabeth, angry at having fallen into a trap. 'I don't believe in it, because it's the Devil's work.'

'Ah, you go a bit far, little one. You mustn't insult the tarot. The cards don't like it. Don't listen to this ignorant one, dear cards. But I'm going to give you some advice, Elizabeth: don't speak to Miss Llewelyn.'

She pronounced it 'Liouline', but Elizabeth did not smile.

'I have no desire to do so,' she replied.

'Nor to Jonathan.'

Outside a bell rang, close to the house.

'That's the first supper bell,' explained Souligou. 'You've just got time to get ready. A flick of the comb through your beautiful hair. As for the rest, good luck. Everything will be alright if you listen to me.'

Elizabeth stood up and went out without a word.

As she was going down the narrow staircase, no wider than a ladder, the mildly ironic voice of the seamstress called out:

'And another time you might say thank you to "widow Trottereau", née Souligou, who is fond of you all the same.'

'Oh, sorry and thank you!' shouted Elizabeth.

But the attic door, slammed with force, cut off these words at the first syllable.

Downstairs, the bell began to ring again.

36

As Souligou had advised, Elizabeth went to her room to see to her hair, but she was too upset to think about what she was doing, and the comb went so many times through the thick mass of golden hair she could not stop herself. Then she noticed that she was trembling.

'Fate,' she murmured. 'What does she mean with her horrid cards? I don't want to see her any more.'

At table, she sat next to Susanna, who gave her her usual lovely, rather melancholy, smile. Elizabeth took no notice, for Aunt Laura's attentive gaze was resting on her, with eyes brimming over with questions. It took no more to make the girl feel guilty and unhappy. She turned her head towards Billy, who was whispering to her things that were embarrassing and out of place.

'We don't see you any more. Where do you hide yourself, you naughty girl? How pretty you are this evening . . .'

'Billy, stop it immediately,' ordered Aunt Emma. 'Your grandfather is speaking with the Lord.'

Indeed, William Hargrove was soliciting blessings from on high for all those present, and for the country in an exceptionally fervent tone. Perhaps without wishing to do so, he sowed disquiet by asking for peace for all the states of the Union. Beads of sweat shone on his anxious face, and his voice became more and more monotonous.

When he fell silent and sat down, his son Joshua asked:

'Have you heard something, Father?'

'No, but I'm wrong to believe in premonitions. It's a weakness, and I'm wrong. One ought to keep one's intuitions to oneself.'

A deep silence followed. No one moved and, frozen to the spot in their gold-braided cotton livery, the servants opened their eyes as wide as saucers.

Suddenly, Elizabeth, who like everyone else was motionless, was seized with a kind of terror as she heard herself being addressed by Mr Hargrove for the first time in two weeks.

'Elizabeth,' he said with some effort, as if the very name caught in his throat, and stopped.

'Have you heard something, Father?' said Douglas. 'You are upset, pull yourself together.'

Mr Hargrove made a gesture with his hand as if to wave his son aside, and continued in a firmer voice:

'When you arrived here, Elizabeth, Calhoun had just died a few days previously, on the 31st of March.'

These words rang out like a funeral bell, and again he interrupted himself, then repeated slowly, as if to convince himself of what he was saying:

'Calhoun died.'

Once again he fell silent.

'You'll frighten our young cousin,' said Joshua.

'Oh, no,' said Mr Hargrove, 'Elizabeth doesn't know who Calhoun was. Calhoun was the South. He defended us in Congress with a courage that filled our opponents with admiration. I saw that man in the street in Savannah. Tall and thin, with pointed features and eyes like a bird of prey that you can't bear to feel looking at you, deep blue, giving a magnificent beauty to his emaciated face. The thick mass of his hair that stood up on end added to his strange appearance. What he wanted,' continued Mr Hargrove, 'was for the South to be on an equal footing with the North, which is more powerful and much more densely populated. That was the price of Union.'

For some moments Elizabeth had stopped following the speakers, but she noticed that they were beginning to converse very quickly. She saw Aunt Augusta making signs to the servants, who covered the dishes and took them back to the kitchen. 'What's going on?' she wondered worriedly. 'Has there been some misfortune?'

Suddenly, Aunt Emma's flat, careful voice forced a passage through the male voices:

'I think we should turn our thoughts to other things than the absence of Calhoun, it's over a month since he died.'

'Be quiet, Emma,' said Joshua, 'let my father speak. For a start, you understand nothing of politics.'

'I understand very well that we are here to have supper, and we are not having it.'

'Bravo,' exclaimed Billy.

'Another word out of you,' said Uncle Joshua, 'and you'll have your supper on the grass outside.'

William Hargrove seemed to hear nothing of these peripheral disputes, any more than what his two sons had said. In a voice that was now loud and strong, but strangely monotone, he continued:

'We fought with Mexico in '48, we took California from them, we have a right to California, and the Washington people will only accept it without slaves. We're falling into the trap of our victory, they've stolen it from us.'

'Father,' said Douglas seizing him by the hand, 'the gold miners, the famous "forty-niners", the California squatters, want no coloreds, freemen or slaves, on their territory. They're making the law.'

'What law? Peace in shame and humiliation.'

'But we're being offered compensation!' exclaimed Joshua. 'The North undertakes to return our runaway slaves.'

'Oh, such foolishness!' William Hargrove thundered. 'Do you really imagine that they are going to give those wretched slaves back to us, with that pack of abolitionists who are stirring up public opinion?'

Again Aunt Emma launched forth into the tumult:

'I am sorry that we are not having supper, but I am glad that the servants are in the kitchens and can't hear you.'

Douglas suddenly let out a peal of mocking laughter:

'And to think that slavery is flourishing in the District of Columbia right in Washington where the sale of slaves is carried on? On the very steps of the Capitol.'

At that moment young Fred, who never said a word, gave his opinion in his turn, conquered by the emotion of his elders. His usually pensive face was suddenly inflamed:

'Yet it's true! They forget it, they who never stop preaching to us, their pastors who'll stay at home with their Bibles and their slippers if there's a war, but we shall be off to it.'

'I shall be off with you!' cried Billy. 'We'll be the first on the first day.'

Suddenly overcome, he had drawn himself up, pushing his chair back, and stood there, on the point of delivering a speech. All the reddish gold of his hair was aflame in an untidy mass of rebellious locks. Joshua, sitting next to him, forced him to sit down again.

'The whole South will set off as one man,' proclaimed Douglas. 'Young and old, rich and poor. A mass uprising will take place of its own accord.'

The servants, who were coming in with the dishes, turned tail in horror, back towards the kitchens, and Aunt Emma, with her eyes closed and her head tossed back, begged, with a groan, to be brought some laudanum.

William Hargrove finally stood up, with both hands leaning on the table. Amidst his abundant gray whiskers, his deathly-pale face was losing its composure in terror. He had evidently not foreseen the catastrophic effect of his praise for Calhoun.

'Listen,' he said, 'listen to me, for Heaven's sake.'

Something in his demeanor and in the whole of his person gave him the disturbing appearance of some apparition, and silence was established.

'You forget,' he said in a flat voice, 'that in 1832 there was a rebellion in South Carolina over a question of tariffs imposed by the North. General Andrew Jackson, President of the United States, sent troops and ships to Charleston, and South Carolina had to give in. It seceded, but the South did not follow suit.'

There was a heavy silence, and William Hargrove continued:

'With no army, no weapons, without a single factory in the whole of the South, how could we have fought?'

'A national uprising always finds what's needed,' replied Fred.

William Hargrove turned his head towards him and looked at him for a moment.

'Think carefully before you speak in that way,' he said.

'The North's superiority is crushing. It's like three against one.'

'I believe I am right, in spite of everything, Grandfather.'

'The facts are as they are, Fred. On the 1st of February 1832, the South was obliged to capitulate before the might of the enemy. And to risk the future of a nation for a mere taxation problem . . . for we are a nation.'

Again Douglas took hold of his hand:

'Father,' he said gently, 'you're English.'

'Agreed, but my children are sons of the South. I am for the South.'

The boys cried: 'Bravo!' and there was a sort of shuffle all around the table. William Hargrove's eyes seemed to be fixed on a spot at the back of the room, and he remained silent. It was Joshua who spoke:

'We are evidently heading for a compromise. We have no luck with our presidents. General Andrew Jackson resorted to force. Why does the President have to be a military man once again? President Zachary Taylor fought in the Mexican war. He finds the Compromise acceptable.'

'When shall we stop retreating?'

'The time's not ripe,' said Douglas crisply.

Did William Hargrove hear these words? He continued:

'Calhoun couldn't see the South's future . . . The last time Calhoun was seen in the Senate, he was dying, so weak that he had to ask one of his younger colleagues to read his speech in his place. The text was terrifyingly lucid in a supreme effort to expose the secret trap of a possible compromise. He saw things clearly.' His voice sounded almost strangled: 'Calhoun listened without budging. Behind his magnificently ugly face, the deep blue eyes seemed to plunge into the void in an endless cry of pain and despair. He took a last look at that gathering of men in black who were seeking to bury his country, and went home to die.'

When he had finished speaking, William Hargrove remained motionless, with his eyes turned towards the open door leading to the hall, as if expecting someone to appear.

Uncle Josh stood up abruptly and said firmly:

'We shall get out of this dead end and go forward to peace. In the meantime, I am of the opinion that we should have supper.'

'A warmed-up supper . . .' exclaimed Aunt Augusta. 'For the first time in my life. My word, we're starting to live like the poor. I'd rather die first.'

'Calm down, Augusta, and let me speak. I propose that we have a cold supper. There is everything here that we need to make it perfect, and we'll have it in the cool, on the big lawn, beneath the stars. And we'll have champagne. I'm sure that you are in agreement, Father?'

William Hargrove did not answer.

'No answer implies consent,' said Douglas suddenly in a jovial tone of voice. 'That's an excellent idea of yours, Josh. Noah,' he said to one of the servants, 'go and have a long table carried out in front of the house. A large white table-cloth, and a dozen wicker armchairs. Melons to start with. Virginia ham. Four big bowls of mixed salads, the cake that was planned for this evening, plenty of fruit, and to finish off, ice-cream and cookies. Off you go quickly, and no arguing. I'm not ordering anything impossible, but I don't want to have to wait. So, to the armchairs facing the great avenue, immediately. Off you go, quick, quick.'

'Not forgetting the champagne!' Uncle Josh shouted after Noah, who had already disappeared, panic-stricken, towards the kitchens.

In the dining room, a hubbub of approval welcomed the decisions that had been taken, and nearly everyone got up, but not William Hargrove at one end of the table, and at the other end, Elizabeth, who was looking anxiously at the immobile man with bushy whiskers. For a few moments she had been wondering whether he was not about to die. She had only ever seen one dead man in her life: her father. To her mind, Mr Hargrove looked like a dead man.

The chair legs grated on the tiles as they were pushed back, and the young people were already bustling towards the door. Doubtless as uneasy as Elizabeth, Josh and Douglas were speaking to their father. In vain. His face was of an ashen paleness and no longer seemed to express any emotion, and his hardened features were becoming frozen, but his breathing could be heard, short and constricted.

The two brothers exchanged glances and went to support him under his arms. They then felt the dead weight of his body.

'We'll help you outside, Father,' said Joshua. 'The fresh

air will do you good, it's much too hot in here.'

In a hoarse whisper, he answered:

'Leave me.'

Again the two men exchanged a quizzical look.

'He'll pull himself together,' said Josh under his breath. 'It's tiredness, and emotion.'

'Go outside,' said Douglas in the same tone of voice. 'I'll stay with him for a bit.'

At that moment Aunt Laura came back and said:

'No, I will.'

Josh and Douglas were too amazed to speak. She leaned towards William Hargrove. Her long, rather melancholy face almost touched that of the motionless man, and imploringly she murmured:

'Father.'

He quivered, seeming to gather up his strength by an act of will:

'Go away!' he said.

She stood up straight and covered her eyes with her hands without saying a word.

Elizabeth fled.

She stopped for a moment on the verandah steps. Her heart was beating so hard that she had to lean on the rail, but even in her distress, she breathed in the perfume of the magnolias. It intoxicated her, as on the evening of her arrival at Dimwood. She made an effort to calm herself and everything seemed to be on her side; the coolness of the night air on her face and the sustained and gentle sound of the tree-frogs. She closed her eyes. Nothing had seemed comprehensible to her. At last she began to walk slowly towards the lights in the direction of the great avenue. Uncle Josh's voice greeted her from some distance:

'There you are! Come on, you're the only one we're waiting for.'

A little dazzled by the brightness of the lamps, she let herself be led. The table on the lawn was set with the usual luxury. On the blinding white tablecloth shone expensive glasses and solid silverware. There was a strange discord between this ostentation and the silent grandeur of the night.

Uncle Josh said threateningly. 'I wonder what our cousin

from England can be thinking of us. She's as quiet as a judge. You must try and understand us, dear Elizabeth, we're going through difficult times.'

'But I don't judge you,' said Elizabeth politely. 'I just feel a bit lost in all your discussions.'

'I'll explain everything to you,' said Billy spiritedly.

Suddenly there was silence. Beyond the great avenue, singing of a bewitching sweetness rose in the starlit night. So clear were the men's and women's voices that the words could be made out by the little group of people on the lawn in front of the house: in their own way, the slaves were recounting the sadness they bore within themselves.

The young Englishwoman was struck by this tender, plaintive melody and she made an effort to grasp its meaning. She could make out these words:

'Dere was an old Nigga.'

When the voices fell silent, there was an emotional pause. Aunt Emma discreetly blew her nose, and the servants in their red livery sniffed as they passed the silver salad bowls. Uncle Josh, addressing Elizabeth, explained the meaning of the words:

'It's about an old Negro, a good, hard-working man, Uncle Ned. Uncle Ned died a long time ago. No more white hair on his head, no more strength in his hands, no more eyes, no more teeth, and as for the corn fritter they put down in front of him, he had to leave it. Master was very unhappy when he died, his tears fell like raindrops. Mistress went quite pale, and very sad at never seeing Uncle Ned again. No more spade, no more hoe for him. No more hard work for poor Uncle Ned, he's gone where good Negroes go.'

'Very touching,' said Fred. 'Words and music by a White from Pittsburgh who's making a fortune out of it. That Stephen Foster is very skilled at provoking tears, which are a guarantee of success for a popular ballad.'

'Very possibly, but adopted by the Negroes and sung with fervor.'

There then followed something singular. It was as if nobody wanted to talk any more and that everything that had to be said had been said. Perhaps they felt some inexplicable formless and faceless presence, as vast as the night. Supper was finished in silence.

4
JONATHAN

37

*E*lizabeth could not sleep that night. She experienced for the first time the horrors of insomnia. She felt as if she were wandering in some unknown land where danger awaited her at every step.

A little before dawn she got up, relit the lamp and began to write. Her hand ran over the writing paper of its own accord. But she had to start again several times. Now too long, now too short, or too abrupt, she finally wrote out these few lines:

> Uncle Charlie, I don't know how to explain to you what's going on inside me. I am too unhappy at Dimwood. You told me I could come and see you. You'll have to fetch me. I could never announce my desire to leave to Mr Hargrove. I think about you, and all you told me.

There was great uncertainty. She did not know how to end. A quarter of an hour went by, a quarter of an hour verging on despair, because the words she needed to find were like some insurmountable obstacle. She got up and looked in the mirror. In the soft lamplight, the mass of her hair shone gloriously around a face made smaller by tiredness. She fixed her attention on the blue eyes that returned her motionless gaze, in which she read one thing only in the very depths of her being: fear.

Where should she go now in this room that seemed to be lying in wait for her? What to do with her body? With herself? Go back to bed, where she would not close her eyes? Risk going out on to the verandah? She did not dare, because a nightlight always burned in Aunt Laura's room. She might see her, come out suddenly and question her. One day, as she was going by, she had seen, through the half-open window, a black cross on the wall over the bed, and she had run away.

The cool air caressed her face. In the woods, the sound of the peaceful and timid tree-frogs had ceased.

She returned to the table, glanced at her letter and esteemed it to be clumsy: 'It doesn't look like a letter,' she thought. Suddenly seized with impatience, she signed it, in spite of everything, with her Christian name, omitting any form of ending, even the simplest. The letter was slid into an envelope as it was and the address written in a firm hand, angry almost, for she was fed up with her hesitations. In a way, she was fed up with herself too. The letter would go later on, with the mail that was collected at about eleven o'clock. With that decision taken, she felt relieved of an enormous weight and leapt into bed. The birds were beginning to sing, but she did not hear them.

The noise of Betty pouring hot water into the tub woke her. She immediately thought of her letter. The simplest would be to give it to Betty, who would make sure it went off. She could be relied on. First of all she must seal the envelope that was still open, on purpose, so that she could re-read her letter once more and make sure that she had really got the point across. Her father, who was scrupulous to the point of punctiliousness, had taught her that.

In her nightdress and with her hair spread over her shoulders, she pulled the letter out of its envelope and re-read it carefully. 'It's crazy,' she said to herself. 'It's a cry for help, I'm imploring him. And to start with, it's not dated.'

Betty's anxious voice called her from the adjoining room.

'Miss Lizbeth, this water's goin' to get cold if you don't come on now.'

'I'm coming.'

She took the pen and wrote: 10 May 1850; that looked better, in any case, more normal . . .

'Now,' an inner voice said to her, 'seal the envelope and have the letter go this morning.'

Elizabeth knew that secret, imperious voice well, having heard it since her childhood. 'Agreed,' she said under her breath and went to wash.

Betty, who had disappeared, came back just as the girl was getting dressed, and chose for her the dress that Miss Lizbeth would wear that day. It was a kind of ritual that Elizabeth accepted out of affection for the black maid. The latter was bustling around the room like some great bumblebee, opening drawers, delving into cupboards.

It was a periwinkle-blue cotton dress that was imposed on Elizabeth, although she would have preferred to be in white;

but she let herself be persuaded, as usual, and made no objection when Betty knelt down in front of her and put on her feet the cornflower-blue shoes that she thought garish. By a quirk of her wildly independent nature, she liked this submission to the tyranny of the big-hearted black woman.

'Miss Lizbeth, she more beautiful than the others,' Betty was saying as she put on her shoes, 'than all the Misses of Dimwood. Everybody say Miss Lizbeth, she's the most beautiful.'

The girl was listening to this sweetly childish chattering distractedly, when the voice she had heard a moment earlier insisted:

'The letter, give her the letter.'

The letter was within reach on the table at her side. She grabbed it without saying anything and slid it into the opening of the drawer.

Five minutes later, she was at her place in the dining room, where the usual appearance of people and of things resembled in every detail the previous day's breakfast, for nothing ever changed at Dimwood. The supper beneath the stars evaporated like a rather absurd dream. This morning, everything was back to reality. Mr Hargrove stood up to say the customary prayers. His flat voice implored peace so sadly that one might have wondered if there was not already fighting on the frontiers ... Despite his black suit and his long white cuffs, he was more like a poor man on a street corner. Elizabeth had the feeling that something had happened inside him. He had doubtless not slept. Seized with pity, she decided to put off sending the letter to Uncle Charlie until the next day.

When he had finished his prayers and the servants began to pour tea and coffee into the cups, Uncle Josh stood up in his turn and began to speak in a joyful tone that contrasted with his father's pious murmurings.

'My friends,' he said, 'the telegraph informs us that the chances for peace with the North are becoming clearer. Our great Henry Clay is addressing the Congress to make a declaration of capital importance. In agreement with Douglas, I'm asking our father for permission to give a ball. Not a great ball, but something to liven up the passage of time at Dimwood a little. There are still young officers in the neighborhood, and young officers ask for nothing better than to come and dance with pretty girls at Dimwood. What do you say, Father?'

William Hargrove frowned:

'As long as the news is not confirmed,' he said, 'it is better not to celebrate. I'm superstitious on that point.'

'Well, we'll wait for tomorrow's paper, but we'll make out the list of guests straight away, and warn our little band: violin, cello, double bass and trumpet.'

'And a drum,' added Billy, 'since there'll be soldiers. That'll make it more military.'

'A flute as well,' suggested Aunt Emma in an angelic voice, for she came back to life on learning that peace was being confirmed.

'You'll have all that,' said Uncle Josh, and he continued: 'Lots of flowers, two enormous buffets, for the army has a noble appetite. I want it to be the event of the season for the neighborhood, Dimwood is becoming gloomy. Are you pleased, Elizabeth?'

The girl shook slightly as if someone had woken her up.

'Very,' she said.

'It's a little bit for you that I'm doing this,' said Uncle Josh. 'We can't rival the lavishness of Savannah, but I don't want to see the young people yawning from boredom at Dimwood. I want people to enjoy themselves here and be happy.'

An approving murmur greeted these pleasant arrangements. William Hargrove raised his eyes as if to make the ceiling a witness to the folly of mortals, and breakfast began with the usual conversational futilities. Only Fred retained a sombre appearance, and the young Englishwoman looked perplexed.

'My letter . . .' she thought.

Perhaps she had done well not to give it to Betty. Dancing with soldiers, perhaps even waltzing with soldiers . . . She considered herself frivolous and made an effort to think of something else.

'Now,' said the inner voice, 'now.'

Elizabeth shook her head impatiently and smiled at Billy, who, from the other side of the table, was telling her something that she was not following.

'Are you deaf?' he shouted. 'I'm telling you you're not bad in sky blue, but I like you better in mauve. Sky blue is

— 340 —

for well-behaved little girls just out of Sunday school.'

She turned towards Susanna in a fury:

'Talk to me about anything at all, Billy is annoying me.'

All the same, she decided to change her dress in the course of the morning and put on a peach-colored one, adorned with lavender flowers.

38

*U*ncle Josh had all the trouble in the world getting together a list of ladies and gentlemen likely to accept an invitation, for Dimwood still retained an unfortunate reputation. Nevertheless, a ball at the Hargroves' was a rare thing. Curiosity might be a factor, and there was still that something that nobody spoke about, but the memory of which had not been lost: the most lavish buffets in the district. In any case, the family should under no circumstances risk the offense of a refusal, not even by one single person. Uncle Josh was determined to do things on a grand scale.

Among Uncle Josh's intimate circle, everybody gave joyful approval, except Mr Hargrove who limited himself to nodding his authorization.

They started to clear the ballroom, which had become cluttered with furniture since it had stopped being used for dancing; and in the entrance hall three long tables covered with starched white damask cloths were set up.

There was a kind of over-excitement in the air. The 'children' ran about in all directions, getting in the way of the servants. The grown-ups themselves were coming and going for no particular reason, and as they bumped into each other they apologized amidst peals of laughter. In fact they all emerged from their usual torpor, intoxicated with the prospect of something happening, a party, a ball that would chase away the boredom.

This happy waiting concealed, however, a worry that no one admitted to: what if, by mischance, tomorrow's newspaper did not confirm such a great hope . . . How demoralizing it would be to have to put all the furniture back, to fold up the tablecloths, to dismantle the decorations, the pretty decorations . . .

In spite of herself, Elizabeth felt herself caught up in the general excitement, pretending not to hear Fred's little sniggers, as he kept up his role as harbinger of misfortune. He was slim and perfectly elegant in his black suit. He wore in all seasons his white, silk cravat, skilfully rolled beneath his handsome faced with its pale-colored eyes. He was already a man, and he was always finding himself, as if by chance, in the path of the young Englishwoman.

'So, you too?' he muttered passing close by her.

'I don't know what you mean.'

'Nothing, if you don't understand,' he said with a strangely pleasant expression.

She turned her back to him and went up to her room. With his cryptic language, Fred, like the others, she thought, treated her like a little girl. Without waiting, she put on her peach-colored dress and went downstairs again.

This time, it was Billy who was waiting for her at the bottom of the stairs, bantering and gallant at one and the same time. At this hour, there was nobody about in that part of the house.

'I don't feel like talking to you,' she said to him. 'Let me pass, Billy.'

He was, in effect, blocking her way by jumping from right to left.

'How disagreeable you are,' he said with a wicked smile. 'But that dress suits you wonderfully, and the more horrid you are, the more one feels like kissing you.'

He came up to her and, seized with fear, she slapped him. He did not move.

'If it gives you pleasure . . .' he said with a smile.

'Leave me alone, or I'll call out.'

'Alright, Miss Escridge,' he said in a formal tone of voice, and bowing, he added: 'If Miss Escridge wishes to be alone, quite alone, she will be left to herself in her corner.'

And he moved to one side. She ran off to look for

Susanna, who was becoming her confidante, and whom she found in the dining room. Without explanation, she made signs that she should follow her, and went with her on to the porch.

'What's the matter?' Susanna asked, taking her by the hand. 'You look upset.'

'That's possible,' said Elizabeth, gently freeing herself, and added abruptly: 'I never ever want to talk to Billy again . . . nor him to talk to me, never ever.'

'I won't ask any more questions, but I think you'd do well to avoid him and all the other boys.'

'Why all the boys?'

'Well, him above all. We know that he runs after Negresses in the maze. They're dangerous.'

'Dangerous? I don't understand.'

'Sick. Often. That's what they say, I don't know any more than that. His father is going to send him to a military college next year, to get him trained. They'll never manage it. Be wary of him.'

'I don't really understand what you mean. If one needs to be wary of everyone at Dimwood . . .'

'Billy could get sick too.'

'Oh, I don't want Billy to fall ill!' Elizabeth exclaimed. 'I don't want anything to happen to him.'

'Don't tell me you're in love!'

'I didn't say that. I'd rather talk about something else. Is there any news?'

'News? What are you thinking of? We shan't know anything until the paper comes. Everybody is waiting.'

'Waiting? Waiting for what? Not for war?'

'Oh, no. Papa says there won't be a war, but we'd like to be sure, do you understand?'

'Are they not sure there won't be a war? Everything you say is frightening . . .'

She gave a heavy sigh.

'You didn't even notice that I changed my dress . . .'

Susanna went into ecstasies over the dress, by way of apology.

'And those mauve ribbons . . . I noticed all that, you realize, as soon as you came to fetch me, poor darling . . .'

At these words, Elizabeth nearly flung herself into her

arms. She held herself back, instinctively. It was the first expression of tenderness shown to her at Dimwood. Even the audacious Hilda had not permitted herself such freedom of expression. Yet Elizabeth was afraid of effusiveness, and she limited herself to furtively touching Susanna's face, without suspecting the gauche enormity of this innocent gesture, for there was no better way of fanning an incipient flame.

'Susanna,' she simply said, 'we must go in. They'll wonder what we're up to here. Aunt Laura might question us.'

'Oh, Aunt Laura is neither nasty nor nosy,' she said.

'I have the impression she's spying on us.'

'I don't think so. You don't know her very well. She's mysterious. You remember the day young Armstrong came prowling around the house with the lady in white? You weren't here.'

'No. Let's stay on the porch a moment longer.'

'Are you interested?'

'Yes, I admit I am, a little.'

'Me, too. Perhaps not for the same reasons as you.'

'I don't understand it properly, but tell me.'

One would have thought that Susanna suddenly found a strange pleasure in teasing Elizabeth in her naivety.

'Well, that day I happened to be in my room, and I saw everything from my window, and do you know who was next to me?'

'How do you think I should know? Carry on, I beg you.'

'I adore your impatience! I'm impatient too, and it pains me. Anyway, it was Aunt Laura. She had come, as she does sometimes, to see if everything is tidy . . .'

'She comes into my room too, very often.'

'When the two of them arrived, him on horseback, she in her carriage, she flung herself to the window, and started to watch. I've never seen anybody watch like that, standing up quite straight and so still, it was frightening, really.'

'What then?'

'She waited for them to go round the house and to come by again, very close this time. You could see them almost as clearly as I can see you. At that moment, without a cry, Aunt Laura fell backwards, stiff as a board. I was crazy with panic. I ran through the house, met Uncle Douglas in a corridor.

He came. I thought she was dead, but he brought her round, and told me to leave the room.'

'And then?'

'Nothing. Everybody at Dimwood ended up knowing, except for those who were in Savannah; you, Billy, Uncle Josh and Aunt Emma . . . and Grandfather who arrived a day before you, but too late. Uncle Douglas made us promise not to say anything to anybody, but you see, I haven't kept my promise with you . . .'

She added with a deep sigh:

' . . . out of weakness.'

Quite close to the two girls, the magnolia was heavy with fragrance, spreading around them its languorous, sweetly sensual perfume. Elizabeth looked at the pain in Susanna's face and had a premonition that another surge of feeling was threatening. In a reasonable tone of voice, she declared:

'A promise is all very well, but you didn't swear on the Bible.'

'Oh!' said Susanna shocked, 'in the South, a promise is a promise, Elizabeth.'

'As everywhere,' said Elizabeth. 'The South didn't invent that.'

Cross at her blunder, she moved away abruptly.

'We haven't time to argue, Susanna, I'm going back in. Stay here for a minute. It's better that we don't go back in together.'

'Why?'

But Elizabeth was already back with the grown-ups in the ballroom. She was so annoyed at having appeared ill-mannered, so annoyed at her unworthy pronouncement on the Bible, that she decided to avoid all conversation with Susanna in future.

Uncle Josh was giving the servants instructions for cleaning the windows and for polishing the parquet floor afterwards, and he wanted it polished to excess.

'Your dancers will slide,' said Uncle Douglas.

'I'm counting on it. Like ice skaters. The little red chairs arranged along the walls, for the mothers.'

'The mothers with their age-old problem,' muttered Aunt Emma.

'Don't start,' said Uncle Douglas. 'The daughters will all

be married off. Where are you going to put the band, Josh?'

'In the sitting room, next door, with all the doors wide open, naturally. I'll add our old piano. A tuner should be coming this afternoon.'

'I wish the tuner courage,' said Aunt Augusta. 'But you're seeing to everything, Josh. Do you still believe in the Compromise?'

Elizabeth ran off. The very word 'Compromise' awoke all her anxiety. In vain did she affirm that an Englishwoman was afraid of nothing: she was pretending, she was afraid like everybody else.

Having sought refuge in her room, she flung herself into the rocking chair to think. Betty, who was tidying up, was silently moving her duster over the furniture, and then lingered by the door, sighing.

'Give me a fan,' said Elizabeth. 'And if you've finished, leave me alone.'

Betty handed her one of the palm leaves, which could be found in all the rooms at Dimwood. As light as a feather, the graceful object created the illusion of a little coolness. Elizabeth was waving it gently in front of her face, when she was stopped by the inner voice:

'The letter, give it to Betty.'

'Absurd,' thought Elizabeth, 'with all the preparations for a party, it's too late.'

'Betty,' she said aloud, 'why are you pulling such a sad face? Is it because I changed my dress?'

Betty nodded.

'Don't you think my peach dress is pretty? As pretty as my sky-blue dress? I'm fond of you, Betty, but you must let me do things in my own way, don't you see?'

In her white apron, the black woman retained the dignity conferred on her by age, and without a word she bowed and went out. A vague feeling of unease took hold of Elizabeth.

'I shan't tell her I'm sorry, all the same,' she said to herself. 'It's rather to Susanna that I should . . . But no! You'd think they were fixing everything to give me a bad conscience. And my letter, my stupid letter . . . What a good job I didn't send it . . . What should I look like, calling on Uncle Charlie for help, just when they're going to give a ball . . .'

The letter in question was still in the drawer. She pulled it out and hid it in the bottom of her travelling holdall, with the love letter that that hateful person had written. She despised him, but the love letter was a love letter, the first, the only one so far. She had not had the courage to destroy it. The other letter would wait to be sent at a more suitable time.

At dinner it was agreed that politics would not be discussed so as not to interfere with the pleasure of eating, but five minutes had not gone by before the Compromise and the chances of peace were raised. The day seemed long gone when these same people were proclaiming secession in an outburst of crazy excitement. The rumors that were going around now pointed towards an agreement. Those present, now they were reassured, gave themselves the pleasure of dismantling it: it was a shameful slur on the honor of the South, but one more political swindle, and Calhoun would be turning in his grave.

Elizabeth was once more given up to despair and turned towards her neighbor, Susanna, who had decided not to notice her and was looking straight ahead. It was to her profile that Elizabeth spoke:

'Susanna, I've something to say to you.'

'Something hurtful?' the profile asked.

'Not at all,' Elizabeth groaned, 'on the contrary. Just now, you should have understood: I feel terribly alone in your South . . .'

'Well, you should have left with your mother,' replied the profile.

'Oh! That's hard of you. If you were in my position, you'd be suffering as I am.'

No answer. The hubbub of the arguments washed over what they were saying. Then a kind of violence took hold of Elizabeth and she suddenly said, in a quick, clear-cut voice:

'Listen, about the promise and the oath on the Bible, it was disgraceful of me.'

These words had the effect of an electric shock on the over-emotional Susanna. She turned suddenly to her neighbor, with tears flowing down her radiant face:

'Oh, no,' she said in a strangled voice. 'Oh, no!'

Elizabeth rewarded her with a choice smile and everything was understood.

39

*T*he afternoon was gloomy. The air was heavy. The excitement at dinner gave way to a more or less general desire for a restorative nap in some quiet corner. Even the valiant Billy gave in to the temptation to go and snore on one of the sofas in the large drawing room.

The newspaper would only arrive at six o'clock, and until then there was nothing to do at Dimwood. The ladies withdrew to their rooms. Elizabeth did the same, after having gratified Susanna with a slight squeeze of the hand to console the inconsolable.

Settled in her rocking chair, she closed her eyes and wanted to sleep, but the political chatter had taken away her appetite, and she had barely tasted the dishes. No need for a siesta. She opened *The Last Days of Pompeii* and closed the book almost immediately. She found its story of love in the shadow of a catastrophe oppressive.

For the twentieth time, she mentally rewrote her letter to Uncle Charlie. Of course, there was the ball which was complicating matters, but how could a party at the Hargroves' rival the dazzling, luxurious folly of Savannah? She was already casting rather jaundiced looks on the modest festivities that were being prepared at Dimwood. It was all very well to increase the number of garlands, make the rooms larger by moving out heavy pieces of furniture, but spacious splendor was lacking, there was no gallery for the musicians, there would be no banquet. The only serious thing in the forthcoming evening's favor was the presence of the army in uniform, soldiers . . .

Emerging suddenly from her dreaming, the girl esteemed

such considerations to be vulgar, but the days spent in Savannah had awakened in her an instinctive taste for luxury and a full and brilliant life. She was still too close to the memory of London's icy streets, the wretched lodging house, where she shivered at night, with her mother silently in despair.

She took a few steps out on the porch. The sky was clouding over without bringing coolness, and the monotonous grating of the cicadas tore through the silence of the woods. This sustained sound had something stubborn and evil about it in the long run. Elizabeth waved her palm fan around her face and her neck in vain, she was sweating. Back in her room, she closed the shutters at the window, plunging the room into semi-darkness.

The heat was drying out her mouth. She rang. Betty came in almost immediately, as if she had been waiting at the door, and seemed worried.

'Bring me some nice cool water, Betty, I'm dying of thirst.'

'Yes, Miss Lizbeth,' stammered Betty.

'What's the matter with you? Has something happened?'

'No, Miss Lizbeth. I'll be back straight away.'

Indeed, she was back five minutes later, carrying a carafe of water and a bowl of ice cubes on a silver tray, which she put down in the middle of the table. She wanted to talk, but fear made her eyes larger, and she stood motionless and dumbstruck, with her big, black hands flat against her white apron.

'You look like someone who has seen a ghost,' said Elizabeth with a laugh. 'My poor Betty, make an effort and tell me.'

'If anyone come by here, Miss Lizbeth, don't open the door . . .'

'I don't understand a word of what you're saying, Betty. Nobody comes here, except you and Aunt Laura. Has somebody told you something?'

'No, Miss Lizbeth, but I's afraid. I's afraid . . .'

'Afraid of war?'

'Oh, Miss Lizbeth, I ain't said nothin' 'bout war.'

'If you don't want to talk, Betty, run off. You'll end up disturbing me with your mysterious airs.'

Betty gave a look that was heavy with reproach and left the room. Overcome with scruples and with curiosity,

Elizabeth followed her on tiptoe into the corridor. She saw her throw her apron over her face, which was a great sign of distress amongst the Negroes.

Unable to hold out any longer, she ran after her and grabbed her hand. The apron suddenly fell back down and Betty let out a cry like an animal caught in a trap.

'Enough,' said Elizabeth severely, 'I'm very displeased.'

And in a threatening voice that was unfamiliar to her, she declared:

'If you know something and refuse to talk, the Lord will punish you.'

This sentence was barely out of her mouth, as if spoken by somebody else, and she was almost as surprised as Betty, who was leaning on the wall, petrified with fear.

'Souligou,' she muttered, 'it's Souligou.'

'Mademoiselle Souligou,' corrected Elizabeth, 'well?'

'Mamzelle Souligou seen somethin' in the cards, and she done told Nero . . .'

'Well, Betty, what did she see in the cards?'

'The house full of soldiers.'

Elizabeth made as if to laugh, but her laughter had a false ring to it.

'My poor Betty, Mademoiselle Souligou saw the ball.'

'The ball, Miss Lizbeth?'

'But yes, the ball, you know perfectly well that there is to be a ball at Dimwood. You people know everything, you listen to everything. You don't need Mademoiselle Souligou's visions to know that there will be a ball . . .'

She was speaking quickly, much too quickly, as if carried away by the sound of her words.

'Mamzelle Souligou, she didn't say nothin' 'bout no ball,' said Betty. 'She say: "Savannah, Miss Lizabeth is goin' to Savannah."'

Again Elizabeth felt dryness in her throat, but this time from a sudden surge of fear.

'Betty,' she said at last, 'I want to know the truth; you've been going through my drawers, you saw a letter, you took that letter. If you've stolen it, I forgive you, I shall say nothing, but I want to know.'

Betty's face underwent a sudden transformation at these words. She was becoming a different woman. Her enormous black pupils fixed the English girl straight in her pale eyes, and she said slowly, in a serious voice:

'I ain't never stole in my whole life.'

Confronted with this unbearable look, the girl was overcome with dizziness, and she thought she was going to faint. She barely had the time to say in a whisper the words that flowed straight from her heart:

'I'm sorry, Betty.'

Running to her room, she shut herself in and heard Susanna calling her from outside:

'Come quickly, Elizabeth. There's news.'

With her head still spinning, she staggered to the adjoining room.

Bent double over the wash-basin, she tried to be sick but did not manage it.

A few minutes later, Aunt Laura came into her room and found her stretched out on the bed:

'What's the matter Elizabeth? Do you not feel well?'

'Tired, that's all,' the girl said as she got up.

'You're quite pale. It's the first time I've seen you looking so poorly.'

Elizabeth hesitated before replying. What Susanna had told her about Aunt Laura came back into mind, as did the memory of that painful moment when William Hargrove had sent her out of the dining room. How could she maintain such an appearance of serenity?

She found the strength to smile and said:

'Aunt Laura, I shall never get used to the South.'

'You don't know it well yet, but you'll end up becoming attached to it, like all of us. It's the heat that makes you uncomfortable. We're going to have a storm which will cool us down tonight.'

In a casual manner she suddenly said:

'I thought I heard you talking with Betty in the corridor, very close to my room. I hope that she is always obedient and respectful towards you.'

Elizabeth answered straight off:

'Betty is very good and I like her very much.'

'Everybody likes Betty. You see, it's important to remain on friendly terms with the servants. They expect a lot, and they pass judgement on us in their hearts.'

These softly spoken words made Elizabeth prick up her ears. She suspected that, without listening at keyholes, this woman of such mysterious simplicity had nevertheless overheard her conversation with Betty.

'I know,' she said with resignation.

'Well, let's go into the drawing room where they are waiting for us. My father wishes us all to be present.'

Everyone was gathered together in the drawing room, as if for some religious ceremony. The lowered blinds softened the light and heightened this impression. The servants were standing by the door, separately from their masters, and Elizabeth recognized Betty amongst them. Their eyes met. A broad, affectionate smile lit up the maid's face, and Elizabeth also smiled, but more discreetly.

Uncle Douglas unfolded a newspaper and announced in his special occasion voice:

'My friends, I believe we may rejoice, without, however, shouting out and crying for joy. Our great Henry Clay has made what he so nobly calls the union of hearts prevail. As a consequence of his speech, an agreement between us and our brothers from the North is in view.'

The word brothers aroused mutterings amongst the men and 'shushes' were immediately to be heard from the women's clique.

Uncle Douglas continued firmly:

'California's accession to the ranks of the Union will be as a free state.'

Dull mutterings and more desperate 'shushes' from the women.

'Moreover, the Washington government undertakes to persuade runaway slaves from the South to return to their homes. This is a summary of the principal conditions of the agreement. Peace, which has been threatened for so long, is today assured.'

This affirmation was greeted by a heavy silence. In an even more solemn tone, Uncle Douglas continued:

'The Savannah newspaper only gives a broad outline of the news. Tomorrow's will give Mr Clay's great speech in full. I will now hand over to the head of the family, who is going to ask for the protection of the Supreme Being for all of us.'

This title, reserved for life's great occasions, gave a foretaste of a formidable chunk of eloquence. Consequently there was great surprise when William Hargrove moved forward to the middle of the room, and began in a voice of almost childlike simplicity:

'Our Father, who art in heaven . . .'

There then took place that indescribable phenomenon, a wave of emotion that passed through those present with the force of a hurricane. Without knowing it, this little flock of humanity was making real for a moment the union of hearts, of which a politician had dreamt for the whole nation.

The light was fading fast, and raindrops were already pattering on the roof of the porch when the final *Amen* resounded.

It was in silence in the half-light that they all went their separate ways. No one felt the need to speak. Confused feelings of the aftermath of defeat hovered over the announcement of peace.

Servants brought torches, escorting their masters, who seemed not to know where they wanted to go. This mute disarray took on a funereal appearance.

Then the clear, cutting voice of young Fred could be heard in the clatter of rain beating against the house:

'And that's how a war is lost without a shot being fired.'

No voice was raised to contradict him.

40

*T*hat night the violence of the storm intensified, and the lightning unceasingly scribbled the country's future across the sky in indecipherable language. That, at least, was what superstitious souls believed, especially amongst the Negros who hid themselves, preferably under the furniture, with each new clap of thunder.

In the smoking room, the men were having their sober, after-supper chat behind closed shutters. Despite his youth, Fred was permitted to join his elders. His opinions seemed curious to them, and they were sometimes shocked by them.

'Uncle Douglas,' he said with all the customary respect, 'I have the impression that you watered down the truth when you said that the North would use persuasion to return runaway slaves to the South.'

'You are right, but that was necessary in front of the servants. The North undertakes to send them back by force.'

'And do you really imagine that they will do so?'

'No, but the matter is presented as a compensation for California, which we have lost.'

'A consolation prize, a gilded paper crown on the temples of a temporary peace. We've been cheated and made ridiculous in the eyes of the world.'

'Get rid of that illusion. The world applauds, and I shall be very surprised if the California squatters aren't celebrating their victory tomorrow.'

'We can count on ten years of peace,' said Uncle Douglas.

'Ten years! That's something,' exclaimed Uncle Josh.

'The North needs it, in fact, to reinforce its position,' said Fred, 'and to prepare some underhand deal for the future.'

'You ought to get yourself better informed. The people of the North have no wish to dive into war. What they want is to work and get rich. Uncle Charlie, who knows the North well, will tell you that you shouldn't confuse the eloquence of abolitionist pastors with the corner shopkeeper's desire for a quiet life.'

'Very good, Douglas,' said Uncle Josh, 'but let's leave politics and talk about ourselves a bit. This very morning I sent couriers bearing invitations to ten of our neighbors.'

'That makes ten families,' said Uncle Douglas. 'You were taking a gamble.'

'I was betting on good fortune, and then I was sure that the Compromise would get through.'

'It'll take at least four days for the answers to come through.'

'Positive or negative,' muttered William Hargrove.

Huddled deep in a winged armchair, he was keeping

— 354 —

silent and seemed lost in thought.

'You can rest assured, Father,' said Joshua. 'All these people are dying of boredom amid the solitude of their plantations. Not one will fail to respond.'

'All the same, we should have held consultations,' said William Hargrove.

This sentence was spoken with the sadness of an old man. Henry Clay's victory had apparently dealt him a blow. Each of his grandson Fred's remarks made him nod his head approvingly.

'Ten years of peace, think about it, Father,' Joshua said by way of an answer.

'Yes, my boy, I am thinking about it, and I recall Calhoun's last words on his deathbed: "South, poor South . . . "'

'Those are the words of a great patriot who has seen disappointment and lost a sense of reality.'

'They are the words of a visionary,' said Fred. 'But it won't be the North who will want to fight, it'll be us.'

'Oh, Fred!' groaned Uncle Josh, then he suddenly added jovially: 'I am of the opinion that in order to cheer ourselves up, we finish this rather serious evening with a last glass of this excellent port that comes to us from so far away.'

The proposition was accepted, and the bottle of port, having circumnavigated the Cape, went round the table. Only William Hargrove abstained:

'My heart's not in it,' he said, so softly that he was barely heard.

Joshua, who was standing up, leaned towards him:

'Father,' he said to him gently, 'peace is here, we're heading for better days.'

There was no response to these words. Despite Uncle Josh's efforts, a heavy sadness weighed down on all of them. A brief moment went by, and one after the other the men left the room. The glasses, which had been barely touched, remained on the table.

That was the moment the servants had been waiting for behind the doors.

41

*T*he replies to the invitations arrived even more promptly than Uncle Josh had foreseen, and, as he was hoping, all accepted, in accordance with the South's timeless forms of politeness, with the exception of a single family, which declined the great honor, etc., etc., on account of a too-recent bereavement.

With the threat of war set aside, leave was granted at Fort Pulaski with great liberality, and the young officers obtained all that they asked for.

At Dimwood, the avalanche of favorable replies meant that people went somewhat wild — to start with. The ladies especially became aggressive as soon as it was a question of choosing flowers, and, according to the mood of this one or that, the flower beds were laid waste. Uncle Josh, who was taking charge of arranging the rooms, had the furniture moved twenty times before obtaining the desired effect. For their part, the girls were changing their dresses from morning until evening, without managing to find out whether they were prettier this way or that. It was, in fact, their first great ball at Dimwood. Until then, there had only been dances that were scarcely to be taken into account. And at least two young ladies were thinking, without daring to say as much aloud: 'Men, there will be men . . .'

Somewhat blasé after her experience in Savannah, Elizabeth kept herself apart, but was nonetheless thinking about the soldiers. There had been a whole load of them at Uncle Charlie's party. Some of them were not bad-looking, but Elizabeth became hard to please. While she was mad about uniforms, she had a high opinion of civilians, but they had to be perfect. Even the despicable person who had written her a love letter exerted, in spite of everything, a dangerous attraction. She preferred, however, the little architect, who had only to give up his eye glasses in order to seduce her with his angelically blind beauty.

As for what she would wear to the ball, she was inclining towards a quite simple white dress, not too long and without any ribbons. In spite of everything, she would seek Betty's advice, having made her peace with her. Betty approved:

'You don't need nothin' more, Miss Lizbeth. You is always so beautiful, just as you is.'

The naivety of these compliments excited Elizabeth's pride, and an idea, an unfortunate one, came into her mind.

'Thank you, Betty. Nothing, nothing and nothing is still the best there is, and yet if Miss Susanna or Miss Minnie were to lend me a ring with a little sapphire ... I like sapphires so much, and they have so many rings ...'

Without being aware of it, she was stirring up the conflict, well known amongst Southern families, between the black servant and the young white mistress. One or the other would have to give in.

'No,' said Betty, 'you is still too young for jewellery.'

'Too young? Sixteen!'

Firmly Betty insisted:

'No, Miss Lizbeth, jewellery, that come later.'

And she added:

'You listen to Betty now, I knows.'

Again she looked Elizabeth straight in the eyes, suppliant and imperious at one and the same time.

Elizabeth did not answer.

'I knows,' the black woman repeated more gently.

At that moment a thought ran through the girl's mind. In whose eyes would she ever see more love, and, above all, more goodness than in those great pupils as black as night? She conquered her emotion and was satisfied with a smile, but deep down she had a premonition that she would no longer be the one in charge. Perhaps she would pretend, but that would be all.

Another three days went by in feverish preparations. The men remained cool-headed, but this had long since ceased to be the case with the ladies and the 'children', and squabbling alternated with frenzied making up. The most valuable jewels were brought out of their cases.

The day before, Uncle Josh undertook a sort of general inspection and declared that he was almost completely satisfied. The ground-floor rooms looked very grand. By good fortune, the great storm a few days previously had lowered the temperature. Thus there was reason to hope that all would go well. There remained one night and one day to be got over. It seemed a long time. The over-excited young people were advised to keep calm, and the serenity becoming their rank in society was recommended to the ladies, but Uncle Josh did not feel completely calm himself. He did not forget that there was a shadow hovering over Dimwood. The mysterious disappearance of the two Armstrong brothers was now part of local legend. It was stupid, but after all the Hargroves' invitations had been well and truly accepted. There were grounds for supposing that the younger generation in any case would not let itself be intimidated by these old wives' tales, and that memories of a happy evening at the Hargroves' would wipe away Dimwood's sad renown. He nevertheless took a good sleeping draft before going to his bed, not suspecting that all the adults at Dimwood were taking exactly the same precaution. Aunt Emma resorted to laudanum to fortify her serenity.

Elizabeth took very early leave of her cousins who would have liked to chat with her until dawn. She preferred to be alone and dream at her leisure of the pleasant surprises that were perhaps awaiting her, for she knew that for all girls the purpose of a ball was to find a *beau*, if they were unfortunate enough not to have one. Crazed with a curiosity that she was careful to conceal, she was working out her chances of success. What she wished for with all her might — but how could she say so and to whom? — was to fall madly in love. She gave herself up to the delights of imagining her ideal. In uniform, if possible. 'Fort Pulaski,' she repeated the name to herself under her breath.

A short visit from Aunt Laura interrupted the flow of her meditations. Sliding like a shadow in her eternal pale gray and white striped dress, she came to say good night to her. With her usual gentleness, she asked the questions that always disturbed the English girl: for example, had she read her Bible, for this strange Catholic wanted her to be a faithful Protestant. 'Be on your guard,' her mother had told her, 'you can never tell what ulterior motive is in the back of their mind . . .'

'Not yet, but I'm going to read it before I go to bed.'

'Very good, and where have you got to?'

'To Jeremiah's curses of Moab. There are three pages of

them.'

'I know them well. A real avalanche, isn't it? But their grandeur and diversity are magnificent. And a chapter from the gospels as well. One must go to sleep on that — on account of tomorrow.'

'Tomorrow?'

'Yes, the ball tomorrow. The enemy of us all has not been invited, but he'll come all the same.'

'You mean the . . .'

'That's it. The Devil, Elizabeth. You are right to avoid your cousins, they'll be chattering until midnight, instead of resting. You are more sensible, you are not thinking about it too much, I hope.'

'I don't know about "too much," but I am thinking about it.'

'It's nothing, you know, noise, moving about . . .'

'I know, I went to a ball in Savannah.'

'Of course. And did you like it?'

'Yes at first, a lot less afterwards . . .'

'I understand, it's so tiring, I knew all that when I was young. I warn you not to take seriously what the young men might say to you. They don't believe anything of what they come out with . . .'

'I know.'

'Especially their compliments.'

'I know, Aunt Laura.'

'You know a lot of things for your age . . . but I'm not worried about you. You won't see me at the ball, but I shall be thinking of you, I shall be thinking about you the whole time.'

Elizabeth looked at her in stupefaction.

'All the time . . . thank you, Aunt Laura.'

Aunt Laura then gave that mysterious smile that aroused mistrust in the girl's heart.

'Sleep well, Elizabeth.'

'Sleep well, Aunt Laura.'

But Aunt Laura had already disappeared. Elizabeth just had time to see her tall, elegant silhouette on the porch, the fluttering of her pale gray dress.

What did she mean by 'I shall be thinking of you'? And for the whole time of the ball? This final detail was enough

to make one uneasy, like a warning of some invisible surveillance. There were times when that woman annoyed her.
In her memory, however, she could see again that handsome, serious face, the depth of the gaze that never left her
throughout their conversation. She used to go to balls when
she was young. A strange admission that did not quite fit in
with the image Elizabeth was forming of her. Aunt Laura . . .
just Laura, dancing . . .

She shrugged her shoulders and got undressed. The shy
and steady little song of the tree-frogs reverberated softly. It
was a rather melancholy sound. Elizabeth was getting used
to it and listened out for it after the long, strident grating of
the cicadas.

In her nightdress now, she hesitated about getting into
bed, not feeling at all like sleep. There was a range of
dressing gowns in her wardrobe. She took the simplest one,
of white silk, then went to look at herself in the mirror.
White suited her, but she wondered for the hundredth time
whether she was as pretty as the others, all the other girls,
the Dimwood ones, and especially the Savannah ones. She
had been told that she would grow more beautiful in time.
Would she have to wait months and months? When would
she have a *beau*? In the light of the oil lamp, the gold of her
hair was aflame with a kind of splendour that she found
somewhat reassuring, but no one was there to see her, to
admire her . . . She sighed.

Finally, and, as if regretfully, she put out the lamp and
went to bed. She wanted to carry on with her thoughts in
the dark, but she slid almost immediately into sleep.

42

T he following day promised to be one of chaos. No other
word could describe this frenzied panic. Everybody was

going in and out of rooms in a crush that resembled some lunatic's pastime. People wanted to see if there was any change in the decorations, and the servants who were being hindered in their work, finally ran off to complain in the smoking room where William Hargrove was holding counsel with his two sons.

Uncle Josh, who was directing operations, had to take matters in hand. Having gathered everyone together on the porch, he advised the ladies to go on a sight-seeing carriage ride round the district or go for a nature walk in the great avenue. As for the boys and girls, they were ordered to spread themselves out through the countryside, on foot or on horseback, as they wished.

Judging his little band of musicians to be too countrified for what he hoped would be a memorable occasion, Uncle Josh dismissed them, not without elaborate compensation, and had a professional orchestra hastily summoned from Savannah. Many of its members had shown their worth at Uncle Charlie's, and they all knew by heart Lanner's waltzes which were all the rage in Vienna, Paris and London. They came by night and were put up at the house of the steward, who was somewhat refractory, but Uncle Josh used gold to close his mouth.

Finally, as the light was fading, the guests arrived. Gigs and carriages lined up behind the house, while ladies in pastel-colored outfits entered via the principal door on the same level as the park. With their crinolines spread out, they moved forward like giant flowers, mingling with the black suits of the men, like elegant crows. They were welcomed by all the Hargroves with the necessary exclamations. There arose from the whole group a kind of confused clamor, which at a distance was reminiscent of the noise that a well-bred aviary might have made.

Out of a concern for politeness, the young officers gave pride of place to this wave of civilian elegance, and so their appearance in the drawing room was all the more dazzling. The prestige of a well-cut uniform, with gold braid on navy-blue cloth, was already wreaking havoc in the classic manner. Having come close to war, however briefly, this conferred a hint of heroism to their military bearing, so dear to those who will never have to fight.

The guests were received in a vast, round drawing room, which had not been in use for many years, except for substantial celebrations. It was a green and gold model of harmonious simplicity, as favoured in England under George II. Padded seats were arranged around the edge of the room, but nobody was thinking of sitting down for the moment. Whether they were young or old, the ladies wore on their hands and at their necks emeralds, sapphires and rubies that would be the envy of the royal courts of Europe. Elizabeth, whose person was adorned with not a single jewel, was letting herself be naively dazzled, as at Savannah, by this display of wealth which, in spite of everything, she found strangely showy. She felt lost in this crowd, and was playing hide-and-seek with Uncle Josh, who was looking for her in order to introduce her. A venerable old lady, whose withered bosom was dripping with diamonds, managed to pin her to the spot for a moment, but the English girl succeeded in taking flight, and, as she was looking for Minnie, happened on Susanna, to whom she said:

'Be nice, I don't want to stay here, get me out. I'm not dressed . . .'

'You're ravishing. I'm the unhappy one, I hate dancing . . . especially with soldiers.'

Several sub-lieutenants began to hover around them. One of them in particular wanted to come up to Elizabeth. His large, wide-apart eyes made him look like a schoolboy on holiday, and he smiled with an irresistible kindness that obliged the young girl to look at him. She shook her head and stammered in embarrassment:

'I'm sorry . . . I believe I guess . . . but I do not dance.'

And smiling as well, she turned away and sought Susanna's hand:

'Shall we go away from here?'

But Susanna did not answer.

A young woman of delicate beauty came up quite close to Elizabeth and said with a smile:

'Excuse me for interrupting you, but your delightful English accent is the reason. Would it be too indiscreet to enquire if you are not Miss Escridge?'

As she spoke these words, she assumed a false air of mystery, as if she were unveiling some secret. Her brown hair fell in light curls around her face, brightening the whiteness of her skin. From between long, black eyelashes, violet-colored eyes sought out the gaze of Elizabeth, who was lowering her head in a sudden fit of shyness. The voice that was speaking to her was not lacking in a certain singular charm; gentle, and at the same time frail, as if it might have snapped all at once. Similarly, her extremely slender features spoke of delicate health. She was also dressed in white, with just a hint of pale blue, and her only adornment was a magnificent sapphire embellishing her bosom in its generously low-cut frock, in the Parisian fashion.

'I am indeed Elizabeth Escridge,' the girl finally said in resignation.

'And I am Jennie Boulton,' the lady with violet eyes said gaily. 'My brother is somewhere in the crowd. I hope you will not refuse to dance with him.'

'Oh, I dance so badly . . .'

As they spoke, neither of them noticed the martyred face that Susanna was turning towards Jennie Boulton. The latter noticed it by chance, while looking right and left to see where her brother was:

'Oh, Susanna,' she said distractedly, 'good evening. What a charming mauve dress . . . I'll leave you both. You absolutely must meet my brother, Miss Escridge. It's his first visit to Dimwood, and he is undoubtedly going through the nightmare of introductions. I'll be straight back. Don't run off, for Heaven's sake. He has heard about you, Elizabeth, and wants to meet you at all costs.'

She disappeared immediately like a phantom. Susanna seized Elizabeth's hand.

'Did you see?' she asked in a voice made hoarse with grief. 'She barely looked at me . . .'

'Well? I don't understand . . .'

'Oh, you don't understand anything, not anything . . . I'm going to try and leave, it's too painful.'

These words were still on her lips when Uncle Josh appeared in front of the two girls.

'Don't stay there in a corner,' he said to them, 'into the middle of the room, quickly! People want to meet you, Elizabeth. Why that long face, Susanna? It's for all of you that this party is being given.'

Susanna looked at her father tearfully.

'I don't feel well . . .'

But her voice was immediately drowned by a clap of thunder. In the next room, a melodious outburst announced the ball. Uncle Josh took Elizabeth and Susanna by the hand and dragged them off to where, all chattering having ceased, soldiers were bowing gauchely to ladies, and partners were being selected amidst good-humored confusion. About as many civilians as officers were competing for favors, and the English girl, weaving her way from one group to the next, began to look for her sub-lieutenant from earlier on. She was displeased to see him accompanying a middle-aged woman with an imperial profile, sumptuously adorned with emeralds. A little mustachioed lieutenant tried to pursue the fugitive Elizabeth. She crossed the whole drawing room and stopped short in front of a tall officer, who was talking to one of the prettiest girls, her pale blond hair piled up on the top of her head like a crown. Her dark blue eyes were half closed as if she were already plunged deep in happiness, while her conquest, who bowed towards her from time to time, was casting looks of impatient curiosity about him. His face appeared to Elizabeth very noble, less on account of the features, which were perfectly regular, than for the blue eyes in which an almost regal power to dominate could be made out. He was walking unhurriedly, with that pride characteristic of officers, and not without a disdainful suppleness. He noticed Elizabeth standing still in front of him, and with an amused air he asked her in a very warm, good-natured voice:

'You seem to be looking for someone, young lady. May I help you in your search?'

The English girl shook her head in terror and fled.

'Who was that?' the officer asked the blonde beauty leaning immodestly on his shoulder.

'No idea, I've never seen her before.'

The music became softer, like a caress in the Viennese manner, with that trace of melancholy that presages sentimentality.

Two steps divided the drawing room from the large entrance hall, where three long tables draped in white offered for inspection everything that hunger and greed might desire, but the guests were imperceptibly speeding up the pace in the opening bars of the waltz, and it would have seemed ridiculous to stop.

Quite in spite of herself, Elizabeth felt herself caught up in the crowd that she was seeking to flee, and suddenly a strong arm gripped her round the waist. She saw that she was the prey of a dashing young officer, who raised his eyebrows as if in reaction to some enormous surprise:

'Don't you think it's amazing? I am ignorant of your name, as you are of mine, and here we are, dancing together!'

He had an impertinent, pretty face and she could only smile.

'You are terribly sure of yourself,' she told him.

'Aren't I? Everyone tells me so. It's a bad fault, which I hope never to be cured of.'

The orchestra cut short this banter. The waltz was getting faster, and in its supremacy, it caught up the couples in a gentle dizziness. It was not the impetuous whirlwind that Elizabeth had experienced in Savannah, where the champagne had had its effect on the dancers before they had taken a step. In the great drawing room at Dimwood, respectability had not yet fallen prey to such headiness, but intoxication was doing its work with a delicious slyness. The ladies' feet barely touched the ground, sliding towards the abyss, when they rose up again light-headedly, fell back down, and floated off again in complete abandon.

Obliged by their age to remain apart from this voluptuous entertainment, the mothers, in their lace bonnets and dull taffeta dresses, walked with confident and worthy step towards the buffet. To start with, they considered the three tables with a hint of disapproval. Could the Hargroves shoulder the burden of such expense? The word 'extravagance' hovered on their lips, then they discreetly tasted one delicious morsel after another. They were offered a glass of Chateau Talbot and did not refuse. With appetite aroused, they allowed themselves to be tempted by treacherous little wild strawberry tarts and other sweetmeats of a similar kind and of amazing variety. As one of these ladies perceptively remarked, all tastes were catered for, and this earned their unreserved admiration. Soon a good dozen plates had been emptied, only to be immediately replaced, 'as if truly by a miracle', declared a venerable grandmother with shaky hands.

For as long as the waltz lasted, they made up for what they called the fatigue of the journey. So as not to be caught in the act of laying waste the trays, they withdrew before the final bars and returned sedately to the round drawing room, where they sat down on the padded seats and fanned themselves with palms while swapping comments.

'Obviously,' said one of them as she wiped the corner of her mouth with a minute cambric handkerchief, 'the expense is considerable, but they have daughters to marry off, and if only one of the four were to be fixed up, it would be worth all the cost.'

'Do you see four of them?' said a smiling little old lady, whose face was lost in the depths of an enormous bonnet with lace flaps. 'For my part, I number five of them, with that mysterious English girl, whom all the young men are looking at a great deal.'

The conversation suddenly became more lively.

'That little blonde doesn't belong to the family.'

'It would be vexing to see her carry off the prize.'

'What prize are you talking about? Apart from my two sons, I can only see fortuneless whipper-snappers . . .'

'. . . but with good breeding. Old Hargrove will have to round up the dowry, and the happy winner, once returned to civilian life, will find himself in the horrible situation of having to work.'

'Work! What are you thinking of? To work is to lose one's rank.'

'Wrong. He can become a barrister or professor without cheapening himself.'

'Perhaps, but to what desperate solutions our aristocracy sees itself reduced . . . Work . . .'

'I don't call that imposing character with such a proud look a whipper-snapper.'

'Lieutenant Boulton? A newcomer to Dimwood, but well known in Savannah. He's the catch all dream of. Rich and perhaps of royal blood . . .'

'On the wrong side of the blankets,' barked several voices.

'See for yourselves! He's a Tudor. Haven't you noticed that people instinctively step aside when he passes?'

'Not especially young, your Tudor. A good five and twenty years chalked up.'

'Not so loud, ladies. We can be heard; they're all at the buffet. With what shocking greed they're demolishing the pyramids of sandwiches.'

'Where are the good manners of the old days?'

'Yes, indeed. We would have been whipped for such gluttony.'

At the buffet, where everything had been restored to normal, a polite commotion reigned, close to being a scuffle. Glasses of champagne were offered to the men and to the ladies if they wished. Not one of them refused, and soon the gaiety became exuberant, while plates were emptied with a speed verging on the prodigious. That very formal, respectable behavior that had survived the languor of the waltz gave way now to that familiarity that passes for dangerous. Couples moved away from the buffet in order to say all kinds of interesting things to each other in some corner.

Towering head and shoulders over the crowd of guests, Lieutenant Boulton praised the champagne that had come straight from the wine cellars of Rheims, and insisted on being introduced to the mysterious Elizabeth. The latter had attempted several escapes, in league with Susanna, but Uncle Josh, who was keeping an eye on everything, had brought them back almost by force to the buffet.

Elizabeth, blushing, appeared before Lieutenant Boulton who bowed and, to the surprise of all present, could find only the most banal words to say to her. He had barely looked at her when his eyes wandered elsewhere, and his gaze fell straight on the unfortunate Susanna, painfully shy, lowering her eyelids and turning her head away, seeking in vain to hide behind Elizabeth. She was pale with emotion and leaned against the young Englishwoman. Tears all ready to burst forth brightened her shining pupils.

With a feeling of horror, she saw this imperiously masculine man take a step towards her, then bow very low, announcing himself in a respectful voice:

'Lieutenant Boulton.'

Susanna tried to smile, not knowing how to answer. So

great was her agitation that she had almost forgotten her own name.

'Would you do me the honor of granting me the next waltz?'

She murmured that she danced too badly and he pretended not to hear:

'Thank you,' he said.

He bent down a little towards her and, as if in a nightmare, she could see only the pale blue of his tender eyes.

A moment later the orchestra vigorously struck up a military tune with a devilish rhythm. The champagne having relieved them of their remaining scruples, the ladies gave themselves up with melting eyes to this unexpected pillage. Lieutenant Boulton carried off his victim like a feather, her head fluttering against the square shoulder of her abductor. She had no idea how much more beautiful her despair made her look. A pearly paleness gave her face the delicacy of an expensive cameo, but between her long, black eyelids, her eyes seemed on the point of expressing revulsion, and her partner believed he could read in them a desperate admission of love, whereas she was hovering on the verge of fainting.

The music was now *accelerando*, announcing a frenzied gallop, enough to take the breath away, then gliding suddenly into a slower, caressing passage. That was the moment for sentimental daring and heavy heartbeats. The fathers and mothers of large families were, needless to say, counting on these traps, so innocent in appearance. But this dreaming did not last, and the waltz came jovially to an end with a sober, everyday jollity.

It was then that Lieutenant Boulton, not without a squeeze of the hand and a sigh from the depths of his soul, moved away from Susanna, who could barely stand upright. Boulton entrusted her to the care of Elizabeth, who, suspecting something disagreeable, had headed in her direction.

'What's the matter?' she asked her as she guided her towards a corner of the buffet. 'You are quite pale.'

'I hate that man, I don't want to see him again. Where is he?'

'I don't know, he went to the back of the room and disappeared.'

Elizabeth made her sit down and gave her a glass of orangeade, but Susanna would not touch it.

She said, 'I should like to be dead.'

The last waltz was short. Slow and insipid to start with, it became more and more insidious, building up gradually to a tempestuous and shattering conclusion, a diplomatic way of turning the guests out of doors.

Lieutenant Boulton's absence was noted. That of Susanna went unnoticed. Only Elizabeth knew that she had locked herself in her room, like some hunted beast. In the reception rooms, there followed minutes of perplexity that seemed endless. How could one take leave of the hosts if they were not there? And where were they? What was to become of the farewell ceremony with its thanks and proliferation of politeness? They went to the cloakroom, got ready, and waited. The men were standing with their silk hats in their hands, the women in their black or gray taffeta capes.

The delightful Miss Jennie Boulton found a means of coming up to Elizabeth, taking hold of both her hands, and in a waft of perfume said mysteriously into her ear:

'Never mind, my charming little one, life is full of disappointments, but you won't be short of *beaux*.'

Having murmured these Sibylline words, she disappeared like a fairy.

In order to prevent all these intrigued and chattering people from becoming impatient, the conductor of the orchestra had the good idea of getting the musicians to play the serenade from *Die Entführung aus dem Serail*, the magic of which took instant effect. Mozart silenced everybody, and when the piece was ended, someone said: 'Encore!' The orchestra struck up again, and once more ears were strained to those soft sounds that spoke of nothing but escape and liberty, when suddenly there was a distant if stifled cry.

This sound, that fitted in so well with a scene from the opera, made the listeners shudder. The orchestra fell silent. People asked questions, quietly at first, prolonging the *sotto voce*, then louder. Something was going to happen, they were waiting for it, as for the curtain to rise in a theatre.

43

*S*uddenly seized with terror, Elizabeth left the room. She was trembling for Susanna, and wondered what she should do. Something held her back from going up to the first floor. A much stronger instinct directed her towards the porch.

As she crossed the hallway, she reached the small entrance and pushed the door, imagining she was emerging from a prison. Closing her eyes for a moment, she breathed in the cool air on which floated the fragrance of the pine trees and flowers that surrounded the house. The song of the tree-frogs deepened the silence of the night rather than disturbing it. For a few seconds she experienced the elusive presence of an inexplicable happiness. She was suddenly wrenched from the world and transported to a region where peace lasted for ever, and when she came back to her senses, for that mysterious joy did not last, she had the impression that her soul was giving way beneath a weight of heavy sadness. She was taken with the desire to seek out a little of that lost joy close to the magnolia tree that had welcomed her that first evening, at the top of the steps, and she took a few steps in that direction, then stopped abruptly.

Somebody was there leaning on the rail, quite close to the magnolia. A man. Tall and dressed in dark colors, he held in his hand a riding crop that he was tapping against his boots. When Elizabeth appeared he bowed slightly, then said beneath his breath:

'Don't be afraid, Miss Escridge.'

She drew back. He continued to tap the leather of his boots with his crop.

'I'm Jonathan,' he said naturally, almost with indifference. 'Does that mean anything to you?'

'I don't know,' she stammered. 'Yes, I think so, but I must go in, excuse me.'

'I'll wait,' he said.

Out of a scruple of politeness, she left the door half open and ran off. Jonathan . . . the one they did not wish her to see, the one who had gone around the house. She decided to say nothing about it and ran to the hallway.

To her great surprise, it was empty. Everybody had gone back into the ballroom. In the adjoining room, with the doors wide open, Uncle Josh was standing on the platform making a speech. The orchestra had withdrawn to make room for him, and he was speaking up in a voice that was half serious and half jovial. Near him were standing William Hargrove, Aunt Augusta and Uncle Douglas. There was Aunt Emma too, sitting on a chair, and Susanna, also seated, with her head bent a little to one side. Finally, behind her, towering over the assembled company like a monarch, was Lieutenant Boulton.

This whole group provoked a strange malaise, as much by its seriousness as by its total immobility, with the exception of Uncle Josh who seemed agitated. His white lace ruff contrasted with the severity of his black suit of studied elegance, and despite polite smiles, he was very pale:

'Once more,' he was saying, 'we beg our dear guests to excuse our absence, which must have seemed inexplicable.' A little forced laugh was heard at this point. 'We have to admire the charming wiliness of this human life of ours. Happiness was being hatched in secret before our eyes, and we had not the least notion of it.'

Here he laughed again just as unnaturally as before, then he continued joyfully:

'I have the honor and enormous pleasure to announce to you the engagement of my dear daughter Susanna to Lieutenant Boulton of the 20th Regiment of Heavy Artillery.'

A great 'Ah!' rose up to the ceiling, then bravos mingled with congratulations.

'I propose,' Uncle Josh proclaimed, 'that we drink to the health of the happy engaged couple.'

There followed a festive tumult, amidst a great buzzing of exclamations and comments. The Hargroves came down into the room, and there was another movement in the direction of the hall and its three miraculous buffets. The champagne went round again. In the general confusion, the family group was besieged on all sides, and they became separated from one another. Susanna, frighteningly pale, stood for a moment beneath the braided wing of her conqueror, while all around them, glasses were raised together, and a deafening hurrah reverberated through the now stuffy air.

The military gentlemen went *en masse* to besiege their victorious brother-in-arms, while the ladies and the civilians pressed towards his blessed bride-to-be, who stammered in a strangulated voice words bereft of sense. People were pushing and shoving a little in good-humored disarray, polite manners having been put to flight. Hands were squeezed, and kisses fluttered over lips that had not been expecting them.

It was then that Susanna managed to slip through the crowd as far as the small drawing room off the hall where Elizabeth, who had been watching out for her, managed to get to her with the feline agility of youth.

Susanna pushed the door and threw herself, sobbing, into the arms of the young Englishwoman:

'It's not fair,' she groaned.

'But why did you accept?'

'You can't imagine. Papa was horrid. He came to look for me in my room. He forced his way in. He told me that it was an unexpected piece of luck for the whole family, that he ordered me to say yes, that to disobey one's father was to disobey God, and that to disobey God meant Hell, I was afraid . . . I've never seen him like that . . . He was red, I thought he was going to kill me . . .'

She had no time to say any more. A forceful arm opened the door.

It was Uncle Douglas. He looked shattered and, leaning towards Susanna, he kissed her:

'Be reasonable, my girl,' he said, 'it's your happiness that we wish for.'

Uncle Josh loomed up behind him. His ruff was askew, his forehead and his cheeks were bright pink. In a voice that was both low and firm he said:

'Some day, Susanna, you'll thank Providence on your knees for what it's doing to save you. Follow me immediately and join your fiancé who is looking for you everywhere. Behave like a Southern lady.'

Grabbing her by the hand, he dragged her off with him as she cast a last, distressed look in the direction of Elizabeth.

It was getting late, and a semblance of order was returning to the hallway. In groups of two and three, the guests were taking their leave of the Hargroves, and showering compliments on the queen of the ball, a somewhat dumb-struck Susanna, who was making a heroic effort to play her role as a proper Southern lady, while her true nature would have induced her to scream in rage.

Lieutenant Boulton was puzzled by that face, so transformed by pain.

'Our dear Susanna is very sensitive,' Uncle Josh was repeating to him, 'any emotional upheaval makes her cry, such as this evening's great surprise, do you understand?'

Lieutenant Boulton protested that he understood perfectly and gave the smile of a man who has understood nothing.

Quite in spite of himself, Uncle Josh took on the appearance of a clumsy card player, cheating for the first time:

'It does happen,' he explained, 'that excess of happiness can provoke tears. Such cases have been known.'

Boulton nodded, his masculine vanity deliciously flattered:

'Your daughter is greatly in love,' he said in a voice full of conviction.

With the last guests gone, the great doors on the ground floor were closed, and the Hargroves, yawning a little, went into the round drawing room where they dropped on to the seats. Only Aunt Emma remained standing: feeling inspired, she wanted to say something noble. In a rustling of puce-colored taffeta and pious thoughts, she headed for Susanna, who was in a state of collapse:

'Susanna,' she said, 'Heaven . . .'

In one leap, Susanna was on her feet:

'Oh, Aunt Emma,' she said forcefully, 'have pity! I'm dying of fatigue and am going up to bed.'

These words were spoken so resolutely that no one moved, and she left the room with rapid steps.

There was a moment of bewilderment, then William Hargrove made a gesture stopping Uncle Josh, who looked as if he were going to go after her.

'You must leave her,' he said sadly, 'she's unhappy.'

'But I want to know why,' exclaimed Uncle Josh, 'I want to get to the bottom of it,'

'Don't try, she's in pain. She has a right to silence.'

'The best match in the whole of Georgia!' declared Uncle

Josh. 'It was beyond our hopes. If ever she falls in love with some little whipper-snapper with no future such as you meet with in these parts . . .'

'Have no fears. And she has said yes, isn't that enough for you?'

'But an engagement can be broken off, Father.'

'Josh,' William Hargrove said softly, 'go to bed.'

At that moment, a servant in red livery announced that Mr Jonathan Armstrong wished to present his respects to Mass'r William.

Immediately the master of Dimwood and Douglas stood up. Josh was already on his feet, and the three men looked at each other with the same worried expression.

'We can't keep him waiting, he is of a much more ancient family than ours,' said Douglas.

'I'm obliged to see him,' said William Hargrove, 'but where? All the rooms have been switched about in the changes for the ball, but never mind.'

And speaking to the servant, he said:

'Show him into the ballroom.'

'That man brings bad luck,' said Aunt Emma when the servant had gone. 'I don't want to see him.'

'You won't see him,' said William Hargrove. 'I shall take him to my study. Josh and Douglas, you'll come with me. The reason for his visit is all too clear. He's trying to ruin us before the due date in '52. He won't succeed.'

'Charlie Jones wouldn't permit it,' said Uncle Josh.

As they spoke, they headed for the hall. Elizabeth, who had not moved since the beginning of this exchange, followed them with her eyes. Her curiosity was such that she had the impression of stepping outside of her body and walking alongside them. One or two seconds went by, and then she watched the man she had seen on the porch come into the hall.

Slim and tall, he was wearing an autumnal brown jacket and chamois-colored breeches. His crop hung from his wrist. His thick black hair highlighted the paleness of the face in which she could not make out the features. He did not seem handsome to her. Her disappointment was extreme. Nonetheless, she admired the unaffected gracefulness of his walk. He greeted William Hargrove with a deep and courtly bow.

The four men were now in William Hargrove's room, that Elizabeth had seen only once and hoped never to see again.

On the table laden with books and papers, a large oil lamp shed a peaceful light. The long rows of books in old bindings covered almost the whole of the walls, and the gilt spines gleaming softly on the dark hide. These studious surroundings fostered calmness. Perhaps on account of this, not one of them ventured to speak. They had all sat down on black wooden chairs, the great carved backs of which were reminiscent of England in the previous century. Everything summoned up forcefully a past civilization, and the present meeting did nothing to dispel that impression.

Taking a rather nonchalant attitude, Jonathan Armstrong expressed himself slowly and disdainfully. His behavior was characterized by an indefinable manner which the Americans used the French word *hauteur* to describe: an arrogant, studied politeness. Where he was sitting, the half-light mitigated the defects in his thin, wilful face. A small, delicately molded nose, a well-defined, slightly mocking mouth might have conveyed a certain handsomeness, if his features as a whole had been better spaced out. The blue-gray eyes, however, made up for everything by the splendor of their gaze.

'Permit me to remind you, sir, that nothing in our agreements obliges you to part with this sum if you consider it too great. I was never taught to bargain. If you prefer, I withdraw my offer.'

'Maintain it or withdraw it as you like,' answered William Hargrove. 'If you maintain it, the sum will be paid to you at my bank in Macon within twenty-four hours. I'm quite prepared to sign the necessary papers on the spot, but I speak in your interest.'

'My mind is made up, sir. I appreciate good advice, but there is nothing for it but to act.'

'Alright. I shall ask you for your signature, which will ratify the agreement, but remember: successively you have made over to me the marshes, the forest called the Wood of the Damned, then thirty more acres of cotton fields. You retain the great avenue, the land extending from the house to the river as far as the edge of the forest, known as the

Indians' Wood, and finally the most decorative part of the whole property, the gardens known as the maze. A house with no garden . . .'

'That's my business, Mr Hargrove. Are you or are you not willing to purchase the maze from me? I am not speaking to you as a beggar, but as the future occupant of this house where we find ourselves.'

Without taking him up on that remark, William Hargrove drew from his pocket a bunch of keys which he held out to Douglas. The latter, from the other side of the table, opened a drawer from which he took a voluminous box file, which he put down in front of him. Papers and books were pushed to one side to make room. Firstly a plan of the whole Dimwood estate was unfolded. A great streak of red ink bearing the signature of Jonathan Armstrong marked each portion of land sold off to William Hargrove, with the date of each transaction. No speech could have recorded better the downfall of a family. The four men, standing near the table, looked silently at this drawing, streaked with crimson in all directions. Finally, without a word, William Hargrove placed his finger on the rectangle which contained the maze.

'Well,' said Jonathan Armstrong in a neutral tone of voice, 'I see it. What are we waiting for to complete matters?'

'Have you thought it over thoroughly?' asked William Hargrove.

'Sir, my decision is taken and we are wasting time.'

William Hargrove opened another drawer and took out an imposing wallet of dark red leather, from which he drew out a check, ornamented with English-style cursive script. His two sons and Jonathan Armstrong drew back, and he sat down to write.

'I'm waiting,' he said patiently.

Jonathan Armstrong's slow and detached voice dropped the figure:

'One thousand.'

On that piece of embossed paper, the goose quill wrote out the figures in words with a little scratching noise, which seemed to fill up the silence. Then the check, duly signed and dated, was handed to Jonathan Armstrong, who took it and bowed. A new goose quill was given to him and, having dipped it in red ink, he signed the deed in a tall, proud hand.

Then two more signatures, witnessing the transaction, were added to the deed. That was the final act of this encounter that came to an end with such ceremony. The master of Dimwood led Jonathan Armstrong back to the porch, where they wished each other good-night, after which William Hargrove went back into the house.

Jonathan Armstrong went down the porch steps and stopped by the magnolia, whose perfume was hovering on the still air. There he stood and waited.

44

*B*ack in his library, William Hargrove found his two anxious sons.

'You gave him a considerable sum,' said Douglas.

'Perhaps, but I was expecting much more. Everything is still well balanced and he is the loser. He will never consent to live in a house whose grounds no longer belong to him. Nor will she. That woman has made him lose his head completely.'

He fell silent and sat down at the table scattered with papers.

'I'm sorry for Jonathan,' he said. 'I find his vanity exasperating, but he is not a bad man.'

'You are weary, Father,' said Joshua, 'you must rest.'

'It's true, but I can't stop thinking about her. It would have taken me ten minutes to fix everything, to set everything to rights. To think that she was here, and that Miss Llewelyn was unable to keep her here . . .'

'She couldn't,' said Douglas. 'If there is anyone in the world who cannot bear Annabel, it's the Welshwoman — but she wants this house.'

'Oh, I would have given it to her!' exclaimed William Hargrove. 'She would have married, been part of society.'

Joshua and Douglas protested at these words, then both spoke at once:

'You surely wouldn't think of that! Reflect on what you're saying, Father.'

'I know, I know, but she's a woman of rare beauty, she's exquisite, refined.'

'We're not in Europe,' said Douglas, 'nor in the North. Here, in the South . . .'

'It's too hard,' groaned William Hargrove, 'we're all too hard.'

'We're not complaining,' said Joshua. 'With her we run the risk of scandal, and a ridiculous scandal at that. Then living here with her, no. None of us would tolerate it, except . . .'

'Enough!' William Hargrove exclaimed suddenly. 'You're making me suffer to no purpose. You don't know the reasons I have for loving that woman.'

'Forgive us, Father,' said Joshua, 'and let us instead rejoice over the engagement of Susanna and Lieutenant Boulton. Marriage will save her.'

At that moment, someone went by on the porch. The light of the lamp filtered through the shutters, and a silhouette was visible for one or two seconds.

'Don't speak too loud,' said Joshua under his breath, 'we might be overheard.'

'It can only be Miss Llewelyn,' said William Hargrove, 'she listens in and spies.'

Douglas went over to the window and very gently opened the shutters a little. He saw a woman moving away like a shadow.

'It's Laura,' he whispered.

William Hargrove shuddered.

'Leave me alone,' he said.

Far away, at the other end of the verandah, Elizabeth was walking back and forth in her room, unable to make up her mind to get undressed and go to bed. After the noise of the ball, the orchestra, the chattering of the guests, the fluid song of the tree-frogs seemed to be trying hard to tell her something unfathomable, and she listened to it in spite of herself, for it seemed to lighten her heart, but she was disappointed. Several times she looked at herself in the glass above the fireplace to see if she was as pretty as people sometimes told her. She even stood on a chair to get a better overall impression of herself. Could she, for example, compete with Miss Jennie Boulton? The mirror told her clearly: 'Yes and No.' She sighed.

As far as *beaux* were concerned, she had only been able to mobilize the army in the person of the little sub-lieutenant, who, moreover, after one round of the waltz, had left the English girl to take his smiles and his compliments elsewhere. She was thirsting for compliments, for tenderness, and quite simply for love, but she did not admit as much to herself. As for Susanna, she had conquered the soldier who was the most admired, but what tears her victory had brought. That was a mystery. Elizabeth did not fully understand. Without feeling the least attraction for that conceited character, she could well see that in the eyes of parents with daughters to marry he would be much sought after, yet Susanna wanted nothing to do with him. He was presentable for all that, and as one had to get married . . . She, for her part, trembled at the thought of remaining an old maid, but dreamt of an ideal marriage with some creature who was at one and the same time a ravishing young man and an angel. Lieutenant Boulton was not sufficiently repulsive to justify the disgust of his intended . . .

For her, the foreigner, the outsider, it had been a rather humiliating evening. She felt that she was being left to one side, and that no one was interested in her. No one, that is, except the ill-fated Jonathan Armstrong for the space of two minutes in the darkness of the porch. She had caught sight of his strange face in the distance. Instinctively she put him out of her mind, but with a sort of perverse obstinacy, he kept coming back.

'Don't be afraid, Miss Escridge . . .'

She thought she could hear the sound of that barely audible voice in the solitude of her room, a voice that was half respectful and half mocking. And then:

'I am Jonathan Armstrong . . .'

Close to the magnolia, her magnolia with whom she sometimes spoke in secret, less than fifteen paces from her room. Finally those last words that seemed to have no meaning:

'I'll wait.'

The absurd desire to go as far as the porch came to her, to that place where the insignificant dialogue had taken place. A little girl's whim, she told herself, making fun of herself and dispelling her vague scruples. Inquisitive, yes, she knew she was inquisitive — and then?

She gently pushed the shutters and ventured to look in the direction of her neighbor's room, Aunt Laura's. No light. She was undoubtedly asleep.

Was it forbidden to take the air in the gallery, late as it was? She slid out on tiptoe, and headed for the magnolia.

Of course there was no one there. The moonlight fell on the tree, carving out each flower and making the long black leaves shine. Elizabeth drew close to the great, fragrant mass. Standing still with her eyes closed, she gave herself up completely to the magic of that perfume, where joy and sadness mingled, when suddenly a voice made her heart bound . . . It was only a whisper coming up from down below, but she heard it:

'Don't be afraid, Miss Escridge.'

Petrified, she felt like running away, and yet she did not move. How could she not have recognized that same phrase!

'You have nothing to fear,' the voice continued. 'It's Jonathan speaking to you. Come closer. I've something to tell you.'

She got a grip on herself and murmured:

'I have nothing to say to you, Mr Armstrong. Excuse me, I'm going in.'

'Call me Jonathan and don't go in. I shall stay where I am, I shan't touch you, I'm simply asking you to come closer so I can see you. How can you refuse?'

She did not answer, but hesitated, then she moved stealthily ahead and leaned forward a little, the white flowers brushing against her face. Less than six feet below the rail, Jonathan's head was raised up towards her.

With one hand, the young man swept aside the foliage, and the light of the moon struck him mercilessly, full in the face.

She looked at him and remained dumbstruck. As if he were reading her thoughts, he smiled and said:

'I'm not handsome, am I?'

'I didn't say that,' she said animatedly.

'I am saying so. But we're not playing at Romeo and Juliet, although the moon, the balcony and the whole set-up are propitious. Admit that I have a strange face and that it displeases you.'

'I admit nothing, there is nothing to admit,' she said, feeling more and more disturbed, for the voice, ironical at first, was becoming almost plaintive in its slowness.

'Lean to one side then, towards me. I shall see you for one minute, that's all I ask, there's no harm in that.'

'One minute and I shall go in.'

'Yes, I shall stay where I am, I promise you. What do you have to fear?'

As he spoke, he kept his eyelids half closed, as if the brightness of the nocturnal light dazzled him. It was that and the whispering of all these sentences that worried Elizabeth most, while at the same time keeping her riveted to the spot. She was possessed by an insane curiosity to hear what he was going to tell her. She took a step to one side, and, in her turn, brushed aside the leaves hiding her.

'Elizabeth,' he said.

She moved her head forward a little. Their eyes met and she felt that she was lost. From the depths of those pale eyes, there rose up an appeal, terrible in its forcefulness.

She thought confusedly of souls in distress, perched on the edge of the abyss that cuts them off from life.

In a voice so low that it was like a breath, he said:

'Listen to me, Elizabeth.'

Despite the terror that was choking her, she admired his eyes that were pale and full of light, and in which mortal anxiety could be discerned.

'I saw you just now through the half-open door. Your innocence, it takes only a glance to guess at that disturbing, wondrous presence. It puts you in danger.'

'In danger, why?'

He raised his head a little higher.

'The day will come when you will be looking for me, Elizabeth, and you won't find me.'

'Why are you saying these things?'

'I'm not here to make love to you. You will only love me when I'm far away. You don't love me now.'

'I haven't said anything,' she murmured, 'I don't understand . . .'

'You can't understand. Beware of all these boys and their formal politeness. They speak of love and don't know what it is. Wait. I'm going, Elizabeth.'

A word that the girl could not hold back slipped out:

'Why?'

'I couldn't bear to hear from your lips a word that I fear.'

'But I have no wish to hurt you.'

'Just say my name, and I shall take that away with me as a talisman. Say "Jonathan".'

With her heart pounding, she hesitated, then softly murmured:

'Jonathan.'

'Elizabeth, I shall always hear the sound of this voice speaking my name on this May night. Now say those words that will be like a cut from a knife, because what can never be must be brought to an end.'

'Why are you talking like that? You're frightening me . . .'

'Well, just say: "Jonathan, I shall never be able to love you."'

'I don't like what you're saying, I shall not say that.'

'Why, Elizabeth?'

'I don't know why, but I can't. Farewell, Jonathan.'

Casting these words almost aloud, she fled and returned to her room. There she fell fully dressed onto her bed, with her face buried in her pillow to stifle the sobs and, suddenly, just as in a faint, she fell into a chasm of dreamless sleep.

45

The days after a party are never without some shadow of frustration. Everyone had enjoyed themselves, and suddenly the boredom of country life resumed its reign. The waltzes, the music, the champagne were all being missed. The house was tidy. The drawing rooms and the hall could remember nothing. People yawned and suffered as before, each enclosed in his or her own personal and secret little tragedy.

Susanna wished to speak to no one and took her despair for solitary walks along the river, as far as the edge of the Indians' Wood. Sometimes she ventured quite a distance beneath the dark foliage of that place which had such a bad reputation, where the disturbing cry of some bird rang out from time to time. She wished that death would suddenly come and deliver her from herself. She suffered especially from the offhand way in which she and her freedom were being disposed of, just as one might in the case of an animal. She was going to belong to a man because her father wished it to be so. Penetrating a little further into the darkness of the forbidden woods, she entertained the wild hope that some lingering Seminole Indian would pierce her heart with a flint arrow, if only in order to plunge the family into the torments of guilty conscience. She would finally return home in time for dinner.

In the heart-rending pangs of first love, Elizabeth too sought refuge in solitude, but chose her bedroom as the scene of her suffering so that nothing might be noticed. She wavered between trembling hope and absolute despair. She did not know how to deal with her body in such circumstances.

This unfamiliar problem presented itself to her with an insistence verging on obsession. She did not cry, she simply wished not to exist. Jonathan would not come back, she believed that for certain, so if there were no Jonathan, there should be no Elizabeth either. But the body remained, with Elizabeth's head, Elizabeth's arms and legs, the chest and throat of Elizabeth, and all that was her: useless. She may well walk up and down in her room, in every possible direction, but for the first time in her life she thought she would die in her longing for the presence of a man, Jonathan. Repeating his name under her breath did not make him appear. She could find nothing else to help her. When he was close to her, among the foliage of the magnolia, she could have told him that she loved him, but she had only realized when it was too late, when she had said that crazy farewell. Now it was over. She had the feeling that she had plunged into the depths of his eyes, as if into a lake. She should have gone bravely down to him. A coward, she had been a coward. All those absurd questions that he was asking her meant one thing only. Her body knew it. So, *farewell Jonathan* was stupid. She had gone back several times at night to the place where he had stood — to see what? To see if he was still there? 'Fool,' she said to herself. And yet she went, leaning into the foliage, and with her arm out-stretched, her hand sought out in the void the face that was no longer there. Touch his face with her fingers . . . She could have done so. Only the face counted, the body was the presence, she could not conjure up any more detail, except for the arms clasping her to himself, she knew no more, nor as yet felt anything else. He had spoken mockingly of Romeo and Juliet, and for her that was what it was. She had read Shakespeare's play in the expurgated version frequently used by families. Juliet had not run away, but, like Juliet, she was keeping her love a secret, and she put in an appearance at every meal. Nobody knew.

One day, however, towards the end of the afternoon, Aunt Laura came to see her. Always serious and smiling at one and the same time and always graceful in her gray and white dress.

She made Elizabeth sit down next to her on the couch and took hold of her hands in a gesture of affection.

'Elizabeth,' she said, 'something is wrong. Do you under-stand what I mean?'

'No.'

'I was expecting that answer. All questioning is indiscreet, but I'm very fond of you and I can see that you are eating less and less.'

'It's too hot,' the girl said rather too readily, as if in self-defense.

'That's true, but you no longer talk at meals, I know you

have always been rather quiet . . .'

'Oh, yes, Aunt Laura. You are, too, I think.'

That was a direct hit, and Aunt Laura did not answer straight away.

'I am indeed, and have been for many years; it's even on account of that that I am undoubtedly the only person who can understand you. You're not happy at Dimwood.'

'That is so.'

'I won't ask any questions. What's the point? There is evidently something wrong.'

These last words made the blood rush to Elizabeth's face, and she said in her most precise, English voice:

'With all the respect I owe you, Aunt Laura, I shall not conceal the fact that I feel as ill at ease as if I were undergoing some interrogation. I don't know how you manage to ask questions without appearing to do so.'

It was the first time she had spoken to Aunt Laura with this brutal frankness. Her mother's words haunted her: 'Catholic, beware.'

Without the slightest movement, Aunt Laura turned pale and continued with a smile:

'I understand your annoyance, Elizabeth dear. You have nothing to fear from me, but it looks clear to me: you are in love.'

Elizabeth stood up abruptly:

'Aunt Laura,' she said, her eyes shining with anger, 'I don't know why you are speaking to me like this.'

The answer came in a calm tone of voice, but with a sadness that thoroughly bewildered the girl:

'Because I was in love myself at your age, and I never got over it. Even today, as I speak to you, I feel that the wound is still there and will not heal. Falling in love can be a great joy or a very great misfortune, but it's not our choice, do you see, it's a mystery.'

There was such nobility in her face when she spoke these words that Elizabeth felt ashamed:

'I didn't know,' she said at last. 'I'm sorry I spoke to you as I did.'

'No excuses, Elizabeth, you reacted like an Englishwoman. I would perhaps have done the same in your place. We're all English in this corner of the world. That's what the North will never understand. Come back and sit down.'

With her heart beating, Elizabeth resumed her place, and again Aunt Laura smiled at her.

'Above all,' she said, 'don't imagine I'm trying to find out things I shouldn't know. If you are in love, watch out. You might have danced with several young men that evening.'

'Only one, a little sub-lieutenant of no interest.'

'I'm rather sorry about that. They are all from quite good families. If it's someone who was there but not dancing, I tremble, and having said that, I've said all there is to be said. You are in danger, Elizabeth, if it's the man I'm thinking of. But perhaps you're not in love after all.'

'Alas!' sighed Elizabeth.

'Do you feel strong enough to leave Dimwood to spend a few months in Savannah at Uncle Charlie's? I could arrange it.'

'It's not worth it. He won't come back, I'm sure of it.'

'I know the man. If we're thinking of the same person, it's better for you to know that he is madly in love with the lady . . .'

She hesitated for a moment and closed her eyes.

' . . . a lady whom you haven't seen, and who came here with him one day in a carriage, while you were in Savannah.'

'The lady in white?'

'They told you . . . There is no point in thinking about him, Elizabeth. He is enjoying making you suffer, but it's not you he loves. Pray to Heaven that he won't come back. I have no right to know any more, but I shall think about you tonight.'

She was going to get up when Elizabeth told her, with uncharacteristic timidity:

'She must be extremely beautiful, that lady in white, for him to love her that much.'

'Extremely beautiful, yes,' said Aunt Laura.

There followed a brief silence, during which each was lost in her own thoughts. Elizabeth felt all the harshness of the humiliation she had brought upon herself. Aunt Laura seemed to be looking into the void, at some invisible face.

'She's an exquisite woman,' she said under her breath as if speaking to herself. 'The little veil she wears to protect her complexion has made her a mystery woman in people's minds, and it's absurd. Similarly the long white gloves to save her pretty hands from the sun. Everything about her is so delicate . . . You would like her if you could see her. One can't help it, but it's difficult to get to her.'

Never had Elizabeth seen such a surge of tenderness in Aunt Laura, and it came as a shock to her, as if she had come upon some secret she was not supposed to know. Finally, rather annoyed, she spoke out:

'If she is so beautiful, I suppose she is married.'

'No.'

'The man who came in the carriage with her is going to marry her?'

'Oh, no!'

That 'no', so categorical, made a flicker of hope gleam in the young Englishwoman's mind.

'If I have understood correctly, he is in love with her, but she is not in love with him.'

'That's more or less it.'

'So, perhaps he will marry someone else?' she asked naively.

Her thoughts could be read so clearly in her eyes that Aunt Laura leant towards her and kissed her.

'My dear,' she said, 'what are we playing at? For a quarter of an hour you've been talking to me about a man you do not wish to name, and for that quarter of an hour I have been listening to you, I have been aware of Jonathan Armstrong's face. I'm not asking you if he is the one in question, but if it is him, beware and flee. He can only bring about your unhappiness. I don't want to hurt you, but I can't hide the truth from you either, and truth is sometimes harsh.'

This speech, proffered in a very gentle voice, devastated Elizabeth's heart, bringing her to the brink of tears. She restrained herself, however, and as Aunt Laura stood up, she stood up too.

'At the present moment,' continued Aunt Laura, 'you don't love me, and you are cross with me.'

'No,' said Elizabeth coldly.

'Yes, but listen. When I was your age, if someone had spoken to me as I have spoken to you this evening, my fate would have been quite different, but there was no one, and you see before you the most unhappy of women.'

She had spoken with a kind of awful stillness, and her whole person seemed clothed in a majesty that cut her off from the world.

Shattered, the girl could only murmur:

'Aunt Laura . . .'

'It's alright,' said the latter as if to hold back any effusiveness, 'have a good night and remember . . . I'm going to try and sleep a little, but I will think about you as well.'

Without another word, she kissed Elizabeth and disappeared.

Left alone, Elizabeth got undressed, blew out the lamp and went to bed, but too many contradictory thoughts were colliding in her head for her to be able to sleep. Emotion, perplexity, irritation aroused by the mysterious phrase concerning the intention to think about her, all that had an unpleasantly disturbing effect on her. The name of Jonathan kept returning to her lips with an irresistible force, in a whisper that seemed like a call. She suddenly fell into sleep, and dreams took possession of her with the powerful strength of hallucination. She groaned and struggled. The door of her room opened gently and let through unknown people, who came up to her and looked at her, speaking some incomprehensible language. Suddenly her father leaned over her and said: 'It's our own language. The rest of you don't know it.' He spoke without moving his lips, and his words came forth from his motionless, ivory-colored face. She tried to cry out, and twisted the sheets around her. After a while, she felt the gentle caress of a hand on her forehead; it barely stroked her and then positioned itself with a cautious delicacy.

She woke up, and in the early-morning light recognized Betty's face.

'Don't be afraid,' the latter said, 'don't be afraid, Miss Lizbeth, there ain't nothing wrong.'

'Oh, what are you doing here, Betty?'

'I heard shouting.'

'Shouting? Did I shout? When?'

'In the middle of the night, I came . . .'

'Where did you sleep?'

'There, on the floor. You musn't be afraid, Miss Lizbeth.'

'On the floor, poor Betty. You must go, go and sleep.'

'No, I's goin' to stay with you now.'

Elizabeth asked if, in her sleep, she had said anything, and Betty began to speak a kind of gibberish to her, which she used as a refuge from unpleasant truths. It seemed dangerous to the girl to insist. Yet she could not resist the desire to know:

'Just answer one question: did I say somebody's name?'

'Oh, yes, Miss Lizbeth!'

'A lot? Often?'

'Yes.'

'Mr Jonathan?'

Silence.

'You won't tell anyone?'

'No, Miss Lizbeth.'

'You swear it on the Bible?'

'I ain't got no Bible, Miss Lizbeth.'

'Strange,' thought Elizabeth, 'but never mind . . .' and aloud:

'You don't like Mr Jonathan, Betty?'

'Don't nobody at Dimwood like Mass'r Jonathan.'

'Why, Betty? I want to know.'

'His two brothers.'

'I don't understand. What do you mean?'

She hesitated, then the answer came in a horrified whisper:

'They's in Hell.'

The words were followed by that furtive gesture which annoyed Elizabeth. Betty looked as if she were wrapping her face in some invisible veil.

'That's absurd, Betty. For a start, you don't know, nobody can know.'

'Everybody say so, Miss Lizbeth,' said Betty.

Without answering, Elizabeth drew her sheet up over her head.

'Close the shutters,' she said at last, 'I'm going to try and sleep.'

Betty obeyed immediately, and as she plunged the room into darkness, she murmured:

'How come you so restless this morning? On account of. . .'

'On account of nothing,' said Elizabeth, cutting short what

she did not wish to hear. 'I'll call you later, you go and sleep as well.'

Betty drew close to the bed and gave the girl a long, compassionate look. Then a corner of the sheet moved aside just enough to show an angry, blue eye:

'I told you to go,' said a voice from the depths of the pillow.

'You ain't angry with me, is you?'

'No, of course not, and I thank you for having slept in my room, but I want to be alone.'

Betty left the room with her heavy step and closed the door, muttering something that might have been a prayer.

46

*E*ach week Susanna would find under her door a note in which sentences, traced out in a firm hand, quivered with desire and the warmth of feeling. The missives arrived with a promptness that was quite military, by the eight o'clock messenger on Tuesday mornings, and it was Jennifer, Susanna's maid, who made herself responsible for sliding the mysterious envelopes under the door.

As soon as she received the very first letter, Susanna rushed to Elizabeth and, her face wet with tears, she could say only two words:

'Read it.'

Elizabeth made as if to scan it from end to end and laughed with an embarrassed look as she handed it back:

'It's only a love letter. Very personal.'

Susanna gave a little cry of despair:

'Do you think I don't realize that? His letter is disgusting.'

'Really? I didn't notice anything very improper.'

'But it's the tone, Elizabeth, the tone. And then he refers

to my mouth.'

Elizabeth blushed and sat on the edge of her bed. If only Jonathan would write such things to her . . .

'Let me see,' she said.

Susanna handed her back the letter and collapsed into the rocking chair.

A more careful second reading revealed a fiery temperament. Elizabeth felt jealousy tighten her heart, and she could not hold back a spiteful tear, of which she was ashamed.

'Indeed,' she said with a slightly trembling voice, 'he goes a bit far.'

'A bit far! He says he felt my body against his during the waltz. To start with, well brought-up people don't have bodies.'

'But . . .'

'No, no. One doesn't talk about one's body, one talks about one's person. Oh, I am unhappy, Elizabeth. What is he going to do to me? Answer, say something.'

'I don't know what married people do amongst themselves.'

'Horrid things.'

'But you aren't married yet. Something might prevent it.'

'What might prevent it? He might die? Die in war. If there were a war.'

'Obviously.'

'A war would settle everything. If there were a war, Elizabeth!'

'You're going off your head, Susanna, but I can understand that. I wouldn't fancy your lieutenant either. When I think that Jennie Boulton came to console me for his not liking me, her brother, that is . . .'

'Oh, if only it had been you! Perhaps if he were to see you again . . .'

'Not for anything in the world. Thank you very much.'

'But it seems he is of royal blood.'

'That doesn't make him any more attractive. He's enormous. He's more of a statue than a man. I like them slim.'

She thought of Jonathan's elegant silhouette, which made her stifle another sigh, deeper than its predecessors.

'So,' Susanna said through her tears, 'you're unhappy as well?'

But the young Englishwoman kept her secrets to herself and did not answer.

As for Susanna's lamentations, they were suddenly interrupted by the quiet appearance of Aunt Laura, who said pleasantly:

'It's charming to hear you chattering, and I'm sorry to interrupt you, but I have letters to write, and your pretty voices are distracting my thoughts. You tend to forget, Elizabeth, that we are neighbours and you, dear Susanna, I have asked you several times not to visit Elizabeth.'

'Oh, Aunt Laura, I'm not happy,' exclaimed Susanna in an appeal to the lady in gray, who was still smiling.

'How many girls in the South envy your success,' said Aunt Laura, leading her gently to the door. 'In a year's time, in six months perhaps, this brilliant marriage will make you one of the queens of society. It's an unexpected grace . . .'

This little speech provoked tears until the door was closed behind the fiancée.

Elizabeth wondered what dark irony was concealed behind those fine words and, as if to confirm this impression, Aunt Laura turned to her and said:

'I sometimes wonder if we are on this earth to be happy.'

The letters continued to arrive in the mornings with a regularity that turned Susanna's life into a long nightmare. She handed each one of these letters to Elizabeth:

'Read it,' she would say, 'and keep them all. Tell me if there's anything new or, if, by a stroke of luck, he has changed his mind and wants nothing more to do with me.'

At the beginning, Elizabeth hesitated a little; reading a letter that was not addressed to her . . . Sooner or later, curiosity got the better of her scruples and she would devour these passionate missives, as one might devour a romantic novel. Even the slow passages were to be savored, and certain repetitions were suggestive of passionate gasps. She was learning things; she was suffering too, imagining her Jonathan in place of this over-excited soldier. The lieutenant knew how to write. The art of delicately hyperbolical implications was his strong point. Speaking about the body was offensive to respectability, he had sensed that — too late —

and kept a watch on his style from then on. It was worse. You had to be an idiot not to understand.

'No hope?' asked Susanna.

One Tuesday, Elizabeth said to her:

'Ominous tidings, my poor Susanna. In this morning's letter, he's threatening to visit this summer.'

'Oh, no, no, I shan't be here, I shall have left, I shall be ill, I shall be dead.'

They wept together for different reasons. That brought relief to both of them.

Events followed their course, however. Uncle Josh would unfold the newspaper and give a reading of the soberly printed headlines, but he avoided any commentary. He undoubtedly found Fred's presence awkward. Fred saw things too clearly. For some time he had been saying nothing, but his very silence, sometimes embellished by a bitter smile, caused a strangely uneasy feeling.

Having more or less reached agreement on the principle of a Compromise, Congress was still battling through the means of putting it into practice, and storms remained a possibility. One could only hope that peace was in sight, that was all.

After the explosion of joy, anxiety gave way to a discomfort that people did not admit to. The South was far from being satisfied with the delays in high places, and divisions were in the offing. After having favoured the admission of California, President Zachary Taylor, with his military abruptness, declared that he was opposed to it. The representatives of the South were, in effect, protesting against the abolition of slavery in this new state. To which the President replied that California would be a free state, and that he, General Zachary Taylor, would hang with his own hands any man who expressed disagreement with his policy. Faced with such an attitude, Congress's fluctuations were understandable.

At Fort Pulaski, leave was again becoming a rare thing, as in all times of crisis. Susanna was the last one to complain about that.

Elizabeth could not manage to finish *The Last Days of Pompeii*. Her attention was constantly elsewhere, and by one of the quirks of fate, she languished for Lieutenant

Boulton's letters. He at least was faithful, and he could be counted on. If he put the unfortunate Susanna into a rage, he instructed Elizabeth on the extent to which violent hungering for love in body and soul could go in a man. He was maturing her, as the sun ripens a fruit, and he was gradually becoming Jonathan. With a humility surprising on the part of a warrior, he complained timidly of his beloved's silence, he begged for an answer, however short. Twenty times he gave his address, written out at the top or the bottom of the page. A line, he implored, a note, a sheet of paper on which her dear hand would have rested to write, tracing out the delightful curves of her adored name.

'You ought to write to him,' said Elizabeth one day.

The answer came in an indignant look, then Susanna said in a voice muffled by anger:

'Why are you making fun of me?'

This cry of despair made Elizabeth tremble.

'Forgive me,' she said, 'I was dreaming. It seems to me that I'm no longer really alive, but only dreaming since I've come to this country.'

'What do you mean?'

'I'm not sure.'

That evening she arranged all the lieutenant's letters in a box at the back of a drawer, having read through them once more. There were six, and she could have recited whole pages in which the voice of brutal sincerity rang out, and that was what she wanted to hear, for she was no longer taken in by the subterfuge of language. These sentences contained a vibrant energy, frustrated by too long a wait.

Putting these words into Jonathan's mouth, she felt herself victim of a dizziness that perturbed her as much as it delighted her. She was becoming a different person without understanding how. It crossed her mind to write to Boulton the letter he desired to read above all others and to sign it in Susanna's name. She knew how to make him lose his reason and to bring him, like a madman, to Dimwood within twenty-four hours. And what then? . . . This foolish plan was set aside almost immediately in a surge of good sense, but she nonetheless carried these missives to her lips before stashing them away in the 'treasure' corner of her drawer. Would she have dared to write to Jonathan? What else did she do in her imagination from morning till evening? Her daring went no further. He did not love her. His ironical remarks about Romeo and Juliet had hit home. 'Beware,' Aunt Laura had told her.

With the drawer closed, she sat down at her table and began a letter in a studied hand:

You forget me, Jonathan . . .

She crossed out this sentence and replaced it with these words:

Jonathan, how can I call you anything else? Your name alone makes you present in my solitude. It seems to me that you are there when I speak it aloud, as I am speaking it now . . .

At that moment there was a very discreet knock at her door, but it was so late that this slight noise was amplified out of all proportion by the total silence, and the girl dropped her pen with a little cry of fear. Letting a second or two go by, she asked under her breath:

'Is that you, Betty?'

The door opened very gently. There appeared a rather thick-set woman, smiling and dressed in dark gray serge. Elizabeth did not recognize her at first, she was so repelled, then she found the strength to take a grip on herself, and said in a voice that she intended to be firm:

'Miss Llewelyn, I am on the point of going to bed. I beg you to leave me alone.'

'Alone to finish that letter that must be so important, as all letters written at midnight are when one is sixteen years old . . . is that not so?'

The smile remained pleasant, and the voice was surprising in its charming intonation which contrasted with the physical appearance of the intruder. Elizabeth remembered what she had often been told at Dimwood: do not speak to Miss Llewelyn on any pretext.

The unfinished letter was slipped into a drawer, and, her throat choking with fear, Elizabeth said softly:

'Leave me alone, Miss Llewelyn.'

Without answering straight away, Miss Llewelyn closed the door silently.

'I have something to say to you, Elizabeth Escridge.'

The tone was serious and confidential.

'And I,' said Elizabeth firmly, 'assure you that I have nothing whatsoever to say to you.'

'The day will come,' continued Miss Llewelyn, 'when you'll have a lot to say to me, and that day is not far off.'

Without adding anything, she walked over and closed the window that gave on to the porch.

'You'll forgive me,' she said in a louder voice, 'but I think we shall chat more at our ease if we don't have to whisper like conspirators.'

These words were accompanied by a broad smile, which revealed a row of white teeth. Coming back towards Elizabeth, she placed herself in front of her, as if ready to be examined. Her powerful bosom stretched the fabric of her dress, and her wide hips emphasized the impression of a solid mass. The square face was like a peasant woman's. Her graying black hair was tied back and knotted at the neck into a heavy bun. A narrow, white collar ringed her powerful neck. She gave off a strong smell.

She smiled and continued in her slightly sing-song voice:

'Don't be afraid of me. I'm not a bad woman.'

'You don't frighten me,' said Elizabeth, whose heart was nevertheless beating faster than usual, 'but if you have something to say to me . . . I feel tired.'

This discreet invitation to leave as soon as possible was not taken up. Like a woman with something weighing on her heart and who is determined to relieve herself of the burden, Miss Llewelyn continued:

'I'm the one who is being shunned. Occasionally an imperceptible nod from the far end of a corridor or the corner of a path, that's all. It's all the same to me. Having no pretensions to superior rank, thank God, I know of things that I oughtn't to know about everybody, about Dimwood, and about what happened over there . . .'

'Over there?' murmured Elizabeth, suddenly goaded on by curiosity.

'Yes, over there, little Englishwoman, amidst the blood

and fire of a fine night in the West Indies. But I've already said too much, and Miss Escridge wants to go to sleep.'

The irony of this last half of the sentence accentuated the strange intonation. Elizabeth would have liked to tell her to stay, but did not know how to set about it, and stayed silent.

'Before I take my leave,' said Miss Llewelyn, 'I must tell you that I am Welsh. My accent will undoubtedly have told you as much. I hope you have nothing against the Welsh, although you are English.'

'Oh, no,' said Elizabeth with alacrity, 'nothing at all.'

'That's fortunate. Shall I sit down again?'

Without awaiting permission, she had already settled herself in an armchair, while the girl sat some distance away on an upright chair.

'I don't want to meddle with what is no concern of mine,' said Miss Llewelyn, 'but we Welsh have special gifts, premonitions, visions, etc.'

This intruder alarmed Elizabeth, who became all the more attentive.

Miss Llewelyn, however, in her armchair gave herself an important air, with just a hint of insolence. She was a different person from a few moments previously.

'Common,' thought Elizabeth. But it was her smell that importuned her the most. She smelt. On account of that, Elizabeth remained at some distance, but in spite of everything, sickening effluvia wafted as far as her delicate and disgusted little nose. Now it was too late to show her out, and she had the disturbing intuition that this massive woman was settling down into a place in her life just as she had done in the armchair. She had been told never to speak to her ... And despite all the discomfort of the present moment, she felt an irresistible curiosity about what she was going to say.

The Welshwoman looked around her for a moment with her small green eyes. 'I'm no Mademoiselle Souligou, I don't read cards and I need no tarot to see into the future.'

She waited, then, faced with Elizabeth's silence, added:

'Of course you went to see Mademoiselle Souligou, as all the young people at Dimwood do.'

'Yes.'

'She mystified you. Was it interesting?'

'She didn't say much, she didn't want to.'

Miss Llewelyn gave a mocking smile.

'The sly old vixen. She doesn't know anything. She shows you two cards and hides a third, the card that tells you everything.'

'Why?'

'To make you come back. She expects her little souvenir.'

'Her little souvenir?'

'Yes, the next time you go to Savannah, you'll remember her. Mr Jones will explain to you what you have to do. We're all fond of our old Souligou. And that leads me to tell you that you would do well to go and visit Mr Jones, for a good long visit of three weeks. He would be pleased.'

'I don't feel like going for the moment.'

'I know you don't, but you're wrong. Flee from Dimwood, Elizabeth. That's the advice I came to give you.'

'Why?'

'Should I tell you the truth, or do you prefer to know nothing and, as they say, harbor your illusions?'

'I want to know.'

'Well, it's useless to hope that he'll love you, and you know very well who I'm talking about. At the very most he is satisfying a whim.'

Elizabeth blushed with anger and stood up.

'I have absolutely no idea what you are talking about.'

'And I know,' said the Welshwoman, 'that you know perfectly well. So, calm down and I'll tell you. He's madly in love with the lady in white and is ruining himself for her. She likes luxury. He's selling his land in order to give her what she desires. Excuse me for telling you that you don't count for much in his eyes.'

'I'm not obliged to believe you, if we're talking about the same person.'

'Alright. Do you know what a passing fancy is? No? He'll teach you. You're going to suffer a great deal, Elizabeth. I know Jonathan. He's heartless. You won't hold on to him.'

As if that name spoken aloud had transformed her at a single stroke, Elizabeth said in a voice deadened by emotion:

'We shall see, Miss Llewelyn.'

47

*T*he summer set in savagely with the pitiless grating of the cicadas. They all longed for the moment of dusk and that little breath of fresh air from far away. Elizabeth suffered, bewildered and indignant each day at the return of that heat that came down like some divine curse. From seven o'clock in the morning the shutters were closed to guard like a treasure the slight wave of coolness that passed at dawn, but the confined air became stifling by afternoon. The only relief was iced drinks served in the darkness of the ground floor, beneath the humming of fans stirring up the warm damp air. People dragged themselves from one corner to another, clutching palm fans, and when the young English-woman asked why the Americans had not had the good sense to settle in the hills where the temperature was supposed to be more favorable, hateful looks were her only answer, for natural predispositions become harsher. Servants dressed in light cotton passed around mint juleps which enabled them to survive.

One evening Elizabeth had a visit from Aunt Laura. With her customary gentleness, she spoke to her of the day's little events. Despite the heat, Mr Hargrove had received calls from some of the guests at the ball. People were forgetting the shadow of evil that had hovered over the pretty mansion of Dimwood until then. As for this crippling wave of heat, it would come to an end within the next three days. A good storm was forecast.

As was her custom, she walked about the room, to assure her-self, so she said, that Betty was doing her housework properly.

'By the way,' she said, 'I didn't tell you that on the night of the ball, two weeks ago now, I took it upon myself to write to Uncle Charlie, advising him to invite you to spend some time with him. You must be bored here, apart from the ball, which was quite exceptional. Oh, I know you are too well brought up to agree . . .'

'But I don't want to go to Savannah,' exclaimed Elizabeth spontaneously.

Why? She would not have been able to tell in any precise way, especially not to Aunt Laura. The latter opted for not answering straight away. In her gray dress floating elegantly around her, she continued her little tour of inspection and uttered these words:

'If you want flowers in your room, Betty will make you wonderful arrangements. She has excellent taste. Flowers bring a room to life.'

'Thank you, Aunt Laura, but I have never asked to have flowers in my room.'

'I know, I know. So your little trip to Savannah is fixed for next Tuesday, in five days' time . . .'

'Fixed! But nobody asked me . . .'

'My dear Elizabeth, my father thought my idea was excellent. It will hurt him immensely if you refuse, not to mention Uncle Charlie who awaits you with impatience. Think of all they have both done for your happiness since you arrived in this country . . .'

Elizabeth could find no answer. She cast a look of silent indignation in Aunt Laura's direction. There were days when she felt like confiding completely in this woman, and others when she detested her. It seemed clear that the Catholic woman had been spying on her, and Betty must have talked. The servants knew everything that was going on.

'I shan't go,' she said at last.

Aunt Laura gave her a broad, affectionate smile.

'We'll see. You will go, my dear girl, and you'll be delighted with it. This time Aunt Augusta will accompany you, and Fred will be the knight in attendance.'

'Oh, no!' cried Elizabeth.

'A little too serious, perhaps? Well, we'll add Billy, who in any case would make an infernal fuss if anyone tried to keep him here. I hope he will behave like a gentleman.'

'But Aunt Laura . . .'

'Good night, darling, go to bed without delay now, I have stayed much too long.'

As she reached the French window her dress floated around her, giving the illusion that there was no body inside those yards of gray cotton cloth.

Mysterious Aunt Laura.

Alone in her room, Elizabeth, having lost control of her nerves, began to prance in front of her mirror.

'You let them put upon you!' she repeated to the image of the girl who was red with anger. 'What are you waiting for, Jonathan? Don't betray me!'

She had the greatest difficulty getting to sleep and was sorry that she was forbidden to use laudanum. Only adults were allowed to have the little phial in their cupboards. In the darkness she thought she could see Jonathan's face, his eyes betraying a prayer that she had only understood when it was too late, but she had understood everything too late, and her 'Farewell, Jonathan', that romantic cry, did not correspond at all to what she desired.

'On the contrary!' she confided to her pillow in a strangled scream.

What was to be done? He would come back and find her gone. She knew only too well that she had to obey Mr Hargrove. She was still doomed to be the eternally grateful poor relation, expected to submit in good part.

She had the idea of consulting Souligou. Perhaps it would be possible to make him come back by some magic trick . . . With that fragile hope, she slid into the abyss of sleep, until the birds' desperate clamoring cried out to her that the world was still a wonderful place.

48

A strange visit was to overturn the sleepy placidity of afternoons at Dimwood . . . Towards five o'clock, an elegant yellow carriage stopped in front of the house, and a moment later, a servant came to announce to William Hargrove that Mr Robert Toombs was begging leave to pay his respects, and was waiting on the porch.

Mr Hargrove, who was in the smoking room with his son Douglas, stood up abruptly and had to lean on a table in order to avoid falling:

'The most dangerous man in the South ... We can't receive him.'

'We shall have to, Father. You forget that he is one of the country's representatives. Jeremy, have Mr Toombs shown into the drawing room.'

'That man means war.'

As he spoke these words, his face turned ashen, and his son was ashamed of him.

'Pull yourself together,' he said authoritatively. 'All will turn out for the best. I'll send a message to Josh to have all the servants off duty until eight o'clock. There's no need for them to hear. Come, come.'

Crossing the hall with rapid step, they found Robert Toombs standing in the drawing room waiting for them. Dressed with evident care, he was wearing a black suit that showed off to advantage the admirable proportions of his body.

His handsomeness was of an aggressive kind and had earned him the nickname Apollo. His dark eyes flashed a fearsome intelligence, and his mouth had something distinctly mocking about it. He was pleasantly polite when he judged it necessary; at other times he bellowed with a fury that had become proverbial.

Having bowed to William Hargrove and his son, he apologized for what he called his intrusion.

'I am on my way to Savannah where I am to visit my friend Mr Charles Jones, who is putting me up for the celebrations on the 4th.'

'He may be a subject of Queen Victoria, but he is a faithful friend of the South.'

'I know,' said Robert Toombs with a smile. 'I am not unaware of the irony of the situation. I have been asked to celebrate Independence Day at Jasper Square. I expect Charlie Jones will stay at home.'

'He is spirited enough to defy his embassy and sit next to you during your speech.'

This remark of Douglas's aroused general laughter which made the meeting easier. A servant brought a tray with four juleps in tall glasses, a sprig of mint decorating the crushed ice like a cockade.

Joshua came in at that moment, and introductions were

made in the flowery style of the Southern states, after which the conversation slid irresistibly into the politics of the day. William Hargrove had regained all his assurance:

'Mr Toombs,' he said, 'formerly you were in favor of the Compromise, but it seems that you are no longer so.'

Robert Toombs placed his glass carefully on the table, and Uncle Josh waved to the servant to go. In a quiet and almost confiding voice, the traveller answered William Hargrove:

'You can be sure of it. I found the entry of a free California into the Union natural, but when some representatives of the South reminded me that originally she was a slave state, and that it was important for the interests of the South for her to remain . . .'

He took his glass and drew discreetly on the straw, then he finished in a tone of voice that was even more confiding than before:

'Well, gentlemen, I changed my mind.'

A flame suddenly began to gleam in his eyes and, with a careful gesture, he plunged his fingers into his mass of black curls. Then his loud and furious voice resounded in the drawing room:

'We are constantly repeating that slavery is a curse for which we are not responsible. Very good, gentlemen. That stills a little the murmurings of our conscience. Unfortunately for our moral well-being, that voice is not one that can be reduced to silence, because it comes from silence and is made of silence. Elijah heard it on Mount Horeb. The tempest rose. The voice was stronger than the tempest. Then the earth began to quake, and the voice was stronger than the earthquake. A curse for which we are not responsible. I'm ready to agree. So who is preventing us from freeing ourselves of it? You don't answer!'

Nobody wanted to answer. Seated between his two sons, who were exchanging looks of consternation, William Hargrove opened his eyes, like an animal caught in a trap.

The speaker let a few seconds go by, then once more thunder rolled over the gilt moldings:

'By what right do we wrench from their homeland men and women who have a body and soul like us, because they have a black skin and we need them to work on our plantations?'

Douglas let his clear, dry voice be heard.

'It's not us who capture the slaves. We buy them at the price that is asked.'

'Like cattle, all in all.'

'The comparison is inaccurate,' said Josh, 'we don't treat them like cattle.'

'I concede on that point. Cattle have no souls. We don't take into consideration the violence done to the souls of the Negroes, depriving them of freedom. We shall have to answer for it.'

In his turn, William Hargrove summoned up his strength and pronounced in a trembling voice:

'Mr Toombs, your eloquence would be admired by a Northern preacher.'

'It's achieving a lot in the South. As for the North, let's leave it to thrash out its own moral responsibilities.'

He started to thunder again:

'We pretend that our hands are clean because we have left to others the dirty dealing that has soiled them. Noble England would not lower herself to hunt game herself on the Ivory Coast. She waits for the natives to capture for her men, women and children who can't run away. She is rich, she pays well, she takes delivery, and the ships, crammed full of slaves, crazed with fear, set sail for American ports where she unloads her merchandise, for which she charges a high price. The profits are enormous, as is witnessed by the great wealth of our mother country.'

At that moment, the door was half opened, and Fred slid silently in and took up position behind the piano.

'But let us come to the principal supplier whose name I speak with regret, for we owe our independence in part to her: France, with its Revolution, which at first forbade slavery, then turned a blind eye to the heavy trading of its slave dealers. Gold flowed into the coffers. If prosperity is a sign of blessing from the Lord, I would have nothing to say. Rochefort, La Rochelle, Bordeaux could answer for me, and Liverpool, etc., etc.'

Amidst his words of fire, his short locks shook themselves into the battle, and his black silk tie made a line across his neck like an angry signature.

'As for us people of the South,' he continued, 'our ancestors taught us, but our own long acquaintance with slavery
has dulled in us the sense of gross injustice which is the
basis of our institutions. We accept slavery as the corner-
stone of our society. Some day we shall have to extricate it,
and deep down inside ourselves, we are aware of this . . .'

'Deep down inside ourselves!' Fred suddenly shouted,
rising up from behind the piano and coming into the middle
of the room. 'We all know it, Mr Toombs, but we do not all
desire it.'

In his slender face, taut with emotion, his pale eyes shone
with a brilliance that made a different man of him. With his
fists clenched he cried:

'If we don't put an end to this evil of slavery, the North
will see to ridding us of it.'

His sharp voice seemed to be battling against a storm, and
he was drinking in a spirit of combat so violent that one
could already imagine his thin, quivering body girthed in
uniform . . .

'This Compromise can only fool the simple minded,' he
continued despite William Hargrove's frantic gesturing,
'these ten years of peace that are promised us, do you think
they'll use them to read the Bible, or rather to get their
factories working to make cannon, for they have factories,
while we . . . Mr Toombs!'

For a few seconds, Robert Toombs had been looking at
him in bewilderment mingled with admiration. In his deep
voice, that filled the room, he thundered:

'Young man, if you're not killed in the war, you'll be
another Calhoun. The way in which the North intends to
destroy slavery is to invade the South, and so, you listen to
me, it will be useless to decree a mass uprising. It will
happen of its own accord and at a single stroke.'

Douglas stood up and tried to give his opinion, but in
vain, for the two speakers were fighting to get a word in.
This unleashing of rhetoric was turning into an uproar. The
door opened once more, and Billy appeared.

With his cheeks afire, he had caught his brother's closing
words and thought that secession was already underway.

'I shall set off with you!' he exclaimed. 'In the cavalry. I
shall sign up tomorrow. With our sabres drawn, we shall lay

into them!'

Douglas and Joshua set upon him to restrain him.

'You will keep quiet,' cried his father, 'or I shall put you outside.'

Billy struggled between the two men.

'I have the right!' he howled. 'I have the right, I'm nearly sixteen.'

'Don't be a fool,' said Uncle Josh, shaking him, 'there is no secession, and there won't be a war. We're at peace for ten years.'

'Another word and you're out,' said Douglas, shaking him with all his strength.

Billy freed himself and ran to take refuge behind the piano. From this stronghold, which he was determined to defend, he stood up to his father and his uncle with his burning blue eyes.

'I'm staying,' he cried.

The two men shrugged their shoulders. Joshua put his fingers in his ears.

'To think that it would be like this everywhere if there were a war,' he groaned.

All this racket attracted the girls and ladies from their siestas: first Mildred, then Minnie and suddenly Elizabeth, emerging from her dreams, feverishly inquisitive, and with an excessively attentive eye. Finally the ladies turned up, looking scandalized by this upset but secretly delighted. Aunt Emma had to be dragged to a sofa where she was quite at ease to simulate a fainting fit.

'My family,' said William Hargrove to Robert Toombs.

And he accompanied this brief introduction with a slight gesture of helplessness.

Without anyone paying attention, the door opened again, and Aunt Laura wandered to the back of the room, like a ghost. Her face was alarmingly pale. She managed to find Mildred who was hiding in a corner crying shamelessly like a little girl. Aunt Laura seized her by the hand.

'Stop crying,' she told her, 'and tell me where Susanna is.'

Mildred raised towards her a face that was almost disfigured by tears.

'I don't know, I've been looking for her everywhere, I think she's gone.'

'Gone! What do you mean? When did she go?'

'When Papa sent all the servants off duty until eight o'clock, she ran off then. I ran after her and she shouted to me to leave her alone. I don't know what's the matter with her.'

'Where was she going? Speak, Mildred, it's important.'

'I've no idea, I was hoping she would come back here when the shouting started.'

In a sudden burst of energy, Aunt Laura made her way to Uncle Josh and tugged at his sleeve until he turned towards her:

'Josh,' she said in a strong voice, 'Susanna has disappeared.'

'Disappeared? What are you going on about, Laura? She's undoubtedly sulking in her room, as has been her custom since the ball.'

'She's not in the house.'

'Well then, she's walking alone beneath the willows like Ophelia. Listen to what this man's saying, Laura, it's the voice of the South.'

'She's your daughter, Josh.'

'You're dreaming, Laura. Where do you think she can be if she's not at Dimwood?'

'I don't know, but she hasn't been here for an hour now.'

'And what do you want me to do about it? Send servants all over the place looking for her?'

She could not answer. Douglas's loud, dry voice resounded brusquely, with the strength of a man who has been put into a rage:

'But, Robert Toombs, you know perfectly well that some planters in our country are giving the slaves their freedom. It's becoming the fashion, as in Russia, where the serfs are being gradually liberated, but what do you want our poor slaves to do if we send them away? They are like our children, they count on us. If they want to run away from Dimwood, they are free to do so. They know it. One of them fled to the North. He was welcomed as a brother and set to work immediately, and what work . . . The climate nearly killed him. He came back. Who will give them the food that we give them? Who'll look after their children? The North? Let's be serious. The North welcomes runaways as brothers and sets them to work in the factories. After a few months, they come back to us for care.'

'They come back to you because William Hargrove has the reputation for being good and humanitarian. Oh yes, everybody knows as much, but there are a number of brutes amongst the planters . . .'

'They are the outcasts of society,' shouted Josh, 'and they live in fear that their slaves will cut their throats, as happened in the West Indies. Ask my father.'

William Hargrove was getting ready to answer when a young servant rushed into the room and headed for the master of Dimwood, amidst indignant protestations from the people he brushed aside.

'Are you mad?' exclaimed Joshua. 'You were told not to show your face before eight o'clock. What's that paper?'

The boy was, indeed, holding in his hand a sheet of paper which he held out to William Hargrove. The slave's face turned to the gray of terror, and his teeth were chattering.

William Hargrove seized the paper, cast his eyes over it and gave it to Douglas:

'I don't understand,' he said feebly.

Douglas read these words written out hastily and clumsily:

'Too unhappy, Susanna.'

He passed the paper to Joshua and seized the servant by his arms, as if to prevent him from escaping.

'Don't be afraid,' he told him. 'No one is going to hurt you. Tell us what this paper is and where you found it.'

In his turn, Robert Toombs came up to the frightened boy:

'You have nothing to fear,' he said in a thunderous voice which he was unable to soften, being still so caught up in the oratorical jousting. 'You are with friends of your race here. Speak, I wish you to do so.'

'Down there,' said the boy in a strangled voice.

He waved vaguely in the direction of the door.

'But where? Where?' cried Joshua.

'The river, Mass'r Joshua.'

'Well? Speak, boy!'

The boy rolled his eyes.

'On the grass, by the water, Miss Susanna's big hat, and the paper on the hat, and a stone on the paper.'

These words, uttered with the panting of an animal, fell into a horrified silence. Two of the ladies present fainted. A piercing howl came from a corner of the drawing room. It was Mildred's voice:

'Susanna has drowned herself!'

In the sinister hubbub that followed, Uncle Douglas, who had kept his wits, took the young servant by the arm and made his way to the door:

'You will take me there,' he said through his teeth.

William Hargrove collapsed on to a chair:

'What have I done for God to strike me like this?' he groaned.

Joshua touched his shoulder:

'Father, we expect you to give us an example of courage. Don't stay like that. Stand up.'

Robert Toombs bowed before the master of the plantation with the stiffness of a man wearing armor:

'Sir,' he said, 'if I can be of any use to you in such painful circumstances, do consider me your servant.'

Joshua took a step towards him and said gently:

'You are a great man, Mr Toombs, but you can't give me my daughter back.'

Once more, Robert Toombs bowed, and Joshua accompanied him to the door that opened on to the verandah. The temptation to come out with some well turned phrase was too strong for the orator to resist:

'Mr Hargrove,' he said, introducing moderation into the most famous voice in the South, 'if Providence has seen fit to cut short a poor human life, for reasons that we cannot fully appreciate, we can do nothing but remain eternally silent, but the union of hearts, which has been so much talked about just recently, is not a vain image.' And taking hold of Joshua's inert hand, he shook it forcefully. Joshua did not answer and watched him go down the porch steps.

'Susanna,' he said under his breath, as one awakens someone sleeping deeply, afraid of startling them. 'Susanna . . .'

He waited, unable to decide to go in.

The tree-frogs were weaving their twilight song with calm indifference. He felt the heavy perfume of honeysuckle and gardenias, with which the porch was overgrown, wafting up towards him. In this enchantment of the declining day, he had the feeling that his whole life was in danger of sinking, and that the image he had of himself was being destroyed. Susanna's imploring face appeared as if in a hallucination as he closed his eyes, and he heard his own voice speak those words, impossible to expiate: 'By marrying this man, you will restore your family to the highest rank in society . . . You have no right to refuse . . .'

He groaned and hid his face in his hands when, quite close by, a gentle step made him start. It was Elizabeth. Too upset to speak clearly, she said to him:

'I left the drawing room when they talked about the war, I can't bear the war.'

'There won't be a war, Elizabeth. What are you doing here?'

'I was hiding in my room, I met Susanna, she cried out to me: "You'll never see me again." Oh, Uncle Josh, you mustn't force her to marry . . . She has run away . . .'

'Be quiet, Elizabeth, I beg you.'

'But I'm telling you the truth. When the servants left, she ran away . . .'

'Elizabeth, don't say that again. I am very unhappy. Leave me, go back to your room, I'll explain things to you later.'

The girl suddenly seized his arm and began to speak as she had never spoken in her life before; she had the strange impression that someone was speaking in her place:

'You must be merciful, Uncle Josh, do you understand? You must, you must . . .'

He returned to the drawing room and found it half empty.

During his absence, in fact, there had been a rush towards the hall. Nearly all of them seemed to imagine the girl's body carried into the middle of the room, dripping with water with weeds caught up in her hair.

Aunt Augusta remained stretched out on a carpet, her face simulating the white severity of marble. Her mouth was open, as if to let out a mother's cry, but this detracted in no way from the nobility of her proud face. Aunt Laura had come to kneel silently beside her. Having slid a cushion under her head, she rubbed her forehead and cheeks gently.

'Grandfather,' said Fred suddenly, 'don't give up all hope. Boats are going to search the river. Everything possible will be done.'

At that moment, a plaintive lapping rose up in the silence.

'Poor Susanna, we loved her dearly.'

This lamentation came from Billy, the breaking of whose voice made this little funeral oration seem sinisterly comic.

At this point, William Hargrove cut short any show of emotion:

'It's my fault,' he said, 'I could have prevented it all. I knew it was a mistake.'

Fred broke in authoritatively:

'Sir,' he said, 'allow me to tell you what I think about this drowning business. Do you permit me?'

'What are you going to tell us that is more frightful than the truth?' groaned William Hargrove.

'This: that I don't believe it.'

'Are you mad? This paper in Susanna's writing . . .'

'I listened, but I know Susanna. She's a coward.'

'A cowardly person driven by despair can easily throw herself into the water.'

'It's possible, but if there's something that frightens Susanna more than the black water of the river, it's the alligator that was seen passing by there last week, and that was perhaps not the only one. That paper is pure lies, intended to give her time to slip away. Billy, instead of crying your eyes out, run to the stable and count the horses. If they're all there, I'm willing to be considered a half-wit until the end of my days.'

After a moment's bewilderment, Billy came out of the corner behind the piano and bounded towards the door without asking for explanations, while Aunt Laura, lifting up Aunt Augusta, helped her to sit down in an armchair:

'What's the matter?' she asked. 'Where are they all?'

'Don't ask questions,' Fred told her, 'and keep calm if you can. There's no cause for alarm.'

'Fred,' asked William Hargrove, 'what makes you talk in this way?'

'My good sense, Grandfather. I maintain that Susanna isn't dead. Have patience and wait for Billy's return.'

'In your place,' said Aunt Laura, who had said nothing until now, 'I should be afraid of rekindling hope without being sure. The disappointment would be atrocious.'

'I'm not asking you to believe in a miracle, Aunt Laura, I'm appealing to your reason.'

'That's all very well,' retorted Aunt Laura, 'but it would be wiser to appeal to God.'

'I can't understand anything of what you're saying,' exclaimed Aunt Augusta with annoyance.

William Hargrove's voice made itself heard, this time with the force of barely restrained indignation:

'It is quite simply about your daughter, of whom we do not know for the moment whether she is alive or dead. Have you already forgotten her, and can you not remember the tears she shed when she asked you and Josh not to force her to marry Lieutenant Boulton? We are all guilty, and you, her mother, just as much as the rest of us . . .'

Anger and fear turned Aunt Augusta's face crimson.

'I'm leaving,' she said.

'Just as guilty if not more so,' continued William Hargrove, beside himself. 'Where was your mother's heart when you pushed your daughter away? You have drawn the wrath of God upon us.'

'Father, this talk is unbearable and I shall not stay a moment longer in this room. My bonnet, Fred.'

Aunt Augusta's headdress had come away from her head during her fainting fit. Fred found it again without difficulty under an armchair, barely ruffled. Only the long, white lace ribbons were a little creased, but the little flaps of starched lawn had kept their austere elegance intact. With her hands trembling crossly, Aunt Augusta put this monumental object back on her head and gave her father-in-law a furious look.

'According to you,' she said, 'I led that unfortunate girl by the hand and pushed a daughter, whom I brought into the world, into the water. No girl was ever married against her wishes. The law is there to defend her, right up to the foot of the altar. My heart is wounded, but my conscience is clear.'

With this speech, she had regained that strange calm, well known to theatre people, who switch from one emotion to another by a kind of inner transformation. They acquire complete sincerity from the power of persuasion in the text they are speaking. In that amazing moment, Aunt Augusta was carried along by the sentences issuing from her mouth, and in her long, puce-colored taffeta dress, she gave the impression of a statue, an effect accentuated even more by the elaborate headdress.

'Have you ever read,' she continued, 'in that Bible that is so dear to you, as it is to us all, a single verse that justifies the murder of an inexperienced soul by a father's fanaticism, that would kill it not once, but every single day of its life, by imposing on it his tyrannical will?'

She suddenly stopped, exhausted by the effort, and moved backwards towards the door, as she saw her father-in-law's face turn pale, like that of a man fatally wounded.

Even stranger was Aunt Laura's attitude. At the point when the Bible was referred to, and the violence done to a soul day after day by paternal cruelty, this woman, usually so self-effacing, came and stood resolutely in front of William Hargrove, in silence. She looked straight at him with her great motionless eyes. He made an attempt to face up to that unbearable gaze, but suddenly turned his head away violently.

'Go away,' he said in a flat voice.

She did not move. With his head still turned aside, he continued:

'I do not wish to see you, I order you to go.'

And suddenly he shouted:

'Go, both of you, I wish to be alone.'

He had stood up to speak these words, but, as if caught up in a dizzy spell, he waved both his hands about, looking for something to lean on, to avoid falling.

Fred ran to his aid and helped him to sit down, while Aunt Laura and Aunt Augusta headed for the door.

They did not have to open it. Billy came in, his hair standing on end and a shattered look on his face.

'My father has gone off with Uncle Josh and the steward and twelve servants, all in boats, to explore the river in every direction.'

'How many horses in the stables?' asked Fred.

'All there. Not a single one is missing. No hope on that front.'

William Hargrove looked angrily at Fred, who remained unperturbed.

'So much for your reasonings and intuitions, you little

fool. And to think I was clinging on to your peremptory way of explaining things. She's dead; Susanna is dead.'

Aunt Laura made the sign of the cross and went out of the room, followed by Aunt Augusta, who was walking with hesitant steps and stopped suddenly. Fred's imperious voice resounded, shattering the silence:

'I tell you she is not dead. She could have gone off on foot.'

'Shut up, Fred,' cried William Hargrove. 'Susanna is dead.'

Augusta was standing still at the door and, after some uncertainty, went out in her turn, walking with majestic slowness. Through the open door, her large, defiant outline, gradually merging with the dusk, could be seen moving away along the verandah. Suddenly, a hoarse, dreadful cry, like an animal howling, broke the silence and made those left behind in the drawing room shudder. They looked at each other silently, but they were visibly struck with both horror and compassion.

49

Supper, served at the usual time as was only right, was dismal. There was mingled with it, however, that satisfaction, that could not be admitted to, of being still alive when Death had just passed by. Known as the grim reaper, the gust of wind created by his sickle had whistled over the heads of these diners, who huddled together for moral support.

William Hargrove had to take a grip on himself to say the prayers that were expected of him, but he was so upset that he could only produce a single sentence.

'Lord,' he murmured, 'have mercy on us in our distress. Amen.'

Neither Aunt Augusta nor Aunt Laura put in an

appearance, neither did poor, unconsolable Mildred. Aunt Emma, who had got over her successive fainting fits, had a comfortable meal served to her in her room. The men were all present, showing proper grief that had no effect on their natural hunger.

Minnie arrived late with red eyes, but took her place alongside Fred, and conducted herself with dignity there. On her left, Billy was silently doing justice to the corn fritters. Finally, at the end of the table, Hilda, subdued and silent, with glazed eyes, did not touch any of the dishes, but seemed, by some strange phenomenon, to have become quite small.

On her right, as motionless as a statue, as if she were not there, Elizabeth was striving to get a hold on her tumultuous thoughts. Like her neighbor, she declined all the dishes that were offered to her. Susanna's tortured face would come into her mind, then Jonathan's amongst the foliage on the porch and the whiteness of the magnolias. Nothing could expel from her mind the thought that these hallucinatory apparitions were part of the real world, whereas this sinister supper was nothing other than a nightmare.

It was Uncle Douglas who was the first to break the silence during the dessert, and that in a slightly learned tone of voice:

'I apologize for bringing up the subject which concerns us all so cruelly, but as we are here, almost all of us together . . .'

He repeated:

'. . . almost all of us together . . .' and resumed after a brief pause:

'. . . well, I'm not quite sure how strong the poor girl's religious convictions were . . .'

'She used to read the Bible,' said Joshua gently and firmly at this point. 'Her mother saw to that. Like all of us, she went to church for the major festivals, and that was sufficient. We have never taken the outward show of piety to extremes in our family.'

He stopped for a moment and continued:

'A member of the Anglican Church . . .'

These words seemed to be the extent of his strength.

He fell silent, and Uncle Douglas took over. Unawares, he assumed the tone of voice of the clergy of the Church which represented the aristocracy.

'We shall have to have a funeral service in the cathedral. With all due pomp, it goes without saying. Black drapes, choir boys in little black cassocks and white surplices.'

Fred cut short this flow of words:

'You'll save the price of a coffin, since you have nothing to put in it.'

'Fred!' his father exclaimed.

'I beg you to accept my apologies, sir. I ask your permission to stay.'

'Very well, but another word and I'll send you out,' said his father, snorting furiously.

He let a few seconds go by in order to resume the tone he esteemed desirable, then continued confidently:

'The organist with the finest reputation in Savannah, Mrs George Wilkinson Howard, will be quite able, if I may say so, to strike the right note of spiritual recollection.'

Again he paused, and with a smile of tenderness, he added in a smooth voice that was unfamiliar coming from him:

'I think the poor girl would be pleased.'

An unexpected explosion greeted these words. Elizabeth had sat up straight all of a sudden, and began to shout in a strangulated voice.

'But it's not true! It's Tuesday tomorrow, and a letter for Susanna from Lieutenant Boulton will come, as usual, and she will give it me to read, and will tell me to put it with the others, and then she will go and cry, and there won't be any black drapes in the church and . . .'

She had turned quite red, and put her hands to her throat, as if she were choking. Uncle Josh, who had got up hurriedly, ran towards her and supported her in his arms.

'My girl,' he said, kissing her, 'calm down, I'll take you to your room, and I'll stay with you, if you like.'

She sat down again almost immediately and freed herself by an effort of will.

'Tell me that she is not dead,' she said.

'Elizabeth,' he replied in a low voice, almost as if he were speaking to someone ill, 'listen, Elizabeth, you must accept it. You must have mercy. It was you who told me that.'

These words fell into an awesome silence.

Uncle Josh leant on the back of the chair. Struck dumb as

if still in the first moments of shock, he was searching in vain for something to say.

Minnie suddenly got up and came towards him.

'Do something, Minnie,' murmured Elizabeth. 'I should like to die.'

Without answering, Minnie took her by the arm and led her out of the dining room, stunned with pain.

'Dead,' she said several times. 'It's not true.'

Taking advantage of the general commotion, Hilda followed them and took flight like a frightened little animal. Amongst the men, left alone, there was at first an embarrassed silence. William Hargrove and his two sons, who usually dressed in black, seemed to be in heavy mourning, as if their clothes had decided to speak the appropriate language and take part in the drama. Billy, in his short navy-blue jacket with brass buttons, found himself immersed in solitude when confronted with a salad of crawfish tails and avocado pear which he ate stealthily, while pretending to follow what was being said around him. Between two hasty mouthfuls, his pink face took on an air of careful attentiveness. There was, moreover, no hypocrisy in his furtive ways, for the disappearance of his young cousin upset him to the very depths of his being, yet his healthy appetite held out against everything.

Joshua had sat down in his place again, next to his father, and Douglas coughed quietly, to announce that he was going to speak once more:

'It seems to me,' he said gravely, 'that the news will have to be, alas, conveyed to the neighboring families, and principally to the press, in very careful terms, and in a guarded style, to silence malevolent whisperings. I hope I make myself understood . . .'

'We can read between the lines,' said Fred soberly. He too was locked in an austere solitude, the product of icy scepticism, his arms crossed over his iron-gray suit.

A furious look was cast his way by his father, who continued:

'I see things more or less in this way: our dearly beloved Susanna sits down on the edge of that pretty river, of which she was so fond. She is a little weary, she watches the water flowing by, she leans forward. A sudden dizzy turn, and she falls into the river, she struggles, but the current carries her off as far as the confluence of the Ogeechee river and then . . . does that seem suitable to you?'

William Hargrove and Uncle Josh nodded. It seemed suitable.

'Who witnessed these things?' asked Fred.

'Fred, keep in mind what I'm about to tell you. In a case such as this, the probabilities are so strong that witnesses can be dispensed with.'

'But there's that strange piece of paper and its eloquent phrase.'

'Nobody will ever see it. The servant who brought it can't read. The more I think about it, the more it seems to me to be the truth.'

'What is truth?' asked Fred.

Uncle Douglas leapt to his feet and shouted:

'I'm ashamed of you, Fred. There is no sense in what you're saying.'

'Father, I'm only quoting one of the best known phrases in world history.'

'Do you think we don't know it? What does it have to do with Susanna's disappearance?'

'This, that you've got the wrong truth, and that Susanna isn't dead.'

'You'll be sorry for this stupidity when you hear the Bishop of Savannah say farewell to the departed on behalf of us all. He knows the family, he is fond of us, he won't refuse.'

'Well, Father, on that day I shall ask you to forgive my bold obstinacy, but I shall retain some shred of hope of finding myself face to face with my cousin again.'

'You'll never see her again in this world,' said Uncle Josh, lowering his head.

Fred stood up, bowed in a not very ceremonious fashion and said quietly:

'I ask your permission to withdraw and wish you, despite the circumstances, a truly restful night. My presence among you can only be a cause of discord, I'm sorry to say.'

Having delivered this little speech with cold politeness, he left the room with his customary rapid steps, which, in their precision, were reminiscent of a soldier's.

'That boy sows discord,' said Uncle Douglas sadly. 'I know

he is intelligent, but I admit that I shall be happy to see him go off to university.'

Night was falling. The master of the plantation had sent the servants off to bed some time ago. The candelabras on the table were casting long shadows on the walls, enveloping the four lingering diners, and the silence had become so profound that nobody seemed to want to break it. Finally William Hargrove said under his breath:

'It's over. Our little one has sought refuge in death and has destroyed our world. We shall never say the same things again, because we shall never be the same again. We all know things that it would have been better to remain ignorant of until the end. Dimwood will look at us as if we were strangers. When Jonathan comes to claim his house back, I shall give it to him.'

Carried away by a flow of words of which he was no longer in control, he seemed to be giving in to some veiled inspiration, originating in the most secret places of a tortured conscience.

After a while his sons took him gently by the arms, and led him away with them. He let them, without stopping to speak, but more and more softly, as if whispering some long, incomprehensible prayer.

Billy, shattered, followed them out furtively.

A storm rumbled in the night. Without rain, it swept away the overpowering heat of the previous day. The morning brought a coolness that would have been a relief in other circumstances. Never to be varied, breakfast was served, and the same people, except one, all appeared around the table. No one said a word, each face remained expressionless, the eyes as silent as the mouths. Seeing them, one might have thought to be at some strange gathering of corpses; the simple movements they made in order to swallow their food did nothing to change this impression. Their frozen features and empty gaze seemed to take them from the land of the living.

William Hargrove occupied his usual place, and they waited in vain for the grace that he was so keen on saying. His weighty side-whiskers, which joined up with the bushiness of his mustache, highlighted the yellowy paleness of his skin, and the purple-tinged black rings around his eyes spoke of a night of cruel insomnia. Uncle Josh tried hard to make him eat, without success. He managed, however, to get him to take a large cup of tea in his hand, and his father raised it to his lips, not without some trembling in his arm.

Suddenly, William Hargrove's fingers let go of the handle of the cup, which fell on to the saucer and broke with a noise that was enormously loud. The yellow liquid spread over the white tablecloth in all directions.

A servant hurried over to set this little disaster to rights. Nobody moved. The servant did what had to be done. It was better to pretend to have seen nothing, nor add to the humiliation of the head of the family by inappropriate fussing. William Hargrove himself seemed unaware of this accident. In less than three minutes, everything was back as it should be, and large white damask napkins covered the traces of the unfortunate little incident, the sinister dimension of which did not escape either Joshua or Douglas, who exchanged worried glances.

Their father suddenly began to mumble words that were more or less unintelligible.

'He's saying something,' said Uncle Josh. 'Can you hear him?'

'Yes, but I can't understand it. I thought I heard "Dimwood".'

Breakfast came to an end, and Uncle Douglas, who was keeping his cool, said with apparent calmness:

'I propose that we all get together in the drawing room to see what it is appropriate to do in respect of yesterday's events.'

No objection was made. Stricken with a general apathy, these people, who were usually so loquacious, silently followed the determined man whose calmness reassured them.

They found themselves now in the large drawing room where the ball had been held, but were they barely settled in the armchairs when Aunt Augusta fell to one side, without uttering a cry. She had to be laid down on a sofa and given smelling salts several times, but she came round only with difficulty, and remained lying in the same position, with a cushion under her head and her eyes closed.

Josh and Douglas led their father to an ample easy chair,

from which he would have been able to observe all that was going on around him if he had had the curiosity to do so. His extinguished gaze revealed exhaustion of body and soul. There issued forth from his mouth, from amongst his bushy whiskers, inarticulate sounds in which shreds of sentences could sometimes be made out. At one point, the two brothers thought they heard the name Laura.

Now all the family was waiting. Seated on red velvet chairs, all had their eyes fixed on the master of Dimwood, their curiosity mingled with fear of some imminent new peril.

Only Fred remained impassive in his dark gray suit, made more severe by a black tie. He had intentionally sat next to Billy, ready to calm him with a thump, should his young brother start to speak. But the boy, who was usually boisterous, seemed weighed down into good behavior by the silence and consternation all around. Sitting on Fred's right, Aunt Emma sniffed discreetly from time to time, but did not have a fainting fit this time.

Minnie was sitting next to Aunt Laura, who was holding her hand affectionately, and was quite still.

As for the girls, the 'children', they were lined up on large chairs, motionless, crushed by sadness in their pretty dresses of pink, white and mauve cotton.

Suddenly William Hargrove's eyes alighted on Aunt Augusta, who was still laid out like a corpse on the sofa, wearing a black satin dress, with long, straight folds that shone in the happy morning light. For some reason that he kept to himself, but which could be guessed at, he looked for some considerable time at her and muttered something. A glimmer was starting to come to life in his eyes.

'He said "Poor thing,"' whispered Uncle Douglas.

'I didn't hear anything, I think he understands nothing.'

'No, Josh. There is hope.'

As he was saying that, the door opened soundlessly, and Susanna came in and sat down near a small table, on which an album of engravings showing some of the artistic wonders of Europe lay open. She began to turn over the pages so perfectly naturally that for a few interminable moments nobody noticed her, although they could all see her.

Aunt Emma was the first to utter a loud, hoarse cry, and she fell into the arms of Fred, who set her upright again.

'An apparition!' she said. 'She's getting her revenge; oh, I know her!'

'Be quiet, Mama. She has never been dead. Susanna!'

Susanna raised her head.

'What's the matter?' she asked.

'Don't play games,' said the young man harshly. 'Stand up, come over here.'

Susanna obeyed and left her place amidst a storm of bewilderment mingled with nervous laughter, a demented gaiety, which produced discordant sounds. Nobody dared draw close to the amazed young ghost. The men turned out to be the most cowardly, the girls huddled together, but when Susanna had reached the middle of the drawing room, her mother, aroused, leapt on her like an animal:

'Little wretch,' she shouted in a flood of tears interspersed with hysterical laughter, 'what trick have you played on us?'

'Trick? What trick?' said Susanna, struggling.

Uncle Josh came right up to her and said:

'My darling,' he stammered, 'I make no reproaches, but why?'

'Yes indeed, why?' asked Uncle Douglas with a hint of anger. 'You don't realize the trouble you've caused.'

Susanna groaned: 'What have I done wrong?'

'Where did you run away to?' asked Fred with the tone of an interrogator.

'Run away? I didn't leave the house.'

Now closely surrounded by the family, it was Susanna who began to be frightened.

'Leave me alone,' she cried. 'I haven't done anything.'

Aunt Augusta drew herself up abruptly and moved away from her.

'You'll tell me the truth,' she said in a voice that had regained its firmness. 'This is your mother speaking to you. I want to know the meaning of that piece of paper placed on your bonnet by the water's edge.'

'Paper?'

'Yes,' said Aunt Augusta, tapping her foot with rage, 'this paper.'

'I have kept it,' said Uncle Josh, holding back his tears.

And with his wallet in his hand, he drew out a piece of paper, carefully folded in four.

'You see, I kept it, there it is. So?'

A sudden change seemed to come over Susanna. Looking determined she simply said:

'So, what does your piece of paper say?'

'Impertinent thing!' exclaimed Aunt Emma suddenly. 'Did you hear her? *Your piece of paper!*'

Uncle Josh turned towards her:

'Emma, for goodness sake, leave us. We thought Susanna had drowned herself, and here she is alive.'

'Yes, go away, for Heaven's sake,' said Aunt Augusta. 'She's my daughter, not yours.'

Uncle Josh raised his voice:

'I'll read your paper to you, as you ask me to: "I am too unhappy," signed: Susanna.'

'Placed on the bonnet with a stone on it, so that it wouldn't blow away,' added Fred sarcastically.

'Silence, Fred,' said Uncle Josh. 'What did you mean by it, Susanna?'

'That I was too unhappy on account of my engagement to that lieutenant.'

'And having written that,' said her mother, 'you led us to believe that you were going to throw yourself into the river.'

'And where did I say in that note that I was going to throw myself into the river?'

Fred burst out laughing.

'I take my hat off to you, you fooled us all. I didn't think you were as subtle as that.'

Uncle Josh and Aunt Augusta looked at each other.

'One has to admit that she is not wrong,' said Uncle Josh.

Tearing up the piece of paper, he threw it joyfully into the air.

'Shall I have some champagne brought in?' asked Fred.

And without waiting, he opened the door, almost knocking over a black servant who had been listening. The latter jumped in the air and stammered:

'Yes, Mass'r Fred, yes . . .'

'Boy, run to the pantry and tell them to bring champagne for everybody immediately. And be quick about it. Hurry!'

In the drawing room, Fred's cheerfulness had chased away the fear, giving way to laughter and exclamations. Everybody wanted to kiss Susanna, to the point where her parents had to push her behind a table, where they made a bulwark with their bodies. As usual, it was Uncle Douglas who spoke up forcefully:

'You're going to frighten her with your shouting. Silence, for Heaven's sake. The important things is that she is here, alive, and in good health. She is going to calm down, and tell us quietly what she wants, and why she disappeared. Aren't you, Susanna?'

They all fell silent, struck dumb this time by extreme curiosity. Then the girl's clear and determined voice broke forth as she stood with both of her hands on the small table:

'I do not want to marry Lieutenant Boulton.'

'That's agreed,' her father said. 'The engagement will be broken off. Do you agree, Augusta? Broken off.'

'Broken off,' said Aunt Augusta. 'Are you satisfied, you naughty thing?'

'Happy, Mama, very happy,' the voice answered with angelic sweetness.

'There will be an interesting moment,' said Fred, 'when the eleven o'clock messenger brings the usual love letter. The dear man is still living in a rose-tinted dream beneath his gold-braided soldier's cap.'

'Fred, be quiet and leave the room,' said Uncle Josh. 'Susanna, my child, you can tell us now where you hid yourself. There will be no punishment, but I'd like to know.'

'I gave my word of honor that I would tell no one,' said Susanna, 'except Grandfather and Aunt Laura.'

At these words, all eyes turned towards the back of the room where Aunt Laura was standing perfectly motionless beside her father. Never before had this woman's deeply serene face offered to the gaze of the curious such an image of anxiety. Then she said in a voice that was making an effort to be clear-cut, but which choked her:

'Susanna, I know of what you are speaking, and I forbid you to reveal anything. I forbid it in both my name and my father's.'

William Hargrove, in the depths of his big armchair, was observing everything in a distracted way, as if he were watching a play, the meaning of which eluded him from time to time. Short, incomprehensible sentences fell from his lips, and Aunt Laura would bend towards him to try and grasp them, but each time she straightened herself up again with a look of despair. After she had imposed silence on Susanna, she leaned towards William Hargrove and said something in his ear. He listened, and then shook his head joyfully to indicate assent.

'My father is as opposed as I am to your revealing the name of the person who sheltered you.'

She looked uncertain for a moment and made an effort to smile.

'He loves you very much, Susanna. Do you want to say something kind to him? That would surely do him good, he has been upset on account of you, do you see?'

Susanna looked questioningly at her father and mother.

'We can't refuse,' murmured Uncle Josh. 'Laura might be right, who knows?'

'Go on,' said Augusta to her daughter. 'Try not to say anything silly.'

Aunt Emma, Fred, Billy, Mildred, Hilda, all moved to one side, as did Elizabeth, who had time to slip this into Susanna's ear:

'He'll want to kiss you. Watch out, it prickles!'

Somewhat emotionally, Susanna crossed the space that separated her from the master of Dimwood, gave him a curtsey, the customary little bow, and William Hargrove's face lit up with a pleasant smile. Leaning a little towards her, he asked her in a soft voice, looking amused:

'And who are you, young lady?'

50

*B*reakfast took place as usual, but William Hargrove did not put in an appearance. He stayed in his room. Uncle Douglas announced this as head of the family. His father's place remained empty. Very few words were exchanged. The programme for the day had been finalized the night before, not without some difficulty. At all costs, William Hargrove was to be surrounded with a wall of silence. Aunt Laura would not go to Savannah, which aroused in Elizabeth secret hopes of seeing Jonathan again, but these were to be immediately dashed. Aunt Emma would simply replace her at Uncle Charlie's, and supervise the young Englishwoman, as well as a very guilty and very repentant Susanna. Uncle Josh would stay behind with his wife. Uncle Douglas would not leave Dimwood either.

The problem of the boys was more intractable. Fred was chosen as being the more serious, and he would serve as Elizabeth's body-guard, while Billy saw himself forcibly supplanted. Suddenly there arose such vociferous protestations from this quarter, that they gave in out of weakness. The ebullient young man, always at the ready, be it for love or for war, had not forgotten the delights of the big town, nor the agreeable Dorcas, with her coffee-colored charm. To be sure of his keeping calm, he was allotted a place in the same carriage as his mother, next to Susanna.

The atmosphere of that morning had nothing funereal about it. William Hargrove let himself be fed docilely by his daughter Laura.

Uncle Douglas had taken on the task of writing the letter to Lieutenant Boulton breaking off the engagement. It was courteous in the extreme, but a blow to his self-esteem as well as to his amorous aspirations. His letters to Susanna were carefully parcelled up and were returned to him. His bellowing was soon to be heard throughout the barracks.

A little before ten o'clock, the travellers climbed into the two four-horse carriages that were waiting in front of the house. As on the most auspicious occasions, the coachman, in his elegant red livery with gold trimmings, sat enthroned on the seat of the first carriage, the second was entrusted to another of the servants selected as the most competent and good-looking.

Aunt Emma, Susanna and Billy got in first, then Elizabeth and Fred took their places in the second vehicle. Uncle Josh came to wish them a good journey, as if they were leaving on some long expedition. Behind him, standing at the base of the porch, the three perpetually forsaken ones, Minnie, Hilda and Mildred, were waving sadly. The moment that the doors slammed to, he came right up to each of the carriages in turn as if he did not want to see them go. Due to the unfortunate events of the previous day, a surge of affection drew him towards his own kin. Perhaps he had never known how much he loved them, but he knew it at that moment. Naively he tried to hold them back, reassuring both them and himself.

'Papa is better,' he told Emma and the children. 'He'll get over it, you'll see.'

Aunt Emma raised her eyes to heaven beneath her mauve parasol.

'Pray for him,' said Uncle Josh.

Moving to the second carriage, he leaned on the door. His face was furrowed with a weight of tiredness, which drew, as if with charcoal, shadows under his eyes.

'Why are you all going away? Everything will be sorted out and then, listen ... I read in the newspaper this morning that the Compromise is on the point of being concluded. Peace is here. We can be happy at Dimwood again, since Father is better.'

'Uncle Josh,' said Fred, 'you know that there are other reasons for this journey, and when peace is given the name of Compromise, it must be pretty sick.'

Uncle Josh made a vague gesture and gave a last look at the travellers before moving away. After a few paces, he turned back with unhappiness in his eyes.

'Don't stay too long down there,' he said.

His voice was lost amid the noise of the wheels and the whips which crackled in the air like pistol shots.

Soon Dimwood disappeared from view. None of the travellers felt like talking, each becoming progressively immersed in their dreams, when a horseman appeared at the end of the long avenue of oaks.

Mounted on a beautiful black horse whose coat was shining like jade, he was galloping at full stretch towards Dimwood. When he was level with the carriages, he slackened his pace and cast an inquisitive gaze at the first. With perfect gracefulness, he made his animal suddenly do a complete about turn, and found himself alongside the bewildered travellers. His black-gloved hand raised his broad-brimmed panama with which he waved a lavish salute. It was Jonathan. Elizabeth felt her head spinning, for those magnificent gray eyes that she saw in her dreams were fixed straight at her, with imperious earnestness. His black hair fell in curls along his cheeks, highlighting the paleness of his skin. With the infallible speed of the female eye, she ascertained that it made him miraculously more handsome. When he smiled she thought she would faint, but he was already looking towards Fred deferentially.

'I heard,' he shouted, 'that Mr Hargrove was indisposed, I am hurrying to Dimwood to enquire after him.'

'You can save yourself the trouble,' replied Fred with authority. 'My grandfather has recovered — otherwise I should be at home with him now.'

'I shall nevertheless go and pay my respects.'

'That you can dispense with also. He is very busy this morning.'

'In that case, I shall limit my excursion to this noble and venerable avenue of oaks, which will always be dear to me. Your servant, sir.'

These last words were spoken in a tone of polite irony, the undertones of which were so obvious that Fred was seized with a desire to strike the insolent fellow. He did not get a chance to do so. In another about turn, more audacious than the previous one, Jonathan moved his horse off with a jab of his spurs and launched forth into the avenue, after a final wave of his broad hat.

A moment passed. The carriage was going at a good pace to catch up with its companion, which had raced ahead. Fred's dry voice declared:

'That man is a cheeky fellow. He's hoping to take advantage of the situation. Money, money, he's always in need of it.'

Huddled up in a corner of the carriage, Elizabeth was trying to follow this indignant monologue, the meaning of which eluded her. Everything around her began to spin. Jonathan's face appeared to her amongst the foliage of the magnolia, with his eyes full of an all-devouring hunger. Then, suddenly, he was riding alongside the carriage, seeking her out like some prey with a look that wrenched her away from herself and flung her after him. A cruel trick of her over-excited memory made her see again his curly hair, rolling down as far as the collar of his chamois-colored suit; then his hands, gloved in black leather, which made them look unrelenting. By some incomprehensible quirk of her shattered constitution, the horse's magnificent body, shiny with sweat, summoned up in her a violent image of nakedness that made her quiver with horror. For a moment she lost her sense of the reality of things and no longer knew where she was.

Raising his voice, Fred said to her jovially:

'You must have nodded off a bit, Elizabeth, there is something sleepy about the monotony of the landscape, but if you look to your left, you'll see a cotton field that we had rented and which is ours now, because we have bought it, so my father told me on the night of the ball,' he clarified, 'but that story is of no interest to you. Look at it.'

The night of the ball . . . Mechanically she turned her head to the left. The plants, laden with green leaves, stretched out for a great distance, in unending parallel rows. Here and there, little white patches could be made out beneath the greenery. The night of the ball . . . Again she felt dizziness coming over her, but she got a grip on herself.

'Not much like England's greenness,' continued Fred's sarcastic voice. 'It's not very pretty yet. You have to wait for the flowering in August and the ripening in September, but do you see, it's that plant that makes it possible for us to hold out. The whole of Europe needs our cotton, and the North. That's why it secretly puts up with black labor while damning it in the eyes of the world, to salve its conscience. For the North loves moralizing, and what annoys them is that slavery is permitted by the sacrosanct constitution, which it cannot abide . . .'

Elizabeth was not listening. This speech was drowned by the noise of the wheels and the clip-clopping of the horses. She had heard it all before. Only the name of Jonathan dominated this confusion of arguments.

'I shall never be able to love anyone else,' she told herself despairingly. 'He has taken in one go all that my heart had to offer.'

5
FAREWELL

51

*I*n the heat of the afternoon, the carriages were rolling along the avenues of Savannah, and memories were already flooding back into Elizabeth's mind. Even in the confusion which afflicted her, she could not fight off a feeling of attraction towards this town that was friendly and proud at the same time.

Uncle Charlie was waiting for the travellers on the porch of his house, and he received them with a gaiety that wiped away, amidst peals of laughter, all the worries of the moment, although it did seem a trifle forced. Fred took from his pocket and handed him a twelve-page letter that Aunt Laura had entrusted to him. A light meal was served in the large dining room, which was cool and dark, after each of the guests was led to his or her room to recover from the fatigue of the journey.

When Elizabeth saw that she was in her usual room, she had that disturbing sensation of lost time, brought about by returning to places that have been forgotten. Nothing had changed. The small table was still in its place next to the rocking chair, the portrait of Uncle Charlie in the full flush of youth was back on the wall, as was the big window, where she had leaned out to listen to the conversation coming up from below on that spring night, together with the exquisite fragrance from the garden and the strong cigar fumes. Happy and unhappy by turns. There had been a duel over her at dawn, when she had believed herself to be in love with that pretty boy — what was his name? Was it really she, that Elizabeth? What was Jonathan's Elizabeth doing in yesterday's setting?

A quarter of an hour later, she found herself with her travelling companions, sitting at table between Fred and Uncle Charlie. Despite her imprecations against Savannah, which she judged to be immoral, Aunt Emma did not seem any the less pleased to be far away from Dimwood. Susanna, whom she had taken under her wing, did not utter a word and looked gravely at the pyramids of Virginia ham sandwiches, made with thin slices of white bread, together with the fruit juices in their cut-glass decanters, the wild

strawberry tarts, the heaps of thin pastry flavoured with sassa-
fras, and green, red and white ice-cream, imprisoned by ice
cubes. Elizabeth was satisfied to nibble at a piece of pastry,
kept silent throughout the meal and asked discreetly for a
cup of tea. Nobody said anything.

There hovered an aroma of mystery over this group of
people, who were usually so talkative. They felt that this visit
to Charlie Jones was something quite different from a pleasure trip. In vain did the master of the house himself risk a
facetious remark about the frivolity of the present day and
the folly of the newspapers. His gaiety was turning to arti-
ficiality. He was visibly in a hurry for the day to come to an
end, keeping in reserve they knew not what for the evening.

Dinner was quite late: delicious as one might have expected, but with no effect on the mood of the guests who
remained serious and spoke almost in hushed voices. Only
Billy's never-changing appetite led him boldly through this
rather difficult time in which they felt a kind of unease
setting in, something akin to fear. What was going to
happen to William Hargrove?

In the flickering light of the candelabras, Elizabeth could
see Charlie Jones's face clouding over as the meal drew to a
close. His stormy blue eyes, that previously she had so much
admired, aroused only anxiety in her now. Every other minute
they lighted on her, as if he were seeking to understand
what was going on inside that head beneath its mass of
golden hair. Since their first meeting, which already seemed
distant, he had shaved his side-whiskers off, and his beardless, dusky pink face briefly regained the freshness of youth
in the dancing light of the candles, flickering in the breeze
of the fans.

As his guests were passing into the drawing room, he
came up to her and said with a smile intended to be affectionate:

'If you can spare me a moment, come with me into my
retreat, my little library, where I try to forget the world.'

She followed him, intrigued, wary nevertheless, sniffing
out trouble. As they were leaving the room, Fred caught up
with them and took Charlie Jones by the arm, as if to hold
him back:

'Have you read Aunt Laura's letter?' he asked under his

breath.

'Yes, hastily.'

'I think, Uncle Charlie, there are things that it is better to keep quiet about for the moment.'

'She is of an age to understand.'

'I'm not entirely sure.'

Although this brief exchange was made in almost hushed voices, Elizabeth guessed that it was about her and became annoyed.

'I can go away if my presence is awkward,' she said aloud.

'A thousand pardons,' exclaimed Charlie Jones with a laugh. 'We're very rude. We'll see later on, Fred.'

'Yes, later,' said the young man as he walked away, 'even if it's two o'clock in the morning.'

Without answering, Charlie Jones led Elizabeth to a small room at the far end of the antechamber.

A row of books on a mahogany shelf barely justified the name of library, but there reigned within these walls a quietness whose charm was immediately apparent. A low sofa, covered with Indian cloth with a red background, was obviously used for resting on. Two armchairs, one of them a rocker, faced each other, both upholstered in black horsehair cloth. In the middle of one of the walls, the portrait of a pretty woman, wearing a large lace bonnet, was the only decorative feature in this place, where the feeble light from a small globe lamp seemed to spread silence.

Charlie Jones pointed out one of the armchairs to Elizabeth and took his place in the rocking chair.

'My young and charming compatriot,' he said with a graceful smile that explained his success with women, 'we're going to do some straight talking, like two true English people. If you think me indiscreet, you'll very gently tell me to be quiet. Agreed?'

'I have no desire to tell you off, because I'm counting on your not being indiscreet,' she replied firmly, for she expected the worst.

'A good answer!' he said with a laugh. 'You are very intelligent, and we're going to be able to tackle the problem head-on. Do you know what a fallen woman is?'

She gave him a surprised look.

'Oh . . . yes.'

'When I say "fallen woman," I'm using current parlance, I make no judgement on the profession.'

'Nor do I.'

He looked surprised in his turn.

'Have you known any?'

'No, but there's Mary Magdalen in the gospel.'

'Indeed, indeed, but she was an exceptional woman. There are fallen women in the world today, as at all times, but they are not all of the same quality. Did you know that? They sell their bodies and earn their living in that way.'

Silence.

'Are you shocked, Elizabeth?'

'No, but why are you talking to me about these things?'

'Because the one they call the lady in white is a fallen woman.'

The girl stood up abruptly.

'I don't understand why you are talking to me about this person whom I do not know.'

He answered in a calm, slow voice:

'I'm sorry if what I'm saying upsets you, Elizabeth. Why are you trembling? I am here to help you, not to frighten you.'

'I don't like what you're telling me, and I think you're wrong. And anyway, the lady is of no interest to me.'

'She is very rich.'

'That's all the same to me.'

'And like all rich people, she wants to be richer still.'

'Well, do you think I'm interested in that?'

'It will interest you in a moment.'

'With your permission, Uncle Charlie, I should prefer to leave.'

'Unfortunately I can't permit it, because I have a duty to speak to you. Sit down, please.'

He looked so majestic as he spoke these words that she did not dare disobey.

He resumed, quietly:

'Aunt Laura has written me a long letter about you. There are certain things that you must be aware of. The lady in white is hoping to make a place for herself in good society, by means of the wealth she possesses. She leads a life of luxury in a state neighboring ours. I'm not making anything up and I'm not giving away any secrets. These are matters of public knowledge.'

'Once again, Uncle Charlie, I have no desire to know what that person wants.'

Charlie Jones continued as if he had not heard.

'She is by no means a dreamer. She is quite aware that all the luxury in the world won't get her over the threshold of a Southern drawing room, but what cannot be had with money might be obtained perhaps through marriage. What is known as a good marriage ... to a gentleman from a great family. For two years or more, she has not exercised her ... profession, but the memory of it is not wiped from people's minds. I apologize for the language I'm using, but there's only one way to say certain things. She is no longer for sale, but is nonetheless marked by it. She is attempting the impossible by getting herself married to a member of the old English nobility. She has made him crazy with love, but will only be his if he makes her his wife. From that moment, she will be received, as they say. That is what she imagines anyway. Some cases of such audacity have been seen to succeed ... in the North. But here ... am I to go on?'

She looked at him, dumbstruck and pale-faced, and did not answer.

He waited for a moment and continued:

'The man in question is hesitating. His pride goes beyond anything one can imagine. He will give in, however, and she will make him a very rich man. Do you want to know his name, Elizabeth?'

'No,' she said in a flat tone of voice.

'No point, in fact. You know it as well as I do.'

'If he's proud, as you say, he won't marry her. She'll always be a woman of low estate.'

'She's not of low estate, she's a lady. That's another story ... But what cunning that woman has! She's ruining that man so as to be able to buy him at a lower price later.'

'I don't understand anything of what you're saying. A man doesn't sell himself.'

'Not like a slave, of course, but when he has nothing left, she will offer him her hand and her fortune in exchange for his name.'

'I hate that woman.'

'You'll change your mind some day. You'll get to know her. She's exquisite.'

'That horror? Never! If that's what Aunt Laura had to tell you about me . . . Does she even know what love is?'

'My girl, you have no idea what you're saying, she knows very well that you're in love, and she understands you.'

'I didn't say I was in love!'

At these words, he stood up and, coming over to her, took her hands in his. Never had she felt such strength, a feeling of human warmth spreading throughout her body. The storm-colored eyes gave her the impression they were taking hold of her, and a smile of ineffable goodness lit up that face restored to youth.

'Elizabeth,' he said in a voice charged with affection, 'has your presence not taught you anything else for the last hour, and are you really afraid that I won't be able to understand you?'

Incapable of quelling her emotion, she began to tremble, but did nothing to free her small hands which were imprisoned in his.

'Uncle Charlie,' she stammered.

He continued, without loosening the grip of his hands:

'Laura is an admirable woman who knows as well as you and I what love is. We will never talk about that, but she believes, as I do, that your place is no longer at Dimwood. It's not the place for you to be happy in any more, since the master has been struck down.'

In a flash of panic, she saw all her hopes of love with Jonathan collapse, but she had strength to say only:

'But I like Dimwood.'

He smiled rather sadly.

'A young Englishwoman fleeing from the truth!' he said and gently let go of Elizabeth's hands.

She felt the burning of shame.

'I love that man in spite of everything they might say about him.'

'That's the Elizabeth I admire,' he said. 'But be careful.'

'I'm sure he loves me.'

'Don't be too ready to believe what men tell you, that one especially.'

'He didn't tell me, but he gave me to understand it so

clearly.'

She was on the point of telling him about the encounter on the road to Savannah. Something held her back.

'Listen,' he said after a few moments, 'I have something to tell you that won't make you too sad, I hope.'

She waited.

'You haven't forgotten that young man who behaved so unpleasantly at the ball and was the cause of a duel.'

'Oh yes, Philip Hudson.'

'He got himself into some more trouble a week ago. Convinced that aping arrogance would put him in the first rank of society, he spoke with haughty insolence to a young man who did not know him and who challenged him to a duel immediately. You can guess the rest, or rather the end. He took on one of our most reputed swordsmen. You won't see him again.'

'Oh!'

The shock was all the greater, for that very morning, before leaving Dimwood, she had torn up the letter from her imprudent admirer.

'They say,' continued Charlie Jones, 'that he was afraid the day before that stupid duel, but it was too late. If he had refused to fight, notices pinned to the tree trunks would have informed passers-by that Philip Hudson was a coward. The South is unrelenting on that point. The poor devil had his chest pierced with a sword in the gardens of the colonial cemetery. He had barely recovered from the previous duel . . .'

The girl remained silent for a moment, then murmured, as if she were speaking to herself:

'He told me he loved me.'

'Others will tell you the same thing. Don't be too ready to believe them. Wait till they give you proof.'

'What sort of proof?'

'It's late, Elizabeth. I think we ought to wish each other a good night. Tomorrow I'll take you to see my house in Madison Square.'

Bending towards her, his lips brushed against her forehead.

She remembered with embarrassment the portrait in her room. She was filled with a vague feeling of happiness.

'Forget Dimwood,' he whispered as if telling her a secret.

The new day began under the auspices of an officially enforced joviality, Charlie Jones being quite determined to rid the house of any shadow of melancholy. A light blue, cloudless sky seemed to smile on his arrangements. In reality, no one had slept well, except Billy, who, in Ned Jones's canoe, had enjoyed peace and quiet and rich images of voluptuousness.

Breakfast restored them all to some semblance of good humor. In her plum-colored dress, her head adorned with an architectural assembly of lace and mauve ribbons, Aunt Emma deigned to be amused at Uncle Charlie's facetiousness. She declared that she was going to rest in her room to recover from the fatigue of the previous day's journey. Fred risked a few humorous anecdotes and promised to entertain his Cousin Susanna by taking her for a walk in the colonial cemetery, or in the direction of Bonaventure. As for Billy, he proposed examining in greater detail all the sights of that interesting town.

The day was planned meticulously: Uncle Charlie took Elizabeth to Madison Square, as he had promised. Ten or so slaves dressed in grayish blue cotton were working at a moderate pace beneath a ferocious sun, against which broad-brimmed straw hats offered some protection. She was able to see that the walls had risen by three feet since her first visit, and expressed surprise as was expected, but trembled inwardly on seeing the face of her blind angel turn towards her. Fortunately he did not see her, sheltered as she was by her parasol, which she used as a shield, but her heart was pounding. She admired as much as she could the promised things of beauty that Charlie Jones pointed out to her in the empty spaces.

'We are waiting,' he explained, 'for a cargo of expensive Elizabethan bricks, but the merchant ships are so slow ... Each one of these bricks is wrapped in cardboard to protect it from any unfortunate knocks. Think about it for a moment, Elizabeth. It's pure England that's sailing towards us.'

'I would rather sail towards her, Uncle Charlie. It's too hot in your South.'

'One day, soon I hope, I'll take you to Virginia, where you'll find your old homeland again. I have a few country houses there, one of which will delight you.'

Having climbed back into his gig with Elizabeth, he began to dream aloud:

'When I think that we let our colonies get away from us! Today we would be the most powerful nation in the world . . . But don't go repeating that, my dear. People wouldn't understand.'

'I promise.'

Elizabeth accompanied Charlie Jones on his visit to the offices of his trading company on the Savannah estuary without enthusiasm, for nothing bored her more than the world of commerce. She forced herself, however, to play her role gracefully. In her pale green dress, she was full of the freshness of adolescence that heralded beauty to come, but she was unaware of that and feared being still taken for a little girl. She had only ever received one love letter, torn up the previous day, whereas the unfortunate Susanna, who wanted nothing to do with them, already had half a dozen of them, passionate ones too. The young Englishwoman still awaited the miracle of a letter from Jonathan.

The obsessive memory of his voice and his eyes prevented her from hearing properly everything the affable, jovial voice, that sought to instruct her, was saying as the carriage drew to a halt on the quayside:

'This great, solid door, flanked by two columns, always makes a big impression on visitors. Let's go in. The monumental wooden staircase could take the weight of a regiment. The enormous bannister is like an invitation to slide down, for Billy for example, but that isn't the company's style. Do you follow me?'

'Yes, Uncle Charlie, may I take off my bonnet?'

'What a question! But you'll turn all the heads of the clerks in the offices. On these white walls you see portraits of the illustrious founders, who all look flushed with success and the fortunes they have piled up. None of them is handsome, let's move on.'

This chatter led them to a room of imposing proportions, where gentlemen in elegant summer suits were bent over account books, or were dictating letters to secretaries, more simply dressed in cotton cloth.

Two enormous fans stirred up the air slowly, like the large wings of weary birds. The two servants responsible for activating them were sparing with the effort they made and, constantly on the brink of falling asleep; from time to time they toppled over into it. Betrayed by the ceasing of the monotonous creaking of the pulleys, a slap then restored them to their duty, but the atmosphere remained just as heavy.

There was a reaction of general curiosity when Uncle Charlie came in with the young foreigner. Two or three men in open frock coats and white waistcoats came un-hurriedly towards them. Charlie Jones cut short the intro-ductions:

'I'm just passing through the office this morning with my young compatriot. She must get a glimpse of the harbor, which is our pride and joy. I'll see you later, gentlemen . . .'

Cutting short the conversations, he dragged Elizabeth off to the verandah, which ran along the whole length of the façade behind tall windows left half open. A wooden ceiling protected it against the sun.

Beyond the river banks fading in the light, the ocean, with its gray-green infinity, its apparent immobility and its im-probably excessive scale aroused feelings of awe. But that in itself attracted Elizabeth and made Charlie Jones dream too, both aware of the eternal challenge of that passionate, unquiet element.

Silently they walked to the end of the verandah. A gentle breeze, laden with the odor of brine, reached them from the open sea, bringing a little coolness. At their feet, in the harbor, men were coming and going around the vessels, loading great bales of cotton, wrapped in cloth and tied with ropes. Several of them, bare-chested, showed muscles shiny with sweat, but Elizabeth instinctively turned away and looked elsewhere, without being able to give herself a reason for doing so. Charlie Jones suddenly appeared to be reading her thoughts:

'You're not seeing the harbor at its best. This blinding sun leaves no room for dreams. How pleasant it can be to walk along this verandah in the twilight, with the person one loves . . . In the rays of a setting sun, the vulgarity of things is modified. Everything speaks a different language. Can you imagine it?'

With her heart ready to burst at the memory of Jonathan

and the verandah at Dimwood, she said simply:

'Yes, I can imagine what it must be like.'

'Come on,' he said, 'let's go in. We're expected at home.'

They went back down to the quayside and got into the carriage.

As they were driving down large avenues, shaded by sycamores, he suddenly said:

'You must know that I am engaged. They've told you, I'm sure.'

'Yes, Uncle Charlie.'

'The marriage will take place here, then in September we shall go to Virginia, to the house the children call the dream house. Once you're there, you'll never want to leave it, you'll be so happy.'

She was alarmed for a moment and replied:

'But Uncle Charlie, I shall be at Dimwood.'

He did not answer. The pretty, narrow houses of pink brick or white stone watched them gravely from behind smiling flower beds, for each one of these dwellings exuded pride.

Charlie Jones continued as if he had not heard what Elizabeth had said:

'When you see the one who is to be my wife, you will be aware, I hope, of the gentleness and goodness in her eyes. The old house will welcome you like a mother. I shan't wrench you away from Dimwood, you can go back there if you want, but it will be to take your leave of it.'

Elizabeth, in her turn, was silent for a moment.

'What about Savannah and the house you're building here?'

'Oh, the Savannah house, my dear, is the bastion for the future, an inviolable corner of England. There are clouds hovering over the future.'

'Do you think there'll be a war?'

'I didn't say that. It sometimes happens that clouds disappear. Nations have their destiny. Let's leave it at that. Have you ever seen anything more charming than this great avenue?'

They were, in fact, driving along one of the most famous walks in the town. Beneath the shade of four rows of trees, elegant gentlemen in top hats with their elegant ladies in light-colored dresses with billowing pleats were walking and chatting all along a pink brick path. Here and there, a scarce ray of sunlight penetrated the layers of light foliage, sprinkling patches of golden light, and the ladies' multi-colored little parasols waved about like flowers.

'Admire the freedom from care that peace brings and remember this image. It's deceptive, for if ever the North were to attack us, the whole of the South would be turned into a wasps' nest.'

'When you talk that way, Uncle Charlie, I have the impression that you can foresee some misfortune.'

'I'm no prophet. It's possible that I'm reading incorrectly the signs I see engraved on Belshazar's wall.'

She laughed nervously and exclaimed:

'If it's come to Belshazar's wall, I would prefer to go away for good.'

'Come,' he said, laughing in his turn, 'let's say I'm wrong, and catching the others' pessimism. We'd hoped that every-thing had been settled, but Congress can't agree. The 4th of July is quite close. You and I, the English, we don't celebrate it. What a pleasant surprise if peace could flare up from the fireworks and the bangs of the squibs! There's nothing against believing in miracles. You, Elizabeth, who have kept your faith and read your Bible every day, ask Providence for a miracle.'

'And what about you, Uncle Charlie?'

'Oh, me . . .'

As he spoke these words, he jumped down lithely from the gig in front of the house, and came round to help the girl out, but she was already waiting at the front door, with a slightly mocking air.

52

June was drawing to a close. The few days that followed were not marked by special rejoicing in Charlie Jones's house. The preparations were quite modest, for the national festival evidently left him indifferent. Enthusiasm was paralyzed by political indifference. The notorious union of hearts requested by Henry Clay was far from being fulfilled. Accepted in outline, the planned Compromise was being discussed in detail; specifically the difficulties raised by representatives of the North in ratifying the law on runaway slaves that the government authorities were to arrest and return to their masters. No abolitionist was prepared to accept humiliation on such a scale. On the Southern side, there was an equally serious problem: soldiers from the South had fought for the conquest of California, slave territory, and now the planned Compromise had proposed the new state under the Union be a free state. The South made play of the fact that the Constitution not only authorized slavery but declared it to be legitimate. The abolitionists replied that the constitution was an agreement with death and a pact with Hell. Moreover, the California squatters, who now formed part of the population, did not want slaves at any price. The South was furious at seeing herself robbed and deprived of her conqueror's rights. According to her way of viewing the situation, she had fought for the Union and, more especially, for the North.

President Zachary Taylor could act, but what was he thinking? What did he want? If ever there were a Gordian knot to be cut, this was a perfect example of it.

It was at this point that the force known as chance, fate or the will of the Almighty intervened. The 4th of July Independence Day celebrations proceeded in the year 1850 entirely according to plan: flags and tricolor streamers, speeches and banquets. Especially banquets! The kitchens excelled themselves. There was a lot of eating. Zachary Taylor ate too much. The heat was extreme. The President was taken ill with indigestion, complicated by a violent outburst of anger against his Secretary of State for War, Crawford. This latter was accused of trading on his influence with the Secretary of State at the Treasury, and all of this with the blessing of the Attorney General. This scandal dealt a great blow to the President, who had always been proud of his scrupulous honesty. He decided to reshuffle his cabinet. The anger brought on apoplexy, complicated by an attack of typhoid fever, which eventually led to his death. The outcome would not be in doubt, and the few days that followed the celebrations were overclouded by a general anxiety; the future looked bleak.

That night, Charlie Jones took the decisions he judged to be necessary. Aunt Emma would return to Dimwood with Susanna the very next morning. It was better for them to be at home in the unlikely event of things taking a turn for the worst. The two boys could wait a while. Billy had disappeared, obviously fearing an enforced departure.

Fred remained cool-headed and calmly analyzed the chances of imminent conflict. Vice President Fillmore could make no declaration while the President was still alive, and how can one know what a politician has in mind when he does not usually know himself? War could, however, be envisaged. That was Fred's wish. In the meantime, he had to take care of his mother, who had to be calmed with laudanum and port on several occasions.

Charlie Jones viewed things with exemplary equanimity. According to him, the North was in no state to launch into a military venture that would be costly in terms of both human lives and dollars, and the people did not want it. It was the same in the South apart from a minority of over-excited fanatics. People wanted peace, so long as it did not take on the appearance of surrender. It was not certain that Zachary Taylor would accept the Compromise. Vice President Fillmore, his successor, was a man of the North.

Sitting in his big winged armchair with a julep in his hand, Charlie Jones was looking at Elizabeth who sat opposite him on a red velvet sofa. Neither said a word, but this was a heavy kind of silence that follows hard discussions. The girl was sitting up very straight in her white dress, her hands primly folded on her knees. Her face betrayed no emotion, but her unspeaking, tightly-clenched lips spoke nonetheless of stubborn determination.

Suddenly, Charlie Jones leaned a little towards her and asked her in a pleasant tone of voice:

'Will you have another julep with me to make peace?'

Elizabeth half ventured a smile:

'You and I are not at war, Uncle Charlie, but I have to admit that one julep is enough for me. It's refreshing, but it goes to the head.'

'Believe me,' he continued, as he put his glass down on a small table, 'I understand all the objections you have raised. I do not have the right to keep you here against your will if you want to go back to Dimwood.'

'The Hargroves wouldn't understand my living somewhere other than with them, as my mother requested.'

'Of course, but the unfortunate event of last week changes things somewhat. In the present circumstances. . . .'

'Have you had bad news about Mr Hargrove?'

'On the contrary. His condition is improving noticeably each day. I received a note from Aunt Laura this evening. She is very optimistic. I have her letter in my pocket. Here it is. I'll read you a few sentences from it, listen:

He is beginning to recognize everybody, as if he were emerging from a dream, and it is very moving. I, alas, am the only one not to have been restored to his memory. I look after him, and he calls me 'My angel', taking me for a stranger. When he becomes aware of his mistake, I fear it may be dreadful.

He folded the letter up again and added:

'It is more, in view of the exceptional circumstances, she insists that I keep you here as long as possible.'

'I don't see the connection.'

'Do I need to remind you of what you confided to me the first time you dined here?'

'Please, don't. You know that Mr Hargrove does not speak to me any more — no more than he does to Aunt Laura.'

'For different reasons.'

'Very obscure ones, it seems to me,'

'Very. The problem with Aunt Laura is very involved.'

'The problem with Aunt Laura is not my business. Mine should be simpler. I never knew what I had done to Mr Hargrove.'

'Elizabeth.'

'Well! What have I said that is so surprising? I beg you, Uncle Charlie, be clearer. What's wrong?'

'Well, you are sixteen, and I thought you had more intuition, were better informed.'

'Then treat me as an idiot and explain things to me.'

'I don't like having to tell you these things. My old friend

Hargrove is undoubtedly sorry about your absence, but it's that which is helping him to regain his . . . how shall I put it? . . . equilibrium, the peace in his soul.'

'I find it charming to hear such things, when one has been welcomed with open arms by the family of which he is the head.'

'Don't get cross, Elizabeth. Just tell me if you've understood.'

'But of course. I suspected something of that kind when I saw him here in the antechamber, passing by like a ghost and looking at me when he thought I was asleep. I was lying on a sofa. He stopped.'

'What's all this? You didn't tell me anything about it.'

'Why should I have spoken about it?'

'He stayed here, in fact, for one day and one night, looking for someone he was trying to help whom he wants to save, as he puts it. And seeing you lying down, he looked at you.'

'For a long time.'

'Poor William!'

'Poor Elizabeth. He is as he is, and I am as I am, and I want to go back to Dimwood.'

Charlie Jones looked a bit deceitful and turned a deaf ear. Then, in an even voice, he continued:

'I have no need to tell you who the person was that he was looking for in order to save her. You guessed that some time ago.'

'Frankly, no.'

'The pretty lady in white, don't you see?'

'The one you call the "fallen woman?"'

'The very same. And what must have been William Hargrove's disappointment when he learnt that she had passed by Dimwood, while he had been looking for her in Savannah?'

'That woman again!'

'If I'm telling you about her, it's because Aunt Laura told me in the note that came this morning of a rumor that's circulating concerning her. The fallen woman is said to have declared that the time was not very far off when there would be a great change in her life.'

'Oh?'

'Yes. Worthy souls thought she was going to withdraw from the world and enter a convent. For you are not ignorant of the fact that she is a Roman Catholic.'

'That's the last straw! They get everywhere, don't they?'

'You are not versed in the ways of the world. The Catholics now have a bishopric at Macon, and a religious community near Savannah.'

'My mother always told me to be wary of those people. They find a way in everywhere . . .'

A flash of joy suddenly lit up her anxious face, and she added with a slight laugh:

'That would be the best thing she could do, since she subscribes to that way of thinking. In a convent. Locked in a convent, far from the world, dedicated to prayer and penance. It seems that for every fault a nun commits, she has to go down on all fours in front of the Mother Superior and make a large cross with her tongue on the floor.'

She was stammering with pleasure as she poured out these strange notions, when Charlie Jones interrupted her:

'I'm sorry to have to disillusion you, my girl. This fanciful view of religious life is a Protestant invention. Those who are less romantically inclined interpret differently what the lady in white calls the "great change" in her life. They see quite simply her intention of getting married.'

Elizabeth turned pale.

'We've already talked about that absurd plan,' she murmured. 'She won't succeed in it.'

'No one will be able to prevent her from marrying whomsoever she wishes.'

'She will never be admitted into society.'

'Perhaps she has given up that ambition simply for the sake of marrying the man she loves.'

'Some man of no rank then . . .'

'But we know nothing of it, Elizabeth. Perhaps she wishes to marry . . .'

She stopped him short:

'Don't say his name, I don't want to know.'

'I shan't say it, but it's clear that we're both thinking of the same person.'

As he said these words, he had the feeling of playing a cruel trick on this girl whom he was reducing to despair, and who was so unable to look after herself. At the same time, however, Elizabeth was again tempted to reveal to him the episode of her encounter with Jonathan on the road to Savannah, but once more she resisted.

'You're spoiling your future,' he said sadly, seeing her so silent and determined. 'What do you want to do?'

'Go back to Dimwood as soon as possible.'

'You can leave tomorrow morning, if you want, with Aunt Emma and Susanna.'

Elizabeth spent a disturbed night, taking a long time to get to sleep. One minute she was glad of the decision she had taken, at another she worried about what awaited her at Dimwood. Every hour, dragged from sleep by frightening dreams, she would get up and lean at the window, watching the night. No sound came up from the town, and never had the starry sky seemed to her so laden with mystery, nor so strangely attractive. Looking at those countless specks of light, she gained the impression that an unknown universe was spinning around in her head. The earth had disappeared, and, by some irresistible force, her whole body became ethereal and, raised gently, was floating in the void. An indescribable joy took hold of her, total oblivion of everything in her life that was tormenting her. Nothing else existed but a feeling of peace, in which the memory of all her fears, as well as all her aspirations, was blotted out. It lasted no more than a second but took on the dimensions of eternity.

When she came to herself in a state of bewilderment, she began to laugh quietly. Everything about that blessed moment was beginning to fade away, and she retained only the impression of having, in that brief instant, lost all sense of personal reality.

At that moment, she heard a bird singing, just a few notes, but joyful ones. A minute later, the same little tune resounded further away, just as clear, but with a slightly different intonation. She listened. Undoubtedly the bird was singing in the garden. He struck up this time in quite a different vein; slow, melancholy, repeating each phrase several times, stopping, correcting himself and modifying his plaintive warbling, as if trying to bring it to perfection.

Then the girl remembered the mocking bird that she had been told about in England. The curse of those who cannot sleep, it imitates the calls of all the birds of the neighborhood and is only satisfied with a perfect rendering; it is only put off by some arrangements of notes that are rather too complex, like those of the nightingale, which it leaves alone.

The persistence of the invisible little singer amused Elizabeth, restoring her equanimity. Returning to bed, she fell almost immediately into a heavy sleep, from which Nora dragged her at about eight o'clock. The old servant was in tears:

'Miss Lizbeth, Mass'r Charlie say you got to get up, if'n you want to leave.'

Elizabeth rubbed her eyes:

'Leave? Oh, yes, Nora, I'm leaving.'

'Oh, Miss Lizbeth, why? Ain't you happy here?'

'Oh yes, yes, but I have to. Quickly, prepare the bath.'

Jumping out of bed, she cast her eyes around that room in which she had suffered and sometimes hoped, and, by one of those tricks that inanimate objects play, the room seemed attractive to her, full of unsuspected charm and silent affection. It was as if the walls were trying with all their strength to keep her there, as well as the furniture with all its commonplace familiarity.

When she had finished washing and dressing, she gave a last look at the garden with its masses of flowers that gave off a fragrance full of the joy of living in the freshness of youth.

All of these impressions combined in secret to affect Elizabeth's attentive mind, and suddenly she was afraid of sombre Dimwood.

The two carriages were waiting in front of the garden gate when Charlie Jones begged Elizabeth to follow him into the small drawing room.

He was smiling, but the smile did not extend as far as his eyes, which were looking gravely at the girl. She had a premonition of something unpleasant and sat down on the edge of the red sofa.

'My dear,' he began, 'I'm sorry to see you going so soon, and I wouldn't like to leave you with a reproach. Listen.

Aunt Emma, who likes dramatic situations, described to me your encounter with a horseman on the way to Savannah.'

'Well,' said the girl, irritated, 'I don't see what concern that is of yours.'

'Really? You might at least have mentioned it to me.'

'What would have been the point?'

'Your silence was more revealing than you think. If you had told me about that encounter, I would have told you that the person in question had come to Savannah to see me. Our conversation did not last more than an hour. It's my turn to be mysterious, but I don't have the right to say any more. Just remember this: beware of that man.'

She recoiled, as if someone had hit her, and she stood up abruptly:

'But why are you saying that?' she exclaimed. 'He didn't behave badly. He is a gentleman.'

'I'm not saying he isn't, but he is a man who is no longer in control of himself. If you don't want to suffer, avoid seeing him at all costs. I've known him for years. I know what I'm saying.'

Elizabeth looked at him without expression.

'Remember that if ever things go badly at Dimwood, you drop me a line and I'll send someone to fetch you. The Hargroves will always be in agreement.'

'Am I to understand that I am not wanted there?'

'There's a more diplomatic way of putting it. Everybody is fond of you, but there's William . . .'

'I know,' she said in exasperation, 'for whom I am the devil.'

'My word, Elizabeth, you say some startling things. But your travelling companions are getting impatient. Shall we embrace?'

She held her cheek to him mechanically, and his lips brushed across it.

'You're nobody's nightmare here,' he said with a laugh, 'and they're very fond of you too, especially Uncle Charlie.'

Without answering, she left the drawing room and ran to the carriage, towards Jonathan, but, once she was sitting down next to Fred, she was sorry for her coldness. Leaning over the door, she waved her hand to Uncle Charlie and called out:

'So am I, Uncle Charlie!'

53

*A*t Dimwood, she found herself in a silent house. There
was only the grating sound of the cicadas in the trees
that seemed to be sawing through the hot air. Uncle Josh
welcomed the travellers at the foot of the porch steps. There
was no exuberance on either side. Voices were lowered more
than usual, as if they were afraid of waking someone or,
even worse, disturbing the sleep of the dead.

'He is very well,' Uncle Josh repeated reassuringly. 'You
wouldn't even guess, really . . .'

'Well, then,' asked Fred, 'why all this mystery?'

Uncle Josh gave a nervous laugh that was not like his
usual good humor:

'There's no mystery at all. He's talking a lot, he says the
prayers — interminably long at breakfast. In fact, everything
is as it was before.'

'What a relief,' exclaimed Aunt Emma. 'I admit I was
having palpitations just now, in the avenue. Well, shall we
go up then?'

'Yes, of course, only . . . Elizabeth and Susanna. We had
hoped, we had thought, that Uncle Charlie would keep
them longer, so . . .'

There was an embarrassed silence. The tender perfume of
the magnolia hovered around them as they now paid careful
attention. Elizabeth's heart, laden with memories, felt tight.

'What are you saying?' she asked in a voice that she hoped
was calm.

'Oh, nothing,' said Uncle Josh, 'it's fine for you to be
here with us. I'll speak to my father. Unfortunately, Laura is
away, she has gone to visit a small community in the
neighborhood.'

Only too happy, deep down, to put off the inevitable encounter with Mr Hargrove, Elizabeth withdrew, followed by a docile Susanna, struck dumb with terror.

Aunt Emma and her two boys accompanied Uncle Josh, who led them to Mr Hargrove.

The room overlooked the gardens from two windows hung with dark green taffeta. Seated in a large rocking chair, William Hargrove seemed to be listening to Uncle Douglas, who was reading the newspaper to him. It was obvious that the master of Dimwood was elsewhere. His appearance had not changed, except for his side-whiskers, which were even bushier as they merged with his thick mustache. Right beside him a table, untidily scattered with books, gave a studious air to what was a small drawing room, in which the two tutors usually exchanged their confidences. Both of them had returned to their respective states because of the impending dangers.

He gave a big smile when he saw Emma and the two boys and said to them gaily:

'You're back from Savannah then! What had you gone down there for? Don't you like it here?'

'A change of air never does one any harm, and Charlie was delighted to see us.'

This explanation was proffered nonchalantly by Aunt Emma who took off her bonnet and sat down on the chair that Uncle Douglas offered her. The latter looked at her questioningly, and then directed his eyes towards the door.

'Fred and Billy behaved themselves,' she continued, 'Fred especially. As for Billy, I can only assume so, for that town seems distinctly immoral to me, and our Billy, who lacks experience, risks serious danger there.'

'I'll put the fear of God right into the marrow of his bones,' said William Hargrove. 'His religion isn't being sufficiently taken care of. Who looks after Billy's religion at Dimwood? I shall see to it myself. You will start, my boy, by learning the Psalms, all of them, by heart.'

'There are one hundred and fifty of them,' Fred remarked with a subtle smile.

'No more trips to Savannah this summer.'

'But I did nothing wrong in Savannah!' exclaimed Billy. 'I

went horse-riding around the outskirts of the town.'

'Where's the other one?' William Hargrove suddenly asked.

'Father,' said Uncle Douglas, 'I thought I had told you that she had gone to visit a community in the neighborhood.'

'She should be here. She's an angel, my angel.'

Uncle Douglas exchanged glances with Aunt Emma. They both nodded their heads sadly.

'Why isn't she here?' asked William Hargrove in a plaintive voice. 'It upsets me.'

Aunt Emma managed to change the conversation by talking about Charlie Jones and his planned holiday in Virginia, in the family home.

'That great rambling place,' sighed William Hargrove. 'I spent pleasant times there in the past.'

For several minutes he walked through that dream house, and, getting lost in his imaginings, he became calmer. The boys took advantage of it to leave with Uncle Josh, while Aunt Emma, suddenly seized with compassion, stayed with William Hargrove. For the first time in her life she forgot her thousands of personal requirements and felt close to the drifting human being that their father had become.

Elizabeth had fled to her room, where Susanna followed her with the obstinacy of a lost dog.

'Alone with you!' she exclaimed, throwing herself into Elizabeth's arms. 'It's providential!'

'Oh, no you don't,' said the English girl pushing her firmly away. 'Anything you like, but not that. It's just too tiring. I want to be alone.'

'Horrid thing!'

'I'm sorry if I'm unkind. I'm worried.'

'Love worries, perhaps? Just like me, do you understand? On top of everything else, I'm not wanted anywhere. Uncle Charlie was not in the least bit interested in me, and I have to hide here ever since that business of the piece of paper at the water's edge. Everything is my fault. I wonder if they wouldn't have preferred to see me drowned.'

'If you want to make me feel sorry for you, you're wasting your time.'

'. . . or eaten by an alligator . . .'

'You make me cross with your alligator, everything you say makes me cross.'

'I thought as much, but you're wrong. I know all sorts of things. I learnt some good ones all the time I was in hiding.'

'Whereabouts?'

'Nosy. Wouldn't you like to know? Everybody would. I gave my word not to tell — but now that everything has worked out . . .'

'Indeed.'

'Do you think it's alright to tell?'

'Only you can know.'

'Well, if you swear not to repeat it . . .'

'Alright. I swear.'

'On the Bible!'

'Oh, Susanna, there are times when I want to grab you by the ears and bang your head against the wall . . . for hours on end. Alright, yes, yes, on the Bible.'

'Well, nobody has the right to go to Miss Llewelyn's. She has two rooms, right next to the attic where Souligou works. She explained to me why I should never marry. Thrilling. I'll tell you about it. She knows everything. She knows too that Lieutenant Boulton is to come on Sunday to take the engagement ring back. Papa will receive him.'

'You're making it up!'

'Not at all! You'll see, what's more. Do you remember when we were still in the great avenue, and we overtook a man on a black horse?'

'Yes, what about it?'

'He was going in the direction of Savannah, but as soon as he saw us in the first carriage, he turned round after casting a glance inside, as if he were looking for someone.'

'Carry on.'

'What's the matter with you? Do you mind me talking like this?'

'On the contrary, I want to know . . .'

'Afterwards, I don't know. I couldn't see him. You must have seen him go by, didn't you?'

'Yes.'

'Well, the Welshwoman told me that he came here and asked to see Grandfather, but Grandfather was ill, so Papa received him with Uncle Douglas. All three were speaking in loud voices. The man wanted them to sign a document for him with Grandfather's signature, and Papa's and Uncle Douglas's. Miss Llewelyn heard it all.'

'She had her ear to the door, quite by chance.'

'I don't know, I don't think so, she just knows everything. She must be a witch, like all Welshwomen. The man began to shout, because he wanted Grandfather's signature most of all, and they refused him. He stayed for an hour talking.'

'And then?'

'Then he set off down the great avenue, heading for Savannah.'

Elizabeth let out a cry of despair:

'For Savannah! He was there when we were!'

'It's possible. When he was going down the porch steps to get back on his horse, the Welshwoman heard him say to Papa: "Next time I come here, I shall be returning home, and I shan't be alone."'

Elizabeth did not answer. She looked shattered and Susanna finally began to be worried.

'What on earth is the matter with you?'

'Nothing. You'd better run off, my dear Susanna. If Aunt Laura were to find you here . . .'

'Aunt Laura's not here.'

'I'd like to see Miss Llewelyn.'

'That's not difficult. She's always wandering about the corridors and on the verandah. You won't tell her I've spoken?'

'Of course not.'

At supper the three empty places visibly disturbed William Hargrove, for he kept counting and recounting those present with his eyes. He nevertheless said, with remarkable dignity, a few personal prayers for the general pacification of the country. He was evidently finding his feet again and gave orders in a calm, natural voice.

Towards the end of the meal, however, he looked sad and, as if speaking to himself, said slowly:

'It's strange, I had the impression there were more of us. And where is the lady who looks after me?'

'Father,' said Uncle Josh, 'do you not remember? Laura's

gone to visit a community.'

'A community, ah yes. Get them to ask her to come back. What about the others?'

'What others?' asked Aunt Emma, sitting next to him in the very place Aunt Laura usually occupied.

'What others,' he repeated mechanically. 'I don't know. It's a mistake . . . a mistake.'

Paying more attention for the last few minutes, Billy was overpowered by some unknown premonition. For the first time, he guessed at the presence of a mystery he did not understand. Hilda and Mildred stifled a nervous laugh in their napkins.

The supper came to an end almost immediately.

54

*A*lone in her room, Elizabeth wondered what fate had in store for her at Dimwood and, in some way, she was not bothered about it. There was no change as far as essentials were concerned: she must stay here at all costs. The superstitious notion that her presence would attract Jonathan took a hold on her and, as night had not completely fallen, the dusk still permitted weak rays of light to fall at her feet. She lit the lamp and flung herself into the rocking chair.

With a vigorous click of her heel she set the chair in motion, making all the floorboards groan. She felt elated, which calmed her great uncertainty. Nearby, at her elbow, she could see her black Bible, closed and full of silent reproaches, but the girl felt in no mood to read it. Through the open window wafted the fragrance of magnolia, haunted by a man's imploring face. In her waking dream, she imagined Jonathan appearing suddenly before her. In the absence of Aunt Laura, who would have stopped her, and then . . . She arrested the chair by gripping the edge of the table. Her heart was pounding. He could be there, in front of her. What would she say? Her imagination was already getting the better of her when she heard a knock at the door and only just stopped herself crying out from nervous tension.

It was Betty, standing worried and timid in the doorway not daring to take a step forward. A red and blue striped kerchief was wrapped round her head, hiding her gray curls, but in her black skirt and white apron she retained that dignified air that always struck the English girl:

'Come in, Betty,' she told her, 'don't stay there.'

'You ain't upset with me?'

'But of course not. Come now. Talk, I want you to talk.'

'Mass'r Jonathan . . .'

Elizabeth leapt to her feet.

'Why do you wish to speak to me about that gentleman?'

Her face red with anger, she was standing in front of the servant, who took a step backwards.

'Everybody knows, Miss Lizbeth.'

'Everybody knows what? I order you to answer without trying to lie, do you hear?'

Seized with terror, Betty threw her apron over her face in accordance with the custom that goes back to the invention of aprons.

'Mass'r Jonathan wants to take back the house,' said her stifled voice.

'Where is he?'

'I don't know, Miss Lizbeth . . . Far away . . .'

'Are you telling the truth, Betty?'

This question was followed by a silence that seemed interminable to Elizabeth. She bore the motionless gaze of those deep black eyes that she saw clouding over with tears.

For a few seconds they looked at each other without moving, each of them waiting for some word that did not come, then Betty withdrew slowly, closing the door very gently behind her.

Elizabeth stared at that door in consternation.

Standing now beside the lamp, she opened her Bible and read a few verses at random, but that night there was not that indefinable communication between herself and the book she had known from childhood. She closed it again in disappointment.

In the half-light, the splash of white that was her bed caught her eye for a moment . . . Sleep . . . No question of it. Nothing seemed to have any meaning any more. Keep the lamp alight . . . 'Like a lighthouse!' she thought with that bitter irony which never left her. Betty had said: 'Far away.' He was far away.

Inspired by despair, she went out onto the verandah, and dragged herself as far as the magnolia. Despite her weariness, she discovered in it the intoxication of memories. In the darkness, full of fragrance, the whole earth seemed to be in love, speaking to her only of Jonathan. The cold and mysterious light from the sky enabled her to see the row of trees along the edge of the river, all along the field, as far as the forbidden forest. She let her eyes wander in that direction, when she suddenly noticed something gray moving slowly at the edge of the wood.

She moved back instinctively, as if she had seen a ghost, but the gray shape had nothing of an apparition about it. A more careful look allowed the girl to recognize the outline of Miss Llewelyn, and she got a shock. But what was so strange about the Welshwoman going to take the air in the grounds of the house? It was true that the massacre of Indians had given them a sinister reputation, but memories of killings hovered over the whole of the Dimwood estate. It was better to tell oneself that all that was not true.

She remained immobile, not without a premonition that she was making a mistake. She was suddenly surprised to see Miss Llewelyn turn in her direction and wave her arm.

Automatically she did the same and, although she was fifty yards away from the Welshwoman and in poor light, she could make out the features and her smile. This very precision made her feel uneasy, as if this strange woman were being drawn closer to her by some magical power.

Her first reaction was to withdraw into her bedroom for the night. Even if she had wanted to go down the porch steps and join Miss Llewelyn, she would have had to throw a coat over her shoulders. She was still wearing a light cotton dress, and the air was cooling down. The temptation to talk to her whom everybody avoided became clearer. Miss Llewelyn had, of course, said disobliging things to her about her amorous aspirations, but now the Welshwoman was there, waving and smiling. A call, a godsend, perhaps . . .

Elizabeth wrapped herself in a dark green shawl. She took a few calm steps on the grass and almost immediately ran towards the person who was standing still, waiting for her with the same smile, sure of herself and of her prey.

The sky had never seemed vaster or deeper, with its millions of specks of light and their indecipherable message. The earth seemed to be questioning, plaintively, through the tinkling little voices of the tree-frogs.

'Well,' said Miss Llewelyn, seeing the girl rather out of breath before her, 'when people are unhappy, they come and look for that awesome Maisie Llewelyn to patch up their love life.'

There was a kind of music in her Welsh intonation.

'I didn't know you would be here . . .'

'Of course, it wasn't me you were waiting for next to your magnolia, but let me tell you that he won't come, not tonight, nor any other. Courage! That man is not for you. I've told you already, and I tell you again.'

Elizabeth gave her a defiant look.

'You're mistaken,' she said. 'Jonathan loves me. I know it, I'm sure of it.'

'In the meantime, he's getting married.'

'It hasn't happened yet. I want that man.'

Miss Llewelyn began to laugh quietly.

'I admire your obstinacy in spite of myself, Miss Escridge. Shall we go for a little walk?'

'Gladly. Is that why you waved to me just now?'

'Not exactly. It was just a way of saying good evening. You ask a lot of questions. Too many, perhaps. Can you smell all the good smells coming from the wood? Shall we go that way? It'll be a quieter place to talk, and we don't risk being seen.'

The girl wondered what the Welshwoman had in mind, but accepted the invitation nevertheless.

A moment later, they were both embarking on the beech-lined path, the trees rising upon either side like columns, dazzlingly white in the darkness.

'You see,' said Miss Llewelyn, 'all young girls of your age wish to catch a man, to use the vulgar expression of these parts. Pretty as you are, you can aim for the best, and there are many pleasant young men in this area.'

'I want Jonathan,' said Elizabeth angrily.

'Wanting isn't enough. You have to be able to get what you strongly desire.'

'But how?'

'There are ways.'

'I'm ready to do all that's necessary.'

Once more the Welshwoman's bright laugh was to be heard, ringing out unfamiliarly in the darkness of the woods. The sand on the path was the only thing that could still be seen.

'You amuse me, Miss Escridge. What you call necessary requires serious study and gifts and is not to be learnt by rote, like German.'

Feeling that these bantering remarks were wounding the girl's pride, she added:

'But you have the gifts. People like me, we can sniff these things out first go. We're getting on to dangerous ground here, though, and I don't want to upset you.'

'I assure you that I'm not frightened of anything.'

'By upset I mean overturn your ideas about the world. But listen to that melancholy little cry. There is a charm in the solitude of this place.'

An owl had begun to hoot, and its call filled the whole of the night with a dreamy sadness that obliged one to pay attention.

In spite of herself, Elizabeth felt ill at ease. She made an effort to appear calm.

'An owl,' she said. 'I like those nocturnal birds, but I like all birds. As for my ideas about the world, don't be afraid of overturning them, Miss Llewelyn, all I want is to hear yours.'

'Let's go a few more steps. I find these woods enchanting.'

'So do I,' said Elizabeth in a lively voice, 'but I admit that I can hardly see anything any more.'

'Take a fold of my sleeve and follow me.'

The girl took in her fingers a fold of the rough material, the gray color of which was familiar to all the inhabitants of Dimwood, and she felt a vague feeling of disgust.

'We live in a world of which only a part is visible,' said Miss Llewelyn. 'Some people have at least an idea of the other. You for example. Come, I can tell that it's so dark you are afraid. Yes, you are. Don't say you're not. It's quite natural. Take my hand and we'll go back.'

Elizabeth hesitated for a second, and suddenly felt Miss Llewelyn's hand groping for hers and taking hold of it: it was a small, chubby hand, but singularly strong.

Together they walked with slow steps through the darkness, and with every step the girl could hear the gentle sound of Miss Llewelyn's dress on the sand. Neither of them spoke, as if the silence had taken over from their conversation. They stopped when they got within sight of the house. Here and there, a few reassuring lights burned in the windows.

'Up there,' said Miss Llewelyn, 'is good old Souligou and her tarot. Lower down, to the right, that's Susanna, who can't sleep and is reading a novel of which she understands nothing. Far over to the left, William Hargrove is reading theology and struggling with his conscience again.'

'How do you know all that?'

'It's not difficult when you know Dimwood as I do. Don't go imagining I'm a witch, although there are some very competent ones amongst us. I have gifts, as you do, and I get by as I can in the world of the occult.'

'The occult?'

'I'll explain it to you another time. Now, if you think I'm the Devil, you must go in and read your Bible and have nothing more to do with me . . .'

'I never said you were the Devil.'

'Alright. That's enough for this evening, I think it's time for you to go to sleep.'

'But Miss Llewelyn, you know what I want, and you said there are ways of getting it.'

'There are, indeed, but they affect the fate of two people, three perhaps.'

'I'm ready to accept anything.'

'It's very serious. Think about it tonight. I'll come by tomorrow.'

'At what time?'

'Never mind what time. I'll be there. Go in without me. It's light enough for you to see. I'll continue my walk. Sleep well, Miss Escridge, do your best to sleep.'

55

*T*he day passed. In a corner of the entrance hall, the atrociously slow ticking of the tall, slim, old clock could be heard. Elizabeth came every quarter of an hour to check the time. By one of those cruel turns of life, she was awaiting the Welshwoman with a lover's impatience whereas, in her heart, she hated that woman who inspired in her as much disgust as fear. Miss Llewelyn was certainly not the devil, but she would have made one believe in him, if one were not already sure.

She came a little before dusk. Suddenly she was there, in the room. She had entered from the verandah without a sound. Elizabeth could immediately smell the pungent odor that she gave off, which came less from her person than from her gray dress, from that dry, coarse cloth that was as unpleasant to the touch as to the smell.

The heavy face with its green eyes turned towards the motionless, surprised girl:

'I frightened you,' said the woman. 'When will I stop frightening people? I'm only there to help them. Have you thought about the warnings I gave you yesterday evening?'

In her lilac-colored dress, her hair like a golden mist in the half-light with the closed shutters, Elizabeth looked guilty in front of the Welshwoman, who suddenly seemed enormous to her.

'Warnings . . .'

'Two destinies, if not three, including yours.'

'I remember very well,' answered Elizabeth, clasping her fingers, 'I have not changed my mind.'

'In that case, you will write down for me on a piece of paper what it is that you wish, then you will fold it and wrap around it a lock of your hair. Have you not got anything that comes from him, some object, a souvenir?'

'Nothing, alas.'

'"Nothing, alas",' repeated Miss Llewelyn in a dull, indifferent voice. 'Write it down, please, and don't keep me waiting. The light is starting to fade.'

Elizabeth sat down at the little desk, took out a sheet of writing paper and remained undecided for a moment.

'State clearly and simply what you want,' said Miss Llewelyn. 'I shan't watch, but be quick.'

'I wish to be loved by Jonathan,' wrote Elizabeth straight off. And, suddenly worried by the thought of the three destinies that this simple phrase risked overturning, she added:

'. . . but I do not wish any harm to come to the lady in white.'

'That's very long,' said Miss Llewelyn, who was standing next to her, like a statue.

By way of an answer, Elizabeth placed the paper under a blotter, then removed it to fold it, rolling it up like a table napkin.

'And now . . .' said the Welshwoman, pulling a pair of scissors out of the pocket of her dress.

Coming close to Elizabeth, she cut off a lock of her hair with a dexterity that plunged the girl into bewilderment. Skilfuly and quickly, the woman plaited a small, golden cord, which she wrapped around Elizabeth's message and gave back to her immediately. She explained briefly:

'A message from you to an unknown destination which will be entrusted to the earth.'

This word cast alarm into the girl's mind, for she exclaimed:

'To the earth! How will that be?'

'If you ask me any more questions, I shall leave you,' said Miss Llewelyn severely, 'and you can work things out for yourself. It's very simple. From now on, you obey me until the end of the rite. Yes or no?'

'Agreed,' said Elizabeth. 'I shall follow your instructions.'

The word 'obey' would have choked in the throat of the proud girl, but the Welshwoman was satisfied with that fine-spun promise.

'It will take place in the wood to the left of the great avenue,' she began.

'The Wood of the Damned?'

'What they call the Wood of the Damned. It frightens only timid souls. It's preferable for us not to go there together. I'll go there now. You'll find me easily at the foot of one of the biggest trees. It rises up in the middle of a large clearing, at the end of a wide avenue. You can't go wrong. I shall be there. Wait for nightfall. It promises to be a clear night.'

Having spoken these words, she withdrew as abruptly as she had come, and the girl, left alone, dropped on to the bed, a prey to worries that drew from her garbled words, mixed with groans. What had she done, and on what evil adventure was she embarking? What did it mean, to affect the destinies of three people? And all that on account of a sentence on a piece of paper . . .

Minutes went by. She had to wait for the night. Why? Suddenly, she left her room and ran to the end of the verandah, to see which path the Welshwoman would take. She arrived just in time to catch sight of her as she was going round the edge of the gardens, dazzling with splashes of color beneath a blue sky that was still light, but her gray silhouette alone was enough to cast a shadow over the landscape.

Elizabeth saw her moving further away, feeling that nothing could stop her and, suddenly horrified at herself and at what was in store, she turned back towards her room.

Passing by Aunt Laura's, she could not resist going in. What struck her first of all was how empty the room seemed. That strange woman had not been seen at Dimwood for several days, and nothing remained of her presence between those walls. The little cross that the English girl had noticed one evening was no longer above the bed, with its blanket folded in four, which seemed, in spite of everything, to be expecting the return of the absent one. And, for the first time, Elizabeth felt she needed her serious look and her calming, gentle voice.

If she had to wait for night to join the Welshwoman, she would wait there, in that uninhabited room, rather than in her own where she had already suffered too much. Here, in some inexplicable way, there was peace. The world and its vexations were far away.

The light was already hesitant in the sky, the birds were singing all around the house with a kind of frenzied passion, as if the shadows threatened to engulf them for ever. Elizabeth could not help but hear a warning in that. The long, oblique rays of sunlight brushed over the ground. The path that led to the woods was perfectly visible. She decided to set off. There was nobody on the verandah. People were waiting for it to be cooler before coming out to rest and chatter in the rocking chairs. She slid out, edged along the side of the gardens and headed for the Wood of the Damned.

She stopped under the first branches. Her heart was pounding so much that she had to lean on the trunk of one of the giant oaks that cut out the light above her head. She had never before ventured that way at twilight. Too many sinister legends came to mind for her to have dared to walk beneath those black trees when the sun was no longer shining, and the curtains of gray moss were waving in the long avenues. That moss was never completely still. On the hottest days, it could be seen, a kind of pale hair hanging from the shadowy branches, waving like the breath from large, invisible mouths. Elizabeth did not even wonder whether she considered it beautiful or not, that mysterious plant, sown by the wind throughout the South. Its long, fringed veils quivering in the silence filled her with a sudden terror, and she was tempted to turn and run.

She resolved, however, somewhat ashamed of her cowardice, to go as far as the end of the avenue, but now the shadows were growing thicker, and she could barely distinguish one tree from another. She began to walk more quickly, until she reached the great clearing, where three other avenues of the Wood of the Damned met up. There she stopped, casting her eyes around to right and to left, without managing to pierce the darkness.

Agitated as she was, she was talking to herself, repeating in a rather tremulous voice: 'Perhaps she's waiting further on . . . in another clearing . . .' These words fell into the heavy silence. No rustling of leaves or creaking of branches disturbed the extraordinary calm of that place. Despite the fear that deprived her of serious thought, she was aware of the beauty of that moment, leaving alive only her panic-stricken heart pounding in her breast.

Suddenly she heard a whispered call and trembled.

'Yes,' she said, 'where are you?'

The answer did not come straight away.

'We mustn't speak too loudly, men sometimes come this way.'

'Men?'

'You see them working in the woods. There's nothing to fear, but I'd rather not see them.'

'What do they do?'

'Who knows? That's of no interest. They are generally only to be seen when the moon is high in the sky. It's only just rising, we must be careful. Come forward a little. Can't you see me?'

'No.'

'You don't get those long, glorious sunsets here, like we get at home in Wales.'

'And like at home in England,' said Elizabeth crossly.

'In their South, night comes down like a curtain.'

She had barely said these words when a feeble light rose up around them, and the girl could make out Miss Llewelyn a few paces from her. The Welshwoman was standing motionless, and her solid outline gave her the appearance of a cromlech. Only her face remained in the shadows.

'Do you have the little object?' she asked.

'Of course,' said Elizabeth.

And with the tips of her fingers, she made sure that the paper, rolled up with a lock of her hair, was still in its place, tucked into the belt of her skirt.

'What do we have to do?' she asked.

'Wait a minute or two for it to get lighter. I used to walk here with the children in daylight. But nobody has come here for years now. They are afraid. You'll see. There's something about it.'

In common accord, neither of them spoke, as if bewitched by the depth of the silence and, gradually, they saw at their feet rays of light still hesitant, but casting their shadow over stony ground.

The girl suddenly held back a cry of surprise when the light got stronger. In front of them, in the middle of the clearing, rose a tree of prodigious size. The giant stretched out over their heads monstrous arms garlanded with moss. As if the better to bear the brunt of storms, it bent backward a little, pulling out from the ground huge, black roots, the enormous folds of which seemed to be moving. Nothing grew in its shade. There was not a single leaf to be seen, by way of foliage, amongst the complex tangle of its branches.

As high as the eye could reach one could make out only rows of gray rags floating noiselessly from one level to the next, with the sinister splendor of ragged standards flying from the battlements of a ruined fortress, still retaining a frightful majesty.

Elizabeth looked at it, dumbfounded.

'This is the place,' said the Welshwoman simply. 'Follow me.'

They went right to the foot of the tree, and there, lifting up her skirt with the greatest of care, Miss Llewelyn knelt down and began to dig at the ground with the pair of scissors which had been used to cut the lock of golden hair. With her back rounded, she stretched her gray bodice, the material of which molded the shape of the muscles of her powerful torso. From time to time, she gave a little sigh of irritation when a stone got in the way of her efforts.

Standing next to her, Elizabeth was looking at the woman with revulsion and contempt, and she despised herself for being there, in that horrible place, involved in that shamefully weird spectacle, yet, in spite of everything, a part of her believed in it.

Now rays of moonlight were filtering through the dead branches, and she could see clearly the Welshwoman bent double at her feet, busily scratching at the earth. Mentally she compared her to a woodland animal hiding its stock of hazelnuts for the winter, with this difference, that a squirrel was nothing but sweetness and innocence, whereas this massive person seemed to her to be an incarnation of evil.

When the hole was judged to be deep enough, Miss Llewelyn stood up, wiped the scissors on a handkerchief and pushed her skirt down with a flick of the hand.

Without a word, Elizabeth, in her turn, kneeled down, as if someone had pushed her quite roughly by the shoulders. With a movement of horror, she threw the little parcel into the bottom of the hole.

'It's done,' she said under her breath.

'Fill in the hole with your hands, but first of all think carefully about what I told you. It's a message. You are sending it to someone. Think carefully about what you're going to say before you put the earth back.'

'To whom, Miss Llewelyn?'

'That doesn't matter. Your questions risk making everything misfire. Stay on your knees and fill it in.'

She moved a dozen or so paces away in order to leave the terrified English girl alone, bending over the hole. Her hair formed a curtain over her face to protect her from curious glances, and she whispered as if into someone's ear:

'Earth, I entrust my love to you. Give me Jonathan . . .'

She hesitated for a few seconds, then finally added:

'But spare the lady in white, do not harm her.'

With both her hands, she put back into the hole the earth that the Welshwoman had put to one side, and, red with embarrassment, she stood up.

'You were a long time,' said Miss Llewelyn. 'Let's go. This is the time when those people slip through the trees.'

Together they headed at a good pace towards the end of the avenue. Not a word was exchanged but, when they could once more see the windows of the house shining in the distance, Elizabeth cried out with relief:

'I shall never go back there!'

'Oh yes, you will,' said Miss Llewelyn with a scornful little laugh. 'You'll come back in the daylight to get the answer.'

'There'll be an answer?'

'Yes, in one form or another. I made a little heap of stones to mark the spot so you won't have any trouble finding the place again.'

'Will you come with me?'

'No, Miss Escridge. You will go alone, preferably in the morning, unless your traditionally English daring tempts you to face up to the dark.'

The girl did not react to that piece of impertinence, and they separated a few minutes later.

56

*T*hroughout all these wanderings in the Wood of the
Damned, festivities of almost regal magnificence were
being held in a Palladian mansion twenty-four miles from
Dimwood on the border of South Carolina. Miss Annabel
Darnley and Mr Jonathan Armstrong were, in fact, celebrating
their recent wedding.

A suite of gilded drawing rooms was lit by countless
candles but, with the clever use of lampshades of darkened
metal, they bathed the festivities in softened light.

The whole of the local gentry had replied to the unexpected invitations, the prestige of those two names acting
as forcefully as a call to arms. From a gallery in the largest
room, musicians played in muted fashion compositions from
yesteryear, and the nobility of these old tunes added to the
indefinable charm of the dream-like atmosphere. Consequently, the voices of the guests were not raised above a
whisper, creating mystery and harmony.

Lackeys in silver-edged sky-blue livery moved around carrying trays laden with glasses of champagne. Gradually the
noise increased. In their flounced crinolines, ladies,
adorned profusely with jewels, laughed discreetly behind
their fans, while officers in full-dress uniform leant over
them as if confiding secrets.

Such was the crowd that getting to the mistress of the
house was a kind of victory. It must be said that when she
sent the bewildering invitations, Mrs Jonathan Armstrong
hoped that one in six would accept, for she knew only too
well of the rumors that circulated about her in the district,
but she was counting on her husband's name to attract a few
people, thus avoiding the crushing humiliation of being
generally rebuffed. She had, however, reckoned without the
enormous curiosity that she had aroused since she had
bought that architectural marvel, her refuge, as she called it
amongst her intimates.

Nobody knew when nor where the marriage had taken
place. The invitation did not mention it.

By birth Jonathan Armstrong was an Anglican, and she,
for reasons that were not fully understood, a Roman

Catholic. But this difference of religion did not alter the fact that in some corner of America their marriage certificate was valid in due and legal form; and at the back of the great room, bright with all its gilding, the newly-weds were proffering smiles and thanks, without losing sight of the fact that beneath all these antics of refined society they were being subjected to serious examination.

Dressed in white from head to foot, and with a cross of sapphires on her breast, she had no trouble disarming those haughty aristocrats with her dazzling beauty. Her jet-black hair highlighted the milky whiteness of her face, whose exquisite slenderness was almost concealed in the faint light in which she stood. The way she held her head was enough in itself to endow her with a sovereign grandeur. Young and old, the men admired her as they passed by the perfect roundness of the arms, that were bare as far as the elbow. The word 'goddess' went around discreetly, alternating with 'mysterious birth'.

On her left, her husband had the bearing of a great lord, with all the naturalness in the world. By the attractiveness in her stance, even in her supple stillness, she conveyed charm to the least of her movements, but by way of contrast he appeared haughty, even when making an effort to appear pleasant, and there was a glimmer of condescension about him. His outrageously tight black suit was impeccably cut and showed off his handsome figure. The men, a little annoyed by such fastidiousness, were of the opinion, in their private conversations, that if the wife was radiantly beautiful, the husband, on the other hand, was nothing less than ugly in his facial features. The ladies thought differently on this point. There were too many curls around the forehead and cheeks, but his domineering look was pleasantly disturbing, and his mouth was worthy of praise.

Who could doubt that some drama was being played out in front of this gathering, bereft of illusions? The wife was evidently one of those women whose attraction was a force approaching violence, and the man's presence was self-explanatory. He would turn towards her almost every minute with a fiery look, as if he feared that the Devil might carry her off at a stroke, but she did not even seem to be aware of his presence and smiled irresistibly at everyone else. In that light that was both tender and shady, she gave the impression of doling out her love with majestic indifference. And in his heart the man hated her already, because he belonged to her, like some choice animal that she had paid a high price for. Stepping outside himself, he was able to glimpse, half hidden amongst the foliage and heavy flowers of a magnolia tree, a young, innocent face, with its halo of untidy, golden hair. But what good was love if desire kept him elsewhere?

Nothing of that was to be seen on the outside. The man was envied, everyone wanted his wife — the women wanted her husband ... Openly, they were admired, and jealousy raged in secret. One single guest retained a degree of well-bred scepticism, muttering that the beauty of the wife and the pride of the husband needed to be taken down a peg or two. In the deliberately dimmed light, he discerned a purpose that he kept to himself out of charity, but he hinted subtly that he knew the West Indies well and left the end of his remarks in suspense. With his head covered in white curls, heavy-chested and short-legged, he was the image of pink-cheeked ill will. No one, however, was in need of his explanations that evening. The wife's long, slender, beautiful hands gave her away, despite desperate attempts at dissimulation. Southern eyes quickly recognized the slightest drop of mixed blood. At her side, Jonathan seemed attentive to the polite intonation of all these voices, and only he could hear a rising whisper of disaster drawing close to him.

57

*E*xtreme agitation reigned at Dimwood. In the large drawing room, the whole family was gathered together, except for Billy who was prowling around in the gardens, and Elizabeth who had taken refuge in her bedroom, still atremble after her sinister escapade. The latest edition of the Savannah newspaper, sent by Uncle Charlie, announced the death of President Zachary Taylor. Vice President Fillmore was taking his place.

'He may very well be from the North, but he won't do anything unwise,' declared Uncle Douglas. 'Peace is not in danger.'

'How shall we look in the eyes of the world, with a President who died from eating too much on Independence Day?'

Thus spoke Aunt Augusta.

'A fine business!' exclaimed Aunt Emma. 'That indigestion was intended by Providence. Taylor was a hothead. He would have plunged us into war.'

'A war that we would have won,' said the chill voice of young Fred. 'The fate of the country is in the hands of a man from the North. There's still a chance of war.'

Uncle Douglas tried to reason with the agitator.

'What you don't know is that the man from the North wants to take into his cabinet Daniel Webster from the North, that fiery defender of the Union, and guess who else: our own Henry Clay, partisan of the union of hearts. Reconciliation will go ahead.'

'And that's how to lose a war on a billiard table,' said Fred scornfully.

'Be quiet, Fred,' all the ladies shouted together.

William Hargrove paid particular attention to Fred. That pale little face with its sharp look already exerted an authority that was unusual in a boy barely seventeen years old. So it was not without a certain unease that he saw his grandson coming towards him, ready to throw him into confusion.

'Fred,' he said patiently, 'I don't know any more than the rest of you. The future is hidden from us.'

'Grandfather, if we put our eyes out so as not to see any more, we are done for.'

'I don't like what you're saying, Fred. I believe that God is watching over us. We are his children after all.'

'The Northerners say that they are his children also, but they have cannons, and we don't.'

'Leave my father alone, Fred,' commanded Douglas.

That night, Elizabeth experienced once again the horrors of

insomnia, with sudden falls into unconsciousness peopled with nightmares. At dawn, she was overwhelmed by nervous exhaustion, and so was unable to recover fully even with the daylight. Then began oscillations of will, with decisions to be taken. Miss Llewelyn had confirmed that there would be an answer in one form or another, that in the morning she could take herself off to the foot of the great tree to look for it at the bottom of the hole, but when? Was it necessary to let a few days go by, as one gives a letter time to reach its destination? But to whom had she sent it it? She was afraid of asking herself too many questions. She feared the Wood of the Damned, but was impatient to go there that very morning. She did not dare. The morning went by without her shifting from the house.

Several times she met the Welshwoman in the corridors. She did not say a word to her, but gave a conniving smile, screwing up her little green eyes.

Life carried on around her, and she felt as if she were at the center of some commonplace dream whose meaning escaped her. Mr Hargrove had resumed his habit of saying interminable prayers at the beginning of dinner, his sad voice stifled in the undergrowth of his mustache. Then they talked politics, and Elizabeth took flight in her imagination, to wander along the paths of the Wood of the Damned. At the bottom of the hole, a message, an answer . . . Suddenly the name of Jonathan Armstrong, spoken by Uncle Josh, gave her a jolt.

'If this news is true, it will spare us the trouble of his visits and endless offers of sale.'

'Married or not,' said Uncle Douglas, 'he came the other day to get a check out of us. Who told you he's got married?'

Douglas gave his brother a slight wink.

'A rumor,' he said.

'I don't believe rumors.'

Nodding imperceptibly in their father's direction, Uncle Douglas dropped these words under his breath:

'Not even spread by a gray dress?'

William Hargrove had caught 'gray dress'.

'Why are you talking about gray dresses? I don't want to see that woman.'

'We were wondering,' said Uncle Josh hypocritically, 'if

she has always worn a gray dress.'

His forehead red with anger, William Hargrove banged his fist on his armchair.

'Always. I detest that woman. She even wore gray in the West Indies during the night of terror. Why are you talking about those awful times?'

'But it was you, Father . . .'

'In those days,' continued William Hargrove, 'she used also to wear a white collar and cuffs in order to look like a lady. She couldn't, she's common and she used to steal. On the night they set fire to the house next-door to ours, she was going through the drawers looking for gold coins.'

'You must try and forget all that, Father. We keep an eye on her here.'

'How much did you give her on the first of the month?'

'The same amount as usual, what you give her yourself.'

'It's shameful, she has no right.'

'You must reduce the amount.'

'I can't, she insists . . .'

In spite of herself, Elizabeth was listening to this exchange. It filled her with horror, although she understood almost nothing of it, other than that Jonathan had eluded her for ever, and that in this inner drama Miss Llewelyn was cropping up again in the guise of a reprobate. An icy coldness filled her as the men unveiled another piece of the mystery. She was on the point of fainting, but she rallied with a surge of pride. Sweat formed in beads on her forehead, and she suddenly stopped hearing, and this attack of deafness was a refuge for her. She felt Minnie, sitting next to her, take her hand and say something to her.

Suddenly, the impression of being caught up in a dream was stronger than ever. She saw William Hargrove stand up brusquely from the table and leave the room with his two sons.

The following day, her first inclination was to run to the Wood of the Damned in the hope of finding an answer. It was ten o'clock in the morning. She was likely to be seen. It was better to wait until noon, when everybody at Dimwood would be out of the sun, but the waiting was a torment to her.

'I'm no good at waiting,' she kept saying to herself in her room.

In such cases, it was customary to open the Bible at random, and the book would speak, giving advice with quasi-magical accuracy. That day, however, she hesitated. The book frightened her, although she loved it with an almost fanatical love that she had inherited from her mother. She loved it as she might a person.

Stretched out on her bed, she felt doubts slipping into her mind as to the effectiveness of a message entrusted to the earth. Gradually she calmed down, but remained wary about that corner of the world in which they believed in witchcraft and fairy stories concerning the Devil. She would have desperately loved to be elsewhere, in her homeland on the other side of the Atlantic. Here, everything was closing in on her, like a prison. The constant grating sound of the cicadas was becoming a wall of iron. Jonathan would never come, he had been caught by that woman.

Beneath a merciless sun, she eventually went along the edge of the gardens in order to reach the road to the Wood of the Damned without being seen. Despite the heat, she was running more than she was walking and was bathed in perspiration when she reached the first of the avenues that led to the heart of that God-forsaken place. The hangings of gray moss offered a grave welcome to the unsuspecting visitor in that disconcerting solitude . . . Lacerated here and there, that drapery retained a funereal grandeur, brushing the ground with its unquiet fringes. The powerful branches of the dead trees seemed to be writhing in laughable efforts to bear the weight of those intangible veils . . . Not a bird sang in that wood, not a cicada scraped its sides. The silence was so profound that Elizabeth had the impression she could hear in it an endless whisper.

With her heart beating, she moved forward, rather ashamed at finding herself there after having convinced herself that those superstitions were only any good for servants, or for people as simple-minded as the Welshwoman. But something told her that Miss Llewelyn was not at all simple-minded.

And so she went straight ahead down the avenue which

seemed to her interminable, and suddenly, in the distance, she caught sight of the giant oak, the memory of which had haunted her dreams. It seemed less frightening in daylight than it had at twilight two days ago, but it dominated all the oaks around it. It gave the effect of a dead king reigning over corpses dressed in splendid rags.

A glance was enough to tell the girl that the heap of stones had been moved, or more precisely scattered, as if by impatient hands, and she approached the hole in the ground with a mixture of horror and curiosity.

The message was there in its ring of golden hair. She seized the object. At first sight, the paper seemed intact, but as soon as she held it in the palm of her hand, it came apart of its own accord. At the place where it had been tied, it was torn, and there was nothing to suggest that the two halves had been read.

A shudder ran through her. She had a definite impression of some invisible presence; with the two fragments of the message clenched in her fist, she fled.

Her eyes were a little red at dinner that day, but nobody noticed. Sitting very straight in her chair, she pretended to look as if she were following the conversation, which, of course, gravitated towards politics. Peace seemed more or less certain, despite the remaining dissensions in Congress over points of detail. The perfect agreement was still far off, but it was becoming unthinkable to set things in reverse. Mr Fillmore, the new President, was turning out to be as understanding as a man from the North could be.

To celebrate this good news or for other, more secret, reasons there was a great set-piece flower arrangement in the center of the table. Masses of flowers had been selected with an exuisite sense of shades of color. The mauve of violets nestled alongside the dark splendor of wallflowers and the innocent blue of forget-me-nots, and the whole range of rose pink and heliotrope. Freesias and jasmine added the finishing touches to the stunning fragrance and bewitching spectacle. The effect was that one half of those present could not see the other; in particular, Elizabeth was concealed from William Hargrove.

The latter seemed attentive to all that was being said

around him and gave his opinion with moderation. He had regained his previous appearance, thanks to the scissors of his barber, who had trimmed his whiskers and mustache. Gone was the overgrown stray and, to heighten this impression, he once again smelt of the Russian eau-de-Cologne that he preferred above all the other reassuring odors which battle with the perfume of flowers.

The ladies barely concealed their joy at seeing him restored to normality and joked cheerfully with Uncle Josh when the occasion arose. Only Uncle Douglas still looked anxious. As for Elizabeth, if something was capable of cheering her up during that long meal it was that floral edifice that hid her from the view of the man she feared. Not without some disquiet, she wondered if this happy obstacle were permanent, but the memory of the hour spent in the Wood of the Damned rendered futile any preoccupations of that order. It was impossible to imagine any kind of tomorrow. The future faded from view. It was her ardent wish to cease living.

Fred, sitting on her left, had been watching her for some time and saw her change color. With a sympathetic reaction that was just like him, he brushed her hand with his own and whispered:

'Don't you feel well, Elizabeth?

She withdrew her hand.

'It's nothing,' she said.

'You're not happy,' he added, 'but never mind, there'll be better days.'

She shook her head and he, perplexed, did not insist.

Less than an hour later they had all returned to their rooms where the delights of a siesta awaited them. All, with the exception of Hargrove's sons. Douglas stopped his brother on the stairs, and asked him to follow him to the smoking room.

In the small, round room with its blinds pulled right down, it was a little cooler than elsewhere in the house, and the half-light was conducive to sleep in one of the vast, padded armchairs. But there was no question of sleeping.

'I received a letter from Milledgeville this morning,' said Douglas. 'My name is on the envelope, but inside there is another, bearing our father's name, and it is open. I have read it. It's strange. Like me, you will recognize Laura's careful handwriting.'

'Come, Douglas, not so much beating around the bush. Give me the letter.'

He took the letter that Douglas handed him and, in order to read it, sat next to one of the windows where he raised the blind a little.

Dearest Father,

When you receive this letter I shall be far away from Dimwood, and already far from the world. You will no longer have the daily ordeal of seeing me sitting at your left, in silence but not in resignation.

Many years have passed since the day you found the courage to accuse me, without proof, of an unspeakable action. Your conscience commanded you to keep me with you, not so much as your daughter, but as some guilty woman who had to be kept prisoner.

I saw my young husband killed on that dreadful night when the very ground itself seemed to catch fire. We had been married secretly, and I had foresworn my Protestant faith to be received into his, and become a Catholic. Three months later, and already a widow, I was dragged off when our family fled, accompanied by a few faithful servants and, unfortunately, that woman whose very name makes me sad. I shall never forget the long journey, those wanderings around the South until our arrival here, and, to finish, the event that made me an object of disgust in your eyes, the birth of my little girl whom you refused to believe legitimate, and who, on your orders, was taken away because she offended your religious convictions. I was not proud of you that evening, Father. My distress was to no avail, nor was charity, for you did not find it easy to forgive — and what was there to forgive? In order to believe me, you would have needed papers signed by the priest who had united us. Papers in a town on fire!

Uncle Josh put the letter down for a moment.

'She expresses herself quite well when she's moved,' he remarked.

'How can you smile at a letter as heart-rending as that? Do you have no feelings?'

'I'm not smiling, I'm appreciating it, but we know all this.'

'Not all of it. Carry on.'

From that moment on you seemed to have lost all memory of my existence, even to the point where, in my anxiety for your recovery, you take me for I know not what angelic fantasy of your imagination.

There remains my daughter from whom you separated me, and whom I shall always love with boundless affection. You know her fate as well as I do, and, like me, you have suffered on account of it. Who pushed her in that direction? By what odious absurdity could you believe that it was I, her mother? Before Him, to whom I have given myself for ever, and who will judge both of us, I swear to you that this is false. That person, that prowler in her gray dress, could speak up if her own self-interest did not keep her mouth closed ... She lives a lie, she frightens you, and that fear has made her the real mistress of Dimwood.

Forgive me for causing such disarray in your soul, which is so intent on its own integrity, so anxious to justify itself. Perhaps you will not be in a fit state to grasp the implications straight away. My brothers will enlighten you as to what is essential.

One evening when I was away from Dimwood, you gave a ball in the hope of marrying off at least one of your grand-daughters and, at the same time, getting rid of the unfortunate little English girl who puts up bravely with your hospitality. In doing so you almost drove young Susanna to despair, as she saw herself offered a prey to Lieutenant Boulton, whereas she was not suited to marriage with that man, nor with any man in the world, but I prefer to keep silent on that point. Your charity, which is made much of, was not capable of making the effort to ask yourself why she refused so frenziedly, but let us leave that. When your last guests had gone, including Lieutenant Boulton full of vain hope, someone else came to visit you, in quite a cavalier fashion, so I am told: your noble neighbor, Jonathan Armstrong, still taking the trouble to satisfy the whims of that woman who has bewitched him, who is always in need of money and more money, although she already has more than enough. He finally obtained my daughter's hand. He must understand now that in selling her his great name, he has at the same time sold his person and his freedom. She has bought him.

The marriage took place a few days ago in the strictest secrecy. I learnt the general outline of these events from my daughter, who wrote me a simple and affectionate letter, for she still loves me a little, although she does not dare to see me. How can I explain to myself the fact that she hides from me? Why can't I see her so that I could tell her that I forgave her long ago? It wasn't me who sold her, when she was fifteen, to that unscrupulous millionaire. What a world where girls are sold and husbands bought!

At this point, Uncle Josh put the letter down again and declared:

'I find that sentence shocking, coming from the pen of a woman as religious as Laura.'

'Let's be honest. The truth has given you something of a shock . . . But carry on. You're going to learn some fine things.'

With what love I would have clasped her in my arms, with what tears of tenderness I would have put my head on her shoulder! When I saw her pass by beneath our windows at Dimwood, I thought I would die of a seizure, but she left . . .

Is there any need to remind you that I was not present at that ill-fated ball? I had left the house to seek refuge a few miles away with a small community dedicated to prayer, and I spent the night there, praying that the Devil should not come close to the 'children'. Perhaps I made a mistake, and my place was in my room, close to our English girl, whom I feel to be perpetually in danger. It was there, in fact, that the enemy of souls exerted himself the most.

When I returned, the woman in gray revealed to me with a smile that, during my absence, Jonathan Armstrong and young Elizabeth had had a secret meeting on the corner of the porch where the magnolia flowers. I did not wish to hear any more about it. I was wrong, I chased away the unworthy tell-tale, not wanting to believe her. Everybody knew that Jonathan Armstrong had eyes for nobody but the lady in white. So what lies was this ill-willed person pouring out to me? She thinks she has a right to everything, because she held my little Annabel in her arms . . .

'That's where she has her hold over our poor Papa,' exclaimed Josh. 'I am of the opinion that we should burn this letter.'

'What crime is there in bringing a little girl into the world?'

'The difficulty doesn't lie there. Our father has confused everything, instead of quite simply stating the truth: his daughter married a colored man.'

'He need only have said creole.'

'Laura's husband was of mixed race, as close to the Whites as it's possible to be, and remarkably handsome, so they say. She loved him to distraction; he seduced her, then married her. But as to proof of the marriage! Papa is as finicky as a lawyer about it. Then there's the drop of black blood that can come out in the children later. He wasn't wrong on that point. It's that tiny bit, a speck, of black blood, that makes Annie so perfectly irresistible.'

'Don't call her Annie, I beg you,' said Douglas.

'What, are you afraid as well?'

'Don't be absurd. I'm ashamed, that's all. Ashamed of the twist our father gave to the story. He didn't believe what Laura told him, she who's incapable of telling lies, and he began to hate her. He didn't want to see the child who was born in secret.'

'There's only one person who knows what happened then,' said Josh, 'but she does nothing but tell lies.'

'The Welshwoman . . . She can keep secrets. If the marriage to Jonathan Armstrong has really taken place, things would sort themselves out. The husband's name would cover up everything in the eyes of society.'

'I'm less sure than you, Douglas, but we shall see. I'll finish reading the letter. There are only a few lines left.'

Now I am leaving the world, which has brought me nothing but suffering and disappointment, except for a few hours of joy, all too brief, the memory of which only inflames my wounds. Within me there rings out constantly a call to religious life, where I am convinced that peace awaits me.

I should have liked to keep an eye on Elizabeth, but the voice of grace is pressing, and I fear that, if I don't take heed of it, I may silence it for ever. What I advise you most strongly, my beloved Father, as well as my brothers, if you read this, is to entrust her to the care of Uncle Charlie who has more than once expressed the desire to take charge of her and make her life happy. I feel strongly that a threat hangs over her at Dimwood, and perhaps in the whole region of the South. Further to the North, though without leaving the states of the South, she might perhaps discover another England, close to the one she misses so bitterly.

I give a tender embrace to each of my brothers, as I do to you, dear Papa, may you be restored to health, but you will never again see your 'angel'.

Laura

'Well,' said Josh as he folded the letter up again, 'those are pages that we will not show to dear Papa, if you agree.'

'Entirely, but we won't burn them. I'll lock them in my strong box.'

Josh handed him the letter.

They looked at each other in silence for a moment.

'Laura,' Douglas said simply.

58

*E*lizabeth, who had left the dining room together with everybody else, did not know where to go. The usual refuge that her bedroom offered suddenly seemed to her like solitude haunted by long hours of disappointed hope. Once again she asked herself the strange question: what can one do with one's body when suffering? Where to take it? How to bear its presence? For it was through the body that her heart was being tortured. In her limbs, her legs, her arms, and even her hands and the tips of her fingers, there was an intolerable malaise, a weight, a heaviness. This was unhappiness. Jonathan was no longer for her. She could feel it in the whole of her body. What was the point of talking about her soul? Her soul had become her body.

In her distress, she went and hid herself at the back of the entrance hall which was deserted at that hour, but someone had quietly followed her. She gave a cry as she turned round and saw Fred looking at her attentively. His narrow face was not like the one she saw every day at table. An invisible hand seemed to have passed over those sharp features, wiping away the harshness, and she read in his steely gray eyes something that had the effect of an insult on her: pity.

'Leave me,' she said.

'Listen,' he said softly. 'I can see well enough that you're upset. You can't be happy here at Dimwood.'

'That's nobody's business but mine.'

'You must go to Savannah, to Uncle Charlie's, and he'll take you to Virginia.'

'You all want me to go away!' she exclaimed furiously.

'Oh, no, you don't understand.'

'Indeed. But I'm not in danger.'

He then said something that left her dumbfounded:

'If you were in danger, I would give my life to defend you.'

Perhaps he had let slip words he had not intended to say, for he colored slightly and, as if in a flash of lightning, he appeared handsome.

'Fred,' she whispered at last.

At the same time, instinctively, she shook her head.

'Excuse me,' he said immediately.

And turning on his heels, he strode away. Her eyes followed him as far as the door. Even in summer, in the hottest weather, he gave the impression of being strapped into his clothes like a soldier, and finding this striking, it made her sorry for having shaken her head, that absurd 'no'. He had made a brief but brave declaration of love. She did not deserve it.

Rather embarrassed, she slid out of the house without lingering by the magnolia that was already full of memories from another existence. Crossing the field with rapid steps, she took the little path that went along the river's edge. There was a fascination in the quiet stirring of the dark waters which led her to confused dreaming. Fred had declared that he was ready to face death for her! A soldier's words. She ought to have found something kind to say to him in reply, but did she not risk betraying Jonathan?

She imagined him walking beside her. He towered head and shoulders above her, and she imagined his black curls around his neck, and the fragrance of that hair. The illusion was so strong that she stopped, worried and disappointed:

'Alone,' she thought, 'there's nobody.'

The strong odor from the woods on the other side of the water reached her, amidst the eternally strident cicadas that seemed to be shouting something to her. She remembered little Susanna and her mysterious surges of tenderness, always rejected.

She reached the edge of the wood and the long path edged with tall trees, which led to the forbidden, enchanted gardens. She saw a dull, gray mass which she took to be a rock. A few more paces allowed her to see it moving.

After some uncertainty, she decided not to go any further. Then, suddenly, the rock straightened itself up, took on a human shape, appearing in the guise of Miss Llewelyn.

'I was picking herbs,' she said with a laugh, 'and was thinking of you, but I had a job to get you to come this way.'

'I came here of my own free will,' said Elizabeth, a shade irritated, 'but I've had my walk. I'm going back.'

'How sensitive we are, Miss Escridge. I admit that I am impatient to know what answer you received.'

She took a few heavy strides towards Elizabeth who, out of

self-respect, did not move, although she was tempted to flee from the presence of the Welshwoman.

'There wasn't an answer,' she said drily.

'What were you expecting then? A letter written in runic script? Did you find your paper again in its ring of hair?'

'Yes, cut in two, if you want to know; the paper had apparently not been unrolled or read.'

'Isn't that enough for you? You have broken two destinies, which should have remained only one.'

'That was not what I wanted at all. I wanted Jonathan, but I did not want any misfortune to befall the lady in white.'

'Jonathan is all very well, but you shouldn't have mentioned the lady in white. You've separated them. They were married a few days after the ball at Dimwood, but Jonathan came that very evening to sell some new piece of land to Hargrove. After which he hid, and he saw you.'

'When will you stop spying on me!'

'I am here to help you, Miss Escridge. I don't spy. I go about the place, agreed, at any hour of the day or night, and I see a lot of things. You made Jonathan fall in love.'

'Oh, Miss Llewelyn! Do you really think so?'

'Ah, when I'm spoken to more politely, I'm ready to share confidences, I receive them and I give them out. He is madly in love with Elizabeth, and he has married the lady in white because he desired her.'

'And what about me,' exclaimed Elizabeth, 'not me?'

Miss Llewelyn did not answer straight away. With her small, green eyes, she scrutinized the girl's gaze, as if to search her soul.

'No,' she said at last.

With her knowing eye, she observed the face which was suddenly overcome with despair.

'Come on, be brave, don't let's stay here where we might be seen. Let's take the big path and go towards the gardens.'

'I'd rather not go so far, but we can take a few steps as we talk, don't you think? I'm not afraid. Tell me why Jonathan prefers the woman in white.'

The ageing woman was finally moved by so much innocence, familiar as she was with all the whims of the body and the heart. Perhaps that corner of the forest was having an effect on her, making her relive some moment of her adolescence when she had believed in love. She had the feeling that the trees were bending towards her, counselling silence. Pushing her scruples aside, she asked coldly:

'Do you know what is meant by desire?'

'Yes, love.'

'Not always. To desire is not necessarily to love. But you don't grasp the difference.'

'Better than you think,' said Elizabeth with a sudden assurance.

'How's that? Could you explain to me . . .'

'It's very simple. Do you remember the story of Tamar and Amnon?'

'Not very well. I don't always have my nose stuck in the Bible like the rest of you.'

'It's not a long story. Amnon was in love with Tamar. Now Tamar was his sister. You know what happened?'

'No, I don't. Carry on. I'm curious.'

'He pretended to be ill and when he was in bed, he asked Tamar to make him some cakes. She made them, and when she brought them to him, he seized her and took her by force. After which he stopped loving her, he hated her.'

'Well,' said the Welshwoman somewhat aghast, 'I can see that the Scriptures instruct little girls wonderfully well.'

'I'm not a little girl.'

'Sorry. I'm beginning to realize as much, but your story goes much further than you think. You see things very clearly. Love and desire are not interchangeable, and the one can exist without the other. There is someone who is very aware of that today, to the point of bitterness.'

'Who?'

'Do you want to know his name?'

Elizabeth did not answer.

'Jonathan,' said Miss Llewelyn softly. 'But you mustn't think about Jonathan any more, because Jonathan is married to the woman he wanted, in the way that Amnon wanted Tamar. And, like Tamar, she brought him cakes: a considerable fortune. And like Amnon, it is probable that he no longer loves her. It's you he loves.'

The deep blue eyes were suddenly overwhelmed with violent pain. They stared for a moment at Miss Llewelyn who remained quiet, for the first time disconcerted at the effect of her words.

'She's more beautiful than I am,' said Elizabeth in a low voice.

'Oh, it's not quite as simple as that. There was the money, too.'

'I don't want to believe that.'

'Jonathan's not a saint. Amnon asked for cakes.'

'I don't like you joking about Jonathan.'

'I know that kind of man. Crazed with desire, they behave in the clumsiest way. He loves you with quite a different love, one which is quite imperious. How can I get you to understand? You are a kind of ideal for him.'

Elizabeth cried out:

'I don't want to be Jonathan's ideal, I want to be his wife.'

'That's speaking your mind, Miss Escridge,' the Welsh-woman said, slightly awed. 'Unfortunately it's too late.'

A long silence followed. The distress in Elizabeth's eyes had moved Miss Llewelyn. Thoroughly disillusioned as she was in everything concerning love, she remained speechless before this breaking heart. As if to add to the cruelty of things, a bird began to sing on the branch of an oak above their heads. It was a thrush. So much joy burst forth from that little throat that the girl could not refrain from listening to it with a tender expression.

Miss Llewelyn seemed to be thinking, then she said calmly and almost affectionately:

'Look now, Elizabeth, you should marry someone more serious than that madcap Jonathan.'

'But I love him the way he is.'

'You'd be happier with someone less strange. You're very pretty, you'd have no trouble finding somebody in this part of Georgia, a young man capable of great love. Even here, perhaps, since you seem so set on staying at Dimwood.'

'I have my reasons for wanting to stay at Dimwood.'

'Only marriage will fix you here for good.'

She waited for a moment. Elizabeth was already preparing her obstinate look.

'Fred,' said the Welshwoman.

Elizabeth looked at her without answering, then she shook her head, as she had done an hour earlier in the hall at Dimwood.

'I shall never love anyone but Jonathan,' she said at last.

Miss Llewelyn did not seem disconcerted by this obstinacy.

'Fred admires you, as all the boys do. You only have to see the way he looks at you — Billy too, what's more, but Billy would be impossible as a husband. Fred is different. Fred is already his own man.'

'Perhaps he will turn out to be somebody, but he'll never be Jonathan.'

'Jonathan is married. It's over.'

'No, he'll leave that woman, he'll hate her like Amnon hated Tamar, and he'll come back, he'll come back here.'

'You're going out of your mind, Elizabeth. You're ruining your chances of happiness. I can see into your future only too clearly. As the years go by, you'll turn into the old maid whose presence at Dimwood is borne out of charity, grudgingly.'

Elizabeth was numbed by these words. Deep inside herself, she could hear her mother's voice crying out: 'Poor relation . . . Every mouthful of bread out of charity . . .'

She gave Miss Llewelyn a furious look.

'What is that to you?' she asked brutally.

Miss Llewelyn's answer rooted her to the spot just as she was getting ready to leave her there.

'What is it to me? I'll tell you. People can't help loving you. You'll make many men fall in love, some of them will be insane with love, and you'll make a very good marriage, but you don't have that white lady's almost diabolical power of attraction. I don't know if I'm making myself understood.'

'I'd have to be stupid not to understand.'

'Pointless to tell you that I keep my distance from all these things. My life is behind me. They have made me into a sinister figure, suspecting me of all kinds of shady practices. I don't care. Believe them or don't. It's all false, but you should know this at least, that I too am fond of you.'

The seriousness with which these words were spoken moved the English girl to silence. A ray of sunlight fell on the Welshwoman, illuminating her from head to toe, as if to show up in all its ugliness that solid body imprisoned in gray cloth.

The merciless light deepened the wrinkles in the heavy flesh of her face. A glimmer of tenderness was the only thing to shine in the small, green eyes.

Elizabeth searched desperately for some pleasant phrase that would not be a lie, for she could hardly get the better of the revulsion which that woman inspired in her. But she was touched by her avowal and the delicacy of her moderation. She blushed:

'I thank you very much, Miss Llewelyn.'

She accompanied these words with a smile, and in exchange received only a rather sad, somewhat wounded look.

Clumsily, she declared that she wanted to go back, to rest in her room, and moved away, with slow steps at first, then more and more rapidly, giving the appearance of flight.

A few minutes later she was in her rocking chair, hiding her burning face in her hands. Such behaviour seemed unworthy to her. Why had she run away so quickly? What had the poor Miss Llewelyn said that was so awful to deserve such a barely disguised rebuff? She was not very pleasant to look at, she was even repulsive on account of her odor that was both sour and stale, but she had said those words of discreet friendship, and she, Elizabeth Escridge, like a heartless, badly brought up girl, had left her standing there for no reason. 'If one could die of shame,' she thought, 'I should be dead, they would find me dead in this rocking chair.' And the unbearable idea suddenly came to her that she owed some reparation to Miss Llewelyn. The humiliation was considerable, an obstacle on her path. Which path? She was not long in finding the answer and, kicking her chair she stamped her foot and cried:

'No!'

And as the chair was still rocking, she shouted to it:

'No!'

This outburst of ill humor calmed her down and silenced her scruples. Only the risk of meeting the Welshwoman, who could spring up at any moment, held her back from walking on the verandah. She took the precaution of closing the large shutters and even turned the key in her door. After which she again flung herself into the rocking chair, took up again *The Last Days of Pompeii*, and ruined her eyesight reading five or six pages which she did not comprehend. She fell asleep.

59

S uch was the torpor of the season in this part of the country that it seemed to dull all activity and to slow down the passage of time. The grating of the cicadas was so loud that they seemed to be weaving strands of iron wire.

One day, however, respite came. A breeze began to blow from the woods, making it possible to breathe, at the same time heralding a storm for the following day.

It was in that blessed hour that an event took place which moved the pieces on that motionless chessboard of country life. The afternoon was drawing to a close, when a noise of wheels and horses rang out in the avenue of oaks which the sun pierced with its last rays. A luxurious black carriage, drawn by white horses, cantered up to the house and stopped in front of the porch.

In an instant everyone was at the windows behind the half-closed shutters, except for William Hargrove, who was sleeping soundly in his bed.

A groom in pearl-gray livery trimmed with gold jumped down from his seat and ran towards the door which he opened, raising his hat. Then the lady in white could be seen climbing down with regal slowness. Pushing aside the gloved hand that was offered her, she advanced towards the porch disdainfully, when a sudden hesitation made her slow down.

A thin veil from her bonnet hid the top half of her face, but everything about her bearing revealed a natural gracefulness. This was the secret of her life and the attraction she exerted over so many men. She undoubtedly knew that she was the first victim of that power of which she was always conscious, but which could not make her happy, because she could not control it and, sooner or later, she was going to make someone suffer. Deep inside herself, she still kept, like a missed vocation, a simple longing for the human love which had been denied her.

Uncle Josh, who was watching this unexpected arrival from his bedroom, launched himself down the corridor, looking for his brother. They almost bumped into each other, and their exchange was brief:

'Did you see?' said Josh. 'I can't believe my eyes. Can we receive her?'

Douglas rounded on him abruptly.

'Why not?'

'But . . . a prostitute . . .'

'What does that matter? Not to open the door to Laura's daughter? Are you insane?'

'You're right. Let's go down quickly.'

The two brothers suddenly found themselves in front of her and, by some irresistible force, she flung herself into their arms without a word.

All three were having difficulty restraining an emotion which none of them had expected. The young woman had pulled off her bonnet to get a better look at them, and her large violet-colored eyes plunged into theirs with avid tenderness. In a voice that choked in her throat, she suddenly murmured:

'They were horrible.'

'It was to be expected,' said Douglas. 'You won't change them.'

'They have no soul,' said Josh.

'No soul,' she repeated like an echo.

Helping her up the porch steps, they led her to the small drawing room. They closed the door. In the half-light of that room, she appeared radiantly beautiful, as straight and as motionless as a marble pillar. Douglas asked her if she wanted to lie down. She did not answer. With her eyes lowered, she was making an effort to get a grip on herself:

'It's quite simple. All is lost,' she said.

'Those words are meaningless coming from you,' replied Douglas.

'You're young and very beautiful,' said Josh, 'your life is just beginning, and you are married, Jonathan has one of the greatest names in the South.'

She shrugged her shoulders.

'But does he love me?' she said.

'You're dreaming!' exclaimed Douglas. 'Everybody knew he was infatuated with you.'

She turned towards them a face in which sadness had spread a painful nobility.

'I know only too well what those words mean; just about nothing. Things will carry on, but, all the same, it's over. Something has come to an end.'

Suddenly she asked:

'Could I see the English girl?'

Uncle Josh went to fetch Elizabeth from her room and left her alone with the lady in white in the small drawing room.

They looked at each other, and the same thought came to each of them, phrased inwardly in a slightly different way: 'There she is then . . . how beautiful she is . . . how pretty!'

The daylight was fading, one of the shutters had been opened. They were both standing, and both seemed to be waiting for the word that would break the bewitching silence.

'You seem surprised to see me,' the lady in white said at last.

'A little, I was not expecting . . .'

'Well,' said the visitor with a smile, 'you are Elizabeth, and I am Annabel. That's what children say who are happy with just Christian names and don't bother about surnames.'

Elizabeth smiled politely.

'But if we remain standing,' said Annabel, 'I shall have the impression that there is an invisible wall between us, and I should be sorry about that, for I have a feeling that we have a lot to say to each other. May I?'

Without waiting for the answer she sat down on a sofa, which allowed her to stretch out her legs a little. With the clumsiness of an automaton, Elizabeth sat on a small upright armchair.

'I've heard a lot about you,' continued the visitor in a pleasant tone of voice. 'You are much younger than I imagined.'

Questions began to spin around in Elizabeth's head, and her heart was pounding. This mysterious woman, who did not stop smiling as she spoke, seemed sad, in spite of everything. Her face was not like any that the English girl had ever seen at home, or even in Georgia.

Her extremely slender features gave her an indefinable air of fragility and, in that golden face, as if slightly suntanned, there opened up her two darkly gleaming, melancholy eyes of violet color. Her small ears were adorned with two sapphires, each the size of a drop of water. One could guess that she knew herself to be graced with a rare beauty, and that she breathed in admiration as one becomes intoxicated with the heady perfume of a flower.

'May I speak frankly?' she asked, 'or should I limit myself to compliments on your hair and your complexion?'

Elizabeth was expecting the worst.

'I don't care for anything but the truth,' she said, flaring up.

'Very well. It's about Jonathan. Who else could it be about, and what would we be doing here, face to face, otherwise?'

'If you say so,' said Elizabeth, swallowing.

'Some day you will know life and its pitfalls better, the mistakes to avoid, the giddiness of temptations.'

She began to speak softly in a voice of a pure and moving intonation that was reminisent of a song whispered among shadows. The accent came from somewhere far away. In spite of herself, Elizabeth fell victim to the charm of those inflections that were becoming almost affectionate, as if to soften the meaning of the words, for there promised to be explanations:

'The day is not far off when handsome young men will start hovering around you. With your deliciously innocent look — yes, yes, I say deliciously, and, believe me, that's an advantage for some . . .'

'We said we would pass over the compliments,' said Elizabeth, annoyed.

'Quite right, so let's come back to facts. Your name, first of all, Miss Escridge. You belong to that part of society known as the aristocracy.'

'I assure you that it means nothing to me.'

'All praise to your good sense! For what are their titles after all? Where are their ancestral lands? What remains for them, other than their grand posing, that notorious arrogance . . . Far from blushing about it, they claim for themselves extra nobility . . .'

She was gradually letting herself be carried away, and her dark glittering eyes began to flame.

'I am part of them on my mother's side, and through the man whose name I bear today. My father was a remarkable man. I never knew him, but the nuns who took me in never stopped telling me so once I was old enough to understand. They knew, they were from the same country, having taken refuge here at the time of the disaster.'

Seeing the girl's perplexed expression, she stopped:

'The story is complicated,' she said. 'He was a lieutenant in the government army, in the West Indies, very handsome, very much in love with my mother, whom he married secretly.'

'Secretly?'

'Because he was a Catholic and my mother a Protestant, like her father, who would have opposed the marriage. The young couple were infatuated with each other. There were battles, three months later, around the English plantations, slaves rising up against the Whites. My father was killed. My mother, pregnant, fled with her father and her brothers, and a few servants who remained loyal. The governess too, a Welshwoman . . .'

Elizabeth trembled.

'You know her, of course,' said Annabel. 'Avoid talking to her, she is dangerous. Eventually I was born. My birth was a secret and kept hidden, because my grandfather wanted it that way.'

'Why?' asked Elizabeth in a daze, and full of curiosity.

'"Why" is a word one should use with care, Miss Escridge,' said Annabel softly.

'Sorry.'

Annabel pretended not to hear and continued:

'My mother might have been dead too. She suffered a great deal, and now she is gone.'

A suspicion ran through Elizabeth's mind, but she remained silent this time.

'And that,' continued Annabel, 'is where you come in, Elizabeth.'

'Me?'

'Yes, you and the man you love.'

Elizabeth stood up, red with emotion.

'I don't understand. How do you know that I'm in love with somebody?'

'Oh, my dear girl,' said Annabel with a smile, 'don't you know that a woman always ends up finding out what she wants to know? Listen, I'd get a stone to talk, if necessary.'

'I've been betrayed!' the girl exclaimed.

'Oh, no,' said Annabel in a look which mingled tenderness and compassion, 'there has been no betrayal. It's just that I'm good at guessing, because I know men, and I know how to observe as well, without saying anything and to listen in silence. Don't be surprised: I should like to be able to love him as you do. Unfortunately I can't. To be loved, yes, but to love, I have never been able to do that. What he himself took to be love was something different.'

A cry rose up from Elizabeth's breast, for she could control herself no longer:

'Then why did you take him from me?'

Annabel lost neither her calm nor her gentleness.

'You have taken his heart from me, Elizabeth, I have taken his person and his name. Think about it, Elizabeth. I did not know him. He came to me, he implored me like a madman, with all the vehemence of desire. Desire was everything. Desire is not love. You have no idea what desire is. I can tell from your eyes.'

Elizabeth remained dumbfounded, searching in vain for an answer.

'You are love. For Jonathan, it's you.'

'Jonathan . . .' murmured Elizabeth.

'You say his name as he said yours one day in the same voice and with the same look, and he thought I had not noticed, because men are naive. That intoxicated look gave him away. Don't think I'm jealous. Far from it. I envy you.'

'I understand hardly anything of what you've been saying for the last few minutes.'

'I'm trying to talk to you woman to woman. I should have liked to have been in love, just once, to see what it is like. I

— 497 —

have never been able to inspire love in the way you do. But it's always the same story: there was no love, there was only desire. I am made for desire.'

She looked so sad as she spoke these words that the girl asked timidly:

'Are you happy?'

To her bewilderment, the answer came amidst a peal of laughter containing no gaiety:

'No, I'm rich! I have what I want. Everything. Don't look so shocked. I'm not wicked. My mother is the only person I love, but she frightens me, for she is just what I am not. But night has fallen, Elizabeth, and we are talking in the dark. I can only see your shining hair.'

She stopped for a moment, and the girl heard her sigh, then suddenly she resumed:

'There are some things that it's easier to say in the dark. It's funny, isn't it? I shouldn't like to say anything that would hurt you, because I like you. I can't make out too well the woman you will turn out to be. For the moment you seem more like an ideal than anything else. For Jonathan, for example. I feel that you don't understand, and there are certain words that I don't want to use. Have you read *Romeo and Juliet?*'

'Of course.'

'Well, you would be perfect in the balcony scene, but inside, in the bedroom — for it has to come to that with them — your victory is doubtful. What's known as temperament . . .'

Elizabeth interrupted her:

'I don't like what you're saying.'

'I don't like it either, and you would not be what you are if you did like what I'm saying to you, but you are ill equipped for life, my dear. Your innocence is terrifying. I'm going to tell you something sad now. That is why I came, and I've been putting off this moment in cowardly fashion, because you will hate me: you will never see Jonathan again.'

She had been expecting some cry, but only profound silence greeted these murderous words.

'Say something, Elizabeth,' she said.

'No,' said a determined voice. 'What you're saying is not true.'

'Yes, it is. We are leaving the country for a long time. I shall have no regrets, neither will he, I'm sure.'

'But why? Why?'

'This country disappoints us. A bitter experience . . . We shall travel, perhaps we shall go and live elsewhere, in Europe. We shall be happier there — even without that love which everybody talks about.'

'Even without that love' . . . As if in a flash of lightning, Elizabeth remembered what Miss Llewelyn had told her: 'You have shattered two destinies that should have made one whole.'

She trembled with fear. She groped her way towards her chair and, having found it, leant on it, ready to dissolve. Annabel's gentle voice continued, a monologue amidst the shadows, of which the girl caught only snatches of phrases:

'. . . I feel that I have pained you . . . I did not intend to . . . If Jonathan knew I were here . . .'

'Jonathan . . .' said Elizabeth.

'Jonathan has been in Savannah since yesterday, to organize our departure. He will know nothing of my visit . . . until months have gone by, nothing about our confidences. Now I must leave you, Elizabeth. I have twenty-five miles to go, and the roads are bad. You're going to help me find my way out of this pretty drawing room.'

Their hands groped for each other for a moment, then Elizabeth guided Annabel to the door, which she opened. In the light coming from the hall, the visitor suddenly seemed cruelly beautiful to her, at one and the same time hard and exquisite in her perfection. Almost immediately, a delightful smile restored her gracefulness and her strange charm.

'How wicked life is, dear girl,' she said.

This remark provoked no response.

'Will you allow me to kiss you?' asked Annabel.

Elizabeth remained silent and did not move. A few seconds passed, and then she felt the warmth of a kiss on her cheek. Straightening herself up, Annabel took a few steps.

'Goodbye, dear Elizabeth,' she said tenderly.

And she added in a whisper:

'Don't be sad. Forget, forget.'

Elizabeth turned her head away.

Left alone, she pulled a small handkerchief from her belt and furiously wiped her cheek.

60

S he did not appear at supper that evening. Uncle Douglas had decided that she was to be left alone. Having taken refuge in her bedroom after the departure of the lady in white, she flung herself on to her bed and pulled the blanket over her head, her distress signal ever since childhood. No tears nor sobbing. She simply wanted to die. Not knowing what to expect, she remained motionless, simulating death.

Through the thickness of the blanket, she heard the sound of the carriage bearing the visitor away, the multiple hammering of horses' hooves on the ground in the avenue of oaks, where it became lost in the silence that closed in around everything.

She made an effort not to think about anything, to wipe out from her memory all the hours she had spent in the South, but she was powerless against a single name that kept coming back to her, with every beat of her heart.

Interminable minutes went by. The night's first tree-frogs were uttering their shy little notes in the trees around the house.

The door suddenly opened and someone came in. The girl lifted the edge of the blanket and cried:

'Is that you, Betty? Go away! I want to sleep.'

'It's not Betty,' said a very calm voice, 'it's Maisie Llewelyn come to see how you are.'

'Oh, Miss Llewelyn, leave me, I beg you. I'm resting, that's all — and I should like to sleep.'

The voice resumed, firmly and quietly:

'I am the governess in this house, Miss Escridge. I'm doing my duty.'

With an impatient gesture, Elizabeth pulled away the top of the blanket that was covering her tousled golden locks and turned towards the Welshwoman, who was standing near the small table. The light from the globe of the lamp lit her from head to foot. Her shadow fell behind her, reaching up to the ceiling, and that vast, black silhouette was like a projection of all of her authority.

After a little uncertainty, Elizabeth regained her strength and her voice was trembling with indignation:

'Miss Llewelyn, I beg you to remember that this is my room.'

'Try to be a little less English, Miss Escridge. What I have to tell you is of major importance to you.'

These slow, clear words seemed to drop from the top of the shadow on the wall, and the girl was struck dumb.

'The way things are,' the voice continued, 'it's up to you to take your destiny in hand. Your future is at stake. Do I stay, or do I go?'

Elizabeth jumped down from the bed, fully dressed.

'You've creased your pretty dress,' Miss Llewelyn observed. 'If I were you, I should take care of my clothes. Life has its unexpected changes.'

The girl was gripped by a vague worry, and the memory of those bad days in London came back to mind.

'You had something to tell me?' she said.

'Yes, Miss Escridge, you left me so abruptly in the woods that I was only able to tell you the essentials.'

'I was overwrought, I'm sorry . . . Do you want to sit down?'

Without hesitation, the Welshwoman settled herself in the rocking chair, which she set in motion with a click of the heel.

'You are quite forgiven, Miss Escridge. But just remember that I'm not a servant.'

She was rocking away energetically while she spoke these words, and behind her her shadow rose and fell on the wall.

'I am the mistress of Dimwood,' she said.

Without saying a word, Elizabeth sat down facing her on the small sofa. Miss Llewelyn let a few minutes' silence elapse and then resumed:

'Annabel was talking to you for an hour. She must have recounted her version of her misfortunes.'

'She told me everything.'

'Everything? I rather doubt it, but we'll see. Such a to-do over a drop of black blood! I was there, in Haiti. I knew the boy well. As white as you and me, clean-shaven. There must have been mixed blood on his mother's side. It was not obvious. A young Englishwoman fell in love with him and became a Catholic to marry him. Are you with me?'

'That's not what I'm interested in, it's Annabel's marriage.'

'Very well. I'll go on: born of that marriage, the daughter is as beautiful as an angel but surprisingly shows the traces of mixed blood. It can jump a generation, but is never eliminated completely. To marry Jonathan, that was her idea. The mistake was to show herself, to appear in public with her noble husband in high society. A strange reception followed by total silence, not a single call was paid, nor the least note scribbled on a visiting card as is the custom, nothing. High society said no. They're leaving the country.'

'I know that too, alas.'

'You know everything then.'

'I know too that they don't really love each other; she told me.'

'Their union is nonetheless indissoluble.'

'What's to stop them separating if they don't love each other?'

'The Church. I see that Annabel committed the sin of omission in informing you.'

'I don't understand.'

'In order to marry Annabel, who is a Catholic, he became a Catholic himself.'

'That's shameful!'

'Call it what you like, but what is done is done. The Roman Church does not allow divorce.'

Elizabeth looked at her in consternation. For her, religion was something one did not talk about, which occupied a private place in life. By turns something terrifying, reassuring or mysterious, it was not to be touched upon. At a stroke, her image of Jonathan was more than troubled by it.

'I don't say your Jonathan sold his soul to the Devil for

that woman, but it wouldn't do to tempt him, and she tempted him.'

'Horrid woman!'

'Oh no, she has an irresistible attraction for people, as her father attracted a Protestant who became a Catholic in order to marry him.'

'But who was Annabel's mother?'

'You're being inquisitive; when will you learn that there are questions one doesn't ask at Dimwood? Listen well: I've received a message from Jonathan.'

The girl leapt to her feet.

'Sit down, Miss Escridge. It's me he's writing to, not you.'

Elizabeth sat down again, her face as red as if it had been slapped.

'He wrote me this letter from Savannah the day he met you on the road. In the carriage, do you remember? Ah, I see that you remember! He'd undoubtedly gone there to put into the bank account of the woman, who had bewitched him, the money he'd got from William Hargrove for the sale of a piece of the plantation. That's what Joshua and Douglas Hargrove suppose. One day, by the greatest of coincidences, I was passing by the smoking room where they were talking, and I caught a few snatches — on the hop, as you might say — and in spite of myself, you might also say.'

'Oh, does he mention me in that message, Miss Llewelyn?'

'There now, you're still interested in him . . . That reprobate has not the nerve to want me to serve as intermediary between you and him, but he proposes that, if ever — may Heaven forbid — you absolutely had to write to him, you send the letter via me.'

'I could write to him this evening . . . but you're here. I send the letter via you? I don't understand.'

'If you were somewhere other than here. Your message has to be brief — and respectable, do you understand, very respectable.'

'But what are you thinking of, Miss Llewelyn?'

'I'm not thinking of anything, I *know*. I'm quite familiar with human nature. If they turn into love letters, I'll stop the whole thing. We're already on the verge of guilty encounters, and from there to adultery . . .'

Elizabeth stood up.

'Why are you saying such terrible things, Miss Llewelyn? In the Bible, adulterous women are stoned.'

'That's not done any more. And then he would be the adulterer, not you, poor Miss Escridge. But that man is a ravenous wolf. Beware. I am here to keep an eye on things, to supervise, to read and to tear up if necessary. And what would you have to say to him, I wonder?'

'Oh, lots of things!'

'You see, it's getting off to a bad start. I was wrong to let myself be moved by his urging. I took pity on him. I said yes. He gave me his next address, and the others will follow, for I imagine they'll be moving around quite a bit, our two fugitives. And you yourself won't be here much longer either. You're leaving.'

'What? They don't want me any more, I suspected as much.'

'They'll put it nicely. The climate here doesn't suit you. You'd be better off somewhere else. You must have noticed what the real reason is. Your presence troubles William Hargrove's conscience. There you are. The most charming man in the world will take care of you from now on. You know him: the great banker of Savannah, Charlie Jones — the banker of everybody down there, and Annabel's and Jonathan's. He'll take you where the air isn't so stifling, and where there is more to talk about than duels and future wars. You'll be happier, but in your letters, if you write them, keep respectability and morality in mind. Good-night.'

She got up from the rocking chair abruptly. It jolted like a horse relieved of its rider and, without further ado, Miss Llewelyn withdrew.

61

*T*hat night, Elizabeth experienced the ravages of night-mares in which there flared forth the word 'adultery', but shortly before dawn she was sleeping so soundly that Betty had to shake her by the shoulder in order to wake her.

An hour later, she took her usual place at breakfast and smiled at everyone, without being able to speak a word. Something inside her had been destroyed, and she came to wonder what she was doing there, in that room, where people all around her were chattering away without her being able to grasp what they were talking about. She refused every-thing she was offered to eat, but drank several cups of tea that put her more or less back on her feet. All the horror of her conversation with the Welshwoman appeared to her in devastating clarity. Her life was a bad dream that she could no longer manage to wake from. Behind the enormous bouquet of amaryllis in the middle of the table the old men who no longer wanted her in their house were hiding. They were reality. Jonathan did not exist.

A hand was placed on hers. It was Susanna. Elizabeth gave her a vacant look. Susanna kept repeating the same phrase:

'Don't go away.'

The English girl smiled without answering.

Suddenly there was the great din of chairs that heralded the end of the meal, and the girl got up with the others. In that rarefied state in which she still found herself, she noticed the beauty of the light, filtered by the blinds, gilding the walls.

She went out of the dining room and found herself in the hall. She stopped there, undecided. Nothing made sense any more. Whether she shut herself in her room or went out, it all amounted to the same thing. Only her body was moving. The person who inhabited that body remained equally indifferent, as if she had been deprived of her own self.

She suddenly realized that Uncle Josh was next to her and was leading her to the back of the hall. She let him. They were both walking quite quickly, and soon a door opened and closed again after them. Then she found herself once again in the small drawing room where she had seen Annabel.

Sitting in a large, padded armchair, she felt vaguely pleased at not having to choose where to go. Uncle Josh was sitting close to her and was talking a lot and with great gentleness. She would have liked to have gone to sleep but he laughingly raised her head with a delicate hand, making a game of it, and he was so good-hearted that she ended up laughing with him, without knowing why. That cheerfulness dispelled the sadness and the girl's eyes brightened. The first grating of the cicadas could be heard in the trees.

'You must recognize that noise,' said Uncle Josh. 'The temperature is going to rise, it will keep us shut up indoors until nightfall. Summer is a curse in this country that we love so much. Do you hear me, Elizabeth?'

The answer was a smile. He continued:

'Here at Dimwood we all believe that you would be happier in Virginia. It's hot there, but less so than in Georgia, and it is more reminiscent of England.'

She looked at him and said simply:

'Do you want me to go away, Uncle Josh?'

'No,' he said animatedly, 'we're all fond of you, and you can come back whenever you wish. The winter can be delightful here.'

Having gradually come to herself, she stared gravely into those good, brown eyes that were lying.

'When am I to leave?'

He shook a little with perturbed surprise:

'But . . . when you like.'

'It's all the same to me, Uncle Josh. Everything is the same to me.'

'Oh, don't talk like that. We shall all be sorry.'

After some hesitation, he resumed:

'I should tell you that three days ago we received a letter from Uncle Charlie who wants to show you Virginia, where he has several properties. He proposes . . . the day after tomorrow, but if you don't want to . . .'

'Oh, yes, I have no choice. I'll do whatever suits you.'

With her pride cut to the quick, she stood up, and he did likewise. She did not take her eyes off him.

'How is your father this morning?' she asked.

He blushed a little.

'Fine, Elizabeth. But you were at table just now . . .'

'I couldn't see him, you know, with all those flowers between us.'

He could not conceal his embarrassment and said, making an effort to laugh:

'Yes, all those flowers. It's a bit ridiculous.'

'All those flowers,' she repeated with a smile in her turn.

They left the room. In the hall, the sound of a discussion in the smoking room reached them through the closed door. Uncle Douglas's vehement, rather flat voice was engaged against that of his son, which was clear and cutting and could be distinctly heard:

'Father,' he cried, 'do you call that Southern hospitality!'

Uncle Josh, startled, gave Elizabeth a worried look. She smiled, and they passed by without a word.

The day passed without incident. Except for William Hargrove's two sons, nobody knew yet that Elizabeth was to leave in two days' time. She herself displayed the greatest calm and kept the secret, but she was nevertheless thinking about preparations for departure.

Her first act was to take *The Last Days of Pompeii*, and put it back in its place in the bookcase in the drawing room. That was a small beginning, and she was surprised at the extent to which she was glad of it.

She had the idea of going discreetly around the house, as if to say a secret farewell. At the very end of an interminable corridor, she came to the linen room.

She went in and, as if in a dream, saw Mademoiselle Souligou sitting at the same long table in front of a heap of shirts and underclothes.

'Oh, it's you,' said the old woman without turning round. 'I was expecting to see you sooner, but people abandon Souligou when they have no use for her any more.'

'Oh, no,' said Elizabeth, caught unawares.

'Oh, yes, but it is of no matter. Sit down there. I've got things to say to you. As soon as it starts to get hot, I stop working on the top floor. It's stifling under the roof in my dear attic. I miss it a bit, because you can see everything from up there.'

A mauve and green checked cotton kerchief was tied

around her head, blossoming out at the top in a great, war-like knot. The face, the color of boxwood, turned towards the English girl, and her cunning little eyes looked her up and down.

'Still the same schoolgirl face in a thicket of gold, but be careful of imprudent behaviour.'

'I don't behave imprudently.'

Mademoiselle Souligou took up again a shirt that she had put down, and began to sew a button on it.

'That's what you think, but it's imprudent to walk along the edge of the wood with Miss Llewelyn, for example.'

'What? Are you spying on me as well? Everybody spies on everybody else at Dimwood.'

'Don't let's exaggerate. Am I not allowed to look out of my attic window to admire the view? And if I see Miss Escridge in conversation with Miss Llewelyn, is that spying? Now I tell you, and I tell you again: that woman is dangerous.'

'I have nothing to fear from Miss Llewelyn.'

'I hope not, I hope not. What you might have said to each other is your affair alone.'

'That's my opinion too,' said Elizabeth drily. 'I'm sorry I disturbed you in your work.'

As she said these words, she got up to leave. Again Souligou looked at her, and the corners of her mouth stretched out into a broad smile.

'Still just as proud, our nice little aristocrat! But remember this: the Welshwoman is ready to undertake the most sordid of jobs, provided the price is right. She loves money and is rich. Now there is something about rich people, they never have enough. She pockets a good part of Mr Hargrove's income by threatening to reveal all she knows about his daughter Laura.'

'Aunt Laura!'

'The very one, a saint, or almost. That's not enough for our Welshwoman. She doesn't let any occasion to make a little profit pass her by. Sometimes she sells silence. Hers comes very dear. Sometimes she busies herself making her talents as go-between bear fruit, but as that involves a risk the price is higher.'

'Mademoiselle Souligou, I don't understand a thing of what you're saying.'

'I'm not surprised, but all that will do its work in your memory, and will be useful to you some day. As for the Llewelyn woman, the hour will come when she will give up her villainous soul, which will go straight to where they're expecting it. But she has the constitution of a horse, and she's keeping the devil waiting. And you make sure you take care. Be good enough to pass me those gentlemen's 'unmentionables' over there, on the end of the table. I'm old. It wearies me to get up . . . Thank you. It seems to me that we've said everything we had to say to each other.'

'I'm sure of that,' exclaimed Elizabeth. 'I had no intention of coming to visit you, it was by chance . . .'

'Well, I won't detain you, Miss Escridge.'

The girl was on her feet in a moment, and passed behind Mademoiselle Souligou's armchair. Fuming at seeing herself dismissed, like an inferior, she was tempted to pull the ends of the cotton kerchief, sticking up like a pair of mocking ears, but she got a hold on herself and found herself outside, all pink and trembling with emotion.

She did not pursue her farewell visit to Dimwood any further. The memory of sinister stories she had been told came back to her: some ancient malediction weighed down on this house, which had such a rare kind of beauty, making happiness impossible within its walls.

The fear of encountering Miss Llewelyn prevented her from going to walk in the woods. In the same way, she avoided the company of the 'children', in whom she could confide nothing of all her latest worries, and she got impatient at their emotional outbursts, especially the frenzy of Susanna, which she found incomprehensible and judged to be childish.

Such was her desire for solitude that she decided to seek refuge in her mother's room, where no one had set foot since Mrs Escridge's departure. There, in the great rocking chair, she could give her soul up to the pleasurable rumination of her various mortifications since her arrival at Dimwood.

She was tormented by these thoughts for quite a while, and finally she fell asleep. At dinner-time they looked for her just about everywhere. It was Betty who found her, and the girl appeared at table as usual, but remained silent.

The rest of the day passed by in the rather mournful quietness of very hot days, with the general weariness of the afternoon. Supper-time came.

Elizabeth felt herself prey to an unexpected sadness. For the first time, she cast all around her a melancholy gaze at that dining room, where she would still be taking her evening meal tomorrow which would be the last time, and never again. She then experienced in advance what nostalgia for the South is. The softness of its voices, the mystery of its dark forests, and the exquisite perfumes of its fairy-tale gardens, all that had found its way inside her.

At the end of supper, she stood up, along with everybody else, and as she passed behind William Hargrove's sons in order to get to the hall, she heard Josh telling Douglas in a confidential tone of voice:

'Do you know what he said just now? I couldn't believe my ears. He asked, under his breath, where Laura was.'

'Yes, everything's falling into place in his memory. He'll soon be himself again.'

'Well then, it's high time for that departure to take place.'

She moved away without being seen and came back into the dining room, where she lingered for a moment. 'That departure . . .' What a hurry they were in to see her leave the pretty house, to which, by a last minute change of heart, she was becoming attached. The little poor relation would go elsewhere . . . In her confused state, she had dropped on to a chair and closed her eyes, to the amazement of the servants who were clearing the table. One of them came up to her:

'Is you feelin' poorly, Miss Lizbeth?' he asked timidly.

Without waiting any longer, she went and shut herself in her room, and went to bed, having assured herself that nobody could get in, either through the door, the window, or the verandah. Tiredness came over her all at once. After the emotional upset of the last few days, she wanted nothing more than to get undressed as quickly as possible to get to sleep in order to forget. She had barely got into bed when she began to savor the delights of the oblivion of sleep.

A persistent knocking at the door finally woke her. She

opened it, and it was Betty who entered, in tears. Too upset to say anything intelligible, the old servant was wailing and uttering little cries like a cat miaowing.

'Miss Lizbeth,' she groaned.

Bent double, she seemed ready to fall to her knees before Elizabeth.

'Come now,' the latter said impatiently, 'pull yourself together and speak. What's wrong?'

'Miss Lizbeth, you ain't leavin', is you? They's gettin' down your big trunk.'

'Well, yes, I'm leaving, I'm leaving tomorrow.'

'To go to Mass'r Charlie's. Not for ever?'

'Yes, I think so, for ever.'

At this point Betty began to cry unrestrainedly, and she suddenly collapsed in a heap at the feet of the bewildered girl, imploring her:

'Miss Lizbeth, you ask Mass'r Josh and Mass'r Douglas to sell me to Mass'r Charlie.'

'Sell you to Mr Jones! You're mad.'

'No, I wants to stay with you . . .'

'They'll never agree, Betty, and you're fine here.'

'No, no, everybody say you go to Virginia with Mass'r Charlie. I wants to be Mass'r Charlie's.'

With a mixture of pity and indignation, Elizabeth looked at the old woman wrapped up in black, imploring her to be sold to a new master. This strange supplication shamed her.

Bending down, she touched Betty's shoulder and said to her:

'Get up, it upsets me a lot to see you there like that. I'll speak to Uncle Josh.'

The groanings gave way to effusive gratitude, as if the transfer had already been agreed to, and the English girl was nearly late for breakfast. She waited for what she judged to be the most favorable moment to make her request, but preparations for her departure were already beginning to turn even the most ordinary of activities to a frenzy. Elizabeth had the impression that they were going off their heads on her account. They had to make the 'children' keep quiet, as their exclamations risked informing William Hargrove of what must be concealed from him, for he seemed to have forgotten the very existence of the fateful

young beauty who had done violence to his precious conscience. Stems of seringa were added to the amaryllis to
thicken out the protective screen, eliminating temptation.
Eyes shining with tears turned towards Elizabeth, and pretty
little hands were stretched out over the plates of pancakes
with maple syrup, as if to keep her there. Even Billy looked
ready to join the weeping chorus. Only Fred retained an
impassive face, looking straight ahead.

That very morning, the large trunk purchased in Savannah was installed in Elizabeth's room, and this was the
occasion for another scene of despair. Betty was opening
the armoires to get out the dresses of Miss Lizbeth, who had
not yet brought the news so desperately longed for, and she
placed the delicately colored dresses in the capacious interiors with sinister little cries. She had already pictured herself
dressing her mistress for the ball in Virginia, and now ...
Elizabeth, annoyed, kept telling her that before the afternoon was out she would speak to Uncle Josh, but she felt
rather cowardly at putting off the difficult moment in such a
way, and she would not have been able to bear a refusal.

Something else was troubling her also. Although she
appreciated all this emotion around her, she remembered
the days when people barely paid any attention to her at all.
Did they love her that much then? Undoubtedly she had to
be removed from the sight of that venerable and scrupulous
gentleman who, in his library, searched for ways to avoid the
thousand and one tricks of the Devil.

The half-full trunk was left open in a corner of the room
until lunch-time.

This meal promised to be more or less like all the others,
when suddenly there was an incident like a clap of thunder
in a clear sky: Uncle Douglas was sufficiently imprudent to
talk about the latest news. The discussions over points of
detail of the Compromise were holding back the final, solid
agreement that would settle the problem 'for ever'.

'Congress is asleep,' said Uncle Josh, 'it must be hot in
Washington.'

Fred's clear, harsh voice made everybody jolt.

'You are right to say they are asleep, Uncle Josh,' he
proclaimed, 'and while they sleep, we're losing the war. It's
now, now, that we should move ahead.'

'But Fred,' said Uncle Douglas, 'you forget that the Union has an army.'

'The American army! Eighty thousand men, and most of the officers favor the South. The North has no desire to fight. But it's in our blood. There would be a spontaneous mass uprising to run to the frontiers.'

'What makes you think that the men of the North aren't just as brave?' asked Uncle Josh.

'Oh, I don't say they're not, but they're a race of shop-keepers, they'd have to be dragged away from their counters, whereas each one of us is ready to go as if to a duel.'

'To leap into action!' exclaimed Billy.

'Oh, you would,' said Uncle Douglas in exasperation. 'If you don't shut up, we shall have one of those talks that you don't like, in the study.'

William Hargrove's rather mournful voice could be heard, as he was wrenched from his dreams:

'What's the matter? Is it the Compromise?'

'Fred,' said Uncle Douglas, 'you're upsetting your grand-father, and you're casting a shadow over her last day for Elizabeth . . .'

He stopped abruptly.

'Alright, Father,' said Fred, 'since no one wants to hear the truth at Dimwood.'

The ladies, in their turn, stirred themselves.

'All the newspapers affirm that there's a Compromise, and that there's peace in our time,' said Aunt Augusta.

'The newspapers!' exclaimed Fred scornfully.

Again William Hargrove's voice was to be heard:

'Have the newspapers come? I hope all is well. I heard Fred shouting something.'

'He always shouts when it's hot,' said Uncle Josh, 'ever since he was a child.'

'Ah?' said William Hargrove politely. 'I'd never noticed.'

And he drifted off into reverie while he ate.

'A duel,' thought Fred. 'A duel with the North, that will be our war.'

62

E lizabeth regretted that she had not had a chance to plead Betty's cause and, as she sometimes lacked a sense of occasion, she chose the moment when the two brothers were making their way, after dinner, towards the smoking room, both of them irritated at what Fred had come out with.

'I fear, unfortunately,' said Uncle Josh, 'that there is a foundation of good sense in what he says in an outrageous manner. Perhaps we are heading towards a disaster.'

'We've been heading towards a disaster since the Constitution was drawn up by the Founding Fathers. The seeds of war were already sown, and they knew it, but it's still a good way off.'

'Do you think so?'

The girl who was following them plucked up her courage:

'Excuse me,' she said, standing in front of them, 'I have something to say to you.'

A little surprised, they looked at her with amused indulgence, but also with affection. Uncle Douglas opened the door and stepped aside to let her pass.

In the smoking room, with its lowered blinds, Elizabeth sat down in front of these two men whom she found slightly intimidating, but she nevertheless put on a determined expression.

'Here,' said Uncle Josh jovially, 'you are in the secret lair where ladies never set foot, but you have nothing to fear from our cigars, we don't smoke in front of young ladies. Speak.'

She brought out all at once the sentence she had carefully prepared:

'I'm asking you to give Betty to Uncle Charlie, so that she can accompany me to Virginia.'

Uncle Josh looked at his brother.

'Give Betty away?' he said.

'Or sell her,' said Elizabeth, 'since she wants to be sold.'

'But we're fond of Betty,' said Uncle Douglas, 'and she is very useful to us.'

'And then,' said Uncle Josh, 'she's a bit old to be sold.'

The girl was starting to become agitated.

'Betty is a person,' she said, 'not an animal.'

The two men raised their eyebrows.

'We should have to know,' said Uncle Douglas with a smile, 'whether Charlie Jones is prepared to take her into his service.'

The point was clarified with passion:

'She wants to be bought and to belong to him for ever.'

She stood up abruptly:

'If I had any money, I would buy her from you myself, since slaves are bought and sold.'

'Even if we want to keep her?' asked Josh calmly. 'For she is ours, after all.'

'She isn't anybody's,' replied Elizabeth, 'she belongs to herself.'

Without answering, Uncle Josh and Uncle Douglas exchanged looks of amazement.

'The same assurance as Fred,' murmured Uncle Josh.

'It's the new generation,' said Uncle Douglas in the same tone of voice.

'I'm opposed to slavery!' exclaimed Elizabeth, who was losing her self-control.

At these words, the men stood up to put an end to this stressful discussion. Uncle Josh spoke up:

'My dear English girl,' he said quietly, 'you will never oppose it as much as all of us who hate it. If you can find a means, a method, a system, whereby we can be rid of it without ruining the country, I undertake to have it presented to Congress in order to have done with this plague. Put down in writing the solutions that you propose. In the meantime we'll send Betty to Charlie Jones with a letter. We'll give her to him purely as a gift. Do you agree, Douglas?'

'Perfectly, but I can see from here Charlie's embarrassment at receiving the present of a servant, whom he does not need and perhaps does not like.'

'But I like her,' said Elizabeth spiritedly.

'Well, my girl, it's you who'll explain everything to Uncle Charlie. Remember, however, before indicting us in the court of universal morality, that it was your homeland, together with France, that sold to the American settlers the first slaves, whom you, like us, feel sorry for. With the passage of time, the Negroes began to die in the North, where the climate killed them. Not lacking in business sense, the North resold the slaves that Europe had never stopped supplying. To enlarge your knowledge, ask Uncle Charlie to take you on a visit to Mr Toombs.'

'Oh, Mr Toombs,' exclaimed Elizabeth.

'"Oh, Mr Toombs",' repeated Uncle Douglas, 'that's what we think of that eloquent gentleman too. We'll see you later Elizabeth, we're going to light our cigars now.'

Without a word, she blushed and disappeared.

She had barely crossed the hall when she heard someone running after her. It was Uncle Josh.

'We took leave rather abruptly,' he said to her when he had caught up with her. 'You are quite right about Betty. I will accompany you to Savannah myself, and I will explain everything to Charlie Jones. Betty will leave with you in the morning. She'll follow the carriage in a little cart.'

'Why not in the carriage with us?'

He smiled:

'Things haven't come to that yet,' he said.

Elizabeth returned to her room and rang for Betty to let her know the good news, and the scene of that morning was repeated, but in reverse this time. The old servant once again threw herself at the girl's feet with cries, not of despair, but of gratitude. Beside herself with happiness, she was laughing and looked as if she were about to roll about on the floor, when Elizabeth touched her on the shoulder:

'At your age, are you not mad? You're behaving like a child. Get up and finish packing the trunk.'

There was an atmosphere of over-excitement throughout the house which William Hargrove's two sons had difficulty in keeping in check. Indeed, their father must not have the least suspicion of what was afoot. As Elizabeth had disappeared from his horizon, he was likely to want to keep her if he suddenly saw her re-emerge. That did not prevent purposeless comings and goings and frantic whispering in the corridors, far away from the drawing room where the master of Dimwood was dreaming in his winged armchair.

The ladies, in their black or plum-colored taffeta

dresses, gave commentaries under their breath on the event of the day from behind their fans. In obedience to Uncle Josh's instructions, Elizabeth stayed in her room with the door locked. From time to time, the girls launched a raid in that direction, but without success. Then they would gather together on the verandah and shake the shutters of the bedroom. The iron bar holding them in place put up a valiant resistance. The English girl, who had perhaps been too much admired, maintained deep silence, and the implorings of her former companions remained in vain.

She wanted to be alone, alone to contemplate her strange life, and to think about that cruel Jonathan, who had gone far away.

Nothing disrupted supper. The girl, in her usual place, had the impression that people were talking less, and more softly, than was their custom, as if someone had departed this life. Fred did not say a word, staring at some invisible point in space. From time to time, Susanna would sniff discreetly.

The only voice to be heard was William Hargrove's as he proffered opinions on the temperature and the chances of a good harvest in the cotton fields. He seemed to be in an excellent mood, in no way aware of the somewhat funereal atmosphere that prevailed in the dining room.

In Elizabeth's mind, one thought dominated over all the others: to flee. Her nostalgia the previous day seemed to her false now. It was with transports of delight that she thought that this was the last time she would see those gilt moldings, those servants in scarlet cotton livery, all of those faces of male and female diners that she never wanted to see again. 'Ungrateful!' cried out an inner voice. 'Why ungrateful? They received me in spite of themselves and in spite of me. The poor relation is going away to other climes. Rejoice, oh poor relation!'

As soon as it was possible to slip politely away, she returned to her room and rang for Betty, who arrived immediately, quivering with zeal and cheerfulness.

'Betty, wake me in the morning at seven o'clock. I want to be ready before everybody else. At what time are we leaving?'

'I don't know, Miss Lizbeth. Not before breakfast.'

'Why breakfast? But take no notice. Seven o'clock. Do you

hear? The trunk is packed, it's being left open overnight. Go now! Good-night.'

'Good-night, Miss Lizbeth.'

Left alone, she locked the door, barred the shutters and got undressed. Once again the same voice as earlier on cried out to her: 'Ungrateful!'

She was suddenly overcome with shame, but she did not linger over these fascinating uncertainties and, sliding between the sheets, she plunged into sleep as one might plunge into the waters of a lake . . .

In the middle of the night, she was woken by the singing of a man's voice, soft and sad, accompanied by a few notes on a mandolin.

She got up and went to listen, with her head leaning against the shutters. The voice seemed to be coming from the porch, and the crazy idea that it was Jonathan raced through her mind, but that was impossible. Jonathan's voice attracted her by its disturbing deepness; this one was clearer and its beauty was very moving, as it rose up pure and almost childlike in the night, with its melancholy overtones.

The words were constantly repeated as in some grave and plaintive recitative. It sounded like a serenade for someone dead.

63

B etty came to drag her out of her sleep at seven o'clock, and did not hesitate to tell her off, for she had not slept under her blankets. The girl looked at her in a daze for a moment, unable to wrench herself from her dreams. She washed and put on a green dress and left her bedroom.

Then there began throughout the house a silent rush of little happenings. Elizabeth's departure had quite simply to be camouflaged . . . No sighs, no spontaneous flights of affection for the girl they were about to lose. Closed in on himself, the master of the plantation was nonetheless suspicious. That morning, as if to delay the activities that were planned, he considerably lengthened the prayers that had to be sat through before tucking into the buckwheat fritters.

'He's doing it on purpose, he can sniff something in the air,' whispered Mildred to Minnie.

A kick under the table silenced the imprudent one, and Uncle Douglas glared terrifyingly in her direction.

At the end of the meal, William Hargrove allowed himself to be persuaded that a nap on his bed would do him good, for, like the previous ones, the day promised to be hot.

The carriage was waiting in front of the porch, and everything was ready for the departure, but Uncle Douglas wanted the family to gather together in the drawing room, amid the greatest silence, to say farewell to Elizabeth. The latter, who was wary of shows of affection, would have been happy without this sentimental gathering, but a minute later she found herself, to her horror, alone in the middle of the drawing room, facing the Hargroves, who were standing in a semi-circle around her . . .

'I propose,' said Uncle Douglas, 'that each of us, one after the other, comes to kiss our Elizabeth. She will be taking away with her some of the *joie de vivre* from our house.'

'Douglas,' whispered Uncle Josh, 'cut it short, it's already looking like a funeral procession.'

Uncle Douglas gave a start and said:

'Very well. We'll begin with the eldest. Emma, would you like to . . .'

Aunt Emma, in tears, went and hugged the girl, who struggled politely.

At that moment, Fred opened the door noiselessly and slid out.

Then came Aunt Augusta, in control of her emotions, and, proffering a few platitudes, she placed a brief kiss on Elizabeth's forehead, and whispered in her ear:

'I've hidden a present in one of your valises, a surprise, in memory of happy hours at Dimwood.'

This disconcerting ceremony nearly turned into chaos, on account of the 'children' who could not control themselves. Susanna especially began to howl unrestrainedly, and her cries had to be stifled. Billy took advantage of the occasion to give the English girl a kiss on the mouth.

Feeling harassed and embarrased, the girl climbed into the carriage with Uncle Josh; she was keen to be on the way now. Behind them, taking her place in the baggage cart, was Betty, exhausted from a long evening of farewells to all her colored companions. Azor, in his elegant red livery and his little straw hat pulled down over one eye, was waiting for the signal to be off. He had been told to go at walking pace until he was half a mile from the house. They considered trying straw to the horses hooves, to ensure total silence.

Elizabeth, however, out of inexplicable capriciousness, wanted to have a last look at that elegant house where she had suffered so much. She turned round sharply, and regretted it straight away ... At one of the windows on the second floor, she saw Miss Llewelyn, standing with one fist on her hip and, with her other hand, waving her forefinger in an admonishing gesture. 'Morality' seemed written across the whole width of her ashen face.

Elizabeth put her tongue out at her.

She was about to sit down again next to Uncle Josh, when she nearly let out a cry. Lower down the house, at one of the drawing-room windows, motionless like a portrait in its frame, William Hargrove was looking at her.

She dropped down on to the seat, Uncle Josh turned his head for a second towards the house, then, touching Azor's back with his cane, he said to him in a loud voice:

'We're off, Azor, and quickly. We'll begin to gallop in the avenue.'

The whip cracked in the warm air, and the four horses set off at a rapid trot.

'Don't be upset, Elizabeth,' said Uncle Josh calmly, 'there's nothing extraordinary about all that. Douglas made a few mistakes in the arrangements. My father has always been wary. There was too much silence around him this morning. The first mistake ... Then too much activity on the stable side. One may well think of everything, but one can't stop horses neighing ... Papa guessed that something was afoot. In my opinion he has got all his wits about him again but is remaining very secretive. Has he started playing along with us? What is he thinking? Is he relieved to see you go? I apologize, but it's possible.'

'Oh, it's all the same to me, Uncle Josh, everything's the same to me, provided I can go away.'

'I'm sorry to hear those words, but I understand . . . I'll explain everything to Charlie Jones. He's an angel in banker's clothing.'

Not finding an answer to that, Elizabeth retreated into her corner and let her gaze wander over the rows of the slaves' white cabins and then, over to the other side of the road, over the high, black wall of pine trees, edging the river. This landscape seemed austere to her, despite the blue, cloudless sky. A vulture accompanied them for a few seconds, beating the air with his outstretched wings before returning to the fields. Her eyes followed it with a mixture of admiration and horror. The noise from the wheels and the horses' hooves followed the thoughts in her head like a monotonous discourse. A memory haunted her, that of the singing she had heard in the night.

'And now,' the wheels and the horses' hooves on the road seemed to be saying, 'the beloved, whom Uncle Josh abominates, is on the road to exile with his beautiful mixed-blood wife who has made him lose face and whom he does not love, because it's you whom he loves, and Miss Llewelyn, the go-between, girt with morality, is quite ready to launch the two of you, you and him, into a guilty, adulterous correspondence, and you will not reply, but yes, you will reply, you will not reply, but yes, you will reply, you will not reply . . .'

'Well,' Uncle Josh exclaimed cheerfully, 'so young, and already muttering to yourself? If you have worries, my girl, you should confide in your Uncle Josh.'

'Worries? It's the noise of the carriage and the horses' hooves that are making me talk to myself, like when I was a child in England.'

'Come now, I'm not in the habit of wrenching people's secrets out of them. Don't be sorry about leaving our rather austere Dimwood. I think happiness awaits you in Virginia. Azor, I can see your head nodding. If you fall asleep, we shall end up in the river. A good crack of the whip and gallop on to Savannah.'

'Yes, Mass'r Josh, at the gallop.'

The whip cracked like shots from a pistol, and Azor set his team off at such a pace that Elizabeth jumped from her seat.

She had barely three seconds to cast her eyes over the mysterious pond, sleeping in primeval solitude. As on the first occasion she had seen it, some inexplicable call seemed to come from those dank waters. The unease that she felt was just as hard to get rid of as it had been on the first occasion.

64

*L*ess than an hour later, she found herself in the shady avenues of Savannah, and the radiant, tranquil beauty of that town wiped the bitterness of the last few days from her mind. Everything promised happiness in that light softened by sycamores and the flower beds at the foot of the white houses. She suddenly felt regret at not being able to stay there, since they were going to take her off somewhere else, to Virginia, of which she knew nothing at all. Another England, they told her, but can you replace your native land?

Charlie Jones welcomed them in radiant good humor, which he had the gift of sharing with everybody. That morning his dark blue eyes were lit up with the cheerfulness of a young man. He kissed Elizabeth, who did not pull away. The smile of the portrait in her bedroom came into her mind, like some apparition swathed in eau-de-Cologne.

'Josh,' he said, 'you old villain, there's no need to explain things. Laura has sent me an enormous letter, containing the whole of the chronicles of Dimwood and the events that she foresaw. Your father will recover. As you don't read the *Savannah Gazette*, you won't know that I led my fiancée discreetly to the altar of Christ Church. Everything took place very quietly. I shall introduce you to my wife,

Elizabeth.'

'Oh, what good news that is, Charlie!'

And as they were going up the steps towards the front door, amidst an exchange of compliments and teasing, Josh suddenly stopped and asked:

'Where is Betty?'

'Yes,' repeated Charlie Jones, 'where is Betty? And to start with, who is Betty?'

'She was following us with the trunk and the valises and is coming here to stay. We make you a present of her, she begs to be allowed to accompany Elizabeth and to stay with her. There you are.'

'I agree to everything, but as she's yours, I'll compensate you for her services.'

'You couldn't, she's priceless, she's yours purely as a gift.'

'Many thanks. I expect something splendid.'

'Hmm,' said Uncle Josh.

'Say no more, I get the message, accepted in advance, angel or she-devil, today we're having a party.'

As he spoke, he led them to a small, rounded drawing room, where light filtered through the blinds of three windows which gave this room the appearance of the interior of a lantern. Gilded panelling with a matt finish brightened up the pale green of the walls, softening the severity of the decor.

As they entered, a woman got up from an armchair and came towards them, smiling. The beauty of her gaze and the gentleness of her large brown eyes were very striking. Her thick, brown hair, parted down the middle, covered her temples and gave added seriousness to a face which shone with intelligence and goodness. Wearing a dress of violet-colored taffeta that reached down to her feet, she intimidated Elizabeth to the point of speechlessness. Incapable of uttering a word, the latter confined herself to a little curtsey.

'How formal we are!' exclaimed Charlie Jones. 'Amelia, may I introduce my friend Joshua Hargrove of Dimwood, and our dear Elizabeth Escridge who comes from England and is good enough to agree to live with us — if we are well behaved!'

The lady in violet taffeta held out her hand to Uncle Josh,

who gave a low bow, and then she kissed the girl, who blushed with emotion.

There was still an hour before lunch, and the travellers decided to rest.

In her room where nothing had changed, Elizabeth leaned out of the window. Bright red birds, which were known as cardinals, were flying among the trees in the garden, encountering blue jays, whom they seemed to be seeing off with a click of the beak. Filled with wonder, Elizabeth watched them for some considerable time. With the perfume of the flowers in the garden rose up memories of the times she had spent in Savannah: the ball, the duel, the great house rising up from the ground, the harbor, the long verandah from which could be seen the ships setting sail for Europe, all that made up a little dream-like life story. She wondered where she was heading now. Virginia: the name had an enigmatic beauty. Jonathan . . . where would Jonathan be, what would he be seeing? Jonathan . . .

Lunch took place in a small dining room that she was not familiar with, and she was struck by the simplicity of the service. The servants were not in livery, but wearing white jackets, and fewer courses were offered than previously. The food, on the other hand, remained exquisite. No wine, cold mint tea taking its place.

They spoke little. Amelia sat straight on her chair and seemed not to notice the smiles that her husband was lavishing on her. He exchanged the occasional word with Uncle Josh on the chances of a good harvest in the cotton fields. September promised to be fine. Quite in spite of herself, the girl was watching Charlie Jones. Was it happiness lighting up his face? He looked more and more like the portrait that she had seen previously in her room and which, she suddenly realized, was no longer there. It had been taken down. The splendid face had disappeared, and she was rediscovering it, in a rather hallucinatory manner, the stormy eyes, pink cheeks, youth . . . Her eyes crossed Amelia's attentive gaze, and the latter gave her a smile full of amused affection. Caught in the act of admiration, the dizzy girl smiled in her turn, lowered her head, and then turned to look at Uncle Josh, in whom she was not the least interested.

After lunch, Charlie Jones took her to one side and led

her to a little green and gold drawing room, in which she had never set foot. The house contained some fairly small rooms, made for mystery and secrets, which paralleled the rooms of stately proportions that served for receiving guests. As she went in there with that man against whose powers of attraction she was defenseless, she had a feeling of being in the wrong, but could she do other than obey? She tried to fix her attention on the pictures of Rome and Venice while he spoke to her, but she did not succeed. Likewise, the memory of Jonathan was no help to her, faced with those dark blue eyes that riveted her to the spot, and that firm, fleshy mouth that spoke disturbing words.

'Sit down, Elizabeth. I have a few things to say to you. See in me a friend who wishes your happiness. You must not think about Jonathan any more. He is a married man now. You no longer have the right to encourage his love. You must change your life. I am saying this in brutal fashion because at Dimwood the two of you were on the brink of scandal. You were seen by that Welshwoman who is much too inquisitive, I agree, but you should be aware of the fact.'

This was a different tone of voice. Inwardly she fought against these phrases that, one by one, struck at her heart.

'We didn't do anything wrong, and Jonathan wasn't married. Where's the scandal in that?' she cried out. 'I hate this spying.'

'Where I am taking you soon, there will never be any. I can understand your indignation. Here you are, turned back into that fighting young Englishwoman whom I'd lost sight of a while back.'

A charming smile was on hand to soften that insidious remark.

'What self-satisfaction,' she thought, fuming, but how handsome he was . . .

'There has not been any scandal as yet,' he continued in a gentler voice, 'but it was beginning to be known . . . So, Miss Escridge, try not to put people into uncomfortable situations. At Dimwood, they feared the suitor would return. The ladies especially, all bristling with virtue.'

Again a smile slid over his features, a smile that made him irresistible in vulnerable Elizabeth's eyes.

'Why are you looking at me in that strange way, my girl?

I'm not your enemy.'

'I know you're not my enemy,' she replied, bewitched, 'but I'm worried.'

He got up, very straight in his well-cut morning coat.

'We'll sort all that out,' he said, and he ran the palms of his hands over his hips with the air of a well-contented man.

At this she felt surprise, mingled with a vague disgust.

'What's the matter with him?' she wondered. 'He's not the same as he was a month ago.'

'Just one more thing,' he said gravely, 'not being up to date with the comings and goings of that character . . .'

'Which character?'

He continued:

'Not being up to date with the comings and goings of . . . Jonathan Armstrong . . .'

'Jonathan is not a character,' she riposted in an animated tone of voice. 'Jonathan is Jonathan — and a gentleman.'

As if he had not heard, he proceeded calmly:

'If by some very unfortunate circumstance your paths were to cross, you would not speak to him, not forgetting that he is a gentleman, and, I do not deny it, you are a lady.'

'*If your paths were to cross* . . .' She had to lean on her chair. Her love came flooding back to her all at once, making her heart pound. In a voice that was hoarse with emotion she replied:

'Do you really believe I am in need of your advice?'

'I leave it to your honor,' he said majestically. 'You would be discredited.'

Opening the door, he stood to one side to let the girl pass by, dumbfounded, and in the antechamber he stopped. Once again he gratified her with his charming smile.

'My dear child,' he said, 'I fear we have had a rather too serious conversation. Be reassured. There are good years ahead of you in Virginia. We'll stay here another ten days or two weeks, and I hope you won't be bored. There are delightful walks to be had in Savannah. My wife will accompany you, or friend Josh, for a young lady never walks on her own in town. Now, why don't you go and take a turn about the garden? There's a whole bed that I've had planted with new flowers. You can tell me what you think of them.'

This little speech was made in an affectionately solicitous

tone of voice, but Elizabeth did not go to the garden. As at Dimwood, she preferred to go to her room. For his part, Charlie Jones went to look for Uncle Josh in the smoking room.

'Josh,' he said as he sat down in one of the padded leather armchairs, 'I've just had a talk with our English girl. Without lecturing her too much, I let drop the great word "honor".'

'Well, now.'

'It was necessary. At first I had thought of talking to her about the Devil and the traps he's famous for.'

'That can be kept for later, we mustn't terrify her too quickly.'

'Tame her rather. I'm thinking about the problem. I noticed that she was looking at me very attentively, I have an idea, but let's leave all that.'

'I think things are going better. So?'

'So, you must know that Jonathan is about. He's seeing to the final details for his departure with his wife. The tickets, the money for the journey, the choice of cabins.'

'I should like to think that the two of them were far away.'

'Crazy as he is, he'd come looking for Elizabeth, if he knew she is here.'

'Where would he see her?'

'I don't know, but she will never go out alone. Sometimes Amelia will accompany her, and sometimes . . . you.'

'Thank you. In normal circumstances, I would have turned that job down, but I accept because I'm afraid for the girl. At Dimwood, they were all of a tremble that that fellow might spring up like a jack-in-the-box on the verandah. This is why we hastened the young lady's departure. We knew everything that was going on. Douglas organized a farewell gathering. He excelled himself in funereal sentiments, he is the most Scots of all of us. We were on the brink of tears, for we're all fond of Elizabeth. Events took a dramatic turn: just as we were getting into the carriage, my father, whom we thought to be resting in his room, appeared at a window. I'd rather not know what happened after that. We left at a gallop.'

'Don't have any worries, William has been back in his right mind for some time in my opinion, but as he is cleverer than you think, and taking pains to conceal his hand, he let you get on with it. It was a relief to see the departure of the principal cause of his inner torment: the little golden-haired nightmare. You can be quite calm on that front.'

'Laura has left, you know.'

'I know. She was right to do so, she wrote to me. She is the saint of the family.'

'As for that wretch Llewelyn . . .'

Charlie Jones burst out laughing.

'If the devil would buy it, she would sell her soul to him, but she has been his for some time, and he's watching his money.'

'That's the third time we've mentioned the Devil.'

'That's because he's everywhere. Certain aspects of human wickedness can't be explained any other way. But let's leave him to his affairs and come back to our own. This evening you will meet Amelia's eldest sister who is dining with us. She's an exquisite little lady who never wished to marry. Armed with good cooking and her religion, Miss Charlotte Douglas is unbeatable at all Southern recipes and could outdo William Hargrove on points of moral complexity, but she is too well brought up to make a show of her knowledge unprovoked.'

'I can't wait to meet her.'

'She'll be delighted to act as chaperone to Elizabeth in her walks, for she loves instructing and directing young people.'

'And it's with unalloyed joy that I give up that role to her.'

'I expected no less from your courtesy,' said Charlie Jones with a wide grin. 'Finish your cigar in peace. I'll go and join Amelia. We're dining at six, quite simply. My wife, you understand . . .'

In her room, Elizabeth found Betty and Nora doing battle over her wide-open trunk, each of them claiming the English girl as her personal property.

'She may be your mistress back there, but here she's mine!' clamored Nora in a piercing voice, with her arms outstretched over the trunk.

'But now she's mine for ever,' riposted Betty in the same tone of voice, 'so be quiet, you old fool!'

'I lives here, so you be quiet!'

The dispute was accompanied by parrot-like shrieks and was becoming so animated that they did not notice the presence of Elizabeth who was watching them in silence. On the point of coming to blows, their small black noses, the nostrils dilated with rage, were already touching.

Elizabeth stamped her foot.

'Silence!' she ordered.

The adversaries gave a start.

'Miss Lizbeth!' they both said together.

'I don't want any more whining; you'll obey me.'

Her ears rang with an unfamiliar pleasure. She suddenly guessed at what the intoxication of power might be, the satisfaction of seeing terrorized human beings give in before one, and she immediately judged herself unworthy. Indeed, the two old servants, bewildered, were bowing with lowered heads.

'Miss Lizbeth is upset,' murmured Betty.

Nora, who was older, hid her worn face in her long, narrow hands and said nothing. More ashamed than both of them, Elizabeth said good-humoredly:

'Come now, don't stand there like that, you're going to work together. Betty will hand the dresses to Nora, who will put them in the armoire. Empty the trunk, and put to one side the two valises, which are for the journey.'

Straightening herself up, Nora gave Betty a vanquishing look.

'Miss Lizbeth is goin' to stay in Savannah,' she said.

The reply came immediately.

'Hush up. She say we is goin' to Virginnia.'

'You're not going to quarrel,' said Elizabeth, who once more played the angry mistress. 'Do as I tell you. We're staying, and then we're setting off, I don't know when.'

They exchanged cross looks, and suddenly burst out laughing, like two wizened children.

At exactly six o'clock the five diners entered the small dining room, and Charlie Jones introduced Elizabeth to his sister-in-law, the former giving a hint of a discreet curtsey. In her dress of black Tussore silk, Miss Charlotte's head was proudly crowned with a large, white bonnet, the flounces of which fell down to her flat chest. Without being excessively given to smiling, her face was mobile and vivid of expression, with a slender, inquisitive nose and a thin mouth impatient to utter opinions. Gentle gray eyes lessened the unease initially provoked by her odd appearance.

Not daring to look too closely at her, the girl glanced in her direction and wondered what kind of life was in store for her in the company of these three people. A smile from Uncle Josh, as if to reassure her, awoke in her a nostalgic regret for Dimwood. She was wary in advance of the 'dream house' that she had been promised and, in a lightning flash of memory, she again saw Jonathan, brushing aside the magnolia branches to draw his face closer to hers . . .

As soon as the soup came, she had a feeling that the meal would be frugal. The solid family silver shone, nevertheless, on a cloth that was like a great expanse of snow, as if for a banquet. Vegetable broth was followed by two fried chickens and a great dish of steaming rice. On the very exact advice of Amelia, Elizabeth saw herself being given a piece of breast, and had to have a second helping of rice, which was considered to be more nourishing than bread, in rather short supply. Then, to complete the meal, a generous dish of stewed fruit; Amelia advised Elizabeth to help herself twice, but with moderation. From time to time, the servants poured water into the crystal glasses amidst a clinking of ice cubes.

In some indefinable way, the conversation reflected the prudent limits that had been set on appetite. Uncle Josh and Charlie Jones exchanged opinions on the actions of Congress. The final objections had been removed. General agreement was no longer in doubt. Everybody admired the competence of President Fillmore, who was on the point of obtaining a definitive and favorable vote. Doors were opening onto peace and happiness for the Union.

Having no vote in the matter, the ladies listened in silence. Only Miss Charlotte, obviously eager to contribute, limited herself to smiling pleasantly at the English girl sitting opposite her.

At the end of the meal, they all placed their hands on the edge of the table and, with bowed heads, thanked the Lord, in low voices, for his bounty.

As they were leaving the dining room, Uncle Josh slipped

his arm in Charlie Jones's and said:

'All things considered, my dear old Charlie, I think I'll head back to Dimwood tomorrow.'

'So soon, Josh?'

'And with regret, believe me, but I feel duty calling me to be with my father. That sudden appearance at the window, when I thought he was asleep in his room . . . He knows everything. How is he taking it?'

'Badly.'

'I think so, and we shall pay for it in some drastic fashion.'

'Rather. I know Willie, he plays to the gallery: he suffers, and he wants people to know it and suffer along with him. Don't worry too much, but I was counting on you to act as bodyguard for Elizabeth.'

'She'll have your wife and her charming sister.'

'Very well. Let's be frank: you don't like our cuisine.'

'Charlie!'

'It's quite natural. My dear wife, you understand? A Scottish Presbyterian, with strict principles . . . Farewell to the frivolous feasting and luxuries of yesteryear. It's all the same to me. I'm deeply in love with her, and she makes me happy.'

'She is adorable . . . but I assure you, you are wrong as to my motives . . .'

'We are what we are, Josh, and I'm fond of you as you are. What time do you want to go?'

'After breakfast.'

'That's settled then. I'll see to everything. Shall we join the ladies in the drawing room?'

And so they headed in that direction. It was one of the formal drawing rooms and seemed all the larger for the company being reduced in ranks: Miss Charlotte, Amelia and Elizabeth, each sitting on an upright chair in preference to the capacious, gilt armchairs, which remained empty. The heavy curtains of sky-blue silk, which were draped and held in place with solid cords plaited with silver threads, gave this room an insolently splendid air. One might have expected a party, a ball, an invasion of beautiful women in crinolines, and handsome young men, instead of which two servants in white jackets were going round offering herbal beverages: a choice of mint or camomile. Placed on a marble table, a simple globe lamp gave out a modest light which did not reach to the heights of a ceiling heavily shrouded in shadow.

'Happy to have you with us,' said Amelia. 'Provided you undertake not to light your cigars. We took refuge here from the noise of the street. I counted at least six vehicles during dinner. Sit down.'

Uncle Josh sat docilely down on a sofa, whereas Charlie Jones showed his independence by walking back and forth:

'You have to let the thoughts circulate,' he said.

'Do you want some herb tea?'

Neither of them did.

'Instead of frittering away the time that is allotted to us in this world,' continued Amelia, 'I propose a topic of conversation that is both interesting and instructive.'

Silence. Elizabeth gave Charlie Jones a look of desperation as he passed by her, but he simply smiled and put his finger to his lips.

'Tell me,' said Amelia gravely: 'is man perfectible in a century in which he is carried away on a tide of progress? The Atlantic is being crossed by steam ships, telegraph links us to the old world, railways are travelling at the terrifying speed of thirty-five miles per hour, just think of it, that's almost as fast as a galloping horse.'

'Amelia,' said Uncle Josh with a somber air, 'Indians on horseback can catch up with and overtake trains, stop them and kill the driver, not to mention the passengers . . .'

'Let us see in that a curse from Heaven upon the railways. In his senseless pride, which is constantly being augmented by his sense of his own power, is not man putting his chances of salvation at risk?'

At this point, Miss Charlotte got up and began to speak. Her high-pitched voice created a strange impression of excess, for it seemed too much for her small stature to reach right up to the shadowy ceiling.

'A good Protestant has nothing to fear from this demented modern world,' she proclaimed. 'He knows for certain that he is saved, and if he does not believe that he is, then he isn't, it's quite simple.'

Uncle Josh stood up in his turn and took a few steps

towards Amelia.

'Dear Amelia,' he said, 'as I was saying to Charlie a moment ago, my father's health worries me, and I am setting off early in the morning for Dimwood. Forgive me if I withdraw, I must rest before the fatigue of the journey.'

His black frock coat and the solemn tone that adorned these words made of him such a majestic personage that Amelia found nothing to say in reply. Her large brown eyes rested affectionately on him.

'I understand,' she said, 'and I'm sorry about this sadly premature departure. Good night, Cousin Josh,'

A deep bow was her reward for this gracious dismissal, and Josh headed for the door with firm steps.

A cry could be heard, but it did not stop him in his flight.

'I'm tired too, Uncle Josh.'

Amelia turned to the girl in distress.

'My girl,' she said, 'at your age, I took pleasure in obeying. I ask you to stay for a while and tell us about your voyage in a steam ship, about the impressive thrashing of waves as they attacked your boat. Was there not in that grounds for quaking fear, as much as for admiration?'

'It takes more than the thrashing of waves to make an English girl quake.'

The vivacity of the tone of voice made Amelia start. Charlie Jones intervened right away:

'Darling, the dear little thing is falling asleep and is in no shape to take part in a conversation that promises to be so compelling. I ask for Elizabeth to be excused.'

Amelia gave her husband a long and tender look.

'Granted,' she said.

Without waiting a second, the girl said thank you with an almost imperceptible curtsey and left.

'Our conversation seems under threat,' said Amelia, 'but thank God you are here, and you will stay with us.'

'You know that I'm not up to much in these animated exchanges of religious views . . .'

'But it's a question of the future of the world, Charlie.'

'My dear, you will settle all that very well between yourselves without me who understands nothing of it. You and I will see each other later, but I think it more reasonable to withdraw now.'

'And I think you are going to stay with us, there in that big armchair, because I ask you to, and as yet you have refused me nothing.'

The large brown eyes fixed on him with an implacable gentleness. With a slight gesture of resignation, he sat down in the big armchair.

65

The following morning, Uncle Josh was alone in the large drawing room awaiting breakfast and reading the newspaper. His haste to see Dimwood again had got him out of bed earlier than usual. Now he was trying to interest himself in the latest news from Washington, without being entirely successful. His attention wandered constantly, he could already see himself galloping down the long avenue at Dimwood, when his dreaming was interrupted by the sudden arrival of Elizabeth. She ran towards him and exclaimed:

'Uncle Josh, what a piece of luck to find you alone! I slept badly last night, I want to go back to Dimwood with you.'

'I've never seen you so upset, Elizabeth. Calm down, what's the matter?'

'I don't want to go to Virginia.'

'You don't know what you're saying. I envy you the stay that awaits you in that paradise.'

'It won't be a paradise with Amelia.'

'Wrong. That woman is an angel.'

'I shan't be happy with her, and Uncle Charlie isn't at all the same. I preferred him as he was before. Yet he looks pleased with everything. What's the matter with him?'

'The matter with him is that he's married to a woman he adores. The soul is happy because the body is calm.'

'I don't see the link. He hasn't changed his body.'

'Let's pretend I said nothing, dear girl. I was speaking in a daze. In any case, there can be no question of my taking you back to Dimwood.'

'Oh, Uncle Josh,' she begged.

For a moment he was tempted to go back on his decision, quite simply to bring joy to that desperate little face, but he knew only too well that Douglas would be firm — and that, as soon as they had arrived, he would take the weeping girl back to Savannah . . .

'No,' he said, 'I'm sorry, but I can't, I . . .'

He stopped. Amelia, on her husband's arm, was making her entry into the drawing room. The smile on their lips seemed to illustrate Uncle Josh's remarks on the matrimonial state and the satisfaction that it brings to body and soul . . . Echoes of a wedding march would not have been too much out of place. Miss Charlotte came behind, making up the procession.

'Good morning,' said Charlie Jones, 'Breakfast is served and awaits you.'

Feeling betrayed and bored at one and the same time, Elizabeth followed everybody else and sat down at the place pointed out to her, between Amelia and Miss Charlotte.

In contrast with the previous day's dinner, this morning's meal was copious. Scrambled eggs with bacon, buckwheat fritters with maple syrup, stewed fruit, heaps of toast, honey and marmalade; everything was there for the taking and in abundance, surrounding a monumental silver teapot and a coffee pot that was no less impressive. Ten people would have been able to satisfy voracious hunger with what was on display, but Amelia's ideas on diet were the rule, and she wanted them to begin the day like an army about to set off on a campaign.

Elizabeth contented herself with a cup of tea and nibbled half of a piece of toast.

'You'll be hungry,' Amelia told her.

'No I won't,' said Elizabeth.

Amelia bit her lip and looked away.

'Pretend, dear,' whispered Miss Charlotte into the ear of youthful disobedience, 'it would be easier.'

In a flurry of good sense, Elizabeth mastered her English pride and finished her piece of toast with noisy ostentation.

Amelia rewarded her with a smile:

'There's a good little girl,' she said.

'That's what's in store for me,' thought Elizabeth, 'good, obedient little girl.'

Exasperation welled up inside her as she felt a bird's talon place itself in friendly fashion on her left hand.

'Patience,' said Miss Charlotte in another whisper, 'I'm here.'

The farewells were brief. No show of emotion: that was the rule. Uncle Josh kissed the ladies and shook Charlie Jones not by the hand but by the arm, saying 'Thank you' in as warm a voice as circumstances required, then climbed into the carriage. But then there was an unwelcome surprise. Azor jumped down from his seat and ran up to Elizabeth; with his hat in his hand he bowed in front of her:

'Miss Lizbeth,' he said in a flow of fervor, 'God bless you, we all love you at Dimwood. Come back soon.'

'Will you have done, Azor?' cried Uncle Josh. 'This is absurd.'

Struck dumb with emotion, Elizabeth did not know what to do, and, losing her composure, she seized hold of the hesitant black hand and shook it. Uncle Josh got to his feet instantly. Seized with terror, Azor hastily put back his hat and his white cotton gloves and was back on his seat almost immediately. The whip cracked.

Using his hands as a megaphone, Uncle Josh leaned over in Elizabeth's direction. The horses set off at a trot. He just had time to shout:

'That's not done, but you did well all the same!'

'What are things coming to?' groaned Amelia when the carriage had disappeared.

Charlie Jones burst out laughing.

'Darling,' he said, 'what is History coming to?'

The shock of this departure affected Elizabeth profoundly. For a good while she remained dazed by this final blow inflicted on hope. Dimwood remained for her so intensely associated with the memory of Jonathan that, in some strange way, the black hand held out, then immediately withdrawn, became an image of separation.

Amelia and Miss Charlotte went inside the house, while Charlie Jones lingered hesitantly on the porch. Looking grave and very attentive, he was watching the motionless girl, her eyes fixed on the avenue where the carriage had driven through alternating patches of sun and shade, before disappearing around a street corner.

Going down three steps, he came up to her and spoke gently:

'Here you are, all aghast, as if you had not been expecting all that, my little Elizabeth. I can understand you very well. Departures are not always without some shadow of sadness, but you are too young to be sad. From now on I shall take charge of your happiness. Do you have confidence in me?'

'Of course,' she answered briefly.

'You have my word. Remember. Today, the 8th September 1850, at eleven o'clock in the morning beneath the trees at the bottom of the steps to my house, I undertake on my honor to do everything to make you happy. Does that reassure you?'

Struck by the solemn tone of this speech, she looked him straight in the face.

'I don't really see what you can do, but I believe you will try. The place, the day, the date, the time, and your word; you can be sure that I shall forget nothing of all that. If need be, I'll remind you of it.'

'You're not English for nothing, Elizabeth, and you're already talking like a woman.'

'I already told you I am not a little girl.'

'A young girl.'

'If you like, but a young girl without too many illusions.'

They went back into the house. Some minutes of indecision followed. Elizabeth maintained a silence that he was not quite sure how to break.

In the drawing room where he led her, he indicated to her to sit down and said:

'If I didn't have to go to my office this afternoon, I would have suggested a carriage ride around the district, but tomorrow we're expecting the arrival of a ship from England. You can't imagine what that means in terms of paperwork and orders to be given. Would you like to go for a walk in the park at the end of the afternoon?'

She made no objection.

'My wife or Miss Charlotte will be happy to accompany you.'

'Oh, I can go out alone.'

'Elizabeth, we live in a formal society. A little too much so, in my opinion, but this is an aristocracy that's closed in on itself. It has its rules and customs. A young lady does not go out walking in town without a chaperon.'

'Agreed,' said the poor relation at last, rebelling in silence, 'I shall do as you ask. Who will chaperon me?'

'Amelia, perhaps. You'll discover that she's a wonderful woman.'

A little after six o'clock, Amelia was walking in the long avenue in the park, with a majestic slowness. Her long dark green dress skimmed the sand with its flounces, and emphasized the impression of imperturbable dignity that emanated from her person and her movements. Her gestures were few and measured. A light mauve silk sunshade cast shadow over the upper half of her face. She was tall, well built and imposing.

At her side, an Elizabeth in a white cotton skirt seemed like a graceful and insignificant little creature escaped from some fairy-tale world, and her golden hair, catching the last rays of the sun, seemed aflame.

People looked at them a good deal. From time to time Amelia would nod towards a pearl-gray top hat that was raised as she passed by, or some group of elegant women, who were as reserved as she was in their politeness, returning smile for smile, and no more. She was evidently not inclined to join in conversation with people she knew only a little.

Beneath the noble shade of centuries-old oaks, which had seen arrogant officers in scarlet pass by, she took the English girl for a walk, as she had undertaken to do.

When they reached a place that was not much frequented, where giant willows bent over a shallow pool, they sat down on metal chairs and watched the fountain in silence. That kind of contemplation can go on for some time. The endless splashing of drops of water has something fascinating about it. Suddenly, Amelia drew herself up straight.

'Goodness knows what I was dreaming about,' she said. 'I

imagined I was already up there in Virginia, in the old house . . . you'll see, you'll fall for it too . . . you'll love it. There's no resisting.'

The girl looked towards her, amazed at seeing this strange woman become human.

'In the meantime, we're here,' continued Amelia, 'in this town, and I don't like towns, you can't breathe. Nature, I long for nature.'

The willows sought to console her in vain, surrounding her with their long, green drapery. The town was too near.

'Another three days,' she sighed. 'Tomorrow it won't be me who'll take you for a walk. My sister Charlotte will take my place. You don't know her yet. Don't judge her on appearance, she has great qualities.'

'I don't judge her at all,' said Elizabeth with conviction.

'That's good. Her life has been sad. She wanted to get married. The man she loved seemed quite ready to contemplate the union. She loved him deeply and perhaps let it show too much, but she loved him with a wild love, like an animal, do you understand?'

Incapable of saying anything, Elizabeth shook her head vigorously.

'Those things are far ahead of your years, but you can take my word for it. I was there, I saw her, we were all living together, and I was fifteen years younger, but I could understand. One day our father received a visit from the man in question. They talked for a long time, then the man went away, and he never came back. The engagement was broken off. And yet Charlotte was beautiful. Her despair was frightening. We thought she was going to die. For months she lived in a hospital — I daren't say an asylum — hovering between life and death for months on end. Her beauty faded, like a dried-out flower. And do you know why the man took back his word?'

She waited, striking the ground with the point of her parasol in an effort to overcome powerful emotion. In a different, cold voice, she suddenly said:

'Because she was very small and he quite tall. He had second thoughts at the last moment, afraid of looking ridiculous at her side.'

A long silence followed. With a lump in her throat from

this tale of suffering that rang so true to her, the girl searched for something to say.

'Poor thing . . .' she began.

'Yes, poor Charlotte,' Amelia interrupted as she raised her head, 'but perhaps it was better for her not to marry such a cowardly man. Often we only understand a long time afterwards what is God's will. When my sister was restored to health, she was no longer the same person. Pain had changed her — how shall I put it? — given her greater depth, perhaps. You and I know that there have been no more saints since the time of the apostles. The last pages of the Bible are written! Yet my sister . . .'

'At Dimwood, they told me that Aunt Laura was a saint.'

'Laura Hargrove!' said Amelia brusquely. 'My husband has spoken to me of her, but she's a Catholic. Those people would fill the world up with their saints if they could. It's different with Charlotte. Be kind to her. Listen to her.'

She stood up.

'Let's go back,' she said. 'You've had your walk. Keep what I've told you to yourself.'

'I'm not a chatterbox.'

'So much the better. Charlotte talks enough as it is. Let her talk.'

'I promise you I will.'

Slowly they retraced their steps home, still encountering the same raised hats and the same smiles.

Silent in their emotion, they were so absorbed in their thoughts that they no longer noticed that the shade of the sycamores was thickening at their feet. Dusk fell on the brick-paved streets and when they reached Charlie Jones's garden the first street lamps were being lit. It was then that Amelia let out these strange words:

'Night already. The return was rather long, but we had so much to say to each other; it seemed short.'

66

At about eleven o'clock the following morning, Miss Charlotte was on the quayside with Elizabeth. Charlie Jones had shown them the spot where they should stand in order to be able to see everything, and the elderly spinster could not contain her impatience. She did not know Savannah well, and her curiosity was as lively as a little girl's. In such circumstances, chaperoning Elizabeth seemed to her a boon.

The English girl viewed the morning's activities in quite a different light. She could not feel happy in that place, where boats were leaving for her native land while she saw herself condemned to remain ashore for an indeterminate length of time, in the South where she had no attachments, except for the memory of Jonathan, and Jonathan was far away.

With a heavy heart she followed Miss Charlotte, who was energetically making a way through the crowd for them. Out of a concern for her looks, at which Elizabeth dared not smile, she had raised her large, white lawn bonnet by fixing it to a little silk turban which she wore around her head, adding four inches to her height. This, she thought by some crazy logic, set her destiny to rights and made her like everybody else, obliterating that awful shortness. The absurdity of this ruse underlined the sadly comic aspect of her figure . The girl, aware to the point of occasionally letting Miss Charlotte go on ahead without her, distanced herself from her, ashamed to be seen with that small person who gave the impression of a dwarf done up for a circus act. Suddenly there came into her mind a thought that frightened her, inspired, as it were, by the Devil: 'I can understand the breaking-off of the engagement, I can understand that man.' She felt her face become scarlet. An inner voice called out to her almost immediately: 'So understand that other man, Jonathan, who preferred a woman more beautiful than you. Give up that ghost of a lover, look elsewhere.'

She fled to get away from the crowd, away from Miss Charlotte.

A great murmuring was rising up from the throng, and the slaves in their gaudy cotton outfits grouped themselves in one corner of the quayside, where they did not risk mixing with the Whites. The steamship was heralded in the distance by a gray plume, and was already being greeted by a chorus of acclamation. The smoke was applauded. The boat entered the mouth of the immense, mud-colored river, and the hurrahs rang out as for a victory.

Curiosity getting the edge over anxiety, Elizabeth headed for the mass of spectators. It was at that moment that, breaking away from a group of ladies a little to one side, a panicking Miss Charlotte ran up to her making wild gestures:

'Where on earth were you? You frightened me. Come on quickly, I'm with some charming people.'

The over-excitement had brought patches of red to her face, and her monumental headdress, as if it too were in the grip of emotion, was lurching from side to side in dangerous fashion. The thin, forceful little hand seized Elizabeth by the wrist and dragged her off.

She let herself be carried along and found herself almost immediately in the company of four or five ladies who smiled at her through their little veils and said a few words to her that she could barely make out. The shouting of the crowd was making all conversation impossible, and Miss Charlotte, stretching up on tiptoe, still could see nothing but the heads and shoulders of men and women.

The girl had become resigned, but sought nevertheless to get away from those inquisitive people who were now behind her, for they were coming from all directions. She fought her way through, finding this closeness to other people a real trial. She felt revulsion when she heard whispering in her ear and imagined the worst. Private things . . .

She turned her head in fury and recognized Jonathan. The blue-gray eyes plunged into hers, as they had on the road to Savannah, with the same authority, greedy for domination.

'Don't be afraid. I saw you just now, but I was with Annabel. I can't stop, she's only a hundred yards away, she and I are setting off tonight. She thinks you're at Dimwood. Say something to me, Elizabeth, I'm very unhappy, tell me something I can take away with me in my heart.'

'Not in this crowd, not here, but you ought to know . . .'

She was gasping.

'I'll come back,' he said, 'I'll come back . . .'

'I'll wait for you . . . all my life . . . Jonathan.'

Suddenly his face, which was aflame, came close to hers. She could see only his eyes, and she lowered her eyelids. A burning mouth placed itself on her mouth, and she thought she was going to faint.

When she opened her eyes again, Jonathan was no longer there.

She had time to see him disappear. His black curls fell on to the shoulders of a chamois-colored spencer. Then she looked for him desperately and lost him, but caught sight of Annabel in a gig at the far end of the quayside. A little apart from the crowd, she was straining to follow the course of the boat making its triumphant progress. The *Bonaventure* entered the port of Savannah.

6
PASSIONS

67

*B*ack home, Elizabeth set about looking for Amelia whom she found reading in a corner of the drawing room. At first the girl was unable to speak despite her enormous effort to get a grip on herself.

'Well,' said Amelia putting her book down, 'what's the matter, my dear?'

With her hair parted in the center, falling over her forehead like two brown wings, she was the very image of placidity.

'You look all upset,' she continued. 'Has something happened?'

Her concerned glance, already full of questioning, rested calmly and gravely on Elizabeth's worried face.

'Nothing disagreeable, I hope?'

The very gentleness of her insistence restored Elizabeth's equanimity.

'The crowd,' she said, 'there were far too many people.'

'How well I understand you! I too suffer from feeling like a prisoner in these great gatherings of strangers. One can't move. But sit down.'

Elizabeth sat on the straight-backed little chair that Amelia pointed out to her. The latter continued:

'The arrival of the good ship *Bonaventure* arouses as much enthusiasm as if it had been built in the town's shipyards. The South had it built at its own expense in Liverpool and now owns it, but Savannah is always ready to claim victory. When you arrived, I was immersed in reading a thrilling book which you perhaps know: *The Pilgrim's Progress*.'

'Yes,' said Elizabeth feebly.

'Well, you'll have the joy of re-reading it at our place in Virginia: that gem has a special place in all Protestant households.'

'I feel very tired . . . If you permit, I shall go up to my room and rest. I should prefer not to have dinner.'

'Well, that's agreed,' said Amelia quickly as if taking a sudden decision. 'You don't feel ill?'

'Not at all.'

'I won't keep you, my child. Charlie will be back a little late, on account of the *Bonaventure*, and I'll explain it to him. Sleep well, and don't forget your prayers. Your dear Betty will take care of you.'

Once in her room, she got undressed with all haste and called Betty. It was Nora who came.

'No,' said Elizabeth, 'not you, Nora. I want Betty.'

Nora bowed a defeated head and withdrew.

There was a muffled altercation behind the door, then Betty came in puffed up with pride.

'I need you Betty, you must obey me.'

The voice had become firm and precise once more and more English than ever.

'Yes, Miss Lizbeth,' said Betty, quite prepared to bow in the face of power.

'In the small cabinet in the adjoining room there is a bottle of laudanum, a blue bottle. I don't know exactly how you take it. You'll get some ready for me in a glass.'

'Oh!' exclaimed Betty, 'not for Miss Lizbeth, laudanum's bad for Miss Lizbeth.'

'Silence! My mother takes it, Aunt Emma takes it, everybody takes it everywhere. Obey, or else I shan't speak to you again, I'll have you sent back to Dimwood, and then it'll be Nora who'll be with me.'

Noisy sobs shook the faithful Betty, torn between duty and fear.

'You need port, Miss Lizbeth,' she groaned amidst a flood of tears.

'There must be a bottle of port in the pantry. You will bring me the bottle and a glass, or you'll pack your bags tomorrow and go back to Dimwood. Go on, quickly!'

In terror Betty bent herself double and disappeared. Elizabeth had the impression that she had curled herself into a ball and rolled out. Again she savored the dubious pleasure of seeing herself obeyed by a slave, simply by raising her voice.

'How easy it is!' she muttered to herself, a little ashamed in spite of everything.

The bottle of laudanum was indeed in the adjoining room in the cabinet, as she already knew. A label gave information concerning the number of drops it was advisable not to exceed.

'Only advised,' she said aloud.

The determined air that she forced herself to adopt did not prevent her feeling anxious. In her white nightdress which reached down to her feet and with the bottle in her fingers, she evoked an image of Juliet preparing to take her sleeping draught, but she was not thinking of that at all. The memory of her mother had been haunting her for the last hour. In her moments of despair, her mother insisted on having laudanum brought, her liberating drug that was on sale without prescription in all the pharmacies of the United Kingdom . . . But what was Betty up to? Had she been prevented from fetching the bottle of port without permission?

If the port did not come, she would drink her laudanum in a little water. Anything at all to be rid of the insomnia which she felt was on its way.

A quarter of an hour went by, feeling like several eternities joined end to end. Elizabeth tried to put on a brave face, but waiting killed off even the desire to live.

'I'm no good at suffering,' she thought, 'they never taught me how.'

She had to force herself not to think of Jonathan.

Suddenly the door opened. Miss Charlotte appeared without her headdress but followed by Betty, looking sheepish and holding a bottle of port and a glass on a silver tray.

Elizabeth shot out of the side room like an arrow.

The little procession stopped in front of her in the middle of the bedroom. With her gray hair unadorned by anything except the chignon at the back of her neck, Miss Charlotte had regained her natural dignity:

'My dear child,' she said with a kindly smile, 'your Betty tells me that you'd like to drink a little port. Splendid! There's nothing like it for getting you back on your feet after the fatigue of the day, and you'll sleep all the better for it. I shall have the pleasure of pouring you a measure of it myself. It's the best port in town. You can be sure it's been round the Cape, for Charlie Jones has to have top quality in everything. Let's sit down. Come forward, Betty.'

Her voice with its fast flow of words betrayed a vehemence that sounded a secret alarm. In her autumn-brown taffeta dress she quivered nervously.

She settled herself in the armchair, while Elizabeth, with some consternation, let herself drop onto the edge of her bed. Betty held out the bottle of port to Miss Charlotte who poured some into the glass, but so clumsily that a few drops were spilled on the tray.

'My eyesight gets worse and worse,' she said. 'Perhaps I've given you too much, but drink it, drink it all the same. Take all this away, Betty.'

Betty withdrew with the bottle and tray.

Elizabeth tasted the port with the tip of her lips, the first she had ever been offered, then she swallowed a very small mouthful of it.

'What do you think of it?' asked Miss Charlotte.

'Delicious.'

'Isn't it? I'm not allowed to have it. In my family, we are all under threat of gout. When I was young, I used to drink a little port at my grandfather's in Aberdeen. Young and happy. That's long ago. But carry on drinking.'

'She's worked it all out,' thought Elizabeth, 'she won't leave me a drop for my laudanum. What shall I do?'

'Perhaps I could put my glass down there, on that little table, and finish it later,' she said slyly.

'No, no, my child. I want to be sure that it does you no harm, but take your time. I want to tell you the plans for the journey we are to make. Our cabins are reserved on board the *Neptune*. We're leaving the night after tomorrow . . . But where's Betty? Betty!'

'Yes, Miss Charlotte,' said a voice from the back of the room.

'What are you doing?'

'I's wiping the tray, Miss Charlotte. There's some drops on it.'

'All that time to wipe a tray! Come here.'

Betty ran up.

'Where were you?'

'Over there, I cleaned it with a bit of water.'

'Over there? What do you mean, over there? Do you mean in the washroom?'

'Yes, Miss Charlotte, to get the water, Miss Charlotte.'

'What a fuss for a few drops of spilt port. And don't try to get around the truth with "yes, Miss Charlotte", "no, Miss Charlotte". I shall go and have a look "over there" in a moment, to see for myself.'

'Yes, Mi . . .'

'Stay there, and don't move. Elizabeth, my girl, you're not drinking.'

'Sorry, but I am. Look . . .'

'There's a bit left in the bottom. Drink it up, my child, and I shall let you go to bed.'

Without arguing, the girl swallowed the last drop. The spite she felt at having been tricked did not stop her from feeling an undeniable well-being, an exquisite burning in her chest and without a word she handed the glass to Betty.

Miss Charlotte stood up.

'Come now,' she said cheerfully, 'I see the port has gone down well. You can get into bed. To the washroom, Betty! Walk ahead and I'll follow.'

Elizabeth watched them move away. The imperious silhouette of the elderly spinster struck her like a premonition of what awaited her in Virginia. She sighed as she waited. Time went by. There was no sound from the washroom, and the desire to sleep was already making her nod her head when she again perceived the chattering sound of taffeta, and Miss Charlotte was suddenly standing before her.

'Well, my girl, it's perfect, everything is in order. You can say your prayers and slide between the sheets. Your good Betty will sit with you. Sleep well, dear Elizabeth. We breakfast at eight.'

This little speech having been poured forth in precise tones that drilled through the silence, Miss Charlotte headed for the door, accompanied by the rustling of her flounced dress.

Alone with Betty, Elizabeth came to again, very angry.

'Betty, you're clumsy and a fool. I don't want to see you any more.'

'Oh, Miss Lizbeth! Why?'

'Why, why? She obviously saw the blue bottle, what did she do with it?'

A broad smile was her answer.

'Miss Charlotte not see bottle. I put it right up on top of cupboard. Miss Charlotte too little to see. She open cupboard and not see the blue bottle. It's there.'

'Oh, Betty, I am pleased. Go and get my laudanum ready

for me straight away.'

'Miss Lizbeth! You has to drink laudanum with port.'

'It'll mix inside, idiot. Will you obey me or go back to Dimwood?'

With groans of horror, Betty ran to the little room.

'If Miss Lizbeth get sick, they sell Betty. They put her on a boat and send her down the Mississippi.'

'Silence, for Heaven's sake! If you cry like that, she might hear you and come back. Off you go, and quick!'

She was tempted to go herself to the washroom, but whether it was the motion, or the port, or both of them, she felt weak in the knees and was afraid of an indecorous fall in front of Betty.

A moment later the latter returned, sniffling, and handed the glass to her mistress like a cup of hemlock in ancient times. She had, in spite of everything, mixed a little water with the laudanum.

Elizabeth swallowed it all down in one gulp and dismissed Betty immediately. Lying down on her bed, she remembered that she had neglected to say her prayers.

'Never mind,' she thought, 'I'll say them in bed. The Lord will understand.'

She had barely said half a dozen words and her tongue was feeling heavy. Betty came and shook her by the shoulder:

'Oh, Miss Lizbeth, you not dead, oh tell Betty you not dead! Wake up!'

'Betty, how dare you wake me when I was going to sleep?' said Elizabeth in a rage.

The black face lit up with a broad smile:

'Thanks be to God, Miss Lizbeth, it's seven o'clock.'

Quite alarmed, Elizabeth looked at her and immediately pulled herself together.

'The sun!' exclaimed Betty, ecstatic with joy. 'The sunshine is in the room.'

'Well, then, lower the blind,' said Elizabeth coldly, 'and go away, I'll get dressed on my own.'

'Yes, Miss Lizbeth. Thanks be to God!'

'You'll buy a bottle of laudanum for me,' the girl cried out to her.

Betty ran off.

68

L ess than three days later, Elizabeth found herself alone
in the spacious cabin she was to share with Miss Charlotte
on board the *Neptune*. Sitting on a black padded-leather
bench, she tried in vain to restore to herself a sense of
reality. Since that night, when the liberating brew had cut
her off from her own self, she knew that she could extinguish
consciousness and had come to question the reality of everything. This worrying thought made her afraid of losing her
mind. She could not get away from a disturbing certainty
that, during the time the laudanum was effective, she had
simply ceased to exist, and she was horribly afraid of that
nothingness. With all her might she desired to live, to believe
once more in people and in things, to believe above all
that Jonathan was real, a man of flesh and blood, who
would come back, as he had promised, and that some day
she would breathe in the odor of his skin and taste the
burning of his mouth.

She was not moved by any desire to look at the cabin; the
whole gave her the impression of comfortable prosperity
with all its brass and dark mahogany. Her trunk was not
there. She had seen it earlier on, swinging through the air
on the end of ropes to be put she knew not where, what did
it matter? It would be all the same to the disillusioned girl,
all of it, if the world did not exist. Alone in a corner, her
two cabin bags spoke to her of solid, commonplace matters,
and she looked at them with a vague gratitude, as witnesses
that could not lie and would drag her out of her dizzy spell.

Suddenly the door was gently opened, and Charlie Jones
appeared, pink and smiling in an elegant coffee-colored
suit. His black hair was dishevelled on his forehead, making
him look like a young man, and he exuded happiness.

'Is everything alright?' he asked. 'You look caught up in
your dreams still. Are you waiting for us to set sail to come
back down to earth?'

'Would that surprise you in an English girl?'

He burst out laughing.

'Ah, there's the Elizabeth we love again, and as we are
alone and shall not sail for another two hours, I'm going to

give you a little advice. You're not completely a Southerner yet.'

'I never said I wanted to be a Southerner. I am what I am, and shall remain so.'

'And aggressively so, it seems to me, but I like that. You're emerging from your vapors.'

'What vapors?'

He pushed towards her a heavy, rounded armchair and settled himself in without taking his eyes off her. A little worried, she rallied, despite everything, so as to remain unperturbed.

'Elizabeth,' he said with a slight smile, 'you don't yet know how to take your laudanum like a Southern lady.'

She contented herself with raising her eyebrows and remained silent.

'I'll explain that to you later. You shall have your laudanum, but you mustn't abuse it. If necessary, I shall prepare it for you myself. As for Betty . . .'

'Betty only obeyed me,' said Elizabeth in animated fashion, 'you mustn't touch Betty.'

'I never thought of doing so but, between the two of you, you managed to get you not intoxicated, but drunk.'

'Shocking!'

'I don't think so, because it was only natural. You are very innocent, my dear Elizabeth. You didn't realize the other day that, in your comings and goings on the quayside, you were being watched as if you had been on the stage of some theater.'

She looked at him:

'So I shall always be spied on!'

'*Spied on* is quite a nasty phrase,' he said calmly. 'I was at my office window, a glance was enough to understand what was going on, and I felt a tightening in my chest. There is no worse despair than the despair of youth, because it's all so unexpected. I've known times of despair.'

She stood up brusquely and went to the back of the cabin, towards her two valises, so that he should not see she was upset.

'What are you getting at, Uncle Charlie?'

'Just this, that I left you like a tormented soul on the quayside, and what I feared might happen occurred. A gig drew up at a street corner leading on to the square. You weren't looking that way, but I immediately recognized Annabel and her husband. I knew that he was around . . . They hesitated for a moment, then he drove the gig a little further on, to a spot where they had a better view of the sea.'

'What are all these details to me, Uncle Charlie?'

He carried on without answering:

'He jumped down, leaving her alone to watch the *Bonaventure* manoeuvering. At that moment you started to look for Charlotte. He did not dare to run after you, through fear of being seen, but he walked in your direction, and I think he must have caught up with you. So do you know what I did?'

Exasperated, she answered in an ironical tone of voice:

'I suppose you asked for your binoculars.'

He looked at her in silence.

'My girl,' he said at last, 'I quite simply moved away from the window. I didn't want to know, and if something happened keep it to yourself.'

She burst out:

'What do you think could have happened in that crowd?'

'That's what I find saddest of all. I understand you, Elizabeth, I understand the laudanum after an experience like that, and I understand very well that you are in love, and that he has lost his head, but he's far away and he's married. You must give him up.'

'Never.'

'If he doesn't give you up either, you will both suffer for the rest of your lives.'

'I'd rather suffer than give him up. He'll come back.'

'He won't.'

'He promised.'

'Why did he marry Annabel if he was already in love with you?'

'I don't know, I don't want to know, it's all the same to me. I love him.'

'I'm very sorry to hear all this, but I understand you, in spite of everything.'

He remained silent for a moment, then resumed:

'I'm going to have to leave you until this evening. Can you

hear all that noise on the bridge? The final preparations for departure. Charlotte wanted to wait in the saloon with her Savannah friends. She'll be coming soon. You get on well with her, I hope?'

'Very well. She knows what it's like to suffer . . . in love.'

'Did Amelia tell you?'

'Yes. If anyone can understand me, it's Miss Charlotte.'

'But the whole world can understand you, Elizabeth.'

As he said these words, a black porter entered and put down a large trunk buckled with solid straps. Charlie Jones pointed to the place where it was to be put. The porter obeyed and disappeared.

'Your bunks are one above the other,' he said. 'As I know Charlotte, she'll give you the choice. Let her have the bottom one, will you?'

'But of course, Uncle Charlie,' she said impatiently.

'Forgive me.'

He smiled affectionately.

Alone once more, the girl looked through the porthole at the long black line of forest that bordered the river, all along its vast estuary. Beneath the sky that was beginning to darken, she was struck by the austere nature of the landscape. She was not taking with her the happier image of the South that she kept within herself, the enchanted gardens at Dimwood, the noble avenue of oaks and the sudden heart-rending memory of the corner of the verandah, where heavy, white flowers bloomed amidst the nocturnal foliage.

A high-pitched, chatty voice wrenched her from the cruel delights of nascent nostalgia. Already full of exclamations and little pieces of advice, Miss Charlotte ran up to Elizabeth and, grabbing her by the arms, gazed into her eyes:

'It appears that things are not too good!' she exclaimed. 'But it's all over now. We're not sad, the two of us. For a start, melancholy comes from the Devil. I'll read you a splendid sermon on the subject. You'll clap your hands. We're going to have fun. What do you think of my travelling outfit?'

As if in a sentry box, she had disappeared inside a long woman's coat the color of verdigris. With her bony hand, she raised one of its flaps to show off the lining that was

was black and dark green plaid in the Scottish style.

'Do you recognize the Douglas tartan? That's our clan. With that on one's back, one feels at home in a storm.'

Miss Charlotte gave her a delighted look:

'Doesn't it?' she said. 'Oh, I know it's only an illusion, an appearance with no thought of deceiving anybody — but after all . . .'

'It suits you.'

'I think so. I must take it off, however, I can't dine and sleep in it. How lucky you are Elizabeth, tall, slender, pretty. Happiness is within your reach.'

Elizabeth smiled without answering.

'I'll tell you in confidence,' continued Miss Charlotte, 'that this coat used to belong to Amelia who gave it to me. I had the sleeves shortened a little . . .'

A long bellowing noise silenced them as it filled the sky with its enormous voice. Soon they heard the footsteps of the last of the visitors, hurrying over the gangplank to return to the quay. It was that noise that stirred Elizabeth's emotions much more than the black clamoring made by the siren. Something in her life was being torn apart.

Dinner was served in a low-ceilinged dining room reserved for the proprietor of the vessel. A long refectory table brought the other passengers together, and the murmur of their conversation was heard only on the occasions when the door was opened for a moment.

This arrangement, which was indispensable for family conferences, favored especially the uncontrolled chattering of Miss Charlotte who always had a thousand interesting things to say. Only Amelia had the knack of erecting a barrage, if only temporarily, against this flow of syllables. In a tone of voice special to her, it was sufficient to say:

'Charlotte.'

Sitting before a damask napkin, Elizabeth was calling to mind the darkest hours of her ocean crossing, the misery of an icy cabin, the indescribable things that were put onto her plate, and above all the stiff face of a woman walled up alive by grief and shame, her mother. By what dubious trick of fate did she, Elizabeth, now find herself in this teak-wood room? Having been placed in a fairy-tale setting where she had experienced first love's stirring, now that same fate was wrenching her away from there, bearing her off to other regions of which she knew nothing.

With a kind of fatalism, she accepted and renounced everything, except love. Beyond the distance that she placed between herself and the world, she could hear Uncle Charlie's even-toned voice talking politics, and the word 'Compromise' recurred, laden with all the weight of boredom.

'The agreement seems final this time,' he was saying.

Only the youthfulness of his smile enabled him to get away with a phrase that had become such common coinage, but he added this:

'When we're off Charleston, I shouldn't be surprised if the telegraph doesn't transmit the news to us of Congress' total approval, which will put a definitive end to all the infernal teasing of uncertainty.'

'Bravo for "infernal",' exclaimed Miss Charlotte in a voice that brought the waiters up with a start. 'The Devil is present in the whole of politics. I can demonstrate the fact to you with the help of forty quotations from the Scriptures.'

'Charlotte,' said Amelia.

Charlotte fell silent.

Well-versed in the cunning of elementary diplomacy, Charlie Jones launched forth:

'I hope that you are satisfied with your cabin. The furnishings would have been perfect if I had been able to add a rocking chair, but we all find ourselves, if I may say so, in that vast rocking chair that is the sea. You'll be able to make your mind up about that in a few moments, Elizabeth. I hope that you've got your sea legs.'

'I am English,' replied Elizabeth.

'And laconic,' remarked Amelia.

'A little later on,' Charlie Jones resumed, 'I shall give you a few details concerning the care we shall take of your sleep on board the *Neptune*.'

'Oh, now, let's have the details now,' said Miss Charlotte.

'They can wait, let's eat our dinner.'

The cream of asparagus soup was followed by a truffled omelette. Then came Italian ham sliced very thinly, accompanied by avocado pears in French dressing. To add body to the menu, a joint of roast beef was served cold with jellied carrots.

This delicate fare imposed silence all round, disturbed only by the clicking of knives and forks. Claret was refused and then accepted by the ladies, who at first only dipped their lips in it, and then suddenly their glasses were empty.

'I think we're being excessive,' declared Amelia.

'We're accepting what is offered us,' said Miss Charlotte, 'I don't see where the sin is in that.'

'The traveller is required to take substantial nourishment,' said Charlie Jones. 'The innocence of the dessert will set your consciences at rest.'

Then appeared the 'chef's triumph', which was quite simply a large pineapple filled with exotic fruits marinaded in maraschino.

To mark her disdain for the world, Elizabeth had secretly resolved to spurn all food that evening, but she had eaten so little for the last two days that she gave in from the soup course onwards. With each dish, she regained a little of her taste for life.

When the meal was finished, Charlie Jones suggested a short walk on the deck:

'The equinox is passed, we can hope for calm seas, but a bit of pitching and tossing wouldn't frighten us, would it?'

No one was afraid.

On deck, Elizabeth held out her face to the wind, which ruffled her hair and filled her nostrils with the smell of the open sea. The black waves unfolded without violence beneath a sky that was full of stars as far as the eye could see. She immediately felt dizziness from such a multitude of stars and, as there is nothing like a good meal for predisposing one to the sublime, she persuaded herself that by some mysterious attraction part of her was being gently raised up towards the celestial heights.

A pleasing sensation of giddiness . . . As she was closing her eyes to give herself up to such a rare joy, someone drew close to her. It was Uncle Charlie.

'My dear girl,' he said almost under his breath, 'I should be sorry to disturb your charming dreams.'

'You're not disturbing anything of the kind.'

'So, I feel quite at ease to talk to you about practical matters. Just now, I didn't want to go into details concerning the quality of sleep on board this boat. I considered that one does not talk about certain things during dinner, which I hope you found tolerable.'

'Very tolerable as far as I'm concerned, and even more than tolerable.'

'Thank you. What I have to say will take only a few words: there are no fleas nor bedbugs on board my *Neptune*.'

She did not react.

'You always respond in the way an Englishwoman should: manfully.'

'I don't know if *manfully* is a compliment.'

'It is coming from me. Did you have fleas and bedbugs on the boat that brought you and your dear Mama to America?'

'We did.'

'Alas, the same is true of the whole American fleet. It's a national plague. In that respect at least, the Union has been achieved to perfection. But once again, no fleas nor bedbugs on board the *Neptune.* You won't have to scratch yourself tonight. We're sailing towards the future on board a boat that is clean and new. As for the future, I don't know. A conflict was narrowly missed. Is it peace? Everybody is relieved and nobody is satisfied.'

'I find it all very complicated.'

'Yes and no. The South considers itself frustrated, because California won't be a slave state. The North is fuming because slavery is still permitted elsewhere. We'll be passing by Charleston during the night, but it will be too late for you to catch sight of it. Moreover, I very much doubt that it will be lit up, she still bears in her heart her unfortunate attempt at separatism in 1832, and the armed intervention of the North. All the same, the Compromise has brought a truce, and a truce can go on for a long time. There are many happy years ahead of you to be lived in the most sensible state in the South, our dear Virginia.'

'Happy?'

'Yes, happy, I pledge myself to it. Have you forgotten my promise?'

'On the 8th of September beneath the sycamore in front of your house? Do you think that could be forgotten? Such a promise as that?'

'I renew it this night of the 20th of September, on board

this ship, which . . .'

'Has neither bedbugs nor fleas, I know, Uncle Charlie.'

'So if you don't sleep, it won't be my fault. Good night, Elizabeth.'

'Good night, Uncle Charlie, I'll do my best.'

Elizabeth went to her cabin almost immediately and found Miss Charlotte already asleep in her bed. Rolled up in her blankets, she was snoring gently like a cat. In that wrinkled face her underlying nature could be made out, that of a little girl with gray hair. There was a great innocence about her, and so strong was this impression that Elizabeth had the feeling of not having the right to know more: but what secret was there to be taken by surprise? The whole of the poor spinster's life culminated in this flight from the world.

Getting undressed immediately, Elizabeth climbed up to her bunk by means of a small pair of steps and stretched out on her back, with her eyes wide open. Sleep seemed impossible to her, she was not even thinking about it.

She was tempted to get dressed again and to slip out, as if to go to a rendezvous, as if the deck were the verandah at Dimwood, but did she want to risk seeing passengers there who would destroy the dream with their platitudes? The boat had been pitching a little for some time, and she could hear in the distance the sad bellowing of a foghorn calling out like some lost animal.

In the silence of the night, she strained her ear to the creaking of the ship and the dull sound of the engines that were thudding in the depths. They were echoing in her heart. Closing her eyes, she saw once more the starry sky, in which she made an effort to read her fate and Jonathan's. Somewhere in this abyss, their lives were written out. Could she live without him, and could she bear to do so?

In the bed beneath her own slept that small person who, for her part, had been forced to bear it.

69

The three days that followed were spent in a monotony which stretched them out to infinity. Too far from the coast to be able to look at the landscape, the passengers grew weary of calculating how much time there was until the next meal. Conversation lacked imagination. The intricacies of the Compromise, finally wrenched from the vacillating Congress, had been thoroughly examined, and at meal times attention focused on the delicious things which filled the plates.

Elizabeth would have been bored like everybody else if Uncle Charlie had not come to her rescue by letting her have a pair of binoculars. And so she was able to discover all along the South Carolina coast lush rows of palm trees, their broad leaves waving in the wind.

Uncle Charlie sat next to her on the deck and guessed that she was thinking of Georgia.

'Our Virginia landscape will come much closer to your English heart. Look beyond the palm trees.'

She could see nothing, the palm trees fascinated her and hid everything else.

'Look right into the landscape. Can you see any water?'

'Yes, lakes.'

'They're not lakes, they're marshes where cypresses and reeds grow, and black bears come to catch fish there. All around you can make out giant oaks hung with grey moss, as in Georgia.'

Elizabeth lowered the glasses and turned an ecstatic, child-like face towards Charlie Jones.

'Bears! Are you sure there are bears?'

'And other animals, almost too many to number, white-tailed deer, raccoons, opossums that pretend to be asleep when you catch them, and you wake them up by tickling them.'

'That's disgusting.'

'Isn't it? Shall I carry on? Foxes, rabbits, to say nothing of the birds, larks, nightjars, horrible buzzards that vomit in the air all over travellers . . .'

'Oh, that's enough, Uncle Charlie.'

'Everything that can be killed, eaten, skinned, that sets

apoplectic gentlemen in red jackets galloping off on horse-back. Everything that starts the hunting horn blaring, the gun shots firing, the hounds yelping . . .'

'What about the flowers, Uncle Charlie, the flowers . . .'

'Too far from the coast for you to see magnolias jostle together by the thousands . . .'

'Leave the magnolias and give me back the glasses,' she said sadly.

'Do flowers bore you? It's true that you saw enough to be sick of them at Dimwood, but carry on looking. The scenery won't always be the same. I'm going to look for my wife and leave the South to bid you farewell with its usual profusion of riches.'

Left alone, she gave herself up once again to the natural inclination of her dreams. Twenty times she put down the binoculars, twenty times she picked them up again, and the strange thought went through her mind that these glasses were helping her more and more to search out within herself the memory of Jonathan. Gradually, the landscape changed without her realizing it.

Pine forests appeared, tall and straight like fences. Thick darkness prevailed between the leafless trunks that were like gigantic pencils. Made suddenly attentive by the serenity of the scenery, she wished she could hide in there, in that blackness, lose herself in it with the demented hope of finding love again inside it.

For several long, hallucinatory minutes, this dislocation of the imagination delighted her as much as it tore at her heart. She convinced herself that Jonathan would come back to her, but a surge of common sense pointed out to her the reasons why that would not be possible.

She was suddenly brought back to her senses by a vigorous bang of the gong announcing dinner.

This meal was barely different from that of the previous day. Miss Charlotte made vain attempts to tell what she had been doing all day, and on each occasion was reduced to silence by Amelia's brief call to order.

'Let's keep these memories for our evenings at home in Virginia. We shall have need of them.'

The answer was a smile that contained no malice. Miss Charlotte cheerfully accepted being treated like a little girl by her younger sister. Even Charlie Jones spoke little. A kind of rule of silence became established during the meals, in contrast to the impassioned chattering at Dimwood, and the memory of Fred's clear, warlike voice came back to Elizabeth.

She withdrew very soon after dinner and was followed a quarter of an hour later by Miss Charlotte, who let her get to bed without wearying her with her conversation. After a little while, she felt the delicious approach of sleep, rocked by the even-toned murmuring of Miss Charlotte at her prayers, saying them with an imploring slowness. The boat rocked gently. From time to time, the foghorn cast its hoarse call into the distance.

Towards dawn, caught up in the confusion of a nightmare, she was wrenched from her sleep by a cry so clear that she sat up on her bed and looked around the cabin in horror:

'I would let myself be killed for you!'

Hoarse and desperate, the voice was that of a drowning man. She did not recognize it, but the words stuck in her throat. Never would she be able to forget them.

With both hands she wiped her face, running with sweat, on the sheet.

'Fred,' she said aloud.

There followed a silence, heavy with trepidation, then from the bed beneath hers there rose a whisper that woke her completely.

'You've been having a bad dream, my little one. You must pray to the Lord.'

'Pray to the Lord,' repeated Elizabeth mechanically, 'yes, but don't worry, I shall go back to sleep again.'

A brief silence and the whispering voice resumed:

'If it's problems in love, the Lord will give you peace, but you'll have to be patient.'

'It's not love problems . . . in the personal sense.'

'Wait and wait . . . sometimes years.'

Suddenly Elizabeth had a strong feeling of hearing a prophetic voice.

'Years!' she exclaimed. 'But life goes by during those years . . .'

'Yes, life goes by, but youth is not the season of happiness

'. . . not always . . . not for certain.'

'What's the point of praying then, Miss Charlotte?'

'Because later on, with the passage of time, it's easier to accept things, to be at peace, the Lord's peace.'

'Oh, Miss Charlotte, life is too sad.'

'One has to accept things, little Elizabeth. Would you like us to say a psalm together? I propose number 13: "Lord, how much longer will you conceal your face?" '

'No, oh no, Miss Charlotte, I can't, there are days when one would be happy to die.'

'I know, my dear, but the saddest thing is that we don't die, we get used to things. I think day is breaking. You must try and get to sleep again by turning your face to the wall, like the characters in the Old Testament.'

She fell silent, and two minutes had not gone by before Elizabeth heard gentle snoring, peaceful and regular. It surprised her almost as much as the rest.

The sun shone in holiday mood, and general good humour reigned on board the *Neptune* that morning. Most of the passengers were commercial travellers, accompanied by their families. Some of them betrayed their origins with the accent of the Northern states, which provoked a smile, but apparently the Compromise, signed at last, had rounded off the sharp corners, and the somewhat naive, fine dream of 'the union of hearts' seemed achievable. It was also something to do with that particular mentality that is created on board ship, even for a journey of a few days. Friendships, sworn to be eternal, spring up spontaneously and fade away no less quickly, in spite of the exchange of addresses made as soon as feet touch the quayside.

Far away from the chattering crowd, Elizabeth was keeping herself apart, curled up in her deckchair. The landscape failed to hold her attention. Her binoculars offered her a view of nothing but vast marshes, and a never-ending wall of pine trees, tinged with pink by a dazzling sun. The *Neptune* gradually moved further away from the coast, and she put down the binoculars. Her thoughts returned constantly to her conversation with Miss Charlotte in the early hours of the morning. It seemed to her that the secret of life had just been revealed to her by that strange little person. Pray to the Lord, wait and wait yet more, accept . . .

The arrival of Charlie Jones suddenly interrupted the flow of this gloomy meditation. Never had he seemed so radiantly full of the joy of living, to the point of indiscretion. Elizabeth saw a kind of insolence in it that made her feel uneasy at first.

'I guess you are bored, Elizabeth dear, and I can understand that. May I sit down beside you for a moment? I shall try to amuse you, since I have promised to do everything in order that you may be happy.'

'Happy?'

'To keep sadness away from you. That is also amongst my attributes. Listen to me. At the moment we are passing some distance off Cape Hatteras, where in the bad season all the storms from the surrounding area meet up, like the witches in *Macbeth*. There are innumerable reefs. Tomorrow we reach the port of Norfolk, the gateway to Virginia. Let me amuse you with a few words about that town barricaded with ships on the ocean side. Do you like history?'

'At times,' she said absent-mindedly, 'it depends on the circumstances.'

'Right. Have you heard of Captain John Smith?'

She gave him a steely look.

'How many times do I have to tell you that I was brought up in England, not Peking?'

'There's me put in my place,' he said with a laugh, 'but I asked for it. Captain John Smith, on the orders of His Majesty James I, landed in Norfolk Bay at dawn on the 27th of April 1607.'

'So?'

'His wonder knew no bounds. One of his companions wrote down the impressions of the sailors while they were still fresh in their minds: vast meadowlands, vigorous growth of trees, fresh water flowing through the woods, everything aroused wonder. The beach of fine, almost white sand could barely be seen for oysters of enormous size. Unable to restrain themselves, our men opened some, and in many of them found . . . what do you think?'

'No!'

'Yes, pearls. The oysters themselves are delicious, their reputation has survived and they are much appreciated. I won't tell you the history of the town. Fine brick houses were built, and the Puritans sought refuge there, creating the ideal climate for the appearance of the traditional witch on the broomstick.'

Now paying close attention, Elizabeth would have been glad of further details of this kind, but Uncle Charlie fell silent.

'That's all I have for the moment,' he said at last, 'and I'm afraid that, on arrival, you'll be disappointed with Norfolk as it is today. Rows of fine houses have disappeared in the name of progress, the oysters that are served in restaurants no longer have pearls in them, the witches on broomsticks have become fortune tellers, but the surrounding countryside still dreams of its former paradise. I must leave you — my wife, you understand? If I'm away for ten minutes, she thinks I'm at the bottom of the Atlantic. A little piece of advice. Don't chat too much to Charlotte. I know her story, she doesn't know yours, but she must suspect something. She is both joyful and depressing at one and the same time. She greets her daily despair with a smile.'

'She accepts,' said Elizabeth sadly.

'You gave yourself away there, my girl. When I saw your tragic little face just now, I guessed everything. Believe me, don't listen to her too much. Life isn't that bleak.'

He suddenly leant towards her and hugged her in his arms. She received, as in a breath of warm air, all the natural tenderness of that man whom she was incapable of assessing properly.

'Wake up,' he whispered into her ear, 'come out of your nightmare, Elizabeth.'

Straightening himself, he looked at her. Sitting upright, flushed with anger, she was tempted to humiliate him by telling him to put straight his tie, which was askew, but he disarmed her with a smile:

'You know my old story,' he said. 'I was madly in love with your mother who wouldn't have me. I married someone else instead of blowing my brains out like a fool. One doesn't accept, one keeps one's head up — in England.'

Elizabeth trembled, and a sudden start flung her backwards like a thoroughbred horse that was being broken in. This commonplace image came into her mind, and she felt herself to be ridiculous in the eyes of the man with his pink, satisfied face that invited a slap. At times she could not bear him. She searched for some hurtful thing to say that would cut him to the quick. The words formed spontaneously on her lips.

'Your love life is undoubtedly thrilling, but it's no concern of mine, and I assure you that it leaves me cold.'

'Bravo!' he exclaimed with a peal of laughter, 'a good answer. I'd have been disappointed if you'd said nothing. Do you know that you are delightful when you're cross? Forgive me for teasing you, but provoking your fury is a pleasure I never tire of.'

'It might be amusing to provoke the fury of your wife too, just to see what it's like.'

'You're being naughty now, but in that respect too I find a fellow countrywoman. My adorable Amelia does not need to be put into a rage to be the most beautiful of creatures. But dream on this, exquisite Elizabeth. If your mother had married me, I would be your father now.'

'Well, I have been spared that blow; Heaven is just.'

He suddenly gave a nervous laugh.

'I'm off,' he exclaimed with a giggle, 'I lose track of myself when I'm with you, I'm afraid!'

She saw him take flight, agile, like a mischievous young man.

Holding the glasses to her eyes, she wanted to act out indifference to herself. What did he mean by his teasing? She didn't take it seriously. Men spoke to her in such a strange way . . . They made her say things she did not want to say.

Those heavy binoculars allowed her to see nothing but a dark line, beyond which one could guess at the smoky blue hills. Yet the *Neptune* was drawing imperceptibly closer to the coast and, with a little more patience, she would have been able to see the landscape change; but, overcome with lassitude, she had put the binoculars down on her lap.

Only Jonathan could understand her. Jonathan would have spoken to her as a woman.

70

*T*hat night, she was woken by the sound of voices. Something was happening outside. Slipping on her dressing gown, she tiptoed out of the cabin and stood by the door that opened on to the deck. Riveted to the spot in surprise, she saw a forest in flames on the coast. Pushed forward by the wind, long flames were unfurling like red waves at ground level through the mass of undergrowth, and wrapping themselves around the trees, which were enveloped in a cloud of white smoke. Many were still standing, others were rolling over with a kind of majestic slowness, bowing their burning brands of foliage, as if in some funeral rite. Seeing the fire run almost joyfully through the rows of trees, she felt herself prey to a sudden exaltation, as if all the strength of her youth were responding to this devastating explosion of energy.

The following day, towards nightfall, they reached Norfolk, and the passengers had the choice between a last evening on board or an immediate return to dry land. For Charlie Jones, there was no hesitation. A large carriage with four horses in harness was waiting for him on the quayside, and he had all his party climb into it with the authoritarian courtesy that was usual with him in such cases. Much more modest than the imposing black vehicle, a solid cart transporting Betty and a mountain of luggage followed. With his customary good nature, Charlie Jones had proposed to the servant that she make the journey by rail, but she had preferred the cart, in which she was settled on some mattresses.

The first stage, which was to be the shortest of the whole journey, brought them to Suffolk in less than an hour.

Barely had Elizabeth set foot on dry land than she found herself settled in the carriage next to Miss Charlotte. People ran about in all directions in a new setting, and she lost all sense of reality, perceiving it only through the incoherence of a dream world. Her impression of Norfolk was dominated by large sailing ships against a reddening sky and, on the corner of a square, the dark brick façade of an old house. Here and there gas lamps were being lit, showing her nothing but the confusion of a crowd talking and shouting amidst inexplicable comings and goings. The horses went at a trot through noisy streets, then reached a quieter avenue, and finally a silent road, and Elizabeth got a shock when they set off at full speed into the growing darkness. The carriage lamps prevented her from seeing the landscape as they left the town, but suddenly she had the feeling of a presence that she had been expecting for weeks, something that was both mysterious and familiar: the coolness of fields at the approach of night, the smell that rises up from the ground like the delicious breath of the earth.

For a few moments, she experienced the joy of a redis-covered childhood, and her gaze searched in the half-light for the color of the grass, the friendly stillness of the trees, but she could make out almost nothing. It all rekindled in her the lost happiness of those years before the sufferings came, and tears hovered momentarily on the edges of her wide-open eyes.

Then, suddenly, there was the dazzling brightness of lights, voices shattered the silence, and she was being shaken gently amidst much laughter:

'She's asleep! We've arrived, Elizabeth, we're getting out of the carriage.'

The little town of Suffolk boasted no large hotels, but decent rooms had been reserved in a spacious inn dating from Jefferson's time. Long and low with a red-tiled roof, the house, which was painted white, was embellished with a porch with twin columns and a sign which read: *Ye Olde Virginia Tavern.*

Dinner was served in a low-ceilinged room lit by gas. Suddenly there floundered in Elizabeth's soul the hope that the journey would be one big party, but here they were in dismal surroundings. The tablecloth was white, however, and the food pleasant. Buttered corn bread was served with fried chicken followed by a pike of splendid size. Placed in an elegant S-shape, which suggested death agonies in boiling water, its head was turned towards the English girl and was giving her an angry, open-mouthed look. Countless little white potatoes, as round as marbles, made a sort of bed for it. The whole lot disappeared and was pronounced good, despite the inconvenience of the bones. A bottle of Pouilly had been placed on the table. It was straight from Uncle Charlie's cellar in Savannah. The two Scottish women saw in it one of the sins to be endured with men. Elizabeth was wary of the whole world since her arrival in this inn, and her discomfiture was so blatant that Charlie Jones undertook to make fun of her:

'Since you know the name of the young English seaman who came here in 1607 was John Smith, I'm going to tell you about his adventure with the very beautiful Pocahontas.'

'Charlie, I hope it's decent,' said Amelia. 'Wine can make a just man stumble.'

'Have no fear, Amelia. This just man knows how to drink like a gentleman. Without following John Smith step by step, having set off in search of the Chikahominy river quite some way to the north-east of here, let's assume he arrived hereabouts, in this very district, which was populated by Indians.'

'Whose home this happened to be,' said Elizabeth, suddenly full of indignation, as she always was when Indians were mentioned.

'A difficult problem,' conceded Charlie Jones, 'but don't scupper my fine story for me. I continue: John Smith ventured too far with his musket-bearing soldiers into the territory of King Powhatan. The Indians set a trap for him and caught him. They made him appear before their chief, surrounded by his warriors. Powhatan condemned him to death. Forced to kneel down, he had to place his head on a stone; John Smith was waiting . . .'

'Bravely,' said Elizabeth. 'He was English, after all.'

'. . . was waiting bravely for the heavy Indian clubs to come down on his skull and reduce it to a pulp.'

'I beg you, Charlie,' said Amelia, 'not at dinner.'

'I'm sorry, but the facts are as they are. The clubs, then, are already in the air, it would have taken no more than the wink of an eye, when the most beautiful Indian girl in the world came on the scene. In bewilderment, and quick as an arrow, she found herself kneeling beside the condemned man with her exquisite bare arms around his head . . .'

'And how old was your heroine?' asked Amelia severely.

Caught on the hop and looking slightly sheepish, Uncle Charlie answered:

'Thirteen.'

Without a word, Amelia seized the bottle of Pouilly and placed it out of her husband's reach.

'What next?' said Elizabeth and Miss Charlotte with one voice.

'So the clubs did not come down, and King Powhatan granted mercy. He went as far as to permit John Smith to explore his lands, on condition that it was not done in a spirit of conquest. That lasted a year.'

'And Pocahontas married John Smith?' suggested Elizabeth timidly.

'She did not marry him, she loved him.'

'Charlie,' said Amelia, 'I don't like the turn your story is taking, it's an affront to good taste.'

In her turn, Miss Charlotte risked a question:

'How do you know she loved him?'

The narrator continued unperturbed.

'Having found out that the king, her father, the suspicious Powhatan, had only released John Smith in order to set a trap for him, she warned the foreigner, who was dear to her, and saved his life a second time. Yet it was not him that she married, but another.'

'Another?' said Elizabeth.

'One of John Smith's companions: John Rolfe. Later on she went to England, where she was received as the daughter of an emperor of the Indians. No trouble was spared to do honour to the royal blood that flowed in her veins, her gracefulness and her beauty.'

'Charlie,' interrupted his wife, 'it's time we were going up to bed. Dinner is over.'

'I conclude,' he said in a firm voice. 'She was converted to Christianity in Virginia itself, and several of the finest families of the Union are proud to be descended from her. The highest aristocracy in America boasts of the Indian woman Pocahontas.'

'She should have married John Smith,' said Elizabeth.

'Whether it's the man or the woman,' sighed Miss Charlotte, 'someone is always denied happiness.'

71

*T*he visit to Suffolk on the following morning was limited to the main street. This was straight and wide, and owed its nobility to tall, solemn trees hovering over rows of modest houses. Small gardens, tended with care, were spread out like multicolored carpets and raised the general tone. Almost opposite the inn, however, a house of grand appearance was adorned with white columns that proclaimed the South, and the two storeys with tall windows set this dwelling apart from the ordinary run of the population.

'An old family lives there,' Uncle Charlie told Elizabeth, 'and it is not everybody to whom the door is opened. I would add that in Virginia you won't find the obsession with family connections that you have seen elsewhere. Here we have a more reserved ancestor worship, which runs as deep as it is silent. The tranquil shade of the plane trees conveys quite a true image of it. We shall set off for Petersburgh shortly. It will take the whole day, but we shall stop on the way. I would have liked to let you visit Smithfield, which isn't far from here. But it would be a detour, all the same, and would take us an hour. Does the name Smithfield mean anything to you?'

'Certainly: the temple of Virginia hams.'

'Merciless memory of sixteen years . . . It would have been good, too, to have a look at the Great Dark Marsh, which is almost on our doorstep. It's the king of all American marshes, the largest and most sinister, the most mysterious.'

'You describe it in such glowing terms that one feels like hurling oneself into it straight away.'

'What need is there to go to that trouble? We all carry within ourselves a Great Dark Marsh. But let's leave this banter. You'll be shown it some day, now that you've become a Virginian. Time is short. My wife has only one idea, to get there and see herself at last in the Old House, never to shift from it again. So, you understand . . . We're setting off shortly for Petersburgh. Have a good look at the countryside.'

Half an hour later, Elizabeth found herself once more sitting next to Miss Charlotte in the carriage that set off rapidly in a northerly direction. The two Scottish women had scarves wrapped around their bonnets which were knotted under their chins, and Charlie Jones was holding his wife's hand in his own.

Still dazed from the haste of the departure, the girl followed Charlie Jones's advice and was on the look-out for the beauties of the landscape that had been promised her, but fields of potatoes gave way to fields of beetroot, and her disappointment was turning slowly into resentment when she suddenly made out a vast expanse of long, broad leaves of a dull green, bending down towards the ground under their own weight. They were stirring slowly in the wind, and the whole plantation showed feeble signs of an indolent way of life.

She turned towards her neighbor:

'Tobacco,' said the latter laconically. 'Horrible cigars, pipes, horror!'

'One of the riches of our state,' corrected Uncle Charlie. 'Admire the beauty of these great leaves.'

Elizabeth admired nothing at all and opted for closing her eyes. The sight of conjugal bliss displayed before her annoyed her without her being aware of it. She had a vague feeling of something indecent that turned her in on herself in a sleepy disgust.

Suddenly she felt her hand being touched and, as she woke, she saw Uncle Charlie smiling at her:

'*England,*' he said.

Startled, she had a view of a great undulating plain rolling down towards a river edged with willows. The wind flattened the grass as it swirled by, and in the distance the woods made irregular black patches against the deep green of the meadows. Its very spaciousness gave this landscape an attractive impression of endless freedom. In the distance, it was bounded by a delicate blue line of hills that merged with the horizon.

Elizabeth felt a lump in her throat, but managed to keep a hold on herself and said simply:

'Indeed, there is something of that about it.'

She now paid more attention, trying to carry everything in her memory so she could lose herself in it later as she recalled it to mind. Here and there amongst this solitude she caught sight of a flock of sheep grazing not far from a small farm, and suddenly she noticed that even the soil on the road was a dazzling rusty red, like some cry of glory.

Slowly there grew up inside her the first intuition of physical love for this new land. Not one of the little farms scattered throughout the countryside escaped her notice, and she admired the vast fences that formed the borders of the fields. They seemed to be made of intertwined tree trunks, some of which had slipped out and were lying on the ground, while others remained parallel or were leaning, half upright, against their companions in neighboring fences. Amongst the confusion of this assemblage was a hint of unexpected centuries-old tradition. There was no trace of negligence, just a haughty disdain for symmetry.

The two days that followed were more like a gallop than a journey.

As gentle as she was imperious, Amelia would countenance no stopping in towns except to spend the night. Travelled through at great speed, Petersburgh's historic and noble colonnaded houses recalled the days of English splendour.

It was the same with Richmond and its elegant avenues that justified its name of capital, its houses lost amidst gardens, the white columns shining through masses of laurel and magnolia. All of this sped by like some happy vision. Meals were taken at country inns where the vain rushing of the towns would not cast unrest into the sensitive soul of the newly-wed bride. She took her siesta in the padded depths of the carriage, in the shade of a mauve parasol held in place by a vigilant, husbandly hand.

Miss Charlotte slept in her corner, rolled up in a ball with that feline gracefulness that made her fragility touching, whereas Charlie Jones sat bolt-upright like a Greek god a little past his prime. Only his gravity prevented him from looking ridiculous in his role of parasol bearer, which he accepted submissively.

In this mad excursion in which the nights became confused with the days, Elizabeth no longer knew where she was. The names of the towns, large and small, were becoming confused in her mind, and she ended up not caring, in spite of her innate desire to find out. Nature restored her to peace with the generous unfurling of meadows and the appearance of large bewitching woods. Sometimes, people on the road would give a friendly wave to the hurrying travellers; Elizabeth would remember for a long time a young man digging the red earth in a field. Wearing a large straw hat with frayed edges, he saw that the pretty girl was looking at him and pulled off his wretched headdress, waving it cheerfully.

She thought of Jonathan. There was no link between him and this young unknown, but both of them aroused in her, with equal violence, a desire to love. She was not betraying Jonathan, but she accepted his greeting in its zest for life. Even the wretched straw hat added in its own way an absurd, but charming, appeal.

Instinctively she turned her gaze towards Amelia, who was dozing, and Uncle Charlie with a sunshade in his hand. She was ashamed of the question she found herself asking: was that what love led to? She was disturbed by confused thoughts: she had before her the image of a perfect marriage, and she shuddered.

As if he were reading her thoughts, but not quite accurately, Uncle Charlie waved at her with his free hand to lean forward. Bending over towards him, she heard a murmur in her ear:

'You too will be happy some day.'

She nodded politely, then went back to contemplating the countryside. Georgia and the resplendent richness of its colors seemed ever further away. What Virginia had to offer was limited to the more serious hues of wood, wheat and grassland beneath a quiet sky, a touch of magnificence being added by the vigorous red of the clay.

72

*T*he moment finally came when the horses slowed their pace. The sky was filled with an enormous silence. The carriage turned into an avenue that ran alongside a vast lawn stretching as far as the eye could see.

Elizabeth looked. She was expecting some venerable dark brick dwelling, half hidden by ivy, like those in her own country. She saw a house of light gray wood with a red-tiled roof, but this house was alive. She loved it instantly, as one loves a person.

What she saw seemed to her as simple as a child's drawing. Two gabled houses, one to the right and one to the left of a central block, set back a little, which linked them. At the base of each one of the houses was a bow window, and above it a window with shutters; behind the windows, white curtains and, right at the top, beneath the gable, was a tiny little window, assuredly that of an attic.

She was already living in it, had explored every nook and cranny. It was a house in which every childhood in the world might have been spent. Anybody might see it and recall memories, his own memories, those so ancient that language is superfluous.

Standing near her when they had got down, Charlie Jones saw that she was in transports of delight.

'You have understood,' he said. 'It always appeals to simple hearts. You will never feel alone within its walls.'

'What's it called?' Elizabeth asked.

'Great Meadow. Well before the revolution of '76, this lawn was a race course, one of the greatest in Virginia. There were skirmishes with a few shots fired during the War of Independence, then a battle, and the house that was on this site was destroyed. My first wife's father had another built according to his own ideas, a house in the fields, such as you see.'

'And the first one?'

'Oh, the first one was Elizabethan, in fine brick from our part of the world, dark red, all adorned with ivy. But why are you looking so serious all of a sudden? You were smiling . . . Aren't you pleased?'

'Oh, yes, Uncle Charlie! I was just dreaming.'

'The children call it the Dream House. The house one dreams about. The children undoubtedly have their own reasons which they don't divulge to adults and eventually forget. But let's go in.'

A birch tree stretched upwards over the two gables in front of the central, recessed part of the house. A verandah, concealed in the shade between the two wings, opened up.

'We come here when it's too hot. They bring cushions for the ladies. You shall have your cushion along with the others, and a palm fan. In general we don't talk, just fan ourselves. The benches are hard. Life at Great Meadow is of Spartan simplicity. My wife knew nothing else during her youth in Scotland. She came here to nurse her sick cousin who was my first wife. They are from the same clan. Follow me.'

He pushed a door, and they both went into a modestly-sized room, into which light penetrated through layers of white tulle curtains.

'If you move the curtains to one side, you'll see one of the bow windows.'

'Naturally there are long benches going around the inside.'

'Yes, how do you know that?'

'It's always been done that way in England.'

'Indeed.'

They went over to the bow window.

'You'll notice a long, flat cushion. The ladies sit there to take their coffee, when there is coffee. The gentlemen stand and say the things that are usually said in such circumstances.'

Elizabeth moved the curtain and gave a cry.

'Uncle Charlie, I want to live here until the end of my days.'

Without a word he came and stood behind the girl and looked at the landscape, trying to see it as she did for the first time, in all its newness and freshness. He did not succeed. She alone could reveal it to him.

'Is it that beautiful?' he said softly.

She hesitated.

'Beautiful, yes, but there's something else.'

From where she was, kneeling on the window seat like a little girl, she could see the black shape of an immense tree, the crown of which was so tall that she had to bend her head back to see it. This giant was growing some way away from the house, on the lawn that was swept by its low branches.

'That fine, black tree keeps watch over Great Meadow,' said Charlie Jones. 'It's a cedar of Lebanon. It's there like someone protecting this bit of the country. I think it must be a hundred years old. It was there as a young tree in the days of the Old House. It hasn't stopped growing since. It has been struck by lightning several times and has lost a few branches, but, as you see, it's still going strong. Are you interested in it?'

'Yes.'

Again she looked into the distance, her eyes wide with insatiable curiosity. At the edge of the meadow she could make out a row of small, low houses, painted yellow and irregular in shape, which in the vast expanse of the deep green field had the effect of a pool of sunlight.

'Is there a village?' she asked.

'Oh, no. The largest of those houses, the one in the middle, was a school in my youth. It was extended on either side, a two-storied wing has been added. It's dreadful. But it's charming. Some relatives of my first wife settled there at the time of our marriage. They were very keen to leave Scotland . . .'

'And then?'

'The house is full of cousins. You'll see them.'

'Why don't they live here?'

'That's tricky, very tricky. Family matters, Elizabeth, are a hornets' nest! The rule is not to ask questions, here as in England.'

She bit her lip and did not reply. The little yellow houses that Charlie Jones found charming troubled her. Without them, the meadow would have seemed singularly familiar to her, and she was sure she had already seen it, but that kind of trick which memory played with time disturbed her, and she was only half enjoying it. She got to the point of wondering whether a little hereditary madness was not about to get through to her from her father's side. She did not want to be a strange person. In this slightly confused state, she heard Uncle Charlie's voice:

'We can't stay here musing over the old race course. I'm

going to show you around the house a little, since it's yours as much as ours from now on. It's more spacious than it seems, though the trees that surround it make the downstairs rooms a little gloomy.'

Elizabeth followed him, and it seemed to her that she was entering an enchanted world. The reduced light allowed her to make out, first of all, shelves of books along the walls, alternating with red velvet chairs that were both heavy and ornate. Another room offered a less severe aspect. Indeed, one could see a sofa with a light-colored canvas cover. Wide and low, it had a hollow in the middle, like the bottom of a boat, an invitation for a siesta. A round table, with an olive-green cloth bore the weight of a large family Bible in dark-coloured leather with a steel clasp. A pair of glasses that someone had left behind told a story in its own little way, beside several letters half pulled from their envelopes. The whole put one in mind of a riddle, an impression reinforced by the portrait of an enigmatic personage dressed in black up to the chin, but with the face sinisterly lit up by a dubious smile. He was watching them go by, and the girl had the unpleasant feeling that his eyes were following them.

'Who is it?' she asked Charlie Jones.

'A Scottish Presbyterian,' he said briefly. 'On my wife's side!'

A corridor decorated with colored landscapes gave them a rapid tour of the European capitals and brought them to a part of the house where the afternoon sun filtered through the delicate foliage of the birch tree. Elizabeth was struck by the tall, spacious room to such an extent that she stood motionless by the door and asked:

'Where are we?'

'A curious question, Elizabeth. We are at the very heart of the house.'

A heavy oak table occupied the whole length of this room, surrounded by about forty red chairs like those that Elizabeth had seen a moment earlier. The effect was that of dreadful boredom, which is proper to rooms that only come alive for the time it takes to eat a meal on ceremonial occasions. The upright chairs, whose backs were carved with more patience than taste, conjured up a picture of an assembly of hard-faced judges.

'Nobody ever comes here,' said Charlie Jones. 'In former times, in my father-in-law's day, a banquet was given here once every twelve months in honour of the clan Douglas. People came from all around. Charlotte can remember it. Then the old gentleman died, and everything came to an end. The decor is sumptuous but rather morbid. It frightens the servants.'

'What is there so frightening about it?'

'The only frightening thing about it is what they project into it, that is to say nothing, but they swear that on the night of the 1st of November every seat is occupied, except one. One chair remains empty, always the same one. Do these foolish tales amuse you?'

'I admit that they do, though I don't believe in them.'

'On each chair then, except one, a person in mourning garb is seated. Dead or alive? Who knows? They're waiting.'

'For whom are they waiting?'

'Who can say? Perhaps the Devil. As nobody comes, they wait until dawn, and at that hour, suddenly . . .'

'Why have you stopped? To tease me?'

'A little, I can't help it . . . anyway, they wait and suddenly, they're not there any more.'

Elizabeth gave a nervous little laugh:

'Has anyone ever had the courage to go in and sit on the empty chair?'

'Yes. Do I have your word of honor that you'll keep this a secret?'

'Yes.'

'The Douglases are afraid of nothing, not even the Devil. One Douglas went in. They all stood up, with the Douglases' traditional politeness.'

'All of them Douglases?'

'Every one of them. He greeted them and sat down.'

'What then?'

'Then, when the first glimmer of dawn came — they all vanished.'

'But that's a horrible story! The live Douglas disappeared too?'

'That's what the Negroes say. People who are better informed say that he was found alone, sitting at the long table, and that he died years later in Washington, in what

— 581 —

the Americans call an "institution". Americans have a taste for euphemisms. Do you understand?'

'I understand very well, but you're spoiling a good story. Disappearing without a trace would have been better.'

'Ferocious little English creature! That young Douglas had a name.'

'Young? What a shame!'

'Isn't it, and a lad with a bright future ahead of him, but ambitious. You see, it's dangerous to sit down in the Devil's chair.'

'Who would have such a crazy idea?'

'He had it, and be under no illusion: it's a place much hankered after by the great men of this world, a choice seat for statesmen, presidents, prime ministers, financial wizards, kings of the gutter press, heads of supreme courts of justice, respectable preachers, anyone who bears a shadow of power in their hands, "because all that is mine, And I give it to whomsoever I wish".'

Elizabeth shuddered:

'That's what Satan said to our Saviour in the desert, in order to tempt him.'

'Do you think I did not have that in mind when, at the age of thirty-eight, I found myself master of one of the greatest fortunes in America?'

She looked at him, stupefied at these strange pronouncements. This seemed so little like the other image of the man with the florid complexion, in the full flower of the happiness of this world.

'Where does money come from?' he asked her abruptly.

'I don't know . . .'

'Neither do I. When you don't have any, you imagine it will rain down from Heaven in times of need. When you have much too much of it, you wonder — sometimes, a little.'

'That poor Douglas who went mad simply wanted to know what was going to happen at this table.'

'What? To hear what dead people say in their own jargon, in what Shakespeare calls their gibberish? He revealed nothing at all, he maintained his silence until the end of his days, but he must have found out something. Let's go up and have a look at your room. It's directly above.'

Leaving the great room to its shades, they took a staircase

so narrow it seemed made for children. In the same way, the room they entered surprised Elizabeth by its smallness. Charlie Jones only had to raise his hand to touch the ceiling, which he did with a smile:

'The whole of the upstairs is like a doll's house,' he said. 'It was the old gentleman who designed the plan of the house, and he intended to give more space to the second storey without having to raise the roof. He was an amateur architect, but he kept to his idea. To compensate, we wanted to make this room the most welcoming in Great Meadow. Do you like it?'

Elizabeth cast her eyes around her:

'I shall like it,' she said, and she added: 'Perhaps too much.'

'That's curious. Your first reaction is the same as that of all who enter here. One wonders a little at first. Fondness comes later and then only increases.'

Through the open window she looked into the distance, beyond the great expanse of green as far as the horizon, underlined in blue by a range of hills. Trees planted here and there shaded a path like a ribbon of red ochre.

'The silence,' she said suddenly, full of wonder.

'Yes, the house has always been surrounded by it. It is so profound that sometimes one would be glad to hear the noise of a carriage. The silence of the countryside. No sound penetrates this far, except for the murmuring of the wind and sometimes the whispering of the pine trees, when a storm is on the way.'

She noticed that the furniture in the room was of light-colored wood: the rocking chair with its outsize back and, in a corner sheltered from the light, the bed, hung with white curtains. Everything was smiling in this room that had a breath of the joys of childhood about it. The walls, painted in eau-de-Nil, were covered with engravings, primitively colored in by hand, panoramas depicting streets and gardens of foreign towns with bold, blue skies, and strollers dressed in old-fashioned style, like exotic birds.

Elizabeth's attention was drawn from one corner to another as she tried to imagine what her life would be like between these walls. The charming decor spoke volumes. 'That's what he thinks of me . . .' This reflection, made to herself, kept her motionless in the middle of the room.

Seeing her looking pensive, Charlie Jones assumed a jovial tone and asked:

'Do you imagine that your silence cannot be read like an open book? You see yourself placed here like a little girl, but at the northern corner of this house there are noble rooms for adults: high-ceilinged, serious and favorable to meditation. A word, a single gesture and you can move in up there. I want you to be happy at Great Meadow.'

'I'll stay here for the moment,' she said firmly. 'Yet the room is so small that I don't see where I can put my luggage, my big trunk.'

'In a room adjoining this one. Do you see that door?'

She saw the door.

Brief and to the point, the conversation was coming to an end when Elizabeth asked one last question:

'You said that this house was located on the site of a ruined castle?'

'And so?'

'In what part of that castle would I be now, if it were still here?'

'In the centre. Directly above the great hall. Does that bother you?'

'Not in the least. I should be less bothered by the sound of living guards than by your forty Douglases talking gibberish with the Devil!'

This sentence which she let slip all of a sudden made her blush violently.

Charlie Jones burst out laughing:

'You have nothing to fear from the one or the other. In any case, my wife intends to give orders for the door to be locked on the night of the 1st of November.'

Again Elizabeth felt herself driven to say something she did not wish to, and all the morbid curiosity of childhood came to her aid:

'And if someone dared you to spend some time in the great hall next 1st of November?'

'I should organize a little party,' he said unperturbed.

Taken by surprise, she laughed without answering. He continued:

'Why play about with the dead? It's much more amusing to play with the living — and more profitable.'

'There is only one living person who interests me, you know that.'

'He is far away now, sailing towards Europe . . .'

'He'll come back.'

'. . . and if I may say so, he's not sailing alone.'

'I know that too, but I have his promise.'

'In that case I can only maintain silence. Young people never listen to their elders, and sometimes they are not wrong. But do listen to this, and store it somewhere in your memory that's all cluttered up with dreams.'

She gave him an imploring look:

'Yes, dear Uncle Charlie?'

'Life will not grant you what you ask. I know what it's like, life is cunning and ill-humored.'

'I ask for happiness, and I ask for Jonathan.'

'His wife wants Jonathan too, and she's holding on to him.'

A terrible sadness rose to Elizabeth's face, like a shadow that came over her eyes, and in a changed voice she let out a few words:

'Telling me such things on such a fine day . . . What's become of your promise to make me happy? That promise made in front of your house in Savannah?'

Standing still before her, Charlie Jones waited for a moment.

'I'm sorry,' he said.

'It is not for me to forgive you,' she said. 'You might just as well tell me that I'm not at home here, any more than I was at Dimwood.'

They stood facing each other in silence. Suddenly she exclaimed:

'Oh, say something, Uncle Charlie! You make me feel horribly uncomfortable, standing there in front of me like a judge.'

'Elizabeth,' he said gravely, 'you have understood nothing. At Dimwood, as here, we are too fond of you . . .'

'People always say that to me, to set everything to rights, but what use is it to me to be loved too much, if the one I love is taken from me by someone else?'

He continued in a steady voice:

'. . . and it's because we are too fond of you that we

tremble for your future. You may not know it, but you make people fall in love with you.'

'Don't start all over again, I beg you.'

'Well then, let's make peace, shall we?'

With the disloyalty of a man who knows himself to be irresistible, he had recourse to the most winning smile in his amorous arsenal.

The instant reply was a look that took his breath away.

'I belong completely to Jonathan, Uncle Charlie.'

The blow was delivered so deftly to its goal that Charlie Jones tossed his head back, as if it had hit him full in the face. He recovered almost immediately, a little pinker in the face than usual, and said playfully:

'If ever I took you for a little girl, Elizabeth, I made a great mistake. Do you still want to keep this room with its childish decor?'

'That's really the only favor I ask you.'

'It's yours for ever!' he exclaimed with a loud laugh that had a hollow ring to it.

She answered coldly:

'Will you have my valises brought up for me?'

This time he could not contain himself:

'I'm quite happy to cross swords with you a little, it keeps me young, but you're going a bit far this time, my dear girl. Who do you take me for? A hotel porter?'

'For a gentleman — usually,' she said, with studied gentleness.

'You are hard, Elizabeth. You take after your mother, she could be hard too. I knew her well in my youth, I admired her, everybody knows about that old story, perhaps I admired her too much . . .'

'Was she so beautiful?'

'Something of it remains, despite . . .'

'Something!' interrupted Elizabeth with a cry of protest. 'Mama is still very beautiful.'

'I know that. She didn't want to come to Savannah. I was engaged to Amelia — my dear Amelia.'

With a premonition that he was going to say something else, Elizabeth remained in profound silence.

'When your father died and disaster followed,' he said after some hesitation, 'if only she had turned to me . . . but out of modesty she did not want to, she wrote to Hargrove, a distant relation . . . She remained so proud . . .'

Suddenly emotional, he added:

'You know she's a very fine woman, your mother, Elizabeth.'

The girl raised towards him a face shining with the joy of childhood:

'Those words have made it up between us,' she said cheerfully.

Without a word, he went downstairs and gave orders for the valises to be taken up to Elizabeth's room. He then went off to indulge his anger at leisure in the room where the great family Bible was kept beneath the portrait of the Scottish Presbyterian:

'Beaten!' he mumbled through his teeth. 'And by a girl of sixteen! It's always the same: at first I humor the little girl who knows nothing of life, and then I find myself face to face with the mother, who puts me in my place and insults me . . .'

He stamped his foot.

'How could I have been so stupid to put her in a child's room? The woman is already there, raising her head. It's time she was married. I shall make her happy, in spite of herself and her ridiculous Jonathan . . .'

At that moment, the family Bible received a formidable punch, giving off a dull sound. Charlie Jones gradually pulled himself together, took off his jacket which he put down on a chair, and pulled on a red cord on the end of a chain.

A tall, smiling servant appeared.

'Mass'r Charlie.'

'Fix me a mint julep, and bring it to me here. Off you go.'

Left alone, he flung himself onto the sofa. Buried in the hollow of this worn-out piece of furniture, and with his feet over one of the arms, he contemplated the ceiling:

'Thank Heaven,' he thought, 'that she doesn't have the terrible hold over me that she has, in all innocence, over William Hargrove. I have no experience of that giddiness of the senses, but I can understand very well that Willie does not wish to see her any more. That doesn't change the fact that she's becoming dangerous. I can see the day when she'll be the beautiful Englishwoman, and will turn all our boys' heads.'

The mint julep not having arrived, Charlie Jones stretched out an arm behind him to reach the red bell-pull, on which he pulled three times.

The tall, smiling servant reappeared almost immediately:

'Yes, Mass'r Charlie.'

'Do you realize, Barnaby, that if I'm found dead from thirst on this sofa, the house will be closed up, and my wife will sell you?'

'No, Mass'r Charlie.'

'What do you mean, no?'

'No, sir, because the mint julep is on its way.'

Alone, Charlie Jones resumed the thread of the confidences he was addressing to the ceiling:

'Unfortunately she has what sets certain men ablaze, the coolness of an untouched young girl. What is to be done, what is to be done? I don't wish anything to happen to Jonathan . . . Let us cast aside that wicked thought. But he is married, and he is far away. She takes no notice of the fact. She isn't in the least bit sensual, but has a heart that's a veritable furnace.'

The arrival of the mint julep put an end to this confused meditation. Half an hour later, a philosophically resigned Charlie Jones was walking beneath the tall, tranquil trees around the house, smoking a cigarillo. Amelia only permitted him this weakness out of doors, and the joy of obeying her was, for the incorrigible smoker, an added refinement, the sweetness of the conjugal yoke.

73

*E*lizabeth glanced around the room adjoining her bedroom and smiled in amusement. Pink walls, cupboards
right up to the ceiling.

'It only needs,' she said to herself, 'dolls in the corners.'

It was a strange place, with a superabundance of cupboards around the walls, leaving free only a square window
that overlooked woods and meadows. A stream meandered
through the grass. Nature had nothing more to offer in this
corner of America, and Elizabeth was exhilarated by a surge
of love for it. What she had been searching for for months
she suddenly found, and it brought refreshment to her soul
and to her senses.

Facing the row of yellow houses at the edge of the large
meadow, her bedroom window showed her an image of
gentle peacefulness, but without the other room's naive
simplicity which made this wasted box-room the starting
point for all kinds of nostalgic dreams. The girl had the
feeling that a little bit of England had been given back to
her, a small plot, a gift from the fairies.

That exquisite moment was disturbed by the clatter of a
trunk that was being dragged up to her room on the narrow
staircase, accompanied by groanings and cursings. Would
the trunk go through the door? Barnaby, who was carrying
the chest on his enormous shoulders and playing the martyr,
swore that it would not, but Betty, who was following and
invoking the Lord, maintained that the walls would move
aside if necessary. Eventually the trunk went through.

It was put down in the middle of the room, and Betty was
charged with emptying it. Exhausted from the journey in
the cart, she was nonetheless overflowing with zeal. She was
full of smiles in this new life in Virginia, and her heavy body
was bouncing up and down out of happiness. The cupboards opened on to deep interiors lined with paper of
floral design, and the old servant raised her arms with a cry
of admiration:

'Miss Lizbeth, things here sure is better than what they is
at Dimwood!'

'Leave Dimwood alone and do your work,' replied

Elizabeth impatiently. 'I'm going downstairs for a moment, and I want everything to be nicely put away when I get back.'

At that point, Barnaby looked as if he was going to make himself scarce, but the girl called after him:

'You, stay here. What's your name?'

'Barnaby, ma'am.'

'Barnaby, when this trunk is empty, take it away.'

He was still quite young and had a laughing, childish face, but his big round eyes suddenly took on a melancholy look.

'What's the matter with you?' Elizabeth asked him. 'Didn't you hear me?'

'Maybe you'd like to keep the trunk here, ma'am. It's mighty hard to take it down.'

'You are a lazy bones, Barnaby. It came up, it can go down. Do you understand?'

With what strange pleasure she spoke in that Southern tone of voice . . . Each time she felt it, she became a little worried.

'Who do you belong to?' she asked thoughtlessly.

'Mass'r Charlie, he bought me in Richmond. I reckon I was sixteen.'

She bit her lip: her question was stupid. The boy could only be Charlie Jones's slave. Seeing her silence and guessing vaguely at her unease, and with the instinctive complicity of youth, he came to her rescue:

'I think Mass'r Charlie's goin' to give me to Miss Amelia, but I's hoping to stay here.'

'Do you like it here?'

'Yes'm.'

She gave him a smile which he returned, showing the full whiteness of his teeth.

'I'll be taking this trunk, ma'am.'

She felt herself turning quite red with embarrassment.

'You still don't know how to talk to slaves . . . These people who are bought and sold, and are given away as presents, like objects . . . I bullied poor Betty . . .'

She was so upset that she had to sit down on one of the steps.

'What does it all mean? What does the world mean? What does anything mean?'

Standing up brusquely, she went down the few remaining steps that led her to the door, and she remained undecided. The sun was shining full onto the roofs. No noise troubled the midday silence. She had made up her mind to walk beneath the trees and go round the outside of the house, when she caught a glimpse of Charlie Jones in the distance, smoking his cigarillo in the shade of the pine trees. She did not want to speak to him, even after his praise of her mother. It was that, in fact, that made her uneasy.

'He courted Mama,' she told herself, still amazed at all she had found out over the last few months. Suddenly she had to hold back a peal of laughter at the thought that if her mother had married him, instead of a certain Cyril Escridge, she, Elizabeth, would be his daughter now, and would be called Miss Elizabeth Jones . . .

He had his back to her for the moment, and he looked very youthful, slim and elegant in his pale gray linen suit. He only needed to turn around to catch sight of her. Taking a step backwards behind a corner of the house, she spied on him, curious to observe him while he believed he was alone.

'He has been in love several times,' she thought. 'He ought to understand that I'm in love with Jonathan. It's not my fault if Jonathan is married, that doesn't change anything. Don't be so obstinate, Uncle Charlie . . .'

He was savoring his cigarillo and was slowly pacing up and down in front of the house. At times, his thoughts coincided with those of the girl, but imperfectly, as in a fruitless attempt at dialogue.

'Dear little Elizabeth,' he said to himself, 'how infuriating you can be! I promised to make you happy, I didn't promise to give you Jonathan. He is taken. So, farewell Jonathan . . . Can't he be replaced? Couldn't you love a bachelor? If only my son were more attractive! He's not a bad boy, but so clumsy . . . But they would make a very presentable couple, in spite of everything. But what's the point of dreaming? The political situation is getting worse. The Compromise is holding war at bay. But it's nonetheless certain, certain and absurd. Only a pretext is missing. They'll find one. The Constitution forbids neither slavery nor secession. Never mind that! The preachers know what needs to be done in such cases, and there will be fighting. The South is outnumbered three to one. An archaic, refined civilization against a modern power of great wealth. Where will the provocation come from? I don't know, but I can feel it coming. I shan't leave the South, to which I owe my fortune, but I tremble for you, Georgia, for your worrying, carefree youth that wails out love songs to the mandolin, or plunges Hell for leather into duels when a disaster might be just around the corner ... "Poor South!" groaned the great Calhoun as he was about to die. My word, I'm getting gloomy, and my cigarillo is burning my fingers. A julep, quickly, damn it!'

'Barnaby!'

Silence. He called again, much louder:

'Barnaby!'

Elizabeth made for a more distant corner behind the house, where she could hear Charlie Jones coming closer and vociferating:

'Where is that great lout of a fellow? I call and no one comes, I get no service. Barnaby!' he bellowed. 'Do you want to be sent away? To take a trip down the Mississippi?'

At that moment he appeared on the doorstep, ungainly and smiling.

'You ain't goin' to sell me South, sir,' he said as he came forward.

'What if I wish it?'

'No sir, the julep on its way too.'

And with a movement of his hand, he pointed to the verandah between the two parts of the building. Charlie Jones had time to see a small black boy place a julep in a tall glass on the table and disappear immediately.

'Miraculous!' said Charlie Jones. 'Explain that to me, Barnaby.'

'There's four juleps out in the kitchen ever since you got here, Mass'r Charlie. I knowed how it would be. I said to Tommy, "When you hears Mass'r Charlie shout, 'Barnaby' real loud, you take a julep and put some ice in it and bring it on out to the verandah."'

'The cook's son is not growing fast enough. Why did he run away?'

'Tommy's shy, sir, he frightened.'

'Frightened of what, the little devil? Have I ever beaten

— 592 —

anyone here?'

At that moment three people on horseback were cantering up the avenue waving their hands. Two boys and a girl.

'Hello, Uncle Charlie!' they cried out joyfully.

'Halloo!' he replied in similar vein.

And he added under his breath:

'I know what that means.'

In an instant they were standing before him like something out of an old master painting. The boys in white jerkins and yellow pants, and the girl in a riding-habit, wearing a man's hat with a black veil fluttering gaily. All three held themselves admirably straight and supple on their mounts.

There followed a small outburst of exclamations and laughter:

'We were expecting you yesterday! Did you get lost in the marshes? How could we contact you?'

Suddenly the English girl emerged from her hiding place, and three curious pairs of young eyes looked her up and down. But Charlie Jones held out his hand to the horsewoman who happened to be in front of him.

'Elizabeth,' shouted Charlie Jones, 'come and let me introduce you to my wife's nephews and niece: Harry, Dick and Elsie.'

Raising the edge of her skirt, the latter went over to Elizabeth, who stood still. With the crop hanging from her wrist and her elegant hairstyle, Elsie created an impression of authority which was enhanced by the flashing of her dark blue eyes and the fine black line of her arched eyebrows. Her head was drawn back by the weight of her thick, raven hair.

'They've been telling us about you for so long! That gives me the right to kiss you, Elizabeth.'

'Us, too,' cried the boys.

Elsie brushed them aside:

'It'll be your turn later,' she said.

'Yes, later!' repeated Elizabeth as she struggled laughingly. 'Let me go!'

Dick, the eldest, a dishevelled blond boy with black eyes, turned out to be the most determined and took hold of Elizabeth's hand, while his younger brother, with his short brown hair and numb with admiration, fixed his honest brown eyes on the scarlet face of the beautiful stranger.

'I love your English accent!' exclaimed Dick.

'Leave her alone!' scolded Charlie Jones. 'That's an order, children. You're behaving like Sioux and Iroquois Indians around a victim tied up to a post. You haven't even thought to tell me why you're here.'

'We've come to you for lunch,' said Dick. 'We're dying of hunger.'

'I might have guessed as much,' said Uncle Charlie. 'What's happening at your house?'

Elsie put on a worldly tone of voice:

'If it's not possible, Uncle Charlie . . .'

Dick cut her short:

'It's quite simple. Mama says she is fed up preparing meals that have to be followed by another as soon as they've disappeared, and so on until she dies. So when she knew you were here, she drove us out of the house.'

'I recognize the boss woman there,' said Charlie Jones.

He began to yell:

'Barnaby!'

No answer.

'He's going to make me wait because he knows it annoys me,' said Uncle Charlie. 'He's hiding, he can hear me perfectly well. I've spoiled him for ever by setting his father free, and giving him a little house and a field. He imagines he's going to get the same treatment, but I shall give him a fright in a moment.'

Once more he thundered out Barnaby's name in a furious voice. After a silence, Barnaby was suddenly standing behind him:

'Yes, Mass'r Charlie.'

'Where were you?'

'Here, Mass'r Charlie.'

'Impertinent as usual. Listen, Barnaby, for the last time. On the Mississippi, there are pleasure steamers, and other boats that have nothing to do with pleasure, on which disobedient servants are sent . . .'

'Yes, Mass'r Charlie.'

'. . . or lazy ones, or insolent ones. Understood?'

'Yes, Mass'r Charlie, but they's always going to sail without Barnaby!'

'Silence . . .' In a steady, firm voice Charlie Jones gave

orders:

'Barnaby, wring the necks of all the chickens, steal all the eggs, empty the pantry and go and tell Miss Charlotte that we have guests and that we insist on a miracle.'

Barnaby bowed and went.

Turning towards the young people:

'Children,' said Charlie Jones, 'that's where the weakness of masters leads. If that man were not basically good-natured, I'd not sell him, but give him as a gift to a neighbor.'

'Oh, Barnaby is very nice, Uncle Charlie,' cried Elizabeth.

'Quite possibly, but one day when I was shaking the day-lights out of him a bit roughly, he threatened to complain to his Papa, because he has become a holy man with a Bible who repays my patience by first of all showering blessings upon me, and then talking to me about my conscience. He has caught religion like other people catch a cold.'

'How's that?' asked Elizabeth, suddenly interested.

'I don't know. You should ask my friend William Hargrove, he suffers from it too, but his is not such a serious case.'

Elizabeth blushed and fell silent.

'What time is lunch?' asked Dick.

'The bell will summon you, impatient sir. You have time to go for a good ride in the woods.'

'For my part,' said Elsie, 'I should ask for nothing better. Won't you come with us, Elizabeth, if Uncle Charlie lends you one of his bays?'

'My father had stables, but I haven't ridden since his death, and I don't have a habit.'

'I have three at home, I can give you one. Didn't you ride at Dimwood?'

'Well, no. The boys did, but not the girls. Billy Hargrove was always on Rumpus.'

This name was greeted with a great peal of laughter:

'Rumpus!'

'Yes, the girls went for carriage rides.'

Uncle Charlie calmed the general mirth by saying in an anxious tone of voice:

'My friend William always worries that if the girls set off at a gallop, they might get lost in the woods around Dimwood.

He has notions . . .'

He ended the sentence with a vague gesture.

'It seems his place is rather gloomy,' said Dick, looking well-informed.

'It's very beautiful,' said Elizabeth loyally.

She had been feeling ill at ease for some moments. Elsie, standing straight in front of her, had not taken her eyes off her and in that pretty, adolescent face the large, dark pupils spoke strangely of things beyond her years.

The English girl was suddenly seized with horror. In a flash she thought she could see shining in the depths of those magnificent blue eyes the intensity of Jonathan's gaze. The illusion was so strong that she felt her heart tighten, as if some hand were crushing it.

'What's the matter?' asked Elsie with a smile. 'Don't you like my hat? I tip it forward a little as the men do. It's my fiancé's hat. I stole it from him.'

'Your fiancé . . .' stammered Elizabeth.

'I'll introduce you to him. He's coming to visit us. You'll see, he's charming. We're going to get married next year.'

She laughed, revealing small, white teeth like grains of rice.

'I warn you that I'm very, very jealous — like a real tigress.'

'Oh, I assure you, you have nothing to fear. I never asked to see your fiancé.'

Elsie continued in all innocence:

'He's kind, if only you knew . . . He is still at the University of Virginia where he's working like a madman, so he tells us. So he *tells* us,' she repeated with a laugh. 'He's studying law. Are you going to get engaged soon?'

'I don't know,' said Elizabeth drily.

'Pretty as you are . . . you must have a *beau* . . .'

'That's nobody's business but mine,' said Elizabeth, whose patience had run out.

Elsie let out an incredulous laugh:

'But all the girls of our age have a *beau* — or else . . .'

'Well, if you must know, I do have one.'

Her voice was hoarse with emotion, and her eyes shone as she hurled these words at the impertinent girl, but the latter did not give up. With impassioned inquisitiveness she insisted:

'What's his name?'

'That's my secret.'

'And so perhaps a secret wedding. Oh, Elizabeth, how romantic you are ... I am too. I feel we're going to be great friends. Does your fiancé come from Virginia? Shall we see him?'

In her anguish, Elizabeth suddenly had a lump in her throat and, to her own amazement, she heard herself speak these words:

'Never, he's very far away from here . . .'

'Ah?'

The over-excited chatterbox was already opening her mouth to ask another question when the bell rang out behind the house.

'Quick!' cried Uncle Charlie clapping his hands, 'put your secrets off until later, young ladies! One doesn't keep Miss Charlotte waiting.'

74

S he was waiting, despite everything, in the dining room some of whose windows looked on to the row of little yellow houses, others towards the woods which, two hours earlier, had filled Elizabeth with delight. A tablecloth, provocative in its whiteness, gleamed on the oblong table.

The guests entered by one door, and Amelia by another, as if some kind of ceremonial were being observed. Wearing a plum-colored taffeta dress, and with her head gripped by a simple lawn and lace cap, the mistress of the house smiled and said gravely:

'Always happy to receive the young people who come to us from the other side of the lawn.'

That was the name she had given Great Meadow. Charlie

Jones was only half pleased about it, but he made no objection. She directed each of them to their place with a regal gesture: a girl, a boy, a girl, a boy, and the solid chairs scraped on the marble as they were pulled back. She herself took her place on her husband's right, and little Miss Charlotte, raised up on cushions, was on Charlie Jones's left.

'Grace,' said Amelia.

There was silence. Then Charlie Jones, with his head bowed, let out some pious mumbling that seemed to be addressed in confidentiality to his tie, then a briefly murmured *Amen* ran round the table. Barnaby made his entrance, wearing white gloves. With a proud smile, he was carrying an imposing joint of roast beef on a heavy silver dish, which he put down on a small table near Uncle Charlie. The latter immediately began to speak:

'In England it's the custom for the eldest son to carve the meat, but as my son isn't here, the privilege is yours, Dick. I suppose your father has taught you how to tackle it.'

Dick leapt to his feet and immediately took up his position by the small table. Barnaby handed him a knife with an excessively large blade and a fork with aggressive-looking prongs. Gripping these weapons, the young man took on, quite unawares, a ferocious air that looked natural, together with an attentive expression, which, like that of a conscientious executioner, completed the picture. He felt all eyes on him, and he set about the task with the care of an artist.

Nobody spoke during this operation except Amelia, who uttered these words in a neutral tone:

'Very thin, the slices.'

They were very thin and fell, one at a time, to be gathered up in an enormous blue porcelain dish with lavishly gilded coats of arms which Barnaby was at last able to place in front of Charlie Jones. The latter nodded his head and, speaking to Dick, praised him.

'Not bad, my boy,' he said.

Amelia then gave her opinion, *sotto voce*, but distinctly:

'The Commodore has trained his children well. That's typical of him. He will always be the same at home as on the bridge of a battleship. The watchword is: obey. My dear sister got the husband she deserved.'

'Let's forget all that,' said Uncle Charlie in the same tone of voice, and a little louder he asked:

'You like it on the pink side, I believe?'

'Rare,' she said softly, 'rare, my dear.'

The scarlet red slice was placed before her on a very hot plate. Amelia looked at it with evident satisfaction then, raising her head, she declared:

'Children, although it's quite contrary to good manners, I agree to permit conversation during this meal. It's something of a celebration, as it's our Elizabeth's first lunch beneath this roof.'

Elizabeth blushed and smiled.

'Your turn, Elizabeth,' said Uncle Charlie as he raised the knife. 'How do you like it? Red?'

'Pink, please,' she said.

'Bright pink like the cheeks of a beautiful English girl!' he exclaimed.

'My dear,' said Amelia, 'there's something a little unsuitable about your comparison.'

'*Honi soit qui mal y pense,* my darling. Pink for you, Elsie, of course.'

'Oh, no. Rare, like Aunt Amelia.'

'You'll give her bright pink, like Elizabeth,' said Amelia crisply. 'A girl of her age needs moderation, and to start with, Elsie, you can take that man's hat off.'

With a defiant look from Elsie the hat remained where it was; the girl's insolence was perched on its upturned brim, just above her little nose.

Amelia contemplated the rebel for a few seconds, then, in a voice that she had inherited from one of her fearsome ancestors, she said simply:

'Elsie.'

'My dear girl,' said Uncle Charlie, 'you're so much prettier without that headdress.'

The hat was wrenched off with a furious gesture which undid her chignon, and the hair fell, thick and shiny, like the black waters of a river that seemed to flow defiantly past Amelia. Barnaby was always where he was needed, at the right time. He seized the hat and put it out of sight.

When it was his turn to be asked, Dick opted for rare, and received two slices of meat instead of one.

There remained Harry, sitting modestly in his corner.

Timid and reserved by nature, he answered almost in a whisper:

'Pink.'

At that moment, a piercing voice made all the guests jump:

'I should like to know why you're forgetting the one who bore the heat of the kitchen, supervising everything, so that we should have a decent meal served us . . .'

'Charlotte,' Amelia said.

'*Charlotte* or not, Charlotte's not putting up with it. I'm hungry too. Whether you like it or not.'

'Oh, Charlotte!' exclaimed Uncle Charlie. 'Forgive me, I plead guilty, but your exquisite discretion is the cause of my rudeness.'

'Charlotte,' said Amelia in a loud voice.

'Charlotte is right, Amelia,' exclaimed Uncle Charlie.

'She's a little in the right, but even more in the wrong,' conceded Amelia.

Perched on her cushions, the small woman in black raised the pitch of her voice so much that Amelia made as if to cover her ears with her bonnet.

'Don't you *Charlotte* me any more,' shouted the rebel. 'I'm not a saint. I'll have it rare, too, Charlie, and rarer than the others.'

'Charlotte, we cannot ask this beast to give more than it has. It does what it can.'

'Alright. Come on, Barnaby, quickly, and off to the kitchen to fetch the potatoes.'

A subdued muttering rose in the silence that followed these words. Barnaby disappeared immediately with the litheness of a wild cat, and Charlotte looked all around her with a victorious glint in her small gray eyes.

It was in vain that she had kept her back straight. She was still the size of a child, but anger gave her stature. With her cheeks tinged with red from exasperation, she seemed to be looking for something decisive to say.

'And that's the way it is,' she said suddenly.

Elizabeth could not take her eyes off her and had the impression she was suffering, that it had taken no more than a ridiculous incident to once again put her through the tragedy of her small size and her happiness dashed to pieces. Because of her small stature her marriage had been called off.

Giving way to an impulse, Elizabeth said with a quite British calm:

'Miss Charlotte, there is something I should like to know.'

'What's that?'

'When you referred to potatoes, did you mean what's known as sweet potatoes?'

Faced with that innocent, smiling face, Miss Charlotte felt her anger subside:

'Of course, my dear English girl. That's something you don't have at home ... But I think Barnaby is taking his time.'

She threw her shoulders back and called:

'Barnaby!'

The strident voice brought a grimace of pain to Amelia's face, and in a humbly imploring tone she groaned:

'Charlotte!'

A reassuring echo came from the distant kitchen and two or three minutes later Barnaby reappeared, looking important, his arms laden with a large, oval dish. With an imperious gesture, Miss Charlotte pointed to an enormous silver stand in the middle of the table that was awaiting this much cherished object. A delicious odor rose to the ceiling, immediately dissipating all ill humor.

Charlie Jones breathed in the fragrance and rubbed his hands together, as if in gluttonous ecstasy.

'Not even at Voisin's in Paris would you smell anything as exquisite.'

Amelia pushed her inquisitive nose forward:

'I admit,' she said, 'that just the sight of certain dishes arouses in me a taste for good things.'

'Well, get a grip on yourself,' said Miss Charlotte, 'and offer up my sweet potatoes as a sacrifice if they lead you into sin. The large, silver spoon, Barnaby. I'm serving. What have you decided, Amelia?'

'Well, you can give me just a taste of them. I admit to a weakness on my part,' she added with a slightly mutinous look, as if to be excused some childish folly. 'But,' she said immediately afterwards, 'what a shame to spoil that golden-pink layer on the top ...'

'Caramelized,' said Miss Charlotte, as she dug the spoon into the fragrant mass, filling a plate for Amelia, who did not protest.

On the contrary, she waited not a second before swallowing the first mouthful. Then she put down her fork and regained her usual composure.

'Charlotte, sister dear, I wonder if you have the right to keep to yourself the recipe for a dish of such rare quality.'

Miss Charlotte burst out laughing.

'A secret!' she exclaimed as she moved the heavy spoon back and forth in the dish. 'I find that amusing. Both of our cooks are quite in the know. Barnaby too. Don't deny it, Barnaby, or you won't get your helping. So, then, let's unveil the mystery of the sweet potatoes. I warn you that if you don't remember it, there'll be no point in begging me to tell you again. The dish, first of all. What's it made of?'

'Earthenware,' said Dick with his fork in the air.

'Right. I coat it lightly with palm oil. Are you with me? Every detail is important. If you miss one, you miss the lot.'

'We're all ears, like good pupils,' said Charlie Jones.

Miss Charlotte continued, taking care to pronounce things like a teacher. From time to time a smile of superiority brought a little fold across her cheeks, and she acted as if she had gained control of an unruly class.

'You take your potatoes — they must be pink, no others will do — and you slice them very thinly lengthwise. After that, you make a bed of them, yes, I said a bed, and then on this bed, you put another layer, this time of potatoes cut — how shall I put it? — into little strips. Then you sprinkle it with cane sugar, nutmeg and cinnamon. Then, listen carefully, you make another bed of thin slices, and on top of that, another layer of strips. Sprinkle it with sugar again and add a little butter or cream. Do you think that's all? No, you carry on building up the layers until you reach the top of the dish. Finish it off with a top layer of potatoes cut a little more thickly, covered with brown sugar and a pinch of salt. Into the oven now, an oven that's good and hot. That's how you caramelize the top. An hour and a quarter's cooking time, with a good servant such as Barnaby to keep an eye on things.'

Soon everybody was served. With the large spoon placed alongside the dish, she contemplated her listeners who were still chasing the last vestiges around their plates. The only thing to be heard in the silence was the tinkling sound of cutlery on porcelain. No comments, no questions. There was a kind of joyfulness about this studious greed. They were all sleepy. Conversation, which had been permitted, faded out of its own accord. Miss Charlotte was the first to leave. Amelia let herself be led to her room by her husband, who suggested that the young people take a siesta on the lawn, in the dark and refreshing shade of the cedar tree. Elsie and the two boys accepted gladly, but Elizabeth preferred to slip off without a word and went up to her room.

With the shutters closed, the half-light made everything in her room seem more beautiful. A slight noise in the adjoining room drew her towards it. The open door of one of the cupboards concealed Betty completely, except for her sandal-led feet . . .

'What are you doing there?' asked Elizabeth.

With a little cry of alarm, Betty came out, a green check kerchief tied tightly round her head.

'I's arranging your drawers, Miss Lizbeth, come see.'

The girl gave a glance, and saw that the drawers were, indeed, meticulously arranged.

'Have you had lunch?'

'Sweet potatoes in the kitchen,' said Betty with a broad smile.

And she asked:

'In the trunk they's a present they done hid for you at Dimwood. I just put it under your pillow for you to find later on.'

Elizabeth did not wait. It was a sky-blue package. With a hand unsteady from impatience, she tore the pretty paper to reveal another layer, mauve this time, with a white envelope slipped under a deeper mauve ribbon. Numbed by suprise, Elizabeth had before her eyes *The Last Days of Pompeii*.

Betty, who had run up to her, could restrain herself no longer:

'Ain't that nice, Miss Lizabeth?'

'Leave me alone,' said the girl, 'and go back to your cupboards.'

When she was alone, she laughed hysterically and drew from the envelope a card on which two lines were written in large, sloping handwriting: 'For our Cousin Elizabeth from England, this souvenir of our dear Dimwood, where she was so happy. Aunt Augusta.'

She tore up the card and, closing her eyes, saw again at the end of the long verandah at Dimwood, the magnolia in the corner by the porch. Time melted away. It was not yesterday, she was there now, with her head buried in the fragrance of the flowers, her face leaning forward, searching for Jonathan's face. But their lips did not meet: then she caressed his cheek with her fingertips ... Had she really caressed him? She murmured his name repeatedly without growing weary of it: 'Jonathan ... Jonathan ...' Her breath, at least, brushed against his half-open lips.

Suddenly she let herself fall backwards on to her bed.

'To die,' she thought. 'If only one could, at that very moment.'

Now reality returned her to despair, the reality of the white curtains around her bed, the reality of the walls and the furniture. A bird was producing a monotonous, persistent call that was unfamiliar to her.

Making an effort, she got up and called Betty, who began immediately to pick up all the little bits of paper:

'Leave them,' said Elizabeth. 'There was a box of writing paper in the trunk. Have you put it away?'

'In a drawer, Miss Lizbeth.'

'Bring it to me.'

Left alone for a moment, the girl went to look at herself in a mirror over the fireplace. She was shocked at the paleness of her face, and she felt as if she were looking at a stranger. With both her hands she took hold of her mass of ash-blond hair, gleaming around her forehead, and raised it up on the top of her head.

'Quickly, Betty,' she cried.

The maid reappeared, holding a box which she placed on the table.

'You're going to do my hair for me,' said Elizabeth. 'Like that, on the top of my head. You can make me a large topknot.'

'What with, Miss Lizbeth? You need hairpins.'

'Oh, Betty, you can see I'm waiting. Do something. Use a ribbon.'

In a panic, Betty opened drawer after drawer and came back with a handful of ribbons fit for a party. Then the task began, interrupted by sighs and exclamations, and, after a few minutes' labor, there was in place a ball of hair that might pass for a topknot, but, as Betty kept repeating with anguished cries, it would not stay in place.

The girl gave a long, cold look at this new Elizabeth who did not flinch. A striking transformation: it was a woman who, from the depths of the mirror, was keeping a watch on the English girl, returning look for look, imitating the movement of the mouth which let out a murmur:

'Me . . . That's me now.'

Betty was afraid, as if she had seen a ghost.

'Oh, Miss Lizbeth, it better before!'

Now Elizabeth succumbed to an unfamiliar anxiety: someone else had entered the room, she had called up someone from the future.

'Undo it, take it down,' she suddenly ordered.

Ribbons were pulled in all directions, and the topknot collapsed, setting free the golden tresses. At a stroke, Elizabeth saw herself restored to the full flush of youth, but she remained uneasy. Betty's presence made her ill at ease, and, with a smile, she requested to be left alone.

In the writing case that she had noticed on the table, she found the pens and ink that she needed and, sitting down, she wrote out the opening lines of a letter.

Dear Miss Llewelyn,

Four full days' travelling separate me from Dimwood, and I must admit that I am most keen to have news from there. You may see this letter as a sign of the complete confidence I have in you since we last spoke. That stems above all from the frankness of your answers when I was driven to question you in my times of personal difficulty. I think it is not necessary to elaborate on this point. What you don't know, you guess; that's a compliment I'm happy to pay you.

At this point she put down her pen and wondered if that was the correct thing to write. She had the feeling that the specter of social distinction was looking over her shoulder. The tone . . . the right tone. What would her mother have to say about such familiarity? Suddenly she was ashamed of her scruples, and her pen proceeded rapidly:

Why aren't you here to advise me! I'm not at all ashamed to admit to you that I feel quite alone in this house, which, nevertheless, is most pleasant, and where everybody smiles at me — but what can solitude mean for me other than the absence of someone? I don't want to be more explicit than that. You know only too well what it's all about. And then there are some words that are so painful to write that my hand will not co-operate.

Some days you must have thought that your company made me very distant, but that is not strictly true. Allowances must be made for my natural reserve, but what good is that reserve now? I am unhappy. The woods and fine meadows do not console me. Do you not have any news from over there, any news from Europe?

I don't dare say any more. I already see on this page too many words in place of those that I wish to put and do not dare. Write to me, I beg you, even if there is nothing to say for the moment, for nothing moves at Dimwood, life is motionless there, as it is here, in fact, but, all the same, I should like to know if all is well.

Yours sincerely,

Elizabeth Escridge

Knowing full well that if she re-read this letter she would not send it, she slid it into an envelope which she left unsealed. For perhaps she would have something to add at the last moment. The address was written with a care that made it a model of the calligrapher's art. There remained the problem of franking it. In these grave circumstances, Miss Charlotte seemed the most approachable person, the most human. She decided to set about looking for her immediately in that great house. The letter was slid to the back of a drawer, but was that not imprudent? The drawer had no lock. She only had a key for her trunk which had been taken away on her orders.

Changing her mind, she took the letter out and left her room.

At the bottom of the stairs she could not hold back a cry when she saw the front door open and Charlie Jones coming towards her with a smile. He wore his panama, which he raised ceremoniously. She tried in vain to hide her letter in the folds of her skirt. He burst out laughing:

'What a fortunate coincidence,' he said. 'I'd just gone out for a bit of a stroll after my siesta, and I was just going to have a word with Miss Charlotte.'

'Miss Charlotte . . .'

'Yes, her room is quite close to yours, in the corridor. Didn't you know?'

'No, nobody told me.'

'She wanted it that way . . . She wants to watch over you like a guardian angel, and she is undoubtedly an angel. But I see you are going to send a letter. I could have seen to it for you.'

Furious at having been caught in the act of deceit, like a naughty little girl, she controlled herself and looked straight into Charlie Jones's pink and wily face.

'I don't know where to put it.' She was quite ready to do battle.

'In my office. I suppose its destination is in the United States.'

'Its destination is Dimwood,' said Elizabeth aggressively, 'and it's addressed to Miss Llewelyn, if you want to know.'

'I didn't ask you that. Give it to me, and I'll see that it goes off tomorrow morning.'

A slight tremble came over her, and she was obliged to lean on the bannister, but she did not turn her eyes away, and remained silent.

In a pleasant voice and with a smile on his lips he repeated:

'Give me the letter.'

In confusion she thought: 'It's him or me,' and she remained motionless with the letter in her hand.

'If you don't want to give it to me,' he said calmly, 'I bow to your will, but it won't be sent.'

No longer able to control herself, she flung the letter at his feet. He picked it up and said in the same tone of voice:

'That's the first time a lady has behaved towards me in such a way.'

And holding the letter between his fingers, as if to show

her, he added:

'Learn this, my dear, that one never sends a letter without having carefully sealed it first.'

As he spoke these words, he stuck down the envelope and said gravely:

'You may write every day to whomsoever you choose, none of your letters will ever be read at Great Meadow, nor any of those that you receive either. I give you my word on that.'

His serious air quite transformed him, and she felt herself blush. In a voice somewhat dampened by shame she explained:

'I had left the letter open so that I could add my present address which I don't know for the moment.'

She said more rapidly, and with an embarrassed laugh:

'Forgive me for what I did just now.'

'No need to apologize,' he said immediately. 'I might have done the same in your shoes. There must be times when I'm exasperating. I've never known how to be in the right graciously. As far as Miss Llewelyn is concerned, she knows our address. There was a letter from her waiting for me here when we arrived. It will give you news of Dimwood, some of it amusing, some of it rather vexing. Old Mr Armstrong has left his little property to end his days in Savannah. Fred had a fall and broke his ankle. It has been seen to, but he will have a slight limp.'

'Fred!' exclaimed Elizabeth.

'Oh, it won't be much. Everything works out alright, except when people don't want it to. If I were you, I should set limits to my confidence in Miss Llewelyn. I know her very well. Don't let yourself be taken in by her eternal gray dress. She is very rich and never misses an opportunity to become richer and richer still, but she is both clever and at times not entirely heartless. Having said all that, be wary.'

'Be wary! How many times have I been given that advice since I've been in America . . . One doesn't like to be wary of everybody.'

Then he put on his most seductive smile, the one that was bound to make her feel vaguely guilty and uneasy.

'In that case,' he said, 'never be wary of Charlie Jones.'

'No,' she said, 'never, never again.'

75

*A*t the first glimmer of dawn, Elizabeth got up and ran to the window of the room with the cupboards. The woods were emerging from the dawn mist, beneath the rays of a still diffident sun. That landscape intoxicated her with its very simplicity and its unspoken call to a full enjoyment of life on earth. She lingered for a moment, then returned, shivering, to the warmth of the bed. 'Only the future counts now,' she thought as she fell asleep again.

The day began cheerfully. From the other side of the meadow, the three young people arrived on horseback, not in order to get themselves invited to lunch, as on the previous day, but to take Elizabeth off horse riding. Elsie was carrying over her arm a dark green habit, carefully folded.

'Take it,' she said authoritatively to the English girl.

The latter glanced at Uncle Charlie questioningly. After looking perplexed for a moment he said:

'Yes, of course, if you're not afraid.'

'Afraid, Uncle Charlie? I rode when I was eleven years old.'

'Then I shall lend you my piebald horse. He's calm and doesn't get temperamental unless you over excite him.'

Without wasting a minute, Elizabeth rushed into the house, followed by Betty carrying the habit over her arm.

When the girl reappeared, there was the cry of admiration, which she was expecting, for she knew that the dress suited her wonderfully well, Elsie being the same height and just as slim.

'You should have asked them to plait your hair,' the latter said, 'won't it be awkward for you to gallop with your hair blowing in the wind?'

Elizabeth shrugged her shoulders.

'I've put my hair up in a chignon,' continued Elsie. 'My fiancé came to see us yesterday evening, and he took his hat back from me. He clings to his possessions. I made a terrible scene . . .'

'Come, young ladies, on your mounts!' exclaimed Charlie Jones looking joyful.

He gallantly held the stirrup for Elizabeth, who thanked

him with a smile. Sitting up straight in the saddle, she looked very grand, and she had the feeling of regaining, in the space of a second, the rank that she had lost with her exile. For the first time in months, her heart swelled with pride.

Her piebald horse did her credit with the slenderness of its head-rope, the elegance of its withers, and its coat marked with large patches of black and white. It shook its thoroughbred head impatiently, and the English girl felt an instinctive liking for it. Perhaps something of this filtered through, for a mount is quick to judge its rider.

'Take care of my Alcibiades,' said Charlie Jones. 'He's the prize of my stable.'

The boys cut a fine figure alongside her, Dick on a bay horse, Harry on a chestnut, which gave him added assurance; but Elsie, seated on a pretty mare, gave them all a haughty look and led the way with her nose in the air.

'Where are you going?' shouted Charlie Jones.

'Anywhere!' answered Elsie. 'Towards the hills.'

Miss Charlotte was present at the departure. She especially wanted to see how Elizabeth would behave. She was holding a branch in her hand, and, quite pink with over-excitement, she lashed at the hindquarters of Alcibiades, who set off at a gallop.

Not in the least surprised, Elizabeth remained in the saddle with a gracefulness that aroused admiration on the part of the connoisseurs.

Elsie and the boys set off after her and did not catch up with her until they were on the main road.

'I hope you know where you're going,' she shouted out gaily to them. 'I haven't a clue.'

'Straight on,' called Elsie. 'Towards the woods, I'll lead the way, darling.'

Elizabeth touched Alcibiades with her crop, and he overtook that cheeky girl by a length. The joy of making her superiority felt mingled with the intoxication of the gallop; the idea of possible danger was a stimulant to her. She was more and more drawn towards risk, a desire to face up to something unknown, to take on the future. Behind her, the boys' voices tried to reach her:

'Slow down in the woods!'

She saw large meadows, where the grass bent over lovingly in a breeze heralding the first coolness of autumn. The cry of a lark reached her, but so high that she could barely distinguish it. Nevertheless, it was like a call to happiness.

The trees appeared at last. She had the strange impression that they had just come from nowhere, pine trees in close ranks, with beech and birch more widely spaced.

She headed straight into the blackness. Her small, firm hand guided her mount with an almost magical dexterity between the huge tree trunks gleaming amidst the thick foliage. It was as if the horse avoided those ghostly pale columns of its own accord, and passing between them in frenzied obedience to the delicate fingers clutching the bridle.

In the thickest part of the wood, at the point where light filtered through so feebly that the presence of the trees could barely be perceived, Elizabeth felt that she was brushing against death every minute. Deeper inside herself she was certain that she had done so intentionally. And suddenly she was afraid and determined to live. With every ounce of strength in her she begged for the grace of a miracle.

Jonathan's face kept flashing before her, appearing as if to lure her into an abyss. She thought she would lose consciousness and fall from the saddle, but pride kept her upright, and her hand did not let go.

Guided by an animal instinct that seemed to be infallible, Alcibiades would slow down, moving forward with an assurance that amazed the girl more than anything else. Dead branches cracked beneath his hooves, several times she thought she felt a tree brushing against her shoulder, then at last there was a hesitant glimmer of light amidst the shadows.

Distant cries from her anxious companions reached her on all sides.

'Halloo, Elizabeth! Where are you? Halloo! Halloo! Halloo!'

It was like a children's game, but this time taken seriously in unexpected circumstances.

The shouting drifted around her, becoming more and more anguished and echoing in the silence. Out of a perverse taste for teasing, she did not answer, letting herself be carried along by the gentle trot of her horse, holding the reins gently now, for at this point she was sure that she was safe. A pale blue sky smiled at her once more at the edge of the wood, where her eyes could take in a vast expanse of thick grass heaving beneath the breath of the wind that scattered the shreds of cloud.

She was happy and allowed the coolness of the air to go to her head, while Alcibiades' large head with its pointed ears dropped down to the ground, his nostrils exhaling into the grass which he munched audibly between his teeth.

In the distance, marking the horizon with a long wisp of blue smoke, a range of low hills merged with the sky.

She waited for a moment without stirring. Then Elsie appeared, furious, followed by both of the boys, their faces blanched with worry. They all began to shout at once:

'Where were you? We thought you were dead.'

She laughed mockingly:

'Calm down,' she said. 'What a lot of fuss because I rode through a wood! You should have followed me ... What were you afraid of? I didn't meet a single wolf.'

'There are no wolves in these parts,' said Harry in a conciliatory tone of voice.

'A few foxes,' added Dick.

Elsie came up to her and shouted at her under her breath:

'Rotten beast!'

The answer followed immediately:

'I like being a rotten beast. Call me all the names you like. Come on, Alcibiades, we're going home. Show us the way, you boys.'

'A gallop through the meadows and we reach the road,' said Dick.

'Splendid!' said Elizabeth as she touched her mount with her crop.

Her horse leapt forward and the little group set off through the grass stirred up by the wind. The intoxication of speed reconciled them immediately. In the regular to-and-fro of the gallop, each of them experienced a slightly voluptuous giddiness. They went some distance towards the blue hills and then came back on their tracks round the edge of the wood.

'I quite like your wood,' said Elizabeth; 'my only reproach is that it has made my hair a mess.'

With her heart heavy, Elsie drew her horse close to hers.

'I take back the "rotten beast",' she said, 'because you're a fine girl all the same.'

Elizabeth favored her with a smile:

'Thank you,' she said, 'but I have no need of adoration. A little friendship is sufficient. Do we see eye to eye on that?'

Slackening the pace a little, Elsie let her gallop on ahead, alone, and the wind blew away two large tears from the eyes of the girl with the ebony chignon.

Clutching his julep glass in his hand, Uncle Charlie welcomed them with a broad, cheerful smile:

'Our young people on horseback,' he exclaimed, 'that's the real Virginia for you.'

In his black jacket and white trousers, he seemed to be in excellent spirits.

'Would you like something to drink?'

The boys accepted the juleps, and the girls made their excuses. Elsie disappeared through the verandah door, Elizabeth through the one leading to the stairs.

The men exchanged small talk over the juleps on the verandah. Everybody agreed sluggishly with everybody else over more or less everything. With the sound of the horses' hooves still in their ears, Dick and Harry felt full of that happiness which comes with the peace of a fine late morning in the country.

Elsie and Elizabeth met at the bottom of the stairs. Dressed in pale green cotton, Elizabeth was once more the beautiful English girl they all knew, with her striking freshness. She was carrying, carefully folded over her arm, the riding habit which had made of her such an imposing horsewoman an hour previously.

'My dear Elsie, you were kind enough to lend me this fine habit, and I return it.'

'Oh, keep it, I beg you. I shall have the illusion of being with you.'

'Thank you, but do you see, it's just a trifle too wide for me, it hangs on me rather.'

'Our seamstress could fix it for you, her work is wonderful.'

'I don't doubt it, but please don't insist, please forgive me.'

Her features tense with stifled anger, Elsie took the habit that the relentless Elizabeth handed her and left without a word.

Elizabeth did not join her. She went up to her room again and looked at herself in the mirror over the fireplace. Fatigue cast a shadow under her eyes. She considered that she did not look as good as usual. And she must stay beautiful for Jonathan.

She tried to reassure herself. Her complexion still had its glow, that true English pinkness. She had understood that from the martyred look in Elsie's eyes as she had glared at her a few moments earlier — but there was a price to pay for the compliment.

Motionless before the glass, she convinced herself that if she stayed there long enough, without moving at all, she would see Jonathan's face reflected over her shoulder. It was a childish superstition: if you look at yourself in the mirror long enough, you could see the Devil's face next to your own.

She suddenly went off into the adjoining room to lean on the window sill. The landscape of woods and meadows charmed her just as much as before and restored her peace. Words of love that had been spoken to her came back.

'I attract people,' she thought, 'and that's all.'

That was all, and nothing further happened. Nothing could ever happen except with Jonathan — and what would happen with him? At that point her imagination came to a full stop. She was not very sure and did not care to know. She did not want to admit to herself that she was petrified. That, too, she set aside. What she asked of Jonathan was his presence, to be near her and to hold her in his arms. That was love. She closed her eyes. She would know happiness, but waiting was awful.

Dick and Harry took leave of Uncle Charlie, as did Elsie, emerging from her hiding place with the riding habit over her arm. There was a proliferation of thanks, Elsie's bearing the mark of an almost funereal gravity. Uncle Charlie sensed some painful secret, but asked no questions.

A moment later the guests were in the saddle and left Great Meadow at a trot that was full of regret, and, for one of the riders at least, of despair.

There followed the silence of the countryside, so profound that Charlie Jones, like Elizabeth, was reluctant to disturb it. They were both standing under the branches of the beech with its dense foliage, and they looked pensive. 'I can see there's something not quite right with Elsie.'

'Oh,' said Elizabeth, 'I'm fond of her, but she's a strange girl.'

'Strange is the right word. There's nothing she can do about it, and I know what the trouble is. It passes with time. She's going to be married, and that's a good thing.'

'I'd rather talk about something else.'

'As you like. Your riding habit . . . You don't have one, and you don't want the one Elsie offered you.'

'That's right.'

'I'll have one made for you when we go to town. Amelia, who thinks of everything, said something to me about it. She had kept all her dresses from when she was a girl and the riding habit she used to wear, a bit old-fashioned, but undeniably *chic*. If there are any alterations to be made, Jemima will take care of them. An excellent seamstress, Jemima.'

'Uncle Charlie, how can I refuse?'

'You and Alcibiades seem to get on. Well, he's yours!'

If considerations of decorum had not restrained her, she would have danced with Charlie Jones, She had to be satisfied with smiling at him and thanking him profusely.

But later on, when she was alone in her room, she danced frenziedly until she dropped onto her bed from weariness.

76

She was asleep that afternoon when someone gave three quite distinct, bold knocks on her door.

A tall, thin colored woman came in. A white apron covered her black skirt and blouse. Her features were perfectly regular, leading one to suspect some mixing of blood, and this impression was confirmed by her behavior. There was nothing servile in her attitude. She had a certain haughtiness that was surprising on first encounter. Carefully combed hair added to her naturally dignified air. Folded over her arm was a long garment of autumn-brown cloth, from which the girl deduced that Charlie Jones had kept his word.

The woman closed the door and took a step forward.

'I am Jemima,' she said.

'Well, good morning Jemima. Are you the seamstress?'

'Seamstress is saying a lot, Miss Elizabeth. There are certain jobs I can do with a needle and thread.'

Her careful pronunciation and her correct English surprised Elizabeth, who almost asked her to sit down.

'Did you go to school, Jemima?'

'Yes, Miss Elizabeth, from the age of twelve until I was eighteen.'

She was a little uncertain for a moment noticing Elizabeth's surprised reaction, but then she suddenly unfolded the brown dress.

'Here is the riding habit,' she said. 'Will you try it on now or later?'

'Straightaway. Give it to me.'

'Would you like me to go away and come back in a minute?'

'Why? You can stay and help me. The dress looks long to me, the material is beautiful, but the color is a bit dull.'

'That was the fashion twenty years ago, but the dress is wonderfully cut. Mrs Jones wore it when she was very young.'

Taking off her cotton dress, she put on the habit with the help of two slender black hands of an imposing firmness.

'Turn round, please, raise your arms . . . again.'

She obeyed with docility and cast her eyes around looking for a mirror, but there wasn't one big enough.

'May I make a remark?' asked Jemima.

'But of course.'

'The riding habit will suit you very well. It comes from the best tailor — but you will have a job to breathe when we've buttoned it up from top to bottom.'

'Oh, why?'

'Because when Mrs Jones was seventeen, her waist was slimmer than yours, Miss Elizabeth. I'm sorry.'

The English girl had the impression that she was being struck by a heavenly thunderbolt for what she had said to Elsie about her riding habit being too wide. She blushed.

'Nothing to be done then? It'll have to be given back.'

'Of course not. I'd foreseen that little problem. I can undo the seams and move the buttons slightly. It won't show, I assure you.'

'Alright,' she said as she got out of the habit fuming with rage, 'but I shall need it for tomorrow.'

'Oh, no, Miss Elizabeth. It'll be three days before you can have it.'

'Three days! Can't I hope for a miracle?'

'I don't work miracles.'

'But I was counting on it for tomorrow. What shall I do for three days not being able to ride?'

'You'll wait, Miss Elizabeth.'

As she said that, she picked up the habit, which she folded with care and respect, and went out.

The girl was bewildered and remained standing there in a state of undress. She felt sheepish and furious at one and the same time and looked indignantly at the door that had just closed. As if to annoy her, the sound of little heels clicking down the stairs reached her ears — for that impertinent black woman wore bootees, like a lady.

When her anger had subsided, she got dressed again and went to look out of the window. The serenity of the landscape succeeded in calming her down.

'I still don't know how to talk to slaves!' she told herself. 'That woman may put on airs, but her skin is black.'

'So?' said a voice beside her quite clearly.

She uttered a cry and turned round. There was no one there.

She was almost accustomed to that hateful illusion. It

alarmed her imagination and troubled her conscience.

Without lingering for a moment longer, she left the window, and as if fleeing from a ghost, she crossed the room and went down the stairs. Once outside, she was soon under the trees. Charlie Jones and his wife were taking the air in the meadow and as, soon as she saw them, she turned in her tracks. She found conversation with them boring, but they had seen her, and Charlie Jones waved vigorously at her; she joined them somewhat reluctantly.

The sun was going down. Amelia, wearing an enormous, floppy straw hat, was fanning herself with a palm leaf and walking at a slow pace, as if in some procession. Uncle Charlie waved a letter cheerfully.

'News from your mother,' he said when Elizabeth had drawn close to him. 'I have heard indirectly through my bank in Liverpool and my currency dealers, but here's a letter from her in person. She has just acquired, after a battle royal, a house in the grand style. You'll be able to spend some time with her in four or five months' time, if that appeals to you, but I hope you will stay with us, Elizabeth. Won't you?'

She was unable to speak for a few seconds, the surprise having sealed her lips. Her fate was changed at a stroke. She finally stammered:

'Stay here . . . oh, yes. I don't understand. Why a battle royal?'

She was walking alongside them, at the same gentle pace, so little in harmony with her own state of mind.

'They were asking a ridiculous price for that splendid house,' explained Charlie Jones in a patient tone of voice. 'She negotiated with the banks. Thanks to shares bought at the right moment . . . But the details of all that would be tedious for a young lady. Mrs Escridge has a considerable fortune at her disposal.'

'But how? It's not possible.'

'She knew how to make what she had bear fruit when she arrived back there. Someone helped her with advice.'

'Someone?'

'You are still as inquisitive as a child, Elizabeth. Do you believe in Providence?'

'Of course, Uncle Charlie, but . . .'

'There's no "but". When Providence takes a hand, things happen.'

With a regal gesture of friendship, Amelia fanned Elizabeth's flushed face.

'You're asking a lot of questions,' she said with a smile. 'One ought not to.'

Feeling there might be a difference of opinion, Uncle Charlie intervened:

'She says in a post-script that she is going to write to you soon. Some day you'll visit her in the old country, and you'll come back home to the South, because you are at home here, Elizabeth. That's what your mother wanted, do you remember?'

'At home? Here?'

She looked at him in bewilderment. At that point Amelia declared that she could feel the coolness of the evening around her shoulders.

'I was wrong to leave my shawl behind,' she said.

'Let's go in, Amelia dear.'

With a last effort to clarify the fabulous escapade of Mrs Escridge, Elizabeth exclaimed:

'Why didn't my mother buy back our family mansion?'

'Later,' he said evasively. 'Go in soon, you'll be cold in your cotton dress.'

Without answering, her eyes followed them. They were going so slowly that they looked as if they were not moving their legs.

'Living here with them,' she thought, 'days and days would go by like that, never any faster.'

Turning her back on them brusquely, she had a feeling of being imprisoned in space. Behind her, the giant cedar was waving its branches gently, as if to tell her something, and birdsong rose up as twilight approached. She stretched herself out on the grass and let her gaze plunge into the void. A single idea remained as the only fixed point in the midst of a confusion of hope and despair: the South was Jonathan.

77

*T*he following day passed in that sleepy peacefulness which only life in the country can produce, with its after-taste of boredom so much feared by young people. Quite perturbed by Uncle Charlie's revelations, Elizabeth sought out solitude and went every hour to look at the great clock, ticking away resoundingly in the silence. What was she waiting for? The end of the day? She had no idea. Nightfall would bring nothing new into her life, and such would be the case over and over again. As if in a game, the day would hand her body and soul to night, and the night to day. If anyone had told her that she was waiting for Jonathan, she would have believed that she was being ridiculed, and yet it was that and nothing else.

Two or three times in the afternoon, she went to the stables to see Alcibiades and talk to him. Confiding in him as she would in no one else, she whispered her misfortunes to him:

'I'm going out of my mind, Alcibiades, I'm madly in love with someone who is far away from here, and I want to die.'

As she groaned, she moved her own head close to the handsome horse's face which seemed attentive. Speaking aloud what was wrenching at her heart brought strange relief, but suddenly she was seized with fear at the thought of being overheard and she ran off . . .

The following morning she had a surprise. As she was walking beneath the trees after breakfast, Charlie Jones joined her:

'Amelia is tired and is going to spend the morning in her room,' he told her. 'There are some very important things that I want to tell you. What would you say to a carriage ride with me?'

Her curiosity aroused, she accepted with pleasure and, a few minutes later, she was seated next to Uncle Charlie in a charming black gig with large yellow wheels.

They went at a good pace along the road beside vast meadows where herds were grazing. Once more she admired the long fences made of criss-crossed beams, some of which were eaten away with age.

'They are venerable in their own way,' said Uncle Charlie. 'Many of them saw the heyday of English colonization, long before the War of Independence.'

He touched the horse with his whip and set him off at a gallop. Large clumps of trees soon appeared, bending over the clear waters of a quiet river which was chattering to itself all through a valley carpeted with grass. Attracted by this peaceful spot, the girl suggested stopping there.

'You don't know what a good idea that is,' said Uncle Charlie. 'This place is known for its simple beauty, and a little further on there is a bench.'

The bench was, indeed, to be found some twenty yards further on; it was well situated in the shade of a willow whose long, curved branches offered protection from the sun. While Uncle Charlie tied the horse to a tree, Elizabeth sat down and let herself plunge into that delight which nature never failed to produce in her. 'A moment of happiness,' she thought, 'oh, that it might last . . .'

Uncle Charlie came back and sat down next to her.

'You like this idyllic landscape,' he said. 'It's going to be put to the test, though, for it is hardly in accord with what I have to say to you, but perhaps it will help.'

Elizabeth immediately thought of Jonathan.

'Bad news?' she said, her eyes wide open with fear.

'Oh, no, you can be reassured on that score. Everything is being settled at present. It's about your mother. You went through some terrible times with her without fully realizing what drama lay beneath it all. She didn't talk to you about it. When you lost your father in February last year, she was close to going out of her mind, for she loved him beyond anything you can imagine, and her one thought was to flee for good from that manor where she had known such happiness. Your father had left nothing but debts. There was virtually no money. She went off to London with you and ran to the lawyer who had custody of the will. She went through it with him, and he had no trouble guessing that she did not understand it. It's rare to find a will that doesn't have some element of confusion in it. Now, that lawyer was a rogue. He assured your unfortunate Mama that she could benefit from her inheritance by selling the manor house but that it would be difficult to sell as it was in a poor state of repair. That word "sell" was like a knife in your mother's heart, but she had such blind faith in that man, the family lawyer, and trusted him implicitly in everything. He made her sign a document to that effect. You were not present at that meeting. Your mother had sent you to wait for her in an Anglican chapel a few minutes away from there. Her entire fortune was about ten pounds, which she had found in her husband's writing desk. Armed with those meager resources, she found, in a poor district, lodgings that you have surely not forgotten.'

'I beg you, Uncle Charlie,' exclaimed Elizabeth.

'I'm sorry, but you have to know. She had given her wretched address to her lawyer. Weeks went by. She finally received a letter from him fixing an appointment with two legal men at Lincoln's Inn Fields. Alone, once again — you were waiting in your room — she crossed an icy November London on foot. She was received respectfully, and the three men in black informed her that there was a prospective purchaser. She could probably count on an answer before the end of the month. The men in black declared that they were prepared to negotiate the sale of that "dwelling": they never managed to find the exact term ... Did she give them the power to do so? They made her sign a document. Then another, and then two more. They all said more or less the same thing, except for one or two words, so that they wouldn't be completely interchangeable. She signed the papers, she would have signed twenty of them in her big, generous hand. When she was back at home, she thought she would faint from fatigue. In a state of collapse, on her knees, she told you to kneel down with her and thank Providence.'

'You're dredging up painful memories,' protested Elizabeth.

'I regret, but there are details that you don't know. Events took a certain inexorable course. The month went by without any further developments. Hope subsided, giving way to anxiety. At that point, you were living on credit. It was at the beginning of January that your mother took the decision to call for help and wrote, amidst tears of shame, to William Hargrove, your father's uncle. Perhaps she might have done better to turn to me, more in a position to come to her aid. Out of finer feelings she did not do so. Hargrove answered immediately, as was only right. In the meantime — the mail can be depressingly slow — your mother had an unexpected visit from her lawyer, bearing the sum of one hundred pounds, which he handed to Mrs Escridge, making excuses for it not being very much. The manor house had been sold, the purchaser paying this derisory sum as a deposit. The principal payment was to be made within the month, placed in the hands of the two legal men in black, as Mrs Escridge had agreed in a document signed by her hand. She had no memory of it, but the lawyer reminded her of the papers she had been given for approval and which she had been willing to sign. One of those documents applied strictly to the present situation. She remained a little perplexed and, seeing this, he reassured her: "Have confidence, madam, the law is on a par with the country's honor." And without giving her any papers to sign, he went away.'

'All of that is true,' sighed Elizabeth, 'but what need is there to make me go through it all again?'

'Patience. We're getting there. As soon as William Hargrove received your mother's letter, he came to see me in Savannah and informed me of the situation. We both had suspicions as to the honesty of those legal men. Something had to be done quickly. I gave orders to my bank in London to make available to your mother the money she would need for her passage to America. At the same time, I asked my business associates to make discreet enquiries. They confirmed my suspicions, but you were already on board ship, you and your mother, when those rascals were caught. The lawyer had already fled to Belgium. There was a big search for him, and the day is not too far away when those fellows will join the kangaroos in Australia. They'll make themselves useful breaking stones for the roadways. Your mother had to go back to England to give evidence in court. With the agreement of William Hargrove, she makes me your guardian. Do you understand now why I made that promise to you in Savannah, under the tree in front of my house?'

The return ride in the gig passed in silence. Uncle Charlie ventured a few words of comfort to set the girl's mind at rest, but she had been shaken by this account of her mother's misfortunes and did not open her mouth. To tell the truth, Charlie Jones had told her nothing new, except for a few details that distressed her in her love for that woman whose fortitude she admired. When the roofs of Great Meadow came into sight on the horizon, however, she was beset by a doubt.

'May I ask you one question?' she said.

'Of course, I would have been surprised if you hadn't asked me at least one.'

'It's very simple. When my mother went to see the legal men . . . it seems strange to me that you know in detail what took place. I know that Mr Hargrove is the source of your information, but then he was not present with my mother in the office of the men in black.'

'Quite right. Do you remember that on one of your very first days at Dimwood, two of your young cousins took you into the wood with them?'

'Perfectly, Mildred and Hilda.'

'Profiting from your absence, William Hargrove went up to see your mother, as common courtesy demanded. He wanted to see if she was satisfied with her room and if there was anything she needed. Mrs Escridge had been waiting for that moment. Proud and devoured by scruples, she could not forgive herself for having appealed for help to a relation of her husband, and in a flood of words she unburdened her heart of all that was tormenting her. To justify her course of action, she described in detail the cruelly humiliating steps her distress had subjected her to, in particular her visit to the men in black and the papers she had signed in the grip of despair. He could see her anxiety at the prospect of her daughter being poor. Hargrove spoke to her with kindness and with respect, and that calmed her. You can quite imagine that when he told me all that he had found out, he would not have omitted that crucially important scene. Have I answered your question?'

'Yes, Uncle Charlie.'

'I was only surprised that you didn't say straight away: "How do you know?" '

Elizabeth did not answer. Tears rolled down her cheeks, but she quickly recovered, and a few minutes later she asked in a tone intended to be natural:

'When are you taking me to meet my cousins on the other side of the meadow? I admit that I am curious to know them all — and their parents.'

He hesitated.

'Of course I want you to go and say hello to them,' he said. 'Perhaps alone. Do you mind?'

'Why not with you? I should prefer that.'

'That's difficult, Elizabeth, as you must know, there is between Amelia and her sister Maisie . . . how shall I put it . . . a regrettable disagreement that goes back a number of years. It's a wretched business about interest. However, by a kind of tacit agreement, the young people are allowed to cross the meadow as often as they like, to go from one house to the other, whereas the parents no longer speak to each other, and will never again cross the meadow that separates them for all time.'

'I find that rather awful.'

'Yes, a *never again* between two sisters . . . And of course the husbands are obliged to espouse the quarrel of their partners. But that doesn't stop the Commodore and myself smoking the occasional cigar together, a good distance away, on the road. You will, of course, keep what I have just told you to yourself. You know nothing.'

They were coming within sight of the house.

Nodding her head, Elizabeth appeared to be thinking.

'And what about Charlotte?' she said suddenly. 'Is entry to the yellow house forbidden her too?'

'Now that's an idea! I should have thought of that myself. Charlotte is an independent spirit, who takes on any amount of prejudice. She will be delighted to accompany you. Go in the afternoon. At this hour they'd feel obliged to keep you to lunch, and there are already seven of them . . .'

78

Charlotte, having been consulted, declared that she was quite ready. She put on a flounced cotton dress, white with gray stripes, and on her head a large bonnet of fine lawn strewn with ribbons that looked like sky-blue butterflies about to take flight. In her pale green dress, Elizabeth felt more casually dressed, but were they doing anything other than pay a simple country visit?

Four o'clock was assumed to be the most suitable time.

As they were crossing the meadow, Miss Charlotte gave herself up to the delights of informative chatter:

'They have been there for fifteen years. The house dates from the time of the English colony. It was an abandoned schoolhouse, and the long, single-storied building in the centre was judged inadequate. They added square buildings at either end, one to the left and one to the right. It does not make for a very harmonious whole, but they had quite a lot of people to accommodate, my sister Maisie with her Commodore, and their tribe of children.'

'A pity that the great house could not bring the two families together.'

'Perhaps, but there had been the great split between my two sisters a long time ago when we were all still in Scotland. Have you heard about it?'

'Vaguely.'

'Let's move on then.'

Keeping very straight, so as not to lose an inch of her small stature, she moved forward, through the grass, fanning herself with a palm frond.

'After the Dream House, you're going to find this a House of Chaos. Ten people are crammed into the ground floor, where they are better off than anywhere else. You'll take it all in at a glance. De Witt, the Commodore from an old Dutch family and, alongside him, my sister Maisie, a martyr, with three daughters to marry off. A problem. I don't know how they manage to be everywhere at once. Perhaps they hope to catch a husband while running about in all directions. Elsie, the second eldest, whom you know, believes she has ensnared one, and she's holding on to him tight. You'll see him, and you can form your own opinion, but don't make eyes at him!'

'Cousin Charlotte, what are you thinking of?'

'He himself is prepared to give what's known as lovelorn looks to anything in petticoats. Fanny, the youngest, is a little scatterbrain of fifteen and quite ripe for that spectacular kind of folly that ends in a shotgun wedding. Hell indeed! That leaves the eldest, Clementine, twenty years old, an attractive girl, refined and prudent, intended for solitary pursuits and for virtue. Her confidante is the piano in one of the end buildings. You know the two boys, Dick and Harry, whom their father is going to turn out of the home and send to Annapolis, where they'll be made into sailors, despite what they may think. Finally Teddy, the idol of the family, who isn't always here, who earned his stripes at Annapolis, handsome, serious and calm, impervious to languid looks, a little mysterious . . .'

When they reached the little white fence enclosing the house, they stopped. Miss Charlotte was laughing like someone about to play a joke, and this gaiety upset Elizabeth.

'What am I going to say to them?'

'Nothing. Good afternoon. They'll take care of the rest. Can't you hear them?'

Indeed, a loud sound of voices reached them, with occasional shouts, as if an argument had suddenly sprung up. Still laughing, Miss Charlotte passed in front of the girl and twice firmly rapped the door knocker, and the door opened wide immediately.

With an imperious yelp, Miss Charlotte announced:

'A visit from England. Your Cousin Elizabeth.'

Paralyzed with fear, the girl took one step forward and stood still. She had the impression of countless faces turning towards her, speechless and frozen, like masks. With her head spinning in her shyness, the thought came to her that she was dreaming and that none of it was true. More alarming than all the rest was a silence that she had not expected.

Even Miss Charlotte was taken aback by it.

'What's come over you?' she thrust at them in her high-pitched voice. 'No one moving, no one speaking. Do you imagine I've brought you a ghost from Scotland? Wake up.

This is your Cousin Elizabeth Escridge whom you are welcoming in such a strange way.'

At these words, a woman in black who seemed to detach herself from the wall, came over and embraced the girl with tears:

'My dear girl,' she exclaimed in a voice broken by emotion, 'our dear Charlie Jones has brought you into the family. Charlotte has told me everything! Oh, Charlie, how sad it is that this meadow divides us! You'll give him a kiss from me, Elizabeth. He'll know, he'll remember.'

Short and solidly built, she retained nevertheless a naturally dignified air that made her seem taller. Her handsome face was furrowed around the mouth and across the forehead from all the grief that had tormented her, giving her the appearance of a character from a tragedy, but her great black eyes revealed a virtually inexhaustible fount of goodness.

The tears ran down her cheeks, wetting the face of Elizabeth, who was at a loss as to how to respond to these noisy effusions, when suddenly there resounded a sonorous male voice, showing distinct signs of impatience.

'Calm down, Maisie!'

Not without a certain brusqueness, Elizabeth turned towards an imposing maple-wood rocking chair in which the Commodore was rocking to and fro while smoking his pipe. He was tall and broad-shouldered, his face edged with a small thickness of grey beard; his eyes were relentlessly blue, his cheeks hollow and his nose hard and slender, hooked like the beak of a bird of prey.

In a voice full of despair, Maisie clamoured:

'But I must explain to Elizabeth why she has come into a family that is cut in two.'

'Go on then,' said the Commodore, 'and be brief. We all know your story.'

'It's simple. Come with me, Elizabeth.'

Dragging her off into a corner of the long room encumbered with cousins, she made her sit down on one of those back-to-back settees known as 'sulkers'. In order to talk one altered one's position, so as to be almost facing the other person.

'When I left Scotland, in order to follow my husband to

Virginia where he wished to settle, I had already, alas, been at odds with Amelia for some time. No point in lingering over that. Disagreements amongst us are fierce. We do not forgive. It's dreadful, I know, but in Scotland they say that when we hate, we do it well. So she stayed over there. Charlie Jones had married a Douglas and was living with her for at least part of the year in the old house opposite. The father of Aminta Douglas, Charlie's first wife, had ordered that fine dwelling to be built on the ruins of a castle destroyed during the War of Independence. Every day I would cross the meadow to see them, for the first Mrs Charlie Jones was our second cousin. When she fell ill, long after the birth of her son Edward, I nursed her lovingly. There were very strong family ties between us. My sister Amelia, over there in Scotland, hearing that our cousin was at death's door, hurried over to see her. I gave up the post immediately, and my sister found herself for the first time face to face with Charlie Jones at the foot of his dying wife's bed. Life plays strange tricks on people. It is certain that Charlie Jones adored his first wife and that her death nearly overwhelmed him with grief, but it is equally certain that he remained in touch with my sister Amelia, and that after two years of mourning he asked her to marry him. From the day Amelia came to Great Meadow, it was decided that neither of us would cross the space separating the two houses. I have not got over the hurt. The children may, if they wish, come and go at will between the small house and the large one. I recognize that I have been partly to blame in this matter, and I am prepared to be reconciled with my sister, who is just as much at fault as me, but she must make the first move.'

When she had delivered this speech in a firm tone of voice, she got up from the back-to-back sofa and called her children over in order to introduce them to the newcomer. Elsie pushed everyone else aside in order to be first and gave Elizabeth a look full of charm. Seeing straight away that it was producing no effect, she had recourse to her winning smile, but the English girl cut it all short with a brief 'Hello, Elsie.'

Then came tall Clementine who, with no fuss, hugged Elizabeth, muttering vague words of affectionate welcome. She was both dignified and reserved, and everything about her spoke of a soul in secret torment. From her clear blue eyes flowed waves of tenderness.

'Clementine is musical,' said Maisie. 'She has a touch like an angel on the piano, and it is she who plays the organ on Sundays at the Presbyterian chapel.'

'Oh, Mama! You make me die of shame,' said Clementine, trying to make herself scarce in her long, mauve skirt.

Dick rushed up to Elizabeth next, who gently rebuffed him.

'Hello, Dick,' she said. 'We've met, we've been introduced, and hello to you too, Harry.'

This latter, with his hand on his heart, was getting ready to say something in line with that romantic posture, when a charming girl of fifteen positioned herself in front of him, pushing him away with her backside.

'Fanny,' she said, 'I'm Fanny, and I'm crazy about England. What a pity they didn't win the war and stay on.'

A pink-faced brunette with sparkling eyes, she seemed to be bubbling over, making gestures with the pretty hands of a lazy girl. She was dressed in pale blue, quivering for some unknown reason, and she stammered when she spoke.

Her father's voice called her to order:

'If you say things like that again, I shall confine you to your room.'

She burst into tears and disappeared.

'Emotional,' said Maisie, 'it's her age. But I should like you to meet my big boy, Teddy. Why is he staying in his corner? He is strange.'

With her hand in Elizabeth's, she led her to the end of the room where, standing near a door, was a young naval officer. It was his gravity that struck one first. In his blue uniform that was almost black and showed off his natural elegance to advantage, he seemed anxious not to be noticed, but when the girl, led by Maisie, was in front of him he bowed graciously.

She got a shock. Never had she seen such a handsome man. The regularity of the features was not sufficient explanation for the indefinable majesty of the face. The large, dark eyes lowered their gaze onto her, accompanied by an imperceptible smile:

'When I saw you assailed on all sides by the family, I did

not want to inflict another introduction on you.'

'That's a good one,' said his mother with an incredulous little laugh. 'I'll leave you.'

A few minutes of embarrassed silence followed. She had to raise her eyes to look at him, for that tall, slender boy towered over her and she was still fascinated by that hint of a smile hovering around his mouth with its admirable contours. To the girl's mind, he represented all the nobility of the South, without the barely disguised arrogance of those charming inhabitants of Georgia whom she had known.

Seeing her reduced to silence, he began to speak to her in a rather subdued but warm voice, different from that of the deep South, whose drawl was so moving — perhaps like Jonathan's, thought Elizabeth.

'As you are one of us now,' he said, 'you'd better know my real name. They call me Teddy, and that's fine, but my real name is Daniel De Witt.'

What would she have given for a smile to crease those suntanned cheeks! She searched desperately for some amusing reply and, flushed with embarrassment, she said with a laugh:

'That makes one think of the dykes in Holland ... but what I'm saying is absurd!'

'Less than you think, Miss Elizabeth. My father is convinced that we are descended from the Grand Pensionary of Holland, who gave the order to give the land up to the sea, in order to drown the invaders.'

'A famous name.'

'That doesn't mean anything. Holland is full of De Witts. You can convince yourself of anything you like. My father insists that we are directly descended. I doubt it, but then I don't care one way or the other.'

Elizabeth did not doubt it. She could see that magnificent personage, standing beside his brother Cornelius, ordering the breaking of the dykes in order to drown the invaders.

He added:

'I shall not have the chance to see you often, Miss Elizabeth ...'

'Elizabeth,' she corrected him with a laugh.

He gave a slight bow.

'Elizabeth, seeing as you permit it. I am on forty-eight hours' leave, and have to go back tomorrow morning.'

'Far?' ('Why all these questions?' an inner voice asked her.)

'Yes and no, Annapolis. I don't come very often. Apart from the family, there is nothing to keep me here.'

'Nothing?' she said in a daze. 'What about the country? Virginia . . .'

He looked at her for a moment in silence which she thought would go on for ever.

'No,' he said, 'not even Virginia, but I shall come back at Christmas. Will you be here at Christmas?'

'I'm almost certain I shall be.'

'Almost, Elizabeth, only almost?'

'No, certain, I'm absolutely certain.'

'You're making my departure less difficult, Elizabeth, but Christmas seems further away than it did a moment ago.'

She tried hard not to understand. A voice was crying out at her: 'Don't listen to him, get away from him.' Without really knowing what she was saying, she asked:

'At what time are you leaving?'

He gave her a smile that conferred on him a handsomeness that she thought heavenly. That was the way she saw it, and she felt a quiver pass through her. Talking to this unknown stranger frightened her. In a kind of mental daze she heard:

'At dawn, I shall go by carriage to the little station at Gainesville.'

She kept silent, and in a flight of distress her gaze plunged into the young man's eyes.

'You'll be asleep,' he said, lowering his voice.

'No.'

She hesitated and said:

'No, Daniel.'

Then he drew imperceptibly closer to her, seized hold of her hand, and she let him take it; all of the warmth of that man was spreading through her body.

'I shall be Daniel for no one but you,' he said in a whisper.

The following minute was silent. What they had to say to each other was conveyed in the endless looks they exchanged. She suddenly felt the large, firm hand open, releasing her own.

'I think we're being watched,' he murmured. 'Will you permit me to write to you, Elizabeth?'

She nodded her head to signify yes and they separated.

Miss Charlotte came over to them.

'We must be going back, Elizabeth, but first have a word with the Commodore, who wants to speak to you. I'm taking her away from you, Lieutenant, but I hope that one day you'll come and see us in the Great House.'

'I hope so, Miss Charlotte.'

'For you,' she added, 'the meadow is no barrier.'

He saluted and she took Elizabeth's hand to lead her to the Commodore. He put his pipe down when he saw her standing before him, and looked at her with his piercing eyes that seemed to be always on the look-out for some frigate on the horizon.

'Welcome aboard the *Quarrelsome*, my young lady, and, no offense, may I point out to you that, on board ship, one greets the captain first . . .'

'Oh, Dirk,' his wife implored.

'Peace, Maisie . . . I wipe the slate clean and repeat how pleased I am.'

Miss Charlotte came up and took hold of Elizabeth's arm, dragging her towards the door.

'Commodore,' she hurled forth in her highest-pitched voice, 'our young cousin is expected on the other side of the meadow. You will excuse this hurried departure. Good evening to you all.'

There was a noisy hubbub and the Commodore, with an infuriated kick of the heel, sent his chair rocking backwards, almost knocking it over.

Once they were outside in the great silence of the country-side, Miss Charlotte assumed a confidential tone as they plunged into the thick grass. Her speech was accompanied by the rustling of her taffeta dress.

'You must never be afraid of the Commodore. Since he has been retired, he lives in a maritime dream world. His family is his crew and he loves them in his own way. Let's not bother with all that. May I speak to you as a sister? Are you afraid of hearing the truth?'

'Of course not,' said Elizabeth, always on the verge of indignation when her courage was doubted.

'Well, my girl, you are on the brink of something unwise. I don't know what you and Teddy De Witt said to each other, but I could see in his features something that made me afraid. A woman doesn't miss a thing. You know nothing about him. That man with the sublime looks is a child.'

'Oh, don't say anything bad about him!'

'Calm down, I'm here to help you. His life is mysterious. He has never been seen to court a woman and, what's more, he has no friends. He is respected and admired, but the only passion he is known to have is his work. Now, either I am very much mistaken, or I saw in his eyes that you have made him love you.'

Elizabeth took hold of both of her hands:

'Do you think so, do you really think so?'

'I'm sure of it, alas.'

As she walked along she fell silent for a few seconds, and the taffeta of her dress simulated the whispering of some secret.

'At twenty-four, he still has the heart of a boy of fourteen with no experience of love. It was enough for you to look at him, tenderly perhaps, to release in him all the passion he has been bottling up. You're growing more beautiful, Elizabeth. Men will be hovering around you, and that one is going to make a declaration, I'm sure of it. Don't marry him. You'll be unhappy.'

'Why unhappy? Oh, come on, Miss Charlotte, tell me the truth.'

'His family is poor . . .'

'That doesn't matter to me.'

'A sailor does not get rich quickly, and that matters, it matters in spite of everything.'

'Not for me.'

'Alright, but a sailor's wife is doomed to solitude. He'll be away for part of the year. What can that mean for him other than worry; worry at first and, sooner or later, jealousy?'

Elizabeth's throat let out a cry.

'But I shall be faithful, Miss Charlotte.'

The spinster stopped short in the middle of the meadow. Lamps were beginning to be lit in the windows of the Great House.

'Elizabeth,' she said, 'are you mad? Have you gone mad? Come to your senses. You have confided in me a little, perhaps without realizing it. I thought you led me to understand, I thought I guessed . . .'

'No,' said the girl under her breath, 'be quiet, I beg you.'

She would remember all her life that moment in which her inner nature was suddenly revealed to her, making her its victim. Dusk was slowly falling. In the solitude of the nearby wood, a thrush launched forth its sad little note, and bats furrowed through the air.

Miss Charlotte was standing motionless, amazed at the state of collapse brought about by her words.

'My dearest,' she said softly, 'you can believe someone who has experienced and felt herself die of grief occasioned by love.'

'By love . . .' stammered Elizabeth.

'The man was unworthy, Providence removed him from my path, I was nearly demented, but I understood, and I see things clearly now.'

'You won't change me,' said Elizabeth who began to sob.

Miss Charlotte immediately pulled a handkerchief from her waist pouch which she handed to the girl. The latter wiped her eyes with it, then blew her nose.

'Forgive me,' she said.

'Do you want me to tell you the name of the one who did not keep his word? I have never spoken it since that fateful day. In the Bible it's the name of a valiant and loyal man, and I used to say it over to myself lovingly when I was alone. I really believed that he would be mine. I have suffered too much and I don't want you to suffer. They did not dare tell me the truth. They did so, but not soon enough, and the disaster happened. I became hard and I must seem wicked to you.'

'No,' whispered Elizabeth, 'but I find what you say disturbing.'

'You'll be grateful to me some day. Do you want me to tell you the name that still sticks in my throat?'

'No, I don't want to hear it.'

'Let's go back,' said Miss Charlotte. 'I've done what the voice was crying out to me to do.'

That night, in the great, sleeping house, someone was awake, walking back and forth from a bedroom in which the furnishings spoke the language of childhood, to a neighboring room, where her anxious hand opened and closed the large cupboards for no particular reason. The light of the moon, in all its brilliance, flooded in through the windows, and an inky black shadow clung to the heels of the girl in her white dressing gown, who did not know what to do with herself, because her bed wanted none of her.

Through the door, intentionally left half-open, the sound of the great clock marking off the hours reached her ears. Each hour rang out so gravely in the silence that Elizabeth unfailingly trembled at each stroke.

Midnight seemed to her less alarming than the early hours that led towards the chill of that fearsome moment. She wrapped herself up in her blanket and watched the sky through the window of the room with the cupboards. The meadow seemed immense, like some colorless lake beneath the harsh moonlight, and the woods formed a black, compact mass, just like a cliff face.

In her head everything was flying about as the blood thundered through her veins. She saw once more the young officer's mouth and at first struggled against the desire to give herself up to hallucinatory dreamings, in which her fingers would touch those lips that parted to say: 'I shall be Daniel for no one but you.'

But so strong was the illusion of reality that she finally flung herself against that ghostly breast and had the physical sensation of a body of flesh and blood grasped in her arms. It only lasted a split second, but it overwhelmed her.

Dropping to her knees at the foot of her bed, she buried her head in the blanket and began to cry out. The real world was recreated through imagination. She had this gift and was still trembling at that discovery in the invisible world around her.

'I'm going out of my mind,' she thought, 'I'm not like other people.'

In an effort to calm herself down, she mentally recited the Lord's Prayer, because her tongue refused to form the words. Being led into temptation was a terrifying mystery, culminating in that final supplication: 'deliver us from evil'. 'Deliver us from the Devil,' her mother had explained to her.

She stretched herself out on her bed, her head still wrapped in the blanket, as protection against all that prowls in the dark, as the psalmist says with breathtaking accuracy. All of a sudden she remembered Miss Charlotte asking her — why that strange notion? — 'Do you want me to tell you the name of that man who went back on his promise?'

She tore off the blanket and stood up. In the darkness she thought she could see the elderly spinster all ready to give the name of the faithless one. On that normally smiling face, at that moment ravaged with sadness, she read the name of Jonathan.

As if felled by the blow, she slipped on the mat and lost consciousness. There she remained, stretched out, until the cold dragged her out of her sleep. All was dark around her, and she heard that little grinding sound which the clock made as it got ready to strike the hour. It struck five times, resounding deeply and with foreboding. Getting up immediately, she groped around the room and found a shawl on an armchair. Through the window with its unclosed shutters, a hesitant whiteness struggled against the thickness of the dark night. 'Dawn,' she thought. He had said, *'I shall leave at dawn.'*

Her eyes were getting used to the darkness, making out the pale green of the doors. Groping, she reached the staircase and stood at the top of the steps, trying to wrench herself from the torpor of sleep that still enveloped her. The fear of falling made her hang on to the rail when she began to descend, and with nearly every step the name of Jonathan came to her in a whisper.

At the bottom, having cautiously opened the door, she could vaguely make out the shape of the great cedar that stood out like a black giant against the pallid light. She shivered and waited by the half-closed door for the moment when what Miss Charlotte had called the House of Chaos would reveal itself to her. And what would she do then? No answer formed in her mind.

Since she had spoken to Daniel De Witt, events had succeeded each other in no particular order, and her behavior was becoming like an indecipherable story in some book written by a madman. She simply could not understand herself. She was in love with one man and, all of a sudden, another one comes along. Could one be in love with two men at the same time?

The cold made her cough and she went back inside the

house, pulling the door to without closing it completely. Through the gap, she could still see the other side of the meadow.

Time went by. She was afraid of being caught out by Barnaby or some other servant but, with an obstinacy that she herself judged to be fruitless, she stood there with her hand on the brass doorknob.

'I loved you the moment I saw you,' she said to herself beneath her breath, without making it clear to whom these words were addressed.

Eventually she caught sight of lights coming on in the windows of the House of Chaos. Several minutes went by, then a gray carriage pulled up in front of the door. Again there was a pause, then, with her heart pounding ever harder, she saw the door open and recognized Daniel from his height, followed by a servant. They both got into the carriage and the lights in the house went out one by one. Soon the carriage disappeared behind the trees and she thought: 'Over, it's over.'

Something held her back from closing the door. Closing the door on hope. In her place, others would do so, but she did not want to believe that everything was really finished and, in a gesture that looked like defiance, she opened it wide again.

It was still not light, and the wind slowly stirred the heavy, black-fringed branches of the cedar. Pulling her long, gray shawl tight around her shoulders, she was watching the wind shake off the last traces of night when suddenly, almost at the foot of the giant tree, she thought she could see someone standing motionless in the shelter of that shadowy spot.

She immediately understood. Daniel had left the carriage on the road, behind the trees, and was coming to have a last look at the house where, he supposed, the one he loved was still asleep. Not a single light shone beneath the roof of Great Meadow. She imagined his eyes searching for her room among the long row of windows on the first floor. The gray shawl in which she was wrapped concealed her well and, very gently, she started to move towards the inside of the house.

An awful desire to throw down her shawl and go out of the house took hold of her. A few steps forward, a few steps towards him would be enough. In her pale dressing gown, she would be like an apparition. It was so easy that everything in her urged her towards it, and yet she did not move. One thought glued her to the spot: 'Do that and it's a betrayal.' She decided not to move. If he looked attentively, he would eventually notice the open door, the bottom of the white dressing gown would indicate the presence of a woman. 'I'll leave that chance open to him,' she said to herself. 'I was there, he came, I did nothing to make him see me.' Internally she carried on the reasoning: 'You did nothing to make him see you, now do something to stop him seeing you, move far away from the door.' She fought with that thought, but did not move. She thought she could guess that he was turning his head this way and that. What was he hoping to see?

Now she could make out the width of his shoulders and she looked at him with every ounce of her strength. It seemed to her that her soul left her body in order to fling itself against his chest. How could he not feel that she was there?

After a moment he went away and, less than three minutes later, she could hear the wheels of the carriage on the road.

In her despair, she tried to gather up her strength by telling herself that at least she had not betrayed anyone, but she collapsed at the bottom of the steps and could not get up.

A little after six o'clock, Barnaby found her with her knees tucked up and her head in her arms. Instinctively he looked at the stairs, then at her, and thought she was dead. He immediately began to howl, as is the custom among the Negroes in circumstances concerning death:

'Miss Lizbeth gone for good . . .'

At that very moment, Miss Charlotte appeared at the top of the steps, wearing a plum-colored dressing gown and a goffered white lawn bonnet on her head.

'Be quiet, you fool,' she cried. 'Everybody knows that Miss Elizabeth walks in her sleep. It's very common. Pick her up and stop making those animal noises . . . and pick up the shawl that's fallen on the ground.'

She flew down the steps, her feet barely touching them, and put her arms under Elizabeth's legs, while Barnaby held her under the arms. Between them they managed to get her to her room without too much difficulty. Miss Charlotte directed operations with a man's authority. She put Elizabeth down on the bed and sent Barnaby packing:

'Out,' she ordered as she wrenched away the shawl that he had put over his shoulder, 'and not a word to anyone.'

As soon as Barnaby had gone, she locked the door and came back to lean over the girl, who was opening her eyes and looking bewildered.

'Do you have any pain?' asked Miss Charlotte.

'I don't know . . . a little, I think.'

With a flick of the wrist, Miss Charlotte had her clothes off and inspected her body all over, feeling the ribs, the thighs, the back, making no concessions.

'Does it hurt here . . . or here . . . here neither?'

She pressed her finger hard just about everywhere without provoking the least cry of pain.

'Not a single bruise. Nothing. It was a soft fall which is not surprising at your age.'

She spread the blanket over the still-inert girl.

At that moment there was a knock at the door.

'Charlotte,' said Uncle Charlie's voice, 'open up.'

'No point,' she said. 'If I need you, I'll have you sent for. There's nothing wrong with Elizabeth. She sleepwalks, like many girls of marriageable age. She tripped and she fell. I was a volunteer nurse in a hospital in Edinburgh for three years. I know what I'm about.'

'Charlotte, I order you to open the door.'

'Go and give orders somewhere else, Charlie. I shall only open it when I judge it appropriate. I'm obeying the voice.'

This mysterious phrase seemed to produce silence on the other side of the door. A male sigh of exasperation could be heard, then steps moving away with an annoyed stamping of slippered feet.

Sitting now at the foot of Elizabeth's bed, Miss Charlotte was stroking her forehead.

'No temperature,' she murmured. 'You'll get warm under the blanket. A little glass of rum?'

Elizabeth shook her head.

'A sugar lump dipped in brandy, perhaps? I have a bottle in my room.'

'No, thank you,' said Elizabeth, smiling in spite of herself. Her eyes were red.

'My dearest, life is hard,' said Miss Charlotte softly, 'but you'll get over the unhappiness. I shall be here to help you. Your handsome officer would have made your life a torment.'

'I loved him,' sighed Elizabeth . . .

'You fell in love with a handsome face, a fearful trap. If there were only the face — the face and the soul — but there's all the rest that I can't talk to you about, for, thanks be to God, I have no knowledge of it. I allowed myself to say things that kept me awake all night, a frightful, horrible night. Since the Fall, man has been inhabited by a Beast. My sister Maisie let me in on things that people never talk about. I had to make her shut up, I couldn't believe it.'

'I don't understand,' said Elizabeth.

'That's perhaps for the best. Be wary, my little one. I had to seek happiness somewhere other than in married life, and that happiness eluded me . . . I found peace that passes all understanding.'

'But love, Miss Charlotte, what about love?'

The elderly spinster kept silent and passed her finger along the fold of the sheet that framed Elizabeth's face. This gesture seemed to have no meaning. She might have sought to conceal the secret of a whole lifetime.

'Love,' she whispered at last, 'that's all I have deep in my heart.'

Not daring to ask any questions because she guessed at some mystery, the girl drew a hand from under the sheet and placed it on Miss Charlotte's.

'Don't leave me,' she said.

Why had she said that? She would wonder about that in amazement later. It was one of those phrases that she let out without being aware of it.

'My dear,' said Miss Charlotte, 'do you think that it is by chance that our paths crossed? And to start with, is there such a thing as chance?'

She stood up abruptly, seeming to become someone else, the everyday Miss Charlotte.

'We're getting off the subject,' she said cheerfully. 'You're going to sleep again, and I shall come back without making any noise, to see if you are alright. If you're not, I'll mix you a good glass of laudanum.'

She went over and closed the shutters at both of the windows, drew the curtains with care and went out. With her head buried in the pillow, Elizabeth did not even hear the door close.

79

Days passed amidst the warmth of a fine autumn. The charm of country life was still apparent in the gentle fragrance of the boredom of hours dragging by. Peace prevailed, the world was so far away that one might wonder if it really existed. Only Uncle Charlie sometimes revealed an anxious brow when the newspaper arrived from Washington, but his good humor did not falter.

And then one night, after an abnormally hot day, cold descended on this corner of the world, and all the trees of the surrounding woods reddened and bedecked themselves with deep red and copper-tinged gold. The foliage of the maples was edged with violet, and the beeches plunged into pale gold. Walks were taken beneath a sumptuously multicolored canopy, which gave life an appearance of barbaric splendor, protesting against the unrelieved green of summer.

Elizabeth lived in a perpetual state of wonder at this unfolding of strong and delicate colors, but nevertheless carried with her a burden of sadness in the magnificence of that Indian summer. The memory of Jonathan's half-hidden face, lost amidst the confusion of magnolia flowers and foliage in the intoxication of a summer evening, mingled with that of Daniel's face, appearing suddenly like some god in a sitting room full of people. Each one offered love and, amidst a surge of dreams, she, in her virginity, gave herself up to one or the other of them, doing battle with the notions she had of the delights of love.

One November morning, however, the mail brought her a letter from her mother; the writing alone seemed to set everything to rights:

Bath, 25 September 1850

My dear daughter Elizabeth,

The address that you see on this letter will explain nearly everything, except for the details of that fortunate and providential change which has come about in your mother's life. At the moment I am living in one of the most elegant houses in this town famous for the refinement of its society and the unequalled beauty of its architecture. You will be pleased to learn, I am sure, that I am a property owner ... and that my dwelling, one of those on the famous Crescent, which is the envy of the civilized world, belongs to me from its attic right down to its cellar.

If you wish it, Charlie Jones will give you a detailed account of my involvement with the courts and the trial in which I triumphed over three rogues who have been banished for ever from the realm. I can now contemplate the future with confidence and do not propose to end my days in solitude. Interpret this phrase as you will, but I'm telling you that if, some day, you wish to put an end to your American exile, an eight-roomed apartment awaits you on the second floor of my house.

When I took you to Georgia with me, I wanted to protect you from the nightmare of poverty that we had known and, above all, to ensure for you a reasonably happy future and the possibility of a sensibly arranged marriage. Listen to me. Stick to the aristocracy, but with an eye to the financial situation of the party in question. Charlie Jones, whom I have made your guardian, will be able to guide you in your choice and will save you from making mistakes. Be prudent.

For Heaven's sake, do not let yourself be dazzled by

attractive physical appearance. Ask yourself if, day and night, you will be happy to hear that same way of speaking, to look at that same nose, the same mouth, the same round eye. In the suitor see the delicate, silky lining, in the husband the suit cut from sturdy cloth that's rough to the touch. Finally, Elizabeth, try not to behave like some foolish creature in a novel. We are in the nineteenth century.

Here people don't believe there will be an armed conflict between North and South. The Queen would tend perhaps to the Southern side, in memory of the old English colonies, but Albert, the Prince Consort, favours the North. We don't know what the Prince-President thinks in Paris, or indeed if he thinks at all. Charlie Jones will take the necessary measures to avoid your being caught up in the turmoil of civil war. But it hasn't reached that yet. The South still has long years of peace ahead of it. Don't be so foolish as to marry a young whipper-snapper likely to be called up straight away. Maturity has its charms. Think about that. Cast an eye over the world of diplomacy. And read your Bible morning and evening. I shall ask you a few questions some day, for, my daughter, we shall meet again.

Your mother embraces you,
Laura

P.S. Without wishing to give way one whit to sentimentality, I admit that there are moments when your absence weighs down on me. It would not take much for me to shed tears of sadness, but forget that.

Having read the letter, Elizabeth remained pensive. She only knew the Crescent from engravings but, as a reader of Jane Austen, she was not ignorant of the fact that Bath was the meeting place of the best society and a town for fine marriages. Mrs Escridge's phrase seemed clear to her and made her smile, but the choice offered increased her state of anxiety. To leave the South and see England again, three months earlier such a dream would have sent her mad with joy, but now was not the South Jonathan? And after a second she added, not without an inner tremor, the name

Daniel De Witt.

Once more she saw herself plunged into a purgatory of uncertainty and immediately took several contradictory decisions. The most attractive seemed to look for Miss Charlotte and to unburden herself to her — or Uncle Charlie, perhaps . . . She was suddenly seized with a violent desire to be free of her problems, once and for all, in fact, to be rid of everything. She would go to Bath, she would become dizzy with pleasure at the balls, at which she could already see the candelabras shining in gilt and white drawing rooms. There were moments when her life in America seemed empty and stupid, missing out on happiness . . .

So as to be able to think better, she determined to give herself up to a giddy, solitary gallop through the fields at the foot of the hills.

The day promised to be cool but fine. Amelia was lying in after a rather tiring night. Miss Charlotte was picking flowers in her garden, and Charlie Jones was seeing to his letters in his office. For a moment she was reluctant to disturb him, but did so all the same amidst a flood of excuses.

He received her with his unchanging good humor. Sitting at a solid black wooden table all scattered with papers, he crossed his slippered feet, a point which displeased Elizabeth without her knowing why. In the same way she regretted that satisfied look which he wore especially in the mornings. Since his marriage, she thought, he was less and less like the portrait in Savannah. She refused to admit that with time men were likely to change in appearance. The thought of Jonathan ever growing old horrified her, and she struggled against the prospect of such a misfortune.

With his natural gracefulness, he agreed to all she wished:

'I'll go and tell Barnaby to have Alcibiades saddled. If you want a pleasant ride, I advise you to go in the direction of the little valley where I spoke to you some time ago. Carry on along the river, and soon you'll come to a forest with broad avenues going through it. There is a spot in the valley where there is an echo, it's fun. Are you going alone?'

'Yes, alone,' she said in a resolute tone of voice.

'Jolly good, but be careful. That valley reminds me of the conversation we had about your mother. You must have had news from her this morning. Is she pleased?'

'Very. Do you want to read her letter?'

'On no account. It was understood that I shall never read any of your letters, no matter where they come from.'

'As you like,' she said cheerfully.

Suddenly she found that with his pink cheeks and shining eyes Uncle Charlie was not doing too badly with what remained of his youth.

Back in her room she had Jemima called; she arrived after a few minutes. In her dark dress and little white collar, she inevitably put one in mind of an English school mistress. The seriousness of her face was intimidating, mainly on account of the directness of the eyes which did not miss a thing. She was clearly a woman who did not lie.

She was carrying the riding habit carefully folded over her arm.

'Good morning, Miss Elizabeth,' she said. 'I suppose you want your riding habit.'

'Straight away. I'm going off for a ride as soon as I've got it on.'

'Get undressed then, please.'

The door opened suddenly and, without bothering to knock, Miss Charlotte came in.

'Elizabeth, my girl, here you are ready to launch an assault on youthful hearts.'

'Can I go, Miss Elizabeth?' asked Jemima.

'Of course, Jemima, and thank you.'

'No thanks, Miss Elizabeth, that's my job.'

With those quickly formulated words, carefully pronounced, Jemima withdrew.

'My word,' said Miss Charlotte, 'she's even more British than you are. One wouldn't feel inclined to confide in her, but Charlie Jones thinks highly of her. Mysterious Jemima.'

'She leaves me cold . . . Oh, Miss Charlotte, how pleased I am to be going off for a ride!'

'I understand. I too, at your age, often used to go off for a gallop on a lovely red and white pony,' said Miss Charlotte with a laugh. 'But be careful, for the love of God. Going clip-clop clip-clop along the road goes to one's head, so sit tight in the saddle and don't let go of the reins.'

'I promise you,' said Elizabeth as she put on a hat that Amelia had lent her.

The heavy golden chignon that covered her neck pushed the little hat forward over her forehead.

The effect set Miss Charlotte off laughing, half mocking and half in admiration:

'How impertinent you look with your hat down over your nose! That's what drives men wild so, in future, be on your guard against conquests too easily made. Forget the House of Chaos and be back here for lunch.'

On the road that led to the valley, Elizabeth did not waste her time going at a trot. In the first place, she hated trotting, which shook her up mercilessly, and she also wanted to lose herself in the solitude of the forest, where the trees spoke to her in their prophetic silence.

It did not take long to reach the delightful patch that Charlie Jones had chosen as a backdrop to his accurate portrait of the somber battles her mother had had in courts of law. The river flowed calmly alongside the woods, ablaze with all the fiery golds of autumn, and the horsewoman was tempted to make a stop and fill her head and heart with that extravagant beauty, but something was drawing her further on with a force that got the better of her.

She did not dare to admit to herself that she was fleeing from someone. Miss Charlotte's advice could only serve to remind her of the sound of a voice murmuring words of tenderness. So powerful was her imagination that she found herself once more somewhat breathless from emotion, standing in front of the young man begging from her a promise of seeing her again at Christmas-time. As the horse plunged into the stimulating coolness, a thirst for happiness was aroused which she felt throughout her whole body. She wanted to forget, and yet she was giving herself up to a frenzied dream that seemed to her at last to reveal the truth: the man held her a prisoner in his arms and hugged her to the point of suffocation, as the grizzly bear mangles his victims with his embrace. That's what love must be. A god with large eyes full of desperate questions that his magnificent mouth barely puts into words, a strangely graceful creature who possessed the force of a wild animal, she was ready to obliterate herself in him.

Yet in her delirium, her attention remained lucid. Not a single detail of the area she was crossing at breakneck speed escaped her. The fields were receding into the distance behind her and the vale had disappeared, when suddenly there was a forest of trees, like the gigantic columns of some palace of darkness. In the center, an avenue opened up, where feeble rays of daylight penetrated the thickness of the foliage. Here once more an extravaganza of autumn colors was let loose, but amid a darkness that conferred a tragic violence. Bronze, copper and blood mingled their muted tints. Elizabeth had the feeling of intruding into one of those legendary forests in which the enchantment of love and death roamed. Far from being afraid, she let herself be captivated by the bewitching charm and, having reached a clearing, she stopped to take in the intoxication of silence. Beneath those heady vaults only the melancholy call of the solitary thrush could be heard at intervals.

Singular thoughts slipped through her mind, amazing her with their newness and their logic . . . Daniel's face became enveloped in the twirl of luminous fog and finally vanished in the twilight that fell from the trees.

Then, in the heart of this play of light and shade, she thought she could see, taking shape before her eyes, the face of Jonathan. The questioning look of his imperious eyes reached out to her once more just as they had during those first minutes amidst the fragrances of the Southern night and the steady song of the tree-frogs. His voice trembled softly, it reached her, touching her face, caressing her cheeks and her mouth like the fingers of a hand. The hallucination was so exact that Elizabeth experienced the horror of feeling herself vacillate under the assault of incipient madness. Touching her horse with her crop, she sent him charging straight ahead, as if to escape from the horror, but the face did not leave her, she carried it with her. Suddenly a cry rose up from her breast and released her. Then a distant echo replied, and she remembered the echo of the valley which Charlie Jones had told her something about: 'You'll hear it, it's fun.'

This re-assertion of reality chased away the waking dream, erasing those minutes of first love and the face of Jonathan in the foliage.

The relief that she felt was taken from her immediately by an unspeakable despair. It seemed to her that she was losing Jonathan for ever. With a thrust of her whole being she called him with all her might. A second went by, and the distant echo repeated to her the only name that counted for her. Clear and distinct, but distant, the three magic syllables travelled to her, as if to tell her that he had heard her. A strange joy invaded Elizabeth's heart. She called out again and, still with that same imperceptible delay, the voice, full of love, answered.

This game that was both childish and disappointing captivated her for a moment, but she could not but notice that at each new cry her horse pricked up his ears. She stroked him to reassure him. He slowed down his gallop a little, and abruptly, as she shouted a little louder, he sidestepped, almost flinging her to the ground. Getting a grip on her terror, she was able to keep her balance and noticed that, fifteen yards further on, they were heading straight for a precipice.

With a hand that was still steady, she stopped her mount. Sweat was running down her forehead and cheeks, and she could hear the beating of her heart which was bursting her chest.

The thought crossed her mind that the echo had led her to this point for the express purpose of killing her, but she cast it aside ferociously. The echo was Jonathan calling her. How could he wish for her death? But the suspicion returned with a dubious obstinacy. She made an effort to calm herself, chasing away the absurd ideas that she was prey to without respite.

Pulling on the bridle to turn round, she went back up the broad avenue at a calmer pace. Her heart was gradually becoming more at peace, and she thought she could hear an inner voice murmuring with patient obstinacy words that she could not grasp, but which, in their gentleness, filled her soul with a mysterious serenity.

When she found herself once more beneath the giant cedar tree of the great house, she had the feeling of coming back from an unknown land. It took Miss Charlotte's rather brusque brand of cheerfulness to bring her completely back to herself:

'Your hat is askew, your chignon is in a mess and Alcibiades is bathed in sweat — all that betrays frenzied gallopings through fields and woods. Very well, my pretty English girl, but we're having lunch in a quarter of an hour. You've just got time to have a wash and change your dress, otherwise you'll be late in the dining room, and Amelia may well raise her eyebrows when she sees you.'

Elizabeth did not hear the end of this speech. She was already in her room, flinging her hat over the furniture to land behind an armchair, and the riding habit, unbuttoned by small hands trembling with impatience, fell down around the young horsewoman's ankles. A cotton dress of periwinkle blue completed the transformation.

Splashing cold water all over her face, she pulled out the pins from her chignon to release her hair, which poured down on to her shoulders in a stream of copper and gold.

'What's the matter?' she said, with her eyes on the Elizabeth in the mirror. 'Who are you now?'

'And you?' said the mirror. 'Who were you?'

Neither of them was able to reply.

At lunch she said nothing. Uncle Charlie's words reached her ears, but she only caught meaningless shreds of conversation.

'A Constitution drawn up by scatter-brains caught in a panic. The Fathers of the nation, those harum-scarums . . . They made of their Constitution a seed-bed for disharmony . . . including war.'

For some reason that escaped her, she felt happy with a vague, secret contentment, and answered Miss Charlotte who was keeping a particularly close eye on her, with smiles.

As they were getting up from table, the elderly spinster came close to her and slipped her hand under her arm:

'Pleased, Elizabeth?'

'Oh, yes, Miss Charlotte, very pleased.'

'Won't you call me Charlotte? And if you have anything to tell me, I shall be in the orchard.'

'I'm going to rest, Charlotte,' she said as she shook her by the hand.

In her room, she dropped fully dressed on to her bed and closed her eyes immediately.

She slept until dinner-time, and the evening seemed destined to collapse into that amiable monotony which characterized life at Great Meadow in all its seasons. It was a bit too cool to take armchairs out on to the grass and admire nature. Reading aloud was suggested. Miss Charlotte gave a distinguished rendering of her party piece: the heart-rending appeal of Queen Catherine of Aragon to her husband, the awesome Henry VIII, who sought to repudiate her in order to marry Anne Boleyn. She burdened her formidable husband with her resounding eloquence, defending both her honor as a wife and all the rights conferred on her by the title of mother. Humble and proud by turns, imploring and demanding, but always regal and always truly human, she stood up to the man who wished to be rid of her.

As it happened, it was Uncle Charlie, the only representative of the stronger sex, who received the full blow of this powerful rhetoric, and he turned his head to one side, looking embarrassed, but the elderly spinster did not take her eyes off him, searching his conscience with a merciless gaze. He knew that she put into this orgy of grandiose vociferation the terrible failure of the whole of her life, and deep in his heart he suffered on her behalf but was shamed, nevertheless. This party piece of Miss Charlotte's was a nightmare for him.

When she fell silent, her face all sweaty and the corners of her mouth distorted with rage, there was an awkward silence, indicating general embarrassment. Elizabeth was shrinking away in a corner when the monotonous voice of Amelia was suddenly to be heard:

'After all,' she said, 'she was a Catholic idolatress, consequently a danger to the Christian faith. I understand the King.'

Uncle Charlie's face had turned scarlet:

'Amelia,' he said in an unusually commanding tone of voice, 'we're going up to bed. I admire your talents, Charlotte, and I thank you.'

But Charlotte had already left the drawing room in tears.

For her part, Elizabeth slid towards the door and disappeared.

80

A few days later, Charlie Jones had asked Betty to hand Elizabeth a letter that made her shake, for it was postmarked Annapolis. Locking herself immediately in her room, she sat down, reflected for a moment, then tore the envelope and read this:

Elizabeth,

To write your name is to have you before me again, when my face drew close to yours. Nothing will ever take that moment away from me. You are the one I have been waiting for since my adolescence, and I might have ended up believing that my ideal did not exist if you had not appeared.

The world barely exists to my mind, I am bored, dances fill me with horror. I have never been a man for pleasures, I was living for you, for the woman I despaired of ever finding on my journey. I do not believe in chance. I am persuaded that we are made for each other, Elizabeth. It's Providence that brought us face to face in my father's house. Tell me that you think so too, Elizabeth, tell me so that I may live, that the one you called Daniel may live.

She put the letter down on her knees and half opened her mouth in order to speak the name but, by a sudden quirk of will, she could not manage it. She continued reading:

I realize that in speaking to you of myself at such length, I am trying to put off the admission of one of the characteristics of the man I am. It is a love of truth that urges me to write the few lines which follow. I wish to be loyal to the end, otherwise how could I live with a burden of cowardice in my heart? I am jealous, Elizabeth, and passionately so. Someone more adroit would conceal that weakness of which I am ashamed, but I am not adroit. I have never in my life written a love letter. Tell me, Elizabeth, that you could never love anyone but me and that your heart is unattached. Tell me, oh, you whom I adore, I want to know, I cast myself at your feet and beg you to tell me so. I feel brave enough to receive the fiercest blows that truth can inflict on a man — but I must have that truth, for I want you to be completely mine, as I am already completely yours, in body and soul, for ever.

Your
Daniel.

Elizabeth threw the letter on to her bed and thought she would go mad. Not knowing what to do, she began to run from her bedroom to the room with cupboards and back to her bed again, where she looked at those two pages covered with small, even handwriting which revealed a firm character. Her heart pounded and she was surprised to find herself talking to herself in a low, staccato voice:

'First love letter in Virginia . . . that man as handsome as a god . . . at my feet . . . at my feet . . .'

In a trice she kicked off her slippers and looked at her feet with intoxicating vanity.

'. . . there, at my feet . . . body and soul . . . it's not possible.'

A terrible hunger gnawed at her insides, a strange hunger such as she had never known before, a hunger for this creature who was offering himself to her with slavish humility. Suddenly a cry rose from her breast, a wild cry that she stifled immediately. What would people say if they heard her? What would they say if they read that letter? Uncle Charlie, for example, or Amelia? Or Charlotte? Charlotte?

A few minutes passed. She calmed down a little, put her slippers back on and folded the letter, which she slid into its envelope. 'If Mama knew . . .' she thought.

At that moment, there was a discreet knock at the door. Hiding the letter under her pillow she said:

'Come in.'

Miss Charlotte came in and immediately sat down in the rocking chair.

'Good morning, little one. Did you have a good night?'

Not without some surprise, Elizabeth saw her smile so happily that she almost asked her if she was bringing good news. Her face was, in fact, radiant with joy.

'Give my chair a little push, will you? I'm comfortable here, but my feet don't reach the ground to set it in motion, and I feel awfully like rocking.'

She was wearing a dress of pomegranate-colored taffeta and a lace cap with streamers reaching down to her shoulders.

'Oh, not so hard,' she cried out with a laugh. 'Do you want to send me up to the ceiling? Don't you like my pretty outfit?'

'Yes, Charlotte, you look charming.'

'This morning marks the beginning of a day of grace for me. You'll understand. Sit down. There's still an hour before breakfast. Listen.'

The girl sat down on her bed.

'About what happened last night,' said Miss Charlotte, 'you won't say a word to anyone, but you ought to know. At dawn, when night was still lingering in the recesses of the sky, there was a knock at my door — oh, so gently that I might not have heard, but I wasn't asleep. Do you know who it was?'

'Oh no, how could I? . . .'

'Amelia.'

'Amelia!'

'Yes, I opened it and she flung herself into my arms in sobs. She asked me to forgive her for what she had said to me about Catherine of Aragon. Oh, how we cried together! What delightful floods of tears, and grace flowing freely with those tears! It lasted a good quarter of an hour. It was the voice, you understand? The voice had moved her heart.'

'The voice, Charlotte?'

'Read again in the First Book of Kings, chapter 19, verses 1 to 14 inclusive. The shadows have been dispersed . . . Let's talk about something else. There were a lot of letters this morning. All for Charlie, except one for you.'

'Yes.'

'Ah? But it's none of my business. I'll go down. Get dressed quickly. It would be best if there were no clip-clopping today. A day of rest. Stop my chair for me, and be very kind to Amelia.'

Jumping down from the chair, she went out humming. Elizabeth stood there with her eyes fixed on the closed door. A few seconds went by, then, giving in to a sudden impulse, she cried:

'Annapolis!'

There was no answer to that cry. Miss Charlotte had gone down the steps of the staircase with a young girl's lightness of tread and was already outside. What meaning could there be in that strange call? The girl did not dare admit to herself that the letter meant only one thing. She ardently desired to show it to Miss Charlotte. The way the latter had confided in her was partly responsible. Wrenched from a world of earthly love, she saw herself transported to regions in which mysterious voices spoke. Amelia's repentance disturbed her. She felt rather ridiculous with her love letter hidden under the pillow. Mad with pride because a naval officer wanted to fling himself down at her feet . . . As handsome as a god . . . Was Jonathan not as handsome? Jonathan's eyes, when he had looked at her on the quayside in the middle of the crowd . . .

The shock of that memory made her feel faint, and she had to seize hold of one of her bedposts so as not to lose her balance. It seemed to her that for an hour now Jonathan had been around her like a shadow that she could not get away from. She could not see him, but he was there.

She washed rapidly and got dressed. Laying aside with regret the pale-colored cottons, she chose a woollen dress in huntsman's green. More in accord with the season, it gave the Elizabeth of yesterday the more serious appearance of a young lady of Virginia. The riding habit had already made her a slightly different person. Standing in front of the glass, she had the fleeting impression of a farewell to the holidays at Dimwood. Yet she had suffered in Georgia. The sun and the proliferation of flowers surrounded her life with an enchanted garden . . . Amidst the more meditative landscape of Virginia, life did not wear the same smile.

When she put in an appearance in the dining room, she was complimented on her elegance. The dress looked ravishing on her but, as Amelia remarked, it was time for her to put her hair up and have it done like a grown-up. This advice rang like a distant funeral bell in Elizabeth's ears; however faintly she heard it, it was ringing nonetheless.

With a laugh, Uncle Charlie called her 'Miss Escridge', and she could only smile by way of a reply. With her fingertips she felt the letter from Daniel De Witt in a small pocket by her waistband and derived solace from it. She was still Elizabeth for him.

For better or for worse, that's the way it was, and Jonathan would know nothing about it.

81

A little later, Charlotte approached her under the trees behind the house. Like Elizabeth, she had dressed a little more warmly, and her dress of autumn-brown serge brushed against the grass of the lawn.

'We're a little worried, it seems,' she said in a pleasant tone. 'May I be of any help?'

'I am always pleased to see you, Charlotte, but I don't think I have anything to ask of you.'

'That's not bad for a start, but I still think you look just a bit too anxious for your age.'

'I have the impression that my dress puts years on me. What's more, Uncle Charlie wants me to put up my hair and have it done like a grown-up.'

'In short, it's time to get married.'

'Is that the advice you're giving me?'

'No.'

'What do you mean then?'

'I mean that I, Charlotte Douglas, am on earth this day,

the 28th of November 1850, to prevent Elizabeth Escridge doing something irreparably foolish.'

'Something foolish? What?'

'You know as well as I do, my dearest, but if you don't want to confide in Charlotte, she's off to the medlars with a basket carried by Betty. Do you like medlar jam? I'm unbeatable at medlar jam. So I'll see you later on, my dear, and ruminate well on your worries under the trees.'

She made as if to set off. Elizabeth lurched forward and caught her by the arm.

'Don't tease me, Charlotte. He's written to me.'

'That's what I had foreseen, too. If you want, we can go over the situation in all tranquillity in the small boudoir on the ground floor where nobody goes.'

She was speaking in a tone of calm authority which attracted the girl who was usually so rebellious, but she felt that she was at the end of her tether and followed Charlotte in a docile manner.

The boudoir in question was a small room with rounded corners where a vague odor of tobacco hovered. The only furnishings were a few red velvet armchairs and a sagging black leather sofa. There was nothing to hint at those pleasant frivolities usually associated with conversation in a boudoir. It owed its charm to a single window looking out towards the distant, pale blue hills, way beyond the meadows and woods, having a calming effect on agitated minds.

They sat down facing the dreamy landscape.

'Well,' said Miss Charlotte with a smile, 'we've had a letter.'

Elizabeth pulled the letter out of her pocket and handed it to her.

'Am I to understand that you are authorizing me — no, that you are begging me — to read it?'

Elizabeth nodded and turned her eyes to the hills, preferring not to see anything else.

In the bony hands of the elderly spinster, the letter was taken from its envelope and unfolded with particular care, as if it were some document of the greatest importance.

It took a certain amount of time to read, during which Elizabeth suffered a good deal, but Miss Charlotte kept her eyes down. From time to time she moved the page closer to her nose, and once or twice Elizabeth had the impression that she was stifling a slightly sarcastic chuckle . . .

After about ten minutes, Miss Charlotte put the letter down flat on her knees and said:

'Yes!'

Elizabeth quivered.

'Is that all?' she asked.

'My dearest, is that not enough?'

'I admit,' said Elizabeth, who was shocked, 'I'd expected a more varied reaction from you.'

'You shall get it, as that is what you want. First of all, you must know that, in my day, young men phrased their love letters rather more prettily, but your lieutenant does inform us that this is his very first attempt. Then, after a few twirls addressed to his beloved, he starts to talk about himself. He is quite caught up with his own person. With a military man's brutal frankness — but I can't hold that against him — he reveals to us that dreadful thing which would make a whole bevy of beauties recoil. Jealousy. He pretends to be ashamed. Fiddlesticks! He's secretly proud of it and even boasts about it. Passionate jealousy. Can you not see domestic quarrels looming on the horizon? Where were you this afternoon? You received a letter from Paris? Let me see it! Tears flow and pretty hands are wrung. That's not all. He wants to know if your heart is unattached, if you aren't already in love with someone else. Jealous in advance, jealous before the wedding, before the long white veil and the wedding march . . . He can already sniff out infidelity. He's got to have the truth.'

As she spoke these final words she rose, and her face took on a tragic air. She continued:

'There is this in his favor: he is, in his own way, honest, but in spite of his handsome face both a child and monstrously egotistic and cruel. Well may you tremble, my dear. I know men, and my advice is reliable.'

Aflame with emotion, Elizabeth looked at her, unable to speak a word. She finally forced out a sentence:

'And what if I love him in spite of everything?'

'You're done for.'

'But I must answer it.'

'Don't answer.'

'That's inhuman. I owe him some explanation.'

'You're done for.'

Having passed judgement crisply, she turned on her heels and went out. She was a different woman.

82

*T*he English girl spent the morning in a silence haunted by images and voices. A whole part of her life unravelled in her head, culminating in that phrase which had knocked her off her feet. *Done for.* Those two syllables pulled on the most sensitive chord in her soul, sending vibrations that aroused all the terrors of the invisible world.

As she left the house, she went to seek refuge under the branches of the cedar that were gently stirring at this first sign of the coming of winter. No one could see her on this spot where Daniel had stood at dawn to get at least a glimpse of her room, and she had seen him . . .

Did not 'done for' mean that all earthly happiness was doomed by the error of an unfortunate choice? Or did letting oneself be bowled over by an attractive face presage a fate of which her mother had already spoken in terms she could never forget? As a faithful believer she was saved, she should be certain of it deep in her conscience. Even the slightest doubt pointed to a gloomy end. Now uncertainty was beginning its patient work inside her. Was she living like one of the elect? What meaning could she attribute to her passion for a married man and to her sudden infatuation with a young naval officer who had written her that mad letter?

For the first time in her life, she understood what blind panic, in the face of death might mean. Like a flash of fire, the idea came to her that Charlotte had prophetic gifts, and that she had induced her to show her the letter in order that she might receive a final warning.

Throwing herself to the ground, Elizabeth covered her face with her arms and remained motionless. Horror passed over her like a breath of icy air. In the hollow of one of her clenched hands, she crushed the love letter and saw herself going down into the abyss with it in her fist. Shivers ran through her body. At that moment, a sudden peace settled within her, loosening the tightness of her chest with unspeakable gentleness, and she experienced an indescribable joy which brought her back on her feet in bewildered delight. She murmured:

'I dreamt it, there was nothing.'

The inner exultation had come to an end as suddenly as it had begun. She could barely remember those few extraordinary seconds. There remained only a nostalgia for something, a distant light.

She thought that she must have been asleep. It often happened that she recalled what was still lingering in the frayed edges of her dreams, but even that melted away almost immediately when daylight brought a return to the prosaic and the ordinary.

The cold made her sneeze. She ran to the house and only just had time to run up to her room and brush her dress and remove the pine needles caught in her hair. Not without sadness did she pull a comb through that golden thickness, soon to be piled up on her head according to the fussy taste of the world. Would Jonathan recognize her? Daniel even . . . She brushed aside that memory with a convulsive gesture.

At table she ate well. Only half listening, she heard what Charlie Jones had to say about a writer who had been dead for a little more than a year.

'A poet,' he said. 'I admit that his verse bores me, but he is talked about in literary circles. He studied at the University of Virginia, Edgar Allan Poe, an actor's son! People talk about the story of a walk he took in the Blue Ridge Mountains with his classmates in 1827 or '28. He predicted a terrible war between North and South, but the boy had a wild imagination, macabre at times.'

'Why are you telling us all this?' enquired his wife gravely.

'To let you see that this obsession about war is no new thing.'

'There won't be a war,' decreed Amelia.

'May Heaven hear you, but I don't like the incandescent fervor of the Reverend Beecher's sermons. That man is doing wrong, he's preaching violence. What's more, he's not the only one of his kind in the South, alas, as much as in the North.'

'Charlie,' said Miss Charlotte all of a sudden, 'don't cast a cloud over the present moment. An agreement has been signed. The North cares much too much for its possessions to plunge into such a costly venture as a war with the South. What reasons could they give?'

'They'll find a pretext. They only have to stir up public opinion enough. Emotion is an explosive of immeasurable force.'

'Another word, Charlie, and I shall leave the table.'

Amelia made as if to get up. Miss Charlotte attempted a diversion in her high-pitched voice.

'I went apple-picking this morning. Betty came with me and returned limping under the weight of a basket full of the finest pippins in Albermarle county. I shall make you a pie that you won't forget, as big as a cartwheel.'

Suddenly more quiet, Amelia asked:

'When?'

'Let's say in three days' time. I want it to be with a short-crust pastry that will make you hanker after more.'

'Shortcrust?' asked Elizabeth out of the blue.

'Yes, my girl. Like shortbread and flaky pastry at one and the same time. Without the shortbread, the flaky would fly away, do you understand?'

'If you make it as big as a cartwheel,' observed Charlie Jones, 'we shall have to call on our young neighbors oppo-site.'

Miss Charlotte laughed mockingly:

'How readily they will abandon father and mother, even the faithful and plaintive Clementine.'

'Little Mike will be missing,' said Charlie Jones, 'he left last week amidst a storm of cries and protestations. He was calling: "Lizbeth! Lizbeth!"'

He cast a knowing look in his wife's direction:

'The eldest of the family, Teddy, will be absent. He's rarely here.'

Elizabeth remained stony-faced.

There was a sudden short yet interminable silence that immobilized all those present. Then Charlie Jones cleared his throat and asked casually:

'You saw him, Elizabeth. What do you think of him?'

'Me? Nothing. I only saw him for a moment. And then what would be the point?'

Charlie Jones gave a big sigh, and his wife smiled slyly.

'Let's go up,' she said. 'I need my siesta.'

'That's right,' replied her husband cheerfully, 'I need mine too.'

Joking to each other, they left the dining room, holding hands, with just a hint of a swing, which made them look as if they were sailing over the calm waters of happiness.

Remaining alone with Elizabeth, Miss Charlotte looked at her for a brief moment without saying a word.

'Do you realize,' she said at last, 'you frightened him to death with that letter from Annapolis?'

'Why?'

'Perhaps we shall understand some day. He saw the name Annapolis on the postmark. That's what put him in such a bad mood all over the warmongering rumors.'

'I don't see the connection.'

Miss Charlotte shrugged her shoulders.

'He had to take his anger out on someone or something. Your indifference to Teddy restored his serenity. But were you really being sincere?'

'Forgive me, Charlotte, I find your question offensive.'

'Very well, very well, I take back "sincere", but tell me, I see you looking well again. You looked like a corpse this morning. Has something happened?'

'You forget that I was done for this morning.'

A nervous laugh shook the shoulders of the elderly spinster.

'Did I say that?'

'Not only once, but twice.'

'That's because I really believed it. Something must have happened since.'

'Oh, yes! Something momentous that deserves a place in the history books: I stretched out under the big cedar tree and went to sleep.'

At these words, Charlotte drew closer to her and, taking hold of her hand, said with extraordinary gravity:

'My dear, that's perhaps more significant than you think.'

The girl could not restrain her irritated reaction:

'Charlotte, it seems to me that you take pleasure in creating mysteries around the simplest things. You began by seeing me in Hell with that wretched letter in my hand . . .'

'Not in Hell, but on earth, slave to a jealous husband.'

'What is certain is that you frightened me. So, shattered with fatigue, I fell asleep under that old tree, and sleep restored me to peace. What's more natural than that?'

'Do you think so? I don't. You must have heard a voice.'

'No.'

'A voice like a breath.'

'Nothing at all. Oh, Charlotte, don't ask me so many strange questions. I'm a normal person to whom nothing extraordinary happens.'

'And what about the letter, Elizabeth?'

'I don't know what I've done with it. I've lost it.'

A broad smile widened Miss Charlotte's lips.

'I've answered your questions, it would seem you are pleased.'

'Confident.'

She added with a look of complicity:

'We can see each other again whenever you like. I'm heading for the kitchens to give orders about my pie.'

Elizabeth let her go without a word, annoyed by that bantering tone. In her room, she muttered aloud:

'She imagines she is going to console me with her pie as if I were a little girl!'

The letter that had fallen from her hand into the long grass could stay there, waiting for an answer that would never come. The rain was free to turn the ball of paper to a pulp. Elizabeth gave it up. Charlotte had convinced her, and she was angry with her for having convinced her. At times she hated that small person — but Charlotte was always right. To give up Daniel. She said it aloud in that room where only the toys were missing to make it a child's room. Like a madwoman she told the rocking chair:

'I give up Daniel.'

She told the walls, she told the furniture, not forgetting the bed, which received only a furtive glance. She told it again to the countryside that she could see from the room with the cupboards. 'I give up Daniel,' she said to the purple- and gold-tinged woods beneath the gray sky. She said it to the Elizabeth in the looking glass, and that one answered with her silent voice, and each time her heart felt more and more constricted. The unrequited tenderness she bore within her was frustrated. Everything inside her was in a state of rebellion, but she had given him up, given him up, given him up.

Crying was unworthy and quite pointless. She had held out and she admired herself for not having broken down. She did not want people talking to her about mysterious voices, for she could sniff out a pious undercurrent in Charlotte's reasonings and exhortations, and that she could not stand.

There was a knock at her door.

Jemima. A dark leather bag was hanging from her right wrist.

'Master Charlie sent me to do your hair, Miss.'

'Now?'

'Those are his orders.'

'Why all the hurry? And where will you do my hair?'

'Here. It's very simple. It's only a trial, you'll see.'

'Are you a hairdresser, Jemima?'

'I was one for a year in Richmond. Master Charlie sent me to take lessons. He wants me to have a trade, for later on.'

'I don't understand.'

Without answering, Jemima picked up a chair that she set in front of the mirror.

'May I ask you to sit down, Miss?'

The pronunciation was accurate, the language perfectly correct. She spoke like a well-educated Englishwoman of the middle classes. The contrast with the color of her skin was quite violent.

Elizabeth felt ill at ease. The image offered to her in the mirror disturbed her, as if someone — herself — was looking at her for the last time. It was too much like a farewell . . . and, behind her, that inky black outline.

'I don't like what you're doing, Jemima,' she said suddenly.

'I haven't done anything yet, Miss.'

'You're not going to cut my hair?'

'No question of it, Miss. What's more, I haven't brought any scissors. I shall manage with combs and pins.'

Elizabeth closed her eyes.

'I prefer not to see.'

'You'll be surprised, Miss.'

Through the thickness of her hair, Elizabeth felt the long caress of the comb send a pleasurable little shiver, then the long, careful hands picked up, one after the other, strands of the golden, bulky hair, and the girl had an unpleasant feeling of emptiness around her shoulders, while upswept combs and pins were stuck in at the top of her head.

She thought: 'I shall see — oh, horror — some respectable Southern society lady, instead of the carefree girl from England, happy and free, with her riding hat pulled down over her nose, and her hair blowing in the wind . . .'

'You can look now,' said Jemima at last.

Elizabeth opened her eyes and saw someone whom she did not know, but who had a kind and timid smile, not at all a society lady, but a delightful young person wearing a cap of golden curls that hung down in venturesome locks above her ears. Her heart throbbed:

'Hello, you,' she said.

When she finally turned round to thank Jemima, the latter was already half-way through the door.

'My compliments, Jemima,' exclaimed Elizabeth, 'and thank you.'

'Oh, Miss, I was only doing my job.'

She disappeared immediately, and the door closed again.

Elizabeth's sheepish look was revealing, for, if Jemima spurned compliments, it was not a matter of indifference to the English girl. She was so pleased with her new hairstyle that she wanted to show it off at all costs. She had a premonition that a new life was opening up before her. She had thrown off a seductive but ridiculous personality. She would no longer play out on the world's stage the role of a retarded adolescent. With her long dress and this wonderful entwining of curls that clasped her head in a golden bonnet, she could face up to the future. Jonathan would not recognize her.

Jonathan. That name brought her to a halt. She hesitated for a moment then went downstairs. Jonathan was far away, even further away than usual through the simple fact of this transformation.

She saw no one outside. Amelia and her husband were having a prolonged siesta. It was cold. She looked into the distance towards the long, yellow house, memories immediately assailed her and her heart was heavy in her breast. Had she not given him up? She felt the need to say it again, firmly.

The call of crows around the house heralded winter, and the Indian summer's splendid leaves were beginning to be scattered at the bases of the great trees. The melancholy countryside of this time was decked out with a poignant beauty. Exuberance was withdrawing from life. She went back into the house to get a shawl. She already had her foot on the first step when Betty appeared behind her in a red smock.

On seeing her, the old black woman uttered a cry and trembled. In her furrowed face, surprise was turning to fear.

'Well, Betty, what's the matter with you? Anyone would think you'd seen a ghost.'

'Oh, Miss Lizbeth,' exclaimed Betty, 'it's you! You surely does look beautiful!'

In this flight of admiration, Elizabeth foresaw years of happiness. Her only regret was that this first homage had come from the lowest echelons of society, but almost immediately she felt herself blush with shame. Leaning over Betty, she supported her.

'Do you think I look better like this, dear Betty?'

Betty then began to stammer incomprehensible words; it emerged from all this babble that she was proud of her mistress.

'Well then, calm yourself, and be as nice as you were at Dimwood. Go quickly now and fetch my big gray shawl. I'm cold.'

'Miss Charlotte want to speak to you,' said Betty, clutching onto the rail to climb up the steps.

When she was at the top, she added with a laugh:

'The basket full of apples can break your back.'

'You should have told me!' exclaimed the girl.

But the old servant had already gone. Elizabeth could

hear the shuffle of her soft shoes on the hall floor.

She waited. Something was happening inside her: she no longer saw herself as the same person she had admired an hour earlier in her mirror. Extreme discomfort was the result, and she was in a hurry for Betty to come back. She was not long. With the gray shawl folded over her arm, she tripped down the steps with a big, toothy grin.

The girl took the shawl and wrapped herself in it; it was a Scottish shawl, and at the back the point hung right down as far as her ankles.

'You know, Betty,' she said softly, 'there is another maid to take care of me and my needs, but you'll always be my favorite. Do you understand?'

That face, so ill-treated by age and by work, looked up at her. It was almost more than the English girl could bear. Betty's love asked for nothing and gave everything. Getting a grip on herself, she adopted her usual tone of voice:

'Where is Miss Charlotte?'

Betty waved in the direction of outside.

'She was in the kitchen but she gone off,' she said almost in a whisper.

'I'll look for her. You rest, I'll tell them to leave you alone.'

'Thank you, Miss Lizbeth.'

She took a few steps beneath the trees in front of the house but saw no one. The wind had dropped. A walk in the long avenue that snaked around the meadow seemed to her the best means of recovery.

She was longing for a cup of tea. The season, the coolness of the air, everything conspired to this end. She did not like to go back and give orders for tea to be served to her all alone in the sitting room. They would undoubtedly have done so, but the solitary nature of life in the country was becoming a problem. In Savannah, and even at Dimwood, balls were held. She missed the balls. She wanted to show herself off. That was new. Her heart belonged to Jonathan, but she could not hide herself away from the world like some precious object in a glass case. On the tips of her fingers, she counted off the number of men who had courted her since her arrival in America. First of all, the poor blind angel with such a pretty face when he took his eyeglasses off. Then Fred, poor Fred, so determined and so upright, but still poor Fred. Then dazzling Daniel, whose frantic love letter would remain for ever unanswered, poor thing. All three had a right to the same description: they were victims.

She suddenly had the impression that the cold air was rubbing her cheeks in order to drag her out of her dreams and bring her back to reality. In front of her, like some hallucination, she saw Betty's black eyes, speaking of nothing but love in their unfathomable simplicity.

Her disquiet brought her to a sudden halt. It seemed to her that she was being shown all the latent frivolity within her. Her long skirt and her elegant hairstyle changed nothing. Her infatuations were those of a child. Only Jonathan might have made an adult of her, but Jonathan was far away. She recalled once more the passion that burned in his face, in that avid look which took hold of her with the brutality of a wild cat. And then with what tenderness he would fulfil her yearning . . .

'Jonathan,' she groaned.

And as irony always had the last word with her, she gave a sad little laugh and commented:

'Rather ridiculous, a girl in a long dress on a path in Virginia calling out to a gentleman in Vienna . . .'

She turned in her tracks.

As she was going in through the verandah door, she almost knocked over Miss Charlotte.

'Well now!' exclaimed the latter readjusting her bonnet, 'I was looking for Elizabeth and I find myself face to face with a ravishing stranger. Don't let's stay here, it's starting to get cold. Amelia and Charlie are in the drawing room, drinking tea in front of a wood fire.'

Too cross to answer, Elizabeth followed Miss Charlotte and indeed found the two people in question in front of a splendid log fire . . . Amidst a bright crackling, the flames leapt and contorted themselves in the fireplace. The large room had lost something of its showy nobility, becoming alive and almost cosy, for long, red velvet curtains concealed the tall windows, keeping the gentle warmth between the walls.

Seated in large armchairs on either side of the fire-place, Charlie Jones and his wife exuded a mature conjugal bliss. Right beside them, a heavy silver teapot was enthroned on a side table amidst plates full of biscuits, scones and muffins.

Elizabeth was greeted by an astonished silence. Feeling nervous and intimidated, she took a few steps forward, accompanied by Miss Charlotte:

'Here she is,' said the latter with a big smile.

Amelia put down her cup and looked at the English girl.

'What do you think?' asked Charlie Jones.

'Very proper,' said Amelia.

Charlie Jones leapt out of his armchair and took both of Elizabeth's hands in his own:

'My dear child, you are exquisite, exquisitely *chic* and *bon ton.*'

These foreign words made Amelia frown, for they were evocative of Paris, that city doomed to perdition.

'I think you exaggerate,' she said.

A piercing cry from Charlotte went right up to the ceiling.

'Exaggerate! It is completely successful. Turn round, Elizabeth.'

'No,' the latter said, 'I want a cup of tea.'

'Oh, we're unforgivable,' exclaimed Uncle Charlie. 'Charlotte, I beg you, attach yourself to the bell rope and call Miranda.'

He himself drew up two armchairs. Elizabeth and Charlotte sat down.

'We were actually talking about you,' continued Uncle Charlie. 'This tea party is for the children opposite . . . Young Elsie is coming with her fiancé, and a friend whose name escapes me but who, they say, comes from a good family. Will two pies be enough, Charlotte?'

'I shall make three!' exclaimed the valiant spinster.

Miranda appeared. In a white lace apron, this young, pale, coffee-colored woman responded to the demands of the current vogue. Her face was exceptionally slender, and her bearing denied the epithet 'slave'. Grave and silent, she waited for Charlie to give the necessary orders and then withdrew without a sound.

Elizabeth was looking pensively into the fire and did not

take part in the conversation, which hovered between platitudes concerning the season and preparations for Christmas.
According to the farmers who had been watching the behavior of livestock in the fields, the winter would be a hard
one and there would be snow before long. On the 25th of
December there would be turkey, and everyone was counting
on Charlotte for the pudding to be flambéed with rum. Out
of habit, Amelia made some disparaging comment about the
North.

'It will be like this all my life,' Elizabeth said to herself,
'unless something happens and Jonathan comes back. And
what then?' She dreamt of him running away with her . . .
but where to?

At that point, she heard Charlie Jones telling her in his
smooth voice, which was reserved for occasions demanding
diplomatic subtlety:

'My dear wife and I propose giving you another bedroom,
more spacious and more pleasant than your present little
one.'

'But I like my room,' said Elizabeth in a spirit of contra-
diction and independence, 'I'm attached to it as to a friend.'

'Fool,' she thought, 'you hate it. Let them go ahead.'

'You'll change your mind when you see the one we're
offering you.'

'Alongside ours,' said Amelia in a tone that was both
tender and sentimental.

'A witch's brew,' said Charlotte pouring the tea, 'something to give us strength.'

'You would have done well to give some to my poor Betty,
who still hasn't got over her fatigue.'

The reply came like a deafening cry:

'I know, I was wrong, I imagined she was more robust,
that basket of apples will press down on my conscience with
its full weight.'

Charlie Jones waved his arms, trying to get a word in.

'Betty will work no more,' he exclaimed. 'She's at the end
of her tether, I'll see to her.'

Elizabeth suddenly perked up:

'You're not going to take her away from me, are you?' she
exclaimed.

'No, not if you're fond of her, but it would be more

reasonable to send her back to Dimwood.'

'She wasn't happy at Dimwood, she told me so.'

'Can I do any better? I'll give her to you. You can set her free if you want. She's yours.'

'Set her free? Where would she go? She wants to stay here.'

He waved his arms like a barrister:

'That sums up the whole of the slave problem. They run away and a lot of them come back, because they don't know where to go.'

'Charlie,' said Amelia in a plaintive voice, 'let's talk about something else.'

And as if to comfort herself, she added in a murmur:

'In any case, we're sure they'll never rebel.'

'Such has been the daily litany of the South for the last thirty years,' said Charlie Jones, while Miss Charlotte, leaning over the gold-speckled tray, stirred the tea to make it stronger.

'There you are, a slave owner,' she said to Elizabeth with a laugh, 'and what are you going to do with her?'

'She's not my slave, she'll take care of my linen, and I like her company.'

This reply was delivered drily and did not displease Miss Charlotte.

'Bravo,' she said, 'that's straight speaking. Can't I offer you anything?'

'Nothing, thank you, the tea is perfect, but I'm not hungry.'

'I'll say it quietly, but you look glum.'

'Perhaps. I think something is in the offing.'

'A premonition? I have them every day — for something is in the offing every day. A premonition . . .'

Elizabeth had the feeling that the supernatural constituted some kind of threat, and she preferred to keep quiet.

In the large fireplace, flames were dancing more restrainedly now, but with the help of the heat Amelia and Charlie Jones sank into their armchairs, and their steady and ever deeper breathing confirmed that they were at the edge of sleep. Miss Charlotte deemed the conditions right for confidences of a serious kind and she whispered:

'We're going to find you a *beau* — a serious, respectable

one, not like the other.'

Leaning over the tray a little, she ventured under her breath:

'Has your mother instructed you in what every young lady should know?'

Elizabeth recoiled in horror:

'Charlotte!' she exclaimed.

'Alright,' said Charlotte with a smile, 'that's all I wanted to know.'

Quite still, the English girl pretended to be looking into the fire and did not answer. Time passed in silence.

83

The light was fading. Fortified by her afternoon nap, Amelia declared that she wished to take Elizabeth to her new room alone.

'Already?' said Elizabeth.

'Yes, my child. Everything was seen to this afternoon. The clothes, the contents of your chest of drawers and the cupboards, your toilet articles, everything. Oh, you'll be pleased.'

As she spoke these words, she looked and sounded like some munificent but unbending sovereign. Her large, lace-trimmed cap added to the majesty of her mien. In spite of herself, Elizabeth wondered about the amorous passion that she inspired in Charlie Jones, but that was verging on a mystery that was no concern of hers. Young ladies were forbidden to imagine certain things.

What is more, she was concerned with other matters at that precise moment. Actions had been taken without consulting her, as if for a poor relation. Despite the affirmations and formal promises of Uncle Charlie, her status had not changed. Over and above the will of that gentleman who presided over an all-powerful export business, there was the capricious will of this rather imposing lady.

She fumed in silence as she followed Amelia, moving slowly in her flounced brown dress edged in black. Her ridiculous little child's room was like a nest to her, a shelter against the world, almost a hiding place where she felt at ease. What surprise was in store for her now?

As she passed her door she could not refrain from asking:

'Who took charge of my things?'

Amelia was a little breathless.

'Jemima,' she said at last.

Always Jemima! Without another word they entered the long corridor which was poorly lit by oil lamps fixed to the walls. Passing by Miss Charlotte's door, Amelia simply said:

'Dear little Charlotte, I'm sure she's gone back to her beloved kitchens. Charlotte is a saint.'

Elizabeth made no comment. The next door was that of a guest room, empty at present; after which, on the other side of the corridor, and set well back, a wider double door.

'Our room,' said Amelia with almost religious solemnity. A few steps further on, she announced in a slightly amused tone of voice:

'Miss Escridge's room.'

They went in. The room was high-ceilinged and dark. An oil lamp on a side table was doing battle with the onset of twilight, but a log fire in the brick fireplace cast great patches of light that flickered over the walls. Elizabeth worked out that she was in one of the two gables of Great Meadow, and her eyes sought out the furniture in this room of rather disconcerting size. White curtains betrayed the presence of a four-poster bed. The rest was left to her imagination. The thing that was most visible was the side table covered with a red mat. In the softened rays of the little lamp, a thick open Bible invited meditation.

In this large space, voices echoed with a particular intensity and bestowed on the simplest of phrases a gravity which they did not deserve:

'I admit that in this light, there is nothing cheerful about the room, but in daylight you will be delighted. It's the finest room in Great Meadow, along with ours.'

Standing next to the side table, she was making an effort

— 673 —

to smile. Her face, struck by the lamplight, nevertheless remained as motionless as that of a statue. With a furtive gesture, she rummaged in a bag attached to her dress.

'Come here,' she said.

A little unwillingly, Elizabeth took a couple of steps forward.

'My dear child,' said Amelia, 'if I wanted to be alone with you up until this point, it is for a reason whose moral import you will appreciate — yes, moral. Just now in the drawing room, I spoke to you rather unkindly about your hair and your dress.'

'I don't remember,' said Elizabeth, feeling uncomfortable at this embarrassing humility.

'Yes, I spoke coldly and drily, I hurt your feelings, my conscience cries out to me as much. Take this honey sweet and let's make it up, shall we?'

Between her pointed fingers, she held out a sweet that she had taken from a small tin. Elizabeth looked at it and was paralyzed with disgust.

'Take it, my child, else I shan't sleep a wink all night.'

The girl took the sweet and, at that very moment, two words implanted themselves in her mind in large letters: 'run away'.

'Thank you,' exclaimed Amelia, 'thanks be to you and to Heaven that unites hearts in a common purpose of charity. I have been relieved of an unbearable weight. And now, my little one, stay there for a while in this big rocking chair.'

Grasping hold of the lamp, she held it up to show Elizabeth a comfortable chair upholstered in crimson velvet and mounted on huge rockers that promised heady rocking.

'Won't you sit down? To please me . . .'

Elizabeth sat down with the sweet in the palm of her hand.

'Don't worry,' said Amelia, 'I'm going to leave you in the dark for a moment, but don't be afraid. There are no ghosts in this part of the house. I shall be close by in any case. I'm going to have a look at your little washroom, just to make sure that everything is in order and that nothing is missing.'

Elizabeth saw her cross the whole length of the room, and suddenly the little light moving through the darkness disappeared behind a curtain. There was a noise of quickly closed drawers, then that of a door, undoubtedly a little medicine cupboard that stayed open longer. Elizabeth threw the sweet under the table.

At last the lamp began to shine in the room again, held, it seemed, in a less steady hand. One might even have said that it was shaking, and soon Amelia was standing in front of the English girl who gave her a chill look.

'Our Jemima is really perfection,' said Amelia with a laugh, 'she can be relied on.'

She laughed again with evident satisfaction and put the lamp back on the table.

'We dine in an hour,' she continued. 'You can stay here if you wish, or come down to the sitting room. As for me, I shall take a little rest in my room. I am prone, as they must have told you, to strange bouts of tiredness.'

She went slowly over to the door. Elizabeth was waiting only for the moment when she would see her go. Her eyes followed her, but Amelia still had a few pronouncements to make.

'Do you remember, my child, that walk in the delightful park in Savannah?'

Elizabeth remembered it.

'We told each other things that will, I hope, have a bearing on your life. I gave you my affection and requested your confidence. Don't forget: confidence! My dear Charlie and I will take care of you, of your happiness . . .'

She stopped for a moment and added:

'. . . of your honor.'

'My what?' exclaimed Elizabeth.

In the half-light, Amelia turned towards her a colorless face, and her quiet voice let drop a phrase of weighty brevity:

'Your conscience will instruct you, my child.'

With these words she left the room and set off down the corridor that she seemed to fill momentously.

Left alone, the girl flung herself into the red velvet rocking chair and rocked herself violently backwards and forwards for several minutes.

She suddenly stood up and went to pull the bell rope near the fireplace. Time passed and then the door opened . . . At first Elizabeth could see only a long white apron. She recognized Jemima.

'Where are my things, Jemima? Where are the cupboards?'

'There aren't any cupboards here, Miss. I put everything

into two big wardrobes. Do you wish to see?'

'No. Are you going to see to me here?'

'No, Miss. I'm not a chambermaid. Today was exceptional. Mrs Amelia gave me orders.'

'Do you know where Miss Charlotte is?'

'I met her downstairs just now. She begged me to tell you that she would be up to see you, and for you to wait for her.'

'Very well.'

'May I go?'

'Yes . . . No, stay. I don't like this room, Jemima.'

Why had she said that? She was no longer in control of herself.

There was a silence, then Jemima's careful voice asked:

'Will there be anything else, Miss?'

Elizabeth shook her head. Jemima withdrew.

84

Charlotte did not keep her waiting. Fussing and inquisitive, she came in brusquely, with her bonnet askew, a sign of heavy weather.

'So this is where our dear sister has put you.'

Her voice rose up to the ceiling, making Elizabeth shudder as she was immersed in her thoughts in front of the fire.

'What do you think of it, Charlotte?'

'Several things at once. Firstly, without actually being next door to the nuptial holy of holies, you are quite close to it. Secondly — but bring the lamp over — no, I'm not going out of my mind: they've had the lock unscrewed. No more key, no more lock. My dear little thing, you'll be a prisoner.'

'Charlotte, you can see that I'm upset and unhappy, why do you tell me these things I don't understand?'

'You're no stupider than the next person. Think a while. As for being upset and unhappy, I won't be having that. You forget that Charlotte is here to look after you.'

Elizabeth stamped her foot.

'No, Charlotte, do you hear? There are already two of them keeping an eye on me.'

'There now, you're beginning to understand. Anyone can come into your room, as into a public thoroughfare, since there is no lock. There is nothing to protect you from their constant solicitude. A key is a right to a private life.'

'But I was alright in my little room, and they left me alone. What have I done wrong?'

'Nothing, but since then something came. A letter.'

'A letter. Yes, a letter. So?'

'So, that letter made the mistake of coming from Annapolis.'

'They didn't read it.'

'That's as well.'

'But Uncle Charlie told me that I had the right to receive letters from whomsoever I wished . . . Why aren't you saying anything?'

'You can receive letters from every part of the world, but the postmark Annapolis annoyed him.'

'For what reason?'

'Be patient, you'll understand soon.'

'I've had enough, Charlotte, I don't want to stay here any more.'

'And where would you go? To Dimwood?'

'They don't want me at Dimwood. They more or less told me so to my face.'

'Not everybody.'

'I know whom you're thinking of, but I'm not in love . . .'

'Because you love someone else.'

'Be quiet, Charlotte!'

These words escaped her like a cry, and she was just as taken aback by them as the elderly spinster who nonetheless did not flinch.

There was a silence, then Charlotte's voice was heard, but very softly.

'Does that mean that you love him, to speak to little Charlotte like that?'

Elizabeth held back her tears.

'I apologize, Charlotte.'

'You have no need to apologize, I understand very well.'
Elizabeth blew her nose hard.

'In this house, people are apologizing and saying sorry from dawn to dusk. It gets on my nerves. Just now, Amelia, with a sweet . . .'

'What? She played the honey sweet trick on you? It's better to laugh at such things, Elizabeth. I knew you're in love, everything about you tells me so: your voice, your eyes, your gestures, you give yourself away all the time. I've been in love too, I know what it's like, but silence on that score.'

She took the lamp which the girl had put back on the side table.

'Follow me,' she said.

With prudent but careful steps, she headed straight for the washroom. There she handed the lamp to Elizabeth and opened the door of the little medicine cupboard.

She moved the bottles and packets around for several minutes and then suddenly closed the door with a cry:

'That's too much! She has taken away the phial of laudanum that I prepared for you myself. Now I understand why she was so keen to be alone with you. Let's get out of here. Walk ahead with the lamp. I'll follow. I need to go and recover in the rocking chair.'

They reached the middle of the room, and once more the lamp was placed alongside the Bible. With her cheeks even pinker than usual, the elderly spinster settled down in the rocking chair which Elizabeth set in motion.

'I forgive her,' said Miss Charlotte, 'because the temptation was more than she could bear, but I'm ashamed. The drug made her furtive. She's worthy of better than that. You should not judge her.'

'I wouldn't think of it, especially as I can manage quite well without laudanum.'

'Do you take it sometimes?'

'Not really, no more than anybody else. I have bad memories from the first time.'

'Undoubtedly too strong a dose. I'll explain it to you, it's best you know.'

'I thought I was doing as Mama did.'

'Ah, your mother is an expert. She knows. There are ways of doing it.'

'I shall learn them. There are times when . . .'

'That's true, but moderation above all, moderation! When I think of that bottle which was as perfectly measured out . . . I had prepared it as I would for myself, for I don't trust the pharmacy. But I'll make you some more, and I'll teach you how to do it yourself.'

The silence was interrupted only by the creaking of floorboards beneath the rocking chair. Elizabeth had sat down on a chair near Miss Charlotte. The fire was slowly going out, and the lamp created a haven of light around these two women in the large, shadowy expanse.

'Life,' said Miss Charlotte in a pensive tone. 'It's a good job there is laudanum to help us put up with it . . .'

Her gaze wandered over to the large open book beside her, and she gave a kind of jump.

'. . . and the Holy Bible, of course, Elizabeth.'

'Yes, oh, yes,' said the English girl.

She reflected for a moment, and what remained in her of childhood inspired these words:

'I wonder what they used to do in Old Testament times.'

The evening was gloomy. Amelia did not put in an appearance and Charlie Jones seemed disappointed at Elizabeth's silence on the subject of her new room. Did she not like it?

'A trifle dark,' said the girl.

'I'll have two four-branched candelabras put there. Tomorrow morning you'll be able to see how fine it is, a real lady's room, and you'll have Miranda to look after you, a treasure.'

'Oh, no,' said Elizabeth in an animated manner. 'I'm keeping Betty.'

'Poor Betty is no longer up to it.'

'Since she belongs to me, I'll let her decide.'

'As you like, but Miranda has more to offer.'

'That makes no difference to me, Uncle Charlie.'

'I understand, but it was my wife's idea . . .'

7
WOMAN

85

*T*he following morning Elizabeth was in her sumptuous
new bedroom when Barnaby brought her a letter. The
tray not being available at that moment, he presented it to
her in the old style, on his three-cornered coachman's hat.

She dismissed him and settled down in an armchair near
the window. On the postmark she could clearly make out
Macon — and Macon could only be Dimwood. The name
and address were written in a delicate hand, a little on the
ornamental side in imitation of high society.

'It's her,' the girl said aloud.

Tearing the envelope, she had to control her agitated
spirits in order to understand what she had before her eyes:

Dimwood, 5th of December 1850
Dear Miss Escridge,

(*There was a large space to show respect.*)

You do great honor to the Dimwood governess in confiding your personal difficulties to her with such refreshing simplicity. For my part, I shall make every effort to
place myself in your position, for your young soul has a
right to every consideration.

Having said that, your letter is stiff and clumsy! Did they
not teach you in England any elegant turns of phrase, to
keep an eye on the sequence of ideas, to regulate the
harmonious flow of words, in short, Miss Escridge,
how to write?

The South will teach you how to embellish your style.
This evening, your humble servant is going to help you
to see more clearly into your personal life. First of all,
your innocence. It worries me. They have allowed you to
grow up in an ignorance of life that makes me tremble. I
am not speaking of certain trials, the inexorable return
of which is the curse of our sex. You're blushing, you
have understood, I'll move on. Permit me to be brutally
frank, as brutal as the truth.

At this point, the girl dropped the letter and hid her face in her hands as she groaned:

'Horror!' she said aloud. 'Horror! Here I am, dishonored on account of that letter which, in my weakness, I sent her, and she dares to criticize me . . . She herself writes like a scullery maid on holiday, with ribbons stuck in her hair which she thinks will make her look like a lady . . .'

She gave free rein to her indignation for several minutes. Finally she picked up the letter, and, curiosity getting the better of disgust, she continued reading:

First of all, some advice. Without really knowing why, you guess that with your long hair and flowing skirts you arouse the attention of men susceptible to the dubious charm of young girls. Your eyes are popping out of your head and you don't understand. Never mind. Believe me, you urgently need to become a woman.

'It's done, you old wretch,' muttered Elizabeth.

You already have several victims on your conscience. The first one, you know, lives a very long way away from here but can communicate with me. I await news from him about his whirlwind existence. They must without a doubt still remember you despite their pleasures.

Allow me to tell you, however, that what attracts him in you is not a vulgar trick of the senses. Do you even know what that means? He loves in you that unblemished Elizabeth and her girlish arrogance. I know what I'm talking about, you can be sure. For the moment, what dazzles and provokes him is that rarity of innocence which you possess. Understand me (if you can . . .). I am no saint, neither are you, but in the most corrupt of men there remains, somewhere in the depths of their being, a nostalgia for their ideal, and you are that man's ideal. What will be left if you give in to him? The situation is most delicate, and here I am obliged, once more, to face up to your delicate nature.

'Alas,' thought Elizabeth. 'That woman frightens me.'

Face, eyes, all that may be dazzling, it's the sun shining on the façade of a palace. But that's not the real man. It shows what might flatter the eyes and win hearts . . . You only see men dressed. Don't tell me that statues from the Ancient World in museums show them differently, and that you know. You know nothing. Statues lie. I admire the good sense of your prudish English Mamas and the advice they give their daughters on the eve of their wedding: 'Close your eyes and think of England.' Personally, I should prefer to think of the Devil, being Welsh.

Elizabeth jumped to her feet and cried:
'She's the Devil!'
In the large, silent room, these words rang out in an unexpected way, almost rousing from their deep sleep walls that were suddenly listening. The girl took a few steps and stopped in front of the window. Beneath a low sky strewn with gray clouds, the cedar held out its black branches. With her heart in the grip of an inexplicable sadness, she cast her eyes over the pages of the letter that had fallen at her feet. She wondered if it were not better to tear it up without reading it. What that woman was saying seemed both unworthy and obscure.

Several long minutes went by before she regained her calm, then once more the uncontrollable desire to know more made her pick up the letter. Turning her head aside a little as if from some unclean object, she read the next lines that were underlined twice:

. . . for some women, Miss Elizabeth, it is Hell.

Her eyes blurred, she jumped two lines and made out:

too violent a contrast between the face and that horrific sight . . . you would not be able to bear it.

'What does she mean?' she murmured. 'I'd rather not know.'
She noticed that her hand was trembling slightly and thought:
'What am I afraid of? She's not near me. At a distance,

she does not exist.'

She carried on reading, and this caught her eye:

Do you really believe that he will respect your fine and vulnerable soul? Desire makes a man like him lose his mind. You don't know what you're letting yourself in for if you allow him to write to you, nor into what disaster it might lead you, for he will write, you can be sure.

She moved straight on to the following lines:

For my part, I cannot and do not wish to become a party to a correspondence which is nothing less than criminal, given your age and the legal situation of the person who would be writing to you. For it concerns a husband. Think about it before writing back to me. I will, from time to time, let you have news of Dimwood if you so desire, and this is all that your faithful servant can do for you.

Maisie Llewelyn

P.S. You will burn this letter of course. Do not hide the one you will find enclosed. You can leave it open on your writing desk, for example . . .

There was, indeed, another letter inside the envelope. Elizabeth read it immediately.

Dimwood, 5 December 1850

Dear Miss Escridge,

As I gathered that you would like to know what has been happening at Dimwood since you left, it is a pleasure for me to be able to tell you that nearly everybody has been missing you. The young ladies are bored without you and, now that you are no longer here, the grown-ups sing your praises. I should not omit to tell you — and I think you will be pleased — that Mr Hargrove has regained his former composure. He says twice as many prayers.

Prepare yourself now for more melancholy news. Poor Mr Fred threw himself out of his bedroom window when he saw the carriage taking you to Savannah. It's a miracle he was not killed. The edge of the verandah roof broke his fall, but he nevertheless fell to the ground in a sorry state. He was immediately taken to hospital at Macon, where he pulled through after a painful operation, but he will limp all his life. People talk about an accident. They are wrong. He was in love, and he wanted to die. Draw whatever conclusions you like. He has silenced himself and does not talk, the only thing he says is that if he can still get on a horse, he'll go and get himself killed in the cavalry fighting the North, and he is expecting war.

Have I told you everything? I think so. Don't take advantage of your power over boys who are likely to take life rather too seriously. If you feel like dropping me a line, you would give pleasure to

Your humble servant,
Maisie Llewelyn

The girl folded the letter and closed her eyes.

Fred. She had not understood. Without being at all attracted by him, she was aware of his love and had felt a little sadness on parting, although one that was quite quickly forgotten.

'But after all, he's not dead,' she said aloud, as if answering someone.

'In any case,' she thought, 'there's a letter I can show if anyone asks me.'

It was clever of Miss Llewelyn to have thought of that . . . Could one offer one's services so unambiguously while adopting such a moral tone? The very word "accomplice" is a masterpiece of duplicity. An accomplice? That is what she wants.

There followed a moment of singular exaltation. She felt she had become different from what she had been earlier. Instead of the hesitant Elizabeth, facing the future with perplexity, now, walking up and down in that room of such imposing proportions, there was a determined young woman proud of the confidence in herself which she was just discovering.

It was possible to write to Jonathan. She hesitated, however. Her letter would pass through the hands of the Welshwoman, whose role would be to forward it to its recipient, over there in Vienna. It was a dangerous business, for if, as Maisie Llewelyn had vulgarly put it, there was a husband involved, there was also a wife, and what more formidable wife than Annabel? If Annabel were to intercept a letter and read it . . . But even worse, what if the Welshwoman, instead of forwarding the letter from Dimwood to Vienna, kept it herself for some purpose?

Elizabeth suddenly began to flounder in this dubious adventure. It was at that moment that she heard a calm, reasonable voice rising out of the silence to tell her:

'Dare.'

86

The milder turn in the weather announced by Charlie Jones set in that very afternoon. They were able to walk in the countryside with as much pleasure as in October. Coats and shawls were left in the downstairs cloakroom.

Never had life at Great Meadow seemed sweeter in its passive immobility. The approach of Christmas was undoubtedly making itself felt. *Peace on earth.* Great Meadow was, it seemed, playing its part.

Then suddenly, on the 23rd of December, amidst an unimaginable hullabaloo, the whole house seemed full of young men. In reality there were only three of them, but one had the impression that they were all over the place.

With her usual authority, reinforced by her strident voice, Miss Charlotte rounded them up at the bottom of the stairs and headed them off towards the drawing room where Charlie Jones was awaiting them. Most majestic in his black morning coat, but with his pink cheeks furrowed by the traditional smile that retained its freshness despite long years of use, he welcomed them with that paternal *bonhomie* which, a trifle heavy-handed, masked the latent terror of an iron hand. In short, he received them politely.

'Great Meadow is all yours, gentlemen. I hope you will be happy here. Ned, what are you waiting for? Introduce me to your friends.'

Ned came forward. He was built like his father, with the same vigor that broadened the shoulders and gave a bloom to the complexion. His thick, black hair flowed in shiny locks over his ears, and his brown eyes smiled beneath a broad, smooth forehead. A certain gaucheness gave away distant origins on the land that a career spent entirely in the city had eliminated in Charlie Jones. The resemblance between them was surprising, like a well-made copy of a portrait, and the handsomeness of the father was passed on to the face of the son with the full aura of youth restored.

'My friend Christopher Hughes, known as Kit,' he announced.

A tall, flamboyant, fair-haired boy bowed to Charlie Jones. His carefully-cut black suit was not entirely successful in making him look serious. His magnificent blue eyes were on the look-out for adventure. There was nothing he could do about it, even in the formal drawing room where this important gentleman was crushing him beneath the weight of his dignity. He was evidently a born seducer. He uttered his thanks in a slightly sing-song voice.

Another smile from Charlie Jones thanked him, and Ned seized the arm of his second friend who was much shyer and tongue-tied.

'Teddy Brown, quite simply,' Ned announced.

'Why quite simply?' asked Charlie Jones with an almighty frown . . . 'Mr Teddy Brown, it's an honor to see you here.'

What Mr Teddy Brown would have liked above all else would have been to vanish through the floor, for he could think of nothing to say.

'May I ask you to come forward a little? Your modesty is keeping you too far back.'

Teddy Brown came within six feet of Charlie Jones. Thin and quite short, he had an almond-shaped face and would have been handsome if his splendid eyes, like sapphires, had not been too close together. This insufficient distance created an effect that one dared not smile at: Teddy Brown gave a slight impression of squinting. That was the cause of his dramatic and awesome shyness.

Charlie Jones immediately grasped the situation by intuition.

'How long have you been at the university, Mr Brown?'

Teddy Brown made an effort:

'I'm in my second year,' he answered.

'Would it be indiscreet to enquire which profession you envisage entering? If my question is too personal . . .'

'No,' said the voice, which was suddenly firmer, 'teaching, but I'm waiting until the end of my studies to make a final decision.'

At that moment Miss Charlotte, who had been standing in the middle of the room, came up to him, feeling an immediate sympathy towards the young student. She guessed that he was lonely.

'Come,' said Charlie Jones, 'I'm going to get our Barnaby to show you to your rooms. Yours is a double room, Ned, you can share with one of your friends.'

'With me!' said Kit Hughes in animated fashion. 'Won't you, Ned?'

'Since you have already decided the matter,' said Ned patiently.

'You will have the more pleasant room, Mr Brown, the one overlooking the hills, but you will be on your own.'

'I accept with pleasure,' said Teddy Brown.

He had spoken these few words with such charming simplicity that, growing bolder, Miss Charlotte took him discreetly to one side. A little embarrassed, he looked at this small, smiling person whose wrinkled face was looking at him attentively. The boy was intrigued above all by the bonnet, which was large and out of proportion to her slight figure.

'Just now you said you were perhaps thinking of the teaching profession.'

'Yes, madam.'

'Don't call me madam,' she said with a laugh, 'I am doomed to remain for ever single. Your "perhaps" made me wonder whether you had ever thought of anything else?'

Teddy Brown blushed and remained silent.

'It's alright,' she said, 'I understand. One day I'll tell you what I have in mind for you. It will be our secret.'

While this exchange was taking place in a conspiratorial

tone of voice, Kit Hughes followed the trail of his aspirations for the future.

'As for me, it'll be the theatre, acting . . .'

'I would have sworn on it,' said Uncle Charlie with a toothy grin. 'Keep an eye on Barnaby and look after your guests, Ned.'

Ned's and Kit's room had the same view of the woods which had delighted Elizabeth when she had been accommodated on that side. Now she was on the other side of the house

As for Teddy Brown, he was on the top floor, just above the small drawing room where Miss Charlotte had read and ferociously analyzed Lieutenant De Witt's love letter. From his window, the student with sapphire eyes could also contemplate the blue hills that restored peace to troubled souls, but Teddy Brown was not happy. He had few friends at university. On account of that perhaps, he had found himself invited to spend a few days at Great Meadow, one of Ned's foolish ideas, for he wanted above all to please him, and even to make him happier. There was no saying no to Ned.

The case of Christopher Hughes, known as Kit, was quite different. If he was sharing Ned's room, he did so by right. That was his way. The proud aura of youth, a certain prestige due to his glibness of tongue, a foolhardiness always verging on insolence, made some people admire him, while others had a poor opinion of him. His barely concealed wish to get on in the world had nurtured in him an urge to be invited by one of the most famous men in the South. How had Ned managed to give in to his repeated, almost imploring requests? He himself was not too sure; the fear of disappointing, perhaps, and above all of humiliating a classmate by a refusal. Besides, his conversation was amusing.

A little after six o'clock in the evening, Barnaby, wearing his green livery, knocked on the boys' doors, and a quarter of an hour later everybody appeared in the drawing room. Ned and Kit were very elegant in their black suits. Teddy Brown's attire was less well cut, but decent.

Wearing a dress of deep pomegranate-colored silk, Amelia received them hospitably, but without warmth, for she recoiled instinctively from youth which was, in her opinion, ready to spread chaos. Her own stepson did not escape these dark suspicions. She gratified him with no more than a firm smile and told him in a flat voice, by way of a welcome:

'You're looking more and more like your father.'

An almost animal fear seemed to engulf her. She trembled at the thought that there might be more talk of the threat of war, which was rearing its head again.

Charlie Jones, who was observing her out of the corner of his eye, was liberal with his good humor and laughed at everything. A sort of procession was forming to go into the dining room, when Miss Charlotte uttered a stifled cry.

At that very moment, the English girl had slid into the room, as if to avoid being seen. She had just come from Jemima who had redone her hair as a goldsmith works at a crown. A dress of sumptuous taffeta heightened the freshness of her complexion, and, framed by the red hangings in the doorway, her beauty provoked a total silence. Deep emotion brightened the sparkle in her eyes, and an incandescent radiance seemed to emanate from her: through her intermediary at Dimwood she had just had her first news from Jonathan.

The three students looked at her as at an apparition. A kind of embarrassment set in, which would have become intolerable if Charlie Jones' laugh had not shattered the sudden paralysis of all those present. Elizabeth shuddered as if she had been dragged from sleep.

'I'm sorry,' she said.

'Don't apologize, we're delighted,' said Uncle Charlie. 'Elizabeth, I introduce my son Ned ... Ned, our cousin Elizabeth Escridge.'

Ned came over to bow somewhat awkwardly; he was lacking in that gracefulness which came naturally to many of his age.

Then came Kit with his winning smile bearing the blazing mass of his splendid dishevelled red hair.

Finally Teddy, who appeared and disappeared like a wild animal seized with terror.

She looked at them all, but saw none of them. She was elsewhere, in the intoxication of a May night, searching for a face stretched up towards hers, overwhelmed by love amongst the leaves of a magnolia tree. Would she ever recapture that moment? There would be others, never the same, not like the first one ... What was she doing here, sitting at this table, where lamps illuminated people who belonged to this unpoetic world? Lost in her inner vision, she was content to look indifferent, but Miss Charlotte's voice came like a rope to drag her out of her dreams:

'Now, young men,' she said, 'tell us a bit about your university which my sister and I do not know — nor does our cousin from England, Elizabeth.'

'Elizabeth'. Her name aroused the girl at the point when Kit, the clever talker, began to speak:

'Columns, hundreds of columns, there are so many of them that you have the impression they go everywhere with you. In those surroundings, I start to take myself for an Ancient Greek ...'

'A Greek god, perhaps,' suggested Uncle Charlie.

The Greek god shook his empty, pretty head, showing his small, very white teeth.

'I should like to be,' he said modestly.

There was a peal of laughter, the gentle irony of which he did not fully grasp. Elizabeth could not avoid looking at him at that point; the deep black of his large eyes in some indefinable way alleviated the aggressive red of his warring locks. He reminded her irresistibly of the archetypal Romantic poet, if not a genius. In spite of everything, he seemed to Elizabeth worthy of a certain admiration, for she was still incorrigible on that point. Suddenly she recalled Miss Llewelyn's horrible phrase about the brutal realities concealed by a handsome face, and she turned her head in violent dismay.

Her eyes met Ned's sitting less than three feet away from her, and her throat went dry. A feeling akin to fear invaded her. She saw herself once more in her room in Savannah, in front of the portrait that had been taken down from the wall and then put back in accordance with her girlish whims, and which had then vanished; now once more she had it in front of her, but alive and smiling with the awkwardness of youth still lacking experience of life.

She looked at him in silence, made an effort to smile but did not manage it. As she had done a moment earlier, she turned her head aside, but for quite different reasons. With a look of consternation, he tried to catch her eye by turning a little more towards her and, in a timid protest, he murmured:

'Elizabeth, I'm Ned, Ned Jones.'

Elizabeth was on the point of getting up and leaving the room, so strong was her emotion. Only her natural pride obliged her to rally and she did not move.

Charlie Jones was keeping a discreet eye on them. Sniffing out a little drama, he decided to intervene:

'Ned,' he said, 'you're well placed at the university to know what they're saying about Edgar Allan Poe who died last year. Is he much read?'

'More or less. I'm not crazy about his poetry, nor his prose. He was only at the university for a year, in 1826 and 27. Later on he was expelled from West Point. He drank.'

'The story of his life is rather short, as you tell it.'

'I don't know him well. He passed for a genius at university.'

'A genius ravaged by alcohol. There must be people who remember him as a student. Talk to us a bit, Ned. You're not very communicative this evening.'

'I admit to not being very communicative,' said Ned with a forced smile. 'I hesitate to mention his prophecy. It's not very pleasant.'

'Say it all the same. A poet's prophecy can only be dreams. We all know what they're worth.'

'Well, during a walk with some student in the Blue Ridge Mountains which we can see from the campus, he prophesied that, one day, war would break out between the North and the South, and that it would be terrible.'

At this point in the story, Amelia moved her head in a convulsive manner and let out a dull, hoarse, little cry:

'I don't want . . .' she said, without explaining what it was that she did not want.

Uncle Charlie grabbed her hand:

'It's nothing, darling. That mad poet was talking in 1826, and there has been no war. On the contrary, today there is an agreement.'

'I'm sorry,' said Ned.

'No, it's my fault,' said his father, 'I insisted, but what credence can one confer on the delirious visions of a drunk?'

'A drunk? Do you think so?' asked Amelia in a languid voice. 'Charlotte, the salts.'

'I don't have any,' said Charlotte roughly. 'A Scotswoman has no need of smelling salts. Pull yourself together and eat.'

This injunction was answered with a wounded look which surprised everybody, arousing a sudden interest like well placed lines in a play. Even Teddy Brown did not hesitate to turn his eyes inquisitively towards that tall, dark woman who was saying nothing. They expected an outburst, but she seemed to be wrapping herself in silence like a mourning veil. A change was taking place in her.

'Well,' she said at last in a suddenly resolute voice, 'perhaps he was right, your poet. We shall see war.'

'But it's by no means sure!' exclaimed Charlie Jones.

'It is. By dint of talking about it people bring it about, and I am not proud of being afraid of it for so long.'

She tried to straighten herself in her chair. She lacked the strength, however, and her husband grasped her hand.

'Do you want to go up and rest?'

She brushed him aside. Into that motionless face there slid a glimmer of satisfaction. She felt a gasp of horrified admiration rise up around her. In her imagination, a heroine of Scottish legend was being born. Moreover, she still had an old score to settle with her sister.

'Charlotte,' she said in a voice that was intentionally brusque, 'you eat up as well instead of making those round eyes at me.'

'At last!' exclaimed Charlotte. 'That's the blood speaking. In Scotland we fought long enough at the side of the Young Pretender not to be afraid of the nasal song of the bagpipes in battle nor the thundering of the drums. I have beaten the drum myself. There is one slumbering in the attic that dates from the days of the English. Have them bring it down for me, and I swear you shall hear me, my fingers are just itching to get going on a *ratatata*.'

Uncle Charlie leapt to his feet.

'That's set them off!' he exclaimed. 'How on earth can I calm them down? Silence! I request, I demand silence.'

'What for?' Amelia asked him with a haughtiness he had not seen in her before.

'Because, my darling . . . because we are here in order to dine and not to go to war, to dine peacefully, all together as a family — or almost . . . And then, there isn't going to be a war. My boys, I don't suppose you will ever be in uniform. You can rest assured.'

'Sir,' said Ned calmly, 'I am not afraid.'

The unexpectedly heated discussion got through to Elizabeth, and she watched those present with a new curiosity. Until then she had evaded Ned Jones's gaze, but when he began to speak in reply to his father something forced her to look him straight in the face. She read in his features human qualities that were beyond her. This impression was like a flash of lightning and disappeared immediately. He smiled, seeing her so attentive, and that smile destroyed everything. Again he looked like the Savannah portrait, but for less than a second she had seen him differently, and had loved him.

This transient dizziness alarmed her. She was discovering such a strange weakness in herself . . . That horrible Welshwoman was right: a handsome face exerted a dangerous fascination over her. Ned's was distinguished only by a sort of happy affection in his brown eyes sparkling with gold. There was nothing of the romantic hero about him. The term 'good boy' summed him up perfectly. That was how she wanted to see him now. Having got over her whim of a moment ago, she could speak to him without disquiet.

'I suppose your name is Edward,' she said more boldly than she intended, but would she ever be able to resist these impulses? Her excuse was perhaps that she wished to make up for her rudeness at the beginning of the meal.

'Yes, Edward, of course, but I'd rather you called me Ned.'

'. . . you called me Ned . . .' She was taken aback, she had never requested such a thing.

'My father told me that we are related in some way, so I'll call you Elizabeth, shall I?'

'Yes, oh yes.'

'Yes, Ned,' he corrected with his father's irresistible smile.

'Yes, Ned,' she said mechanically.

Had she not said these things already? Was it one of those false recollections that turn up to annoy one's memory?

Suddenly she could see herself once more in the House of Chaos in front of Daniel De Witt: 'Call me Daniel — Yes — Yes — Daniel.' It was beginning all over again. She felt so ill at ease that she was on the point of getting up and leaving the table. He noticed this and, with a rather fearful gentleness, touched her hand. Faced with that look which was overflowing with affection, she did not have the courage to pull her hand away.

'What's the matter, Elizabeth?'

'Nothing, too much noise . . .'

It was true that the conversation was becoming more and more animated all around her.

Amelia, in a harsh exchange of views with Charlotte, had rediscovered the guttural tones of her native land.

'Why are they shouting?' Elizabeth asked.

'It's about Charlotte's apple pies. They told me about it. Do you know about it?'

'The tea party for your cousins from over the way? I was there.'

'Charlotte spoke about the old family feud. She thinks it's ridiculous, and that made Amelia cross.'

'Cannot the quarrel be made up?'

'It could be, but Amelia is relentless.'

As he spoke these words, Charlotte, standing up with her cheeks ablaze, was clamouring deafeningly:

'One wonders what you can be thinking of when you dare to say in your evening prayer that you forgive those who have trespassed against you.' At that moment Uncle Charlie got up from his place and called out in a booming voice:

'You're going too far, Charlotte, I order you to be quiet.'

As if the better to hurl her voice towards the ceiling, Charlotte threw back her shoulders and, moving jerkily, her cap lurched forward.

'Give your orders to your wife,' she howled, 'not to me. She is there for the purpose of obeying you according to matrimonial law.'

Something happened then that aroused visible alarm on the part of Teddy Brown and Kit Hughes, who turned pale and tried to make themselves inconspicuous. Charlie Jones, in his black morning coat, broadened his chest and clenched his fists. He seemed to be increasing in size in an indescribable way, inflated by anger. Elizabeth admired him, he was once more becoming what he really was, a man. One of his lace-cuffed fists came down on the table and the glasses gave a gleeful clink, as if for a party.

'Who is the master here?' he asked in a deep voice that he knew to be splendid, both rich and powerful.

Barnaby, who was handing round a dish, put it down at random on the table and fled, while Amelia, getting up in her turn, showed what she could do. Majestically she ordered:

'Leave it Charlie, it's my business. Charlotte, you will have to account for your words at the Last Judgement.'

Her harsh accent and funereal tone produced an effect of ghastly terror even in Charlotte, who vacillated for a moment. But she got over it almost immediately and gave her response with the force of the fateful trumpet blast:

'I'll see you there, sister dear, I'll have you called for your false charity and that hard flint you are pleased to call a heart . . .'

'No, no and no!' bellowed Uncle Charlie suddenly, 'this cannot go on.'

These words were charged with such energy that they immediately brought about an oppressive silence with the force of a bolt of thunder. Then Amelia's voice slid into suspended animation, softly stubborn:

'Forgiveness will be granted when they come here to ask me for it.'

There was a great muttering from the mouth of Charlotte, proposing the following commentary:

'Not seven times shall you forgive, but seventy times seven.'

'I shall wait,' said Amelia and, getting up from table, headed towards the door.

To everyone's surprise, Miss Charlotte remained speechless, moving ostensibly to one side to let her sister pass.

When the latter had disappeared, Miss Charlotte simply said:

'Now she will suffer.'

Charlie Jones shrugged his shoulders:

'You might have chosen some other time than two days before Christmas to quarrel. I'll go up and see her in a while.'

Elizabeth was struck by his calm, Where was the husband who was all attentive to his wife such as she had seen him since his marriage? Perhaps he had had enough of the devious capriciousness of the implacable Scotswoman.

Barnaby served the dessert, and conversation resumed on more or less indifferent subjects. Leaning a little towards Ned, Elizabeth murmured:

'Without wishing to be inquisitive, nor to ask too many questions . . .'

He smiled his most disloyal smile which was also his most seductive, and leaned, in his turn towards her.

'It's simple,' he said under his breath. 'The two sisters used to live in the same house; Amelia and Maisie took it in turns to keep the accounts. For a mistake in adding up, Amelia found herself more or less accused of dishonesty.'

'For a mistake in adding up? That's not possible.'

'Perhaps the error in the sum was a pretext. There must have been something else between those two Highland lasses. Sometimes hatred can burst out in a split second, like a flash of lightning.'

'Lightning flashes of hatred?'

'Like lightning flashes of love,' he said artfully, without taking his eyes off her.

She lowered her head and did not answer.

The evening was of the shortest. Undoubtedly on account of that painful altercation at dinner, no one seemed in the mood for talking, except Kit, the Greek god, who was anxious to launch into brilliant talk. Anecdotes were in bud on his lips, but faces were looking elsewhere. People were turning the pages of albums lying open on the table in the large drawing room. Uncle Charlie was screwing up newspapers which he threw down one after the other beside his armchair. He finally got up and said:

'I'm tired, my children, I'm going up. Good-night to you all.'

Miss Charlotte followed his example immediately. Never before had she been seen looking so serious. Yet she tried to smile as she said to the guests:

'I hope you will find your rooms. Ned, you will guide the way. Go to bed, Elizabeth, you don't look well.'

The girl asked for nothing better than to go. Anything rather than stay alone with that group of boys. What could she say to them? Having wished them good-night, she took flight.

They took leave of each other of their own accord. Not all in the same direction, however. Teddy Brown went off to his pretty room overlooking the sleeping hills, while Kit followed Ned up to their shared room.

Half an hour later, Great Meadow was swallowed up by the great silence of the countryside. That was the moment when Barnaby, who had hardly any private life, tried to catch up on those of other people. A wild animal's agility had come to his aid on more than one occasion, for listening at doors was not without its risks.

Not all the doors of the house were equally satisfactory. That of the young lady from England was of no interest, nor was Miss Charlotte's, from which emanated nothing but the recitation of psalms. That of Mr and Mrs Jones would have been worth a try, but the danger was awful, for Mr Jones was wary and kept a watch.

That night, Barnaby focused his talents on the guests' doors. To tell the truth, that of the insignificant Mr Teddy Brown was not worth lingering over. But Ned's and Kit's was in itself a question mark, and he glued his ear to it in fervent curiosity. What he heard at first seemed nothing more nor less than a battle. First of all, a heated discussion, albeit in lowered voices that made it all the more dramatic and, suddenly, the loud clatter of an overturned chair and the indisputable sound of a forceful blow. At that moment, the indiscreet Barnaby was seized with panic and headed off into the gloomy corridor, carrying off as a prize this mysterious little piece of stormy student life.

87

*I*n her room, where the embers of a dying coal fire looked like a heap of rubies, Elizabeth, unable to make up her mind to get into bed, sat thinking. She was spellbound by the silence all around her. No echo of the little drama taking place on the other side of the house reached her.

The fearsome words exchanged by Amelia and Charlotte were still ringing in her ears. In this confusion, she sought out what was closest to her heart, Jonathan's face.

Sitting at a little mahogany writing desk, she had her eyes fixed on a blank sheet of paper, as if already reading what she wanted to write on it. A letter from Dimwood had arrived for her during the day, but it had only been given her belatedly. It had not, of course, been opened, but it must have been passed around, and they knew that she was corresponding with Miss Llewelyn. What this latter had to say, moreover, was contained within the space of two lines: 'Bad news. You're being thought about a lot over there. If you absolutely insist on replying, your answer will be forwarded from here. Burn this paper immediately.'

Another letter, one that could be shown around, accompanied the brief missive. Miss Llewelyn informed the girl that everyone at Dimwood was well, but that Fred was having trouble with his foot which had been operated on . . . Mr Hargrove seemed worried: the day would come when Jonathan would demand that the key to the house be returned to him, once the twenty-five years tenancy was up.

'You're being thought about a lot over here.' Into what transports of delight those words had plunged her! She had carried them off in her heart when she had gone down to dinner, and now she could write to Jonathan.

A sudden thought put an end to her intoxication: the woman in the dress the color of dust and ashes was going to read what she wrote, her desperate love calls, with her she-rat's eyes. Never.

She stood up abruptly. She had to think. Having thrown the dangerous missive on the fire, she got undressed and went to bed.

With the lamp out, she lay there with her eyes open. She

went over her problem in the darkness. The only solution was to get Jonathan's address and to write to him directly. Would the Welshwoman give it to her? Nothing was less sure. She would have to insist politely, cajole her a bit, implore even — a little. Or, in case of failure, find the means of giving Jonathan her address at Great Meadow in Virginia.

Her feverish imagination set to work, giving birth to feeble hope. She fell asleep almost happy. Just at the moment when she was about to lose consciousness, she thought she could hear Ned's slightly mocking voice telling her: 'Yes, Ned, yes, Ned.'

The following day began most auspiciously. As after a great storm, the air was cleared. Beneath her broad bands of brown hair parted down the middle, Amelia's face breathed the tranquil joy of a well-balanced conscience, and she smiled indulgently at the chattering of the boys. Kit had an endless supply of wicked little stories at the expense of certain professors, and Ned laughed loyally in the right places, even though the facile verve of his guest sometimes seemed to him on the vulgar side, and he was ashamed of it.

The latter deplored the fact that he would be unable to spend the whole of Christmas day at Great Meadow, having promised his parents to be home in time for the big family lunch. The journey would not take long. He lived six miles away.

'We're almost neighbors, after all,' Kit told Ned with a smile.

He could not have asked more clearly to be taken home in a carriage or a gig.

'It will be a pleasure for our Barnaby to take you,' said Ned, 'and to restore you to your folks who are counting on you to bring the party to life.'

'And as soon as you wish,' confirmed Charlie Jones with barely disguised urging.

'I enjoy little anecdotes,' said Miss Charlotte suddenly, who guessed by the distress in Kit's eyes that he had realized too late that he was not wanted . . . 'You are a first-class raconteur, and I hope that you will come back to Great Meadow.'

Kit turned towards Ned, who confronted him with a broad smile which was so hard it seemed to bounce off him as against a wall.

'Teddy Brown isn't going to desert us, in any case,' said Charlie Jones. 'His parents will not deprive us of him, I hope.'

Ned whispered into his father's ear:

'No parents. An orphan.'

'You are as amongst family here,' said Charlie Jones immediately, imprisoning Teddy Brown's small hand in his own large ones.

The sapphire eyes were immediately raised towards him with a childish gaiety, and the mouth opened to say something so softly that Charlie Jones could not make out a single syllable. He nevertheless shook Teddy Brown's hand vigorously before letting it go.

Elizabeth was watching this scene of which no detail had escaped her, for she seemed to be seeing each of these people in a new light. Without being aware, she was herself becoming the object of a somewhat unflagging attention.

Miss Charlotte at her side said to her softly:

'You can read them like a book, but don't judge.'

The mysterious tone of the spinster moved her and made her smile. Charlotte excelled in talking as if she were telling a secret, but, on the other hand, any allusion to Scripture could only disturb the English girl, who immediately felt guilty and under attack.

'I am not judging,' she said, 'but poor Kit does not look very happy.'

'Well,' said Charlotte, pretending to be surprised, 'you are human after all.'

Elizabeth blushed.

'Don't be offended,' said Charlotte, 'I was only teasing. You'll understand eventually.'

At that moment Uncle Charlie raised his voice:

'I suppose that we are going to be subjected to an invasion from the House of Chaos. Do you have any ammunition, Charlotte?'

'I've been on my feet since six o'clock this morning,' declared Miss Charlotte in her highest pitched voice. 'The whole kitchen is at work. There will be plenty of everything, and plenty of indigestion.'

Peals of laughter greeted these words; everyone got up amidst a great scraping of chairs on the parquet floor. Elizabeth grasped Charlotte's arm and, her eyes enlarged by anxiety, she asked:

'You don't think he'll be coming as well, do you?'

'No. They didn't want to talk about it. He has asked for a transfer to Louisiana.'

88

A heavy wreath of holly hung on the front door of Great Meadow. Like drops of crimson blood, the berries shone in the prickly foliage.

Although a trifle conventionally, perhaps, an atmosphere of innocence and joy spread irresistibly through Great Meadow. Faces wore smiles. In front of the house, moved by a kind, friendly instinct, Ned was insisting to Kit that he should at least stay to dinner and leave afterwards. Kit's reply was a relief: the family was expecting its prodigious offspring, he could not disappoint them.

'Well,' said Ned, taking it upon himself to be nice, 'I shall drive you back myself in my gig, that way we'll have longer together.'

A light gleamed in the green eyes edged with auburn lashes:

'Do you mean what you're saying? You're not cross with me?'

'Fool!' said Ned as he burst out laughing, and he gave him a thump on the shoulder.

This burst of generosity was ended by the arrival of Uncle Charlie.

'I'm pleased to see you're such good friends,' he said cheerfully. 'The university draws young men together much better and more lastingly than social relationships. We're sorry you have to go, Kit, but at what time did you want to leave?'

Kit turned a little pink and answered:

'Whenever you like . . . Shall we say five o'clock?'

'I'm driving him back,' said Ned.

'Oh, no! You're staying here, we need you for the preparations. Barnaby will be ready at five o'clock, Kit. I'll come and say good-bye to you and shake your hand.'

With a smile he turned on his heels and walked resolutely towards the house.

'Never mind,' said Kit sadly, 'but it's been fine all the same, everything has been fine.'

'Everything has been fine,' repeated Ned like an echo.

What Charlie Jones called the preparations existed only in his imagination. He needed a pretext, some word, no matter what, to rid himself of that Greek god whom he did not like. The evening meal was Miss Charlotte's affair, and she certainly had no need of Ned's help. With the calm of a general before battle, she prepared for the invasion of cousins from over the way.

At exactly five o'clock, the black gig with yellow wheels was in front of the house, and Barnaby busied himself with loading Kit's valise. Kit, looking a little somber, was hesitating before climbing on board, when Ned rushed up to him.

'We shall see each other again soon,' he said as he shook his hand. 'We'll meet under the colonnades! You haven't been too bored here?'

Uncle Charlie came up at the same moment, cutting short the question as he cried:

'Happy to have had you as a guest at Great Meadow. Good luck, my boy, and a happy Christmas.'

And, as he had promised, he seized his hand and shook it with a laugh. For his part, Barnaby seemed delighted at this little trip he was to make with Mass'r Kit. He was undoubtedly hoping to engage in a very discreet conversation, to find out what had happened, for the sound of that blow was still ringing in his ears, like a gunshot in the night.

They were barely out of sight when the little flock of

neighbors from opposite turned up. Fanny, with her hair as dishevelled as usual, Elsie, Dick, Harry and tall Clementine, pale and serious.

In a desperate flurry of chatter, Fanny came out with her usual indiscretions.

'Papa has never been too hot on religion, and Mama does everything he says, so they let us come, because for us Christmas is Christmas, so you understand . . .'

'I understand perfectly,' replied Uncle Charlie. 'Christmas without a dinner, for example, would that still be Christmas?'

A cry went up from the little group:

'Won't there be dinner?'

Only Clementine remained silent, but her eyes betrayed worry.

'Rest assured.' said Uncle Charlie, 'your religion will not suffer an affront under my roof, and we shall have dinner in an hour.'

Clementine spoke up softly with her plaintive intonation:

'Teddy has written to us. He is sorry not to be with us.'

'He is doubtless at sea,' said Elsie.

Elizabeth closed her eyes. She saw again in a flash that radiant face drawing closer to hers with a great unspoken cry of love in its dark eyes. How had she been able to cast aside that happiness, that unexpected joy?

Uncle Charlie, who was watching her out of the corner of his eye, broke the painful spell with a firm voice.

'The light is beginning to fade. We'll go in. You're going to be set to work, Clementine. I've had the old piano in the drawing room tuned. You know what that means.'

In the drawing room, Amelia was waiting in a large armchair for people to come and greet her. With her face lit up by the indefinable smile of a good woman, acquired at the cost of much effort, she set about fulfilling her role. By way of a concession to Christmas joy, a dark lilac silk dress replaced the usual black taffeta, setting off her generously rounded figure. An enormous white shawl with a long fringe was crossed, however, over her ample bosom.

In the minds of the girls and boys who came up to her on that evening, she sowed a horror of respectability. She was vaguely aware of it and felt saddened by it, for she wanted to be liked by all these people, especially the young ones. But the constant inner game of hide-and-seek that she played with her conscience confused everything hopelessly. Even Ned found her terrifyingly virtuous.

In a very gentle voice, she wished a happy Christmas to them all and would have extended her good wishes to the parents of the young guests had it not been against her principles. One should not weaken at the memory of an affront.

As usual, Uncle Charlie arrived on time to relieve any embarrassment.

'I'm waiting to hear the steps of the poor children who come to sing their Christmas carols to us. Old customs must be respected.'

Indeed, in front of the house a row of boys and little girls was standing waiting in the darkness. Each of them held a large candle in one hand, sheltering the flickering flame with the other. In their black or blue woollen clothes, they looked rustic rather than poor, but the thick scarves round their necks spoke of poverty, as did their boots with thick and noisy wooden soles. The youngest might have been twelve, the oldest fifteen, and the little light shining beneath their faces conferred on them all a legendary beauty.

Their clear, determined voices rose up before their audience with an almost martial energy. Without knowing it, they wiped clean the slate of a world where rumors of war, political battles and half-pious, half-aggressive sermons raged. Intoning with unaffected purity, they told the story of Christmas:

See the tender, innocent babe,
In the ice-cold night of winter,
Lying trembling in the manger.
Alas! what shame to see him thus!
The inn is full, no man to give
His place to the pilgrim babe.
Lo! the simple beasts stand guard
Beside his cradle bed.
But this stable is a princely court!
This cradle a royal throne!

They were listened to in silence right to the end, when the enchantment faded away amidst a hubbub of words:

'My friends,' said Charlie Jones, 'you have made us believe in peace on earth for those too-brief minutes. You sing wonderfully well, and I shall not let you leave without thanking you.'

With charming good grace, he went up to the choristers and slipped a gold coin into the hand of each. Eyes shone in the candle light.

Suddenly all heads were turned towards the door, and the young singers who were preparing to leave remained rooted to the spot as before some apparition. In her dress with its iridescent pleats, her head caught in the lace halo of her cap, a tearful Amelia, struck dumb with emotion, was standing on the doorstep. Any religious singing stirred up in her a host of inexpressible feelings, where vague sentiment mingled with the heady certainty that she was counted amongst the elect.

She wanted to say something, but she weakened, and she was tottering when two long, ebony-black hands grasped her firmly by the waist, preventing her from falling. It was Jemima who was keeping an eye on her and, without wounding her mistress's dignity, skilfully steered her round towards the hall.

Uncle Charlie had missed nothing of this incident but did not flinch.

'Nothing to worry about,' he said to an alarmed Clementine, who was standing next to him. 'It's just a little attack of piety, such as she gets every now and then. I had foreseen it all, and Jemima was at the ready.'

'But Uncle Charlie, what's she going to do?'

'She'll go back to the drawing room and wait patiently for dinner.'

He spoke these last words with a slight smile and in a loud voice shouted:

'Charlotte!'

The answer came from the depths of the house, distant but strident:

'Send your angels this way. In the pantry they'll find heavenly delights prepared by my own hand.'

Joyful laughter was to be heard, and the angelic choir,

asking no questions, followed Ned who showed them the way.

It was decided that while waiting for the dinner bell the guests would go, warmly dressed, for a walk. Charlie Jones judged it appropriate, moreover, to leave Amelia to her meditations in the solitude of the large drawing room.

Settled carefully by Jemima in a large armchair scattered with cushions, she gave herself up to pious dreams as she looked into the fire. A sincere effort to fix her thoughts on Christmas did not prevent her from raising her eyes from time to time to the bracket clock on the mantelpiece and wondering if dinner time would ever come.

Charlie Jones, for his part, had gone to smoke a cigarillo in his usual place of refuge, where the sagging sofa was an invitation to rest beneath the ever-disapproving gaze of the Presbyterian pastor. He really did not care for that portrait, but too many thoughts were going round in his head for him to pay much attention to it. What worried him more than anything was Elizabeth's correspondence with Miss Llewelyn. He knew well the Welshwoman whose considerable bank account made her one of his clients. What need did Elizabeth have to write to her? The memory of the English girl's farewell to Jonathan came sharply to mind, but the link between the two events remained tenuous. The girl, who was so secretive by nature, would not put up with an interrogation. Moreover, had he not given his word not to ask any questions?

In a few days' time he was to leave the house to go to Savannah where he would be detained by business matters for several long weeks. A visit to Dimwood was inevitable, if he wanted to go over with William Hargrove the thorny question of the lease, which was coming to an end. He would take advantage of that to see Miss Llewelyn and question her adroitly, without appearing to do so. If she was subtle, he was too . . .

And there was still the problem of Ned . . .

Far from suspecting the importance she was assuming in the mind of her guardian, Elizabeth had gone up to her room. Moved by that Christmas carol that had taken her back to the England of her childhood, she wondered if she would be able to write to Jonathan that evening. For she wrote to him every evening, and every evening she burned the letter.

At once cruel and delightful, the time spent writing to Jonathan helped her get through the day with a lighter heart. From 'Dear Jonathan', she had quickly moved on to 'My Jonathan', then to 'My Beloved'! She had reached 'My Love, love of my life'!

Ned's arrival had modified the tone in a curious way. His first look, his first smile had troubled her, and that night the letter to Jonathan had verged on the delirious as she affirmed that she had never loved him so much. The following day it was clear to her that Ned no longer took any notice of her. Had she not caught him out smiling a couple of times at Elsie during the Christmas carol? It was all the same to her, and her love for Jonathan went into paroxysms. The phrases she had in mind were about to write themselves down unaided on the blank paper: 'Jonathan, you are far away and I am dying, Jonathan . . .' But the Christmas carol was still ringing in her ears, and she did not dare go on . . . Jonathan did not receive his letter.

Why did she feel relief? The bell rang and she went downstairs.

89

The dinner was a boisterous affair. No other word could describe it. Things had got off to a good start, however, with a sort of well-bred calm. In the long dining room, decorated with large landscape paintings of Europe and the East, the table was resplendent with its white tablecloth and the weight of the family silver. Amelia sat enthroned, like a queen, opposite her husband. The latter had placed the guests rather at random, although not entirely, for Elizabeth was surprised to find herself next to Ned.

Why did the ten of them round the table seem like twenty by the end of the meal? The first few minutes were indeed exemplary. Charlie Jones, looking majestic with his cravat right up to his chin, stood up and proposed that they say a Christmas grace first of all. There was no objection, but he added a suggestion that provoked a certain consternation:

'The inspiration came to me to ask one of you to say it in my place, and my choice happened on . . .'

Hearts pounded.

'. . . Teddy Brown.'

Teddy Brown stood up immediately to general stupefaction. With admirable dignity, the short young man with sapphire eyes said clearly the customary grace of the Anglican Church. His grave voice pronounced each phrase without pious affectation, but with the emphasis of deep faith.

When he had sat down, there was silence and someone gave a slight cough. Suddenly Miss Charlotte perked up in her turn and trumpeted forth:

'Mr Teddy Brown is destined for the priesthood.'

'Oh,' exclaimed Charlie Jones, 'what a good idea, Teddy Brown, I had not suspected . . .'

A lie. He had set it all up with Miss Charlotte in the naive hope of restoring a serious note amongst these rowdy and frivolous young people.

'But I still have three more years of study to do,' said Teddy Brown modestly.

Conversation resumed in quiet voices at first, then louder, but with a modicum of respect for the future man of the cloth.

First of all a too-heavily spiced turtle soup was served. Large glasses of water were emptied amidst tears and coughing fits, which did not prevent Charlie Jones from whispering a magic formula in Barnaby's ear:

'Chateau-Lafitte Charles X.'

Finally the turkey was welcomed with greedy groans. To see it in its great midnight-blue porcelain serving dish, one might have thought that it was wearing a gilded breastplate. It exuded intoxicating aromas and was garnished with amber-colored sweet potatoes.

'Indeed,' said Uncle Charlie with a long knife in his hand

when the turkey was placed down in front of him, 'this creature doesn't know what it's doing here, for it is in the North that they are particularly favored.'

A dish of cranberry sauce appeared close at hand, then a large bowl of jelly made from the same fruit, sweetened to counteract the berry's bitter sharpness. Carved with expertise and elegance, the various portions found their way onto the hot plates, while Barnaby poured the venerable claret into the crystal glasses, tactfully measuring, according to the age and sex of the guests, giving very little to some, and more to others . . .

Pensive and well-behaved, Clementine seemed to be eating only out of politeness or duty, but the other cousins, let out of the House of Chaos like a pack of wild animals, devoured turkey and potatoes in an unceasing clinking of knives and forks. Once empty, the plates were filled up again almost immediately. Unfortunately, under the effect of the wine, which was rarely served at table, heads began to spin.

Miss Charlotte watched them sadly. Something was preoccupying her mind. But the behavior of the guests went beyond what she had feared. It was Fanny who was the first to begin the barrage of things one ought not to say. With her cheeks red and her eyes sparkling with stupidity, she exclaimed:

'I love turkey! We wouldn't eat as well as this at home.'

Clementine, always silent, corrected her immediately from the other side of the table:

'Be quiet, Fanny. Everything is fine at home.'

The two boys chimed in, Dick especially, with his blond hair dishevelled in anger:

'If Papa could hear you, Fanny, he would take you behind the door. You know what happens when the Commodore takes you behind the door.'

'Oh, you're frightening me!' cried Fanny in a high-pitched voice.

'Calm down, children,' said Charlie Jones at this point. 'I have dined at your house. You have a first-rate cook.'

'A cook!' said Fanny. 'It's Mama who's the cook, yes she is.'

Amelia slammed the palm of her hand down on the table. With consummate skill, which would have been the envy of an actress, she made her face take on an expression of terrifying severity. She was suddenly the embodiment of Justice:

'Fanny,' she said slowly, 'do you like plum pudding?'

'Plum pudding,' spluttered Fanny, already a little tipsy and crazed at the thought of what might be coming.

'Well,' continued the implacable Amelia, 'when it's time for the plum pudding, if you do not fall silent *immediately,* there will be a separate dessert for you which you can offer up to Heaven: a fine, empty plate.'

Fanny forced back tears of rage and lowered her head.

Barnaby, who was waiting at table with his usual zeal, was following this scene with passionate interest, like some theatre-goer. When he drew level with Charlie Jones, the latter let slip into his ear:

'No more wine for the three young ladies.'

Barnaby obediently continued on his journey around the table. Ned signalled to him on his way past.

'After dinner, wait for me by the dining-room door. I have something to tell you.'

'Yes, Mass'r Ned.'

Conversations resumed as best they could. Ned leaned towards Elizabeth:

'Pitiful, these scenes, don't you think?' he whispered into her ear (a little too close to her ear, she thought, without moving away). 'All this is due to the family feud. We could all have lived here together, and it would have worked out. The Commodore lives on his pension. Money is scarce on the other side of the meadow.'

'I think that's awful,' she said in the same tone of voice.

'Why aren't you looking at me, Elizabeth? Are you not content?'

She guessed that the wine was having the same effect on him as it had on her, and it was pleasant.

'Not content? pleased? Of course I am.'

'You didn't look at me yesterday either.'

'That was you. You were looking at all the others, except me.'

'I didn't look at anybody.'

'You did. Be honest.'

Uncle Charlie was too far away from them to grasp a word

of their exchange, but he blessed with a smile of complicity those whisperings that were in line with what he wished for. He was already on his fourth glass of Chateau-Lafitte 1830, and in a pleasant confusion of ideas he searched for some subject to enliven this Christmas dinner. The name Paris shone out in his memory.

'I can understand very well,' he said, 'why Mr and Mrs Jonathan Armstrong did not linger in Paris on their way to Vienna.'

'City of perdition,' observed Amelia.

'It seems,' continued Charlie Jones, 'that cholera has broken out there again, as in '32.'

'Punishment from Heaven,' said Amelia. 'When will those people be converted? What are our Protestant missionaries up to?'

Ned saw Elizabeth change color and wanted to take her hand, but she pulled it back immediately.

'What's the matter, Elizabeth? You're all white.'

The very name of Jonathan produced a terrifying echo in her. For a moment she thought she saw him in Ned's place, and she remained incapable of saying a word.

'Do you not feel well?' he said. 'Shall I help you up?'

His solicitude annoyed the girl. She came to herself and sobered up.

'Leave me alone, please. It's nothing. I'm not used to drinking wine, that's all.'

Uncle Charlie was holding forth:

'What they need is a strong government. Paris is always ready to lapse into convulsions. The Prince-President . . .'

The pudding made its entry at that moment, and the Prince-President faded into oblivion.

The heavy brown sphere, decorated with a sprig of holly, was placed respectfully in front of the master of the house as he stood up. He was handed a bottle of cognac and, with a quasi religious solemnity, he doused the pudding lavishly. Soon the flames were heading up towards the ceiling, joyful, free and provocative. Even on Amelia's face a childish wonder began to shine.

The helpings were generous, filling the hot plates, and the thick brandy butter sauce followed in little silver pots. Soon the clan from the House of Chaos was uttering cries of delight. Almost on the brink of drunkenness, the young ladies were gabbling for all they were worth and generally misbehaving:

'What a pity,' exclaimed Elsie, 'that Teddy isn't here! He's been complaining for years about not having Christmas pudding.'

'Everybody says he is the most handsome boy in Virginia,' exclaimed dreadful little Fanny, now that she had secured her pudding.

'Be quiet, Fanny!' cried Miss Charlotte.

'Why?' said the rebel, gulping down the last mouthful before anyone could take it away from her.

Elizabeth turned towards her neighbour:

'This pudding is making me feel sick, Ned. Do you think the dinner will soon be over?'

'The dinner yes, but there will be the hymns. I have had enough too, but there's no getting out of it.'

She turned her head away brusquely, as if she were cross with him.

90

Ned was telling the truth. They left the dining room, the youngest of the guests staggering. Clementine was led by Uncle Charlie's firm hand to the piano in the corner of the drawing room. The instrument was fairly modest in appearance, a classic upright, with brass candle holders with pale pink silk shades. She sat down on the stool like a martyr. She was not feeling happy because her stomach, more clearly than her conscience, was reproaching her with having indulged too much in everything, and two large glasses of wine did not help the situation; but at home she was always hungry.

Amelia demanded the hymn 'While shepherds watch their

flocks by night' which is the favorite of all the Protestant Churches.

The notes followed each other timidly and then all the voices rang out with that fervent piety that is helped along by an excellent dinner. Charlotte especially produced shrill hallelujas that made them all shout with joy and formidable jubilation.

In a panic, Clementine abandoned her piano and, waving her arms in the air, she requested silence. She was pale with emotion and looked so unhappy that they all fell silent. She said in a faltering voice:

'I can no longer hear myself playing, I'm sorry.'

'She's right,' yelled Miss Charlotte. 'Our hallelujas are too loud.'

'The Lord is not deaf, after all,' declared Amelia sententiously.

'Do you hear,' said Uncle Charlie who was feeling as emotional as all the rest, 'so, softly, you angels, eh!'

They all got the message, and all sang in semi-whispers while Clementine accompanied them in tears.

'Ned has gone up to bed,' said Miss Charlotte suddenly. 'What a shame! Merry Christmas, Ned!'

'Merry Christmas!' they all cried together.

He refrained from answering or from lighting his lamp. They would have thought he was asleep. For the first time at Great Meadow he felt disappointed, not only on account of Kit, who had spoken to him in such a strange way, insisting with his unhappy eyes, and finally that unexpected gesture . . . and then the blow . . .

'How could I have foreseen it? I had no idea.'

But never mind. What was troubling him more than anything was Elizabeth's tortured face at the end of the meal. She had not wanted to look at him, whereas a moment earlier she had smiled at him. It was when the girls were chattering away: 'I feel sick . . .' She had barely touched the pudding. He had said a few words to her and she had suddenly turned away. What had he done to her?

In a sudden burst of anger, he tore his clothes off, throwing them on the floor, over the furniture and, running to his bed, he slid into it quite naked in the darkness. He did not want to suffer, he wanted to sleep.

In Elizabeth's room, the log embers were still burning, spreading their comforting scent which the girl always breathed in with the same delight. That night, however, she did not stop to use the bellows on the flames as she would normally have done, but ran to the table where a lamp was shining, and immediately turned up the wick.

Then, taking writing paper out of the drawer, she wrote these words on a blank sheet of paper: 'Tell him that I love him and have never loved anyone but him.' After which she slid the paper into an envelope which she addressed to Miss Llewelyn at Dimwood.

The sealed envelope was placed in an obvious position in the middle of the table. On the day after Christmas it would be given to Uncle Charlie who would send it off with his letters. He could think what he liked, but he could not open the letter, because he had given his word on it, and the message would go to Dimwood, and from there to Vienna. Was it so difficult to take a decision and put it into practice? She had been ruminating on this gesture which was so simple throughout the pious celebrations. This did not mean that she was unmoved by the Christmas carol of the young village children, and even by the hymn after dinner that had brought tears to her eyes. Her faith remained just as strong. Her love for Jonathan was a separate problem and had nothing to do with religion. All of that could easily be compartmentalized in her conscience, provided one did not exaggerate, but there was something else.

Since yesterday, she sensed that Ned was beginning to be important to her. She looked out for his smiles and was cross if he did not look at her. He often did it on purpose; depriving her was the penance he inflicted on her when he judged that she had been indifferent, inattentive, or distant. In short, he was behaving as if he were in love. In love and teasing her. She, of course, was not the least bit in love. The proof of it was that she had just written to Jonathan, the first love letter he would receive from her.

Such a relief! Such peace! There would be an answer, because there must be an answer. She knew her Jonathan. It seemed to her that life was opening up before her. 'Dare!' a voice had told her coming from the depths of the silence, in this very place, here in this vast room, and she had dared. It would not have taken much to set her singing.

She began to get undressed and was heading towards the bed when she almost cried out in surprise. In a distant corner, half hidden by the showy wardrobes, Betty, on her knees in her red skirt, facing the wall, was lying quite still, all curled up, with a little lighted candle in front of a piece of paper, a picture perhaps.

Elizabeth hesitated. Her first reaction was to withdraw without a word, for she did not know what to think. As strange as it all seemed to her, it was the little candle that intrigued her and, she had to admit, she found it moving. Her poor Betty was as mysterious as white women with their complicated lives. An absurd notion. She did not know Betty well, but she loved her the way she was; yet curiosity got the upper hand, and she leaned forward to see what the picture might be.

To her bewilderment she saw, colored by an unsophisticated hand, a child whose head bore a heavy crown. She recoiled, vaguely alarmed. Betty was mad.

Feeling both sad and perplexed, the girl took several steps backward with the litheness of a cat, but she could not prevent the floorboards creaking and Betty turned round. A broad smile of happiness gave that black face a beauty that wiped away the furrows of the wrinkles, leaving only her splendid gaze.

'Merry Christmas, Miss Lizbeth,' she said without getting up.

'Happy Christmas, dear Betty. Are you saying your prayers?'

'Yes, Miss Lizbeth.'

'In front of a picture?'

'In front of the Good Lord.'

'That child with a crown . . .'

'Why, that's God, Miss Lizbeth.'

Suffocated by this answer that only increased her fears, Elizabeth moved away.

'Good night, Betty. When you've finished, blow the candle out and go to bed.'

'Yes'm, Miss Lizbeth.'

Betty had barely moved throughout this conversation. That was what had struck Elizabeth first. 'In any case,' she thought, 'my poor Betty is perfectly harmless. She carries about in her old gray head some African superstitions inherited from her great-grandparents from over there. It would be better not to say anything to anyone about it.'

As she finished getting undressed to go to bed, she ended up finding that childish brand of madness quite moving. It was only the candle that worried her. A candle in the hands of an old woman who was going out of her mind . . .

The fire died down slowly. From her bed, Elizabeth could see the pink glow from the ashes. The large Flemish wardrobes concealed the old black woman in her mysterious adoration. A great silence reigned in that room and invaded the darkness.

For Elizabeth, the night brought peace. Her letter, as if by a miracle, brought Jonathan across thousands of miles to be at her side. There was something about that thought that made her feel happy and light-headed.

She suddenly realized that she had slid into bed without saying her prayers. Too lazy to wrench herself from the warmth of the bed, she half hid her head under the blanket and fell asleep saying the Lord's Prayer far from suspecting that the old African 'idolatress' was saying exactly the same prayer in the same old-fashioned and piously mutilated language.

91

*T*he following day, Christmas Day, was much calmer. The Commodore's children did not leave the House of Chaos, where the family meal awaited them, a little less succulent, perhaps, but their father's orders were clear: 'Everyone on the bridge for dinner.' The house was his ship.

At Great Meadow, with all the guests gone except for Teddy Brown, it was realized that they had taken their bad manners with them, but also a good deal of life and gaiety. Secretly they were missed. The Christmas meal was as it should be. Everyone behaved well. Teddy Brown was asked to say grace, as if he had become the family chaplain. His modesty made them all well disposed towards him. Uncle Charlie said a few words about peace that should be requested from Heaven. A goose was served in place of the previous day's turkey. The Chateau-Lafitte Charles X was replaced by a home-made beverage, which no one would have been able to describe, for it was tasteless except for a certain sweetness. An Indian name endowed it with a certain rugged dignity.

Elizabeth did not look once at her Cousin Ned, convinced that she did not love him. Her love for Jonathan was enough, as she had proved by the letter written the day before.

Ned, for his part, never once turned his gaze in Elizabeth's direction, as if to punish her indifference, but also because he felt himself falling in love, and that annoyed him, for basically he preferred brunettes.

The English girl, as she sat next to Teddy Brown, engaged him in conversation. She felt sympathy for him, but, in a more obscure way, she wanted to irritate the young Virginian who was looking more and more like the Savannah portrait. This was only apparent at certain moments, perhaps a question of the light or a fleeting posture. That day one might have thought he was doing it on purpose, and it made her uneasy. Consequently, Teddy Brown, an undemanding neighbor, seemed Heaven-sent.

'I was asked yesterday if I was content. Are you?' she began affably.

'Me, oh yes,' he said with sudden fervor. 'I am very happy, today as every day of my life.'

'Every day!' she said with a smile. 'I envy you, how do you manage it?'

'I am happy because I am saved.'

She might have expected it . . . A budding pastor. Unsteady, guessing what would come next, she was not kept waiting:

'What about you, Miss Elizabeth, are you saved?'

Was he mad? But no, she recognized the ways of certain fanatical Protestants. She answered in an unsure voice:

'Oh, I hope so.'

'It's not enough to hope. You have to be sure of it, be convinced of it. Otherwise . . .'

'Otherwise? Oh, I beg you, let's talk about something else.'

'Oh no. The Spirit blows where he wills, here as elsewhere. He is urging me to tell you that if you are not sure about your salvation, it means one of two things: either your salvation is dubious or your conversion needs to be begun all over again. I must talk to you about it. It is not by chance that we have met.'

Elizabeth turned pale and shook her head.

This extraordinary conversation was conducted almost in a whisper, but there was an intensity in those sapphire eyes that obliged Elizabeth to lower her eyelids. Did he see in that movement an admission of guilt? He continued implacably:

'Recognizing one's faults is a step in the right direction. Be brave, Miss Elizabeth. I am here to help you find your way again.'

She folded her hands on the table:

'I beg you, Mr Brown, let us put a stop to this.'

He gave her a look of even more alarming gravity than his words and fell silent.

Sitting on Elizabeth's left, Miss Charlotte had been unable to grasp more than half a dozen words, but she delighted in piecing the whole together, in the same way that an accomplished musician needs only a few notes to divine a favorite score, but she did not rise to the bait.

Quite the contrary. Ned, who was on the opposite side of the table facing Teddy and the girl, was giving way to indignant thoughts: 'That's a bit much,' he said to himself as he wriggled on his chair, 'am I dreaming? There is that cheeky little pastor paying court to that girl before my eyes! He's getting closer by the minute, my word, they'll end up kissing. No, she's moving away a little, oh, only a little, out of decency. It's all the same to me, after all. Let her do as she likes, let her marry him! I admit that she's not bad with her golden hair, but would I really want to spend the rest of my life in a corn field?'

He pushed his plate away in an irritated gesture.

'You're not eating,' his father said to him, 'and you look as if you've got something on your mind. Where's your Christmas spirit? I should have liked to have served you all a drop of champagne, instead of this . . . mixture, Amelia's secret.'

'Are you talking about me?' asked Amelia.

'I was trying to remember the name of this Indian drink.'

'Scuppernong.'

'I shall never forget it,' said Ned rather sarcastically and added in treacherous vein: 'Our dinner yesterday evening was more . . . convivial. Hardly anybody is talking . . .'

'The quiet after the feast,' commented his father.

'. . . nobody, that is, except for my friend the pastor.'

'Very pleasant, what's more. He's deceptively quiet. I know that kind. Once they start, they are unstoppable. At the moment he's telling endless stories to Elizabeth, who looks petrified . . . I'll shut him up for you. Mr Teddy Brown!'

'Sir?' said Teddy Brown.

'I'm going to tell you a secret. They are going to serve ice-cream to us in a little while.'

'I wanted it to be a surprise,' said Miss Charlotte in a fit of pique, 'an ice-cream indeed, flavored with vanilla, the most innocent of all the flavors, for Christmas. *Benn*-flavored crackers will liven up the taste a bit. Do you know what *benn* is?'

'I admit my ignorance on that point,' said Amelia, as if offering her humility as an example to all.

'Can you instruct us, Mr Teddy Brown?' asked Charlie Jones mischievously.

'Yes, I think I know,' said Teddy Brown.

'You surprise me, but we're all ears.'

'The story is a trifle melancholy. When the poor slaves first disembarked on the coast of Georgia . . .'

'Barnaby,' said Amelia, 'go and fetch my smelling salts from my room.'

'Yes, ma'am.'

He disappeared and hid behind the door in order to listen.

'When they left Africa, they carried with them a handful of *benn* seeds which, they had been told, would bring them luck. With what hope they clutched those seeds in their hands God alone knows.'

'Cut the sermon short a bit, won't you?' said Ned.

'*Benn* is nothing other than sesame. The slaves planted it and used it in their food. Their masters were not long in discovering the secret and *benn* immediately became very popular in Georgia and South Carolina.'

'What is Barnaby up to?' asked Amelia suddenly.

For some moments she had been unable to keep still on her chair and seemed in the grip of some violent anxiety. In a harsh voice that was not her usual one, she exclaimed:

'That fool is incapable of finding the most ordinary of objects. I need my salts. I'm going to faint. I can see war.'

Charlie Jones leapt to his feet to hold her in his arms, but she struggled:

'Leave me alone,' she cried.

'Calm down, darling, there's no reason to be upset. Run off quickly, Ned, and look for the smelling salts.'

Ned rushed to the door and nearly knocked over Barnaby who was running in, holding the smelling salts:

'Yes, ma'am!' he said out of breath, 'the salts.'

Wrenching them from his hands, Charlie Jones held the bottle under his wife's nose, and she tossed her head back, like a horse.

Silent and with clenched teeth, Miss Charlotte was holding her sister firmly by the arms.

'It'll pass,' she said in a hurried whisper to Charlie Jones, 'it's her condition, a vision.'

The bottle of salts set the convulsive movement of the head off a second time, and then Amelia came to. Lowering her voice, which was both flat and staccato, she began to speak:

'A column of black smoke reaching right up to the sky . . . the plantations burning . . . soldiers lying on their backs, in rows . . . they won't wake up . . . too much blood . . . too much blood on them, too much blood in the grass . . . soldiers running forward . . . the sun shining on bayonets . . . on the edge of the ditch, a boy of thirteen, almost a child . . . lying on his back, barefoot, his face pure and tranquil, one hand on his stomach, there is a hole . . . a large red hole . . . he will stir no more . . . elsewhere, young men . . . one of them, his head hidden under his tunic . . .

— 723 —

It's over . . . those who won't return are all around us . . . war is coming towards us . . . war . . .'

Elizabeth and Ned were standing together. Instinctively they looked at each other in silence. Without really knowing what she was doing, Elizabeth took Ned's hand and squeezed it. A long smile, laden with tenderness, was his reply.

'Don't be afraid,' said Ned in a whisper. 'She's delirious.'

Amelia had fallen silent. In her agitation she had lost her cap, and her thick, brown hair fell in tresses on her shoulders.

Her face suddenly became less tense. The pious mask fell beneath the effect of an immense pain which seemed to encompass the tragedy of the world. The big, dark eyes were lost in the distance, beyond the present moment, and with terrible simplicity she pronounced:

'All is lost.'

She remained motionless for a moment. As she was about to collapse on to the table, Charlie Jones caught her in his arms.

Miss Charlotte helped him to carry her to the neighboring drawing room. Ned joined them to see her to her room, upstairs.

Teddy Brown had remained motionless but passionately interested, and was still standing at his place. The deserted table, with serviettes strewn across the half-empty plates, was like a comic battlefield.

Seeing herself alone with the young fanatic, Elizabeth decided to take refuge in the drawing room and took a few discreet steps towards the door, but Teddy Brown ran up to her.

'Don't go away, Miss Elizabeth. What you have just heard has a high spiritual value.'

'Frankly, I think she's delirious. That's Ned's opinion and he knows her better than you or I.'

'People said the prophets were delirious too. We shall have a war.'

He looked at her with his steady gaze. The blue of his eyes seemed to be clouded over, but she stood up to him in exasperation.

'If you were really convinced that Amelia saw things rightly, you wouldn't be talking about it so calmly now. In such a black future, what would be your fate?'

'I should be killed, Miss Elizabeth.'

She shrugged her shoulders.

'Don't say that. All that speech is nothing but dreams. She saw a thirteen-year-old child run through by a bayonet. If war breaks out in four years' time, that child is playing marbles with his friends now. He is eating and sleeping, he is happy, growing up in order to reach the spot where death awaits him in a red earth ditch, to put a hole in his stomach with a steel blade! Your religion is horrible, Mr Brown!'

He waited for a moment and said softly:

'The boy was free to go or to remain at home. The Lord sees all of the past and all of the future of the world, but he does not interfere with our liberty. Mrs Jones saw what the Lord sees.'

He was speaking with a politeness that made the girl feel awkward, as if she were being instructed in the art of living. His reasoning made her feel at a loss, she searched for some objection, but found none.

'I see,' she said, 'that you have an answer for everything but, even if you are right, I find it horrible. Everything is arranged in advance.'

'Everything is *seen* in advance.'

'But perhaps she saw it wrongly, perhaps she made a mistake. You can't kill off hope in peoples' hearts.'

'We shall see if she saw things correctly.'

'How can you be so detached?'

And, in one of those outbursts that she never managed to control, she exclaimed:

'I don't want you to be killed, Mr Brown.'

He stood still, as if he had been punched.

'Really, Miss Elizabeth?' he asked gravely.

She made an effort to pull herself together:

'Yes, really, not you nor anybody else, not Ned or . . .' she stammered.

She was going to add: 'nor Jonathan', and stopped. No longer knowing what to say, she asked a question that she had been wanting to ask since her previous conversation with the future pastor:

'Would it be indiscreet to ask whether you belong to the Church of England?'

'No, Miss Elizabeth, I'm a Methodist.'

A Methodist! She might have guessed as much. He certainly did not have that Anglican smoothness, nor the well-bred looks of the clergy at home ... With Methodism one was going down the social scale.

Seeing her confusion, he took pity on her and said with a smile:

'Don't let that upset you. I am a Christian like you. My grandparents lived in Savannah. John Wesley himself converted them.'

'John Wesley ...'

'John Wesley was a saint. He knew how to talk to ordinary people, he brought back to the Lord a whole army of poor people who were on the brink of rebellion.'

Elizabeth maintained an embarrassed silence. Once more she felt that strange unease which religion occasioned in her, attraction mingled with rejection.

'I am happy to have had this conversation,' she said at last as if to bring it to an end.

'I am too,' he said, 'but I shall return some day. Then we shall talk again, in a more decisive manner.'

There was no time to say any more. Two servants came in to take away the empty plates and to replace them with dark blue crockery decorated with golden flowers.

Then came Barnaby laden with a tray bearing a monumental ice-cream which he put down in the middle of the table:

'Miss Charlotte and Mass'r Ned is comin'. Mass'r Charlie is stayin' with Miss Amelia and he say you ain't to wait.'

He stammered a bit as he spoke and his terrified looks proved that he had not missed a word of Amelia's prediction.

Miss Charlotte appeared almost immediately, followed by Ned who gave Elizabeth and Teddy Brown a suspicious look.

'Let's sit down,' said Miss Charlotte, 'and set about this vanilla ice-cream. Where are the crackers, Barnaby? My word, you forget everything.'

Barnaby disappeared immediately and Miss Charlotte took advantage of this short absence to say in a calm tone:

'Perhaps you don't know that my dear sister is expecting a child. It's very early days yet. In that condition, it happens that women are favored — if one can put it thus — with premonitions and visions of the future. It happens frequently at home in Scotland. We are,' she added proudly, 'married or not, young or not, on intimate terms with the invisible universe.'

'Do you really believe that Amelia saw war?' asked Elizabeth anxiously.

'Who knows? We shall find out.'

'As for me,' said Ned, 'I believe that she painted us a detailed portrait of her fears.'

'There's something to reassure you,' said Teddy Brown to Elizabeth, with an affectionate smile that Ned did not fail to notice.

Suddenly Miss Charlotte launched an appeal in a voice that made all present tremble:

'Barnaby, stop listening at the door and bring us those crackers. I shall speak to your father about you.'

As if by magic, a heap of crackers appeared almost immediately on the table, in an enormous round white Wedgwood dish.

'Yes, ma'am, the crackers,' said Barnaby in a fit of zeal.

'Ned,' said Miss Charlotte, 'in the absence of your father, you are head of the family, so you can serve us.'

The ice-cream was savored without comment. The crackers, as they disappeared, revealed a raised inscription around the edge of the dish, forming a garland of gothic lettering. Teddy Brown read it aloud: 'Eat thy bread in joy and gratitude.'

These were the only words spoken until the end of the meal. Funereal silence weighed heavily. Only the slight sound of spoons on plates could be heard. They were waiting for Uncle Charlie. His portion of dessert was melting. He did not put in an appearance.

As they got up from the table, Ned took Teddy Brown aside. Linking his arm in his, he said cheerfully:

'If I am not mistaken, my dear old Teddy, you are interested in my Cousin Elizabeth.'

Teddy Brown answered in a grave voice:

'I want to save her.'

Ned withdrew his hand brusquely:

'Are you mad? She's not in danger!'

'I want to save her soul.'

'Well!' exclaimed Ned. 'You come and play the pastor in our house! Listen, if you want us to remain friends, leave Elizabeth's soul alone. Understand?'

'I shall do what the Spirit tells me to do.'

'Not here, Teddy, not in our house.'

Teddy Brown looked at him firmly and calmly but did not answer. Ned felt himself blushing at the idea that he was acting like a jealous lover in the eyes of a boy who was so aggressive in his austerity. The sapphire eyes did not avert their gaze, but seemed to want to pin him to the wall. Such was Ned's embarrassment that he nearly gave in to a sudden burst of anger, instead of which he got a grip on himself and said with a sigh:

'You must try and understand me. I've always been a bit on the rough side.'

'I can leave this evening if you like.'

Ned burst out laughing and shook him:

'Fool! Don't do that. My father wouldn't understand. He is fond of you, and you are our guest. So let's forget all that. I'm going to go for a horse ride. Are you coming with me?'

But Teddy Brown preferred to go up to his room where he had some reading to do.

Meanwhile Elizabeth was struggling with herself, not because of the attack Teddy Brown was making on her soul, but on account of her letter to Miss Llewelyn or, more exactly, to Jonathan. It was important to see it leave as soon as possible, before being tempted to tear it up, for she knew herself.

The mailman did not call on Christmas day. The following morning he would come and collect the mail that was in the box, but first it was necessary for Charlie Jones himself to put stamps on the letters in his libary, and it was for him to hand them over. That was the rule. Everyone at Great Meadow stuck to it. Usually, Jemima was in charge of collecting letters for posting from each of them. In general it was a thin harvest, but what a torment for Elizabeth! She did not want to entrust her precious and dangerous missive to

Jemima even for a few minutes. Even less to Uncle Charlie, who had given his word of honor . . .

It was painful for her. If she could have slipped her letter herself into the mailman's bag, but then it would not be franked. It was truly painful . . .

In the end she was ashamed of her cowardice and, going up to her room, she took her letter and, with her heart pounding, set about looking for Uncle Charlie. Of course, he could only be with his wife. Crossing the corridor, she knocked timidly on the door of the nuptial temple, as Miss Charlotte called it. At first there was no answer. She needed to knock harder. She still had time to think again and go back to her room with her letter. She hesitated, the whole house seemed dead around her. The tall, wide door was pale grey with its panels outlined thinly in gold. One could not deny that there was something regal about it.

And suddenly it was opened. They had heard, after all, and Charlie Jones, in his black morning coat, was standing in front of a petrified Elizabeth. There was a brief silence, then in a pleasant voice he declared:

'I was not expecting a visit from our dear Elizabeth. You may come in. Amelia is in a deep sleep and will hear nothing until tomorrow morning, but take that terrified expression from your face.'

A mechanical smile hovered on the English girl's lips as she went in. The room was plunged into a peaceful half-light, the shutters at the three windows being half closed, and the long, white muslin curtains filtering into a kind of mist the last rays of daylight. Generously hung with ivory-coloured curtains, the enormous nuptial bed occupied a corner of this majestic room. On a dark green carpet, a large upholstered-leather rocking chair was surrounded with newspapers that had been unfolded and cast down in a heap, like wrecks in a stormy sea.

Settling himself in this chair which he set in gentle motion, Uncle Charlie pointed out a second chair to his visitor.

'And now,' he said, 'I'm listening.'

Each time a ray of light fell on his face, he seemed pinker, calmer. In spite of herself, Elizabeth admired this entirely British placidity in the face of his wife's horrifying vision.

She wanted to speak but couldn't manage it. Without a

word, she handed him her letter. He took it in silence and slid it into an inner pocket of his morning coat.

This gesture, which was so simple and so quick, came as a relief to Elizabeth. Now she did not have to choose any more, there was no more decision to take. Yet her peace was of short duration.

'Tomorrow,' said Uncle Charlie, 'the mailman will call, but this letter will not be given to him.'

'Oh, why not, Uncle Charlie?'

'Because the day after tomorrow I am leaving Great Meadow to go to Savannah, and from Savannah I am certain to go to Dimwood. Now, something tells me that your letter is intended for someone at Dimwood. Am I right?'

Elizabeth's strangled voice answered:

'Yes. At Dimwood.'

'And so I shall be the mailman, and perhaps I shall be a little quicker than him. In any case, there is no risk of your letter being lost.'

He tapped his coat over the spot where the letter was, as if to reassure her.

'It will,' he said, 'be delivered by hand. No franking necessary,' he added with a slightly joking air. 'Satisfied, Miss Elizabeth? Do I not deserve a little thanks?'

'Thank you, Uncle Charlie,' she said in one breath.

He continued in a more natural tone of voice:

'Don't let my dear wife's monologue at table upset you. She has always been haunted by the historic memory of her country's war against England, and in particular the massacre of the brave Scotsmen by King George III's brother, the Duke of Cumberland, the famous 'Butcher of Hanover'. She saw it all again in a kind of waking dream. Tomorrow she won't remember anything about it. That's what I hope, in any case. There you are. Do you think there is any vanilla ice-cream left? I would have liked to have had some . . .'

'Melted,' she murmured, 'I fear it's melted.'

She felt melted herself, melted out of horror. She could suddenly see what she feared: Uncle Charlie handing the letter to Miss Llewelyn and the latter opening it and casting her eyes over it, then raising her eyebrows. Charlie Jones, inquisitive, pretending to look worried without asking questions, and then . . . and then the Welshwoman, feeling ill at ease, would betray her, giving everything away.

For she too had premonitions. That scene that was so clear, she could see it at the entrance to the great avenue of oaks, quite close to the house, not far from the verandah and the magnolia at the bottom of the steps.

'Thank you, Uncle Charlie,' she said as she got up, 'I'm going to have a rest in my room now.'

'Until this evening, then. It's always a pleasure to be of service to you. Have a little siesta, we'll meet at dinner.'

As she headed for the door, she felt as if she was dragging herself along like a sick fly. Outside, she thought she would slip to the ground and lose consciousness. Pride alone kept her upright. If by misfortune Charlie Jones had come out of the room and found her thus, what an admission, and what suspicions would be going round in that man's head.

In her room, she stretched out on her bed and, with her eyes wide open, tried to control her fear. Who had told her that the Welshwoman would lose her nerve? On reflection, nothing was less likely. Unflappable and her own mistress, that woman would, in due course, send the passionate message to Vienna. Days would pass and there would be an answer. She despised herself for having suspected Uncle Charlie's honor. There would be an answer. From now on, she was going to live for that answer, for there would be an answer, there would be an answer . . .

92

The following day was one of general scurrying about in preparation for Charlie Jones's departure. The large, closed carriage with its sprung suspension was cleaned and polished to excess. A team of six horses was made ready. The thickest blankets were unpacked, and the big shawls checked with black and the colors of the Douglas clan. The

heavy cowhide cases were filled with clothes and underclothes, selected in a methodical, almost military spirit, as
were the silver-gilt toilet requisites, the precious phials of
eau-de-Cologne from Russia. The hats were not forgotten in
their impressive leather cases that took the shape of the
headgear in question. Without doubt Charlie Jones travelled
like a king.

Amelia, who had more or less recovered from her
ordeal, shed the flood of tears that was expected of her. Miss
Charlotte turned out to be the most active and the most
useful, keeping an eye on everything with the zeal of a
honey bee. Two servants, chosen from amongst the most
robust, were to sit alongside the coachman wearing thick
Shetland coats. Ned was coming and going, looking busy,
bustling the servants and getting in the way rather than
helping. Elizabeth viewed all of this from a distance. She
remained in her room and only appeared at mealtimes. Her
imagination was travelling a thousand times faster than the
carriage would towards Dimwood, and from Dimwood to
Vienna, her agitated heart passing from hope to despair
with the dizzying regularity of a pendulum.

Dawn finally broke on the day of departure. Everything
was ready. Charlie Jones was wrapped up like a Russian
boyar as he said goodbye to everybody, but just as he was
getting into the carriage he took his son to one side:

'Now, mind you behave well, and no foolishness with Elizabeth.'

Sitting inside he leaned out of the door.

'Or not too much, in any case — if you see what I mean
. . .' he advised.

Ned indicated that he had understood. Elizabeth was standing a little distance away and waved her hand, as was the
custom, but her chest felt tight from anxiety. A minute
previously, she had been lavishly kissed by Charlie Jones
amidst a cloud of eau-de-Cologne. At the very moment when
the first cracks of the whip could be heard, he saw her,
turned towards her and, with a knowing wink, patted his
coat over the spot where the letter was hidden. She
managed a smile and staggered. Ned just had time to run
over to her and catch her in his arms.

The departure of Charlie Jones left a great void. His black morning coat and his permanently good-humored smile were missed. Amelia stayed in her room most of the time, and when she put in an appearance her serious expression never left her. Ned himself seemed to have something on his mind and tried in vain to catch Elizabeth's eye, but she avoided him, constantly immersed in her dreams. From time to time, Miss Charlotte's voice shattered the silence which was settling on the great house.

Teddy Brown had been taken part of the way home to Manassas soon after Charlie Jones's departure, and Ned missed him in spite of his preaching tendencies. After all, he was a friend with whom he could talk.

In the week that followed Christmas, the House of Chaos released its hungry hordes, and once more young people made Great Meadow resound with their amusing clamor. People complained about it, groaned a little, but as soon as they left, their stomachs filled, an indefinable sadness invaded the dining room. It had become too large now and the drawing room too was once more given up to the emptiness of boredom.

Ned hovered around Elizabeth whose somber expression and distant look intimidated him. She was quite aware of his maneuvring and remained determined to take no notice. Basically, what she reproached him with was not that he was Ned, but that he was *not* Jonathan. What is more, the handsome face of the Virginian reminded her too much of his father, who was heading towards Dimwood in his carriage with the dangerous letter in the inside pocket of his morning coat. How could she forget that dreadful wink which could have meant anything?

One day, when they found themselves alone in the drawing room with twilight hovering behind the curtains, Ned took the initiative and approached Elizabeth who was pretending to read in an armchair beside the fire:

'Well?' she said, putting down her book.

He was standing with his legs apart and his hands behind his back.

'Aren't we talking to each other any more? What do you have against me?'

'I don't have anything against you.'

'There is something. You're bored at Great Meadow.'

'Frankly, yes. I should like to be elsewhere. I'm not saying that to be unkind, but since you ask . . .'

Abruptly she let slip a lament:

'I'm not happy here.'

'That's silly. If Papa were here, he would give a ball. I'm a very good dancer. I would have waltzed with you.'

'I don't dance.'

'But with the waltz, you only have to let yourself be carried along. I would have shown you . . . It's heavenly.'

'Thank you. That wouldn't change anything.'

'You forget everything in such moments, Elizabeth. The other day, when I took you in my arms . . .'

Suddenly he was at her side, leaning over her armchair.

'Oh, that was an accident,' she exclaimed, 'I was going to fall, and you caught me, that's all. Let me get up.'

Ned's arm, held across the armchair, was preventing her.

Instead of obeying, he bent down towards her, and suddenly she had before her eyes his face aflame with desire, and she could feel his breath. With both of her hands on his cheeks she pushed him away. Straightening himself up immediately, he said:

'I take nothing by force, but you don't have to say no twice. You find me repulsive.'

'Come now, Ned, not at all. You must try and understand.'

She thought: 'What a pity! If he had insisted . . .'

Night was falling. In the flickering firelight he seemed to her irresistibly handsome.

The next few days passed by uneventfully. Ned had resigned himself to the situation, talking to Elizabeth from time to time about Virginia, about the architectural merit of the university, but the best part of his days he spent on horseback, riding around the district.

'Riding on *my* Alcibiades,' the girl said sadly to herself. But had she not wished for it to be thus? She had defended her honor. A melancholy victory. But then, was her honour really in such danger? How susceptible the young Virginian was, such pride . . .

Now she did not know how to occupy her time. All the

books in the library were boring.

Like a prowling lion, the words 'criminal correspondence' slid into her memory. She shrugged her shoulders in a fury. Faith dealt with everything. Never had she had such thoughts in her head.

In the meantime, Uncle Charlie's carriage was driving through North Carolina. Only an earthquake could prevent him from reaching Dimwood. Elizabeth did not wish for an earthquake — not really.

She should have kept quiet. She had revealed too much. From now on they would see that an English girl knew how to keep quiet . . .

The following day, New Year's Day, was all smiles, greetings and little gifts. Everyone gathered in the drawing room. Beneath the bunch of mistletoe hanging from the chandelier, Elizabeth was the most favored. Amelia gave her a delightful little collection of pious verse. Miss Charlotte, with a great sigh, gave her a pair of lilac gloves.

'I must admit,' she told her, 'that I part with these gloves with a rather heavy heart, they are perhaps a little out of fashion; I wore them when I was your age and still believed in happiness.'

Elizabeth politely made as if to refuse them, but Miss Charlotte insisted:

'Not at all, not at all, my girl. I nag you sometimes, I know, but I'm fond of you.'

Ned turned up with a little bouquet of Christmas roses:

'Happy New Year, Miss Escridge,' adding in a rather laboured French: '*Je vous aime.*'

'What's come over you?' she said rather surprised. 'And why are you speaking to me in French?'

'Because French is the language of love,' he said, making a valiant effort.

'Do you not believe, sir, that one can speak of love just as well in English? Do you enjoy playing the fool on New Year's Day?'

'Well,' he said with a laugh, 'let's put it down to playing the fool, Elizabeth, but do take these flowers. I look ridiculous holding this bouquet.'

She took the bouquet and smiled with a hint of sadness in her eyes. Suddenly he exclaimed:

'And now, my dear Elizabeth, I am going to give you a New Year kiss in front of everybody.'

Throwing himself at her, he took her in his arms and squeezed her with all his might as he covered her face with kisses, the last one placed tempestuously on her mouth.

'That's for the other day,' he said, red with emotion.

Neither Amelia nor Miss Charlotte understood the allusion, but they laughed good-naturedly.

'Everything is permitted beneath the mistletoe!' declared Miss Charlotte.

'I know,' said Elizabeth cheerfully, 'I should have been on the look-out.'

'You dare tell me that you didn't like it,' said Ned triumphantly.

'I didn't say anything,' she riposted, 'but I see that what is refused out of decency can very well be taken by force, Mr Play-actor.'

Amelia, who understood nothing of this bantering, clapped her hands:

'Come, come,' she said, 'I am terribly hungry and lunch awaits us.'

Without adding a word, she headed majestically towards the dining room. In her loose black dress that covered her feet, she seemed to be floating.

Of her own accord, Amelia proposed a toast to peace, but her voice faltered, and tears ran down her cheeks.

Then came the time that Ned was now dreading. His holidays over, he had to set out once more for Charlottesville and the university. An elegant black tilbury awaited him under the tall beeches in front of the house. Wearing a leather trilby, Barnaby was carrying his young master's valise. The latter, dressed in Shetland wool, looked sadly about him, his eyes searching for someone. He had said goodbye to Amelia, who feared the cold, in the dining room and to Miss Charlotte in the doorway.

Suddenly Elizabeth appeared. Wrapped in a white shawl, she tried to smile, but it was obvious that she had been crying.

'Ned,' she said, 'let's pretend, like the other day, shall we?'

He understood immediately.

'Alas, Elizabeth,' he said, 'at the point I've reached, I can't pretend any more.'

'Never mind,' she said. 'We'll pretend we're pretending!'

And she opened her arms. Her shawl fell from her shoulders. Ned ran towards her and clutched her to himself. Their mouths touched and the girl made herself turn her head aside, but he held it with both hands.

'Well, well,' exclaimed Miss Charlotte from the doorway. 'You're going to miss the train, Mr Ned Jones.'

She was laughing very loudly as if at a good joke, but it was easy to guess that she knew, as she had the previous day.

'Write to me,' said Elizabeth as she moved away from Ned.

'I promise, but I shall be back, I shall be back before . . .'

'Before what?'

'Before his return.'

Two minutes later he was sitting next to Barnaby, who whipped his horse. Elizabeth watched the tilbury move away down the long, winding avenue. When it was past the white gate, she stifled a sob.

Miss Charlotte came and picked up the white shawl and put it back around her shoulders.

'Cheer up,' she said. 'It has never been known for a man of this family to go back on his word.'

'But I didn't want . . .' murmured Elizabeth. 'It was in spite of myself.'

93

With the first falls of snow the house became like a tomb. Amelia was not to be counted on for cheering things up. Her hearty appetite which brought her to table at set times, was no obstacle to her habitual melancholy. She was missing her husband. Each day the mail brought her a letter from Savannah, none of the sheets of paper burning with tenderness could replace the physical presence that she needed. She quite often had her evening meal served to her in her room. Then Elizabeth would find herself alone with Miss Charlotte, who chatted pleasantly and did her best to amuse her, but since Ned's departure the girl preferred solitude.

From her bedroom window she looked out on the meadow with its grass hidden beneath the snow, and reflected on her life. Formerly she had seen her life as a road at the end of which Jonathan would be waiting for her, but now the great white plain was a blank sheet from top to bottom. Elizabeth no longer felt herself to be the same person. That face straining towards her in the magnolia foliage was somebody else's dream. The snow wiped away everything. The snow that was falling in this corner of Virginia was the same that was falling in Charlottesville, the snow that Ned was watching. She wanted Ned.

He had written to her on the 3rd of January:

I am at the back of a large room full of students and, through the high window overlooking the campus, I can see a long, white expanse. Why am I telling you this? I don't know. The professor is boring today. I'm escaping from his lecture by looking at the snow, I'm fleeing to be near to you. I tell you in French: 'Je vous *aime*,' like the other day, when we were playing at pretending. I'm going to come back soon, and we'll play at pretending, only this time, what I have to tell you I'll tell you in our own language and then it will no longer be *pretending*. It will never again be *pretending*. I love you.

Ned

She slipped this letter inside her blouse, as close to her heart as possible, like a lucky charm. Her joy would have been perfect for that whole week if she had not received, the following day, an unexpected missive from Miss Llewelyn:

Dear Miss Escridge,
I learn from Mr Hargrove that Mr Charlie Jones is on

his way to Savannah, and that he will come to visit Dimwood. He knows nothing of your interest in Vienna, but if he were to suspect anything through some indiscretion of an ancillary nature, you will take the only line possible in such cases, do what I do, deny, deny and deny relentlessly, again and again.

Your faithful servant,
Maisie Llewelyn

P.S. Put this paper on the fire.

Her first task was to look up in a dictionary the meaning of the word 'ancillary', which she did not know. What she read made her freeze with fear. The allusion was clear. She should not forget that all servants listened at doors. Her talk with Annabel had perhaps been overheard, letting out the secret of her love for Jonathan.

After a few minutes of panic, she threw the letter on the fire and pulled herself together, firmly resolved to lie if necessary: no, and no, she was not in love with Jonathan. An inner voice said to her softly: 'Yes, you are.' So, could one love two men at the same time? And the quiet, reasonable voice answered: 'One can love two men at the same time perfectly well.'

'Mad,' she murmured, 'you think someone is talking to you, and there's no one here.'

She wrote to Ned immediately:

Ned,

There is still time before the *return*. Come as soon as you can. I know by heart my role in the *pretending game*, but if you don't hurry, I might forget it.

Elizabeth.

A week passed, seven empty days, seven deadly evenings in the large drawing room in front of a log fire. Sometimes Amelia and Miss Charlotte were there, the former dozing amongst her cushions, the latter embroidering flowers on a tablecloth that covered her feet like a sheet. Sometimes Amelia stayed in her room, and then the girl would be alone with the talkative spinster. The latter's conversation was full of blood-curdling scenes from Scottish history, and equally thrilling stories of ghosts, and Elizabeth loved them. She listened to these tales avidly, to the point of looking under her bed before going to sleep at night.

Roses, violets and forget-me-nots all came in turn from the fingers of Miss Charlotte, who seemed anxious to amuse the young cousin from England. With her large, white bonnet bent over her work, she spoke with a remnant of the harsh accent of her native land. One evening she said in a confidential tone of voice:

'Snow has been falling more abundantly and we have been prisoners for two days. You must feel a bit lonely in the great house. Do you want me to invite the hordes to lunch?'

This was her name for the young people from across the Meadow, who would have come over on sleigh at the first hint of a call.

'Oh, no!' said Elizabeth.

'I see that we feel the same way. A pity your Cousin Ned isn't here. He's so amusing.'

'Unfortunately his studies keep him away,' said the young hypocrite with a sigh.

Ned had received her letter a week ago now. She was expecting to see him arrive from one moment to the next.

Miss Charlotte maintained a mysterious silence.

The following day was a Saturday. Just as the bell was ringing for lunch, the black tilbury stopped at the front door and, less than a minute later, Ned bounded into the dining room.

'Set a place for me!' he cried joyfully.

'It's done,' said Miss Charlotte, 'look.'

He burst out laughing:

'Thank you, Miss Charlotte. I showed your letter to my tutor. He agreed entirely. "Since family reasons demand your presence, it must be very serious. Off you go, and good luck."'

'It is indeed very serious,' said Miss Charlotte. 'We are all going to die of melancholia if you are not here to liven up our everyday life. Elizabeth especially. She is the worst case.'

Elizabeth put on an artificial air.

'Hello, Ned. What a nice surprise.'

'Ned, my dear,' said Amelia, 'give your coat to Barnaby so that he can shake it outside. You are covered in snow.'

'That's right,' said Ned, letting his overcoat be taken from him, 'I look like a Father Christmas who missed his train.'

'Where are the presents?' asked Miss Charlotte.

'Lost on the way. The Sioux attacked us and took everything.'

'What news from the university?'

'None. They are all like madmen and talk about nothing but war. Each of them has chosen his regiment. I'm for the cavalry, I shall go on Alcibiades. But it will be no more than a military excursion.'

'Silence,' said Amelia. 'We don't talk about war here, because there won't be one. I know it. I'm sure of it.'

The others raised their eyebrows and exchanged surprised looks.

Sitting, as if accidentally, next to Ned, Elizabeth said to him under her breath:

'You're not going, Ned!'

'Calm down. Everything is always settled in the Senate. In the meantime, it amuses them to show us their strength with fine phrases.'

The meal consisted of Ned's favorite dishes: glazed Virginia ham, sweet potatoes, crayfish salad. The whole meal was crowned by a cake in the shape of a domed building, in homage to the university, the library of which was designed by Mr Jefferson as a reproduction of the Pantheon in Rome. It goes without saying that Miss Charlotte had lent a hand with this monumental pastry, which was so splendid that it seemed a shame to cut it.

They were over two hours at table. It was enough to finish anyone off, especially as Miss Charlotte had dug out a precious but very dirty and very dusty bottle of Chateau-Talbot 1830. They each drank half a glass of it, but that was enough to finish them all off, except for Ned, who had never jibbed at a drop of alcohol.

Amelia had to be carried to her room, even as far as her bed. Miss Charlotte was valiantly fighting off sleep, but Elizabeth's eyelids were drooping, and she was giving everyone hazy looks. Ned took her to her room where the vigilant Betty was waiting.

As for the young student, he went to collapse on the sofa of the small library where the Presbyterian pastor in his gilded frame was powerless to counteract a long and noisy siesta.

He woke up as night was falling. His first thought was to rinse his face in cold water, then his pocket comb was pulled through the thickness of his black curls. Judging himself to be more respectable now, he went up to Elizabeth's room and knocked discreetly on the door.

Wrapped in a Shetland shawl, she was standing in front of the open window and holding her face towards the cool evening air, as if to purify her being of the last vestiges of the feasting. A little ashamed of having eaten so much, she was feeling vaguely guilty and the knocks at the door made her start.

When Ned appeared all pink and shining with youth, she exclaimed:

'Oh, Ned, don't come in.'

'Alright,' he said. 'I'll see you downstairs in front of the house, in the snow. It's stopped snowing, the air is milder, the night is going to be magnificent, a fairy-tale setting for the second act of the *pretending game.*'

'Do you think so?'

'I'm sure of it, the script demands it.'

He went down. A quarter of an hour later they were both running along a path that the servants had cleared with shovels. Rugged up as if for a journey, they were laughing and holding hands. The fields spread their whiteness beneath the moon which was rising over the woods.

After several minutes, they reached a pine plantation and Ned stopped:

'This is the interlude,' he said. 'Admire the stage set, the co-operative shadows, the complete silence. This is the point when I say to you: "My beloved, my darling . . ."'

'I didn't think we'd got that far,' she said with a laugh.

'I cut out the long bits that slowed down the action, so come on, act properly, at this point you say in a rush of feeling: "My dearest, my Ned . . ."'

She abruptly dropped her arms that she had folded round his neck.

'No Christian names,' she said.

'Why not, since it's *pretend?* I said "Elizabeth" just now.'

'No.'

'Yes, I did, and if I didn't, I thought it, so come on!'

Elizabeth's heart had been pounding for some moments.

'We can just as well use other names,' she said feebly, 'otherwise the *pretend* . . . runs over.'

'Agreed, I'll take Lizzie, what about you?'

She murmured:

'Jonathan.'

'What a name! Why not David and Solomon while you're about it?'

'Jonathan is fine.'

'As you like. I think about you night and day, Lizzie, I want you to be mine, mine alone.'

'That's not in the script.'

'How badly you're acting! Since it's *pretend* . . .'

She suddenly cried out:

'Jonathan!'

'Is that all?'

'Jonathan, my beloved, my only love, hold me, hold me very tight so that I cannot escape from you.'

'Ah, that's better, you can rest assured, you won't escape from me, and, as for holding you tight, you'll see.'

She thought he was going to suffocate her, so powerful was his embrace, but she was not afraid. On the contrary, she was panting with a strange joy and, as she closed her eyes, thought: 'Jonathan.' On the whole of her face she could feel the fiery breath of the young man, and suddenly he took her mouth in a frenzy.

When he finally let her go, she made as if to push him away.

'Leave me alone,' she said in an altered voice, 'you cheated, that wasn't *pretend* . . .'

'No,' he said, 'I couldn't pretend any more, but you . . .'

She was on the point of telling him that she could not either, and that Jonathan was not a *pretend*. In a flash the warning of the Welshwoman crossed her mind: 'deny, deny again and again . . .' She fell silent.

He stroked her face gently with his ungloved hand:

'Of course you hate me.'

'A little bit . . . Ned.'

'A little bit doesn't kill all hope, Elizabeth, a little bit is good, a little bit is wonderful, but why hate me?'

'You cheated. You didn't keep your word.'

'Elizabeth . . .'

'Let's go back, Ned . . . I'm cold.'

As they left the wood, they took once more the little path between the vast meadows, where not a shadow or a footprint marked the whiteness. They shone beneath the moon as in some other-worldly light.

For several minutes, neither of them seemed inclined to break the silence. Ned had put his arm tenderly around Elizabeth's shoulder, and she was walking close to him, pacified by the magical clearness of the night.

At last he said in a half-whisper:

'Don't be afraid of me, Elizabeth.'

'I'm not afraid of anyone.'

'Well, think about things a little, you are just seventeen, I am nineteen. If we are not happy now, time will steal our youth from us. Let us hasten to live it.'

'That means that you believe in the war.'

'It might be slow in coming, but it casts its shadow over the finest days, our days, yours, mine. Don't push love away, don't play at loving some imaginary being. I will make you happy. Don't you love me a little?'

'A little, no, unfortunately.'

'How can you say *unfortunately*? We're not pretending now, Elizabeth.'

He had quite a long wait for his answer, but seeing her with her head bowed he dared not rush her. In a voice subdued by emotion, she finally yielded up part of her secret:

'I'm unhappy about loving you, because I didn't want to.'

'Oh, why?'

'I can't tell you, and I won't tell you, but I love you.'

'So, Elizabeth . . .'

He hesitated.

'Well?' she said.

'Will you be my wife?'

'What I said should be enough for you, Ned. I shan't say any more today.'

He took her in his arms and pressed her face to his. She did not resist.

94

*D*inner was simple and quiet. Amelia had been sleeping so soundly since lunchtime that no one could make up their mind to drag her from her slumbers. Miss Charlotte spoke particularly about the cold that was beginning to set in around the district, and she congratulated the young people on having had their walk before the ice came and spoiled everything. She turned out to be quite maternal and, when the meal was over, she led them into the small drawing room off the dining room.

It was a charming little room, furnished with upright chairs and two armchairs, a little severe, but in a good, old-fashioned style: straight backs and hard seats.

'They're all signed,' she explained as she drew them closer to a splendid log fire giving off an exquisite warmth.

On the pale pink walls, Italian landscapes charmed the eye: Vesuvius erupting, *pfiferari* singing and dancing in a landscape of vineyards, festooned with bunches of grapes.

'There,' said Miss Charlotte, 'you can rest your fatigue in front of the fire. Barnaby will bring you a card table. You can choose between backgammon, dominoes, drafts — drafts is thrilling, I was crazy about it at your age. No cards. At home in Scotland we say that cards are the Devil's building bricks. Ah, here's Barnaby.'

Barnaby came in and placed a green baize card table between the two armchairs; on it was a mahogany box containing all that was needed for amusing the young couple.

'Would you like them to bring you some tea?' asked Miss Charlotte, 'or perhaps a herbal infusion: mint, lime, rowan-berry? Jemima awaits your orders.'

They both shook their heads gloomily.

'As you wish, dear children. Keep an eye on the fire from time to time, will you, Barnaby?'

Barnaby bowed and went out.

'There we are,' said the elderly spinster. 'I was your age once. I'm sure you have hundreds of things to say to each other, our Ned especially is such a chatterbox, and so amusing. I'll leave you. There are times when one is in the way. A pleasant evening, my dears. Don't stay up too late.'

Left alone, they sat down facing each other.

'Is she doing it on purpose?' Elizabeth asked.

'I get what you mean. She does everything on purpose; that elderly lady whom we adore is a curse, like all people who want to do things for us for our own good.'

'Is she perhaps keeping an eye on us?'

'We'll see. Usually there is a sofa over there by the door. She's afraid of that sofa, she's had it taken away. Likewise — but I hesitate to tell you.'

'You weren't so shy earlier on.'

'Well, normally the wooden floor is covered with a thick, Turkish rug.'

'Ned!' exclaimed Elizabeth, 'does she take us for animals?'

'Those are the reflex actions of someone who has no experience of certain aspects of life, and whose imagination runs riot.'

Remembering one of Miss Llewelyn's letters, Elizabeth made a horrified gesture.

'I understand. No point in speaking about such horrors.'

'I don't know which horrors you're thinking of, there are no horrors . . . love is beautiful . . .'

'I beg you, Ned, let's talk about something else. Do you really want to play backgammon?'

'Are you mad?'

'Drafts, dominoes . . .'

'I'm going to do something else, which might amuse you.'

Getting up from his armchair, he went over to the door on tiptoe and opened it all of a sudden to find Barnaby, who nearly fell over at his feet.

'Mass'r Ned!' exclaimed the horrified servant, 'I was just about to knock on the door.'

Ned forced him to stand up as he held him by the ear.

'Barnaby,' he said, glaring at him fixedly, 'if you were listening to me, I would correct you myself, but you know that no one lays a hand on the servants in our house, and so you take advantage of it, but do you know what I am going to do?'

He had let go of Barnaby's ear, and the servant flung himself to his knees.

'I am going,' continued Ned, 'to go on horseback as far as

the road via the little path, and from there I shall get to the little house of the pastor, your father, and I shall tell him about you and your habits. It won't be the hand of a white man that gives you a thrashing, but the vengeful arm of your Papa.'

'I's sorry, Mass'r Ned,' groaned Barnaby, 'I won't do it again.'

'I'm sure you won't do it again, after the thrashing your father has in store for you.'

'Oh, oh, oh,' cried Barnaby, as if the first blows were already falling.

'I ask you to pardon Barnaby,' exclaimed Elizabeth with a laugh.

'Oh, thank you, Miss Lizbeth,' cried Barnaby.

Suddenly Miss Charlotte appeared. Her high-pitched voice rang out like an alarm signal.

'What's going on? I want to know.'

'What is going on,' said Ned in the utmost irritation, 'is that Barnaby has just been caught listening once too often at doors. I don't know what he was hoping to hear. Did he imagine, for example, that Elizabeth and I were going to say improper things to each other? I have the impression that we are being spied on.'

Miss Charlotte suddenly felt unsteady and had to lean on the wall. Yet she recovered her firmness almost immediately and set her bonnet straight.

'Justifiable anger!' she exclaimed. 'Go away, Barnaby. Out of sight, you wretch! You are quite within your rights, Ned, but a little in the wrong too. A gentleman and a young lady are not suspected of exchanging words that would offend good breeding — and in such an elegant decor.'

'Was it you who chose the elegant decor?'

Miss Charlotte's face turned quite pink.

'It's impossible to lie to you. It was me, but I had received instructions from on high.'

At this point Ned was overcome with such perplexity that he was tongue-tied, for 'on high', in Miss Charlotte's way of speaking, could mean Providence or it could mean Charlie Jones.

Elizabeth got up:

'For my part,' she said, 'you will be good enough to excuse me if I go up to bed. I'm completely exhausted, the walk before dinner . . . Good evening Miss Charlotte, good evening Ned.'

'Let me at least accompany you to your corridor,' said Ned. 'The staircase is badly lit, and you might fall. Good night, Miss Charlotte.'

Alone in the deserted little drawing room, Miss Charlotte cast a melancholy gaze around her. 'Crazy old woman,' she thought, 'I who had managed everything so well. My parents were the same with my fiancé. On the look-out for danger. And on account of that, nothing ever happened . . .'

'Nothing,' she repeated aloud, as if she were speaking to the fire, which was of no use now, but was flickering cheerfully in the back of the fireplace with its slender doric columns.

The narrow staircase that led to the bedrooms was indeed badly lit. An oil lamp on a round table almost at the bottom of the steps gave out an indeterminate light that left the first floor landing in shadows.

'Leave me,' said Elizabeth, 'I'll go up on my own, I know every one of these steps.'

For unclear reasons that always guided her in certain circumstances, she felt that her future was being determined in this rather dark corner of the old house.

'Leave me,' she said again when he wanted to take her in his arms. 'I don't want you to touch me.'

'Are you still cross with me over that kiss in the woods?'

'Frankly, yes . . . a little. You were saying just now: "Love is beautiful." Is that what love is for you, that violence . . . ?'

'I was hungry for you.'

Guessing that he was shocking her, he added immediately:

'I will never be violent again, Elizabeth.'

'All men are violent, I know more than you think.'

She was afraid. Jonathan had talked to her a little in that vein, and the clearer recollection of certain dreadful words of Miss Llewelyn's were floating around in her memory. Greek statues lied, and Ned was a man like all the rest.

'Go away, Ned,' she said suddenly. 'If you become again as you were on that first day, I shall love you.'

'As on the first day?'

He tried to take her hand, but she got away from him and was up the stairs in a few seconds.

He did not follow her.

Night wiped everything away. The following day life set everything back in its place. Miss Charlotte once more forecast ice throughout the district and wondered how Ned was going to get back to the university.

'Perhaps you will have to prolong your stay at Great Meadow,' she said.

'No,' said Amelia dispassionately, 'the butcher, who has two horses shod for ice, collects travellers in distress in his cart.'

'In distress,' repeated Ned under his breath, giving Elizabeth a long look.

The girl gave a little smile of resignation.

'Ned won't miss the train at Gainesville,' continued the impassive Amelia. 'In any case, everything will be in order.'

The buckwheat pancakes with maple syrup were swallowed in silence, and spoons made their familiar clinking sound in large teacups, speaking of a peaceful and uneventful life. Such was Ned's view on the brink of despair.

That very morning, he had waited for the English girl at the bottom of the stairs and told her that because of her he was going to die.

'Die?' she said in amazement.

'Die, because your absence will take away my taste for living.'

'You'll come back.'

'I have the impression that you're still cross with me for that one unfortunate kiss I took from you in the pine plantation.'

'Took? Wrenched in an indescribable manner. I was ashamed. You were like an animal.'

'Oh, no, my love, that's human nature.'

'Well, I think that human nature is disgusting!'

'There's nothing I can do about it, you know. That's the way people kiss when they are in love.'

'Not me.'

'Show me how, Elizabeth.'

'Not here, not now. We might be seen.'

'Do you love me as you did before?'

'I love you when you are kind and gentle, as you were on the first day. I don't want any more of what you call "human nature." Go away, we mustn't arrive together. I don't know what Amelia and Charlotte might imagine.'

'They know very well, you can be sure of that. They're not against it . . . but we are causing them to live in terror.'

'I should like to know what they're afraid of.'

'Foolish things, what are known as foolish things, I'll explain it to you some day.'

'I don't care to know. Go away, Ned. I'll join you in the dining room in a minute.'

The day stretched out into boredom. All walks being impossible, they gathered in the drawing room where a large log fire was burning. Amelia suggested a historical or edifying subject of conversation as a means of waiting for the next meal in a way profitable to the mind. Like Miss Charlotte, she seemed to want to spend this last day of Ned's at Great Meadow in the young people's company.

It was rare to see Amelia in such a good mood and, in her black dress and with an edifice of lace and ribbon on her head, she lost nothing of her majesty. She even risked a pleasant banter, such as was fashionable in those days:

'My dear Ned,' she said with a smile that made her look more beautiful and took ten years off her, 'we are going to monopolize you.'

Disconcerted, but courteous, he bowed deeply.

'Give us the pleasure,' said Amelia, 'of taking us on a walk around that university with its thousands of columns — or if that should bore you, talk to us a little about the great Thomas Jefferson. I imagine his memory still lurks in that place of yours. What sort of a man was your hero? We only ask to see him and admire him.'

Ned, in exasperation, pretended to collect his thoughts:

'Let us praise the architect. He saw the Pantheon in Rome and pocketed the idea in order to build a library according to his own ideas. He placed it at the end of the campus, kept in view by a regiment of columns. In Paris, he noticed the Hotel de Salm, which he slipped inside his flowered waistcoat . . . Once he was back home, he arranged it in accordance with his taste and turned it into his house, Monti-cello.'

'What a man!' said Miss Charlotte.

'As soon as trouble broke out in July 1789, he decided to return to Virginia and missed the French Revolution.'

'What next?' said Amelia pulling a face.

'He was a very great man who tried to see as far as possible into the future of the country when he signed, along with several others, the American Constitution. Did he have doubts about the reliability of that document? One might think so, but how could he foresee that in 1850 a part of the North would see in that Constitution nothing but an agreement with the Devil, and proclaim that moral law is higher than the Constitution? You can do anything you like with an agreement when you set it against moral law. That's very convenient.'

'Your remarks seem subversive to me,' remarked Amelia.

'Forgive me, I feel in a subversive mood at the thought of having to leave tomorrow at daybreak in the butcher's cart. A number of reasons make me feel attached to this place.'

The principal of the numerous reasons sighed.

'They wouldn't put you in prison for two or three days' extra leave,' she said blushing.

'No, but the effect would be deplorable,' declared Amelia. 'The butcher has been warned. You can be sure he will be on time.'

Seeing that the conversation was likely to take a turn for the worse, Miss Charlotte adopted diversionary tactics:

'Poor Barnaby came this morning and flung himself at my feet to intercede with our dear Ned on his behalf. The fear that his father the pastor inspires is truly unimaginable.'

'If the fool had kept quiet instead of making a scene,' said Ned, 'I should have forgotten all about it. I have other things on my mind. But I want to be humanitarian, and I'll cancel the visit to his father. For the moment, at least . . .'

'Bravo,' said Miss Charlotte.

'But,' continued Ned, 'for the sake of example, the next time I catch him, I'll pin him to the door by the ear.'

'Oh, how barbarous,' exclaimed Miss Charlotte.

'Ned,' said Amelia, 'I don't recognize you, you remind me of the horrors of the Spanish Inquisition.'

Miranda, in a white lace-edged apron, came to serve coffee in place of Barnaby who was temporarily indisposed . . . The beautiful West Indian woman always caught Ned's eye. A splendid head of brown hair with auburn tints fell to her neck, where it was gathered up, as in a bag, by a gold hairnet. He could feel Elizabeth's anxious eyes on him, and he turned his gaze immediately away from the maid, whose walk and every movement might charm him with its un-affected grace, but he refused the cup of coffee that she was about to set down in front of him. That gesture restored Elizabeth to life.

The hours dragged by until evening. Kept under more or less discreet surveillance, the two lovers were resigned to their fate until the time came to say good-night at the bottom of the stairs. Of her own accord, Elizabeth stroked Ned's face and whispered:

'It's dreadful, you're leaving.'

'It'll still be dark when I leave. You won't see me, you'll be asleep.'

'Oh, no!'

He wanted to kiss her, she turned away.

'Only on the cheek,' she said.

With the same voracity as on the previous day, he covered her face with kisses.

At that moment, Miss Charlotte's steps could be heard on the doorstep.

'Good-night, Elizabeth,' said Ned aloud.

'Good-night, Ned.'

Without even touching the bannister, she was up the stairs in a couple of seconds.

95

*T*he winter night was very long. In her big four-poster
bed, Elizabeth tossed back and forth unceasingly, her
head full of thoughts that put a certain end to sleep. Ned
had looked at Miranda. He had ostentatiously refused the
cup of coffee. In the pine plantation, he had frightened her,
but she should not have compared him to an animal. She
had humiliated him.

From time to time she could hear pine branches brushing
against the walls of the house with a noise like a broom.
Then she would pull the sheets over her head. She should
not have told him that she found human nature disgusting
. . . There were so many things that she should not have said.

The room became vast in the darkness, like the vault of
Heaven. A red patch quivered in the fireplace, giving off a
feeble glow that allowed one to make out the Flemish wardrobes that had become enormous. Suddenly old Betty crossed
the room without making a sound and threw the last remaining logs on to the ashes. Elizabeth looked at her for a
moment and closed her eyes.

Voices dragged her from her sleep. The coarse and clear-
cut intonation of a common man could be heard outside.
Elizabeth was on her feet instantly.

'Betty, where are you?'

Betty appeared. One never knew where she sprang from.
Perhaps she had been sleeping in a corner of the room in
order to keep an eye on her mistress.

'Get into bed, Miss Lizbeth, it's cold.'

'Quickly, my shoes, my coat, my shawl . . .'

Her voice was so insistent that the maid obeyed straight
away.

A minute later Elizabeth was running along the corridor
towards the staircase which she jumped down two steps at a
time.

An icy cold invaded the house through the open door.
Elizabeth had time to see Ned in a black coat about to take
his seat beside the butcher. Bounding up to him just as he
put his foot on the running board, she shouted to him:

'Come back quickly, Ned!'

He put his fingers to his lips.

She would have liked to fling her soul after him in a cry, no matter what. The whip cracked, she lost her head and yelled:

'Never mind about human nature!'

The hours that followed were amongst the most painful that she had experienced in America. Only the farewell to Jonathan had cost her such bitter tears. Lying flat on her stomach on her bed, with her face in the pillow, the cry that she had let out seemed to her inexplicably absurd, but she had wanted to shout something, and then that stupid phrase had come to her ... Sometimes she disliked her uncotrollable excesses of language.

Crying was a relief however, and Betty, who was watching her from a corner of the room, did nothing to help her. She simply threw a thick blanket over her, for the wood fire had not yet warmed the room up sufficiently. She knew also that the pains of love were not to be cured with words and had quickly understood that Miss Lizbeth was mad about Mass'r Ned, but she kept quiet.

In the house that the stillness of the snow had made even more silent, Elizabeth made an effort to regain a taste for life, but she did not know what to do with herself. None of the books in the library held her attention; novels, poetry, sermons above all, products of another age, seemed to her good only for throwing out of the window. The only thing that might have attracted her was a glass-fronted bookcase that was kept locked, where Charlie Jones kept for his own personal use volumes hidden behind a curtain of dark red silk, the color of crime.

96

The following morning, beneath a dark, grey sky, the
vastness of the snow seemed to be waiting for something
to be written in it. Crows with widespread wings tore at the
silence with their discordant cry.

As Betty was helping to button up Elizabeth's dress for
her, Jemima knocked at the door and came in.

'Miss Charlotte asked me to bring you this letter that the
mailman has just delivered.'

The letter was thick. Elizabeth tore the envelope on which
the fine, careful handwriting of Miss Llewelyn was spread
out.

Settled beside the fire in the rocking chair, the girl told
Betty:

'Leave me alone. I'll call you later.'

She had in fact read, at the top of a large sheet of paper,
these words that made her heart leap:

Palais Wilczeck, 10 December 1850

My beloved,

I have finally made Miss Llewelyn promise that she
would forward my letter, and here I am, at last, at your
feet, in spirit at least. How can I give you some idea as to
the dreadful state of my soul? I am living in a palace and
I am in Hell. One would not find in the whole of America
a dwelling of such magnificence, and all the pleasures of
the world are available to me, but you are far away. I was
out of my mind when I married that woman, tortured by
the idea of having her to myself. You cannot really understand these things, because your soul is pure, and it's
not a question of the soul with her. I doubt if she even
has one. She is a vampire. Whereas you are all soul, she
is all flesh. She has seduced the most blasé city in
Europe, the most difficult, the capital of a vast empire
— but can you even follow what I'm saying? I'm writing
the first thing that comes to mind because I am crazed
with grief, and I want you to understand. My hand does
not obey me properly.

Elizabeth got up from her chair and ran to the window where the daylight was becoming a little stronger. A strange fear welled up inside her. Despite all her efforts, she could not make out all the letters that ran into each other: the lines collided with one another. The whole of the bottom of the page was nothing but unintelligible scribble. One would have thought the words had been scrawled in the dark and at top speed. What added to the mystery was that a furious hand had botched it all with a large ragged line. She waited for a moment, torn between alarm and violent curiosity. Resuming her place beside the fire, she turned over the page to one dated the 12th of December:

The night is over. I'm continuing this letter without daring to re-read the beginning. I would undoubtedly be tempted to throw it on the fire.

Calm has returned to this palace. Everything is mad here, even the staircases are full of statues. There was a party which lasted until dawn, you can't imagine the tumult of music, waltzes and the wine that accompanies such interminable banquets. After which, my wife ... It's not possible to tell you certain things. I don't want to be the slave of that creature who hates me and whom I should like to be able to kill, but we need each other, there is that diabolical link between us. You know nothing about life.

When I think of you — oh, do you remember? — I see you once more at Dimwood, at the end of the verandah. In the white light of the night sky, your face leaning towards mine amongst the leaves that your fingers move aside, and you are like an apparition, a spirit from an unknown world, and, without speaking, you fill me with an ephemeral joy. You are the one I have always searched for, who can wrench me away from this earth. I have lived for pleasure, and I hate pleasure, I cannot free myself from that constantly recurring appetite, ever more voracious, and when I saw you later on the quayside, in the crowd, and our mouths touched, I understood that my life would have no meaning if I had to live without you. It's you I wanted, not that female monster to whom I'm attached by a senseless marriage which I shall break.

If you were to see her, calm and disdainful as a queen, in these salons where all the aristocracy of Vienna gathers, you would understand that there is some evil force inside her. I tell you she is not human. In her white satin dresses, she remains unbelievably beautiful, unsullied by the worst excesses. Unquestionably she is there on account of the name which I gave her. The exotic blood that flows in her veins only serves to make her more irresistibly seductive. With my heart in torment, I realize that in the eyes of Viennese society I am no more than that woman's husband. It would be ridiculous to wonder if she is at least faithful to me. I would kill in a duel the man I suspected of taking her from me, but all of those smiling faces know how to lie, and when she disappears in a carriage for a whole day at a time, where does she go? In the evening she is there again, overwhelming me with her indecent tenderness which I cannot do without. She never asks me any questions. And so I am abhorred, Elizabeth. It is to you that I turn as to my only hope. Marriage . . . Mine has been a trap. The law is clear. It protects that woman whose name I cannot even bring myself to write. If she could die, if someone could kill her . . . I shall try to free myself in order to join you, I shall find some means, I'm thinking of seeing a lawyer, not my own who is too legal-minded, manifestly too much won over to that woman's desires, but one of those shady characters, experienced in all the devious ways of the profession. I know some, this is not my first attempt. So the day will come when I shall get away from Europe and be able to join you over there, to clasp you in my arms, to be yours for ever . . . Write to me, my love, fear nothing, no one will see your letter, I shall take care of that, but for Heaven's sake, write to me or I shall die.

Your Jonathan

At the bottom of this page, where the words seemed to jostle with one another in a kind of panic, a firm hand had written one line: 'My poor child.'

Elizabeth recognized Miss Llewelyn's writing and dropped

the letter. The Welshwoman had read it all before her. She felt as if she had been robbed.

For a moment she remained motionless in her rocking chair, no longer knowing whether she was happy or disappointed. Those cries of love alternating with explosions of hatred disturbed her, pained her. That was not the voice she had been hoping to hear when she opened the envelope, and the fact that that woman's little green eyes had scanned that desperate scribbling from top to bottom spoiled everything. The moment that counted the most in her life, those minutes at the end of the verandah and Jonathan's face through the foliage, all that was no longer her secret, and the governess's pity made her indignant, as if she had suffered some affront.

Other letters would undoubtedly follow and be sullied too by the inquisitive gaze of the governess, unless, giving in to Jonathan's imploring, she ran the risk of writing to him directly in Vienna, and then would begin that sinister business, the name of which caused her a nagging worry: a criminal correspondence.

In any case, she did not have to write to him straight away. The two or three words of love which she had confided to the Welshwoman would reach him soon, crossing with those two rambling pages, he would take it to be an answer . . .

Then in a brusque reaction, she felt ashamed of her prudence and her cowardice. For, after all, it was Jonathan.

She sat down at her bureau and wrote one sentence only:

My Jonathan, a first love remains always the only one, you are that one for ever.

Your Elizabeth

The letter was hurriedly folded and slid into an envelope. She wrote out the address with care and hid the audacious missive in her drawer.

'It's true, after all,' she said aloud, as if answering someone, 'you can't replace a first love.'

That thought restored her courage and silenced the inner voice which was shouting out a name other than Jonathan's.

There was a knock at the door. It was Jemima again.

'Miss Charlotte is worried at not seeing you at breakfast.'

'I'm coming straight away.'

She found Miss Charlotte alone in the dining room and made her excuses:

'It's nothing, but I wondered if you hadn't had bad news from Dimwood.'

'No, none, rest assured.'

How she would have liked to know what was in the fat envelope!

'I hope Aunt Amelia is not unwell,' the girl said.

'A little indisposed, as happens with women in her condition.'

The little meal was fairly gloomy. Miss Charlotte was angry with the English girl for being so secretive and affected a patient expression as she watched her drink her tea, for she had consumed her three cups some time ago.

Elizabeth went back to her room as soon as was possible. In order to send her letter to Jonathan, she would have to ask Miss Charlotte to frank it. She had been rather clumsy with the elderly spinster. It would have been better to tell her anything at all, to invent something even, but not to send her away having said nothing.

And then, there was Ned! Well may she have fled from him — he was there, present, with his smile that brought everything down around her, and his Virginian accent that was as ravishing as a love song. She loved him, she felt herself helpless before him, even when he threw himself on her, as he had done in the pine wood.

Jonathan was different, it was love at first sight in the Southern night, with its enchanting perfumes, and the flashing of two pale, deep eyes, in which a gentle but terrible passion burned.

'First love cannot be replaced,' she repeated to herself. She had to write to Ned and tell him that she had loved another before him, at all costs she must do that.

Again she sat down at her writing desk and wrote:

Ned, my Ned whom I love, I want you to know. Before I knew you, I loved another man.

She hesitated, and in her fury to tell the whole truth, she added on another line:

His name was Jonathan.

This letter, in its envelope, went to join its companion, and the drawer was locked with a double turn of the key.

Days went by, then, one evening, Elizabeth was standing in front of the fire that heated her room. She had a letter in her hand. For a good while, she seemed to be thinking, and then, suddenly, she dropped the letter into the flames. After which she rang to call Jemima.

'Jemima, I need this letter for Virginia University franked, and tomorrow morning you will give the letter to the mail-man.'

97

*T*he simplest gestures are sometimes the most significant. Elizabeth spent an excellent night and, the following morning, the letter was dropped into the mailman's bag, but a surprise awaited the girl.

As she was going into the dining room, she saw Miss Charlotte running up to her looking radiant:

'Good morning, my dear child. We are going to sit beside each other and chat over breakfast. I told Barnaby to leave us. We must be alone.'

Elizabeth had the impression that time, far from flying, as she had thought, had suddenly ceased to exist in these circumstances.

They sat down. Miss Charlotte herself filled Elizabeth's teacup and began:

'I thought about you last night, I was imagining strange things on account of those letters you receive from Dimwood.

I was wrong, your correspondence is none of my business, but I thought I could detect misfortune lurking. You doubtless quite simply feel nostalgic sometimes for the old house with its columns.'

'Sometimes, yes.'

'Say no more, that's enough. This morning, I saw in Jemima's hands a letter for Ned, your letter, dear Elizabeth, and I took the liberty of completing the address: Room 40. Remember it, write to him, you'll make him so happy. Perhaps you are not aware of it, but he is a reserved boy, quite restrained in his feelings. You'll know him better some day. I admit that more than once I have let myself go with dreaming the dreams of a solitary soul deprived of love. Don't miss out on love, Elizabeth, don't miss out on life as I did, and eat your pancakes before they get cold. If ever you see the spark glowing in Ned's heart, oh, do not put it out . . .'

She suddenly hid her face in her serviette.

'I can't fight it off,' she said at last, bringing her fist down on the table. 'These tears are tears of rage on account of my wasted life. I don't want to feel sorry for myself, but the hand of the Lord weighed down on me. If you feel yourself to be in love, put all your strength into it. Amelia doesn't understand me, she is shut up in her own little world.'

Without a word, Elizabeth took the elderly spinster in her arms, knocking her cap askew.

'I can't bear to see you unhappy,' she said at last, 'you know that we all love you, me even more than the others.'

'It's not the same thing,' said Miss Charlotte, 'you don't know what life is like. And you're spoiling my hair, you hadn't even noticed that I'd put a little ostrich feather in my ribbons to celebrate . . . to celebrate what? I don't know what I'm saying any more.'

'But I did notice the pretty feather. The ladies in Savannah wear them sometimes, above the ear, like you.'

But Miss Charlotte would not be consoled.

'I was wrong to move the sofa out the day before Ned left. It was clumsy. I might have known that there would be nothing serious to fear from a boy of fine feelings such as he.'

'I should have had something to say too,' said Elizabeth proudly.

'Of course, but with me the same mistakes would be made as when Jonah . . .'

With a childish gesture, Elizabeth placed her ten fingers over her mouth, as if to prevent Miss Charlotte from saying 'Jonathan', but 'Jonah' remained 'Jonah'.

'What's the matter?' asked Miss Charlotte. 'Jonah is a very nice name.'

Elizabeth nodded and Miss Charlotte continued:

'When Jonah came to visit me . . . Papa was present at our conversations, sitting with us, not opening his mouth. So speaking of love in such circumstances . . . Ah, let's leave all that. Let's forget. I'm going to make an effort to entertain you while we wait for the snow to melt. Spring will return.'

'It's obliged to, in theory,' Elizabeth remarked with a certain bitterness.

'Do you want me to invite the children from over the way? They sometimes wave a white flag to signal us. They pretend that they're dying of hunger, because they're fed up with their mother's cooking. One has to admit that Maisie lacks imagination when it comes to her kitchen range. And then, they're bored.'

'If they really have enough to eat, perhaps you could wait.'

'What a burden you take from my shoulders! If you had insisted that they come . . .'

'I can wait.'

From that moment, the conversation began to flag, and they went separate ways. Then the nothingness of the morning gave way to the nothingness of the afternoon.

There was simply nothing to do at Great Meadow. Everything confirmed as much to Elizabeth as she explored the old house in the hope of coming across something new, some detail in the background of a painting . . . In each room the same silence awaited her, barely disturbed by the sound of steps in the corridor and, at each window, the same unmoving snow and sky. Day after day, nothing moved. This obliteration of life oppressed her. One morning, when she was in the large drawing room, it came to her with the certainty of a revelation that time was passing by like a hurricane in that place where everything bore the imprint of death. No force in the world could stop it, and it was carrying her along without a second's remission. This thought struck her with horror, she wondered what one could cling to in order to stay in one's place and hold on to life, the present moment, youth.

Her letter to Ned had been sent three days ago. She did not dare remember too clearly what she had put in it. How would he react to the truth? And that too was far away from her now, carried along with all the rest.

As for Jonathan, he was so far away that he seemed to be receding backwards in time. She would wait for long weeks on end for him to answer her four or five lines without a signature, crossing an ocean in order to seek him out in some baroque palace.

Waiting and waiting, something inside her could do so no more when, one evening, Jemima brought her a letter.

Ned. She prepared the usual ritual: the armchair by the fire, in her room, the lamp standing close by, and she read:

West Campus, Room 40
30 January 1851

Elizabeth, my love, having said that, I've said it all. With my pen in my hand, I'm as clumsy as a schoolboy, so I hope you'll understand. I say everything straight off, without fine phrases or dressing it up. Your letter came as a shock. If I did not adore you to the point of folly, I would make the trip to Great Meadow just to shake you. You are as naive as you are innocent. What need was there to tell me the name Jonathan? Do you think I was taken in when we were playing at pretending? Did you seriously think that I had not understood when you were addressing passionate calls to that gentleman, that some-one else before me had claimed a place in your heart?

What is disarming about you is your refusal to lie. I don't know anything about your Jonathan, but one thing is clear: he can't have taught you much, and he left you — so what? I don't like to use certain words that can easily seem ridiculous . . . But, damn it all, you are as pure as before. You may look like a young lady, but the little girl in you is alive and well. You have a freshness that I cannot resist. You will see how I shall love you,

Elizabeth, if you can get over your dreams. Don't say no to love, my Elizabeth, don't say no to your Ned.

The girl read the letter once more, then put it eagerly to her lips. She covered it with kisses again and again. These outbursts went on to the point where she thought she was going mad. She came to believe that the sheet of paper retained something of the hand that had been placed on it, the warmth of the palm and of the fingers.

A considerable time passed before she could be separated from the letter which she locked in the drawer of her writing desk, with that of 'the other one', whose name she could no longer bring herself to speak aloud. And yet, just as she was turning the key in the lock, she let out a cry of distress:

'Jonathan!'

98

Miss Charlotte came up to her in the dining room and, without even saying hello to her, immediately asked:
'How is he?'
Elizabeth looked at her distractedly:
'Who?' she said.
The spinster recoiled and supported herself on a chair. A horrible sadness clouded over her face and she was speechless as if from the announcement of some bad news.
Elizabeth pulled herself together.
'Ned is fine, why are you worried?'
'How do I know?' said Miss Charlotte trying to smile. 'I'm constantly in a state of trembling on your account. That's my sentimental nature. And then I'm afraid he's not eating properly at the university.'

'He doesn't mention that.'

'Is he pleased?'

'I suppose so. The letter is very . . . nice.'

'All is well then!' exclaimed Miss Charlotte. 'We can live again and be happy on earth. Sit down next to me.'

Elizabeth sat in her usual place and a thought suddenly went through her mind:

'Where is Uncle Charlie?'

'Probably in Savannah. We're waiting to hear from him. Why?'

'Do you think he'll be going to Dimwood soon?'

'Undoubtedly, but he'll write all that to us. Are you still thinking about Dimwood?'

'I have memories there.'

'We'll take you there one day when it's fine.'

Soon Uncle Charlie would be handing her message to Jonathan to the Welshwoman. She closed her eyes.

'I had these sesame buns made especially for you. But what's wrong with you?'

'Nothing,' said Elizabeth, and began to nibble a bun, then drank her tea docilely.

And so the pretending game continued throughout her daily life.

That evening she wrote Ned a letter that seemed to her a model of wisdom:

My darling Ned. Don't torment yourself. The answer you are asking me for is not one that can be given by correspondence. For that, we shall have to see each other and talk to each other. Now it's my turn to admire your innocence! But have no fears, you will never be made to suffer by the one you already call your Elizabeth.

She felt she had given away less than she might have done. All thoughts of marriage were suspended.

The letter went, and time rushed through every room of the house and over all the expanse of snow, like an invisible tornado, but the answer from Ned did not come.

On the other hand, she received from Charlie Jones a

letter that she opened with her legs feeling like jelly, and yet she was reassured:

Dear Elizabeth, I gave your letter to Miss Llewelyn who used it to fan herself with while we were chatting in the sun in the great avenue on a more or less spring morning, after which she slipped it into her pocket. As you see, I have been the perfect go-between. Charlotte will give you fuller news of Dimwood, where you are still spoken with a sigh. I embrace my charming cousin from England and do not forget the promises made beneath the sycamore in front of my house at Savannah.

Uncle Charlie.

From then on, it was a question of waiting. Ned did not come. If he was sulking, she would sulk even longer and better: in the English manner. Several letters to Jonathan were written in the great silence of the night, and thrown on the fire one after the other. In the house opposite, they were waving the white flag, and that was about the only event in weeks.

Miss Charlotte had really no news of Dimwood to give, for nothing of note disturbed the succession of days there, other than that Minnie had become engaged to a Mr Siverac from New Orleans. Charlie Jones announced in his letter that a friend of his family had been invited to spend a few weeks at Great Meadow: Miss Eliza B. Furnace, a lovely person who could not take the climate of Georgia. She could be expected in the first days of spring.

A black and icy January gave way, amidst a snow storm, to a turbulent February, interspersed with abrupt interludes of sunlight. The winds chased the clouds in every direction in impatient outbursts to have done with winter. Ice cracked and melted in the ruts on the paths, and there were times when the sudden mildness of the air filled Elizabeth's heart with joy.

Amelia stayed in her room now, and Miss Charlotte kept her company. Sometimes she would prepare her a precious potion for which only she had the recipe, sometimes she would hold discourse with her on the soul and the after-life. On one day only was Elizabeth admitted to the room with half-drawn curtains, and stood for a moment beside that woman who was even more majestic lying down than standing. Propped up on three cushions, she had on her cap decorated with lilac ribbons, barely parting her lips to speak with an intriguing slowness about the rigors of the season. These words, spoken with an indefinable kindness, seemed to be offered to the English girl as marks of favor. After which she lowered her eyelids and retreated into herself, dismissing the visitor ... The latter looked at her for a moment until Miss Charlotte showed her out into the corridor.

'Does she stay like that doing nothing for long?' asked Elizabeth.

'From morning till evening. She is a saintly person.'

'I find her a bit frightening. Does she not move?'

'She doesn't move, she says she is in conversation with God.'

'Do you believe her?'

'Let's leave it there, my girl; I don't know any more about it than you. But she eats well. She has two people to feed. It'll be in July ... You've had your visit. It was all very good, very proper.'

99

*I*n accordance with tradition from time immemorial, the month of March had the right either to come in like a lamb and go out like a lion, or vice versa. In the grip of a haughty capriciousness, it both came in and went out like a lion. For thirty days, the wind howled amidst the turbulent clouds and turned chimneys into organ pipes. A sinister and powerful voice announced misfortune to people blinded by black smoke. In consequence, Charlie Jones' return was hailed as an intervention by Providence. A kind of order was re-established with his return. He had porcelain stoves brought up from the cellar, and they were installed in the middle of each of the principal rooms. Interminable pipes linked them to the chimneys, almost managing to domesticate the furious rushes of air.

He himself was as usual pink and full of news, of which he gave little bits at a time, for he spent the greater part of his leisure with his wife, whose condition made him permanently anxious. Like many of his temperament, he appreciated the joys of marriage and feared its difficult moments. He would have preferred to go on a tour of the Caribbean islands and return to the great house to find a handsome child, all new and clean in the women's hands, while Amelia, delivered from the nightmare of giving birth, would throw herself into his arms with sobs of love. Unfortunately, duty rose up before him like a knight in shining armor: a constant and over-bearing pressure.

Elizabeth was almost entirely ignorant of this less amusing aspect of the love between man and woman. She was not unaware of the fact that in the case of Romeo and Juliet, had they lived, their unforgettable effusiveness on the balcony and elsewhere would inevitably have ended in Juliet's suffering, not Romeo's. That gave food for thought and reinforced her rather sulky approach to Ned. The latter's silence allowed the girl to retreat and to discover herself, as she believed herself to be. Previously she had been beset by all the dizziness of innocence. From now on she would be wary and hard to please. The suitors could wait, grow up, Ned in his colonnades, and even her Jonathan amidst the gilding of his baroque palace. In short, she felt herself to be a woman. Soon she would discover that she still had everything to learn.

Wrenched violently from its sleep, nature was stirring in every sense of the word. The snow in the meadow was melting, exposing here and there great islands of blackish grass that grew bigger every day.

Opposite, the distress-call flag was still waving in Clementine's window, but Miss Charlotte remained firm. Elizabeth wondered if the Commodore and his wife were aware of this frenzied signalling. Charlotte assured her that they had no idea of it. The 'children' were served a substantial, but unvaried diet, as in the navy. That shirt on the end of a broom-handle was no more than the emblem of an oppressed greediness. Furthermore Amelia would never have coped with the din made by those rowdies.

At table, Uncle Charlie tried to restore good humor in those last days of a dismal winter.

'The heat is setting in very gradually in that paradise at Dimwood. The flowers are coming out. Dear Minnie is wearing a wonderful sapphire on her finger. Siverac does things well. He was brought up in Charleston and dreams of nothing but secession, a little cloud on the horizon . . . Another problem, and a big one: my poor friend William Hargrove sees the return of Jonathan Armstrong, to demand his house, drawing closer.'

At these words, Elizabeth nearly dropped her teacup and put her napkin to her lips to stifle a cry. She thought she saw the whole dining room, with Uncle Charlie, Miss Charlotte and Barnaby, shake. 'I'm going to faint,' she thought, 'I'm going to give myself away.'

She got a grip on herself, however, and seized the edge of the table with both hands. No one noticed. Uncle Charlie's quiet voice continued:

'He still has a year to go and we shall be there to help him hold out, but he has always lived in terror. It's been like that since . . .'

His eyes followed Barnaby's comings and goings, and he fell silent. A moment passed and he resumed in a more cheerful tone of voice:

'I'm counting a great deal on Miss Eliza Furnace to cheer up the house. You'll adore that woman, Elizabeth, her presence is a ray of sunlight. She promised to come during the first days of April . . . But, my dear child, you are quite pale . . . what's happened to your lovely pink English cheeks?'

'I feel perfectly alright,' said Elizabeth firmly.

Without answering, Uncle Charlie fixed her with an attentive gaze. She sniffed danger and did not flinch. In moments such as these, all of her courage was aroused and, for a few seconds, there was a silent battle between them: what was the opponent thinking? In her girlish head, a suspicion was emerging: the Welshwoman had spoken. As for Uncle Charlie, he remained impenetrable. He finally gave a broad smile:

'Elizabeth,' he said cheerfully, 'I understand that you feel nostalgic for the deep South. Do you remember the sycamore in front of my house in Savannah?'

'As if I were there now,' she said, aiming an aggressive flash of her blue eyes at him.

He bowed his head as if in recognition of the way in which she had parried the blow.

When she was alone in her room, her anger exploded, restoring to her face all the roses of England.

'People lie here, just as everywhere else,' she said to herself indignantly. 'Uncle Charlie is a hypocrite with his double meanings. Miss Llewelyn gave away the secret of our correspondence. All is lost. All I can do is write to Mama that I want to go home.'

Minutes went by. She wrote, not to her mother, but to Jonathan. This love letter of farewell seemed admirable to her. She read it and re-read it, and each time the page became more moving and more beautiful ... A brief moment of uncertainty, then Elizabeth threw it on the fire. That simple gesture calmed her down strangely.

'How worthless it all is!' she exclaimed.

What did she mean? She herself had no idea. The words had taken shape on her lips of their own accord. She felt free. As for Ned ... oh, him ...

One grows weary of everything, even a victory. She had given a lesson in modesty to the student from Charlottesville, and the day came when she surmised that he was getting his revenge by not writing to her. The thought occurred to her that he might have had enough of her teasing, and that he was no longer interested in her. At that her pride began to bleed and she went into a panic. Swallowing her self-esteem, she went to the drawing room and asked Miss Charlotte, in an indifferent tone of voice if, by chance, she had heard anything from Ned:

'Oh, yes, he's very busy. He just has time to scribble a couple of lines. Perfect health. Uncle Charlie got a longer letter as well. You had nothing. No letters, but he's going to pay us a little visit at the end of April. So, patience, my little one.'

'I'm not at all impatient,' said Elizabeth haughtily.

'Perhaps, but you look like someone in need of a good dose of laudanum to calm your nerves. Do you even know how to prepare your laudanum?'

Rather annoyed, Elizabeth admitted that she did not.

'Basically you know nothing about life,' said Miss Charlotte with a laugh. 'As Charlie and Jemima are seeing to Amelia, I have a moment to spare. Follow me, you know-nothing.'

Putting her Bible down on a small table, she got out of her armchair by the fire and led Elizabeth to her bedroom. This was directly underneath the room where Teddy Brown, the young future pastor, had slept during his stay at Great Meadow. The dimensions were the same, but that was the extent of any resemblance. As she crossed the threshold Elizabeth admired the wall hung with pale blue chintz strewn with countless little flowers, with cornflowers and forget-me-nots dominating. The walls alone proclaimed the transparency of Miss Charlotte's almost childlike soul. The elm-wood furniture seemed rather large for this person of small stature. The inevitable rocking chair, upholstered in lime-flower velvet, stood by the window that looked out on to the long range of smoky blue hills. Just above the window, a verse from a psalm in Gothic letters embroidered in petit-point cast a serious note into the softness of the decor:

I lift my eyes unto the hills.
From whence cometh my help?

Is it necessary to add that a double row of pious literature occupied the whole of one corner of the room, where could also be seen a fine steel engraving of a detailed view of Jerusalem?

'There,' said Miss Charlotte with a smile, 'my refuge against the wicked of this world. That,' she said as she pointed to a small four-poster bed, 'is the place where bad memories from the past are wiped away. And now, to work!' she added with feverish activity as she opened a fabric-covered door leading to a washroom next to the bedroom.

The first thing Elizabeth saw was a table covered with an

assortment of phials, porcelain bowls, filters. Stills lent to the whole an appearance of medieval witchcraft that disturbed her slightly. More than all the rest, she was intrigued by a retort, enthroned in the centre of the table, in which a golden liquid slumbered. On closer examination, she noticed a kind of black mud at the bottom.

Miss Charlotte left her no time to dream.

'Listen to me,' she said, 'and remember what I tell you. I don't like repeating myself. What you can see there are poppy seeds from Smyrna, the best. You crush them to make a powder. Evil tongues call it forgetting powder. Are you with me?'

'Yes, so far,' said Elizabeth, already bewildered by this new Miss Charlotte, whom she was newly discovering in this dimly lit place.

'One hundred and twenty-five grammes,' the latter continued as she gave a slight flick to a small pair of scales. 'One gramme of cinnamon essence. That from Ceylon has more body to it. A gramme of essence of cloves, a few shreds of saffron. I'm not in favour of putting a lot in, because it upsets the liver. Finally nine hundred and twenty grammes of thirty-degree alcohol. You leave it to macerate for ten days and stir it every night before you go to bed.'

'Before going to bed,' repeated Elizabeth, who was beginning to lose the thread.

'Afterwards,' continued Miss Charlotte implacably, 'when it resembles water . . .'

'When it becomes quite clear,' suggested Elizabeth, pretending to understand.

'Oh, no. Make an effort to understand. When the liquid and the residue have quite separated, as you can see it is now, I carefully pour the liquid into a still, through a filter.'

With her delicate old hands with their raised veins, she carried out this operation.

'You filter the residue in its turn and press it hard so as not to lose any of its qualities. Follow me now to the other side of the table . . . and watch carefully.'

Then she took test tubes and small flasks, made some mixtures, heated them and poured the result into a still that she filled up with distilled water, then with a liquid that she added while holding her nose:

'Ether,' she murmured.

Without waiting, she shook it all and put it down on the table.

'Rest,' she said addressing the phial. 'On the quality of your rest depends the quality of ours. Oof!'

In all of this handling of bizarre objects, this transferring of one thing to another, this mysterious brand of cookery, there was a seriousness that evoked memories of the days when old women were burned at the stake, convicted of consorting with the Devil. One would have to admit that, with her tall bonnet and her ribbons, poor little Miss Charlotte might have passed for a suspect. The dim lighting in the washroom added to this sinister illusion in Elizabeth's mind. Timidly she asked:

'Miss Charlotte, how am I going to manage to remember all that?'

'I foresaw that question, but don't panic. I've written it all down on this piece of paper that you will keep carefully and never show to anyone. Never, do you hear? Not even to a husband! There are all the secrets: ether, iron chloride, hydrochloric acid, everything. As for the measurements, you can read up the details later. That's the essential, the secret in the heart of the secret.'

'And what's going to happen now?'

'The liquid will separate out in this phial. It will be red in colour, to be mixed with port. One piece of advice, but an important one: don't take too much. It reduces the appetite dramatically. Just one exception, my sister.'

'Ah?' said Elizabeth.

And under the impulse of that demon that lures people into imprudent remarks, she asked in all innocence:

'But, Miss Charlotte, can't you buy that at the pharmacist's?'

Miss Charlotte hurled a terrifying glare in her direction:

'Miss Escridge, what cannot be bought at the pharmacist's is quality, mine.'

Elizabeth apologized, but for a while she could hear the rapid breathing of the elderly spinster whose pride as an expert had been wounded. The girl's look of consternation finally calmed her down.

'I realize that it's not simple,' she said as she led the way back into the bedroom. 'And then you don't know what laudanum means to us. When I was living up there in Scotland, in the Highlands, alone in my room, after the great disappointment that you know about, given up to despair, how would I have been able to carry on living without the help of those few red drops in the bottom of a glass?'

Elizabeth looked at her in silence.

'Oh, I know one could say there's the Bible. In spite of everything, certain days, in really black moments, you'd say that it doesn't speak to us, that it leaves us in our abyss ... on purpose. You will experience such trials, they come to everyone. God is there, however, even when he hides his face. I thank him for being there. We must thank God for being God.'

These words, uttered in a flat, breathless voice, moved Elizabeth so much that she had to lean against one of the pillars of the bed in order to calm down. Such religious exaltation found in her a deep echo, the violence of which surprised her, because she felt that everything about her was put at risk, her future, her dreams of love ... Horror mingled with admiration, and she looked in silence at the little red face, the eyes aflame with intensity.

Suddenly Miss Charlotte flung herself into the rocking chair, turning her back on Elizabeth in order to fix her gaze on the hills. She rocked back and forth in this way for several minutes, and the creaking of the floorboards was the only thing disturbing the silence.

With an abruptness that betrayed an inner state of tension, she finally got up, seeking to get a grip on herself.

'I wonder what you must think of me,' she said.

'Miss Charlotte, I love you the way you are,' said Elizabeth simply.

Miss Charlotte seemed not to pay any attention to that reply.

'I put up no resistance,' she said. 'When the spirit forces me to, I speak.'

Then, in a voice that had returned to normal, she said straight off:

'It's cold in my room, let's go down and have a cup of tea in the drawing room, by the fire.'

100

*I*ndifferent to the strivings of men, spring promised to be all smiles. Buds were scattered along the hedgerows and trees were wrapped in a timid brushing of foliage. This as yet discreet joy seemed not to have arrived at the great house, where the predominant concern was Amelia's rest. Not the slightest sound was tolerated around the room in which she awaited July's 'event' in a haze of laudanum.

Uncle Charlie was in a dreadful mood, seeing the labor pains advancing towards him, as if they had been his own and not his wife's . . . A delegation of the starving from the House of Chaos was turned unceremoniously away.

Fleeing from this austere atmosphere, Elizabeth gave herself up almost every day to the delights of a gallop. On the roads that were dry once more, resounded again Alcibiades' glorious clip-clop invariably carrying his mistress off into the forest where she dreamed day after day of the divine encounter with Jonathan — since Ned no longer wrote. She had even chosen the spot where the reunion would be celebrated: beneath the enormous oak tree whose gigantic branches extended over the road. For he had said that he would come back. For her, that hope, that certainty, replaced the most expertly mixed of laudanums. Her heart emptied itself out under the trees to the accompaniment of impassioned monologues, sometimes even shouts. Who could hear her in this solitude?

Back home again, one evening, she sat down at her writing desk, and with a schoolgirl's careful hand, made a little drawing of the exact place in the forest where the meeting was to take place. The tree was there, on that sheet of paper, with its low branches, each as thick as a smaller tree: it was impossible to mistake it. Together with a note burning with love, that letter was entrusted to Jemima, who handed it to the mailman.

At home, with all the doors closed, mealtimes took an unusual turn. Although he did not spurn the dishes that were always tasty, Charlie Jones gave way to bouts of deep pessimism. Everything in the world was going badly. In

France, the Prince-President, supported by the military, was waging an incipient war on the National Assembly, which was demanding a return to the constitution of '48. In Vienna (an ear pricked up) disruption in the parliament: Prince Schwarzenberg had subdued Hungary, which had been on the brink of rebellion.

'Even in London, Queen Victoria is not much liked; too German ... they're talking about the Eastern question again ... And at home in America, that dangerous fool, Pastor Beecher, has just discovered slavery, about which he had never said a word before, and is throwing himself wholeheartedly into an indictment of the South. His inexhaustible flow of verbiage makes his Northern audiences thrill with virtuous indignation. Southern preachers reply with equal elegance. All of these cretins in clerical dress, in North and South alike, are stirring up public opinion, preparing the way for tomorrow's great slaughter.'

'I think you're going a bit far, Charlie,' observed Miss Charlotte.

'Do you think so? In Savannah I learnt that the official history textbooks are being cast aside, and that Southern children are being taught that their homeland constitutes a separate nation from the North. The North is a nation, the South a different one. We've known that from childhood, but now it's being taught. Secession is starting to come to the boil.'

This worrying speech plunged the two listeners into consternation. They did not read the newspapers and formed only a hazy image of the outside world. Elizabeth, however, suddenly remembered something:

'In London,' she said, 'when I left the country with my mother, everybody was talking about a crystal palace that was going to be built.'

Uncle Charlie turned to look at her and his fury subsided all of a sudden.

'Quite,' he said, 'and thanks to the activities of Prince Albert, that wonder has been erected. In contrast to the periodic convulsions on the continent, England remains calm and in control of herself. From all civilized countries, people are hastening to admire that prodigious diamond set in the south of London.'

Miss Charlotte shrugged her shoulders.

'Still a rebel, Charlotte?' said Charlie Jones with a smile.

'Scots,' she said.

'Do you hear, Elizabeth? She will never care for our England.'

'No,' exclaimed the girl, 'and I understand her, one cannot respect people who fawn to the conqueror.'

'Come now,' he said in a jovial tone of voice that was coming back to him, 'we're going off the rails a bit. I can't remember where I'd got to.'

Elizabeth's mocking voice came immediately to his aid.

'You had been fuming with anger as far as the Crystal Palace.'

He burst out laughing:

'Cheeky little thing, my word! But if I am in a bad mood, I have my reasons. I have my cross to bear too.'

'You're bearing what?' asked Miss Charlotte in a voice that was suddenly high-pitched.

'Oh, Charlotte, spare me!' he begged, and suddenly began to yell: 'Barnaby, if you continue to hover round the table in order to listen to what we're saying, I'll send you down the Mississippi.'

Barnaby disappeared.

'And now,' asked Miss Charlotte sarcastically, 'who's going to serve you your coffee, as you are the only one drinking it?'

'Well, I'll renounce it, I offer it up as a sacrifice . . .'

'And do you seriously believe that the Eternal One will accept your cup of coffee?' said Miss Charlotte.

He gave her a martyred look and went out without a word, looking dignified in his tight morning coat.

'There,' said Miss Charlotte to Elizabeth when they were alone, 'that's how to stand up to men who take themselves for gods. Remember this, they always give in.'

'Do you think so?'

'You can be sure of it. When Amelia has had her baby, Uncle Charlie will be himself again. But why wait to tell you the news? From next week onwards, you will only be here for meals. You're leaving the great house.'

Alarm transformed Elizabeth's face, her eyes widening.

'Tell me, tell me quickly.'

'Don't look so horrified. It's nothing so terrible, the contrary in fact. This morning I received a letter from Miss Eliza Furnace. She's arriving here in a week's time, a charming woman, refined . . .'

'I know, and then?'

'Less than a mile from here is a little house that you can't see on account of the trees hiding it. It's called The Coppice, in fact. It dates from before the War of Independence, and it's a model of comfort and elegance. You'll be fine there.'

'On my own?'

'Oh, no. The attractive Miss Furnace will be staying there too. She knows the house and loves it.'

'And what if, by some misfortune, I do not love Miss Furnace?'

'Impossible. By the way, Ned won't be able to come before May. Too much work. He asks me to give you his regards.'

It had become a normal state for Elizabeth to be itching with curiosity.

The very next morning she had Alcibiades saddled and set off at a gallop over the meadow and, behind a beech grove, she discovered her future dwelling place. With its pink tile roof and grey walls, the little house seemed as pleasant to her as could be. She found five of Uncle Charlie's servants in the process of setting it straight, for the winter had left its mark. Wood fires were burning in every fireplace to drive away the damp. Large buckets of paint were waiting for everything to be dried out before giving a coat of eau-de-Nil to the walls, and a darker shade of green to the skirting boards. The furniture was missing, but the overall impression was pleasant. Everywhere was being swept. Elizabeth did not hang about, but continued her ride with her head full of dreams, still perplexed over Ned who did not write, and the mysterious Eliza Furnace.

The latter, moreover, kept them waiting, having put off her arrival until the last minute.

Uncle Charlie ended up hating her, for he was impatient to get Elizabeth moved out of the great house before the birth, which he foresaw as a dramatic event.

May was triumphant, with its brand-new flowers and

foliage, its blue skies and thousand of birds practising their scales with enthusiasm, and still the lady did not put in an appearance. It was for the best, however, as far as The Coppice was concerned, as the paint had time to dry, but nerves were on edge at Great Meadow.

She arrived at last in the middle of the night, in a manner destined to annoy everyone as much as possible, the whim of a pretty woman. Dressing gowns came to meet her, and polite grimaces attempted to make her believe this pleasant surprise was a joyful occasion. She accepted it all with a smile of infallible charm which Charlie Jones found quite disarming; it even had an effect on Miss Charlotte, but it did not cheer Elizabeth who remained somber. 'She is prettier than me,' she thought, 'and Ned doesn't write to me any more.' What link was there between these two observations? The English girl preferred not to go into the matter any further. She was afraid.

In her light beige travelling outfit, Miss Furnace was a match for any of the elegant women of the South. Her cape had slid from her shoulders down to the carpet, and she had thrown her otter-skin cap on to a sofa. One could not be cross with her for her casual behaviour, her face excused everything. Thick brown hair with copper tints framed a small, exquisitely delicate oval face, in which shone large, violet eyes that at times looked languid and, at others distant.

In his damask dressing gown, Charlie Jones felt himself to be handsome, and he harvested a few dangerous smiles that it was better for Amelia to remain ignorant of. It was at such a moment that Miss Furnace declared in a delightfully pert tone of voice:

'I am really insufferable, but I'm dying of hunger. Dare I admit it to you? A simple midnight feast, a few sandwiches and a thimbleful of champagne — if it wouldn't be putting anyone to any trouble!'

Uncle Charlie looked in desperation at Miss Charlotte, who hurried out.

A strange disruption then invaded the colored people's dormitory as they were dragged from their beds, and the kitchen range was relit.

In the meantime, Miss Furnace was chatting with Uncle Charlie in the drawing room, in front of a roaring fire that made her look resplendently youthful. Sitting in her corner, Elizabeth contented herself with observing the seductive woman in action, bending her ear to the delightful intonation that was sometimes unexpected, as if she came from elsewhere.

'After a long tour around bustling Europe,' she was saying, 'how pleased one is to be back home in the sleepy South. You who have travelled so much, do you not find that one wearies of those brilliant capitals, of the Faubourg Saint-Germain in Paris, of the balls in the palaces of Vienna, the Kinsky Palace, the Savoy, the Wittgenstein, the Wilczeck Palace (at the very name Wilczeck, Elizabeth's heart began to pound, but she remained in control of herself), the Lobkowitz Palace, and what else besides . . . The soul can then be restored in that enchanting Venezia (she put on an Italian accent). The singing of the *gondolieri* on the Gran Canale, the piazza San Marco, the Salute, what a fine dream it all is.'

As she spoke, she held her pretty little feet to the fire, having tucked up her skirt, but not so far as to show her ankles.

'Oh, my four-horse carriage is in front of the house,' she said suddenly . . .

Charlie Jones raised his hand with an angelic smile:

'Have no qualms, Miss Furnace, I will see to everything.'

Seeing to everything meant that Barnaby, who had been kicked out of his dreams, had rushed, half-dressed to the carriage that was led to the stables by a morose coachman. The same Barnaby reappeared half an hour later wearing his green livery to serve the midnight feast. The table was set as if for dinner with a white cloth and a candelabra that made the family silver gleam gently. Miss Furnace sat on Charlie Jones's right and did justice to the venison pie, not to mention the incomparable Smithfield ham, nor the coffee ice-cream that followed, limiting herself to three glasses of champagne, which was 'such as was to be had only at Voisin's restaurant in Paris.'

The problem of a bedroom was tackled head-on by Miss Charlotte. At two o'clock in the morning, Elizabeth gave up her vast room on the second floor and found herself once more in the little room in which she had spent her first days at Great Meadow. She did not complain, accepting everything in indignant silence. But she suffered as only a woman can suffer.

Betty rolled herself up in a blanket and, hiding herself in a corner of the room with the cupboards, kept watch unbeknown to Elizabeth.

Miss Furnace slept 'divinely', as she herself said the following morning.

101

*J*ust as a shout or a stone can trigger off an avalanche, so the arrival of Miss Furnace seemed to accelerate the course of events in the hitherto static life of Great Meadow.

Elizabeth and the guest settled without delay into The Coppice, where everything had been arranged for their comfort. Four-poster beds hung with muslin, upholstered seats and mirrors in all the rooms, nothing had been forgotten, and the beeches around the house already covered it with the light shade of their foliage.

Although hard to please, the great traveller swooned with admiration and uttered exclamations in several foreign languages on seeing her room. The corridor that led to it was cut off by a pretty curtain of iridescent taffeta which screened the rooms reserved for Miss Furnace. Elizabeth wondered secretly to herself, what can the eternal poor relation do in such circumstances?

Miss Charlotte came over in a gig to find out what they thought of The Coppice and was happy to learn that they were pleased.

'The house has a rather old-fashioned charm, perhaps, but everybody likes it here. I think I told you, Elizabeth, that the first Mrs Charlie Jones's mother was born here. She bequeathed it to her daughter, who made a gift of it to her husband.'

'Uncle Charlie.'

'Perfectly right, you're with me. The great house, which also belonged to the first Mrs Jones, was bequeathed to her son.'

'To Ned!' exclaimed Elizabeth.

'Oh, yes. Didn't you know? Ned is sole proprietor of Great Meadow.'

How that simple sentence changed the way everything looked . . . Elizabeth was still stupefied with surprise, and even Miss Furnace was starting to look interested.

Imperturbable, but keeping an eye on everything, Miss Charlotte continued:

'Every day a carriage will come to collect you at mealtimes. Everything is arranged for your horse-riding, you need only say the word. I see they have omitted to put vases of flowers all over the place. Jemima will make good that omission. If you are short of anything, or if there are any difficulties, let me know. I'll see you later.'

Having made this little speech in a calm voice, she gratified them both with a kind smile and left the house. With boyish agility, she climbed into her gig and set off at a trot, leaving them alone together.

Surprises followed one after the other, as if jostling for a place with each hour that passed. That afternoon, Miss Charlotte took the girl gently by the arm and led her under the trees in front of the house. There, with a smile that concealed great anxiety, she drew a letter out of one of her pockets and handed it to her:

'My dear child,' she said, 'this came for you before lunch. I didn't want to give it to you in front of Miss Furnace, who is inquisitive. I myself have neither the right nor the desire to ask you questions, but it is neither from France nor from England. I know nothing, but there is always a scent of danger hovering around you. All that I have to say to you can be summed up in one word: beware!'

The girl took the letter and turned pale:

'Has Uncle Charlie seen this?'

'Yes. He raised his eyebrows and said: "You'll simply have to give it to her." I'll see you later, Elizabeth.'

Feeling too emotional to say anything, the girl turned on

her heels and went to seek refuge in her little bedroom, which was still empty.

Coming from the Austro-Hungarian Empire, the letter, she knew, was from Jonathan, and the writing was almost as untidy as that of the first one. Buried in her armchair by the window, she read as follows:

Victory, my beloved! My marriage has been broken and I am free. Is not that something to be joyful for? But here are the facts: in despair at seeing myself bound for ever to that monster — why trouble to name her? — I consulted lawyers. Not hers, of course — she bought those fops to do her bidding — but serious, thinking men of the law. None of them gave me the least grounds to hope that I would ever be able to disentangle myself legally from those ties. The last one, however, a man of great age and wisdom, took pity on me and advised me to consult a prelate, an intimate of the highest dignitaries of the imperial court. The venerable father received me courteously and, even knowing that I was from a good family, reverentially. After the compliments, the questions . . . Oh, my beloved, why were you not present with me? You cannot imagine the subtlety, the tact and penetrating spirit of these people! I find that they are awesomely clever, and that one feels almost like a small boy when confronted with them. My intimate life was unveiled so easily. He omitted nothing, apologized for everything, but he was making progress, and suddenly, casually, he asked me how I was dressed for my marriage. I immediately gave him a very detailed description, not forgetting a piece of gold braid or a ribbon, for I was wearing the barely altered uniform of my grandfather, who was an officer in the guards under His Majesty George III.

'The sword at your side, perhaps?' he asked.

'But of course, Father, it was in the place of honor in its diamond-studded sheath.'

'Alas,' he exclaimed cheerfully, 'because of that unfortunate sword your marriage is null in the eyes of the Church.'

My marriage annulled! *Ipso facto*, he said. I could have kissed his hands. Divorce is forbidden. My beloved, I am leaving that wretched creature who was never my wife, I am leaving the Wilczeck Palace, I am leaving Vienna and I am coming. Your Jonathan is going to set out and will find you, wherever you are. Oh, no, Elizabeth, your Jonathan will not delay.

She dropped the letter and fainted.

8
MENE, MENE, TEKEL, UPHARSIN*

* Words written by an invisible hand on the wall of the banqueting hall of the palace of Belshazar, as he was giving a feast on the night when Cyrus took Babylon (Book of Daniel).

102

I t took her a long time to recover and, seized with terror, she stood up. She went to look in the mirror, as if to seek advice from the deathly pale girl who was regarding her with her mouth half open.

'What have you done?' she said under her breath questioning her double.

Her letter to Jonathan was travelling towards Europe with the address of Great Meadow, the means of getting there and the little drawing showing the forest, with a little cross marking the great tree with its enormous branches, the place of their meeting. And who could prevent Jonathan from coming, if he was free?

She suddenly tore up Jonathan's letter, not wanting to give herself time to think. And, not satisfied with having torn it, she threw the pieces into the fireplace and set them alight. In that way, she was obliterating everything. There had been no letter, Jonathan had never written. In moments of panic, she managed to convince herself that nothing had happened, that she had dreamt it. If ever he turned up, she would not move, she would stay at home. She would say she did not understand. Yet Jonathan had her letter . . .

The idea crossed her mind that the wisest thing would be to admit everything to Miss Charlotte. The elderly spinster would see to everything. Ned would not have to know. That was the most serious aspect, something which she did not dare to admit to herself.

Walking back and forth, she examined herself and, as she went past the mirror, her reflection hurled at her: 'because the great house belongs to Ned'. She uttered a cry of rage:

'But that doesn't matter to me!'

And, in order to persuade herself once more that it did not matter to her, she said the phrase over and over again. The mysterious effect of words repeated in a whisper like prayers restored her composure. She re-arranged her dishevelled hair, drank a glass of water and left the little room.

Outside, beneath the trees, she met Charlie Jones who was smoking a cigar and seemed calm, but she immediately felt certain inside herself that he had been on the look-out for her.

Indeed, he came straight up to her and said with his air of smooth kindness which was quite familiar to her:

'My dear little thing . . .'

She looked straight at him:

'Yes?' she said, almost aggressively.

'I'm worried about you.'

'You are quite wrong,' she said. 'Why not admit that you are intrigued by that letter from Austria?'

'Don't get into a rage. I wouldn't, for anything in the world . . .'

'It might give you pleasure to know that it seemed so crazy to me that I burnt it.'

He threw down his cigar which he trod out with his heel.

'Oh!' he said with a smile, 'there I see the good sense of an English girl.'

She could not stop herself from being pleased. Once more she had extricated herself without having to lie. Her pride was intact and her conscience at rest.

At The Coppice that night she went to bed late, but slept well once Miss Furnace's chattering had come to an end. Yet that beautiful brunette was amusing to listen to . . . In her pink silk dressing gown edged with ermine, she had taken the liberty of sitting down on the lime-flower velvet sofa that adorned Elizabeth's room and was giving the latter advice as to the line of correct behavior to adopt once she was launched into high society.

'After all, you're not going to stay here and die of boredom, I suppose. Get them to take you to Paris, London, Vienna. What are you waiting for? You should get yourself presented at the imperial court. It's very simple. I managed it without any difficulty, having become, for the occasion, the cousin of an archduke who had paid me a lot of attention. The Empress is an angel. I gave her a very big curtsey, with my top-knot practically touching the ground.'

'I don't know any archdukes,' said Elizabeth.

Such naivety was answered with a pretty smile.

'You must have some in your family. You can make up an archduke in Vienna.'

Each time she heard the name of that city, the girl felt ill at ease. Miss Furnace's talk embarrassed her more and more by its improbability. The great traveller was undoubtedly making it up.

'Of course,' the latter said, 'Virginia has its charm, but I can't see you settling down in this God-forsaken spot, however lovely it may be. And then, alas, there is the shadow of a possible threat of war. For my part, I shall leave in good time, without waiting for the crisis.'

'Things haven't reached that point yet,' said Elizabeth rather coldly.

'Oh, no, no. But you're English aren't you?'

'Yes.'

'It would be quite natural to go back to England. You could make an irreproachable and elegant exit.'

From her seat on the edge of the bed in her white dressing gown, the girl stood up.

'Miss Furnace,' she said, 'I have no desire to go away. One ends up getting quite attached to Great Meadow, you see. Will you excuse me, I can barely keep my eyes open.'

'Oh, dear Elizabeth, you have your own way of saying things, which is unique. I'll leave you. One last little bit of advice that will amuse you and which is passed around amongst the women at Court in London. When you enter a drawing room, for a ball or a reception or whatever, you say first of all under your breath: "prunes and prisms" to give a nice shape to your mouth. Good night, dearest, and think about what I told you. I should so much like to see you happy and far from here!'

She disappeared like a fairy.

Elizabeth went to bed immediately and put out her lamp.

'Far from here . . .' she said to herself in the dark. 'What does she want?'

The following day, after lunch, there was another surprise. Led at a trot by Barnaby, a gig pulled up beneath the beech tree in front of the house. Ned jumped down and rushed into the hallway. In a loud voice he cried out:

'Miss Charlotte!'

Nobody answered, so he cried out once more:

'Is there anybody here? It's me.'

A minute went by, and Jemima appeared.

'Miss Charlotte is in the orchard, Mr Ned.'

'Where are the others? Is my father with Mrs Jones?'

'I think so.'

'Barnaby, take my valise up to my room, with my guitar. Be careful of my guitar.'

Elizabeth came out of the drawing room and entered the antechamber.

'Ned!' she exclaimed.

'Yes, Ned,' he said drily. 'Go up to your room, I need to speak to you.'

She obeyed immediately. Climbing the stairs in a couple of leaps, he followed her and closed the door, turning the key in the lock. With his untidy black curls and his face red with emotion, he stood with his back against the door.

Elizabeth looked at him with a mixture of bewilderment and anxiety, disturbed most of all by his silence. Suddenly he began to speak in a flat but steady voice.

'Couldn't you have told me sooner that you wanted nothing to do with me rather than play-acting with your sighs? We're not pretending any more, you cruel girl, you heartless, wicked girl.'

Elizabeth, her face as white as a sheet of paper, stretched out her arms as if to push him away, although he stood motionless with his legs apart, looking fearsome.

'But, Ned . . .' she exclaimed.

'There's no "but Ned". I wrote you a letter offering you my hand. You answer saying that you can't accept by correspondence. What did you want? That I make a declaration of love in front of a lawyer, with a minister of the Anglican Church and his Bible to unite us?'

She dropped down onto a chair.

'You're going off your head,' she said in a strangled voice. 'I never stopped loving you.'

'What lies are you trotting out this time?' he said with a hollow-sounding laugh.

The English girl felt as if she had received a whip lash across her face. Gathering up her strength, she suddenly stood up straight in front of him:

'How dare you?' she said in an icy tone. 'Are you drunk? I order you to open that door.'

It was his turn to assume a bemused look, then his fist furiously turned the key in the lock.

'Do you realize,' she asked in a scornful tone of voice, 'that you are already behaving like a jealous husband? I would have been mad to marry someone like you.'

In a panic he began to shout:

'Try to put yourself in my place! How would you have put up with that dreadful silence? Each time the mail came without bringing me the letter that would have restored me to life, it seemed to me that you were saying no to me again. *No* three times a day for a month.'

'Calm down,' she said, as to a child. 'This is ridiculous. I never said no to you, and at the moment you're doing nothing to make me say yes. And you're shouting too loudly.'

He took a step towards her and gave her a long look.

'Elizabeth,' he said with a sudden gentleness, 'can't you see that I am sick with love?'

She held back an impulse to rush to him.

'Now you're becoming the Ned I know again, instead of the fanatic of just now . . .'

'Fanatic!' he repeated indignantly.

'Yes,' she said, 'did you even hear what I was saying while you were playing out your tragic scene?'

'What you were saying?' he said, looking perplexed.

'It obviously wasn't worth making a declaration of love to you. When you can remember what I said to you, we'll be able to see things more clearly.'

'Forgive me, Elizabeth, I didn't hear, I was beside myself.'

'Ned, I've just told you that I made a declaration of love, isn't that enough? You're not stupid, are you?'

He flung himself towards her and wanted to kiss her, but she fought him off.

'We're not in the pine wood,' she cried with a laugh. 'Now that the door is no longer locked, anyone might come in.'

'Whose fault is that?'

'Don't let's start again. Let's get out of here.'

'I ask for nothing better. This funny little room was mine when I was a child, but it hasn't been used for a long time.'

'Ah?'

'What does "ah" mean?'

'Can't one say "ah" without you asking questions? What a husband you'll make for whoever marries you!'

'For whoever marries you . . .' he repeated in a panic.

'Ned, for Heaven's sake, be reasonable, we'll talk about all that later. You're going to get your nice room on the second floor back, it's being returned to you.'

'Where are you sleeping, Elizabeth?'

'Not here any more. Your father has thrown me out of the great house,' she said with a laugh.

'Well I never! Am I going mad?'

She explained to him the new arrangement at The Coppice without mentioning Miss Furnace; although she was obliged to tell him when he was upset at thinking of her all alone in that little house.

'Miss Furnace! My father told me about her last year. A strange lady. Fancy inviting her . . . Especially as she clings so tenaciously to people.'

'I have no opinion on that matter. She's a great traveller.'

'Don't make me laugh. I doubt if she's ever set foot on a steamer. Goodness knows how she manages to live, on borrowed money some people say. But she has style for all that. Papa thinks she's a lady. When she's penniless . . .'

'Is that the way you talk at the university?' said Elizabeth scornfully.

'Sorry, when her treasury is ill-disposed — and it happens — she turns herself into a lady's companion in the homes of well-bred people.'

'At her age? You surprise me.'

'She's not as young as you think. And what a fantastic arrangement! Putting you over there with her . . . Why? Why, after all?'

'On account of Amelia. So long as she is unwell, I need to be kept away. They come and fetch us for meals.'

'My father did the same thing when I was born. He sends everybody away, except those who are indispensable. We'll go over there straight away. I want to see what they've done with the old Coppice . . . you can show me.'

Elizabeth was gripped by a strange fear, but she remained unable to respond to these difficulties which she had not foreseen. It seemed to her dangerous to risk being alone with Ned in that little house.

'You go without me and then come back,' she said.

He laughed teasingly:

'Are you still afraid of me? Isn't there a lady companion at The Coppice?'

And if he were to find himself alone with that beautiful brunette?

'You're right,' she said, 'let's go.'

A quarter of an hour's walk and they were making their way into the house, and Ned immediately went into ecstasies:

'They've made a jewel out of the old place! Velvet everywhere, the walls repainted, oriental rugs. In popular parlance it would be called a love nest. Especially as there is a heady smell of perfume about.'

'I know,' said Elizabeth annoyed, 'it's her.'

He took a deep breath.

'A fashionable perfume, Evening Charm, people can't resist it.'

'Not so loud,' whispered Elizabeth. 'She is doubtless in her room and might hear us.'

But Miss Furnace was not in her room, she had gone out.

Elizabeth had the impression of being caught in a trap by some malevolent power which she vaguely called fate.

'Well,' she said bravely, 'here we are, alone together.'

'Alone in a quiet and secluded spot,' he said banteringly, 'the dream of all lovers.'

She gave a nervous laugh.

'I hope that you are going to behave yourself and be a gentleman. Otherwise nothing is possible. We're not in the pine wood now.'

'I beg you to note that I have been very proper so far. Do you want me to get down on my knees and make you a standard declaration of love?'

'I hate operatic posturing. I would die of embarrassment.'

'Well, Elizabeth, look me in the eyes. I have never seen you as beautiful as you are today, with that radiant sunlight in your hair. You'd think the sun was pointing it out to me on purpose, for me to touch. Will you allow me to touch it, Elizabeth?'

'Certainly not, you would mess up my hair dreadfully. Besides your remark about my hair makes me want to ask something that you'll perhaps find indiscreet.'

'Go on, I've nothing to hide from you.'

'One day, when we were in the drawing room and Miranda was serving tea, do you remember?'

'Yes, I think so, vaguely.'

'Miranda is beautiful and her hair is as dark as night. What do you think of Miranda?'

'What do you want me to think about a colored maid? Nothing.'

'Nothing? Didn't I catch a veiled look that was full of admiration?'

There was a silence full of consternation, then the boy, whom the English girl judged to be rather slow, answered in a way that took her by surprise.

'Elizabeth,' he said with a subtle smile, 'are we having a domestic row already? Do you think the prospect of marrying a jealous wife is very appealing?'

She took the blow without flinching, but despite the love she felt for the young Virginian, somewhat against her will, she nevertheless saw the great house drifting away from her, and she wanted it.

'Without being jealous,' she said coldly, 'one has perhaps the right to inform oneself. You like brunettes, and I'm as blonde as can be. I shouldn't like there to be any stupid difficulties between us.'

'Difficulties, my angel! I swear to you . . .'

At that moment, a sound of horses' hooves outside made them both start.

'Let's look natural,' he said in a daze.

'Natural! I'm at home.'

Two or three minutes went by, then the door opened. Eliza Furnace came in with a firm step and her head held high. A red riding habit with black trimmings added to that regal quality she evidently sought to bestow on her person. Her face, lit up by a ride through the countryside, glowed with a striking beauty. She glanced at Ned and said in an indifferent tone of voice:

'Oh, a gentleman.'

Elizabeth introduced them. Miss Furnace took off a small man's hat which she threw down on the sofa, for there was a hint of impertinence about all her gestures. With both her hands she fluffed out her thick brown hair which fell magnificently in waves.

Ned looked at her aghast.

'You will excuse me,' she said, not deigning to look at him, 'I'm going up to rest. After that ride . . . One of you can tell someone to see to the horse.'

Having spoken these words with a haughty casualness, she disappeared. Her crop, which she had dropped on the carpet, still spoke of her, in the way that objects do.

'My word,' said Elizabeth, 'she is excelling herself today. Her coquetry can be quite violent . . .'

'Violent?' repeated Ned in a daze.

'Yes. What's the matter with you? Do you think she's charming? Tell me.'

'Charming? I don't know, I didn't have the time to . . .'

'The time to what . . . ? Admire her?'

'I didn't say that. The time to see her.'

'You will. She's settling down here for good.'

'You're dreaming.'

'I'm not. Come to your senses, Ned! Just now you were talking about her disapprovingly, but it took only one glance for her to bewitch you like all the rest, your father, and even Miss Charlotte included.'

Abruptly he managed to get a grip on himself:

'My love, I am not bewitched, I'm simply amazed at her strange behavior and her singular off-handedness. Come, shall we go back to Great Meadow? On foot, if you like, it's not so far. Or I'll jump on the horse — she took Napoleon, one of the best chestnuts — and I'll go over and return with a gig.'

'If you like, but be quick and come back at a gallop. I have no wish to be alone with that pest.'

'Is she unpleasant with you?'

'On the contrary, but she bores me. I suppose she keeps her scornful pose for men.'

He smiled in agreement and, without another word, went to untie Napoleon. She watched him ride off down the road at a cracking pace and decided to wait for him in the meadow rather than in the house. At the very thought of Miss Furnace, her heart pounded in anger. How could she help but see a rival in this newly-arrived woman who was so full of arrogance and so dangerously attractive?

In the soft light of late afternoon, Elizabeth and Ned rode to the edge of a little wood that edged the road beyond the House of Chaos. It was not the quiet and secluded spot that Ned had dreamt of, and he had to watch his behavior, especially as he had to be pardoned for his admiring glance at the woman who put people under her spell. He had trouble explaining things on that point, but he lavished compliments on the girl as thickly as one might spread honey on well-buttered bread. Moreover, the word 'honey' was constantly on his lips:

'My love . . . honey . . .'

She finally let herself be convinced, allowing him to place his lips on hers, but no more. By dinner-time they were completely reconciled. She had the feeling that a union of souls was already taking place, in the absence of any physical one about which the girl preferred not to think.

Charlie Jones did not appear at table. Amelia was complaining more and more, and as laudanum was forbidden her from now on, someone had to stay with her and try to take her mind off her pain.

Miss Furnace kept them waiting for almost a quarter of an hour. She sat down alongside Ned. Elizabeth and Miss Charlotte were seated opposite. Wearing a dress of champagne-coloured satin, the great traveller described her stay in Constantinople with such a proliferation of detail and so many names of pashas casually dropped that Miss Charlotte declared herself to be carried away in a story from *The Arabian Nights*.

Insensitive to the charms of the story teller, Elizabeth observed her with a mixture of attentiveness and alarm, for it was evident that this woman with her provocative beauty was set on seduction, but of whom? The arrogance of their earlier encounter had given way to smiles that seemed to join together and form garlands. Suntanned, perhaps by the wind on long sea crossings, her amber-colored skin had just a hint of color on the cheek bones, and deep eyes full of gentle cunning shone beneath thick, black lashes.

This exquisite person barely touched what was put on her plate. She sometimes waved her delicate hands around when the tale became exciting.

Towards the end of the meal, she judged it to be a

suitable moment to ask Miss Charlotte discreetly about the county of Virginia in which Great Meadow was situated. She knew the old house a little, noble and simple as it was, but was ignorant of its history.

'Ned Jones would be better able to talk to you about it than anyone, since it belongs to him.'

She turned imperceptibly towards her neighbor. Feeling Elizabeth's eyes fixed on him, he tried to master the unease which that woman provoked in him. The latter had no trouble guessing the situation and immediately gave him that wonderful smile which means nothing more substantial than promises.

'So young and already a man of property,' she said. 'What effect does it have on you to be a property owner?'

He blushed deeply and stammered:

'I don't know, I never think about it.'

'That's a good answer,' she said.

As she spoke these words, she stood up and asked Miss Charlotte to excuse her as she was still feeling tired after her splendid ride through the woods. Could Barnaby drive her back to The Coppice?

'Barnaby,' said Miss Charlotte, a little shocked at this sudden departure, 'leave the dishes and harness the gig.'

Miss Furnace addressed her thanks to Miss Charlotte and took leave of Elizabeth and Ned with a slight nod, the latter making as if to accompany her to the door, but she stopped him with a gesture of her hand:

'I shall wait for a moment outside,' she said. 'Nothing moves the soul like the sight of a starry sky, and this evening the night sky is so transparent that it lifts one up from the earth. I've only ever seen that in Egypt.'

At that moment a high-pitched trembling voice was heard; it could only be Elizabeth's, but not immediately recognizable.

'You have your guitar, Ned. This would be the moment to accompany such a contemplation with one of your fine Southern serenades.'

There were a few seconds of bewilderment, then, with the voice of an Italian prima donna, Miss Furnace intoned softly:

'Not this evening.'

She headed gracefully for the door and moved away under the trees. Behind her floated a perfume that seemed to rise from night-scented flowers.

Miss Charlotte stood up in her turn and clapped her hands.

'Come now, children,' she said, 'don't look so stupefied. The lady has her strange ways, but she is interesting. She's eccentric, that's all. It's all that travelling . . .'

Ned turned imploring eyes to Elizabeth who turned roughly away.

103

*T*he reconciliation did not take place until midnight, this time in the shade of the great cedar tree. Suffocating tears followed little cries of anger, which in turn gave way to groans and words of farewell that the guilty party forced upon his victim with his profusion of words and threats of suicide.

With slow steps they returned to Great Meadow and, as if trying not to disturb the silence of the night, they spoke in whispers as they walked hand in hand. They stopped for quite some time looking up at the sky until they were dizzy, for it seemed to both of them that the stars had never shone with so bright a light.

'My guitar is in my room,' he murmured. 'If you want, I could fetch it and sing to you a Southern song . . .'

'Oh, no!' she said.

'. . . you don't want a fine love song?'

'That woman spoilt everything, don't you see, when she said "Not this evening".'

He did not answer straight away.

'She won't stay long under our roof. I shall speak to my father. I know what she wants.'

'What's that?'

'The house, Elizabeth, she is very cunning . . .'

'Is she mad?'

'I don't know. She has a way of insinuating herself with people.'

'You'll never look at her again?'

'Never . . . Do you hear that carriage on the road? It's Barnaby coming back from The Coppice. Do you want me to take you there?'

'To be with that woman again? Don't think of it. I'd rather go back to the little room I had before in the house.'

'No, you take the upstairs room, and I'll sleep downstairs. No arguing,' he added as he kissed her.

She put her head on his shoulder.

'Get me away from that woman,' she said.

'I shall do everything to rid us of her. My father invited her so that you would not be alone at The Coppice until the baby is born. He couldn't have made a worse choice. It's the most foolish thing he has ever done.'

'Does he do many?'

'He was off his head, but it will sort itself out. You'll stay here tonight.'

'But Ned, all my things are over there, my clothes, my toiletries.'

'Does a young lady need so many things?'

'You don't understand, Ned, your education is incomplete.'

'Very well. I'll go and fetch all that for you in the gig.'

'Are you demented, Ned? If she sees you coming in at this hour she will call out.'

'No one will hear her.'

'Your plan is impossible. I must be with you at least.'

Together they hatched a childish plot and as soon as the gig arrived Ned ran to stop it on the road.

'Did you drive Miss Furnace to her door?'

'Yes, Mass'r Ned. She was a shoutin' "Faster, faster! I want to go to bed."'

'Good. Get down from the carriage and you go to bed too and sleep well. I'm going to drive Miss Elizabeth back home. I shan't need you again until tomorrow.'

Barnaby jumped down from the gig all the more readily as Ned still inspired feelings of terror in him. A few minutes later, Elizabeth was sitting next to Ned on the seat. A slight crack of the whip was sufficient to start the chestnut horse off again after a prompt turnaround.

'Don't let's go too quickly,' said Elizabeth. 'What we are doing is so unwise, Ned.'

'We have to act if you want peace. We'll stop a few yards away from the house so as not to wake the lady up. I'll go in on tiptoe.'

'No, I'll go in. You wouldn't know what to take. You wait outside and I'll bring everything. She mustn't see a man in the house.'

They cantered along, but the horse's hooves disturbed the mystery of the night in spite of everything. The whole country-side seemed to be listening to the clip-clopping. Feeling both happy and anxious, the girl held on tightly to Ned.

'Do you think that woman is beautiful?' she said softly.

'In a theatrical kind of way, perhaps. She's like an actress who does everything to make people look at her.'

'Would you marry an actress?'

'What are you dreaming of, my love? You're forgetting that you have forgiven me.'

A great, meditative silence ensued, then she said with a laugh:

'Nearly all the women are brunettes in the South, that's just about all you see . . . don't you agree?'

'It's true. Blondes like you are very rare.'

'Do you like them as much as brunettes?'

'I only like Elizabeth, you know that.'

Reassured, she thought herself rather stupid for saying that and decided to keep quiet.

The little house gave the impression of being asleep in the middle of the fields like someone tucked up in his dreams, protected against all intrusions by its isolation and its vulnerability. With feline lightness of step they got down from the carriage, and Ned tied the horse to a tree at the edge of the road. There he waited, in accordance with Elizabeth's instructions.

The girl's footsteps in the grass could not be heard. She reached the door which she opened with the key held in a somewhat trembling hand. She went up to her room on tiptoe, but not without endless gropings, suffering a dull thudding in her chest.

When she had closed the door behind her, feeling safe, she began boldly to look for matches, found them at last and lit the lamp. A quick glance showed her that peaceful setting which communed with her in the unspoken language of inanimate objects. She was struck by the strangeness of this moment in her life: the bed in which she would not sleep, the rocking chair that would remain still. But time was short; beginning to panic, she opened the chest of drawers and made a quick selection of things she needed. Then came the toiletries in the adjoining washroom. Everything was put in the valise that she had used in coming to The Coppice. She only had to take the valise by the handle and blow out the lamp, which she did, with her throat dry from fear. Getting out of the house was going to be much more difficult. Her plan was to put down the valise on the steps once she was outside. Ned was to come and fetch it from that spot.

Everything was on the brink of success. She bumped into one or two pieces of furniture, the door opened with barely a creak, then there was only a narrow hallway to cross, four steps to reach the front door.

Yet it was in this confined space that something happened that took her breath away. A very soft light suddenly lit up the hallway, coming from behind the pretty, iridescent taffeta curtain that separated Miss Furnace's apartment from the rest of the house. On the other side of the curtain, a corridor led to the great traveller's bedroom . . .

Fear made Elizabeth freeze into a statue. At that moment, the edge of the curtain was moved aside for a split second and fell back again. As in a vision, she caught sight of a dull, white, expressionless face.

Horror restored to her the use of her limbs; in a frenzied act of will, she dragged her valise down the steps and threw it out having first managed, she knew not how, to open the door.

She ran to the gig and took hold of Ned's arm. All she could say was:

'The valise, quickly!'

Without asking any questions, he disappeared into the darkness and, coming back with the valise, threw it into the vehicle where Elizabeth was already sitting.

As soon as they were on the road, the girl leaned her head against Ned's shoulder:

'Quickly!' she begged.

The whip cracked and the horse broke into a gallop.

'What's the matter with you?' asked Ned.

'Oh, Ned, I thought I would die of terror. In the hallway, a corpse looked at me. The Coppice is haunted.'

'Well that's new,' he said. 'People say that the great house is, but not the small one. Perhaps you imagined it . . .'

'Don't talk like that, for Heaven's sake! I have my wits about me, I'm not mad. A frightful face stared at me for a second. I was paralyzed with terror, and I still wonder how I managed to get away.'

'With the valise,' Ned remarked.

'Oh, don't laugh.'

'I'm not laughing, my love. You will never again set foot in The Coppice. Miss Furnace will have the house all to herself — while waiting for me to make her leave.'

'Are you going to explain to your father that the house is haunted?'

'He would laugh in my face. He is uncompromising on anything connected with the after-life: according to him there is no such thing.'

'But if you manage to get rid of Miss Furnace, isn't he going to want me to sleep down there? I should die, Ned, they'd find me as stiff as a board in my bed.'

'Oh, no. There's no question of you being alone at The Coppice, but that's another problem. What I think is that you saw an old maid belonging to Miss Furnace. She is mysterious. She had her sent for secretly, for she needs to be attended to, like all very beautiful women.'

'Very beautiful, Ned?' said Elizabeth softly.

'Ladies of her kind, preening beauties.'

'She's not a lady.'

'She does her best to make people think she is, but she needs to take lessons.'

Feeling more cheerful, she was overcome with a sudden feeling of exultation.

'Oh, Ned, look at the sky . . . the stars . . . there is still . . .'

104

*I*n the grip of nightmares in which the face of the corpse
recurred looking disconcertingly familiar to her, Elizabeth
spent the night in the large room upstairs, while Ned did his
best to sleep in the short bed in the little room downstairs.

Neither of them looked too good the following morning.
In order to set Elizabeth's mind permanently at rest on the
subject of The Coppice, Ned saw no other solution but to
speak to Miss Charlotte about it.

They found her a little before breakfast in the drawing
room where, as was her custom, she was reading her Bible at
the fireside. Elizabeth immediately told her the tale of the
apparition. Short and to the point, she omitted the circumstances, namely her running away from The Coppice by
night, and restricted herself to a description of the frightful
face behind the curtain.

Miss Charlotte listened to her carefully:

'No one has ever said the The Coppice was haunted,' she
said. 'Miss Furnace has never complained about it. We'll ask
her just now.'

Her sharp eyes suddenly fixed their gaze on Elizabeth's,
as if to seek out the truth of the matter in them.

'My dear girl,' she said, 'there are the three of us here,
and we won't say a word about this conversation to anyone,
but might you not have taken a bit too much laudanum
yesterday evening?'

Elizabeth blushed to her ears.

'Do you take laudanum?' exclaimed Ned.

'A few drops are permitted,' said Miss Charlotte, 'to
relieve a migraine, toothache — or if one is very, very upset.
That never hurt anybody.'

'Well, I never!' said Ned. 'Elizabeth!'

'Elizabeth has only taken it once, under my instructions
and on my advice. You yourself must have a bottle of it in
your washroom, Ned.'

'That's possible, but it would never occur to me . . .'

'It will occur to you some day, as it does to everybody.'

At that point Barnaby appeared in his green livery and
announced breakfast.

'Barnaby,' said Ned in a strict tone of voice, 'you look like someone who has just been listening at doors.'

Barnaby's face turned to a leaden hue and his teeth began to chatter.

'Leave Barnaby,' said Miss Charlotte, 'and let's go and have breakfast.'

As they were heading towards the dining room, Ned whispered in Elizabeth's ear:

'Have you ever taken laudanum?'

'Yes, once, out of love, you beast.'

He assumed a disapproving air but felt a little flattered nevertheless, feeling sure that he was the one in question.

Miss Furnace kept them waiting several minutes but when she appeared in the doorway, with a tiny parasol protecting her head from the sun, she produced a stunning effect. The dark splendor of her hair highlighted her complexion that was colored only by pale pink on the cheek bones. Undoubtedly aware of the admiration that she aroused, she responded with a youthful smile.

Miss Charlotte could not restrain herself from expressing a sense of wonder:

'You really look a picture,' she said with a laugh. 'Standing there, in your pretty peach-colored dress with your little parasol, in a ray of sunlight.'

'My parasol?' she said coming in with light step, 'one of those absurd and irresistible Paris novelties. I hope that everyone slept well.'

A good humor that was in such sharp contrast with the previous day indicated that she could change her mood like those capricious high-society women.

Elizabeth kept her eye on Ned with ferocious vigilance, and the young Virginian did not know where to look; he finally adopted the solution of keeping his head down.

'Miss Furnace,' said Miss Charlotte boldly when the beautiful brunette had sat down next to Ned, 'have you ever had the impression that The Coppice harbored ghosts?'

'A ghost,' clarified Elizabeth in a whisper.

A joyful peal of laughter was the response to that unexpected question:

'If that were the case, I should have told you,' said Miss

Furnace with a flick of her superb curls. 'I only once had an experience of the supernatural. It was in a royal castle in the Scottish borders where I spent the night as a guest of the Duke of Norfolk. I'll tell you about it one evening next winter.'

'Next winter!' exclaimed Elizabeth.

'Oh, yes, dear child; are you afraid of The Coppice?'

This question disturbed the English girl.

'I admit to feeling a bit disorientated there, I had been so used to the great house . . .'

'You set off without me this morning. I called you. No answer. But we all have our little secrets, you mysterious Elizabeth.'

As she spoke these words, she took on a rebellious air that, for inexplicable reasons, gave Ned a kind of sensual thrill which filled him with horror. He suddenly felt certain that a wild kind of happiness was only possible for him in the arms of that woman. So as not to give himself away before Elizabeth's eyes, he turned his head away, but that moment was painful. So far everything in his life had been simple, he had enjoyed a few quickly forgotten amorous involvements. This time, mad with desire, he was discovering that hard, human passion which leaves no illusions. Horrified, he realized that he belonged to that woman and that she knew it. Even worse, he felt intuitively that Elizabeth knew it as well. Elizabeth who, he thought, had taken laudanum on account of him, and the great love that he inspired in her . . . He suddenly felt disgusted with himself and judged himself repulsive. Getting up abruptly from the table, he stammered that he had an unbearable pain hammering at his temples, which was not too far from the truth, and, begging to be excused, he left the dining room without looking at anyone, through fear of giving himself away.

Elizabeth's first reaction was to run after him, but she did not dare and cast a look of desperation in the direction of Miss Charlotte, who shook her head:

'Poor boy,' she said, 'too much work over there at the university. Fortunately the holidays aren't too far off.'

Miss Furnace gave the charming smile of a monarch granting some choice favor.

'I shall go into your garden and pick him a bunch of

flowers which I shall arrange to help him forget his pain.'

Elizabeth's breathing became uneasy, and she pushed her teacup away from her, spilling its contents onto the table-cloth. Miss Furnace gave a hysterical laugh, like a schoolgirl, revealing an admirable set of teeth.

'Such commotion over a headache!' she declared. 'Your sensibility is enchanting, and what an attractive woman you are going to be. I can see from here dukes and nobles at your feet at the English court. In the meantime, as this exquisite breakfast is coming to an end — it had barely begun — I shall go off and do a little gardening, if you are agreeable, Miss Charlotte. Some scissors, please, gloves and a little basket . . .'

Turning towards Elizabeth, she added:

'. . . and to carry my basket, that kind Elizabeth . . .'

The answer came in an angry cry:

'Sorry, kind Elizabeth has better things to do than to carry your little basket for you.'

'How vexatious!' said Miss Furnace sadly, 'but perhaps your Betty will be able to accompany me.'

'Certainly,' said Miss Charlotte, with a disapproving look in Elizabeth's direction.

'Betty is at The Coppice,' said Elizabeth drily.

'Have her sent for,' replied Miss Furnace. 'Is that possible, Miss Charlotte?'

'Certainly,' said Miss Charlotte once more, full of indulgence for the great traveller.

'So,' resumed Elizabeth in a fury, 'you are going to send for my maid at The Coppice to have her carry a little basket for this lady whom Heaven has nonetheless endowed with two hands. For once I can understand the abolitionists.'

'Dear me!' said Miss Furnace.

Miss Charlotte stood up and stretched herself up on tiptoe. In her most deafening voice she shouted:

'Elizabeth!'

Elizabeth stood up. Behind the door Barnaby took flight.

The girl went out without a word and ran right up to the steps leading to the children's bedroom.

She went in without knocking and saw Ned standing in front of the window. He turned round suddenly and she was speechless confronted as she was with a face that she did not recognize, ravaged with anxiety as she was ... They looked at each other in silence for several seconds, then he said almost in a whisper:

'What do you want, Elizabeth?'

'I'm not afraid of the truth, Ned. Talk to me. Do you love that woman?'

He shook his head.

'No.'

As he spoke that word, he looked so grave and so much in pain that she had to lower her head so that he should not see the tears shining in the corners of her eyes.

'She fascinates you, Ned, how do they say, she attracts you.'

'I didn't even look at her this morning . . .'

'You want her, don't deny it.'

'That has nothing to do with love, it's you I love. Do you believe me?'

'I should believe it more readily if you sent her away. You promised me last night that you would rid us of her. Do you remember?'

Before he could answer, she threw herself in his arms with the cry:

'My dear Ned, I beg you, I shall be yours, but send her away.'

She clung to him so hard that he was going out of his mind. His blood boiled in his veins from desire, as it had at table earlier on.

'Lock the door,' she said curtly.

'What are you thinking of? Here?'

'Lock that door,' she commanded.

Half an hour before lunch, they heard people calling them. Ned went out first and disappeared down the corridor in the direction of his usual room on the top floor. Elizabeth tarried a good while longer to rid herself of all traces of disorder and finally appeared at the top of the stairs; seeing no one, she descended unhurriedly and went outside.

Uncle Charlie was pacing up and down in the meadow. When he saw Elizabeth, he hurried towards her.

'What's this I hear?' he exclaimed looking very agitated.

'You don't want to sleep at The Coppice any more because of some ghost you've seen there?'

'That's right,' said Elizabeth in an icy tone of voice.

'My dear child,' he said, disconcerted by the calmness of her attitude, 'we're not going to fight over it. Pull yourself together. Let's go under the trees and talk about it like two rational people.'

In the shade of the beech tree, they sat down on the bench, and there, as always, the English girl remained fiercely calm.

'You haven't seen a ghost, because ghosts don't exist. Is that clear?'

'It's clear, but it's wrong,' she said.

He blushed a little and looked at her gravely. She bore the gaze of his large, storm-colored eyes and could not help comparing them with those of his son. Ned was less handsome, but she could still feel the violence of his embrace.

Uncle Charlie continued gently:

'I'm not used to being answered like that. You will return to The Coppice this evening.'

'Do you think so?'

'I think so, because the state of my dear Amelia obliges me to keep you away from the house so that you won't be disturbed by her cries. It was for this purpose that I had Miss Furnace come, as your lady's companion.'

'I don't like Miss Furnace.'

'Elizabeth, it grieves me to see you so different from the delightful young lady I knew in Savannah, of whom I have pleasant memories.'

'Under the sycamore in front of your house, perhaps!'

'I haven't forgotten the sycamore, but that does not change the fact that you will obey.'

'Perhaps.'

Getting up, he gave her a smile full of charm.

'Where is Ned?' he asked.

She had the impression that he was sounding an alarm, but she did not flinch.

'I saw him at breakfast. Since then . . .'

A vague gesture accompanied that last word, which summed up perhaps the entire future of her life.

'He'll have gone off again on Alcibiades. That's what he

misses most at university. I'll send Barnaby to see where he
has got to. I shan't lunch with you. Amelia doesn't like me
to leave her, but rest assured, dear Elizabeth, I haven't
forgotten the sycamore and I'll take care of your happiness.'

'That's good news, Uncle Charlie,' she said with an acid
smile.

105

The lunch was strange, like the aftermath of a battle.
None of those present was the same person they had
been that morning. Ned, whom Barnaby had finally found,
gazed at Elizabeth without seeing her, so far away were his
thoughts. Nor did he acknowledge the bouquet that was set
in front of him, although it was artistically arranged with
small flowers packed tightly together in a multicolored ball.

Looking more pensive than usual, Miss Charlotte seemed
to be directing her attention towards some inner world, and
she crumbled her toast with distracted fingers. Elizabeth's
sole occupation while she ate was to defy Miss Furnace,
without taking her eyes off her. The latter, still dazzlingly
beautiful, gave the impression of solitary triumph, like a
statue in the middle of a sandy waste.

The silence had become too profound and had gone on
too long for it to be broken naturally. To tell the truth, each
of them was embroiled with his or her own problems, perceiving no need to escape, and so there was general relief
when the meal was over. Miss Furnace went to lie in the
drawing room while she waited for the time to go back to
The Coppice. Perhaps she might have been happy to chat
with Miss Charlotte who, vaguely suspecting something, had
disappeared without a word. The bouquet remained alone
on the table, telling its tale to the empty chairs.

Elizabeth walked with calm steps towards the meadow

behind the house. There Ned, who was a little slower, joined her and took her hand.

They both went and sat down on a bench in the shade of two birch trees, whose light foliage quivered in the breeze. The sky of very pale blue was empty.

'Are you happy, Elizabeth?'

She stroked his face with her hand.

'Didn't I tell you enough this morning?'

He placed his weary head on her shoulder.

'You haven't heard me play the guitar yet,' he murmured, on the brink of sleep. 'Now, if you would like . . .'

She ran her fingers through the thickness of his black curls.

'Normally,' she said with a little laugh, 'people play the guitar *before*, and at night. It's not quite the same thing afterwards, but you have a nice voice, you can sing me a song of the South when we're alone at The Coppice.'

'Alone at The Coppice . . .' he repeated, 'but I'm leaving tomorrow.'

'Somewhere else, tonight, in the countryside.'

'It will have to be very late then. Did you notice that nobody said anything at table?'

'It's because they all know.'

These words made him raise his head.

'What are you saying?' he said, afraid. 'How could they know?'

'There's a part of them that guessed, but they can't believe it yet.'

'I don't entirely understand, but I hope you're wrong.'

'They'll know some day or other, I think.'

'In any case, I'm going to have to tell my father, and he will get terribly angry.'

'The anger will pass, you shouldn't be afraid.'

'I'm not afraid — but I'll tell him in a week's time, I'll come back for that purpose, but not this evening. Night makes everything sinister.'

'You're right, and besides, tonight is ours.'

'Yes, my love, this night is ours.'

'And tomorrow morning . . .'

'Tomorrow morning I shall go back to the university.'

'You won't go back, Ned, my beloved. It will be easier to

talk to your father in broad daylight. If you like, I can fall at his feet to appease him, like in a melodrama.'

'Don't let's play-act any more, Elizabeth.'

'No, not now. I am yours for ever.'

The tone of voice in which she said this made him start. The inevitable marriage was taking on quite a different aspect. He stood up instinctively and she got up too. Both of them held themselves as if in front of an invisible altar. Everything was changing in their world. The night of love made them dreamy. He suddenly realized that he could no longer think of anything to say to this golden-haired beauty who was already his wife.

And yet he loved her, but if loving her became a constraint . . .

For the first time, in the secret of their hearts they asked the same question: 'What have I done?' For him as for her, there persisted the obsessive image of the face of another.

'You're tired, my dear Ned,' she said as she kissed him. 'Go up and rest in your room.'

'I admit that I feel sleepy, but what about you . . .'

'Oh, me . . . You don't have to worry about me. Women are made of steel. When you've rested, I'll get my valise which is in your room.'

Suddenly, in response to a simultaneous impulse, they flung themselves against each other, cheek to cheek, like two children seeking in affection consolation for a faded dream. It was perhaps the only moment in which they understood each other.

Ned went up to stretch out on his bed where he closed his eyes in an effort to forget the nightmare that awaited him the following morning. Elizabeth's phrase haunted him: 'I'll fall at his feet to appeal.' He guessed that she would be quite capable of doing it. She was not play-acting. She had a hold on him. And yet he loved her.

Letting her hair loose on a whim, she went for a walk in the meadow, her skirt dragging in the long grass, which rustled slightly at every step. Jonathan. She kept saying his name in a tone of desperate gentleness, and abruptly she let herself slip down into the grass, her heart pounding and her face soaked with burning tears. After the fire of pain came the shattering invasion of pleasure in her flesh. It was indescribable, beyond any transport of love poetry, and as frightening as a mystery. She would have liked to owe it to someone other than this nice, young Virginian, and the shadow of Jonathan with his wild eyes hovered over it all. She was happy and unhappy at one and the same time, she was lost in visions of what might have been. Was it all still impossible? He was no longer married, and she was yet to be . . .

But Ned had taken her, and she belonged only to him. Yet at that very moment, Jonathan had in his hands the little drawing with the exact spot of their meeting, under the enormous tree. He was on his way, she was certain that his presence here was something which she both desired and feared. It was all too late now.

'Mad,' she said aloud as she got up.

Time had gone by, the light was fading. She decided to go back to the house and knock boldly on Ned's door.

He was no longer asleep, and he welcomed her with a disconcerted look.

'The valise,' he said, 'is no longer here . . . Barnaby must have taken it while we were sitting under the trees.'

'Back to The Coppice.'

'I fear so.'

'Your father doesn't want me in the house. Everything is in a mess again. Ned, I don't want to see Miss Furnace at The Coppice any more.'

In spite of himself, the name of Miss Furnace made him tremble.

'You'll see her at dinner.'

'I'd rather not have dinner. She takes my appetite away.'

'Well, if you lock yourself in your room down there before she arrives . . . It isn't six o'clock yet . . .'

'We have two hours until dinner-time. You can say I went off for a ride and that I'm dining with Elsie.'

'You'll see her again tomorrow . . .'

'Oh, everything will have changed tomorrow when you've spoken to your father. I don't know how, but everything will have changed by then, Ned.'

Faced with the young man's perplexed expression she exclaimed:

'Oh, Ned, we shall be happy, but we must act, you said so yourself. Act, act, act!'

She stamped her foot when she read the distress in his face. 'A coward like all men,' she thought scornfully, 'and capable of leaving me with a child on my hands.'

There was silence, then she said haughtily:

'Don't force me to tell everything in your place. It's not for the victim to speak, but the guilty party.'

'For the victim, Elizabeth?' he said in a daze.

'Don't let's argue about it. Come with me on horseback as far as The Coppice and bring the horse back to the house. Do what you like with it, but go. Don't be seen at dinner. You've warned them that we've gone for a ride. It would seem strange if I went off on my own. She might guess.'

'Such a lot of secrecy . . .'

'Kiss me, Ned. We will be forgiven for this slight distortion of the truth, and it will be the last time. Everything must look plausible. For that, it's enough for us not to be seen at dinner.'

He gradually felt an uncontrollable anger surging up inside him, and in a cold, precise tone of voice he asked:

'For us not to be seen at dinner? You mean for her not to see us, and also for Miss Furnace not to see *me*.'

To his surprise, she answered calmly:

'I'm defending myself. Have the horses saddled.'

'My sweet Elizabeth, I didn't think you were so, so . . . careful.'

'Let me help you. "Wary" is the word you're looking for. You are mine as I am yours. I am looking after our happiness. Don't be afraid in front of your Papa tomorrow . . .'

He slapped her.

This gesture stupefied both of them, as if the hand had detached itself of its own accord to strike the unsuspecting cheek. Elizabeth looked at Ned admiringly: standing there without a waistcoat and his collar unbuttoned, with his legs apart like a soldier. His untidy, black curls added to the spiritedness of the face that was still red with anger, and she found him handsome.

'You asked for that,' he said with a forced laugh. 'That'll teach you.'

'That'll teach me what?' she said putting her arms round him.

He made as if to break away.

'What are you thinking of? You'll spoil everything . . .'

Galloping at full speed, they reached The Coppice. Betty, who was putting Elizabeth's things away in her room, cried out as she saw them come in.

'Mass'r Ned,' she said, 'Miss Furnace be a comin'.'

'Not for an hour at least,' he said. 'They must still be at table. Leave us, Betty.'

The old black lady gave them a frightened look and headed for the door. Elizabeth waited for the red smock to be out of sight.

'And I took you for an angel,' he said with a laugh.

'I'm not an angel, Ned, I'm a woman for whom you have opened up a new world. Now you must go off with the horses, do you hear? The light is fading, I just have time to go to bed without lighting a lamp. Run off quickly, or poor Betty will suspect something.'

'So what does it matter?'

'I don't want her to.'

'Why not? Whether she knows or not, now, a maid . . .'

'I don't want to . . . Not Betty. You wouldn't understand. Go away, Ned. We'll see each other tomorrow morning.'

She pushed him out. When the door was closed, she let a minute go by until she heard the dull sound of horses' hooves on the meadow.

'Betty!' she called.

The maid came almost immediately.

'Betty, I'm going to marry Mr Ned, are you pleased?'

'Mass'r Ned! Oh, yes, Miss Lizbeth. When?'

'Very soon.'

'Very soon?' said Betty slightly worried.

'You're the first person I've told the news to, my little Betty. I'm going to bed to sleep. Now, you must be good and not tell Miss Furnace that I came with Mr Ned.'

'No, Miss Lizbeth.'

'And you can say a prayer for me. You can ask that I shall never see a ghost here again.'

'No, Miss Lizbeth, Betty not ask.'

'What? But why not?'

'Because there be no ghost here.'

'But I saw it, Betty. A frightening face, over there, behind the curtain.'

'Well, Miss Lizbeth must ask.'

'There's no point in me asking, the Lord doesn't listen to me.'

'Then there's no ghost.'

'You're being naughty, Betty. I tell you I saw someone.'

'Someone, yes, someone in the bedroom.'

'Is there someone? Oh, Betty, you're going to make me cross. Tell me who is in the bedroom.'

'Miss Furnace.'

'Of course, and who else? Whom did I see?'

'Betty not sayin'.'

'You're going to light that lamp and take me to Miss Furnace's room.'

'No, Miss Lizbeth, no.'

'Obey!' exclaimed Elizabeth. 'We shall go together and you won't be afraid.'

Unwillingly the old servant lit the oil lamp, then moved to one side to let Elizabeth pass.

'No,' the latter said, 'you go first and lead the way.'

Together they crossed the hallway, then Betty pulled the iridescent taffeta curtain to one side. The young woman avoided touching it as if she was fearful of catching something from another world, from death.

Betty had further scruples in front of the bedroom door:

'Miss Furnace, she not be pleased if she knew.'

'She won't know anything. I shall go in and out. Open it.'

The door was finally opened after a few lingering hesitations. Betty went in, followed by the young woman who cast an inquisitive gaze all around the room. Two large mirrors in their gilt frames reflected the tentative flickering of the lamp which seemed, in some indefinable way, guilty.

'Put that lamp on the table.'

Betty placed it in the middle of a small round marble table.

'We must go now, Miss Lizbeth.'

'Be quiet. I want to look at these books.'

The books were in rows of thirty on mahogany shelves.

Elizabeth read out under her breath the titles of some of the volumes.

'*Journey in Turkey, in Spain, in the Austro-Hungarian Empire, New Journeys in the East, in Prussia, in Russia* . . . Evidently a great traveller, a cultured woman, I admit, but how she shows off her knowledge! Fancy . . .'

She stopped at a small door that she tried in vain to open.

'Locked, Betty, open it!'

'Betty can't, Miss Lizbeth. Miss Furnace, she not want. Miss Furnace's washroom.'

'Do you have the key?'

'Betty can't open . . . Miss Furnace forbid it.'

'You're not Miss Furnace's maid, you're my maid and you're going to open it.'

The maid began to be agitated, clasping her hands and looking at her mistress.

'If Miss Furnace not want, the Lord not want.'

'What's this madness, Betty? You'll open that door, or I'll dismiss you from my service.'

'No, Miss Lizbeth, the Lord punish you.'

'One last time, I order you to open it.'

The old woman burst into sobs, crossed the room and took a key from a hook in a dark corner. Coming back towards Elizabeth, she dropped on to her knees and held out the key.

'Miss Lizbeth be punished some day,' she said, 'think of Betty.'

'What a lot of fuss over a key to a washroom,' muttered Elizabeth as she inserted the key into the lock. 'My word, you'd think we were in Blue Beard's castle . . . Ah, I can't see anything. Bring the lamp closer, Betty.'

But Betty had fled and the young woman had to fetch the lamp herself, which she held level with her head.

At first she saw nothing at all out of the ordinary. A bath tub hanging on the wall, a pitcher for water in a bowl, a mirror high up and at an angle. Then she lowered her eyes to a table on which bottles and boxes were spread out in a confusion of multicolored labels.

Putting the lamp down on the corner of a table, she examined all of these objects ever more attentively, for each of them spoke only of beautifying the skin, the complexion. Careful instructions revealed the method to be followed, the creams needed to be lightly patted on to the skin with the finger tips so as to form a foundation; elsewhere, a liquid cream, barely brushed on to the cheek bones would produce a glow guaranteed to be long-lasting.

Elizabeth was totally ignorant of such refinements, and her blue eyes danced with pleasure as she opened the boxes and bottles she took great pains to return exactly to the right place. It crossed her mind to apply a hint of one of these colors to her skin, but at first the idea seemed ridiculous. With a complexion that all the ladies envied, what need did she have of all that?

In spite of everything, it would be amusing to try on the palm of her hand, for example . . . She chose a peach colour, with just a touch of pink, and was surprised at the result. How wonderful! The skin absorbed that exquisite color.

For several minutes she looked at the fairy-like coloring of her hand that had been white a few minutes previously. She rubbed the mark a little to make it go away, but it would not disappear.

She laughed to herself. One day, when she was old, boxes and bottles of all kinds would come to her aid, and suddenly she stopped laughing. Growing old was inevitable, unless one died young.

Taking the lamp, she left the room, then locked it again. How long had she been there? If ever Miss Furnace had caught her . . . How old might the great traveller be? That thought suddenly flashed through her mind as she crossed the room full of books and mirrors. She had never thought about it. Yet the question remained. It was so interesting, in fact, that when she was back in her room, she kept asking herself over and over again: was the beautiful brunette cheating?

Betty might know something, having undoubtedly seen Miss Furnace when she got up. She called Betty.

The old servant arrived after a little while, but it was not the usual humble Betty, bent double; quite the contrary, she was making an effort to stand up as straight as she could manage in her flame-colored skirt, and she looked at Elizabeth without unclenching her teeth.

'My dear Betty,' said Elizabeth, 'do you see Miss Furnace in the morning when she gets up?'

'Sometimes, Miss Lizbeth,' said Betty, looking displeased.

'How does she look at such times?'

'She look like Miss Furnace.'

'You don't want to answer, that's very bad, you should tell the truth. Is she as nice as when she sets off with me in the gig to go to the Great House?'

'Miss Furnace always very nice, very nice to Betty.'

'Very well. Go away, Betty. I'll get undressed on my own.'

She was surprised to see the maid leave the room without a word, and thought: 'She knows something and won't tell — out of loyalty. I can't be cross with her.'

Taking off her dress and all of her clothes, she lit the candle on her bedside table, then blew out the lamp and got into bed.

Her Bible was within reach, like a mascot. She no longer read it as she used to. The book cast her into anxiety and doubt. If she opened it at random, she would happen upon phrases directed against her, sometimes in so personal and obvious a way that her sleep was disturbed. Yet she wanted the black-bound book to be there, keeping watch in spite of everything.

She waited some time before blowing out the candle, gripped by a childish fear of the dark and of possible apparitions. She did not like the way Betty had changed. What was there between the black maid and that woman? What understanding? Some arrangement, perhaps? Ridiculous. Not with her dear Betty. But there were too many mysteries at The Coppice, too much solitude. So it was with a kind of relief that she heard the gig bringing Miss Furnace back. Having dismissed Barnaby, she came into the house, then stopped in the hallway where Betty came to meet her with a lamp in her hand.

'Good evening, Betty,' said the sing-song voice that Elizabeth usually found amusing, but not that night. 'Light the lamp in my room and go to bed, I'm going to stay up quite late.'

'Oh, Miss Furnace, Betty can wait.'

'Traitor!' thought Elizabeth. 'What zeal! I was right to suspect them.'

A few more words were exchanged, then the young woman almost cried out in surprise when there was a knock at her door.

Miss Furnace came in and smiled.

'I saw the light,' she said. 'Will you grant me a few minutes?'

As she spoke these words, she sat down in the big armchair and favored Elizabeth with another smile. Sitting in bed, the young woman propped herself up on a pillow and looked at Miss Furnace in silence. With the dim lighting, patches of shadow surrounded the visitor like a wall.

'You don't like me, Elizabeth,' said Miss Furnace softly. 'Your eyes tell me so, even if your mouth remains silent.'

'Why do you say that?'

'Because it grieves me. My life is not very happy. Circumstances do not permit me to settle down anywhere for longer than a few months. Here I hoped I had found . . . what? A haven of grace.'

'You travel such a lot.'

Miss Furnace repeated as if in a dream:

'I travel such a lot . . . Why do people travel? Often in order to flee from loneliness, boredom and, perhaps, despair. Come, you're still too young to understand and I'm preventing you from going to sleep.'

Her face spoke of such distress that Elizabeth held out her hand towards her:

'Don't go if you have something to say to me, I shall try to understand.'

'It's not worth it. When you looked at me today, all through lunch, with that triumphant look that I found rather hurtful, I realized that once again I had lost out.'

'Can you explain that to me?'

'Don't be cruel, Elizabeth . . . Your dear Betty, who is nothing in the eyes of the world, showed compassion. She guessed. I did too, as you might imagine. A woman understands straight away. It only takes a glance. I couldn't be angry with you, but you turned the knife in the wound, as they say, oh yes you did, and enjoyed it terribly.'

'Don't say that,' exclaimed Elizabeth, moved, 'I didn't realize, I was wrong.'

Miss Furnace stood up.

'Those words wipe away everything, Elizabeth. You are young and youth is hard, and you know only too well that

— 819 —

you are pretty.'

'I assure you . . .'

'Don't protest, I was your age once. And then you were afraid that someone might take your Ned away from you. Your face said it all. I saw everything. A sideways glance told me the whole of your story. You have no idea. It was yesterday, when you came to fetch your valise. Barely time enough to draw a curtain aside and drop it again. A second . . .'

Elizabeth jumped out of bed.

'Miss Furnace!'

'Well, what is it? You look terrified as if you'd seen a ghost. It's time I went!' she added with a cheerless laugh. 'Good night, Elizabeth.'

With that gracefulness that accompanied her always in even the simplest movements, she hurried to the door and vanished.

Suddenly overcome with weakness, Elizabeth felt her legs giving way, and she dropped onto her knees at the foot of the bed. A groaning rose up from her breast:

'It was her! She was the ghost . . .'

Poor ghost, with the artificial beauty wiped from her face.

The young woman could not bear the revelation of such a sad secret. All of those powders and creams in the washroom should have opened her eyes, but the link with the sinister, bloodless face had escaped her. And the following day, that look of triumph directed at the beautiful brunette . . . If only she had been able to get a glimpse of the truth!

She was ashamed and horrified at herself. Without thinking about what she was going to say, she ran in her nightdress to Miss Furnace's door and knocked.

'Is that you, Betty? Go to bed, everything is alright.'

'It's not Betty, Miss Furnace, it's me.'

'My dear Elizabeth, I don't receive anyone in my bedroom, but what do you want?'

'Nothing . . . I don't know.'

Suddenly she began to knock harder on the door as if to cover the sound of her own voice.

'To tell you that I'm sorry . . . to ask you to forgive me.'

From inside, the voice rang out, a voice without the singsong intonation, but human and anguished:

'I can't open the door to kiss you, Elizabeth, you can't

understand why, but I'm giving you a hug. Be happy. Everything is wiped away, I told you so.'

'Thank you, Miss Furnace.'

106

*T*he following morning the gig came to fetch them for breakfast. Neither of them spoke a word, Barnaby's presence made all conversation impossible. But, in spite of everything, smiles were exchanged that were equally affectionate on both sides.

Elizabeth was making a great effort to remain calm but still had doubts about how Ned might behave; she hoped it would be in a manly fashion. Uncle Charlie could be ferocious at times.

That day, as for some time now, he did not come down and Ned, seconded by Elizabeth, opted for sending him a message entrusted to Jemima. 'Dear Papa, I have something urgent to tell you, something of the greatest importance. I'll wait for you in the drawing room. Ned.'

In the drawing room, the sun was shining behind the trees and sprinkling the big Persian carpet with patches of gold. Many birds were singing in the garden. Everything spoke of peace and happiness, but the young student remained somber.

'Do you want me to stay with you, to fling myself if necessary . . .'

'No, no. Go away, I beg you, I shall fight alone.'

'Bravo, Ned. I was sure that you would do it very well.'

At the moment she was leaving the drawing room, she met Uncle Charlie in his purple silk dressing gown.

'Good morning, Elizabeth. I hope that cheeky young Ned has not forgotten that his train leaves in an hour's time. He just has time for breakfast. What can he want to tell me?'

Being quite ignorant of how to be diplomatic in difficult circumstances, Ned immediately unburdened himself of his secret.

'Father, I did a foolish thing with Elizabeth, and in the fullest possible way. Since yesterday . . . she is a woman.'

Standing in the middle of the drawing room, he awaited the blow that would knock him to the ground. It did not come. Uncle Charlie raised his eyebrows and said:

'What do you expect? We Joneses are all the same. Hot-blooded! I did exactly the same with your mother.'

Ned stood open-mouthed in amazement.

'But tell me, how did you set about it? She can be difficult. Did she put up a struggle?'

'Not at all.'

'In short, full and complete consent on both sides, I imagine.'

'More or less. She wanted . . .'

'There wasn't a lot of point in hiring a lady's companion at a gold-plated price to protect her. And how am I going to get rid of the lady now?'

'At a gold-plated price, Papa?'

'Evidently, but now, my boy, marriage, eh what?'

'Yes, Father.'

'And straight away. I know only too well what happened to me. You see to the carriage. It'll take us to Manassas. The minister will do it all wonderfully well, given that I built his church for him. And the witnesses, we need two of them. You'll go and fetch the Commodore and tell him that I request this favor of him, but without delay. That's one but what about the other? A woman. Damn it! I can't think of anyone but Miss Furnace.'

'Do you think that's wise?'

'Do I think it wise? With all my heart. Given how distinguished and how beautiful she is, she'll make a tremendous impression on that old goat of a Presbyterian.'

'Elizabeth's an Anglican.'

'It doesn't matter. She's a Protestant. The marriage is valid.'

He clapped his hands.

'Quickly, drink your cup of coffee and gather everybody

together, Charlotte will take care of Amelia.'

'What about the university?'

'There won't be any university today. I'll write to the president. About this marriage, does Elizabeth consent?'

'Wholeheartedly!' she exclaimed as she ran up to him.

He burst out laughing as he clasped her in his arms.

'She heard everything. If ears and keyholes were abolished, there would be no more novels and no more plays, but here is my dream come to fruition. Come and let me kiss you again.'

The young woman felt a freshly-shaved cheek make contact with her face in a haze of eau-de-Cologne, and Uncle Charlie's mouth brushed several times against her own.

'Ned!' he shouted to the young man who was on his way out of the drawing room, 'four horses for the carriage. I want everything to be completed by the end of the morning. People will be counting on their fingers . . . You know what they're like. You arrived at just the right moment. And now, to finish making good the damage, my printer will spread this interesting piece of news in Savannah. I'll see to Virginia myself. As for your mother,' he said to Elizabeth, 'she'll know soon enough.'

The day went by as in a whirlwind.

The return from Manassas did not bring all the gaiety one might have expected, despite Uncle Charlie's exuberant good humor. He had no suspicion of the slight cloud of suspicion hanging over their conjugal bliss.

The Commodore behaved impeccably, with imposing dignity. Still dazzling, but more serious than usual, Miss Furnace had played her role with admirable fortitude, keeping until the end a martyred smile intended for her more fortunate young rival.

She turned her eyes away when Ned surreptitiously cast her one last, hungry look.

Of her own accord she announced her departure to Uncle Charlie. The interview took place in the small library where the portrait of the venerable Presbyterian ancestor kept watch over siestas and struggles with consciences. An envelope slid from one hand into another, and the great traveller took her leave with a more or less serene expression on her face.

That very evening, the new bridegroom left the great house to return to the university and his young wife slept in the solitude of the room with the Flemish wardrobes.

One consolation awaited her. Her old Betty emerged from a corner of the enormous room and, throwing herself at her feet, took hold of her hands which she drenched with tears.

'What's come over you?' Elizabeth asked her.

'Oh, Miss Lizbeth, Betty very pleased now. Everything fine, but you not tell Mass'r Ned that she the ghost, Miss Furnace.'

'Come now, of course not.'

To tell the truth, she had thought of it, just to cure Ned of his absurd obsession, but she had cast that temptation aside.

'Some day, Miss Lizbeth is goin' to think about Betty and be afraid.'

'Be quiet, Betty.'

'Sorry, Miss Lizbeth.'

'Come Betty, leave my hands and get up, you're forgiven a thousand times over.'

While this little scene was taking place, Uncle Charlie was sampling a julep in the room where his wife was asleep. Miss Charlotte was with him in a rocking chair, reassured by the turn events had taken, but still somewhat anxious about Elizabeth.

'Calm down,' said Uncle Charlie with a malicious smile. 'The cries she might hear will complete her education now that she's married. She will utter them, too, but on that day, I swear to you, I shall be in Barbados.'

*T*he great house dropped back into silence once more; the only things to be heard were the occasional groans of Amelia, suffering in apprehension of the greater pain to come.

'When will it be my turn?' wondered Elizabeth . . . 'Next January.' She preferred not to think about it. The Welsh-woman had given her to understand that it would be a terrible time. Elizabeth had no desire to inform her of the marriage. She had, moreover, determined to space out her correspond-ence with that woman, but nothing had come from Dimwood so far; it was doubtless too hot down there to write.

Miss Charlotte proved to be less talkative than before. She seemed worried and always on the look-out for the mail when it came to have a quick look at it before Jemima took it to Charlie Jones . . .

One day Elizabeth accidentally overheard an amazing dialogue. Amelia's door had been left open and Charlie Jones's voice could be heard:

'Put the mail down on the desk, Jemima. Still nothing from China?'

'I didn't see anything, Mr Jones.'

The door was closed again. Elizabeth looked at Miss Char-lotte.

'My brother-in-law has agencies in all parts of the world,' the elderly spinster said briefly.

Elizabeth did not insist. It did not matter to her if there was no letter from China for Uncle Charlie. In fact, nothing mattered to her; since Ned's departure, he had not written to her. His studies, Miss Charlotte explained. Elizabeth pre-tended to be cheered up by this. Yet when she was in bed, with all the lights out, there were times when she had a strange yearning for his presence, and the big bed seemed a desert to her. She suffered as she had never suffered before, and in a way that was destroying her. The nights were never-ending, empty and cruel.

When she was dressed, she played tricks on the horror of boredom by leaping onto a horse's back. The forest was her refuge, but she could no longer quite believe that Jonathan would appear there. Marriage changed everything, killing dreams.

A new hunger, unknown during her adolescence, and desire rose up inside her like a devouring flame. She was angry with the young Virginian for having aroused all her senses, for having set a fire raging in her flesh which hitherto had known nothing but langor. By day, exhaustion from her riding took the edge off frustration, but once the night came with its hallucinations, the young woman would roll on her bed stifling cries of rage and despair. She cursed that moment when, in the pine wood, Ned had kissed her mouth by force and begun it all.

Now, when life was resuming its normal course of unbearable banality, she became once more the impassive English girl who chose her words carefully. Her apparent coldness worried Miss Charlotte.

Someone else was keeping a secret watch on the young woman. Slipping into her room in the depths of the night, Betty would huddle in a corner behind one of the big wardrobes and cry silently.

June passed. July broke suddenly like a fire. The heat wave closed up the houses where the cool of the night was preserved like some treasure until evening.

The dry meadow gradually turned to a beige color. Quite soon it became impossible to water the gardens. The strongest of wills underwent a kind of flattening-out.

The ferocity of the sun created a demoralizing climate. Only Elizabeth held out. Having brilliantly passed his exams, Ned was restored to her. She admired and congratulated him, after which she turned her mind to more serious matters. As soon as the evening was drawing to a close, she left Miss Charlotte and Charlie Jones taking their ease on their *chaises-longues* in order to give herself up to the contemplation of the night sky, and then she would go up with Ned to the room which was now their matrimonial home. The lock on the door had been put back in its place and, as was often necessary, Ned had to perform his duty to pacify the golden-haired young bacchante . . . He loved her without a doubt, but she took advantage of him, it seemed to him quite dreadfully. At daybreak he would collapse from fatigue while she was still awake and wide-eyed.

It was in such circumstances that, one morning, they were roused from sleep by the first loud cries of the over-sensitive Amelia. As yet, it was only by way of a prelude. Elizabeth shuddered nevertheless. Ned calmed her with kind words, then, as the cries began to come one after the other, she even regretted leaving The Coppice. She tried to persuade her husband that they would be happier in that charming little house, quiet and intimate . . .

'A love nest!' he said with a laugh. 'Never. I'm at home in the great house, my beloved, and we're both fine here.'

She did not think he could be so firm, it was a surprise.

Is it necessary to point out that Charlie Jones coped very badly with the inconvenience of the situation? If he put in an exceptional appearance in the dining room in his purple dressing gown, a storm entered with him. Why did one event, that augured so badly have to occur one particular morning when his mood was taking a murderous turn?

No one could believe their eyes . . . The Commodore was to be seen coming out suddenly from the House of Chaos. Without hesitation, he set out, like a wild horse on his great legs, through the long grass of the meadow that was forbidden to the heads of the warring families. His gray hair was blowing in the wind and, with a hand raised above his head, he was frantically waving some newspapers.

Charlie Jones came to meet him with his face red with irritation.

'What's the matter?' he shouted. 'You're coming across the meadow! It'll make my wife ill. Has war been declared?'

'No, but it's on the way, believe me. Do you not get the *National Era*? That silly goose Harriett Beecher-Stowe is bringing out in serial form a novel about slavery in the South.'

His emaciated face stiffened with rage, and he surveyed Uncle Charlie's angry eyes as if he could make out the presence of an enemy frigate in them.

'So?'

'She takes pity on the fate of those good slaves whom we treat like cattle, so it appears.'

'It's worthless. I know the lady . . . She's never set foot in the real South and has only seen Kentucky. She has no real knowledge.'

'That's possible, but she has the necessary vulgarity to reach a vast audience and set its sense of indignation ablaze. There have already been two instalments. I'll leave you this rubbish and go back to my warship.'

'Do you not have time to smoke a Havana cigar under the trees with me? It would calm my nerves. Amelia is on the point of giving birth today.'

'Poor old chap. It's hard, isn't it? Maisie already has six children, and she wanted to commit the same folly again, but I called her to order. You need to know how to train women.'

Having spoken these words, he began to run through the long grass once more, this time in the opposite direction, returning to the House of Chaos.

The child was born in the night, after a day that was full of horror for Elizabeth. She was tempted to leap on to Alcibiades and flee into the woods, but Ned put her to shame. No one would understand if she took to flight at a time that concerned the whole family, of which she was now a part. She was not spared a single cry. Conjugal bliss suddenly appeared to her in a different light.

It was a boy. He was called Emmanuel. When he was well and truly born, Charlie Jones immediately became angelic once more and wept for joy.

Restored to life, Amelia smiled with happiness and murmured:

'There's one, at least, that won't die on the battlefield.'

That night Elizabeth proved moderate in demanding her rights and her young husband slept well.

The relentlessly blue sky held out no hope of a single drop of rain, and the heat weighed down as if to suffocate the world and rid people once and for all of their perpetual desire for fine weather.

The inhabitants of the great house dragged themselves from room to room like shadows in nightgowns. None of them felt like eating, and cool drinks, once they had been drunk, did no more than fan the flames of thirst. A persistent humidity made everything worse. It was sufficient to raise an arm for sweat to run down from the wrist to the arm-pit. A sheet of paper on which one hoped to write a letter became a piece of blotting paper.

The days were gloomy from beginning to end, yet care had to be taken of frail Emmanuel, who was suffering like the rest of them. His wet-nurse Ada, a black woman, well built and with a heart of gold, ran with sweat beneath her white blouse, and she hummed melodiously as she fanned the newcomer with a palm leaf. She was greeted from a distance, for she smelt of baby, sweat and milk. Charlie Jones, whose sense of smell was over-sensitive, stood some way off and breathed through a handkerchief soaked in eau-de-Cologne. Nevertheless, he ordered that, for the time being, everyone was to obey Ada, who was so precious. Indeed, the latter rolled her enormous black eyes, full of love, at the tiny creature whom she could hold in one hand.

Three weeks went by in total inertia. Was anything happening in the world? Unopened newspapers piled up in a corner, and barely opened letters were devoid of all interest. Then one day, late in the afternoon, the swallows began to fly low and, as the shadows thickened, bats came in great numbers to flap their wings around the house.

The air remained still, however. The lamps, which gave off heat, were put out and they all went up to bed carrying candlesticks; soon the darkness was complete.

A little before eleven o'clock in the evening, a terrible din woke the sleepers. With an apocalyptic crash, the heavens split apart, and lightning began to strike the earth from a long tear in the sky. The whole countryside, from the hills to Great Meadow, was revealed in a blinding light of supernatural beauty illuminating each leaf, each stone, each blade of grass with a hallucinatory intensity. The almost constant rumbling of the thunder underscored the horror of these moments so evocative of the end of the world. All of the servants were under their beds, except for Ada, who covered little Emmanuel with her arms, deep in undisturbed sleep. Miss Charlotte, standing in her nightdress, was screeching a psalm.

Dazzled with admiration, Elizabeth was standing by the window despite the shouts of her husband who ordered her to join him under the covers. In the stables, the horses were neighing and trying to escape.

At last, the first drops of rain clattered on the roofs with the sound of bullets, before suddenly falling in a downpour. The violence was accompanied by a semblance of rage that spread panic amongst the inhabitants, disturbing the house from top to bottom. Only Miss Charlotte, who had taken refuge in the drawing room, was still singing. In vain did Uncle Charlie who had come down in his purple dressing gown, try to silence her; the elderly spinster did not calm down for a full half-hour. At that moment the rain began to fall with a calm regularity which had the effect of soporific music on all of them. It continued the next day and patiently persisted throughout the three following ones, welcoming with all the good fragrance of wet earth the month of August with its reputation for wet weather.

108

*E*verything at Great Meadow returned to its routine. Amelia reappeared at table, serene and smiling under her white lace cap decorated with a little ostrich feather. In order to avoid disturbing her, Charlie Jones talked neither about politics nor about *Uncle Tom's Cabin*, the third instalment of which had just appeared. He had regained his good humor, and seemed to be proud of his wife for having given him a son.

One morning he took Ned by the arm and took a stroll with him under the trees behind the house.

'My boy,' he said, 'are you happy with Elizabeth?'

'How could I not be? She is always charming, perhaps still a little reserved, but in secret she simply adores me, I assure you.'

'What makes you think that?'

'Her shows of affection. I'll say no more than that.'

'I'm watching her with interest. I'm sure you're right, but she's changing. She is no longer anything like that enchanting girl I knew in Savannah.'

'A lady!'

'Ha, ha, but in her eyes there's occasionally something rather wild — which suits her, what's more, which suits her. There are things I should like to talk to you about. You see my dear Amelia. You must have been struck, like everybody else, by her unflappable calm which makes her appear so majestic.'

'Of course, Papa.'

'That woman is an angel. She cries out in anticipation of pain, and she cries out when she is in pain as well. That's nothing, that's nothing. Now, like a large number of women in America, and elsewhere, Amelia has never really experienced pleasure, what we understand as pleasure.'

'Ah?'

'Yes. That's where her wonderful, almost Olympian, composure comes from. So, you keep an eye on your Elizabeth's composure too. Let her remain like Amelia, who regularly sees her partner in the grips of a crisis of which she understands nothing. Do you see what I mean?'

'Yes,' said Ned as he tortured a little flower he had just pulled from a bush.

'It's preferable for it to be that way with women,' Charlie Jones continued gravely. 'Otherwise, there is a danger of them turning into . . . mmm . . . nymphomaniacs, I apologize for the term.'

'Nymphomaniacs!'

'Things are as I tell you, my boy. Do I need to spell it out more? But this is man to man. They can even become hysterical.'

'Oh!'

'Quite. With the depravity of morals these days, England is full of hysterical women.'

'But that's monstrous, Papa. What do those wretches do?'

'They write novels.'

Ned looked at him in bewilderment:

'Novels! Oh, Papa, how dreadful!'

'But some of them are devilish talented, and the public adores them.'

'I, in any case, shall keep an eye on Elizabeth. She is very obedient.'

'Well, I am quite reassured . . . But these affectionate outbursts, Ned, does she have a lot of them?'

'She wants to be sure of having a child. It's calculated.'

Charlie Jones stopped and looked at his son attentively. Ned did not turn away his eyes, but remained silent. Charlie Jones sighed and Ned, lowering his head, began to contemplate the tips of his shoes.

'Listen carefully to what I am going to say, and remember this,' said Charlie Jones. 'When you are with her, at certain times . . . are you with me?'

'But of course.'

'Be selfish, be short . . . there are women of easy virtue for the rest. Understood?'

The young man blushed and nodded.

'Let's go in,' said the father. 'Have confidence, everything will be all right.'

Disturbed by this conversation with his father, Ned went for a walk on his own. From the very pale, blue sky, light shone gently on the damp earth, and birds were singing at the tops of their voices in the trees. Normally in such weather Ned would have started to whistle, with his hands in his pockets, as carefree as a schoolboy, but that morning he had a bitter taste in his mouth, on account of some of the things Charlie Jones had said to him. Had they not revealed some of the mysteries of the flesh with which he had thought he was quite familiar? But had he ever looked for anything other than pleasure? He was confusing it with love. The most frivolous of his adventures with women had concealed an underlying tenderness. That there should be married women and mothers who were ignorant of physical enjoyment he found confusing. In those circumstances, had he made Elizabeth insane? That thought disturbed him for the rest of the day, and he contemplated the world with a downcast look of angry sadness. He was cross with the absurd education he had received. Instead of teaching boys Greek and trigonometry, it would have been better to instruct them in these essential aspects of life, but they were precisely the things that were not to be spoken about. Experience was supposed to be enough, and experience was gained in a half-light strewn with traps.

He felt alone for the first time.

On the road to Great Meadow, Charlie Jones passed in front of the House of Chaos, from which the Commodore emerged energetically and walked up to him.

'I saw you coming from some way off,' he told him. 'Let's take a few steps together. I have something to say to you.'

Pulling from under his arm the crumpled next instalment of the serial, he began in a flat tone of voice which grew to a bellowing:

'Have you seen it? Not yet? It's enough to make you think that half-wit of a woman enjoys selling slaves. Men and women, she knows all the tricks of the trade. She splits families up to see if it makes them cry, but today she's gone beyond the limits of fair play when she presents us with a black woman and her baby who's ten and a half months old, both for sale. The husband has already been bought. There is a crowd on the boat which is in harbor. She wants to see her husband for the last time, but what to do with the baby? Listen to this. She puts it down in a crib, covers it with a cloth and off she goes. When she comes back, no more baby . . . It's been stolen, she claims, the infant was sought after by slave fanciers! Now, can you imagine a mother abandoning her baby in a crowd, if only for a minute? Do you think she'll get people to swallow that, even the abolitionists in the North?'

'Perfectly well,' said Uncle Charlie calmly. 'They swallow anything at all, and ask for more, when it comes to berating us. The people will applaud her and the pastors will give rapturous approval, she'll bring public opinion up to boiling point where it explodes. Then there will be a holy crusade against these Southern reprobates. And war will follow quite naturally.'

He appeared to be free from all illusions as he spoke, which only made the Commodore's fury rise:

'It doesn't seem to bother you,' he exclaimed. 'Isn't there any way of making her shut up? An indictment for defamation, for example?'

'A court case would be wonderful publicity for her. Can't

you see the headlines in advance: 'New light on Southern iniquities'? I grant that hothead will be adorned with a halo, a halo splattered with blood, but she will have it. And she will continue to say her prayers and read her Bible.'

'You are mad. She almost makes me believe in the Devil.'

'The Devil can be a wonderful spiritual guide. He'll open her Bible for her in all the right places, he knows them as no one else does.'

'My word, you are right.'

Unfolding the serial, he pointed a finger trembling with rage at the beginning of a chapter: 'A voice was heard in Rama, it was Rachel weeping for her children . . .'

'With lines like that,' concluded Charlie Jones, 'she has her entrée into every conscience. While we wait for the next instalment, let's smoke a cigar to restore our calm.'

The Commodore did not have to be asked twice, and soon they resumed their discussion with greater composure. Grave judgements were pronounced and immediately carried away by the breeze together with the elegant blue curls of smoke from their Havana cigars.

Uncle Charlie and Amelia appeared at all meals at the great house once more. Tiny Emmanuel was the prize of fat Ada, who wrapped in fierce love that little creature who grew more handsome each day. The black wet-nurse became his real mother. Miss Charlotte often kept her company, respecting her as she would an angel, giving the occasional sad smile in response to secret thoughts.

109

E lizabeth, seeking to avoid solitude, took advantage of every occasion to walk or ride with Ned. She was growing fond of him. His handsome, open, slightly naive face, his kind, deep eyes that never showed any malice, all of this, together with his natural good nature, nourished in her a tenderness which she tried to pass off as love. But, in reality, she had nothing to say to him and, from that time onwards, their long strolls in the woods held no mystery. Nearly every possible subject had been exhausted.

The nights were quite different, for Elizabeth at least. Ned was placid by nature and had reduced what he called love to that act which she secretly described as prosaic on account of its regularity, devoid of any emotion, but which he undoubtedly considered necessary for his well-being and health. She was there to provide that beneficial effect for him. With an impatience she could barely control, she awaited the little satisfied sigh that marked the end of the operation. After which he tenderly wished her good-night and drifted almost immediately into a noisy sleep.

It was then that her night began. With her eyes wide open, she questioned the blackness. Had he at least found satisfaction in this monotonous mounting? She wondered. Her memory spoke of delirious moments in which neither he nor she was satiated. Shortly after they were married, this happiness had come to an end, like a mysterious paradise that suddenly became the object of a total ban. Why had he opened that portal to her?

What had happened? One despairing night she asked him certain questions with cautious modesty. He simply laughed and, as he covered her face with kisses, explained that their previous excesses corresponded to the fiery impulses of their first encounters. Marriage had brought about good order. There were things that were no longer permitted between husband and wife. He abstained out of respect for her, for her . . . (the word 'dignity' hovered for a moment on his lips, but the furious look she gave him sealed his mouth: she had guessed).

'Very well,' she said, 'but what a dreadful renunciation!'

'You'll get used to it,' he said gently, 'and children will come in due course. Don't upset yourself, go to sleep, my darling.'

The lamp was put out with these kind words, and Elizabeth returned to her renewed perplexity. She remembered Miss Furnace and the hold she had on her young husband.

More than once she had been tempted to reveal to Ned that that fascinating person could count at least thirty-five, but, out of female loyalty, she refrained. The problem was simple. She had married a man who loved brunettes, whereas she had all that gold on her head . . . Had he ever brushed his cheek against her hair which had been so much admired? Had he ever buried his face in it, had he ever fingered the tresses? Was she one of those women that men do not lose their reason over, despite their dazzling beauty? Why had he married her? On a whim. Or had his father secretly driven him to it?

Silently, and in the mourning of yet another night of deprivation, she shed tears of sadness and rage.

In the hardest moments of her distress, a memory came back to her like a flash in the night. With a bewildering clarity she saw herself once more as she had been during those first days at Dimwood. She was suffering then, having been wrenched from her native land, but she had a premonition that the time would come when her heart would find peace, and she lived on that hope. She had been completely innocent in those days. If the soul was suffering, the body at least was calm. The body knew nothing. And for a moment that seemed of short duration, but which lasted until dawn, she was once more the young innocent for whom the world of the senses was a mystery. Without knowing it, she experienced a kind of ecstasy from which she was roused by the rays of sunlight coming through the shutters. The disappointment was awful. She was appalled at herself and cursed that pleasure whose lack made life Hell for her.

Once more, pride got her back on her feet. She had not clearly foreseen the life which marriage had in store for her, but she determined to pretend that, for her, all was going well. She would act out the sinister comedy of conventional happiness, she would be the attentive and smiling young wife, concerned for the well-being of her husband.

How long would this go on? This question of her inner voice was forcibly set aside. The world would know nothing. Only Ned would know.

One morning, when she thought she was alone in her bedroom and combing her hair in front of her dressing-table mirror, she saw Betty at her feet. One never knew where the old black woman sprang from; she would hide in any corner and suddenly she would be there.

'My dear Betty,' said Elizabeth, 'I don't need you for the moment. I'll call you later.'

'Betty stay for a minute, Miss Lizbeth. Betty comb your beautiful hair, please, Miss Lizbeth.'

The young woman could not resist the imploring look of the large black eyes, and soon the comb was going through the supple, golden waves with loving gentleness.

The young woman bent her head back and experienced an almost physical joy in letting her hair be combed.

'Do you like my hair?' she asked, savoring in advance the flattering delight that would console her.

'Oh, Miss Lizbeth, nobody got such beautiful hair, nobody in all the world.'

'Do you really think so?'

'Oh, yes, Miss Lizbeth, but Miss Lizbeth, she's not any more happy.'

Elizabeth gave such a start that Betty dropped her comb.

'Why do you say that?' asked the young woman. 'Tell me, Betty. I want to know.'

'Betty know everythin' when she see Miss Lizbeth.'

'You don't know anything,' said Elizabeth crossly, 'comb my hair, Betty.'

Betty picked up the comb and thrust it once more into the thick golden tresses.

'What do you do when you're not happy?'

'Now Betty always happy. Not before.'

'So, what did you do when you weren't happy?'

'Asked.'

'You asked the Lord, is that what you mean?'

'Yes, Miss Lizbeth, the Lord, He say "Ask".'

'I ask and nothing happens. Why weren't you happy?'

'When Betty younger, she love a man who don't love Betty back.'

At these words, Elizabeth stood up and bent towards the black woman.

'I'm very fond of you, my dear Betty, so you must tell me

what you did.'

'Betty tell everything to Miss Laura. Miss Laura say: "You tell everything to the Lord, and then ask, ask." '

'Oh, Betty,' said Elizabeth disappointedly, 'is that all?'

'Yes, that's all. The Lord, He promise to give, so He must give.'

'And so what did the Lord give you? The love of that man?'

'No, His own love.'

Elizabeth remained silent.

Seeing tears in the maid's eyes, she gently stroked her face and said:

'Betty, they always tell us that the Lord loves us, but that doesn't prevent us from suffering.'

'Not when He stand alongside you, Miss Lizbeth.'

Elizabeth bent down towards the old woman and gave her a kiss on each cheek, her hair surrounding that frizzy little head like a luminous cloak.

Of this conversation, which she judged to be futile, she did, however, retain two things. One was the name Laura, about whom she hardly ever thought, the other an unfamiliar emotion associated with the kiss she had given Betty. It had lasted no longer than the gesture itself, giving unforgettable peace and joy. She explained the matter to herself through her pitiful need to love, her heart full of unsatisfied tenderness.

These reflections inflamed her desire to talk over with Ned the torment she was undergoing.

That morning he had left early to take a solitary ride, which had become a habit with him since their marriage. He always came back in a good mood with his head full of new ideas for his studies, he said.

Elizabeth awaited him impatiently, leaning out of her bedroom window on the look-out for his return. Pretending to meet him accidentally, she went down the stairs as he was coming up and said cheerfully:

'Did you go off to gallop through the fields in order to think about your studies? Oh, when shall I have a husband who has finished his studies?'

'My darling,' he said in the same tone of voice, 'I am your

husband from the top of my head to the tips of my toes. Did you miss me so much?'

She went ahead of him into the bedroom and said to him with a determined look:

'There are certain questions I need to ask you. Will you sit down?'

He shook his head and remained standing, sensing that a storm was on the way.

In her white dress that enhanced her beauty, Elizabeth stood in front of him and tried to put on a look of displeasure:

'Ned, the other evening you spoke to me like a schoolboy.'

'Which evening, and what did I say to you?'

'We were talking about love. I don't want to go into details. There are certain words that I don't like, but you told me that I would get used to the way you behave towards me. Do you remember?'

'Yes, vaguely.'

'I'll be more precise: "you'll get used to it, and children will come along in due course".'

'What a memory! I said that, so what?'

'I find such language monstrous. You take no account of our first encounter in the children's room and all that I experienced in your arms.'

'That was nature, Elizabeth, the irresistible impulse. You wanted it so much.'

'I don't want to argue about it. You introduced me to a joy that you deprive me of now.'

'We shall manage very well without it in the long run, you must be patient.'

'Do you think that Romeo and Juliet restrained their impulses?'

'You're dreaming! In America we don't behave as the Italians do, and then times have changed. Marriage is as you and I are living it.'

'Times haven't changed,' she said stamping her foot, 'and what we did is done all over the world.'

'You're mad, that's your imagination.'

'No. You taught me to experience pleasure and now . . .'

'I shouldn't really have done so.'

She let out a desperate cry.

'And what do you propose to do to make me forget?

Answer.'

'I don't know.'

'Do you really think that Romeo held himself back?'

'Stop bothering me with your Romeo. I'm not Romeo.'

'No, because Romeo was not only a husband, he was a lover too.'

He became red with anger.

'Never say that word in front of me again. If ever you had a lover, I should kill the man to avenge my honor. You're mine.'

'Who's talking about a lover? Why aren't you my lover?'

'It's not possible . . . It's not done in America.'

'Are you trying to tell me that in America men are satisfied with marriage as you present it, with that moderation you speak of?'

'It's not a question of them, but of us . . . You experienced pleasure because you wished to.'

'Me? How could I wish for what I didn't even have any idea of?'

'Ah? Who was it who ordered me to close the door and to lock it?'

She felt unsteady on her feet, but pulled herself together immediately:

'I'm sorry, I had not at all imagined love to be as you revealed it to me . . . with its great joys . . . I thought it was nothing more than the embrace we had in the pine wood, when you clasped me with all your strength and you took my mouth . . .'

'Fully dressed, Elizabeth.'

'I know, I thought that there was something you had to do when you were naked, but without that overwhelming pleasure.'

'You didn't know?'

'No, no one had ever told me anything about that.'

He took a step towards her and, with a radiant smile, held out his arms towards her:

'My love,' he said, 'we behaved like two children, so let's forgive each other.'

So little was she expecting these words that tears flowed from her eyes:

'Oh, Ned!' she said, plaintively.

'I swear that I shall always be faithful to you.'

All she could do was to fall on his neck without answering, while he placed his lips on her eyes.

Charlie Jones was quite ignorant of these heart-rending avowals. His joy flowed over at seeing his family around him with good order established. Little Emmanuel was losing his wrinkles as if his face were ironed each morning, and he would smile at everyone without ever crying. 'A little love,' Ada would say as she held out her breast. Amelia would keep an eye on things, give her approval and move on.

But what delighted Charlie Jones almost as much was the sight of the young newly-weds who sat opposite him at table. They both looked so well behaved and so handsome, she with her royal diadem on her head and he with his avalanche of black curls that gave him the charm of a Romantic poet.

'My children,' he said to them one morning, 'I have some good news to announce to you. My valiant little female workers from China have arrived and are going to be set to work immediately.'

'For the love of Heaven,' exclaimed Miss Charlotte, 'tell us what you mean. Who are these little Chinese women, and what are they coming here to do?'

He assumed a sly expression.

'Allow me the pleasure of preparing for you a surprise which will astound the whole of our century. These young ladies work remarkably well.'

'They'll have to learn English, nevertheless, in order to understand what is being said to them.'

'Charlotte,' he said with a subtle smile, 'they know it already.'

Very satisfied with his answer that said it all but explained nothing, Charlie Jones touched his wife's hand.

'My dearest,' he said, 'I think we have all finished breakfast, and the weather is magnificent; would you like to take a stroll with me under the trees?'

Amelia was looking particularly beautiful that morning. Wearing a sumptuous bonnet of lace that had come all the way from Bruges, her face relaxed, she was smiling kindly at everyone, yet still retaining her superior air, which was so exasperating. With a slight nod of the head, she indicated her approval to her husband and they both stood up.

Elizabeth watched them go out, walking with that measured step which made them so imposing. Amelia was wearing her favourite plum-colored taffeta dress with wide flounces, and she advanced amidst rustling of fabric that was flattering to her ear.

The young woman looked dreamily at the couple and thought: 'That's what lies ahead of me. I shall learn to become calm like her, but did she ever lose her composure in Uncle Charlie's arms? A mystery. How do they manage?'

She and Ned no longer broached the subject and habit seemed to settle everything, except for Elizabeth's insomnia about which her husband knew nothing. Once or twice in his sleep he would stretch out his hand in a half-conscious gesture, as if to assure himself that she was still there. Shortly before dawn, weary of wondering about her fate, she drifted into sleep which swallowed up her despair.

Two uneventful weeks went by. Uncle Charlie was methodically preparing his departure for Savannah, where business called, especially work on his house in Madison Square. He grumbled a little at the thought of leaving Virginia where the heat was becoming bearable, whereas merciless summer was still in full force in Georgia. Amelia would join him later, with the first cool days of October, together with Elizabeth and Miss Charlotte. As for Ned, his return to the university was only a few days off, a week at most. There would doubtless be sighs and tears, for the two children, as Charlie Jones called them, were evidently madly in love with each other. Such was his vision of things, and he found it most endearing.

Elizabeth accepted everything, feeling sick at heart with a resignation that was more like despair. She was no longer angry with Ned. She sometimes saw him following her with his eyes with the worried look of a dog saying it is sorry, but the irreparable damage had been done, and they would perhaps suffer for it throughout their youth and beyond.

She made all efforts not to think about Jonathan any more, but a force within her that was independent of her will obliged her to calculate the amount of time it would have taken her letter with the map of the forest to reach him, and the time it would take him to join her in Virginia.

'I mustn't,' she said when alone, nor knowing to whom she was speaking.

If her calculations were correct, he might turn up in mid-September. Ned would be at university then, and Uncle Charlie in Savannah. She saw that circumstances were conspiring strangely in her favor and, through the natural inclination of her imagination, she arrived at a point at which she saw everything as a secret conspiracy of fate, life's tacit approval. Someone felt sorry for her and was setting an injustice to rights.

Once she was dragged from her dreams, she took fright and thought she must be on the verge of madness. Was it the effect of deprivation? Suddenly, by one of those mental reversals that came naturally to her, she persuaded herself that Jonathan would not come. According to her new way of deciding things, he had had plenty of time to make the journey without waiting for a letter from her. He had said: 'I am coming.' What need did he have of an answer? He would leave immediately — but he had not even left.

110

*T*wo days before Uncle Charlie was due to leave, she decided to make one more sentimental pilgrimage to the wood of the unconsummated rendezvous. Mounted on Alcibiades, she took the long way round.

The sun was shining on the horizon in a sky that was turning pink. The days were growing shorter. Two hours of daylight remained, and then it would be dark. This was the time of day she preferred, when occasional birdsong subtly heralded the silence that would descend on the countryside.

She stopped at the edge of a little vale by a chattering

stream, whose murmur delighted her. She remembered the conversation about Jonathan she had shared there, on a bench, with Charlie Jones. He was the only person in Virginia who knew of her unhappy love, and how happy he was now that this marriage had put an end to all that, or so he thought . . . She sighed and sat down on the bench, having tied Alcibiades to a tree.

Charlie Jones was assuredly one of the best men in the world and generous to the point of folly, but sometimes naive. He had succeeded in everything. A fortune had rushed into his arms like a woman in love. Only the death of his first wife had cast a shadow over his life, but that had not lasted.

She was given up completely to her dreams as she watched the sky that was slowly turning into bands of red behind the trees on the other side of the vale. She could see a certain magnificence in the day as it imperceptibly declined. Here was that magic moment when dreams are aroused.

All of a sudden she heard, in the distance, the sound of galloping hooves coming through the meadows. She stood up suddenly, with such vehemence that she almost fell over backwards. It seemed impossible that she could be wrong. The silhouette of the horseman coming towards her could bear only one name:

'Jonathan!' she shouted

He stopped three yards from her, made his superb black horse rear up on its hind legs and greeted her with a wave of his hat held high.

'Anything can happen, even the improbable!' he exclaimed joyfully.

Jumping to the ground, he tied his horse to a tree some way away from Alcibiades and hurling his hat to the ground, he knelt at Elizabeth's feet:

'Get up, my Jonathan, don't stay like that.'

'You're forgetting you're an angel,' he said as he stood up.

'I'm not an angel, I'm . . .'

He closed her mouth with a hungry kiss and embraced her so hard that she thought she would suffocate, but he did not let her go, and she struggled as best she could in his iron grip.

Slackening his hold a little, he told her breathlessly:

'I'm sorry, but I've been waiting for this moment for ever.'

'So have I,' she said, 'but I'm suffocating.'

He let her go for a few seconds and stroked her face with his hands. She exclaimed:

'My adored one, let me look at you. How handsome you are . . . your fine black curls and your eyes . . . a wild animal's eyes.'

He pulled off her riding hat and with furious fingers unpinned her hair, spreading the flow of gold over her shoulders.

'You are the only one I have ever loved,' he said as he hid his face in her hair, breathing in its fragrance.

'You showed me what love is, Jonathan . . . Do you remember the magnolias at Dimwood?'

'My beloved, I have lived on that moment ever since I saw your face amongst the leaves. You looked ethereal . . . It was you whom I wanted to marry, but there's that woman who clings to me . . .'

'Is the marriage not broken off?'

'Impossible, the law forbids it and she has bought lawyers. I should have to kill her to be free of her. But you belong to me. Tell me, tell me.'

'I shall never be able to love anyone but you, but it's over, I cannot be yours.'

'Not mine!' he exclaimed.

Taking hold of her below the waist, he lifted her up and then lowered her on the grass in the shade of the birch trees. She gathered up all of her strength to push him away, but her resistance could only increase the desire of that powerful man. In vain she struggled and struck him on the face, he took her brutally and she let herself go . . . terrified and happy.

At dusk, they separated. They rode part of the way together.

'What now?' said Jonathan.

'I don't know, but I shall only ever love you.'

'We'll live together, my darling.'

She was silent for a moment and sighed:

'Jonathan, you'll have to know . . . I'm married, like you.'

'Married!' he said furiously . . . 'you didn't wait for me?'

'No more than you did for me . . . It doesn't change anything as far as our love is concerned.'

'It changes everything . . . Who is it?'

'Charlie Jones's son.'

'A Jones! If you want children, he'll give them to you, but that's all. The men in that family are well known for being placid.'

'He hasn't always been that way. The first time . . .'

'The first time doesn't mean anything. Everyone has experienced that initial impulse. Listen. If ever I see that man, I know, I will be capable of killing him.'

Elizabeth uttered a cry:

'If ever you do that, you will kill me at the same time. I couldn't bear it.'

'Do you love him, Elizabeth?'

'Not the way I love you, but in a different way, yes.'

'You can't love two people at the same time.'

'Women can.'

'Well, only one of them can be her lover. I am yours. If you had married me, I would have taken you to live in Europe, in London or Paris. There people know how to make the most of life. I shall be rich in a month's time. I'm going to sell Dimwood. Dimwood is mine.'

'Dimwood is yours?'

'It's complicated, you wouldn't understand, but I'm selling it, you won't guess to whom. To my wife. She is very rich. She buys everything. I shall be free of both of them.'

With one accord, they brought their horses to a halt. Lights were already being lit in the windows of the houses along the edge of the meadows.

'I shall leave you,' he said, 'but we shall see each other again. Every afternoon I shall pass by the spot where we were, at about the same time.'

'Wait for a few days . . . They would be suspicious if I left the house every afternoon and came back so late . . .'

'Don't make your lover pine, my darling.'

'I'll do what I can, because I love you more than my life, Jonathan.'

He drew his horse close to hers and took in his hands the head of the young woman, who had redone her hair as best she could.

'I'm afraid,' she said, 'it's almost dark.'

He kissed her and said:

'Off you go, my love, but don't forget. I shall carry you off.'

She put her fingers to her lips and galloped away.

111

She managed to get home without being noticed, the attention of everybody in the house being caught up in preparations for Charlie Jones's journey. The problem was simple: everything had to be perfect and comfortable. Ned himself, in a fit of enthusiasm, made his contribution by choosing the finest ties and casting his eye over the state of the toilet requisites.

In her room, Elizabeth got undressed and washed herself thoroughly in her bath tub. Betty poured jugs of warm water over her shoulders and the young woman soaped herself with a fury that verged on madness ... She had it fixed in her mind that her body retained the smell of Jonathan, a warm smell ... Not daring to ask Betty to confirm this, she rubbed all the harder, watching the old servant out of the corner of her eye, but she remained unperturbed.

When she was dressed, Elizabeth looked at herself in the mirror. A strange thought crossed her mind: 'It doesn't show, in any case.' The soapy water had washed away something more than the smell of Jonathan.

The torn riding habit was replaced with the finest white cotton dresses, with no ornament but a royal blue velvet belt. Betty combed and coiffed her mistress's hair with minutely attentive gestures that found their inspiration in her heart, but she did not open her mouth throughout the whole operation.

'Did you have a good ride?' asked Ned when he saw her at dinner.

'Very.'

'You look a little tired,' said Miss Charlotte. 'You mustn't overdo the clip-clopping, you know.'

Elizabeth gave an embarrassed laugh.

'Yes indeed, but the weather was so fine.'

She was answering distractedly, in the same way that one brushes a fly aside with one's hand. For the last minute she had been looking at Uncle Charlie as she had never looked at him before. She was trying to understand him. In that calm, pink face, she tried to detect a weakness of character, some vice perhaps, but all she could make out was self-satisfaction, greed in the lines of the mouth, but also irony in the curl of the lips, and that was what troubled her. The eyes, however, were reassuring. The magnificent, storm-colored pupils revealed nothing but intelligence and an evident kindness, which was a little naive, she believed, but she could not gainsay his long experience as a businessman, lawyer and financier. Of course, she was seeing what she wanted to see. Several times, conscious of this mysterious examination of his person, he gave her a handsome smile which betrayed a solid layer of vanity, that of a young man.

He took coffee in the drawing room with his dear Amelia, whose hand he fondled affectionately from time to time, and his majestic wife rewarded him with a sweet smile. They decided to go up to their room as the clock struck ten. It was the same every evening.

That was the moment Elizabeth chose. Going up behind them without a sound, she grabbed Uncle Charlie by the arm just as Amelia was disappearing into the bedroom.

He looked at the young woman in amazement as she raised an imploring face towards him:

'My dear, what's the matter? You see that I am retiring for the night with my wife.'

'I know, Uncle Charlie, but I'm in distress.'

'Come now, what's the trouble? Tell me quickly.'

'Not here, I must be alone with you for a moment.'

'But, Elizabeth, the house isn't on fire, I hope. You've chosen your moment badly. Have you had a quarrel with Ned?'

'Oh, no. It's nothing to do with my dear Ned and he knows nothing about it.'

'Elizabeth, you can tell me everything tomorrow morning, go to sleep and good-night.'

'No, no,' she said, not letting go of his arm. 'My future is in your hands. Oh, Uncle Charlie, remember the undertaking you made under the sycamore in front of your house?'

'What are you waiting for, Charlie?' groaned the offended voice of Amelia from the depths of the bedroom.

With a movement of the hand, Charlie Jones asked Elizabeth to wait and closed the door. There followed a sound of animated discussion in the nuptial chamber. Without a doubt, Amelia did not understand why her husband should leave her all alone, be it only for a moment, and moreover she wanted to know why. Calmed down at last, she fell silent and Charlie Jones reappeared at the top of the stairs.

'Let's go downstairs,' he said in a tone that betrayed his annoyance.

They reached the drawing room without exchanging a word. As they crossed the antechamber, he took the nightlight that was gleaming feebly in the corner of the house and placed it on the marble table in the large, solemn room. The lighting was sinister, but perhaps that was what he wanted. A black shadow concealed the ceiling and the top of the walls. Surrounded by blackness, they sat down opposite each other, their faces appearing like masks in the flickering of the little lamp.

'I'm listening,' he said.

She waited for several seconds as if to gather up her strength and then said straight off the sentence she had been going over in her mind for hours.

'I'm leaving with you tomorrow.'

In bewilderment he pushed his chair back and exclaimed:

'Are you mad, Elizabeth?'

'No, I'm not mad! I am no longer safe here. It's a matter of conscience which I cannot divulge to you, but I beg you to believe me.'

In a flash he could see his journey become impossible, his precious comfort all sabotaged by this importunate daughter-in-law who would take up half of the room in the carriage and weary him with her chatter.

'A thousand pardons,' he said. 'My conscience tells me to leave you here in the protection of your husband . . .'

She interrupted him:

'Ned is leaving for the university in four days.'

'So?'

'A woman of my age ought to be able to count on the protection of a man.'

'But what have you to fear?'

'What if, by chance, someone were roaming around the neighborhood? With goodness knows what intentions. There's no point in elaborating. I'm young.'

'What an insane idea! There's no one roaming around here. People would know about it.'

'Uncle Charlie, it's no longer a little girl you're talking to, it's a woman, and a woman calling for help. Remember your promises. If you don't take me away with you, you and Ned risk never seeing me again.'

'What are you going on about, Elizabeth?'

'I should run away, almost for certain.'

'But why? Why?' he said almost in a fury.

'I've said enough. Do you want me to swear on the Bible that I'm telling the truth?'

He gave a glance at the thick family Bible, lying unmoveable in the place of honor on the marble table.

'No point, I believe you,' he said with the smile of an exhausted opponent.

He stood up abruptly and with a sweeping gesture of indignation that brought out the lawyer in him:

'Oh, obstinate little English girl, I give in, but don't think I'm going to let you bother me in my carriage.'

'Dear Uncle Charlie, I shall make myself very small.'

'You can make yourself as small as you like, but not in my carriage. You'll follow behind in a reasonably comfortable vehicle.'

'With my dear Betty.'

'With your dear Betty and Milton's *Paradise Lost*, and saucepans for making cocoa on the way, and the cook's tomcat and . . .'

'You're too kind, dear Uncle Charlie.'

'I am of the same opinion,' he said, fuming as he took the nightlight.

He passed in front of her and left the drawing room. His enormous shadow hovered for a moment over the walls, followed by the slim and graceful silhouette of Elizabeth.

'Good-night,' she said to him at the bottom of the stairs.

A short grunt was his reply. She went to her room.

In the darkness she found the bed and slid into it so nimbly that the sleeper did not wake, but a little later his hand began to thrash about in the direction of the unfaithful one and stroked her. She was there, everything was as it should be.

'He took me by force,' she thought, with her eyes wide open in the night, 'I'm not an adulteress.' — 'Who called him?' asked the silence. 'I was in love,' she answered each time, 'in love.'

Contrary to what one might have expected, the farewells were not heart-rending. Ned took things in his usual manner, philosophically.

In any case, Amelia was leaving Great Meadow with Miss Charlotte in a month's time, swearing that she would never spend the winter there again and, of course, Ned would accompany them. Would his studies suffer? He would catch up later, if necessary.

Sensitive as women are on such occasions, Elizabeth was ready to supply a few tears, but she held them back in a manly fashion, as she told herself with a malicious smile.

They had been obliged to empty the stables in order to provide four horses for each of the carriages . . . The second one looked something of a poor relation behind Charlie Jones's, which would have been a credit to a president, but Elizabeth had no grounds for complaint, for her vehicle, less well upholstered perhaps, was spacious and its good springs guaranteed a relatively smooth ride.

They finally set off amidst a joyful clattering of hooves, cracks of the whip, cries of 'safe journey' repeated twenty times, and handkerchiefs vigorously waving in a radiant September sky.

Why does life seek at all costs to cast a shadow over the most agreeable scenes? The travellers had barely reached the highway when a scene broke out in Charlie Jones's carriage. He was settling down amongst his padding when he began to look through his mail which had arrived just before he left.

There were a lot of letters, but also a magazine, that infernal *National Era* with the fourth instalment of *Uncle Tom's Cabin*, which he set about reading forthwith.

Each paragraph made him start with anger, and the pages, torn out and shredded into pieces, flew out of the window to be scattered on the road. One after the other the pages, with their breathless sentimentality, were reduced to tiny scraps of paper that fell like dirty snowflakes on the red earth of Virginia. Elizabeth, whose eyes were following this strange phenomenon, thought that Charlie Jones was going out of his mind; then, after a good while, the final shreds floated in the breeze and she finally guessed the cause of such fury. A nervous laugh came over her that set her free from her mawkish thoughts. Such was the only notable incident on the journey which she had first made as a prey to worry, and was now undertaking in the opposite direction with a joy that verged on anxiety. She was fleeing from a love that made her afraid, and that she regretted with every turn of the wheels.

112

They reached Savannah at dusk a week later. It was the time when all the flowers of the town fill the air with their perfume, and the young woman felt a melancholy happiness stir inside her. Too many memories assailed her all at once for her heart not to feel something pulling at it. The sycamores in the long avenues and squares told her the tale of the young girl who had woven her first dreams of love in that place, when she was still ignorant of life's betrayals.

Betty, who saw that she had something on her mind, helped her to her room. Elizabeth felt the intense shock of memories. The woman that she had become could not get used to the timelessness that reigned within these walls, where nothing had changed. Instinctively her eyes sought out the portrait of Charlie Jones in his youth, and saw in its stead a commonplace still-life. Had she forgotten that the handsome young man in his gilt frame had gone downstairs to Amelia's room? She could not restrain a laugh. A ghost welcomed Mrs Edward Jones in her long dress and her hair done up in a crown on her head to this room: the ghost of little Elizabeth Escridge, sometimes happy, and sometimes torn apart by sadness at the thought of her distant England.

Charlie Jones's noisy activity, however, returned her to the present. Satisfied with his journey, he was walking back and forth giving orders and bustling all his people into action. His good humor was restored, he had shared snippets of conversation with Elizabeth, half serious and half playful. When he was alone with her at dinner, he spoke to her amiably, but not without teasing her a little. On one corner of the table, a bottle of champagne was cooling in an ice bucket.

'You didn't have too bad a journey, and now here you are in Savannah as you wished in so dramatic a manner. If I were indiscreet, I might say to you: what now?'

'There would be no indiscretion ... I wanted to come back to Georgia for several reasons, one of which will surprise you: to visit Aunt Laura and have a talk with her.'

Charlie Jones leaned towards her over the table and looked at her as if she had changed into a wild beast.

'To visit Aunt Laura,' he said, almost under his breath, as if it were a secret.

'I said that was one of the reasons.'

He sighed and resumed his normal tone of voice as he leaned against the back of his chair.

'I thought I knew women,' he said, 'but with you I learn something new every day. You are filling the gaps in my education . . . You are quite full of secrets, my dear, and I'm not cross with you for it. I'm too fond of you for that. At Great Meadow I was short with you, and I apologize, but do you know where Aunt Laura lives?'

'In a house of Catholic nuns near Savannah.'

'It's not very near, and not very far away either . . . Between Dimwood and Macon.'

'Betty knows the spot. She'll take me there.'

'I have too much respect and affection for Laura to argue with you, but that's an unexpected plan.'

'Unexpected,' she repeated mechanically.

'Let's remove all obstacles. You shall go . . . That convent was formerly an abandoned farm. I helped those women to restore it, but there's nothing luxurious about it, on the contrary. Laura used to run off there secretly from Dimwood sometimes, to visit them. They used to plot together.'

'What did they used to plot?'

'How do I know . . .? Nothing dangerous. On second thoughts, I'll send you there in a carriage. Two hours to get there, the same coming back.'

'You've taken a great weight off my mind, Uncle Charlie.'

'That's my role on this earth, I spend my time lifting great burdens from shoulders. I call that the nun's side of my character.'

She burst out laughing, and he poured another glass of champagne.

The convent was situated on the edge of a pine wood that bordered a small river. The house consisted of a ground floor only, a long rectangle with white walls, shaded by a plane tree that covered half of the red-tiled roof. A narrow path led through sun-parched fields to a black door that seemed very solid.

Followed by Betty, who had given Barnaby the necessary directions, Elizabeth rang a bell and waited. Time passed, then a little iron grille in a panel of the door was opened. The young woman could make out a face surrounded by black. Behind iron-rimmed spectacles, two brown eyes were looking very attentively.

'What do you wish?'

The voice was neutral in tone, rather short.

'To see Miss Laura Hargrove.'

'Sister Laura!' cried Betty, who was hidden on account of her short stature.

'It's you, Betty!' said the voice. 'Just a moment.'

The grille was closed again and a minute later a bell rang twice inside the convent. The door was half opened. Dressed in black from head to foot, the woman with the large spectacles led Betty and the visitor into a small court-yard where the heat of the day was somewhat less intense. From there they were shown into a small room that smelt of polish and was divided in two by a grille that allowed one to see into another, darker room. The only furnishings in both rooms were two rush-seated chairs. On the wall was a large crucifix which Elizabeth, in embarrassment, tried not to notice. They had to wait another minute or two and then the door at the back was opened and a woman in black appeared and said simply:

'Madam.'

'Sister Laura,' exclaimed Betty, 'it's Miss Lizbeth.'

There was a moment's bewilderment on both sides, then the great square-patterned grille turned on its hinges. The woman in black opened her arms.

'Elizabeth!' she exclaimed. 'I didn't recognize you. You're a lady now. How grateful I am to you, Betty, for bringing Miss Elizabeth to see me! Would you leave us alone for a while? If you go to the kitchen Sister Mathilda will be very happy to take care of you.'

Too moved to say anything, Elizabeth flung herself into the nun's arms and eventually sat down with her back to the large crucifix.

'You're in tears, my little Elizabeth. What's the matter?'

'I'm unhappy,' said Elizabeth.

She blew her nose discreetly and asked:

'Are you happy, Aunt Laura . . . I mean Sister Laura?'

'Aunt Laura wasn't,' said the nun with a smile, 'but Sister Laura is completely happy.'

'What do you do?'

'There are ten of us in the community. We came here, far from the world, to journey towards God, and I think that we are all happy, but talk to me, Elizabeth, what's the matter?'

'I'm unable to confide in anybody.'

'How many times did I ask you to confide in me? Do you not remember our conversations on the terrace at Dimwood?'

With the black veil covering her head and the long black serge dress, she might have looked intimidating, but she still retained the composure of the lady in pale gray that she had been at Dimwood. Her pale eyes made her look beautiful, despite the wrinkles which lined her face.

In sentences interspersed with silences, Elizabeth told her the whole story.

Leaning over her, Sister Laura listened for a good half-hour, then she took hold of both of her hands and asked:

'I imagine you have not forgotten my room at Dimwood, next door to yours?'

'Oh, no! I went back there several times after you left.'

'On the wall there was a crucifix, before which, for nights on end, I called on death. I know what it's like to suffer, Elizabeth. I won't tell you my life story, you know it. I suffered too much on account of love and the fire that doesn't go out, desire. You mustn't see Jonathan again. I'm not telling you to forget him, you won't be able to, we're too much alike on that point; he was your first love with all its tyranny. I too was tortured in my flesh and experienced what it would have been better not to experience. It's a mystery. Certain souls are asked to renounce themselves, make themselves celibate, who are dedicated to the love of God. Why those souls and not others? How can we know? All the saints understood it.'

She spoke in this way for several minutes, but in vain.

'But I don't feel that I'm made to be one of those who renounce,' groaned the young woman.

'You have a husband, Elizabeth.'

Her only answer was a painful, wide-eyed, blue gaze full of perplexity. Sister Laura continued softly:

'You don't know yourself properly yet, but I don't want to insist. Listen. You came here with Betty. Let her ask instead of you. Perhaps you don't suspect as much, but Betty is a woman of prayer. What she asks for, she gets.'

'I want Jonathan's love.'

'Jonathan is the husband of my daughter whom he does not love, my poor Annabel. Jonathan is behaving like a madman. Don't try to see him again.'

'How can I not wish for what I yearn for with all my might?'

'You don't want to be an adulteress. Do you love your husband?'

'I love him in a different way.'

'If he were to die, would you suffer?'

'I should be very unhappy, I'm very fond of him.'

'So, ask Betty to pray for you. God has granted her exceptional gifts, even though in the eyes of everyone she is only a little old black woman, the humblest of all. But flee from Jonathan.'

'Sister Laura, I'm not a Catholic, but I was hoping for something from you.'

'We shall all ask that you might find peace.'

'Peace . . . I have tried to ask for it, I prayed last night, I would have cried out if I'd dared.'

'Your heart was crying out, Elizabeth. God hears those cries.'

'I don't know, I'm afraid, that's all.'

'Christ said: "Do not be afraid." '

'I should like to hear his voice, like you do, like Betty, but I hear nothing, nothing. It's not my fault.'

Sister Laura fell silent and kissed her one last time in the doorway. Words welled up in her mouth, phrases that one always repeats. She knew them all. Faced with the despair of the young woman who was looking at her in expectation of a word of life, she felt ashamed at remaining silent. Something inside her was shaking the image she had of herself.

The door opened and was closed again.

When she was back in Savannah, Elizabeth, who had not had any lunch, had a light snack served to her, which she ate hurriedly. 'That appetite at least,' she thought with bitter irony, 'can be easily satisfied. The other one that springs up all of a sudden is atrocious.' From all that Sister Laura had said to her, she recalled the word 'desire' and she was grateful to her for at least having put a name to her brand of Hell. She was carrying the Hell of desire around inside her. Suddenly she found herself immersed in it. Ned had done that. Jonathan too, a wrecker. And who else would there be? No. There would not be anyone else. 'One gets used to it.' She remembered those words, and those others: 'Children will come along in due course.' In fact, everything would be settled harmoniously!

Evening was falling. It was that most enchanting of times when the breeze from the ocean brought the ladies out of their houses, and they headed in their dozens for the shade of the sycamores on the long avenue that ran through the town. How elegant they were, and how it all contrasted with the heavy silences at Great Meadow!

Preferring not to be recognized, Elizabeth pulled her big straw hat down over the top half of her face. But, more significantly, she had changed since her departure for Virginia. Her new hairstyle and her flowing skirt had transformed her, and she walked a little apart.

Above all, she was struck by the gaiety of these women who twirled charming and completely useless sunshades above their heads. They laughed a lot, but always softly. White, pale gray, eau-de-Nil, pink, the attractive splashes of color of the silk dresses added to the impression of happiness. With a kind of revulsion, Elizabeth saw herself once more in the parlor of the convent, where women in black were fleeing from the world, searching for peace.

That visit seemed strange to her.

What had she gone there for? To talk about the torment of unrequited carnal longing? Undoubtedly, but there was something else as well. Various changes of a physical nature, a break in 'the curse', made her suspect that she had recently become pregnant, but she had not dared to talk about it. An absurd shyness, a horror of expressing certain things . . . Yet if anyone was experienced in such matters, it was Aunt Laura, Annabel's mother. She would have to tell Ned.

That evening at dinner, alone once more with Charlie Jones, she answered as best she could the questions he asked her about Sister Laura. For his part, he did not really understand that communal life, but since it gave those women peace . . .

'One has to say,' he added, 'that they are not content merely offering prayers in front of a cross hanging on a wall. They do a lot of good, they take care of the sick who are brought to them from the surrounding district, and they don't trouble anyone. I would always prevent it if someone tried to evict them.'

Elizabeth kept to herself her thoughts on those rather mysterious words. Charlie Jones continued:

'I fear that your life might be rather boring for the moment, alone for part of the day, but you'll have your Ned for a good fortnight in a month's time, and between now and then, a surprise . . .'

'A nice surprise?' asked Elizabeth, who had become wary.

'But of course. If I've calculated aright, it won't be long.'

'Oh, tell me!'

'No. The surprise doesn't wish it.'

He laughed looking smug.

'The sycamore is still there, in front of my door, and I keep my promise. Uncle Charlie has an eye on your happiness.'

'Is the news any better?'

'Oh, it's not that, alas . . . That silly goose, Beecher-Stowe, isn't capable of making war break out, but she's preparing the right climate for it. Peace still reigns. Let's take advantage of it.'

'If only he knew!' thought the young woman. 'Ned first, then Jonathan . . .'

The days passed, made pleasant by walks either in the colonial cemetery where two men had fought over her, or in the enormous, rather shadowy park, in a deserted corner of which Amelia had given her some good advice, none of which had taken root. That time was already far behind her . . . The body was at peace then, however agitated the heart may have been.

Towards the end of an afternoon full of the heady perfume of heliotrope, lilies, roses and freesias, she was amazed, as soon as she set foot in the house, to hear a joyous sound of voices, interspersed with laughter, coming from the drawing room. She ventured a look out of curiosity, but she was noticed and called over authoritatively. She saw three ladies sitting in large armchairs, and was amazed on recognizing one of them. It was Miss Eliza Furnace, dazzlingly beautiful as usual, beneath an enormous hat in the eighteenth-century English style, with the brim boldly turned up on one side and hanging down almost to the shoulder on the other. The whole thing was strewn with flowers, as if for a queen girt with rustic simplicity. A pale green dress underlined the desired note of freshness. Her opulent brown hair with its tints of gold completed the seductive power of that radiant face. With gestures that led one to admire the gracefulness of her arms which were bare as far as the elbow, she was waving her hands about as she told of her pleasant misadventure at Gizah, where she might have been lost for ever in the sinister corridors of a great pyramid, had not one of the sons of the Pasha come to lead her towards the light.

The two other women were beside themselves with laughter. One of them, with a long face of aristocratic ugliness, was evidently the person to whom Miss Furnace was acting as a lady's companion. Her white curls jumped for joy at every detail of the thrilling account. Dressed in black taffeta, she lost nothing of her noble appearance as she gave herself up to this frank hilarity.

The third of these imposing personages seemed somewhat more singular. She was rather corpulent and wore a dress of daffodil yellow with very full flounces. One hand was laden with emeralds, and the other held a sunshade with an interminably long handle. That was about all Elizabeth could see, for an imposing poke-bonnet held her head prisoner, blurring the profile.

The laughing ceased when the young woman came in. Miss Furnace wished her good day in a pleasant manner, and, bending towards her neighbor with the white curls, said with obvious respect:

'Mrs Edward Jones, Mrs Devilue Upton Smythe.'

A brief silence ensued.

'Naturally, Elizabeth,' said Miss Furnace at last, 'I don't have to tell you . . .'

She was suddenly interrupted by a familiar voice which emerged from beneath the poke-bonnet:

'Well, the stupid little thing doesn't even recognize her own mother!'

Elizabeth gave a start and took three paces towards the poke-bonnet:

'Mama!' she exclaimed, but was repelled with a firm hand.

'No show of emotion, my girl, I can see you are pleased. That will suffice for the moment.'

She stood up and suddenly, although of only average height, she appeared monumentally tall.

'Violetta,' she said, 'and you, dear Eliza, I am obliged to tear myself away from you. I have to speak seriously with my daughter. However, when I saw Charlie Jones on the quayside, he said he was going to return soon and was counting on seeing you. I will see you later, dear friends. Elizabeth, take me to your room.'

They went upstairs.

With a somewhat fearful softness, Elizabeth's intonation betrayed the fullness of her joy in spite of everything. Joy at seeing her mother again, joy at being at last able to confide in her.

'First of all you must know that your mother has remarried ... Lord Fidgety. A very old Norman family. William the Conqueror, 1066, you know. And a large fortune.'

Lady Fidgety's voice was both powerful and precise, like that of a great tragic actress on stage:

'Mrs Edward Jones, née Escridge,' she continued. 'Jones like everybody else. I quite concede that Charlie is a gentleman. I counted him amongst my *beaux* when we were young and he sighed a great deal. A handsome man, but nothing more than a Jones! But we'll leave that. The South respects him, but how many times did I tell you, you little fool, to marry an adult, who could not be called up in time of war? There is a threat of stupid and ferocious war, and you go and join your fate to a whipper-snapper who will set off on the first day amidst the cheering of a hysterical crowd. Sit down if you feel upset. As for me, I prefer to say what I have to say while walking up and down.'

The parquet floor did indeed begin to groan and creak beneath her steps, while Ned's young wife remained speechless.

'A sudden passion, I know,' continued her mother, 'and the marriage seen to as quickly as possible at a Presbyterian church. Charlie told me everything when I arrived. Still, married all the same, to a husband who is still a student. One of those clumsy and exuberant fellows who are capable of the worst kind of folly, whereas a thinking adult who might weigh matters . . .'

'Oh, Mama, if only you knew!'

'If only I knew what? Come now, try to talk like an Escridge. I'm not going to eat you. After all, even if one gives one's daughter a thrashing, there is still what is called a mother's heart. I can see that you are upset . . . You may kiss me, there, on the cheek, but I forbid tears.'

Elizabeth was muttering, but was interrupted at strategic points by resounding exclamations.

'Louder, for Heaven's sake. Don't be afraid, you idiot. I'm your mother, you can tell me everthing.'

'This torture . . . I didn't know, I was ignorant of everything . . .'

Then there was an abrupt outburst that seemed to rend the air with its vibrations:

'Is that why you're putting on that guilty look? Do you imagine that at home we don't all experience what you call "this torture"? What forms the basis of our glorious poetry if not that burning preoccupation, as much from women as from men? Get a grip on yourself, my girl. Life is not as black as all that. Behave like a lady. There are those who behave badly. I don't approve, but we are not maniacal nuns locked up in a convent. Ah, don't make me say what I haven't said!'

'No, Mama,' said Elizabeth in a voice that was already firmer.

'Remember what Shakespeare said: that one needs to keep one's life intact and a spotless reputation . . . Our whole society is built on the granite of that noble principle. Do you understand? Do you really understand?'

'Yes, Mama,' said the voice that had become as clear as crystal.

'And never let that nasty word "adulteress" hover around you. One gets oneself organized. That's all. Let's go downstairs.'

Elizabeth did not go down to the drawing room with her mother. Firstly, she preferred not to see Miss Furnace again, finding her presence annoying, and secondly, she wanted to be alone in order to savor her indescribable relief. With a few words, her mother had brought her back into the mainstream of humanity. To learn that all women suffered as she did made her pain almost bearable. And, lifting her skirts a little, she began to dance a few steps to a popular tune, humming the words.

This joy was short-lived, however. Why did an importunate memory have to spoil it for her? She suddenly saw herself once more in the parlor of the Catholic convent with Sister Laura, whom she secretly admired for having given up everything, and also old Betty who was transported into another world by a picture and a candle.

'Am I mad?' she thought. 'Let's keep our feet on the ground, like Mama.'

There was a casual little phrase of Mama's of just a few of words: 'one gets oneself organized'. 'One gets oneself organized', the whole of life was opening up before her. As yet she did not have any clear ideas as to how, but she had the feeling that a key had been placed in her hand.

Of course, she had not said a word about her love of Jonathan, but there, 'one gets oneself organized' was right to the point. She dreamed about it for a moment, then went downstairs.

When he came back from his office, Charlie Jones talked to those ladies with all the charm he knew how to muster in such circumstances, just as the peacock fans out its ocellated tail feathers. Would he have acted in the same way if Amelia had been present? But Amelia was already rolling along in her carriage, far from here, on the roads of Virginia. Elizabeth intercepted the looks that he was sending in Miss Furnace's direction, likewise the fury contained within the features of Lady Fidgety, who was perhaps jealous after so many years . . .

'Oh, there you are,' he said as he saw Elizabeth. 'I was talking to these ladies about the party I hope to give at Dimwood as soon as my dear Amelia and Ned are with us once more. There is a shadow hanging over that splendid property, and I propose clearing it away. A wonderful surprise will help me to that end. I want it to be grandiose, in a way that will drive away all worries and tears. In order to prepare for it, I shall have to spend a whole day down there. I shall most likely go the day after tomorrow. Elizabeth, I shall leave you in the care of your beloved Mama, who is as beautiful as ever, and it goes without saying that you are all invited to these festivities. It will be towards the end of October. By then my mysterious little workers, direct from Peking, will have finished their work . . .'

At the mention of Peking, Eliza Furnace gave her characteristic start, like a horse pricking up its ears at the sound of the horn, and she stood up:

'The next time I have the pleasure of finding myself among you, remind me to tell you of my visit to the dear Empress in the famous gardens, where she confided in me . . .'

As if by some tacit agreement, everyone stood up and the two visitors took their leave, Eliza Furnace supporting on one arm the frail Mrs Devilue Smythe, who walked with hesitant steps. In a slightly quavering voice, the latter said to Charlie Jones:

'You've teased our curiosity long enough with your mysteries from China. We are expecting a miracle at least.'

And more softly, she murmured into his ear:

'Thank you for having sent me that enchanting creature. I've already put her in my will.'

For her part, the enchanting creature graciously saluted her benefactor, thanking him with a single look that contained a whole speech.

When they had gone, Lady Fidgety cast her eyes around her. She was rather stout around the waist, but held herself very erect nevertheless, with her shoulders well back and her head held high. This stance gave her an aggressive appearance which was in harmony with the firmness of expression, which she had retained throughout all her misfortunes. The nose and mouth, energetically formed, made of her a woman to be looked at as if everyone were obliged to do so. Elizabeth sometimes trembled when confronted with her. However, that implacable mother would have defended her child from the least threat with the ferocity of a wild animal.

'My dear Charlie,' she said, 'you have a charming house where the best of well-bred taste reigns. May I ask you where you intend accommodating my daughter in such an elegant town?'

'One of the finest houses in Savannah awaits her and her

husband in one of the most distinguished squares of the town. It's a present that I'm making them. But I am surprised at the question. Do you have anxieties, my dear Laura?'

'No, memories.'

Charlie Jones guessed that she was thinking of the bad days in London after the death of her husband.

'All that is over, Laura, over for good.'

She made an evasive gesture and added:

'In any case, you will excuse me for not going to Dimwood. I experienced too desolate a time there.'

'I understand you well. I shall not have too many scruples at leaving you here while we're over there. Your name is already being spread around. The whole of Savannah society will be knocking at your door.' In the end she changed her mind.

113

At dawn two days later, Charlie Jones set out on what he called his 'tour of inspection' at Dimwood. He returned the same evening in a state of exultation which transformed him into a young man.

'It will be sublime!' he exclaimed. 'I am dazzled by it all in advance. Ah, if only our poor servants could work with the love and zeal of my little Chinese women! I envy you for not knowing anything about it all yet. I know what to expect, but it will be a surprise for you.'

He continued in the same vein for a while and had champagne served in order to celebrate, if not the party, then at least the success of the preparations, for it would be the event of the season.

'Now,' he said, 'my dear Amelia, Ned and Miss Charlotte must not be delayed on the roads of South Carolina. I'll give them another week, and then just enough time to draw breath, before they are off with us for Dimwood.'

The champagne made him more and more talkative, and he began to verge on the indiscreet. And so Lady Fidgety and her daughter became all the more attentive. Elizabeth especially had a premonition that he was going to give away some secrets.

'The house is all upside-down. They are living in fear of a visit that they dread, but I shall be there, as always, to smooth things over. One little note of sadness, however. Fred has left. He had to undergo another operation which was dreadful; the boy's courage is amazing. His foot gradually regained its normal shape and now he walks like everybody else. After a bout of depression, he decided he no longer wanted to live at Dimwood, and he's gone off to join the cavalry. He is sure that there will be a war, and he is wishing for it with all his might.'

Elizabeth could not prevent herself from muttering his name under her breath, with her heart gripped by sadness.

'Fred!'

She saw once more that brief and painful scene. Face to face at the bottom of the stairs, the anxious look of that boy while she, Elizabeth, had said no, because she could not love him . . .

Charlie Jones continued:

'A real boy of the South, that one, with fire in his veins and not so much as the shadow of an untruth in his eyes.'

He emptied his glass of champagne.

'Quite different to that character whose visit hangs over the Hargrove family.'

'Some drama?' said Lady Fidgety out of curiosity.

'A complicated situation. In short, Dimwood had been leased for twenty-five years. The agreement expires in three months' time, and the owner of the plantation wants to move back into his property.'

'But I'm perfectly well aware of all that,' said Lady Fidgety. 'Everybody at Dimwood knows the story. It's Jonathan Armstrong, a name that's very highly thought of in England.'

The blood drained from Elizabeth's face. She remained perfectly still. Uncle Charlie cast a glance in her direction and added rather hurriedly:

'We shan't see him though . . . Hargrove is expecting him from one day to the next. He will have left before we arrive, he's only coming to sign papers. A sad business. It's getting late, ladies. If you are in agreement, I suggest that we go up to bed.'

'Willingly,' said Lady Fidgety. 'You look rather pale to me, Elizabeth. Like me, you need your sleep. Thank you for that thrilling evening, Charlie.'

Elizabeth did not sleep. Twenty times she was tempted to wake her mother to confess her relationship with Jonathan. Her affair. She did not dare to say her adultery.

Not entirely adulterous, she reasoned, since he had taken her by force. But if the body had not been adulterous, the heart indeed was. Who had written the letter and fixed the meeting under the big tree? Had it not happened under the big tree? Absurd! Adulteress. In the gospel, the woman taken in adultery, who was going to be stoned to death, was forgiven. How many women had quoted her example without going to the end of the quotation: 'Go in peace and sin no more'?

'One gets oneself organized.' What exactly did her mother mean? She did not want to hear that nasty word 'adulteress' buzzing in her head . . . So? It was better to keep silent. Nobody knew. Things would sort themselves out. She would not see Jonathan any more. She was going to die. She tossed and turned in her bed until dawn and then suddenly fell asleep.

The day that Uncle Charlie had been awaiting so impatiently arrived. Amelia, Ned and Miss Charlotte climbed down from their carriage in front of the house, all of them hungry, exhausted, and dissatisfied with their long journey. They had only one idea: to take refuge in the washrooms and to change their clothes. Lady Fidgety observed them with interest and introduced herself with a single, perfectly pronounced, sentence. Her voice, with its ultra-British intonation did not fail slightly to intimidate the three travellers, who were incapable of doing anything other than mumble the usual compliments. Servants in red livery surrounded them and ushered them out.

Indeed, when Charlie Jones arrived back from his office, he was surprised to see that they had arrived a day early. He was quite full of his plans for the party at Dimwood, and he waited until dinner-time to lay it before them with that Southern eloquence at which he excelled. Dropping with fatigue from the journey, the three travellers heard him propose that they leave the following day at dawn in order to avoid the heat, and to spend a whole day quietly in the paradise that was Dimwood. He was met, however, with mutterings of rebellion and the expedition was postponed.

The delicious dinner was gloomy. Plates were emptied, but conversation threatened to die out at every turn. No, nothing was happening in Virginia. The tobacco was growing well, the nights were cool, an unknown man on horseback had come and asked for Mrs Edward Jones, and when they had told him that she was not there, he had galloped off and vanished . . .

Ned, who was dozing over his meringues, seemed not to hear, but Elizabeth felt Charlie Jones's eyes on her and turned away.

'A mysterious stranger on horseback who gallops off and disappears,' said Lady Fidgety, 'I quite like that romantic touch, like something out of Sir Walter Scott.'

Amelia groaned her request to her husband to help her upstairs, for she was tired out.

'Charlotte,' she muttered, 'no potion this evening. No point.'

The dinner came to an end.

Less than an hour later, Elizabeth was stretched out in the dark alongside Ned who was desperately sleepy . . . Through the open window, she could hear distant voices of young people singing to guitar accompaniment.

She thought over her life, about the horseman who had come looking for her, who was, perhaps, galloping through the countryside at that very moment . . . She did not see him. Adultery . . .

There was a name that she would have liked to speak aloud in the night . . . She did not do so. With Ned at her side, whose regular, childlike breathing she could hear, it would have been unpardonable. That night the inert hand did not flail about in her direction as it usually did.

Through the white hangings that surrounded the big bed she could hear the humming of mosquitoes.

A thought suddenly flashed across her mind: 'Romeo and Juliet . . . People always forget that they were married. Would that impede impulses of desire?' But there was no Jonathan, no adultery. Her life was becoming complicated in spite of herself. What would happen if Jonathan saw her at Dimwood? She feared that encounter, yet she was yearning for it with all her soul.

If only those guitars would be quiet . . .

114

*A*fter a day's rest, Lady Fidgety, who was usually quite reserved, suddenly took over the general conversation at breakfast:

'Charlie,' she said, 'not feeling inclined to sleep, I found five issues of the *National Era* that were sent to you here while you were away, and I read the pieces called *Uncle Tom's Cabin.*'

'We're all anxious to know what you think of it. You may not know that the author has never set foot in the South, and her imaginary descriptions of slave cabins make even the Negroes laugh. She's making it all up, making it up.'

'I'm not capable of passing judgement on that, but when she paints a picture of the poverty of the South, I am far from laughing, I get very impatient, for that lady on her moral high horse, has no idea what poverty is. But I know. Elizabeth knows. There is no shame in revealing these things . . . I recognize wretchedness when I see it. I'm familiar with the smell of it, and the pangs of hunger and the permanent shivering of the skin caused by cold.'

'Laura,' said Charlie Jones, 'those memories are painful, and all that is far behind you now.'

'Thanks to you and William Hargrove, but I insist on

denouncing that woman's impudence. Whoever has not seen the bleak poverty of certain areas of London in the middle of winter has not plumbed the depths of despair.'

'The cold and poverty of New York can rival London's icy Hell,' said Charlie Jones. 'I sometimes go there several times a year on business, and I assure you that the cold bites just as hard and that slow, agonizing hunger does not let up its ravages amongst the poor for a minute.'

'There are charities,' said Miss Charlotte.

Lady Fidgety shook her head and continued:

'So when this woman, in her husband's comfortable vicarage, shows us your Southern poverty . . .'

'We do have our own poor Whites,' said Uncle Charlie in a changed tone of voice, 'and what worries me as much as the threat of war is that the South despises them. It comes to their aid but does not respect them, and is not ashamed to call them the dregs of the white race, Poor White Trash, an expression that makes me squirm, because it's going to bring down thunder on our heads.'

'You can't count the families that cling to you for support,' said Miss Charlotte forcefully.

'That doesn't change the problem at all. Laura, you have driven me to say what I have kept hidden inside myself, because I love the South as if it were my native land. Oh, I know! With its enormous wealth, the South acts very charitably, but it does so as one pays taxes and in order to be rid of the protests of outraged conscience, or does it . . . with . . . I can't find the word.'

The same word was on the tip of every tongue: 'love', but so great was their embarrassment that no one dared to say it.

'Come,' said Charlie Jones, 'I'm letting myself be carried away by rhetoric.'

'Let us say, rather, that you are being sincere. For my part, I shall be so until the end. I have been poor and I have suffered on account of it. I no longer am, and I'm pleased about it. That's not saying much. My satisfaction is scandalous. My husband's ancestors, like many of our great English families, made considerable fortunes in the eighteenth century in the slave trade, buying Negroes and reselling them to your farmers in the North. But the Negroes could not stand the climate in the North, and their masters, who had their wits about them, resold them to the South, where they were much in need. How much gold was passed from one white hand to another!'

'Does that not bother you, my dear Laura?'

'One sets things to right, as one can,' said Lady Fidgety simply. 'But I'm making you late with my unpacking of truths. I've finished. Off you go. The sun is beginning to warm up.'

Two carriages awaited them. Lady Fidgety, Amelia and Charlie Jones took their places in the first, Miss Charlotte and the two newly-weds in the second.

They had undoubtedly been moved by what Lady Fidgety had to say, and nobody uttered a word but Charlie Jones who pointed out to the coachmen the route they should take, which was different from that usually taken for going to Dimwood. It was at that moment that a horseman rode up at a gallop and stopped in front of the house. He appeared to be a common man and, raising his straw hat, he said to Charlie Jones:

'Sir, I have a letter for Mrs Edward Jones.'

'Give it to me. Where have you come from?'

'I am the Sisters' gardener. One of them asked me to bring this letter. Urgent, she said.'

Charlie Jones took the letter, cast an eye over the envelope and, to Amelia's surprise, got out of the carriage.

'Elizabeth,' he called, 'can you come here for a moment?'

The young woman joined him immediately on the road. Charlie Jones handed her the letter.

'I admit,' he said, 'that I don't care for these messages that arrive just as we're setting off. They're writing to you from the convent. It must be Aunt Laura. I hope nothing has happened to her.'

With a trembling hand, Elizabeth tore open the envelope, read the letter and gave it to Charlie Jones.

'I don't understand,' she said.

He cast his eyes over the letter which consisted of only a few lines. There was a little cross at the top of the page.

Elizabeth, my dear child, I prayed for you last night. In the name of Him who died to save us, don't go to Dimwood. I have very grave premonitions. May God keep you.

Sister Laura

rel. ind.

'I don't understand,' she said again.

'What can she be afraid of? Those nuns are so strange with their superstitious fears. Did you confide in her? Forgive me for asking?'

'We talked about religion,' said the young woman in a somewhat enfeebled voice. 'About my marriage too, . . .'

'Well, we shall be there to protect you, Ned and I. If you prefer to stay here, stay. If I were you, I should pay no attention to the holy lady's dreamings.'

Elizabeth did not hesitate.

'I'll get back into the carriage then.'

Charlie Jones called over the messenger who was waiting in front of the house and slipped a golden coin into his hand.

'Tell Sister Laura that everything is alright and that there is no answer.'

Standing in the road alone with Elizabeth, Charlie Jones suddenly turned red with irritation.

'I'm very fond of those nuns,' he said with a sudden burst of anger, 'but there are times when they annoy me with their premonitions. Shall we tear it up?'

Elizabeth nodded.

He tore the letter into pieces which he scattered in the wind.

'What shall I tell Ned?' she asked.

'That you talked to her about religion . . . about your marriage. Forget the premonitions. Ah, when we get out of Savannah, you will take note of the road. We're very proud of it. It's paved with oyster shells.'

They separated and, two minutes later, the carriages set off at a canter.

'What was it?' asked Ned. 'I saw you were handed a letter.'

'Yes, Aunt Laura. Advice from a nun. She talks about being prudent. Your father says there is no sense in it. He even tore the letter up.'

'All those Catholics are the same. Laura wants to convert you, I guess.'

'Me? You must be joking.'

'What a shame Papa tore up the letter. I would have been amused to see it . . .'

Although her experience of married life was short, she detected a tone of jealousy.

Miss Charlotte, who had not said a word, looked at her gravely, with her eyes full of unspoken questions.

They were almost past the last houses of the town when the horses' hooves suddenly began to ring on the road surface with a hard and clear-cut sound that made the travellers start. Elizabeth remembered what Charlie Jones had told her:

'Oyster shells!' she exclaimed. 'It's like going over a metal surface.'

Ned leaned out.

'They are enormous,' he said, 'cemented together to form a level surface. Savannah is very proud of it. I'd forgotten.'

He placed his hand on Elizabeth's and, with childish affection, murmured:

'I'm pleased about this little journey with you, darling.'

She smiled. These affectionate impulses of Ned's stirred something inside her. He added nothing else to these words, embarrassed perhaps by the presence of Miss Charlotte, whose lips remained tightly shut.

The young woman wondered why the usual itinerary had been changed. She was sorry not to see again the spot where, from inside the carriage, she had seen Jonathan on horseback when he had given her that imperious look. At that moment he had taken possession of her soul even more completely than on the verandah overhung with flowers. She was his. Later, Ned had taken possession of the body, but the soul eluded him. Now it all seemed horrifyingly simple to Elizabeth.

Along the road, trees were starting to lose their leaves but retained the brightness of good weather days. The deep green was strewn with gold, but what was that compared to Virginia's magnificent Indian summer? The clip-clop of hooves on the road was hammering in her head, as if to tell her something, a name, sometimes hers, sometimes Ned's and Jonathan's, with unrelenting regularity. She was trying to block her ears when the noise suddenly stopped, and she was aware of an odor that she breathed in with delight. The carriage was now rolling on sand, through a pine forest. The reddish trunks formed a mass of columns rising up into huge shadows. Unfortunately, yellow dust rose up from the road, forcing the travellers to cover their heads. Finally, as they emerged from the woods, they embarked on the last lap of the long journey at a gallop and reached Dimwood amidst waves of heat that indicated that midday was not far off. Ned and Miss Charlotte were full of admiration at the sight of the gardens that were like some glorious song.

All the Hargroves were there on the porch to welcome them. Kisses and compliments abounded, together with the customary exclamations, before there was a joyful rush for the coolness of the drawing rooms where the blinds were lowered.

Elizabeth was declared to be more bewitching than ever, and all of the family had to be introduced to Amelia and Miss Charlotte, and Ned to all the family. Lady Fidgety was treated with great delicacy being given an elegant room which was far more sumptuous than her previous apartment, as befitted her new station.

On the first possible occasion, Elizabeth went up to seek refuge in her mother's old room. Unbelievably, everything was just the same as she had seen it on her return from Savannah when she had found the room empty after Mrs Escridge's nocturnal departure. The large four-poster bed, the little table where port stains were still visible . . . In a few seconds she lived once more through those interminable weeks. Like a ghost, she saw herself again in the kilt and all the gold of her hair covering her shoulders, and the adolescent look of surprise on her face. She was suddenly gripped by violent fear and she dropped on to the bed.

'I shouldn't have come,' she said under her breath. 'Laura saw something.'

They were calling her. She got up hurriedly.

Downstairs they were serving juleps in the large gilt and white drawing room where everyone was desperately chattering away. Sitting to one side in large armchairs, William Hargrove and Charlie Jones were talking with very grave looks on their faces.

'I don't understand Jonathan Armstrong's decision at all, Charlie. He has sold the house and the plantation to his wife, who becomes sole proprietor of Dimwood.'

'But why? Did he give a reason?'

'None. There has been an agreement signed between the two of them, and he made me read it. I couldn't believe my eyes. She is offering us a renewal of the lease for twenty-five years, on the same terms as the previous lease.'

'And have you signed?'

'Yes.'

'Dimwood will stay in the family. Your grand-daughter becomes the owner. Perhaps you did right, but I would have preferred to see the contract. My years of experience as a lawyer . . . And the house you bought in Savannah for your departure from Dimwood?'

'I'm intending giving it to my grand-daughter Minnie on her marriage with the gentleman from New Orleans.'

'That seems very reasonable to me, if the clauses are respected.'

'Annabel included an affectionate letter with the lease. She is leaving her husband and will never return to Georgia.'

'After the unforgivable affront she received from society here, I have to say that I can understand her, but America is large. I could very well see her settling down in the West — or in the North. As for Jonathan Armstrong, he was in no way a husband for her.'

'They are separated, not divorced. She is keeping the name.'

'Of course. That in itself is worth a lot. He must have received a considerable sum for that.'

'Considerable.'

'And what is he going to do with his fortune?'

'Fritter it away. He doesn't know how to do anything else with his money. You forget he's a squire.'

'I can't tell you how much that term annoys me.'

'For my part, it makes me smile. If you had seen him this morning riding up on his black horse . . . Such elegance and such haughtiness!'

'In any case, I'm glad he didn't come while we were here. We're well rid of him.'

'I hope so, for frankly I hate him.'

Uncle Charlie frowned.

'You hope so? You are sure of it.'

'Alas, no. He has a lot of friends in the district and wants to tell them all what he calls the "good news." This will allow him to polish his reputation up a little, for it had become rather besmirched. He's going to have a busy day.'

'Why couldn't he have stayed in Vienna!'

'You weren't his neighbor. In what way does he bother you?'

'He doesn't. I just don't care for that character.'

'We had to see each other, he and I, over business.'

'Of course. It's just an unpleasant impression I can't get rid of. Isn't that your dinner bell I hear?'

'Yes. This afternoon we'll put the finishing touches to this evening's party, which promises to be splendid, thanks to you.'

'Splendid,' repeated Charlie Jones with a worried look.

And he added with a somewhat forced smile:

'This party, which was supposed to wipe away the sadness at having lost Dimwood, will celebrate the joy at having kept it.'

The dinner was of the simplest. The evening's banquet would compensate for that. Conversation was loud and cheerful. Several times Charlie Jones begged everyone not to take a look over in the direction of the great avenue before nightfall.

'We shall have a longer siesta than usual,' said Aunt Emma, 'but we are expecting wonders. You're making us die a slow death from curiosity.'

'Hold on until the guests arrive,' said William Hargrove with a smile that was lost in his beard.

Restored to tranquillity by the renewal of his lease, he felt that twenty-five years had been added to his life. That in itself was reason for a feast. The tortured man of former days had given way to someone new who no longer wanted to believe in war and sought refuge in the brightness of the present moment. One of the events of the day concerned Elizabeth. She no longer needed to hide herself behind masses of flowers so that he would not see her. A beautiful young woman now met William Hargrove's indifferent gaze.

Yet there was a shadow hovering over this beatific optimism: he feared that Jonathan Armstrong would turn up to dampen and spoil his evening, strutting around with his nose in the air amidst the revelling, simply in order to be seen, out of vanity and insolence. And how could they stop him? But perhaps it would not happen. He waved his hand to chase away such black thoughts and stood up. The meal was at an end.

There was a rush for the rocking chairs.

In the smoking room, William Hargrove questioned his mentor:

'Charlie, are you sure that the floor will hold under the feet of all those dancers?'

'A double thickness of flooring. What else do you need? It covers the whole area under the trees.'

'Where are you putting the orchestra?'

'At the foot of the oaks, in the avenue.'

'Are you sure that your Chinese women have been sufficiently diligent?'

'They never stop weaving night and day, they are like maniacs. You lack resolve, William. You should read Seneca again.'

'Why Seneca?'

'He was in favor of resolution. I feel like having a sleep.'

'Sleep? While carriages are heading for Dimwood full of inquisitive guests, difficult, full of chatter . . .'

'What is done is done. We have set something in motion. Let's call it fate and have a nap.'

Their tête-à-tête came to an end and the house was silent.

Ned had taken Elizabeth by the hand and went for a little walk with her under the trees that edged the gardens.

'If we stayed here for a few days, I should like to walk with you in the woods behind the house.'

'I went there once with Hilda and Mildred. You can easily get lost if you don't know them well. But there is the great avenue.'

'I shall go wherever you wish. Are you pleased to be here with me?'

'Very pleased, but I don't like all this activity. All those people who will be arriving later on . . .'

'I admit that I don't find it very exciting either, but that's the way of the world, Elizabeth . . . Do you love me?'

'Of course, Ned. I think there are going to be two of us to love you.'

'Two? Do you mean . . .?'

'Yes, Ned.'

'Oh, Elizabeth . . . I've always been clumsy with you. Shall we go and rest in our room?'

'You go and rest, Ned. I'm going to take a walk down by the river. I should like to be alone.'

'Don't go too far away from the house. If ever anything should happen to you . . .'

115

They parted and, although it was forbidden, she walked quickly off in the direction of the porch. Her heart was beating so fast that she had to slow down and, keeping close to the walls, she reached the verandah where memories awaited her. The spot was deserted. She slid along as far as the magnolia, whose flowers were still fully open, spreading their love-laden fragrance. Not daring to touch them, she brushed her lips against the petals and softly told them Jonathan's name. All the intoxication of youth went to her head. Her heart alone spoke, the body no longer existed. She imagined their souls thrust together as victims of the ecstasy of an indestructible love, and the eyes were the means by which they would rush headlong towards the abyss. She sighed. It was over. Today she loved him differently, and it was less beautiful, but she no longer had any choice. She was his, but not completely.

There was Ned . . .

She moved away and, as she suddenly turned round, caught sight of servants in the great avenue, standing on the top of enormous ladders. With tools that looked like bellows, they were sprinkling the leaves of the oak trees with gold. That was the secret that they were not supposed to know. She caught a quick impression of this magnificent idea and ran off towards the front of the house which faced the wild woods where she had walked with her cousins in former times. She stood motionless.

The air was silent. In front of her, the masses of impenetrable greenery had something both malevolent and attractive about them. Indians were sleeping there, beneath the ground, and snakes wound and unwound themselves amongst the tall grasses.

A voice called her. She raised her head and saw a hand waving out of a long, narrow window on the top floor, and that hand was holding a card. A name suddenly came back to her: Souligou.

'Yes,' she shouted.

'Come up,' said the voice.

A moment later she found herself, as in a dream, face to face with the same Souligou as before, sitting with her back to the door in her big armchair, the same dark blue cotton kerchief sticking its aggressive points up from her head. In a face the color of boxwood, the crafty black eyes were watching her.

'My word,' she said with a smile that parted her thin lips, 'a lady, a real, elegant and beautiful lady. Sit down, madam.'

Elizabeth sat down beside her. Souligou's long hand was placed on the card that she had been waving out of the window a moment earlier.

'Do you remember the day when I drew the tarot cards for you, when I had concealed a card from you, the last one? I didn't want to show it to you, to upset you, but we have been unwise, Mrs Jones.'

'Call me Elizabeth,' the young woman said impatiently.

'As you like. Here is the card.'

Elizabeth saw, with horror, a hanged man drawn with brutal naivety.

'I had hoped,' said Souligou, 'that things would be put

right, for the other cards were not too worrying, but this one is decidedly so. It conceals a drama.'

The young woman remained speechless. Her blood was rushing through her veins. In a voice dulled by fear she asked:

'What should I do?'

Silence. The fortune teller lowered her eyes as if to withdraw into herself to seek for an answer.

'You will break hearts. Be prudent. I can see a shadow.'

She looked at Elizabeth.

'You are expecting a child. You must be prudent. This child will be your joy.'

'That is reassuring news.'

'Yes, but it doesn't sweep aside the shadow which I don't like.'

'War?'

'Oh, war . . . That's all people talk about, but it won't be tomorrow, there are years yet.'

'That's some relief.'

'A bit, but the shadow is there, and nothing is shifting it. I don't see anything else.'

Elizabeth cast a desperate look around her. All along the walls of this low-ceilinged room, the spy-windows, not unlike loop-holes, spoke to her of her previous visit, of her ignorance concerning everything in those days, of her confused, adolescent dreams.

'What advice do you give me?' she asked as she turned back towards Mademoiselle Souligou, who was silently watching her.

'What advice should I give you? I see nothing, and that's what bothers me as much as the rest. Nothing.'

Elizabeth stood up looking very pale and supported herself with one hand on the back of her chair.

'Thank you, Mademoiselle Souligou,' she said almost in a whisper. 'I shall come and see you again.'

'Perhaps, Mrs Jones, but I don't think so.'

She moved slightly to one side to let Elizabeth pass behind her and opened the door that gave on to the little staircase as steep as a ladder.

She was worried and waited until the young woman was at the bottom before crying out to her:

'Good luck, Elizabeth.'

It was barely dusk when the first carriages arrived. Having taken the long way round, as they had been requested to do, they skirted the edge of the Wood of the Damned and lined up in front of the stone steps that led to the gardens.

From her window, Elizabeth saw these things with increasing anxiety. As she got dressed for the party, she could think of nothing but her conversation with Souligou, of that shadow, of the prudence that was counselled.

Ned who, for his part too, was getting ready saw that she was worried and did not dare to ask her why. He himself felt uneasy at the prospect of a fashionable evening, which was a nightmare to him.

'You have put your white dress on,' he said with deliberate cheerfulness, 'it is plain, but you are never more beautiful than in white. People will be looking at no one but you.'

'Oh, I don't at all want to be looked at! I swear that I would much rather stay here in this bedroom.'

Then they went down.

116

*I*n the large drawing room with its red curtains draping the tall windows, the ladies were chattering away for all they were worth; there were already quite a lot of them and nearly all wore pastel-colored dresses, in contrast with the funereal elegance of their black-suited husbands. Ned and his wife merged with the crowd, but no one paid any attention to the newly-weds whose faces were unfamiliar. Elizabeth was relieved. She could not fail to notice Ned's awkwardness and found it rather touching. He had retained something of the appearance of a gentleman farmer from his native Virginia.

Outside, the noise of carriages continuously arriving almost drowned conversation, and voices were raised amidst laughter and exclamations in this fashionable din. The Hargroves, who were mixed in with all this confusion, tried in vain to get the servants to circulate with trays of tall, unsteady champagne glasses. The idea had to be abandoned. The carriages were finally assembled at the the back of the house under the strict direction of Azor, who had no hesitation about bullying the coachmen of the most prominent families. With his little soap-leather cap pulled down over his nose at a war-like angle, he managed to get his way thanks mainly to his shrillness, which made him sound like an angry parrot.

Darkness was falling when the double doors swung back on their hinges and Charlie Jones announced, in a loud voice, that the ball was going to begin beneath the oak trees of the great avenue. An ample gesture indicated simultaneously the neighboring room where candelabras shone. With the frivolity of elegant people who revert to a schoolboy mentality as soon as they are in a group, the guests obeyed amidst a tumultuous outburst of noisy gaiety.

When this aristocratic horde had gone the whole length of the ground floor, it found itself face to face with a spectacle that rendered it speechless, then an uproar of genuine wonder rose up towards the stars. The whole of the foliage of the giant trees was shrouded in a golden veil with flame-colored highlights. A double row of servants in red livery stood on either side of the avenue. They stood six feet apart and each of them held, in a white-gloved hand, a stick topped with a lamp. This light rebounded from the tops of the trees which seemed avid for it, as if the purpose of these lights was to scatter trails of sparks through the darkness. In consequence, shivers of awe rippled through the hearts of the guests as if to add spice to their pleasure. As far as the eye could see, the fairy spectacle extended beneath the vault formed by the branches, extending the dazzling tunnel that pierced the black shadows.

Charlie Jones finally divulged the secret that he had kept to himself for so long.

'It's simple,' he said, 'thousands and thousands of spiders, brought from Peking in paper bags. You release them into the trees — they spin webs in the foliage as if demented —

and then you throw gold powder on to the webs. And there you are!'

Such was the fascination of this prodigious feat that no one paid any attention to the orchestra concealed under the oaks, and the crowd jumped in surprise when one of most thunderous of Johann Strauss's waltzes suddenly burst forth. With delightful little shrieks of alarm, the ladies flung themselves into the arms of the men, who instantly whirled them around in time to the music. All were overcome with a joyful giddiness.

Elizabeth, clinging on to Ned, shouted into his ear:

'I don't know how to dance.'

'It doesn't matter,' he answered, 'pretend.'

At the buffet, which had been set up in an endless gallery, there was a superabundance of exquisite delicacies, some piled up in pyramids, others on porcelain dishes bearing coats of arms. Servants dressed in white poured out oceans of champagne into permanently empty glasses, and many a pretty head began to spin.

The young officers in their dark blue uniforms were late arrivals and took double helpings as they made eyes at the ladies.

Elizabeth could not manage to share in the great joy of the ball. She felt at a loss. Her efforts to drag her young husband off to one side were in vain, and she began to feel more and more uncomfortable. But Ned was evidently having a good time, and the champagne having made him talkative, he was chattering cheerfully to one and all, but not much to the women so as not to displease his wife.

In spite of herself, the latter could overhear shreds of conversation: they were talking about the threat of war. She preferred not to listen to them. She noticed that Ned was talking more loudly and more quickly than usual with the officers. The discussion was lively, indeed thrilling to him, and the young woman felt that, for the moment, he had forgotten she was there.

'Ned,' she told him, 'I want to go into the house and rest for a little while.'

Suddenly worried, he turned towards her:

'Where in the house?'

'In my old room, don't worry.'

Somewhat sickened by the smell of food and tobacco that hung in the gallery, she wanted first of all to go outside and get some fresh air into her lungs. For a moment she admired the magnificence of the great avenue shrouded in light. In spite of everything she felt distanced from this ball, from this explosion of joy, for since early evening an idea had taken root in her, and she suddenly began to run towards the porch on the verandah. It was there that she got a strange feeling, like a revelation. It seemed to her that she was beginning her life at Dimwood all over again, in the same way that one can start to read a book again by going back to the first page, and with her face close up against the magnolia, she said under her breath:

'I have come.'

Going up the steps that she had first climbed with her mother, she went straight to her room. She had to grope in the darkness to find the bed again, and she stood there for a moment. She recognized the smell of the room and memories assailed her: nostalgia, worries and the first heart-ache of love. This desire to relive everything corresponded to a need to understand. At the point she had reached, she was trying to discover what meaning her life might have.

She went out. Aunt Laura was no longer there in the next-door room to keep an eye on her. The girl that she had become once more could run to the corner of the verandah where the big leaves of the magnolia were going to part to reveal a face glowing with love. As if a prey to hallucinations, she leaned over once more.

At that moment a sound of steps made her stop short; they were making the floor of the verandah creak behind her, and a voice rose up in the silence, dull and precise:

'You have been a long time, Miss Elizabeth — or should I say Mrs Jones?'

Elizabeth held on to the bannister. In consternation she asked:

'Were you expecting me, Miss Llewelyn?'

The massive silhouette with broad shoulders advanced towards her.

'Do you think a child wouldn't have guessed, knowing your story, what you were going to do? But time passes. I don't like your being here tonight.'

Now the moonlight permitted her to see the thickset face of the Welshwoman and her piercing little eyes.

'It's better to speak clearly. You are in danger at Dimwood.'

'But why?'

'He about whom you must no longer think is looking for you in the gardens. You are an adulteress, Mrs Jones.'

Elizabeth jumped:

'Did you try to prevent it?'

'Who begged me to come to her aid? But let's leave all that. It all started at the foot of the tree in the Wood of the Damned. Do you remember the answer to the piece of paper buried in the ground? Torn in two?'

'What significance do you give to that?'

'One doesn't ask for love from occult forces. They don't know what it is. They destroy.'

'I didn't ask for love.'

'You did. You asked that the woman who was obstructing your love be removed. Now you attract misfortune by your presence. Hide. Don't go out of the house. That's the advice I give you, and that's all I can do.'

'You are a very wicked woman, Miss Llewelyn.'

'I am not a wicked woman, I'm trying to save you . . .'

She hesitated:

'. . . to make amends.'

She turned abruptly on her heel and went down the verandah steps. Elizabeth followed her with her eyes until the gray figure had disappeared behind the house.

A few minutes' reflection sufficed for the young woman to know what she wanted to do.

She went down the steps.

In the distance the orchestra was playing with a wheedling softness that caught her attention for a moment. Something inside her responded to that dance music. She liked love. That summed up everything. The word 'adultery' hurt her like a wound. She fled from that word. Where was she going? For the moment she had no idea. To hide no matter where. In the dark.

As she walked along the side of the house, she was surprised not to hear any noise from the apparently deserted gallery where the buffet was. She was irresistibly tempted to hazard a few steps in the direction of the avenue. In the dazzle of the lamps, she caught sight of the couples swaying back and forth to the treacherous languor of the waltz. How futile it all seemed compared to her great torment in body and soul . . . Ned was in that crowd, holding forth to the officers, drinking rather too much champagne unless he was dancing, but she doubted that.

She turned her back to the avenue and, passing in front of the white columns of the porch that shone like silver in the moonlight, she reached the gardens, but did not dare to go in for fear of getting lost in the maze. The fragrance of the night-scented flowers calmed her down: stock, poppies, gardenias and, above all, honeysuckle that she breathed in with her eyes closed the better to relive her childhood days in England.

Further down, the lawn where older members of the family sometimes walked in the evening spread out endlessly. There was no one there that night, and the young woman felt with pleasure the soft thickness of the grass beneath her feet. The vastness of the sky scattered with stars filled her with that mysterious happiness which brings consolation for all things, but she would not have been able to say how or why. She suddenly felt herself wrapped in an unspeakable silence, and she wondered what she was doing there, in a ball gown, in that corner of the world.

Further on still was the boundary of the plantation, at the edge of the Wood of the Damned that filled her with terror now. She could not stay there. She must go back. They would perhaps be worried at no longer seeing her. And yet she lingered. Deep down she wished that he whom she yearned to see would spring up beside her; perhaps he was looking for her, roaming about in the darkness. They were both, she thought, playing hide-and-seek in their lives as in this darkness . . .

Suddenly she heard someone calling her name, cast forth into the echoes beneath an incredible number of stars on a background of black sky. She began to run across the lawn, along the edge of the garden, and then along the side of the house.

It seemed to her that there were fewer people, the

orchestra was still playing and the avenue still shining, but it had lost its charm, the effect of the surprise had passed. Magnificence had undoubtedly had its moment of triumph but was less imposing now.

Again the young woman waited before drawing close to merge with the crowd of party-goers. She noticed liveried servants bearing trays laden with glasses and plates. Someone caught sight of her and waved.

It was Billy. He was laughing and called out to her more loudly than the others. As she drew closer she was struck by the golden complexion of all of these faces she saw. The light raining down from the trees placed a mask of a gold over the features of each of them. This magical transfiguration riveted her to the spot in bewilderment, and Billy had to run over and take her by the hand:

'Where were you hiding yourself?' he asked her joyfully. 'We've hardly spoken to each other since you came back.'

His young face was aflame. She guessed that he was a little tipsy. Still just as bold, he tried to kiss her, but she easily pushed him aside.

'You're mad,' she said, 'everyone can see us.'

'Oh, they've all been drinking, they're having a good time. Come on now. Wouldn't you like to have a little waltz with me?'

'No, Billy, I'm tired.'

'You never do anything to please your Cousin Billy.'

He shrieked with laughter.

'Do you remember the slap you gave me on the stairs at Savannah?'

'No . . . yes . . . I don't know any more.'

'My cheek remembers it,' he said, dragging her off.

He was laughing ceaselessly under the influence of the champagne, and his cheerfulness was a comfort to Elizabeth.

Having rejoined the crowd of guests, she immediately found herself surrounded. Ned gave her a kiss on the cheek.

'You frightened me,' he said, 'I imagined . . . I don't know what.'

A young officer declared:

'We were all ready to leap on to our horses and hurtle through the countryside to find you.'

'A little glass of champagne?' suggested Ned. 'It won't do you any harm, and it is the best. Papa does things properly. It comes from Paris.'

She refused with a smile. They were beginning to waltz again all around her. The orchestra was resounding with love and the dancers' feet were raised off the ground in a sentimental whirlwind.

The waltz was gently dying down when an elegant silhouette emerged from the shadows and moved towards the light. In black from head to foot, with white silk rolled at his neck: Jonathan.

Elizabeth's heart leapt painfully in her breast and she thought she was dreaming. He was not the man she had known. Fiery violence no longer shone in his pale eyes, but only an immense tenderness which overwhelmed her.

She instinctively seized hold of Ned's arm as if to stop him moving, but he had never seen Jonathan. With his glass in his hand, he gave the newcomer a polite smile.

Jonathan paid no attention to him. Taking a step closer to Elizabeth, he looked at her, overflowing with love. He said softly:

'Elizabeth.'

Suddenly sobering up, Ned exclaimed:

'Who are you, sir, to dare speak to my wife in that tone of voice?'

Jonathan bowed slightly.

'Jonathan Armstrong, at your service, Mr Jones.'

'Jonathan!' Ned repeated.

Seized with fury, he threw his champagne in the other man's face. Jonathan did not flinch. With a smile he let slip the word:

'Clumsy.'

And drawing a handkerchief from his pocket, he wiped it over his forehead and cheeks, and then he added calmly:

'That's easier to wipe away than blood, don't you think, Mr Jones?'

Ned pulled himself up straight:

'I await your orders, sir.'

'In that case, I think the simplest thing would be to settle the matter with pistols tomorrow morning.'

Elizabeth fainted. Three men immediately carried her to

one side and sat her on a chair. There was a doctor close at hand who took care of her.

'I know a quiet spot where we won't be disturbed,' Jonathan continued. 'We'll meet here at seven, on horseback. Does that suit you?'

Ned nodded.

'And we need seconds,' said Jonathan.

The young officers offered their services. The doctor who was bringing Elizabeth round undertook to be present. Everything was settled perfectly according to custom. Jonathan was used to that kind of thing.

The orchestra had fallen silent.

The guests returned in silence to their carriages.

Only the lamps continued to shine for no reason.

Charlie Jones and William Hargrove had been having a rest in the drawing room for some little time when the incident took place. Weary from their efforts to ensure the success of this ball that wanted to be a memorable occasion, they reckoned that the guests no longer had need of them to enjoy themselves. They were contemplating the smoke from their cigars when Joshua and Douglas came to bring them the bad news.

Leaping to his feet, Charlie Jones uttered a cry:

'It's my fault! Laura warned us.'

In his despair, he beat both of his fists against his head. Joshua tried to calm him down:

'But they're not dead, Charlie! You'll see. I can see the report already: "Two bullets fired and no result. The opponents shook hands." It's a tradition.'

'Do you think so?' said Uncle Charlie. 'Do you really think so?'

William Hargrove remained motionless in his armchair. Charlie Jones went up to Elizabeth's room. He stormed in without asking leave.

Stretched out on her bed, the young woman was deathly pale. Her eyes were closed and she did not open them when Uncle Charlie came up to her uttering a deep groan.

'My child,' he said in a voice hoarse with pain, 'it's my fault, not yours, oh, not yours . . .'

At that moment Miss Charlotte sprung up from behind

the bed. Flushed with annoyance, she pushed Uncle Charlie roughly away.

'Are you mad to disturb her with your cries,' she said to him in a ferocious whisper. 'Go away. I'm taking care of her.'

She pushed him, and he let her, like an overgrown child.

'Off you go,' she repeated. 'Out.'

In a somewhat louder voice he exclaimed:

'Oh, Lord have mercy!'

'Go and say your prayers somewhere else,' said Miss Charlotte as she forcibly directed him towards the door which she closed behind him, and she added so that he would hear:

'You should have said them beforehand!'

Back at Elizabeth's bedside, she reassured her in a calm tone of voice:

'Now let us stay quite calm, my little girl. I've got some carefully prepared laudanum for you and you're going to drink it nice and slowly. A little glass of port will sort everything out and you'll sleep like an angel.'

Elizabeth turned her tragic gaze towards her.

'And what about tomorrow?' she whispered.

'Tomorrow you'll be alright and life will carry on as usual, full of birds and flowers.'

With the glass in her hand, she made the young woman drink as she supported her head. After which she made her swallow, in the same manner, a good glass of port. Elizabeth dropped down on to her pillow.

'You are too tired to say your prayers,' said Miss Charlotte, 'but I'll say them for you. I'll read the psalms aloud while you sleep.'

'Sleep,' repeated Elizabeth, 'do you think I shall sleep? Do you think it will all be alright? Do you think . . .'

She could not finish her sentence. Miss Charlotte's laudanum had a shattering effect.

117

At exactly seven o'clock the following morning, eight horsemen gathered in front of the house. Mounted on his black horse, Jonathan spoke these simple words.

'The journey will not be long, gentlemen, but the path is not terribly good. It would have been difficult on foot.'

They followed him without a word, skirting round the house, then the gardens and the lawn, finding themselves eventually at the edge of the Wood of the Damned.

Day was breaking, and the great shreds of moss hanging from the trees stirred imperceptibly. Those greenish-white hangings reached almost down to the ground and gave the central avenue an air of ragged splendor, as if for some secret ceremony, but the trees with their enormous branches had only a sparse foliage. Not a single bird was singing.

Having reached a clearing in which there rose up a gigantic oak clothed in a coat of moss, they saw the first rays of sunlight falling on the gray earth, marking out the favored spot.

The preparations were rapid, each of them playing his role with exemplary precision. A distance of twenty yards between the opponents was judged to be sufficient. Jonathan threw down his hat and stood motionless, holding his pistol against his leg. His face which was both proud and calm did not show any sign of emotion, whereas Ned, who was a chalky white, was having difficulty mastering his extreme impatience.

At the signal, the pistols that had been held at head height were lowered and arms stretched out straight.

'Fire!'

Ned's aim was true. Jonathan fell right back, struck in the heart. Then Ned staggered and had to be supported, then stretched out on the ground at the foot of the great oak. A groan of pain came from his mouth and blood ran unceasingly down his suit, a little below the stomach. Less than a yard from his face, void of all color, the fringes of a moss curtain fluttered softly in the morning breeze.

At about ten o'clock, a great sound of voices in front of the house roused Elizabeth from her sleep. In the half-light of the closed shutters she saw Miss Charlotte leaning over her.

'Well,' said the elderly spinster, 'I hope we've had a good sleep!'

'Sleep? Oh, yes,' said Elizabeth, who was still not properly awake.

She suddenly sat up in bed and cried out:

'Miss Charlotte!'

'What's the matter?'

'They're not going to fight, are they? That duel won't take place?'

'My dear child, I've spent the night in the rocking chair and I don't know a thing. I hope not, but I don't know. Pray to God, Elizabeth.'

'You're frightening me. One prays to God when things are going wrong, but He never answers me.'

'He always answers in His own way. Let's say the 23rd psalm together.'

The door was abruptly opened and Elizabeth's mother appeared, swathed in a green and black travelling rug,

'Bring some light,' she said in a loud voice. 'I want to see my daughter. Where is my daughter?'

Miss Charlotte opened one of the shutters and Lady Fidgety ran towards the young woman's bed.

'Elizabeth! Still in bed at this hour? Are you ill? Why didn't they tell me anything? I want to know. Downstairs nobody is answering, you'd think that everybody was hiding. Speak, Miss Charlotte, for Heaven's sake.'

The rapid outpouring of words made it difficult to understand. She took off her gloves, which she threw onto the bed, and pulled off her bonnet, setting free an untidy wave of locks some of which were silver-gray. The vigorous, handsome face suddenly became like that of a fury. Sitting near the bed, she seized hold of one of Elizabeth's hands and let it drop again.

'No fever. What's the matter with you? A premonition woke me up last night. Something is wrong. Miss Charlotte, I ask you once more to speak.'

'I know nothing, Laura.'

At that moment, the door opened once more and Betty came in. She was in tears.

'Betty has become a real friend to me,' said Lady Fidgety in an almost aggressive tone of voice. 'You can well imagine that I dismiss those absurd Southern prejudices.'

'Betty!' exclaimed Elizabeth, 'why are you crying? Only you can find out what you ask for, so ask and tell me that nothing has happened.'

'Betty can't ask, can't change what is done.'

Miss Charlotte drew closer to Lady Fidgety:

'Yesterday evening, during the ball,' she whispered, 'two gentlemen had a quarrel. I don't know what happened afterwards. I was here. Barnaby told me and then ran off. I don't know anything else.'

Betty had thrown herself to her knees near the bed and was holding her folded hands against one of Elizabeth's.

'Miss Lizbeth,' she said in a strangled voice, 'Mass'r Ned say he want to talk to you.'

'Talk to me? I'll go down straight away. Help me, Mama.'

'No, no,' exclaimed Betty. 'Mass'r Joshua come and fetch you, Mass'r Ned injured.'

At that moment Lady Fidgety sat up straight in her chair and, as if she had turned into another woman, began to speak with irresistible authority.

'I was not mistaken,' she said in a voice that was carefully articulated once more. 'There was something wrong. This is the hour when you're going to need all your courage, my girl. I will be brave for you, I will be brave for both of us if the burden is too great. An Englishwoman stands firm when faced with misfortune.'

'Misfortune!' exclaimed Elizabeth. 'Jonathan. Where is Jonathan?'

'It's Ned,' said Lady Fidgety.

'Betty, where is Jonathan?'

The old woman burst into sobs:

'Betty don't know where Mass'r Jonathan is.'

Lady Fidgety stood up and said in a loud voice:

'Elizabeth, one thing is clear, you must hold firm as your mother herself did when she lost the one she loved. There has been a duel. Your husband is in danger. If he were to depart from us . . . listen to the voice of common sense. I am going to return to England and you shall return with me. Only there would you have any chance of happiness. If your husband pulls through, as I hope he will, of course you can stay despite the threat of war. Go to your poor Ned's bedside, but remember England, Mother England.'

Elizabeth barely understood anything of this speech and asked Betty to help her get dressed.

'Not yet, Miss Lizbeth. Mass'r Joshua goin' to come.'

Miss Charlotte came up to Lady Fidgety and said in her ear:

'I think it would be better to leave her for a while. She can sleep a little longer; I assure you that I'll see to things.'

With her interest suddenly aroused, Lady Fidgety asked:

'Do you have some new preparation?'

'No, the same one, but I have my own recipe — very potent.'

'I should be grateful if you were to entrust it to me.'

'Yes, later. We must let the storm blow over. You know how fond I am of your daughter.'

'Very well. I'll entrust her to you for an hour. What's Jonathan's involvement in this business?' she asked suddenly.

'I suppose it was he who wounded Ned in the duel.'

'And my Elizabeth, beside herself, is ready to kill the one who killed her husband. How well I understand her. Revenge! It's very British, you know. It's not for nothing that Elizabeth is English. Charlie spoke to me about this Jonathan Armstrong. A very bad character, an incorrigible swashbuckler, and he bears a noble name on top of all that, but, my God, how stupid these duels are! Do we know the cause of this one?'

Miss Charlotte made an evasive gesture. Lady Fidgety shrugged her shoulders.

'May she not give way to despair over her poor husband. I don't wish to appear cruel, but in Bath husbands are easily replaced. She will be at home over there, not here. But let's hope, in spite of everything, that Ned will pull through. He looks a good young man to me.'

She went out as abruptly as she had come in.

When the door was closed again, Elizabeth, stiff in her white nightgown, looked at Miss Charlotte and said in a strangely flat voice:

'Jonathan is dead.'

A little later, Uncle Josh came and knocked at the door, which was opened by Miss Charlotte with her finger to her lips. He saw Elizabeth, in a dark green dress, standing with her back to him and her forehead against one of the window panes. At the foot of the unmade bed, Betty was on her knees.

Taking Uncle Josh to one side in a corner of the room, the elderly spinster spoke to him softly:

'She knows everything, she seems very calm, she said a few words but isn't speaking any more now. I admit I'm worried.'

Joshua's face became more and more grave.

'She has overcome . . . What do you want her to say? What strength of character in a woman so young!'

'Perhaps I gave her too much laudanum. She is completely white.'

Without answering, Uncle Josh went over to Elizabeth and took her by the hand. The big, blue eyes were watching him. He looked for what he was expecting to see: pain, despair, but he saw nothing.

'Come,' he said.

She followed him obediently like a little girl and, leaving the bedroom, they went down the stairs and crossed the gallery where the buffet had been. Everything had been tidied away, but as soon as they were in the white drawing room, a smell of ether wafted towards them.

Uncle Josh stopped and said to Elizabeth in a very gentle voice:

'You won't be afraid? Your poor Ned is in the next room.'

She shook her head. They went in.

On a bed placed in the middle of the small drawing room, Ned was stretched out, the middle part of his body swathed in cotton wool and bandages. Close by him a doctor whispered to the young woman:

'You will only stay for five minutes. He can speak a little and is not in too much pain for the moment, but if you tire him he'll pass out, and then . . .'

Elizabeth looked at Ned and for a second wondered who it was. The mass of black curls on the pillow brought her back to herself, and amongst the white flesh clinging to the bones, she looked for the face she had once kissed passionately in the woods in Virginia. An enormous feeling of pity suddenly came over her. The eyes of the wounded man were half opened:

'Is that you?' he said breathlessly.

'Yes, Ned.'

'Have you forgiven me?'

'For everything, my dear Ned.'

He made an effort and said:

'I killed the man you loved.'

She leant over him and placed her lips on his forehead along his hairline.

'I love you too, dear Ned.'

'I shan't see our child. You'll call him Charles-Edward . . .'

The doctor appeared and touched the young woman's arm:

'Don't tire him, he's going to be in pain.'

'Stay,' said Ned, 'I'm not afraid. And listen, don't leave the country. If you go away . . .'

He stopped and resumed slowly:

'You'll suffer over there because you belong to us. Our South will be the dream that will stay with you until you die, the dream of distant lands where you experienced love, and you will cry.'

'I shan't leave,' she said.

He closed his eyes.

'Go now, my love.'

On a sudden impulse, she bent over very low and pressed her mouth to lips that were already dead.

That same evening, her mother came to sit at her bedside. A night light illuminated the room in which the young woman had spent the day in a kind of stupor, trying to understand what had happened. She had a vague premonition that the real test would come later, when memories came flooding back.

Lady Fidgety wanted to speak with the greatest tact.

'My little girl,' she began, 'I have learnt . . . It's horrible. So young . . . We shall all be with you. You won't be alone. As for the future, everything will sort itself out.'

'It's pointless, Mama, I'm staying.'

'Did I hear correctly? Do you realize that the country is on the brink of war?'

'That makes no difference to me, I'm staying.'

Lady Fidgety stood up.

'Elizabeth, out of consideration for your grief, I shall not insist today, but we shall resume this discussion when you've come to your senses.'

'I have come to them, Mama, and I'm staying.'

Lady Fidgety looked at her in silence, then said to her sadly:

'I cannot force you against your will, but remember what I'm telling you: you'll be unhappy here.'

'I would be even more so anywhere else.'

Her mother was on the point of adding something but had second thoughts and left the room, closing the door gently behind her.

She went down the stairs with rapid steps, along a corridor and finally reached her bedroom where she locked herself in with a double turn of the key. There this woman who always appeared to be so perfectly in control broke down. At the foot of her bed, with her face buried in her hands, she sobbed uncontrollably for quite some time; stifled cries interrupted the flow of the tears.

Although exhausted, she managed to get herself to her feet, then washed her face repeatedly in cold water. They had not heard her. She was sure of that. A terrible silence weighed down on the house and the presence of death was everywhere to be felt. One might have thought that all the rooms were empty, for not the slightest sound issued from them, but they were serving as refuge for twenty silent, horror-struck people.

118

*T*he following morning, at about eleven o'clock, a woman in a gray dress was ringing at the door of the little convent.

Time passed before she was allowed to enter, but a moment later she found herself face to face with Sister Laura who was behind the parlor grille.

'Miss Llewelyn,' said the nun, 'what a surprise to see you here.'

'I know, Sister Laura, I don't have a very good reputation in your circles.'

'And yet you were, I think, baptized a Catholic in Haiti?'

Miss Llewelyn nodded.

'In any case, I'll open the grille, which has no meaning for the two of us. It's easier to talk like that.'

The Welshwoman gave a hint of a smile.

'Thank you, but I would have preferred it if I could have brought you other than the bad news that I've come to tell you. Jonathan, your son-in-law, died this morning, killed in a duel by Elizabeth's husband.'

'I'm very sorry, I had begged Elizabeth with great urging not to go to Dimwood. She did not wish to listen to me. Did Jonathan know he was going to die?'

'Killed instantly with a bullet through the heart.'

'Poor unfortunate Jonathan!'

'Forgive me, but it doesn't seem to upset you.'

'No.'

'No! How can that be? How mysterious you are! A duel . . . It's almost murder.'

'Not in his case . . . Without wishing to be indiscreet, I can tell you that he came to see me, we spoke together at length, and I can confidently say that when he left here he had no intention of fighting a duel. He must have been provoked.'

'Provoked, yes, and in the most obvious way, a glass of champagne thrown in his face by Elizabeth's husband.'

'With Southern attitudes he couldn't do otherwise.'

'I am confused. He turned up out of the blue with that strange look of serenity on his face and even gentleness in his eyes, whereas usually . . . there's something at the bottom of that.'

'You're right.'

'But what?'

'Let's say that he had been transformed by love.'

'You nuns know how to give an answer that isn't really an answer . . .'

'Miss Llewelyn, I may be a simple woman inside the walls of a convent, but I haven't forgotten what is done and what is not done in the world. Betraying the secret of a soul is not an honorable thing to do, either here or there.'

'I'm sorry . . . There was a change, that's clear.'

'Call it what you like. I'm convinced he's saved. What about Ned?'

'Dead. Died in the afternoon, it was not possible to operate.'

'Poor boy, so young! And what of Elizabeth?'

'It was a very hard blow. She fainted several times.'

'So young . . . and her husband dead. We shall all be thinking about her. Is there anything else you want to talk to me about?'

A bell rang.

'I'm sorry,' Sister Laura continued, 'we have the office now.'

Miss Llewelyn suddenly uttered a cry:

'The office, the office! Oh, Laura, leave the office and listen to me. I'm not a bad woman as everybody thinks, although they never dare to say so to my face.'

She looked so upset that the nun stood up.

'What's the matter, what can I do?'

'They say it was I who led your daughter Annabel into bad ways. It's not true. In that boarding school where Mr Hargrove had put her, because he didn't want her in his own house . . .'

'Alas!'

'. . . she went unsupervised, she was too pretty not to be in danger, and she fell into evil hands, alone, in town.'

'I know all that, Miss Llewelyn, you're touching on too painful a subject, I beg you . . .'

'A man — shall we ever know who — introduced her to old Jurgen, the millionaire, to whom he offered her. And your father thought it was you.'

'Be quiet, I forbid you to mention that lie again. My unfortunate daughter was a victim, and I have paid my due. That's enough, Miss Llewelyn, let us stop there. Please take your leave.'

The Welshwoman who had stood up dropped back down onto her chair. She put her hands to her throat as if she were having difficulty breathing.

'Forgive me, Sister Laura, it has taken an enormous weight off my mind to have talked to you and confided in you. There's no one else like you.'

'You labor under many illusions.'

'Listen to me, for the love of God. I have loved money, I have done things which I ought never to have done.'

At these words Sister Laura's hands emerged from her long, black sleeves in which they had been concealed and, drawing the Welshwoman towards her, she embraced her.

'Dear Miss Llewelyn, it's not to me you should be telling these things, but I shall think about you now with all my heart.'

She added with a joyful laugh:

'I haven't forgotten that you helped me bring Annabel into the world! Don't be sad any more.'

The Welshwoman held back her tears by blowing her nose and, shaking Sister Laura's hand, went out without adding another word.

EPILOGUE

*T*ime passed in that unmoving hurricane that had previously amazed Elizabeth. Months and years went by and
there was no war. Cotton grew and looked like snow, snow
fell and changed to mud; speeches flowed, rich in poison;
hatred and lies flew from church pulpits, from North to
South and from South to North. Tongues were extremely
busy. Folly flapped its heavy wings over the country, but
there was no war. Fifty-three, fifty-four, fifty-five . . .

Elizabeth was living in Savannah in the house which
Charlie Jones had wanted to give to the two young newly-
weds. She had moved in while she was still wearing her
mourning clothes. Betty never left her now. The house was
simple if a little on the narrow side. The only thing about it
to attract the passing eye was the front door, its panels
sculpted in the Italian style. Neither rich nor poor in
appearance, but quite exquisite, this eighteenth-century
dwelling attracted the attention of connoisseurs. Tall sycamores provided it with their fluttering shade. A great expanse
of flowers girdled it with perfumes that were gentle and
imposing, according to the season.

Inside, the rooms that were slightly darkened by draped
curtains exuded tranquillity and a jealously guarded solitude
under the protection of the old black servant. A visit was
almost an event. Miss Charlotte, however, was always well
received and sometimes came to spend a few weeks in winter.

The cheerfulness of Elizabeth's room, all in chintz with
white net curtains, distinguished it from the rest of the
house where a more formal and solemn style dominated.
From her windows she could see the whole of one of the
most admired squares in the town, surrounded as it was by
pink and white houses, all of which had the traditional shiny
brass knockers adorning their front doors.

Each day she would take a stroll in the great avenue where,
in former times, she had looked at the elegant ladies. How
many naive questions she had asked herself about them!

Back in her room, she could hear in the distance the
long, hoarse sirens of the ships in the harbor, but she
never went in that direction.

The child that Ned had given her was now three years old, and she lavished on him all the love with which her heart overflowed. The boisterous and happy little creature looked at her with such tenderness in its smile that she was often overwhelmed. They loved each other and together experienced moments of happiness that delighted Elizabeth, and sometimes worried her, because of the intensity of the attachment.

He had his father's fine black curls with copper tints. From him, too, he had inherited his large, innocent and laughing eyes. In serious moments, in front of other people, she called him Charles-Edward or, as it was rather long, simply Ned, but when she went to wish him good night and tucked him up in bed, she would ask him in a whisper:

'You haven't forgotten our secret? You haven't told anyone?'

'No, Mama.'

She would kiss him passionately and say to him under her breath:

'Sleep well then, my Jonathan, good night, my Jonathan.'